Chronicles

OF THE

INSURRECTION

Chronicles

OF THE

INSURRECTION

Julie & Ryan Dickerson

TATE PUBLISHING & Enterprises

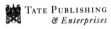
TATE PUBLISHING
& Enterprises

Chronicles of the Insurrection by Julie and Ryan Dickerson
Copyright © 2007 by Julie and Ryan Dickerson. All rights reserved.

Published in the United States of America
by Tate Publishing, LLC
127 East Trade Center Terrace
Mustang, OK 73064
(888) 361–9473

Scripture quotations marked "NIV" are taken from the *Holy Bible, New International Version* ®, Copyright © 1973, 1978, 1984 by International Bible Society. Used by permission of Zondervan Publishing House. All rights reserved.
The opinions expressed by the author are not necessarily those of Tate Publishing, LLC.

This novel is a work of fiction. Names, descriptions, entities and incidents included in the story are products of the author's imagination. Any resemblance to actual persons, events and entities is entirely coincidental.

Cover Design by Melanie Harr-Hughes
Interior Design by Brandon Wood
Cover and Interior Art by Julie Dickerson

ISBN: 978-1-5988640-2-1
07.05.02

Chronicles of the Insurrection is dedicated to the real Ree and Tar.

Some special thanks are in order to the Almighty for his eternal grace and to all of those who have supported us: our parents who have always been there for us, Tate for giving us an amazing opportunity, and all of our friends who read this before it was in its final form—especially Pat Karl and Lisi Klus for combing through this novel with a fine-tooth literary comb.

KURÄK

KEY

▲ PORT
⚑ FORTRESS
▲ MOUNTAINS
🌲 FOREST
⌂ VILLAGE
➤ CAVES
‡ WALL

KROIN ISLES

GONDRABAD
ARMENDOR
MALGER
KHAYNERN OCEAN
OSC
PURNISTON
EARYN
DANRESH
SEA OF WHITE PEARLS
JULON
KAIRI
LASOFEH
VALANCAR
ACOSTAD
URTHIEN
ZABYN
VALLEY OF SOLITUDE
BORDERLANDS
BREL
GASHNERN
FAL-EVEIN
FAL-RUNEN
GEDON
TUAL OCEAN
GRÄFIN REEF
KALTHARNGA
Halfast
FIELDS OF BONDEN-AR
QUANTUS PLAIN
BLACK WATERS
SHALDAN EMPIRE
MENDOR ICE BERGS
TIL-TORG SEA
ANDRATH
N. HEROG SEA
WHITE ICE FALL
N. MENERS
MENERS
FORTOLN
SUNSING INLET
DREÁG COAST
GRÄOIN OCEAN
OROIN
EMLAND
ARTHIAN
TALTHARNIA
S. HEROG SEA

N NW NE W E SW SE S

AN INTRODUCTION TO THE

Preceding History

The specific origin of the Shalkan people will forever remain a mystic enigma shrouded by the fogs of time and distance. Even the most insubstantial vestiges of memories, slivers of the landscape that was their homeland or faint echoes of the urgent call which compelled them to traverse the vast reaches of the seas, elude them. It is as though their pasts never were, as though they materialized mysteriously from the air, and as though they were born that one, unrecorded day when they arrived on the beaches of Kurak.

Stepping from their murky ships onto the luminous stretches of sand, their arms and weaponry vested them with an immutable strength. The weary limbs and salt-crusted lips customary to those at sea did not plague them, and the ease with which they assimilated into society as leaders and warlords was peculiar. The migration of their brethren thus amassed in numbers and momentum but attracted little attention. So competently did they accomplish this feat that the people regarded the Shalkan presence favorably and without trepidation.

There were, however, two men by the names of Turock and Lain, in the high government of Kurak, who refused to overlook or underestimate the significance of the Shalkan existence. Officers of the executive, they circumspectly observed the Shalkans who continued to covertly exercise authority. What the men did not know was that the Shalkans, seeking a leader, had likewise kept a wary eye on them and had come to the conclusion that Turock would become one of their own.

Through various, manipulative, and complex ways too dark and fantastic to describe, the Shalkans infiltrated Turock's thoughts, offering him unimaginable power. For a time, Turock resisted their persistent summons, but he told nothing of the offer to his closest friend and companion: Lain. Equally able in mind and body, the men trained together, honing each other's mental and physical acuities. Meanwhile, the hold of the proposition festered in Turock's mind. As soon as both men and Shalkans gave good testimony of him, Turock knew the time had come to reveal his true motives.

At the Shalkans' request, Turock persuaded Lain to divulge the name of the last people who would resist Shalkan control: the tribesmen of the jungle. Though Lain suspected Turock of pursuing an aberrant path, he disclosed the information, refusing to believe his doubts would give birth to truth. With time, the effort required to conceal the depth and intensity of Turock's transfiguration multiplied, and Lain's misgivings solidified. One night, when the burden of uncertainty assailed him, Lain accused his friend with candor. Turock returned the gesture with an icy coolness.

Soon, Turock's bellicose nature engulfed him. With the Shalkans backing him, he gained totalitarian control of the government. Lain remained his sole opponent—one Turock planned to eliminate. After a harrowing battle, Lain slipped from Turock's sight, taking his remaining, loyal men with him into the jungle.

And so after numerous happenings and years passing, the world of Kurak came to behold a second uprising against the Shalkans, the officials of the land. Those uprising were called the rebels, and their trouble is the story that comes to pass...

Prologue

All was dark. Waves of mist undulated, swirling endlessly. Shapes of many sorts found themselves, in moments less than seconds, to be almost recognizable, but before their forms materialized, they dissolved into the void of nothingness. For truly there was nothing until the Light pierced the shadows with its radiant brilliance, flinging darkness aside. The Almighty had come, Greater than All, Creator and Destroyer, King of Kings.

Everything about the light was good, but some rose against the perfect will of the Almighty in a resistance to His holiness. With time came the dissenting, fire-eating hordes with their blackened blades. Mounted upon a white horse, He met them with His Son wielding a double-bladed sword. A scarlet band encircled His forehead, and righteousness was His shield.

His soldiers, garbed in white robes and carrying staffs which no swords could slice, fanned behind Him. He gave the enemy one chance to surrender, to rejoin with the Light and capitulate their evil deeds. They scoffed at the offer, and with their rejection of redemption, the heavens clashed in an epic battle.

He vanquished the darkness, but as it plummeted from the heavens and unto the earth, it felled many a bright star from the sky. The Holy One sent His soldiers after it, and they marched along the hidden staircase that travels from heaven to the four corners of the earth. Descending onto the land, the soldiers discovered that to destroy this evil they would also have to uproot the Almighty's seeds of light with which the darkness had entwined. Leaving the seeds intact, His soldiers returned, and He contemplated the Harvest. Some of His seeds would die, but others would live. He would not leave His earth unprotected. No, He would wait for the right time to obliterate completely the evil which had corrupted His perfect existence.

Sneering with hate, the fighter wiped his face with a sweating hand. With a thunderous roar and with his steel drawn, he rushed into the town. The lust to kill vibrated throughout his tense body. He was made to fight, to inflict pain, and to revel in death. Orders thrust aside, he concentrated on his target: a lone child. As the thrill of the oncoming kill escalated, he gained speed until the sickening thud of a gun barrel burying into his stomach halted his rage. The weapon belonged to Turock. Groveling on the ground, he whimpered.

"I said no killing!" Turock roared. "We are not strong enough to incur the wrath of the people. Burn their houses and steal their goods, but do not murder yet. The time will come when your hunger for blood is satisfied. As for now, shall I reveal what happens to a soldier when he forgets his master's command?"

The other fighters dropped their weapons and kneeled as Turock fired the gun.

The First Book

Chapter 1

Split. Splat. Thump. A drop of water plunged gracefully from the sky and landed squarely on a human head. The head shook, sending the drop sailing. Falling with a gentle plop, the globule of water landed in a pool and swirled in the current until it was lost.

Above the pool, a glistening waterfall sprayed over a ledge's jagged periphery and played with the stirring ferns. Ripples from the fall slid over the placid water and wrapped around a lone rock. On its far side, the pool bustled into a dancing stream, bubbling and jumping over the pebbly forest floor. It was early, and a layer of mist blanketed the quiet morn. The constant hum of the waterfall blended into the whisperings of the stream, and both sang in harmony with birds' euphonious melodies. The dense foliage rustled with the movements of animals, and the leaves of the canopy swayed in the wafting breeze. Sunlight shimmered on the graceful branches as it rose slowly into the serene, young sky.

A solitary figure crouched pensively on the tiny rock island. Thin layers of droplets covered her, and when she shook her head, they dove into the puddle accumulating under her bare feet. She watched them swirl in and out and around each other before sticking a thin finger into their midst. The water adjusted easily to the stimuli.

Shifting slightly, she heard her feet scuff against the rock and the skins of her clothes brush against one another. Removing her finger from the water, she dried it on her clothes, careful not to drench her bow and arrows. She returned to her spot and mumbled something before drawing a path of mud from one end of the stone to another. She doubled back upon the path and put the tracing finger to her lips, musing at the line's elegant simplicity. Timidly, she added two slender, hopeful lines to its tip. With her eyes, she followed its path; it was an arrow pointing to the future of the forest. She contemplated its destination. Where was she headed?

The muffled sound of a trumpet ruptured Shrie's thoughts, and her head snapped up like a hound responding to its master's voice. Knitting her brow, she leapt from the slippery rock and onto the sloppy bank. Mud seeped between her toes. After two deep breaths, she eased her body into a run.

Scampering through the ancient trees, she strained to hear the trumpet. She did not have to wait long—the same call echoed again throughout the woods, brimming with opportunity. She had not seen a fellow human since her tribe's departure, but she knew a trumpet did not sound by itself. The noise came from a human, and for a human, she was searching.

Venturing momentarily from the back of her mind, images of brightly colored clothing, lazy trails of smoke, and the polished, tanned and ebony faces of her tribe overwhelmed her. Before her eyes, transient children played games among a stand, their mothers laughed, and the men hunted. The measures of a long forgotten music chimed in the distance. They had diminished long ago—left her, long ago. With sad faces and quiet eyes, they had faded like seasons from the forest. Perhaps, like the seasons, their departure did not signify an ending but rather the necessary passing which predicates renewal. They had named her their heir to the old ways, longing to return to her as a circle embraces its starting point. Contrary to Shrie's desire, the years had not brought them back. Even if she could not determine it, she believed a valid reason existed to explain their absence.

Everything has its own song, and fate always has a motive.

Flying through the trees with a grace more animal than human, she became a part of the jungle. Her body beat with the same power that enlivened the woods, and her legs pounded alongside the wild hunters. She, the breathing apotheosis of everything the jungle called its own, ran as her slick temple boiled in unnoticed sweat.

The jungle's passion coursed through her blood; its hope and serenity rested in her soul. The secret havens recognized her, and like brothers they opened their arms to welcome her. The sky and the earth accepted her, teaching her the secrets of peace. From wind and fire she learned to fight and to flee, and the current of water revealed to her a pulsing beauty. The languages of birds and beasts were hers to know, and the wisdom of the trees tingled in her ears. The forest was neither her past nor her present. It simply was, and in its act of pure, unaltered being, it fulfilled its purpose.

The dirt meant to ward away mosquitoes cascaded down her face in jubilant design. Her green eyes sparkled, bending into arched slits as the leaves brushed against her face. From exposure to the sun, her dark skin and black hair glowed. A small, chiseled chin sat defiantly under the curve of her bottom lip, and her thin face boasted of an empowering tenacity.

The trumpet beckoned her.

The humans were close. Her pace quickened in anticipation, and then rapt with the curiosity of the unknown, she lost herself in the warnings of the trees. The woods had been empty of her kind for so long. Aside from her, the trees trusted no one. If the humans proved themselves foes, it would be a lonely, devastating battle. If they were friends, the familiar cycle trapped in its haunting and assuring path, would return.

The ancient songs rang clearly in the reeds, and Shrie slowed to a stop as the throbbing rhythm of the earth directed her. A small escarpment fell away from her feet before abruptly spreading into a clearing. Here the forest regressed. The fields marched ahead, slaughtering anything higher than the waving grasses. The trees resonated in anguish, and the invading music of the newcomers rattled the leaves. Concealing herself behind a leafy bush, Shrie tried disastrously to assimilate her body to the harsh, drumming beat. Beyond their ill-kept fire, the humans argued inside the previously white tents now gray like an illness.

A mutilated piece of meat dangled on a stick, and a shape came to retrieve it. The form was human, though raucous voices snapped and leapt from its throat. His shoulders were slumped and brawny, his legs bowed, and his hair unkempt. She watched guardedly as he sniffed the air and spit into the weakening flames. As he drew a rapier from a dirty sheath, a metallic grating entered his song, and a cruel twist of a mouth darkened his face. Thrusting the blade continually against an imposing edge of rock, he sharpened it. Shrie's eyes studied the unfamiliar move-ment, wavering from the hilt to the dull, blackened blade. The color was strange to her; it was not the bright, cherry blood of prey but a deep scarlet. Human blood soiled his sword. Her eyes narrowed.

Stepping from the foliage, she crouched and snuck behind the man. His sword stopped. She waited for him to turn, but he did not hear her song: the melody of the wood. She squatted in consternation. The strange hissing of the metal suddenly aggravated her. With a swift maneuver, she wrenched the sword from his hand. The hilt felt hot in her hand, but she held it firmly, and the burning sensation crawled into the crevices of her skin. The tip she placed delicately where his neck met his back, stilling him with his own sword point. The voices came from his throat, forced and angry. Shadowy forms burst from the tents. Shrie searched their eyes and found fear—and hatred. The spirit of the wood wavered.

She dropped the sword and turned the burnt palm outwards in a sign of peace. The hand stretched painfully, and smoking gray tendrils rose from an ugly red mark nesting in the skin. Her momentary offer confused them, for they were driven to kill. They raised their shrieking voices. Cruel laughter escaped their lips as they girded their weapons and rushed her, drooling like raving animals in their madness. Metal raced towards her, and the voices surrounded her, pushing her back into the woods.

She desperately defended herself against their swords, matching their blows.

The forest invested its strength into her limbs, and for a time, the darkness was kept at bay.

"A fool's talk brings a rod to his back,
but the lips of the wise protect them."
Proverbs 14:3

Chapter 2

Two years later…

"Curse them," Ree shouted as the wooden frame shattered under his force. Shards of wood pierced his skin, and he yanked the sword from its grave. Vibrations from the Shalkan trumpets rattled the walls of the compound. In response, tipped helmets dipped and rose over black and navy uniforms outside the collapsing building. "Cowards," Ree sneered at the helmets, "all of you are cowards." He launched his sword into a support.

"They may be cowards, but they'll crush us, my friend. We may have destroyed their fort, but now the trumpets have summoned them." A rebel sheathed his sword.

The helmets neared, and Ree watched them in burgeoning hatred. "Two against two thousand—not awful odds." Resentment oozed from his reply, and it held the other rebel in his position. Their eyes locked until a burning timber buckled beside them in a deafening roar of sparks and groaning wood. The command was broken.

"Make that one against two thousand," the rebel cried as he dashed from the blazing compound. "If I were you, I'd leave the Shalkans to wallow in their loss, but let's avoid becoming victims of the Shalkan reinforcements, shall we?"

Lowering his sword, Ree cast a yearning look at the warriors; how his sword ached to penetrate their armor and dig into their flesh! He kicked violently at a piece of smoldering wood, stalled, and then ran from the fort. The other rebel jogged ahead lightly, waiting for Ree to join him. Ree scowled; he did not like to be predicted.

"Where's your unit, rebel?" he asked disgustedly.

"Where's yours?" the stranger asked affably before supplying the obvious answer. "Probably dead with the rest of mine."

Ree knew he was right. The anger burned to the zenith of its ability and then drowned itself in a void. Ree felt nothing. The rebel continued amiably.

"Destroying a Shalkan fort is no small feat. We're lucky to survive."

"Surviving without honor and at the expense of our troops is no feat," Ree added dryly. "Give me your name." He looked straight ahead as he ran.

"Corious." The jungle swallowed them.

When the smoke no longer singed the insides of their nostrils, Ree coldly offered his name. The coldness emanated from the blankness. Ree vaguely heard as Corious suggested setting up camp. He scorned the suggestion. Breaking for camp was as crucial as it was abhorred. It never granted the luxury of sleep; only constant movement would save the runner from chance bullets. If weary limbs refused to move, the woods became perilous.

The jungle's eerie branches blocked their path. Corious stalled, uncertain. Ree hesitated before exposing several inches of his sword, but a resounding crash abrogated the decision. Corious hurriedly squirmed up a tree; Ree remained crouched and ready in the underbrush.

"There are four officials coming this way," Corious whispered into the twilight.

Ree squinted into the settling night; nothing but the maroon shadows of leaves entered his vision. They would not fight officials by night.

Morbid creatures, yes. Assassins and trackers fringed by the nimbus of their cruel hunger; things with gangrene fingers and accusing slits of eyes. Things with lying lips glued to stiff bodies exhumed from fresh graves.

They do not abide by the rules of nature. They do not belong. Their presence: heavy rocks tied about my waist, my wrist, my eyes...all of them pulling, straining, demanding, and hoping to knock me off course. How long will I last?

Sitting pensively, Shrie balanced herself skillfully in the hollow between the spiraling tree branch and its sturdy trunk. Beneath her fingertips, stately tree limbs arched like flying buttresses fanning to support the tall expanse of sky. Gazing into the stained glass windows of rustling leaves, Shrie tossed a small, red berry into the air and caught it delicately in her mouth. With her front teeth, she lightly pierced the thin skin, and the viscous juice, now freed from the cage of the berry's exterior, rolled merrily down her throat. She let her tongue explore the curved roof of her mouth. When no sweet taste of the berry remained, her disappointed tongue relaxed against the center of her jaw.

Many moons had waned and waxed in the navy sky, and tonight marked the date of her last encounter with the men who were neither alive nor dead and who obeyed and loved nothing more than their desire to slaughter. Flawless, clear skin wrapped around their faces like the preserved and unblemished bandages of a mummy, and like a mummy their bodies stank of rotting flesh. Shadows from their helmets cast black sheets across their faces. Shrie saw them for who they were, and their discordant song loomed over the jungle in distorted harmony.

Their ghoulish faces ferried her across the streams of time...

The men marched ahead steadily; their comfortable pace made them easy to track. Foam and vile anathemas bubbled from the sides of their mouths. A pestilence that swarmed its host with plagues, shadows of darkness had replaced their minds. Hovering in the trees above them, Shrie positioned her bow. Should she taint her arrow with their blood? They deserved to be hung from a cliff, to endure an eternal, promethean punishment, but compassion restrained her. They formed a ragged semicircle, and a small, black ball of fur lay before them, squealing in fear. Her fingers did not release. A dark man heaved mightily and swung with a shining blade. The sword hacked into the hatchling's back, and it cried for its mother as blood leaked from its head. Her head hung in shame, but the howling of the tormented lifted her chin until certainty filled her downcast eyes. She would redeem her wrong. Brimming with anger, Shrie loosed an arrow.

The Mali's blood spilt in her mind, and the red berry stains on her fingers sealed the memory. Sunlight glimmered on the surface of the leaves, and Shrie allowed herself to fall into its rocking, sweeping trance. She permitted herself to temporarily escape the horror of the recollection. In her trance, Shrie could see the old myths twirling in the jungle vines and awakening the woods with their ancient words of knowledge. The legends found their refuge and delight in the shifting curves of trees and rivers. But now the forest's song sounded seldom. The wood had retreated into its silence, and it would tell Shrie nothing of this new calamity.

Stretching a cramped leg, Shrie felt the muscle pull happily. The leaves crackled, as though stirred by some mischievous intention. No birds had announced an arrival, but Shrie sat straight, her ears trained. Her instincts told her to investigate.

Leaping from her tree to the next in perfect silence, she heard again the rustling. It was not the quiet disturbance of animal paws nearby but rather the muffled crashing of feet from afar. She strained to see. Peeping above a supple branch, Shrie saw an expanse of swamp unfolding before her. Two spots ran swiftly through the lagoon, parting the reeds and leaving unsightly, muddy tracks in their wake. Burdened with supplies, their strides were long and heavy. *He was running to her, his sweat mixed with the drenching rain. The cobalt night could not hide his pulchritude—his intelligent eyes sparkling with the knowledge of her, his lips firm but soft like ripe fruit, his long fingers sure and able.* They pushed their tall, muscular bodies tirelessly through the underbrush. *The touch of the tips of his fingers on her jaw stilled her, and her eyes on her upturned face closed in ecstasy. His beautiful lips pressed briefly against hers; her entire body tingled.* The usual garb of the dark men did not decorate their beings, and Shrie's curiosity was piqued. She climbed until the leagues of land fled from her range of vision.

A strict triangle of dark figures gained on the fleeing men before them. A rush of adrenaline seeped through her body. The chase and the fight to survive never ceased to thrill her. Today she would consolidate her power as ruler of the forest; and any enemy of the dark men was a friend of hers.

With a nearby vine, she swung herself across a small brook. If she hurried, she would be able to head them off. Sliding through the branches like a fish through water, she covered the distance with an unnatural speed. *"We are one."* She would not be able to outrun him or the pain. He was with her; he would always be with her. Tumbling from the last swing, she leapt and readied her bow. Less than twenty feet from her, the figures pounded forward without recognition or concern for her presence. She kept her ground. No one went past her without questioning.

"You enemy or friend?" she called harshly. The first one slowed to a stop. A dazed and determined expression swirled on his surface features. The second continued to run. So he underestimated her, did he? She let go of an arrow, and he ducked, just in time.

"When the wicked rise to power, people go into hiding;
but when the wicked perish, the righteous thrive."
Proverbs 28:28

Chapter 3

Corious raced through the tall weeds and brush. His companion, Ree, was a stride in front of him. His breath came in rushed flows, and his fingers trembled visibly. He prepared to nock his last arrow to the bow. It was not his arrow, but that did not matter. It was an arrow, even if it smelled of the dead official from whom he had yanked it.

The sabotage on the officials' headquarters had ended in disaster, though the compound had been destroyed. The officials had flanked them, a move the rebels had not expected and that had cost them dearly. Now, cut off from the others, Corious's entire mind was bent on escaping alive. He prayed desperately Ree knew what he was doing. As Corious sprinted ahead, Ree stalled.

"Move," Corious yelled. Ree did not budge, and as Corious neared, he noticed, without true comprehension, that a form blocked his companion's path.

"You enemy or friend?" the figure cried furiously.

Corious did not slow his pace. The strings of the bow relaxed. His chin snapped backwards as the arrow narrowly missed his face. He and Ree were trapped. The vine-clad figure lifted a hand branded with the Shalkan mark. She was their enemy. *She?* He shouldered his way past Ree and inspected their attacker closely; yes, the shape formed was that of a woman's. The shock reverberated up and down his spine. He had not seen a woman since leaving the port of Icostad five months ago.

She was a slight creature, but rather muscular from years of living in the forest. Thin arms held an arrow staunch and steady on the string, and large eyes questioned them. She kept her curtain of wavy black hair tied back from her face with a scrap of leather that matched her rather primitive clothing. Her feet were planted firmly, as though they were the roots of a tree. She glanced at them impatiently.

The appearance seemed somewhat familiar to him—the slightly pointed ears and the determined brow—but that was nonsense; he had never seen forest folk before. Often rebels passed stories around camps of allies hidden in the wood, but the tales, the results of vain hopes, had always died. Corious began to wonder how in vain they had been.

Ree gawked before spitting out words which were incoherent even to Corious. He attempted to push the arrow's point from his forehead.

"Who are you? You trespass into Shrie's wood," the girl said flatly. Ree sneered imperiously before remembering he was the one with the arrow trained on his forehead.

"Shrie is ruler of forest and an enemy of dark men." She paused, unsure of how to offer an alliance. Her question came out, "Shrie like you?"

Corious recovered from the reverie first, his fear forcing him to speak. They did not have much time before the officials found them. Negotiations would have to be brief. "Yes, Shrie like us," he said. Then nervously looking over his shoulder he added, "The officials are close. Can you help us?"

Shrie suspiciously stepped forward. It appeared she either did not understand them or did not feel like responding to his plea. Corious glanced at Ree who shrugged helplessly. Boots pounded the earth menacingly. Shrie lowered her bow. Grabbing Ree's arm, she led them from the path. Corious sighed in relief, praying they were not too late.

We will run forever, Corious thought numbly. *I may die, but I will never stop running.* They careened deeper into the forest, passing palm leaves the size of his face, slithering past ominous, red trees, and swinging through the green jungle air on vines as solid as his forearm. None of the surroundings appeared familiar. Or maybe everything appeared the same.

Shrie finally slowed near a steep embankment. Multitudes of skeletal arms sprouted from a vine, anchoring it to the rock's face. She tested the vine's stability. Pleased with the results, she began to climb. Corious wrapped his calloused hands about a similar creeping plant, tugged on it, and then spat when it flew from its mooring on a loose rock. He tried another, found it sturdy, and allowed his eyes to follow its path up the overhang. Suppressing all thoughts of doubt, he shimmied up the vine. Willing himself to ignore the bits of loose vegetation and rocks which Ree's climbing feet knocked from the earth, Corious let his mind slowly shield his nerves from the dangerous distractions.

Reaching the top with sweat sliding off his forehead, he swung one leg over the edge before the other followed aptly. After taking several, drawn breaths in a prostrate position, he rose when Shrie's hand clasped his sleeve like a hawk clutching its prey. She led him and Ree on what appeared to be a path. Corious would never have noticed it if not for her occasional glances at the ground. Searching for the signs she evidently sought, Corious began to see the outline of odd tracks ruffling the dirt and brush. At a certain fork in the trail, Shrie tumbled onto her hands and knees and then slid on her stomach, moving as an earthworm furrows through the ground.

The men wound their way less easily, stooping beneath jutting mounds of earth and overgrown, drooping plants. Eventually, they too were reduced to crawling on their stomachs. They passed through broad areas of flaccid marsh weeds before finally finding themselves in a dry, sequestered overhang where they caught their breaths. Shrie waited for them to speak.

"We lost the officials," Corious offered. Shrie blinked; it was not what she had expected him to say. Corious bent his head. Letting the obscurity of the meeting settle into normalcy, Corious struggled to find something to say, but no words came to mind. Corious looked to Ree hopefully. Ree cleared his throat and pushed back hard on the cuticle of his right thumb. With what seemed like an enormous amount of energy, Ree sat cross-legged on the ground and placed his weapons next to him protectively; he honored and cared for the items which would guard him in turn. Shrie extended an inquisitive hand to touch them, but then thought better of it. A warrior's weapons were his life, and his alone.

Verbalizing Shrie's thoughts, Ree proclaimed in monotone, "I am a warrior. I fight on behalf of the rebels. I have no home, nor do I need one. My allies are my strength—my foes the officials."

Shrie cocked her head slightly. "Who officials? And who boy sitting next to you?"

Corious rose to protest being called a boy, but Ree abruptly pulled him back down. Shrie was the third presence which united the two men.

"This is Corious. You will respect him."

Corious folded his arms and responded gravely, "Yes, you will respect me." Shrie turned back to Ree; she did not take Corious's comment seriously.

"Who officials?"

"The men we are fighting. They are sometimes called the Shalkans. They were the ones chasing us," he said in a steely voice. "I plan to kill every one that comes into my sight."

"Shrie no like these dark men who chase you. They are invaders of the forests. What you know about them?" The question came urgently, almost desperately.

Ree suddenly realized that he knew no more than what he had said. He had lived his entire life in the barracks, training to battle the officials. The enemy had threatened the small remembrance of a home he had known. When they had killed his family, Ree killed them back. Now he spent the rest of his life hunting them. He had no other reason.

"Is no good—this hate. Righteous anger, yes, but no hate—else you be like them." Shrie's eyes held sympathy, as if she had read his thoughts. Ree saw the pity and abhorred it. He did not want or need pity.

"It is time we leave. Come, Corious." He took his eyes from Shrie's face.

Corious did not rise. Shrie, no matter how offending, was a potential ally. "I believe it well to stay until the officials pass."

Ree sat silently in momentary defeat, though he avoided Shrie's gaze. Shrie turned to Corious expectantly.

"So," Corious cleared his throat gruffly. He felt it was his responsibility to ease the tension. "I met Ree a few days ago. I was raised by a blacksmith but never fully took on that trade. Men were needed to help fight the Shalkans during the attacks. I was transferred to this band of rebels, as we call ourselves, and have been doing my duty ever since." Shrie did not respond, so he prompted, "And you?"

"Shrie rules and defends the forest."

The conversation ended. Shrie sharpened the tip of an arrow shaft, and Corious watched listlessly. The markings on the arrow were distinct; gold, red, and white triangles marched along the shaft, fading into the feathers which sprung lithely from the end. Blinking, Corious reached into his quiver to retrieve the hoarded arrow. The markings were identical. Corious tossed her the arrow. She caught it readily. With a funny gleam in her eye, she shifted her gaze from the arrow and locked her eyes on his. In that moment, Corious knew something had transpired between them. Shrie opened her mouth as though about to speak, closed it, and then simply tossed the arrow back to Corious.

"Keep arrow; you might need it," she said eyeing his empty quiver.

Corious thankfully fingered the lone arrow. Shrie glanced at Ree, as if deciding whether or not he deserved one of her prizes. When Corious encouraged her with a smile, she relented and tossed Ree one.

"I don't use the bow," Ree said, "but I accept." Shrie showed her approval with a tight smile, but a wave of nausea swept over Ree; unease gripped his sides. "Shrie, I need to talk with Corious for a moment."

The jungle maiden motioned them outside. Beyond the small shelter, Ree spoke, until he noticed Shrie watching them. Annoyed, Ree took several steps to distance himself from her.

"I don't know if I like this, Corious. I think she thinks that we've made some sort of permanent alliance with her."

"Haven't we?"

"See, that's just the problem. We don't necessarily want that," Ree said stonily. "She'll slow us down. How are we supposed to return to our unit with her?" he caviled.

Corious quieted. "Who said we have a unit left alive? Or even if we did, why do we have to return? The unit could be anywhere."

"I like order, Corious," Ree's voice rose and teetered on the edge of lost control. "I strive for complete regulation. This situation was unpredictable."

"And fortunate." Corious folded his arms across his chest. "She led us away from the officials and is obviously proficient with the bow."

"How long do we plan on staying then? How do we deal with her?"

"I don't know." Corious shrugged. "Ever have any sisters?"

"No. Did you?"

"No. Well, okay," Corious blundered, "we'll just treat her like a fellow soldier."

"She's a woman."

"She's a fighter. I wouldn't want to come to blows with her."

Ree frowned. "Fine, but how long do we stay? Why would we stay?"

"Look, we both agree it's not a good idea to bring her back to the mangled men who comprise our unit. We shouldn't violate her trust either. Where there's one, there's got to be more. A tribe, maybe."

"Maybe there was once a jungle people," Ree said dismally, "but if so, they have diminished. She appears to be alone."

"We could still recruit her help. We could form our own, independent unit. There are lots of rebels who lived in the wilderness. They were, and are, indisputably the best fighters."

Ree shook his head. "We will stay for awhile and continue to pursue our attackers, biding some time until we collect more information. Until then, we should strike a more concrete deal with her—not one based on furtive glances and indistinct promises." Not waiting for Corious to agree, he stalked back under the overhang as the sky began to darken.

Ree sat in front of Shrie, laying out his ideas which were presented as suggestions but meant to be finalities. Corious followed the serpentine conversation as it wound through differences in dialect and thrashed out the terms demanded by two very obstinate people. To avoid the brunt of the verbal conflict, Corious only occasionally contributed his point of view despite the fact that it was generally and hurriedly dismissed. Without his help, they reached a consensus by midday. Shrie was to hide them and provide for them if they were to drive the evil from her forest. The pact seemed more than fair to Ree and Corious, but perhaps the gods of the sky frowned upon it, for as soon as the lengthy exchange had achieved a sense of resolution, a light breeze carrying rain made the conditions less than appealing.

For the majority of the night, they trekked along the sloppy banks of a halcyon stream spilling slowly onto its banks. Corious's legs felt like a rusted piece of metal straining against the inevitable snap. Shrie dropped back with the hurting Corious, attempting to entertain his exhausted mind with an animated discussion about forest life. Her monologue continued into the night without question or response from her one man audience, and the silence eventually prodded her to pose a most unfavorable question.

"Are you listening?"

Corious, almost asleep, had to give the wrong answer. "You were—talking to me?"

Shrie slapped a hand to her forehead like a true thespian and shook her head of raven hair. "You not listen about Mali-Malis or Snake Land?"

"Mmh, how far is it to your—hut?" Corious said, trying to ease into another line of conversation. Surprisingly, his tactic worked.

"What hut? Shrie have no hut. Where you come from anyway?"

Corious raised an eyebrow and slowly replied, "I reside anywhere the officials are not. I live in abandoned places; sometimes, I am with my rebel unit."

"What 'abandoned' mean?"

Ree, who by this point had slowed his pace in order to walk beside them, answered Shrie's question. "Abandoned means vacant, or not lived in." Ree gazed questionably at Corious.

Corious put a rough hand on Shrie's bare shoulder. "Where are we going to stay tonight?"

Shrie frowned and scanned the horizon like an anxious sailor seeking land. She finally said, "We stay here." As if to show it, she stuck her walking stick blithely into the slushy mud, sending splatters raining down upon them. Shrie enjoyed the mud shower, and her ebullient smile revealed a beautiful row of slightly uneven, white teeth. "We make fern beds and sleep under forest canopy!"

"Where officials?" Ree said thickly, taking on Shrie's broken English. His question blotted out her brief moment of joy.

She bowed her head. "Dark men here tomorrow. The evil things arrive tomorrow."

Ree pursed his lips in thought before gathering ferns and concealing his weapons and loose equipment under the ungainly brush.

"Sleep. We fight tomorrow," Ree said dryly.

That's it? Corious could not help but feel cheated. They had suffered together and shared an inexpressible bond. A yellow in sunlight and purple in shadow striped landscape stretched before him in an eternally alternating pattern. Days ago, Shrie had slunk through this mercurial landscape without another human in whom she could confide. Days ago, Corious had never slept freely under the forest sky. Days ago, Ree had maintained almost as many human connections as Shrie had. *Nothing like the threat of death to connect people,* he joked to himself before feeling foolish. He felt awkward accepting the peace, tenuous as it was, suspended above the trio like a filmy spider web. *I must not get comfortable or complacent.* Corious repeated the deadening, barrack rhetoric until he smiled despite it and lay facedown on the ferns.

"Good night, Ree—you, too, Shrie." He received no reply from his left where Ree now slept, but Shrie was another story.

"What that weapon you carry?" Shrie wondered aloud to Corious. She had taken his goodnight wish as an invitation to talk.

"Shrie, good night."

"Oh, good night, Corious," Shrie responded with a hint of frustration. Corious grinned though her comical character was far from intentional. Happily, he gazed at the stars. He recognized none of the ethereal shapes and patterns formed by the white pinpricks of light, but the foreign sky did not alarm him. Merely living to see the sky filled him with an inexplicable joy. Settling into the ferns, he fell asleep with his head propped atop an arm and with the scent of crushed flower petals stirring in his nostrils.

Corious woke with the rising sun, wiped the back of his hands against his eyes, and yawned like a lion awaking from its glorious slumber. He glanced over his right shoulder at Shrie; her body, wonderfully at home in the wilderness, lay sprawled immodestly across a patch of ground. Paces away, Ree sharpened his hatchet blade mindlessly while cooking something over two Y-shaped sticks and a small fire. Corious nodded in greeting before extricating his equipment from a bush and squatting to pull it on. Crusty, brown seeds scratched the corners of his eyes; sleep hung about him like a robe. Jogging to the stream bank, he splashed the placid river water over his face and arms. His cheeks woke immediately, and his hands shook slightly from the cold surprise as he returned to camp.

Shrie had since awoken and sauntered into the woods to find her own breakfast, but not before regarding Ree's food with disgust. She had not hesitated to profess its hideous appearance. In retaliation, Ree had stared at her blankly, shoving a huge spoonful of the goop into his mouth and letting it drip priggishly down his chin. Corious shook his head, and a droplet of water plopped into Ree's soup.

"Mind if I have some?" he asked pointing to the slop Ree currently devoured.

Ree's eyes barely appeared above the bowl to give his approval, and they ate in an undisturbed silence. As Corious shoved a third bite into his famished mouth, a shrill cry pierced the air. Instinctively, Corious and Ree dropped their food, grabbed their weapons, and dashed toward the noise.

Shrie finished her breakfast of berries as the tenebrous shadows dashed beneath her. She would have missed their presence entirely had she not peered forward and seen the unwelcome glint of Shalkan weapons through the branches. As her hands found a ripe fruit, they dropped it, and her eyes watched with interest as it splattered on the shoulder of an unwary soldier. The force of the unexpected blow prostrated him, and a loud, distressed grunt issued from his mouth. The rest of the party turned, and with a strident battle cry, Shrie dove into the heaving masses below her.

Swords drawn, Ree and Corious appeared seconds later. Charging a tree, Ree planted his foot on its trunk and catapulted his powerful body backwards. Using his momentum, he clothes-lined two officials with his unyielding arms. Corious wrestled another into the river. In his peripheral vision, an official lunged ineptly for Ree.

With the warning cry from Corious, Ree had enough time to thrust his dagger into the enemy's leg and push the bloody body away from his untouched one.

Corious, cornered against a wall of foliage, began to suffocate in a rush of fear as two snarling officials leapt from their positions of skulking into ones of fighting. Ree rushed towards Corious, throwing the attackers into the barbed hedge of vegetation.

An unscathed official placed his lips against his trumpet in one last kiss before slumping over with Shrie's arrow in his back. He would not be allowed to sound a last call. Shrie yanked her unforgiving arrow from the dead man's back.

"Run, Ree," Corious shouted as he took off a step ahead of him. Shrie had been right: the Shalkans had come, and no one knew how close the others were. His unprotected leg stung where an official's steel-toed boot had kicked the skin raw. Corious jumped, grabbed a vine, and swung across the river, landing heavily on his back and drenching his right pant leg in the water. His head spun woozily. A weight shifted in circles behind his eyes; he winced but stood, gasping in painfully short breaths. Ree and Shrie were already far ahead, and to avoid meeting the Shalkans by himself, he would have to put his pain aside. Pulling his feet from the soggy jungle floor, he darted after Ree's fading form.

Shrie mumbled distractedly to herself. Her timing had been off; the dark men were moving quickly. *At least Corious and Ree fought well. In battle they moved swiftly and surely, but Corious is taller, moves with more agility, and is crowned with lighter hair.* He was also younger, though perhaps less impulsive. Contrasting the hard mien which habitually enveloped Ree's craggy face, his wavy hair was cropped loosely over a headband. His sharp chin lines, brown eyes, and strong physique brought the past colliding with the present; he resembled someone she had known well before. A set of footsteps approached her.

"Where are we going?" Corious asked in exasperation.

"To new location," she said.

"I left some of my stuff," Corious protested weakly.

Shrie slowed to a walk. "What you leave?"

"The cooking materials from our survival packs."

"Good," Shrie said firmly and with relief, "now you not eat food that look like animal droppings. Come, we keep going, but we walk now. It takes three weeks to get to safe spot. There other places to stop along the way. The first one we reach after nightfall, so we construct a shelter for tonight."

"Why do we need a safe spot?" Ree questioned.

"To prove as temporary," Shrie fumbled for the right word, "to use as temporary base of operations. We fight dark men, no?"

No one disagreed.

As they traveled, a varying routine established itself. Every morning, Shrie would wake first and dutifully make breakfast. Corious and Ree would spar before accompanying Shrie on her daily hunts. If they had a bad hunt and a dinner's worth of time to pass, Corious or Ree would try to teach Shrie the finer grammatical points of their language or Shrie would enlighten them with the properties of various plants and fruits. After lunch, they would travel to the next location, usually reaching it by dusk. Conversation was generally maintained; rarely, the three reverted to silence when Shrie deemed it necessary or when there was simply nothing left to say.

Shrie once broke such a still moment by plucking a small leaf off a plant, holding it reverently before her, and announcing, "If you eat this, you will become an outhouse." Her comment remained one of the few that could squeeze a drop of mirth from Ree.

Over the course of several days, they encountered no officials, and after the first week, Corious gradually eased from paranoia to apathy. It was something he would hesitate to do again. Five days into the third week of travel, Shrie calmly but abruptly squatted, loading her bow. Alert, but hearing nothing, Corious had not been prepared for the clash of Ree's sword above his head. An icy terror froze Corious into perfect stillness. Ree's wrath halted the officials momentarily while Corious regained his composure. Determined to reach a status quo antebellum, they thrashed the callow enemy in a flurry of furious blows. The officials fell like blades of grass beneath their swords.

The attack had consisted of ten officials, all of whom now lay motionless on the ground. Conveniently, Ree had made defending his fellow rebel second nature, if only for the practical reason of keeping sheer number on the rebels' side. Corious was particularly impressed by his skill tattooed in the red streaks and slashes decorating the arms and breasts of the enemy. Smugly surveying their quick work, Corious gave Ree a vicious slap on the back as Shrie cast him a disappointed look.

"What?" he asked indignantly.

"An official escaped." She sourly kicked at the ground. Corious's pride refused to melt. Counting the bodies, he got to eight when Shrie released an anguished cry.

"He alerts other dark men!"

As if on cue, the sound of a trumpet rang clearly throughout the woods. Pursing his lips in fleeting thought, Corious sheathed his sword and jolted into a jerky run. Behind him, Ree pushed Corious forward with a sarcastic, congratulatory pat on the back. Shrie pulled ahead, and they continued until she gave the signal, diving into leafy brush. Ree and Corious swam through the green leaves after her. Unable to see much past the hand that held back the greenery, they collided with Shrie and stumbled haphazardly into the hidden niche. Cramped against the others, Ree was relieved to hear his breathing was not the sole one to be released heavily. Their bodies stuck together with sweat, and the hiding spot grew steamy. Shrie squirmed to get comfortable. The officials approached. Surreptitiously and with difficulty, Ree unsheathed his sword. The others were squeezed together against his chest, making any movement arduous; he did not know how long he could last. Suspense and raw nerves were teased as the dark men marched feet away, sedulously searching for the rebels' tracks.

Ree focused on the object closest to him; he did not want to attract the enemy with a blatant stare. Gossamer strings of spider webs spread before him. Sparkling with dew, they barely retained their tenuous holds to the dark bark. The spider was not in sight. Corious clenched his sword. His resistance was failing as the urge to swing at the passing boots seized him. A muscle jumped in his arm, but Shrie pressed her shoulder firmly against his upper arm, forcing him to remain immobile. Corious swallowed the desire to attack, but each second dragged; there was no break in the marching rhythm. It was an impressive display of power, and when it finally passed, Ree gently shoved Shrie and Corious off him. Sucking in a deep breath of air, he crawled from hiding.

"How do you do that?" he demanded, directing his brusque question at Shrie.

"Do what?" Shrie stretched her legs.

"You can detect the dark men before us. How?"

Shrie seemed confused. "You not feel presence of dark men?" she questioned affably.

Her nonchalance perturbed him. "No, I do not feel the presence of dark men." His eyes narrowed, absorbing Shrie's arched eyebrows and slightly slanted eyes. He could find no explanation for her prescient insight.

Her mouth moved slowly as she attempted to elucidate. "Shrie feel shadows when dark men are near; she hear their song."

"That could be useful," Corious concluded after contemplating the benefits of building an inner, defensive warning system. When Shrie offered no additional details, he decided there was nothing more to be gleaned.

Sitting back down, Shrie smiled. "This nice place to make camp."

Ree followed her gaze into the tall trees of the jungle. Like stalwart soldiers, they poised firmly against the sky. Leaves exploded to meet the azure sky, and birds chirped without concern. The area exuded a peace Ree did not trust. He stirred restlessly.

"We should keep moving. The officials are ahead of us. Now is a good time to throw them off track."

"Safe place is not as beautiful," she lamented, standing.

Corious rolled his eyes. "But it would be safe."

"We fight dark men from here," Shrie said hopefully.

"It's in the middle of the woods with no protection!"

"Fine," she acquiesced reluctantly, "but Shrie warn you. She not been to safe place in long time. Is in a cave," she added with a touch of awe. "Maybe cave has new creatures in it."

"Then those occupants will have to be removed." Corious twirled his sword in the air. "Where is this cave?" He strode next to Shrie.

"Is by Great River. Shrie say we attack dark men entering Shrie's forest by River. Shrie not know another way dark men enter. She thinks they come in by night, from the north."

"The north," Ree repeated. "So they advance into our realm."

Shrie smiled sadly. "Tribe has gone west."

Something about her sentence sparked a memory. "Your tribe?"

Shrie snapped out of her slight daze and shook her head ruefully. "No, no tribe, now."

"Sorry," Corious offered lamely. The wheels of thought slowed in disappointment. Shrie appeared to be their sole forest ally. As they trekked in a new direction to refill their water canisters, Corious was unable to suppress his curiosity and continued to probe.

"Why are you the only one left?" he asked, not without commiseration.

"The legends demanded it." Her words were tight, as though she would not let more escape from her mouth.

"What legends?" Ree queried.

Waving her hand in the air, Shrie grew frustrated as the words would not come to her. "Legends…ancient history of Shrie's wood…tribe leader…" Flinging down her disheartened hand, she refused to talk the rest of the day. Ree later chastised Corious for pushing the matter.

"She will talk when she is ready. Besides, we did not offer the stories of our unabridged pasts."

"There isn't much to tell," Corious expostulated. "Her information, on the other hand, could prove valuable."

"False. We only believe our past does not matter because we do not wish to remember it. Don't forget it though, Corious," was Ree's caveat. "Use it to propel yourself forward." During his speech, Ree found himself gripping Corious's arm. Corious wrenched his limb from Ree's grip.

"Let's get something straight, Ree. I do not know much about you except for what I've seen in our short time together in the unit. Either way, rebels never talk about their past; they study the present moment to survive it and fight their way to the next."

"Well maybe that system ought to change, Corious. I'm tired of fighting for revenge; I need a purpose greater than that. Shrie possesses a reason to live. If I am blind to all else, I recognize that. I want to be more than just a rebel. A rebel, hah! That makes us sound like insurgent men who love anarchy."

"Like it or not, Ree, that is what we are, or have become. We lack order and fight like animals for anything we can get," Corious continued bitterly, "and who can blame us?"

The air thickened as their wills clashed tangibly. The tension broke when Shrie's voice called to them. Both relaxed. For some reason the moment ended without residual emotion. The taboo topic had been broached. Corious knew Ree's statements contained certain elements of truth. He would watch Shrie carefully. There was something about her that fascinated him, and he could not quite place it.

Hunkering by an enclave of soaring rocks, Corious and Ree discussed the finer points of battle and swordsmanship. A densely woven roof of vines barred the rainy night from eavesdropping on their conversation. It was the horizontal barrier that cut them off from the world, and from Shrie. Despite the weather, she would sleep in the trees above them, as she usually did. Corious had asked if she had ever fallen from her tree abode and had been answered with an inscrutable expression. Somehow nature seemed to keep her drier and more rested than the two men who relied on their sturdy shelter.

Morning rays pierced the camp far too soon for Corious's pleasure. The enveloping comfort of night shrunk from the laughing patterns of light which danced over his clothes and face. Waking, the rebel rubbed his eyes and managed to stumble from the encampment without waking Ree. A thick mist muffled the dull, gray sky and wrapped Corious in an ethereal, white blanket.

"I am a caterpillar in my cocoon," he muttered to himself with a chuckle. As he began throwing dirt over the remains of the fire, Shrie dropped from her tree with an obnoxious yawn and greeted him cheerily.

"Morning, Corious. We go hunting."

Loading his bow, Corious trudged through the forest behind her. At a small scuffling noise, Shrie's ears perked, and she swiveled to locate the origin. Eyeing a small rodent-like animal within the embrace of a tree, she and Corious released their arrows simultaneously. Shrie's arrow hit the target, and Corious's whizzed over hers, less than an inch off target.

Upon returning with his retrieved arrow, Corious found Shrie gone. With a sigh, he made the arbitrary decision to peruse the perimeter of the camp; though he wished to explore the jungle, he did not wish to lose his bearings. After finally shooting a small, ugly bird, he gave up the hunt with the intrinsic knowledge that Shrie had fared far better. The closer he came to the camp, the more tantalizing her breakfast smelled. He considered dismally the pathetic prey he had caught, stuffing it in a small bag. *Who knows if it is even edible?* Something stirred in the underbrush. Blinking away the image, Corious slowed his feet and focused his vision. Through the haze of distance, Corious saw Ree point at what appeared to be a cyclopean spider. As he neared, he could hear Shrie's broken English and Ree's shaky voice.

"How big do Mali-Malis get?"

"This one is very small," Shrie replied in an erudite manner.

Corious placed an iron hold on his stomach; the largest animal in his vocabulary was a horse, which paled in comparison to this jungle brute. Corious felt the gaze of the creature's beady, black eyes on his face. Ree turned slightly pale and frowned.

Corious blanched. *Gross. The fangs would be...* Corious shuddered and edged his way towards Shrie and Ree; he did not want to attract any unneeded attention from the spider.

Shrie turned and addressed him. "Hello, Corious." Then, noticing his bag, she grabbed it from him deftly. Peering inside eagerly, she seemed pleased with its pitiful contents and tossed the scrawny bird in the air towards the spider.

"The Kwaka is the only animal the Mali-Mali eats," she announced excitedly after the demonstration.

"Sure," Corious responded weakly, trying not to be sick as the Mali tore the bird to shreds. Sounds issuing from the waking jungle reminded him of their immediate peril. "Should we not be concerned about the officials?" he asked gruffly.

"Yes, we be concerned." She mused about this for a moment and then called the Mali-Mali to her, as Ree and Corious backed away cautiously. Ree drew his sword, and Shrie literally attacked him in a rage. Flinging herself upon him, Shrie vigorously knocked the sword from his hand as the spider began to rise gradually, swaying and chanting. Corious's mouth relaxed into an oval at the surreal scene unfolding before him.

"You upset Mali," Shrie hissed. "Malis no like fighting. Sword upset him." Shrie pointed to the sword on the ground. After allowing Ree to get back up, she uttered several, crisp words to the Mali-Mali in a strange language. The creature disappeared into the foliage.

Ree took a deep breath. "What did you do?"

"Mali explore situation and warn us if danger be here. We rest now from yesterday's battle."

"That is wise," Ree responded, "but we should move camp."

Shrie shrugged. "Dark men will expect us to do that."

Corious was not impressed with Shrie's tactics and countered, "That is if the dark men know where we are. I doubt they do."

"This is exactly why we should bunker somewhere near here until we know more," Ree said, acknowledging the merit of Shrie's idea. Corious grumbled in protest as Shrie flung dirt in every conceivable direction, hiding the remnants of their camp in chaos. Ree and Corious helped move the shelter to a more secluded area, avoiding the flying soil. When they finished, the camp oozed of desolation.

Corious considered conversing with Shrie about the forest. *I should have listened the first time...* The sight of the giant spider still unnerved him, proving his ignorance of the forest's anatomy. The eyes and fangs stared at him from the corner of his mind, and suddenly he wondered how much he actually wanted to know. Phobias are slow to leave a person. Using his forearm to wipe off the sweat from his brow, Corious rejected any further questioning of Shrie and instead sought Ree's company at the edge of the camp.

As he walked closer, Corious discerned Ree dismembering what remained of an old tent. Mechanically, Corious reached out to stop him; tents were luxuries the rebels did not often see. Ree paused in his work and answered the question already forming on his comrade's lips.

"Shrie wanted it done." Ree paused dramatically. "She said she needed the cloth."

Infuriated, Corious lifted the humble remains of the tent and tenderly attempted to put them back together. Ree crossed his arms and watched, amused by his friend's futile attempts to repair the mangled wood and cloth.

Corious finally threw the thing to the ground. "What does she need it for anyway? A dress?"

Ree smothered a small smile as it began to play on the corners his mouth. He took the cloth and held it out to the sun.

"This is to be used in the making of hammocks," he said dryly.

"Hammocks?" Corious shouted incredulously. "We have no need of hammocks! We sleep on the ground to avoid detection! Why in God's name are we flying our wanted bodies high in the sky for any official to effortlessly pick off?"

The smile that had tried to show itself finally crept onto Ree's face.

"Shrie has found us a cavern in which we may, for the time, inhabit. She insists it is very similar to the safe place. In my opinion, it is the safe place, only she forgot so. It runs underground, and there it will be quite safe to sleep in a hammock, away from the inevitable rats and slime that abide together on a cave floor."

"A cave then, eh? Where would its entrance lie?" he asked, scanning the area and kicking aside the foliage. His foot connected with something solid, which happened to be Shrie's head emerging from a concealed hole. She yelped and grabbed his foot, using it to pull herself over the undergrowth. Corious danced on one foot to keep his balance while Ree stood motionless, watching.

"My apologies," Corious stammered in surprise as Shrie released her grip on his foot and scrambled to her feet.

Shrie grunted, smoothed her excited hair, and gave him a toothy grin.

"You did not expect me there!" she exclaimed in enthusiasm. Her cave was a good place to hide. Corious did not hear her; he was already on the ground, vanishing into the earth.

"Excellent! I have never seen a better…" His muffled voice trailed off, and to the world, Corious no longer existed.

Satisfied with her work, Shrie planted her hands on her hips expectantly. Ree nodded his approval before continuing his work on the mutilated tent. Shrie decided she would oversee his progress, and after a quarter of an hour, Ree completed the requested task. Handing her the mended cloth, Ree parted the grass above the cave's orifice and crawled into the entrance. Shrie glided easily through the tunnel after Ree, but he grunted in exertion. Though the entry provided a capacious amount of room for Shrie, it consisted of solidly packed dirt and stone, and there was little room for Ree's muscled bulk.

She called ahead teasingly, "You too plump for cave, Ree?"

Ree rolled his eyes and did not respond.

Shrie continued, "Too fat or too slow?"

Ree's eyebrows rose at this taunting, but he forged onward without a word.

Corious, who from his ideal spot in the cavern heard the entirety of the dialogue, called to Ree mischievously, "Shrie fancies you, Ree."

Ree snorted. "You would never know it."

"Fancy," Shrie pondered aloud, "what that mean?"

Ree ignored her. An air of humor she did not understand permeated the tunnel. Shrie longed to understand what had transpired, but instead she shrugged and went on her hands and knees as the shaft opened.

"Now there more room for you Ree," she said.

Ree sighed in relief and took his first full breath. "I do not disagree with you."

After traveling through a last section of the restricted tunnel, they came upon a cavernous opening graced with glistening rock formations dangling from the ceiling and spiraling from the floor. Light had somehow found its way into the cavern, and it painted an eerie shine on the surface of the water that dripped down the cave walls. A colossal, serene pool of turquoise water sat in the corner and wound its way deep into the back of the cave and perhaps beyond. By this pool, Corious waited for them.

Shrie spread out her arms and said decisively, "Good cave. No bats, no bad smell!"

She laid the cloth on the ground and took out a sharp rock. Cutting the strong fabric ate chunks of time, but Shrie did not mind. She would be done before nightfall. From a pile of wiry vines, she wove three, taut rectangular meshes and threw the pieces of cloth over them. Securing the ends of one hammock to two rock pillars, she tested it.

"Almost as comfortable as a tree," she stated happily. Ree and Corious looked at each other and then secured their individual hammocks. Corious hung his near Shrie's so that it faced the pool. Ree placed his not far away, slightly in the shadows. Fascinated, Shrie watched him and Corious as they unloaded their weapons and placed them wherever space permitted. Corious rolled his shoulders, enjoying how light they felt without his customary burdens. Running a hand through his sandy hair, he eyed the water and then splashed his face. In the water's reflection, Ree came over, shirt in hand.

"Going for a swim?"

"Don't think it's deep enough," Ree said regretfully, "but at least it's enough to wash and clean my clothes in."

Corious wondered when he had last washed his shirt. When he could not remember, he took it off and dunked it into the water.

Shrie said suddenly, "You two should wash. Shrie beginning to smell...ugh... bad smell! I leave." She jumped from her hammock and threw them some scraps of cloth with which they would rub off the pervasive grime settling into their skin. Corious flexed his muscles at Ree before wading into the pool's shallows. The water sparkled invitingly, mirroring Corious's bright mood. Ree sank into the cool water and let it wash the fatigue from his body. He relaxed.

Corious floated on his back in feckless wonder. The older rebel pulled his shirt over his head and waded farther into the water. The bottom slipped from his feet; the water was astonishingly deep and clear. In several strokes, Ree found himself in the middle of the radiant pool. With a scrap of cloth, he began scrubbing his arms vigorously. The perfectly reflected images of the ceiling's rock formations dissolved into tiny ripples as Ree bathed. The dirt melted into the clear water, revealing tan skin rough from weather and travel. As the mud fell away from Ree's torso, a tight, white scar bubbled from his skin, racing from his shoulder to his lower chest. Corious repressed an exclamation, but his eyes flickered to the scar involuntarily. Ree noticed his companion's reaction but did not offer an explanation. He did not need to really; Corious knew from where it came. Ree tossed Corious a rag, and Corious scoured himself energetically in turn, trying to forget the unpleasant reminder of their pasts. The water was refreshing, and they were clean. Soaking in the water, Corious washed his clothes and laid them out to dry. Minutes later, Ree walked from the pond, dried himself with his shirt, and hopped onto his hammock.

"The full moon doesn't come out until midnight," Ree commented dourly. "Shrie will return eventually. I would hate for her to catch you like that."

Corious grimaced at the thought and threw on his wet clothes uncomfortable though they were. Presently, as if called, Shrie slipped into the cave without warning or expectation. The flaccid bodies of several rodents hung over her back. Fresh fruit and an assortment of plants filled the bags secured to her waist, and in her arms, kindling and brush rested. She greeted the men briefly before skinning and cleaning the animals. She deftly cut away the fat atop the kidneys and fed it to the flames. Hanging the skins and plants with twine, Shrie freed her hands to dig the fire pit and encircle it with rocks.

As Shrie started the fire and placed the meat above the flames, the first stars climbed into the sky and lent their light through a small fissure in the cave ceiling. Stifling a yawn, she tried not to drool. The enticing smell of meat wafted to Corious who hastily rolled from his hammock and onto the floor. His clothes were wet and hot against his body.

"Food be done soon," Shrie informed him.

"Smells good."

Shrie agreed and wondered how Ree could sleep when a meal awaited him.

Removing the sticks from the fire, she handed one to Corious, took one for herself, and laid the other aside. She wrapped her teeth around the steaming food and felt the juice dribble down her chin.

"Thif if good!" Corious said while his cheeks swelled like bloated balloons. "By the way, did we ever find out where the officials moved to?"

Shrie recalled her rendezvous with the Mali. "They go northeast. Many go, but some stay to patrol nearby. Some go west to the shore."

"You said shore?" A furrow formed between his brows.

"Yes. River run into falls and falls into bigger river and bigger river to mountains and beyond."

"So the officials must have a growing navy," Corious mused, licking a piece of stray juice from the side of his face.

"Yes," Shrie said gravely, "tall boats, with black sails and worn figureheads of hideous creatures. I call them beasts, after animal of jungle."

"Animal of jungle!" Corious exclaimed with a full mouth and more than a smidgen of disquietude. The forest appeared to hold many unforeseen dangers.

"Animal of jungle," Shrie repeated, holding back another yawn. Devouring the last bites, she tossed the stick back into the fire and stretched.

"Shrie need rest," she said simply before crawling into her hammock. She fell asleep quickly, but Corious's thoughts would not allow him to slip into the dream world. He remained in a hypnagogic state, letting the story of his life sweep through his restless mind. So many things had transpired so quickly. *Where will we go next?* Shrie's questions about the officials bothered him. *From where exactly do the officials come? Why do they wish to conquer the forest?* Strategically, at least as far as he knew, the woods held no value. The official presence was as unexplained as it was unwelcome. *If I cannot logically elucidate their purpose, then how do I know I'm right? What if my standards are the ones which are incorrect?* The absolutes by which he had lived his life began to dissolve in the waters of useless pondering. The constant ebb and flow of thought eventually coaxed him into a deep but troubled sleep.

In the morning, by the dying fire, Shrie found him slumped with his head in one hand and his half-eaten meat stick in the other. His clothes were twisted about his body, and Shrie tugged them straight with a matronly concern.

"He didn't even use new hammock," she murmured to herself.

Shrie had awoken before dawn, and Ree's eyes opened to see her pulling stubborn clay from the cave's lake bottom, squirming through the entrance, and then returning. Her face and hands were caked with mud. His curiosity piqued, he headed outside. Unfortunately, it was a one-way tunnel, and he met Shrie coming down. Nettled her routine had been disrupted, Shrie wrinkled her face in annoyance as she crawled backwards. Ree suppressed his amusement, and by the short time they were finally outside, he had completely composed himself.

On a nearby stone soaking in the sun's rays, a hefty amount of damp, dripping clay lay. Eagerly, Shrie began to mold the gray lump. "I work out water and air and then make bowls and spoons." Dividing the pile of mud into two, she motioned for Ree to start on the second. He did so hesitantly but quickly found himself relaxing into the rhythm of the work. Once he had worked the bubbles from the soft clay, he handed it to Shrie who in turn taught him to form a bowl. Set in the sun to bake, Ree's handiwork pleased him. He stood admiring it when Corious emerged.

"So Shrie is instructing you on the finer points of housekeeping, Ree?" Corious's voice asked casually.

"At least I'll have something to eat out of," Ree countered. "I'd like to see you do it."

"Fine then. Shrie, hand me some clay."

The master bowl maker's mouth twitched humorously as she tossed a hunk of clay at him. It splattered over his shirt, and he grimaced. He sat down nonetheless and began to sculpt. After the hour-long process, during which Ree and Shrie went hunting, Corious finished. His masterpiece would be functional, and that was the extent of its value. The entire piece was lopsided, had an irregular thickness, and was still indistinguishable from the mud from which it had come. Though Corious knew he was no Bezalel, the piece elicited his pride, and he placed it confidently in the sun. Shrie patted him on the back and kindly told him it was funny but workable. Ree threatened to smash it once it dried. Shrie simply ignored the ensuing bicker and completed the rest of the eating ware with expert hands.

They spent the next months fixing the cave, replenishing their supplies, and training. Shrie educated Corious in the art of aiming a bow and arrow, and Corious and Ree sparred around the campfire. Some nights, Shrie would amuse them with stories of her jungle life. On rare occasions they discussed the officials. It was easier to imagine the Shalkan warriors did not exist, and that this was the life they had always known. During those days in the forest, Corious would often forget his former life, the injustice his family had suffered at the hands of evil, and his responsibility to protect his home. Instead of a physically defensible place, he had company, food, and a good fire. The forest was his home, with Shrie's happy laughter at his inane and jejune jokes, the mud fights, their peripatetic life, the exhilarating hunts, the light of a flickering fire, and the stars shining brightly in the sky above.

One day, Shrie impolitely awoke Corious from his dream. "Time to fight again," she said stolidly.

Corious dropped his eyes to see clearly the spear he had been shaping mindlessly and in good humor. He had heard the words he had long resisted hearing. He had resisted them because he knew they were true.

"We must, I suppose."

"Of course," Shrie said simply. "The Almighty did not put Ree, Corious, and

Shrie here for nothing. Is time to assume duty and protect. We rested; now time to battle. Besides, Mali informs Shrie of dark men movements. We scout tomorrow."

No other words were needed.

Cringing as a loud snore emanated from the black hole of Corious's mouth, Ree forcibly shook his friend awake. "It's time to scout."

Corious sleepily rubbed his eyes while Shrie brought some of their supplies outside in order to set up a more convenient camp. He grabbed a piece of fruit and lethargically, for sleep had not entirely left him, put on his gear, following the others from the cave. As he hauled his lower body from the shaft, he blinked in the brilliant daylight. Shrie's makeshift camp drew his attention away from the cave, and there, he caught a glimpse of Ree's body in the brush. Breaking into a jog, he fell in beside Ree but did not notice Shrie anywhere.

"Where is she?"

Ree hesitated, searched the trees, and squinted, his hand shielding his eyes. Corious spotted several lustrous birds chatting and a lone black monkey picking at the bugs in his fur but nothing more. As he turned away, black tresses gleamed in the sun, and Corious finally saw Shrie crouching in the limbs beside them. Something beyond the tree line absorbed her attention. Ree, assuming Corious had found his answer, threw off his heavy boots and tucked them under some brush.

"No fighting today, Corious, only careful tracking—quiet and careful observation," Ree whispered as he finished hiding his boots. "Troop movements and supply trains—watch for them. We need to make a map and chart it all. From that information I shall decipher future battle patterns. From there, we can plan our ambushes."

"Sounds smart," Corious stated. "Shrie will be in the trees, I guess, and us on land?"

"Your logic is correct."

As Shrie progressed forward, they hurried to catch up. Ree's bare feet, freed from the prisons of his heavy boots and basking in the liberty, molded themselves happily around the uneven path of roots and rocks. The ground, still cool with the morning dew, was soft against his burning blisters and calluses. Ree was pleased to note that Corious could move just as noiselessly as he did through the trees. Ree turned, but no one received his nod of approval. The wood shielded Corious from view. Following the sylvan path, Ree watched for officials and hoped Shrie's height in the trees provided her with a better view.

A twig snapped behind him. Fear leapt into his throat. He twirled, sword outstretched as a fat rodent waddled across his path. Ree sheathed his weapon, disgusted with his unreasoned terror. The knowledge that Corious or Shrie would watch his back had made him lax. Ree clenched his teeth; he did not need anyone to watch out for his safety. With a quick turn, he strode ahead defiantly.

Corious sneaked into the trees away from Ree. He was tired of being told what to do. Tracking and quiet observation he could do by himself.

Hearing the crunch of steel boots against the forest floor, he took advantage of a rock's cover. Minutes later, a unit of twenty officials marched paces from his spot. Corious noted the position of the sun behind him as he waited for the stomping of footsteps to fade away. *A unit of officials at noon passing by...where exactly am I?* He studied the rock pensively. It seemed oddly familiar. Suddenly, he remembered. Below him was the rock overhang to which Shrie had first brought him and Ree. They had been traveling in circles.

The frightening knowledge dawned upon him: the officials were heading towards the camp and the cave. *I'll trail them*, he decided rashly. If they were seeking the heads of the rebels, he would ensure they failed. Corious could only hope the cave would escape their sight. Restraining himself from running ahead, Corious knew he needed balance; he could not get too close or too far behind. Fortunately, if it became imperative to close the gap between himself and the enemy, the brush would camouflage him well. With a fleeting thought, he wondered where Ree and Shrie were before adjusting the spear on his back.

Ree strode confidently through the forest. Another twig cracked behind him. He turned charily. Nothing. He stalked forward again. Not a minute passed before another crackle reached his ear. This time it was closer, and instincts told him it was the distinct sound of human feet passing over the dense foliage. And it came again and again until a steady pounding pervaded the forest. Ree dove into the brush as ten officials burst into the clearing. They bent over, panting hard.

"We lost him," one official coughed, spitting blood.

The commander kicked him in the stomach and sneered, "We lose him the day you die."

The official slumped to the ground, writhing like an animal. The Shalkan's eyes were dilated and blank, and a pink sliver of spittle mixed with blood dripped down his chin. A red and gold arrow protruded from under the official's shoulder blade. Ree's eyes opened wide. It was Shrie's arrow, but Ree did not confirm her presence for fear of rattling the leaves covering his head.

"By the god of six moons," the Commander swore, "it's that same cursed arrow picking off my men! Well," he shouted to no one in particular, "you got him." Bending down to the dead official, he added unnecessarily, "He's dead. C'mon, you feral sons of toads. We have a rebel to catch. And once we catch him, we'll have a little fun with him before we kill him, eh?"

The officials hated their Commander but were now one reduced in number, and his speech had inspired them. They would wait until they caught the boy to lodge their knives into their leader's back. With a shout, they set off running, leaving their companion's body to the scavengers; the arrow was still in his back.

Shrie had trailed the small band of officials and now saw their prey: a younger boy around fourteen years of age. He stumbled through the trees, not knowing how closely death bit at his heels. Shrie's heart went out to him. She must save him, but she had used her last arrow and needed to head back to the camp. Leaping from the trees, she froze. Someone had called her name.

"Shrie!" Ree called, leaping to his feet. "Shrie, it's Ree."

A relieved breath preceded her next sentence. "I run out of arrows, Ree," she said, planting a foot on the dead official's back and jerking out the arrow, "but officials chasing a young rebel. You go and track officials. I get arrows and locate Corious." Without waiting to see if Ree had any objections, she sprinted away.

Corious thought his back would break. He had been bent, stooping to avoid detection, and his sore muscles demanded that they be stretched. To makes things worse, his leg had tightened in an unbearable cramp, but stoic and stalwart, he remained stationary. The current situation would not be conducive to sudden movements. The officials had found the camp and had noticed the rebels' absences. The Commander, deeming it wise to set an ambush for the camp's inhabitants, had surrounded the premises. When he gave the word, they would attack. Corious bit his lip. He had to prevent Shrie or Ree from getting too close and falling into the tediously placed trap.

Shrie raced through the trees, heedless of any obstructions. She desperately needed her arrows. How stupid she felt for not bringing more with her, but she could not think of that now. She had to focus. Flying through the trees, she was almost to camp.

The Commander heard the light, furtive footsteps and smiled. "That would be the jungle maiden." To his lieutenant he whispered, "It will take at least ten men to capture the jungle woman if she is armed. For the others, you will need more. Remember, if possible, capture them and only kill as a last resort. We want them to talk."

The lieutenant smirked wickedly as the girl neared.

Corious also heard the footsteps. He saw the commander lean over and mention something to the official next to him. A muscle jumped in the official's neck. The Shalkans were preparing to jump. Crawling on his hands and knees, Corious attempted both silence and speed. Amazingly, his activity went undetected.

Shrie raced closer. Her hair streamed behind her, and she pushed her legs harder. She was so close.

Corious crouched. He had to catch her at the right time. Just a few more seconds and the timing would be perfect. Corious sprung from his position like a tongue from a famished frog's mouth.

Shrie was twenty feet from the camp when it hit her. She was tackled to the ground and was about to scream when a calloused hand clamped her mouth shut and an arm pinned her to the ground.

She dug her teeth into the hand which released its grip as a familiar voice whispered, "Ow! God! Shrie it's me. There are officials surrounding the camp. They're waiting for us."

"Oh! Hello, Corious."

"Come, we have to get out of here and warn Ree."

Shrie shook her head, "Sorry. Shrie need to get arrows."

She ran straight into the camp.

The Commander heard the scuffle in the brush. Puzzled, he turned to see Corious wave his arms as rapidly as possible over his head before walking on his hands away from the camp. The Commander did not see Shrie slip into the cave, but he did see a lone, male rebel with his legs dangling in the air and with his tanned, bared stomach begging for a sword in its gut. With a shout, he led his men in the charge.

Shrie smiled as she slid through the tunnel. Corious had made a good decoy. When she reached the cavern, she grabbed her extra arrows and proceeded to catch Ree. Corious would be fine on his own.

Ree stuck close to the officials. The soldiers were gaining on the boy. A mere half mile separated them from their prey. *Where is Shrie?*

Corious did a front handspring and rushed into action. Fuzzy blotches of green, pixilated plants streamed passed his eyes as he weaved between trees with a renewed burst of speed. He had distracted the officials well. *Shrie better appreciate this,* he thought numbly as sweat poured down his face. *The amount of pain I am about to deal with for this woman…*His legs aching and stuffed with lactic acid, Corious halted his thoughts, redirecting the energy from his brain towards the muscles maintaining the run.

The officials fanned into position. Corious could hear them crashing tirelessly through the crushed plants in his wake. Abruptly, something gelid and sticky caressed the back of his neck, latching decisively onto his shirt. Corious felt himself levitate in the air, suspended by a hairy leg. Flailing his arms in bewildered retaliation, he screamed in astonishment as several bleary eyes stared at him from behind dark fur. The giant spider which Shrie called Mali-Mali held him in its clutches. The Shalkans, like Corious, had not expected this, and they stopped in their tracks, watching nervously.

An idea flashed through Corious's racing mind, and he cried out hysterically, feigning torture at the hands of the jungle creature. He faked agony, not fear. The

Mali stroked his shoulder in an attempt to comfort him but lugged him higher into the trees. Several officials shrieked in delight while others vomited. When Corious dropped a bloodied shirt to the ground, the officials scattered throughout. No Shalkan would risk death at the expense of obeying a commander. Corious watched in relief. The hairy legs which had arranged the deus ex machina still gripped his shoulders.

"Thank you," Corious said stupidly, "you can let me down now."

The spider ignored his request.

Shrie backtracked. When she finally reached Ree, he shot her a worried look.

"We should have overtaken the boy by now. An official threw a knife at him and just barely missed. They have searched the area and found nothing, not even the knife. I'm afraid they, and we, have lost him."

"We head back to where they throw knife," came Shrie's resolute response.

"Then we do not have far to go." They drifted into the forest, and Ree pointed to a small clearing. Shrie collapsed onto her hands and knees; her inquisitive fingers tickled the tops of the grass while her eyes grazed them. Ree crouched beside her.

"There is trampled grass here. A log rolled this way," she murmured to herself, stepping carefully through the brush so as not to disrupt the tracks. The trees opened before them. "Trails lead to bank of river." Sure enough, a log floated in the middle of the rapids. Shrie yelped in alarm.

"River leads to falls! Come, Ree!"

Ree's will wavered. He was torn between the boy, a lost cause, and gathering intelligence, a verifiable necessity. Shrie understood his dilemma.

"You go; I get Corious. Officials surrounded camp, but if they gone, is good time to move camp."

Without another word, they separated in a flurry of motion.

The spider set Corious down on an isolated tree branch. It rumbled a few words in an odd language and then bounced expectantly next to him.

Corious eyed it uncertainly. "Umm, let's see here. Thank you. You," he pointed to the spider, "very helpful."

The spider seemed to understand this. It chattered away several loud strings of sound and then crawled into the trees. Taking his eyes from the spider, Corious gaped beyond his dirty feet waving in the open sky. Layers of leaves hid any view of ground. A powerful gust of wind rattled the tree, and he swayed in his seat.

"Actually," he yelled to the retreating spider, "maybe you'd like to give me a lift down."

The spider scurried on. Corious blinked several times to clear his head. Only one option remained. Embracing the branch, Corious gradually and painstakingly lowered his feet to the next branch. Swinging his legs, he smiled as his foot skimmed the top bark of a lower branch. He closed his eyes and let go, landing safely. In this methodical way, slipping and sliding, and sometimes falling, Corious made his way to the bottom. When he finally reached the ground, he kissed it thrice in succession. At that embarrassing moment, Shrie chose to appear.

"Quickly, Corious, quickly!" She was nearly screaming, but her voice sounded far away. "Collect the gear! Hurry!" Urgency coursed through her command.

Corious did not feel like moving, and the overwhelming sense of relief which had seized him upon reaching the ground weakened his desire to confront danger. Shrie was already running through the underbrush. Mindlessly, he donned the bloody shirt he had dropped earlier. *And not even one word of thanks.*

"Do not say, 'I'll pay you back for this wrong!'
Wait for the Lord, and he will deliver you."
Proverbs 20:18

Chapter 4

Pound, thump, pound, thump. Tar's footsteps hit the dirt in perfectly measured intervals. His gasping breath sounded rough in his ears as it rasped against his red, raw throat. Salty trickles of sweat stung his eyes, but the pain did not bother him. Why should he care about eyes that could not see? His breath quickened, and his heart palpitated as his mind fought to keep his weary legs moving.

Even in his exhaustion, he could not forget his haunting past...

With the exception of his blindness, his life had begun normally. His family had not ostracized him, and he had enjoyed the love of many friends. With his older brother, he had shared a bond of unfailing friendship, one that would endure the test of time, though they would never meet again in the flesh.

The fire had claimed everything, encircling the small village, mercilessly burning. Anyone who had miraculously survived the flames had been shot by the officials. His parents had been among the unfortunate. *Because I could not protect them.* Tar's hands had ripped the floorboard from its place, bashing its fiery end into an official's face. The same hands had strangled the Shalkan, ensuring its death. His unseeing eyes had shed tears. Another set of hands, his brother's, had pushed Tar away from the blue official lying limp in the orange flames. The hands had thrown him out the door, sacrificing themselves and their owner so that Tar could run.

Tar had fled for two days with his brother's memory pushing him forward. His deep hatred of the officials sought revenge, but now he could barely save himself. Someone yelled behind him. Tar's palms sweated in apprehension. He jerked his body to the right and slipped. Falling face first into the mud, he groaned but hurriedly pushed himself from the mire. As he rose, he groped for the obstruction over which he had fallen and located a hollowed log. It was more than the log he had stumbled upon; luck was also within his grasp. Hurriedly stretching his arms over his head, he squirmed and forced his youthful frame into the narrow space. He barely fit when nine sets of boots plodded tumultuously through the underbrush. A cramp built perilously in his leg. Holding his breath, he silently shifted the scream-ing limb. The log creaked; he tried to move his leg back. Something splintered, and the log began to roll down the small slope on which it had rested.

Unexpectedly, the log groaned as a vibrating knife blade sliced into the bark precious inches away from Tar's neck. Tar turned his body, encouraging the log to move away from the Shalkans. The weakening wood splintered under his elbow and then, in a matter of dizzying seconds, he was airborne.

Wet scratched at his clothes and fingers. A river—he was in a river. The current picked him up, tossing him in the rolling log. Frantically, he struggled to arrange himself favorably within the clammy confines. The water spiraled out of control, converging before him in sickening swirls. It jostled him unforgivingly, and bark fell away from his body; the log would not support his weight. Spray licked at his face. The rotting wood ruptured as he hurtled down stream.

Tar feverishly grabbed at the knife beside him in the water and thrust it towards the bank. The current threw him severely to his right, and the knife slid hopelessly through the water. A large rock loomed before him. Tar reached out with a desper-ate yell; his body cracked violently against the rock. The Shalkan knife wobbled in his hand. Tar weakly held onto the gray stone, but a slippery sea weed had already claimed the surface of the rock. His hands and body slipped off in seconds. He jerked his arm against the current: this time the knife stuck into the slick bank. Tar sighed briefly in reprieve, but the current clawed at his limbs. His face barely rose above the surface. In time, the water would take him.

He bit his lip and waited until the unspoken agony spurred him to risk detec-tion. If they captured him, he would at least have a chance to flee; the water did not offer him that luxury.

"Hello! Hel—"

A swell rose and covered his cries. The crashing water hit him with the force of a battering ram. Flying through the air, his feet flipped over his head, and then he lost any relative bearings. He heard the water nearing him, and then he tasted blood at impact.

"The prudent see danger and take refuge,
but the simple keep going and suffer for it."
Proverbs 27:12

Chapter 5

Emerging from the jungle, Shrie watched the surging water sweep by her. Called the Tashorn by Corious and Ree, the vast river swam powerfully around the edge of the jungle and into the heart of Khaltharnga. Even though Corious breathed laboriously behind her, the roar of the river rang louder. Spray splashed their faces as the current crashed brutally upon a stubborn rock. She worriedly searched the water for the hollow trunk as she ran, but the river's heaving waters were vacant. They were too far down stream to hope for the best, but she forged ahead, and Corious's feet rose and dropped behind hers. He, too, saw the empty river.

"I think we've lost him," he paused carefully. "Should we search the rocks for a body? At least we could give him a decent burial."

Shrie cringed; if the boy had fallen, the water would be his final resting place. Jagged rocks jutted from the base of the falls, and even if he had been so fortunate as to miss those, perilous eddies swirled and churned, binding their victims below and sucking the air from their lungs. The fate was inevitable once the white foam carried its quarry over the edge.

"There he is!"

Peering intently at the watery crag, Corious spotted him. Prostrate on a rock, the unconscious boy's body was contorted awkwardly. The turquoise water tore at his feet and legs, loosening his hold on life. In its eerie, singsong way, the water beckoned the boy to join its mortal plunge over the falls. Sprinting, Corious wrapped his fingers around the boy's slippery wrist just before it drifted out of reach. Shrie took the other and heaved. As his battered body reached land, the boy vomited before returning to the restless blackness that shielded him from the pain of consciousness. Corious threw the boy over his shoulders and traipsed into the jungle where Shrie hastily examined his wounds.

"He bleeding hard but will live."

Corious glimpsed skeptically at the torn body. Involuntarily, the one eyebrow rose slightly over the other, and the corner of his mouth turned up skeptically. Shrie felt strangely irritated by this. *He underestimates me,* she thought as she patted the boy's arm bitterly. She had healed worse than this. A breastplate covered in gore floated to the top of her memory, and the river's siren song played sweetly in her ear before Corious shook her roughly from the past. After carefully ripping a piece of cloth from her tunic, she tied it firmly about the boy's bloodstained arm and forehead.

"You carry him to camp now, Corious. Shrie will fix him; Shrie is the healer," she added indignantly. They gingerly boosted the comatose boy onto Corious's back, and providentially, the three had no trouble slipping silently through the forest. Any noise would have aggravated the marauding Shalkans, who, like a mine, would explode if stepped upon. Shrie strained her senses to their highest capabilities. Taking an extra individual increased the risk of being detected. Shrie presumed the boy was what Ree termed a rebel. He had said that if one was not an official but a human, then one was a rebel: one who fought valiantly against the oppressive warriors from the north. It dawned upon her that she too fit this description.

"So Shrie must be a rebel then?" she asked softly.

From beneath his heavy load, Corious let her hesitant question echo in his ears. Seeing her hopeful expression, he had not the heart to tell her that the rebels were not like her. They did not wear leaves and fur, nor did they live joyfully. "I suppose," he said cautiously, "though you aren't quite the type."

"What you mean?" she asked defiantly but in a low whisper. "I fight dark men; I a rebel like you." A distant clatter chased away her query; Shrie suddenly hoped Ree was keeping track of the officials' paths.

"Yes, but in different ways," Corious explained mischievously. "See, most rebels are skilled with the sword." He grinned, knowing his comment would nettle her. Shrie was constantly attempting to verbally prove her superior strength. Corious thought it a funny and rather ironic argument—one which he usually chose to end by using complicated vocabulary until she was baffled to the extreme. Movement again was heard in the forest, and Shrie ducked slightly as they retraced their path. Tensely, Corious hunched; somehow Shrie knew the difference between her spider friends and the enemy. Shrie began to speak again, and his muscles strained as she started to run. He freed a hand to finger his dagger.

"You sweating, Corious." Shrie quickened her pace. "Maybe rebels good at sword," she smiled insidiously, "but them not very fast."

Corious employed his free hand to shift the boy's mounting weight. He smiled eccentrically, trying to achieve an impish grin. When she missed his attempt, he whispered to her back, "Race you to camp," and then set off at a sprint.

Shrie gave into her pride, and her love of competition took over. She relegated her senses to winning the race, immediately taking to the trees. Yards apart when Shrie took off in a different direction, Corious was left to guess at her whereabouts.

He continued smugly and surely, and then as his burden grew heavier, his steps gradually grew less confident. After several minutes of running alone, Corious stopped among unfamiliar surroundings. He whirled around. Trying to jog his memory, he observed his environment.

"Trees with twisty vines crawling up them," he noticed, "they seem familiar." He turned to his right to see almost the same tree. "Another tree with twisty vines; it looks familiar too. I wonder why?" he asked himself sarcastically. "Perhaps because all the trees have twisty vines growing up them," he exclaimed in frustration. At a loss, he scoured the identical trees, chose a direction, and jogged ahead lightly. *Quiet and careful observation*, Corious reflected upon Ree's words. "Too bad I didn't observe where I was going," he murmured, hoisting the boy higher onto his back.

"Corious!"

Was that him or someone else? The voice came from above him. Arching his neck, he saw Shrie's face peering down at him. To his surprise, the mark of victory was not written over her every feature.

"Corious," she called again, "Shalkans not far off! Hurry, climb this tree."

Corious glanced at her worriedly; it would be difficult to hide the three of them.

"Here, tie boy's hands and feet together so he hangs around shoulders," Shrie instructed while handing him a softened but sturdy rope. Corious adeptly wrapped the vine about the injured boy's hands and feet. Both body parts were rough, as he had been barefoot, and full of calluses from running. Small scratches and bruises covered his arms and legs. Corious shared similar markings. Overlooked pricker bushes, briars, and sunken roots filled Shrie's forest and were determined to rip the flesh of those who passed. The sharp rocks and stones did not bother Shrie however. She had lived with them all of her life, and they with her. It was the trespassers, those like Corious, whom the vegetation despised.

And if the plants are annoying, then the animals are downright hell, Corious thought. Shrie's voice from the past gravely repeated, "Mali-Mali not like you Corious." He had coolly inquired as to the identity of a Mali-Mali. She had grinned wickedly and replied, "Big spider, big teeth." And yet, the Mali had saved him...

"Corious, follow Shrie and not make any noise," Shrie said, interrupting his thoughts. Gracefully, she transferred her weight to another tree branch. Focusing his vision, Corious stepped on the rough bark, shimmying on his stomach to the overlapping branch of the next tree. As he stood upright, he felt the boy slip from the rope holds and rub against his back; Corious's shirt was uncomfortably soaked and stuck firmly to his back. Sweat trickled in tiny beads down his spine, and splatters of blood leaked onto his arm from the boy's wounds. Flicking a piece of hair from his forehead, Corious fought exhaustion. He slid one foot in front of the other and rounded the tree trunk. In front of him, Shrie's figure receded into the leaves.

Shrie was ready to turn back when she felt Corious's body sidle up behind her.

He pressed softly against her shoulder blade, asserting his presence. Using the tree trunk to pivot, she glanced behind her as a gunshot reverberated in her ears. The loud explosion echoed in an omen of danger, a harbinger of death. During the race, the pursuing officials had forced her to find Ree and the new camp. The lack of Corious's direction sense had fled her busy mind; she had had to go back. Even if she had remembered to tell him that the camp was southwest of the old one and closer to the river, he would not have found it. She prayed her peccadillo would not prove too costly.

When Corious caught up again, she leapt to the ground and headed west. She would go through the marsh; the officials avoided its mud and pitiless insects. Another gunshot raced through the air, and Shrie took off as though catapulted by the sound. Corious had known Shrie could race through the trees, but he had never suspected how quick she could be when circumstances demanded it. She waited just until he could see her, and then she was off again. After half an hour of constant running, they stopped. They had lost their trackers.

"Corious, Ree moved camp west and to the south. The officials found cave," Shrie explained between sharp intakes of breath. The evanescent menace of marching boots sounded remotely in her ears. "We almost there, but boy must be checked on first."

Corious rushed to loosen the knots that bound the injured boy to him. *The officials have found the cave then; that's an unexpected blow.* They had thought it to be impenetrable, especially with the decoy camp to distract attention from the cave's entrance. Watching as Shrie used several fuzzy, blue leaves to clear blood from the boy's face, Corious grew anxious. He wanted to get down from the trees.

"He is fine after rest and good food," Shrie commented while taking fistfuls of leaves and berries from the trees. Crushing them in her palm, she dabbed the concoction onto his sores. Corious vaguely wondered how she had learned to mix her healing potions.

"We carry him to camp."

Shrie swept the boy's arms in her own while Corious firmly held the boy's legs. Though it appeared the officials had gone, Shrie and Corious continued to make haste. They soon arrived at the makeshift campsite. Pushing aside the carefully placed, concealing brush, the three entered the sanctuary. Light blue and green mosses covered the ground, and the sun darted through layers of leaves, joining in the gambol of light's enchanting patterns. Lofty plants grew thickly about them, creating an aesthetic illusion of peace. Items Ree had scavenged from the cave were strewn about, and Corious was happy to see that nothing important was missing. Ree, however, could not be accounted for, but it was generally assumed he had gone hunting. They would be safe for now. Leaving the boy in a bed of ferns, Shrie picked some fruit from a nearby tree and craftily slipping the food into the boy's mouth. The movement managed to wake him.

"Your name?" she asked pensively.

He awoke groggily and in pain. He mumbled a one syllable response from which Shrie was able to decipher his name: Tar. Tar reached about him tentatively.

"He's blind," she told Corious sadly as she took the boy's hand.

"Blind but not deaf," the boy responded stolidly despite his injuries. "Who is this?" he croaked. "This is no official's hand!"

"Shrie, jungle warrior. How you feel, Tar? You had bad fall in river. Officials hunting you, but we safe now."

Tar relaxed. "Who else is here? Someone else is here?"

Corious cleared his throat. "I'm Corious, a rebel." Taking the boy's other hand, Corious shook it. "You took a good fall; I'm surprised you made it," Corious complimented. Shrie patted Corious on the back; he had said the right thing.

"Ree, another rebel, will come too; he hunting now."

"It's just you three," Tar probed.

"Yes, but we fight like twenty," Shrie bragged. "Besides, four is not too many to hunt for. You come from far away," Shrie said the question like a comment.

Tar corroborated her statement. "I've been on the run for several days. The officials burned my village." Intensity entered his voice. "My family is gone. My brother was not so fortunate as to run into your path," he lamented. "I should have died, but he gave his life for me."

He paused. Every rebel had a story, a dangerous past that was a nearly healed wound. At the resurrection of memories, the pain would spill from the poorly covered lesion and into the tenuous present. Tar's wound was fresh, and he needed to show it to someone in the hope that they could heal it. Shrie knew the healing could only come from inside of him, but talking helped, and so by the end of fifteen minutes, Tar's story, or as much of it as he had chosen to tell, had been told. Exhausted, Tar soon fell into a deep sleep. Shrie touched the boy's arm fondly. She had seen his strength behind the passing bitterness and anger. He was one of the few who saw with his soul. After a moment of reflection, Shrie began to organize the camp. Corious joined her. Though he had not said much, he also felt taken by the boy, and he was reminded of their original companionship: Ree, Shrie, and himself. Corious turned to Shrie, his usual insouciance fading.

"We should find Ree. We do not know where the officials presently lurk."

"Ree? He is by himself," Shrie said thoughtfully, glancing first at the boy and then at the plants twining about them. Uttering something under her breath that sounded like swaying reeds, she pointed to the boy. Corious thought maybe she was talking to him, but she then addressed Corious. "Tar will be safe here. If you wish, Shrie will come with you to find Ree." Corious's cheeks grew hot as his already injured pride crippled. After watching him get lost in the jungle, Shrie obviously did not trust him to travel alone. Her concern did not embarrass him—the fact that he needed her did.

"Shrie would like to find Ree too," she said diplomatically, ostensibly attempting to preserve some of her companion's dignity.

Corious brushed her aside. "Okay, then. Let's go."

Passing through the brush, Shrie again muttered something in her singsong chant, and the wall of solid brush hiding Tar from sight melted into the rest of the jungle. Corious shook his head in wonder. With Shrie's uncanny sense of direction to guide them, they stumbled upon a brooding Ree within minutes. Despite Ree's unwelcoming countenance, they briefed him about Tar. Surprisingly, he knew of Tar, or at least of Tar's older brother. Corious thought this an odd coincidence. They wisely chose not to inform Ree of his friend's death; Ree did not need additional fuel to add to the furnace of his insatiable anger. After a phlegmatic conversation, Corious and Shrie departed to tend to Tar, leaving Ree to return in his own time. Corious agreed with Shrie: Ree would be fine on his own, at least for a while.

Chapter 6

"Reckless words pierce like a sword,
but the tongue of the wise brings healing."
Proverbs 12:18

Thanks to Shrie's timely warning, Ree had moved camp before the arrival of the Shalkans. Once he had established everything to his satisfaction, he had departed to hunt. Serving as his outlet, hunting provided him with precious time to think. Since game was plentiful, and the need for food constant, he had a ready excuse to indulge his turbulent mind. Letting his thoughts wander, Ree found himself remembering the day he had met Corious, Shrie, and now Tar. Tar's brother had participated in ambushes and raids of which Ree had been an integral part. Though Tar was young, if he was half as skilled as his brother, he would fare well against the officials. Ree felt confident Tar would recover with the three at his aid. Tar's brother had always bragged about Tar's ability to overcome obstacles—at least all of those but his plaguing blindness.

Ree checked his weapons and decided to return to camp. He hoped Shrie and the others would be there. He headed on, and for a moment, the Shalkan warriors did not appear so terribly awful. *You know,* a tiny part of the back of his mind called, *you seem fond of your jungle comrades.* Ree shook himself roughly from his thoughts. He did not let the idea linger within his conscious mind, and so it simmered where it was, waiting to be accepted. *No time to think; return to camp. After all, I could; no, I can and will, rely on my own strength.* Abruptly Shrie's voice countered his thoughts, challenging his resolution. Ree contemplated a response to her imaginary retort before shunning the idea.

Tar woke slowly, blinking and placing a hand gingerly to his forehead. He instantly pulled it away as the skin stung and hissed in response. *It has been hours probably,* Tar thought, *or days since the river*. His upper body cramped in racking pain. A groan escaped his dry lips. *Mustn't lose my bearings*. By listening to and feeling the earth beneath him, he sought to determine his location. A person walked towards him.

"You not get up; you lie down and rest!"

Tar's mind reeled. Somehow the voice sounded familiar, but when he tried to place it, his head swirled. Tar knew he should be cautious, but something told him he was safe.

"Will you tell me your name?" Tar asked in a hoarse voice.

"My name is Shrie. You not remember me?" The voice sounded female and disappointed.

Tar avoided the question. "My name is Tar. I live on the southeastern boundaries of the forest," Tar said preparing himself for a conversation. Shrie seemed inclined to conversation, for after feeding him some fruit, she sat down on the fern bed across from him.

"Meet Corious—he just come too. You obviously not remember our past talk. We know lots about you, but I guess we tell you again about ourselves."

"Hi, Corious," Tar said awkwardly when he heard someone enter.

"Hello, Tar." Corious's deep voice sounded pleasant, and Tar felt comfortable as the lassitude slipped from his body.

"So," Shrie continued, "you remember why you go down river?"

Tar paused as the dark torrents obfuscated his ability to reason logically; he felt the dirt under his nails and the water rushing into his mouth. Then the fire flashed in front of him, its heat overwhelming him, the two people running from the jungle—yes, he remembered.

"The fire," he stammered, trying to explain, "I was at my village; I was running..." he paused, and then the words came to him as his life unfolded before him. Telling his history drained him, and so Shrie commanded him to rest. He did not want to, but the cushioning ferns were soft beneath his body. Drowsily, he fell back and let himself be ushered into the navy world of sleep.

That afternoon, Shrie and Corious returned to find Tar fast asleep and Ree cooking a sizeable hunk of meat over a primitive fire. The second Shrie laid eyes on Tar, she eyed Ree threateningly. He had promised her earlier that he would apply a specific ointment to Tar's skin, and Shrie had left him very clear instructions from which he had apparently had deviated. With a look that seemed to say prepare yourself, Corious patted Ree supportively on the back. Ree grimaced, and sure enough, Shrie began her tirade. Corious suppressed laughter. When he was not the object of Shrie's acerbic words, her rants in broken English were somewhat comical.

"You not put ointment on right," she scolded vehemently. "Tar never be able to train back to perfect health if he not treated right." No one said anything for a while, too worn out to argue with the truth of Shrie's words. After hanging his head in a ceremonial show of remorse, Ree finally began his apologetic discourse. Shrie fell for it.

"Ah, it okay, Ree. Shrie just do it next time." Her hands rested easily on her hips.

"We should move camp soon, move eastward," Ree said solemnly. He did feel compunction for applying the ointment incorrectly. What he knew about Tar he liked.

Shrie agreed with Ree's statement but glanced worriedly at Tar. She did not deem him ready for such a move. "Tar maybe not ready yet," she said, concerned.

"But we should go," Corious noted resolutely, breaking the deadlock. "We've been here for an entire day, and the officials are not far off. It's a mere matter of time before they find us."

Shrie argued against logic, and soon, a small quarrel assaulted the camp. It was probably the noise that woke Tar again, for the sounds of discord among friends resonate louder than the shouts of the enemy.

Several days came and went, and their passing erased most of Tar's pain. Still, Shrie protested the move.

"You not understand! He not fully better! He rest, he sleeps, you train, and then we go. Ok?" Shrie stared at Ree and Corious boldly. "I am ruler here. Tar cannot move camp yet."

Ree's face contorted in irritation. *Shrie's not the only one here who has had to take a life, who has had to rule, and who has had to separate from family. Yet she insists on servitude and control. Or perhaps,* he sighed, *am I simply angry because occasionally she is right, and I hate to be challenged?* Ree could not decide. Taking a deep breath, he turned on his heel to face Shrie.

"Moving camp will be Tar's training. He will have no other until we bivouac elsewhere."

A fire leapt dangerously in Shrie's eyes. She stalked away, stopped abruptly, and then said over her shoulder, "Shrie no agree."

Corious exchanged a fleeting glance with Ree before starting to pack their meager supplies. Shrie glared back at them from the edge of the encampment. Something inside of her raged against her urge to remain at camp; this foreign force coursed through her body, and before she knew it, she had stuffed the exploring gear in a bag and nodded curtly to Ree. She and Corious would search for a suitable spot for their subsequent encampment while Ree went with them to the river. There, he would watch for officials and check on Tar. Together, they trekked for a couple of miles and then broke paths. With the sweat from the exertion slid any resentment Shrie had previously harbored.

"I sorry, Ree," Shrie stated as they parted.

Ree waved them on with a smile. That was Shrie: quick to disagree but quicker to forgive.

Tar woke, yawned, and reached for his knuckle gloves. Stretching his fingers into the coverings, he then jerked a headband over his eyes and fitted it into its contented position on his forehead. Tying his knee high boots with an impressive accuracy, Tar thought of his brother. The blue official burned, and a pair of hands shoved him through a door. Tar fingered the knife that had saved him by the waterfall. He heard talking not far off and moved in its direction.

A freakish whistling preceded his arrival. He bit his lip and felt circumspectly around him. A set of thorns reached his hands, and he withdrew his searching arm from their daggered points. Without warning, a furious cry ripped through the air, and a set of loud snaps succeeded the rustling of bushes.

Tar gasped and tried to run. He leapt over a briar patch, but a rough hand shook his shoulder. Tar's momentum carried the rest of his body forward, and he stumbled into the greenery.

"Whoa there, Tar. Take it easy!"

Tar recognized the voice. Letting out a deep, shaky breath, he extracted himself from the leaves and dirt which now covered his clothes. In the annoyance which stems from embarrassment, he replied, "I'd prefer it if you could refrain from sneaking up on the blind boy."

Clearing his throat, Ree simply helped Tar back to camp. As Tar used his nails to scrape at the mud ingrained in his clothes, Ree informed him that they were traveling to a new location and that Tar was welcome to join them if he wished. Tar acquiesced readily.

"When the storm has swept by, the wicked are gone,
but the righteous stand firm forever."
Proverbs 10:25

Chapter 7

Shrie cocked her head sideways, listening for officials. "They far behind us now," she whispered to her companion, Corious, beside her.

Scouring for a new campsite, they were now high in the treetops of the forest Shrie knew so well. She relaxed. Every single tree had its own song. This particular one, with its smooth bark and welcoming branches was a prime choice for surveying the land. Long ago, she had searched for game within its limbs or gazed into the beautiful shades of green that were the soul of the forest. Now, she often used such trees to scout for dark men, as she called them—the hideous men with demented minds. Breastplates covered their chests, and sharp, pointed helmets rose hideously into the air. Their faces were human, if one could get close enough to peer into their shadowed helmets, but they were distorted. Perhaps the darkness played tricks on her eyes, or perhaps their appearances had been changed by a consuming evil.

Khaltharnga had never welcomed them. The Shalkans had come as invaders from a sea, many seas away, but they had found a leader here whom they feared and respected; they called him Turock. In Shrie's tongue, his name translated to Taberah, and it meant burning. Uttered in their guttural language, his name caught in the air and brought with it much gloom; for it was the name which appealed to the evil nature of all men. Shrie shuddered as a chill enveloped her; even she and the most unbending rebels were not immune to it. She did not fear him, but she dreaded his potential and his desire to rule her forest. *No*, she reprimanded herself. She would not let that happen; the natural cycle of the wood must continue. The animals still listened to the rules of nature and so did her three new companions. She would immediately accept other such rebels into her forest home. A crackling noise spurred her onward.

"Corious, we go up. Machines that make loud boom cannot follow us there."

"I suppose you mean guns," grunted Corious as he struggled to follow Shrie higher into the branches. "Are you sure these limbs will hold my kind of weight?"

"What you say Corious?" she called down from her position in the soaring branches.

"Forget it," Corious mumbled. More noise would only attract more officials. As Corious leapt to another branch, he felt something dart by his head, ruffling his hair. Unexpectedly, a firm hand gripped his tanned shoulder as he slipped. He found himself suspended by Shrie's thin arms.

"Ugh, you are heavy, Corious," said Shrie smiling while attempting to steady him on a branch.

"What would you do that for?" Corious asked heatedly.

"Big snake not like you. He told me he not like your eyes." Shrie pointed to a crafty snake slithering away into the tree. "I tell him you my friend; no worry."

Corious flared his nostrils. *Another creature that isn't fond of me*, he thought miserably.

"So what wrong with your eyes?" Shrie questioned affably as they ascended. "I never see snake act like that before." Shrie paused expectantly. "Look at Shrie, Corious." Corious did so obediently. Looking deep into his eyes, Shrie's nose almost touched his before she turned away muttering, "I see nothing different, nothing wrong. How many fingers Shrie hold up?"

Corious blinked and knocked her hand away. "Four—and my vision is fine."

"Maybe you are blessed by the Almighty." Shrie peered again into his face curiously.

"Hey, cut that out, okay?" Corious demanded. Her scrutinizing gaze unsettled him. "I can see peculiarly well in the dark. That's about it. Some people say I have some form of nighttime sight; other rebels have it too for some reason," Corious continued. "Maybe that Almighty of yours, is that who you believe in? Well, maybe He gave it to us because we are slightly disadvantaged against the Shalkans and any bantam skill helps," he said sardonically.

"That very wise thought." Shrie had taken him seriously. Glancing at him with a new respect she said, "Yes, the Almighty bless you. Shrie once believe in many gods, but she now knows there is only one."

"Oh yeah?" Corious questioned, not particularly interested.

"Yes," she answered gravely. "The Almighty, He is the one the trees talk about, the one the sunset sings to, the one the waves of the sea and the stars of the sky obey." Shrie thought about this. "We stop here." She plopped down on a branch. "The Almighty has plan for each one."

"Yeah—what in the firing blazes?" Corious's mild oath truncated her speech.

An ugly four-legged, hairy bee-like creature raced toward him in the tree; he backed up cautiously as Shrie explained easily, "Cousin of Mali-Mali."

"Doesn't look like a Mali-Mali to me," Corious said with an ashen face; two new creatures in one day were two more than he could handle.

"You not worry, Takelala likes you."

"Oh, wonderful! Just what I was hoping for, really," grumbled Corious, cautiously touching Takelala's bristly fur. A sole, random shot rang in the air, arresting Shrie's movement. Minutes later, Corious heard the rustling of leaves below them. Fearing the noise signified an official, Corious did not dare take a breath. Shrie, on the other hand, scampered one branch higher.

"Corious, Shrie, get down from there or I'll have to come and get you guys myself," a coarse voice called. "I need that tracking information for my map."

"What you say, Ree?" Shrie asked with a puckish grin, scurrying even closer to the canopy. Ree muttered a foul word; he knew Shrie had heard him. She was always trying to prove she was the ultimate ruler, and she immensely enjoyed taking advantage of the fact that his tall, muscular body could not climb a tree. As Shrie watched him fold his arms, she began to say something smug when a smaller figure appeared beside him.

"Tar," Shrie shouted, "you feeling better?" Corious hushed her, but she ignored him.

In response, Tar began to climb the tree. Nimble as he was, Tar went slowly, testing each branch before resting his weight on it.

"Come, Ree, now you have to get us all down. Ha, see! You not so powerful."

At the bottom of the tree, Ree pulled out an ax. "You come down, or I'll take you down. It's your choice."

Corious would have laughed, but Ree was not joking. The situation was no longer funny. Unfortunately, Shrie did not understand this, and thus crossed her arms in utter defiance. Ree calmly took his ax, brought it behind his head, and let it smash into the tree. Vibrations rattled through the trunk. Shrie's insolence disappeared.

"Manure!"

"Shrie! Where did you learn that word?" Corious asked, shocked.

"Ree tell me it a better way of saying 'stop' in your language."

Ree was now smirking, and a look of pure wonder crossed Corious's face.

"That's rather cruel, but hilarious nonetheless," Corious murmured to himself. "Why did I not think of that?"

"Are you coming down now, Ruler of the Forest?" Ree brought the ax behind his head once more.

"Shrie coming down! You just wait and manure doing that."

Corious chuckled as he dropped the last few feet to the ground and said, "You should really tell her."

"No, we shouldn't. It's funny."

Tar joined them on the ground. "Maybe you should tell her and not lose her trust," he volunteered.

"He's right, Ree," Corious said half in sarcasm and half truthfully.

Ree scowled but said, "Shrie, don't say that word. It doesn't mean stop; it means something else—something unpleasant."

"Ok, Shrie now only say that when referring to Ree," Shrie retorted jokingly, hopping from the tree.

In a cheery mood, the foursome continued their search for a camp location. As they walked, Shrie related to Ree what information she could. He wrote it down carefully in a curiously concealed journal and then closed his eyes as if to imagine the officials' movements.

"We'll need a place we can conduct assaults from, at least for a short time."

Shrie did not volunteer her distaste for his plan and for once agreed readily. With Ree's plan in mind, they crossed the river with relative ease. The water, cool and calm, seeped through their clothes.

"Keep low," Shrie reminded them of the constant danger. "I see caves ahead on river bank. What say you, Corious, Ree?" There was no rebuttal, so swimming gently in the small waves and swaying reeds, Shrie let herself float in the ebbing water. Her dark hair floated majestically behind her. Corious was tempted to pull it, but Ree reached around Tar to slap Corious's groping hand. Shrie righted herself and entered the first cave as Corious rubbed his stinging hand and as Tar pushed the unbalanced Corious forward. Corious fell awkwardly, splashing into the water like an ungainly duck. Ree slapped Tar staunchly on the back in congratulations, unintentionally sending Tar into the water right behind Corious. Oblivious to this, Shrie squirmed into the cave and then back out.

"It not go back far enough to fit us." She dipped herself back into the water and swam to the second cave, not noticing as her three companions started to pay less attention to their quest. Almost completely healed, Tar did not fear the river; it was shallow and gentle at this point in its course to the sea, and he enjoyed knocking the others in when he could. In wake of this, Ree and Corious had fun catching him off guard and no longer felt guilty getting him back. Only during these moments, however, did Shrie choose to turn around, and Corious and Ree both received harsh lectures. Eyeing each other after Shrie had entered the mouth of the next cave, both men shoved each other but were soon in the cave behind her. The ceiling of the site hung relatively low, and sand squished beneath their feet. Shrie picked up the mud mixture with her toes and let it run over them before walking forward. Wet rock replaced the grainy sand under her feet.

"What you think?" she asked the dark tunnel ahead. "What ahead of us Corious?"

"The cave must turn; I don't see anything but rock."

"Ow!" Tar groaned slightly, grabbing his head and attempting to quell the frustration welling inside of him.

"What wrong, Tar?"

"I did not know the ceiling sloped so low; I hit my head."

"Sorry, Tar, we tell you next time an obstruction is in your path."

"Thanks."

Ree hushed them. "I think I hear something. Listen."

Hushed whistling echoed throughout the cave.

"That wind, Ree," Shrie stated like a teacher explaining a simple concept to a child. "Keep going. This cave is very long and deep. It make good place to hide, but I not so sure about camp. Something is strange. It feel different, this cave."

Corious shouted suddenly. Everyone turned to look at him in surprise, but his eyes, opened wide, were plastered to the floor. "It's a tomb," he said uneasily. Shrie's stomach turned as her eyes discovered an old skeleton lying in the cave's recesses. Scraps of an official uniform clung to the pearly bone. The sepulchral aura could not be broken.

"They must have turned on themselves," Ree reasoned. "It is the only explanation."

"What's going on?" Tar questioned worriedly.

"There dead officials here," Shrie said. "Maybe we turn back."

"That would be folly," Ree reasoned. "The officials would never come back here, and thus it would be perfect for our camp. Besides, what Corious thought was a turn is the end; the cave really isn't so deep after all."

At that moment, Tar tripped. Shrie caught him, but noticed the odd shape of the block on which he had stumbled. Placing Tar back on his feet, she crouched to examine it. Rubbing her hand over its surface, she found it to be not too smooth, not too rough, but almost white enough to be a…

"A tooth!" she exclaimed, unnerved. "Is a giant fang Tar tripped on." Ree whirled around, startled by Shrie's discovery.

"That's two times I've tripped over an object of interest."

"Let me see that!" Ree demanded. It was too heavy to lift. The color drained from his face. In the process of attempting to gain better leverage, Ree staggered forward, knocking Shrie off her feet. She lurched backwards, her shoulder sliding along the rim of a previously unnoticed opening. In what seemed like an instant, the orifice swallowed her. The remaining trio gaped at the place where Shrie had once been and at the hole from which the wind whistled. Corious called Shrie's name and peered into the hole; nothing but darkness filled the space.

Recovering first, Tar said, "We have to find her. Who knows what's down there. Take a step back," he continued, feeling his way along the edge of the opening.

"Tar, you're crazy," Corious paused. "I'm going with you. I mean, I don't know why we think it's dangerous," he shrugged histrionically. "A couple of dead officials, a large tooth—it's probably nothing. And besides, it was an accident. You know for a fact Shrie can take care of herself just fine. In fact, she lets me know this every single day. I think it would be funny if we left her there a few days. I mean, come on, she'll probably make it back here before we even leave," Corious said smiling.

"Personally, I agree with Corious. However, if Tar goes, I go," Ree headed over to stand next to Tar.

"Well, I'm not going to stand in this cave waiting for you, so I guess I will have to go too," Corious said, attempting a joke.

"It's settled then. Corious, you go first."

Ree never finished his sentence; in a matter of seconds Tar had pushed all three of them into the hole. As he fell, Corious pondered Tar's ability. He was blind, but very persuasive, and a tad too smart for his own good.

Corious groaned softly. Trying to stand on wobbly legs, he bumped his head against something hard.

"So that took us where, exactly?" Corious mumbled incoherently into the darkness. Tar's voice rang through the eerie cavern.

"Corious, Ree! Come this way. I feel a cool breeze. There must be an opening somewhere; the cavern must widen along this passage. Come help me find it," Tar shouted as he sloshed through the stagnant water covering the ground.

Kicking Ree into full consciousness, Corious started after Tar.

Shrie skulked among the swaying, dead grasses of the underground swamp, her body alert. In the caverns, she could barely see the difference between dry land and the pockets of old river water which lay hidden beneath fallen reeds.

"They so dense," she mumbled under her breath. "I say, 'It time to turn back,' but they say, 'That folly!' Now Shrie is stuck in big swamp cavern with big beast. That is where fang comes from." She crouched quietly in the reeds. "Yes, Shrie seems to remember the trees telling her about that once. A giant beast—"

"Beast?" asked an incredulous voice behind her.

Shrie whirled around and shot an arrow; it went wide.

"Sorry to startle you."

"Oh, it just you, Ree. What you doing down here?" she asked in vexation.

"Shrie, we are here to rescue you," Ree began.

"I tell you Corious, Ree, and yes you, too, Tar—you always get me into a mess I always has to get you out of. You here to rescue me? Ha, funny joke, Ree," Shrie retorted.

"Shrie, you cannot get out without our help," said Corious, attempting reason.

"Shrie do fine on her own. Shrie ruler of forest! You three are silly boys with many weapons."

"Maybe many weapons will help stupid men and high and mighty Shrie get out of this place," Corious suggested.

Shrie quieted for a moment, her eyebrows knit together, pensive. She appeared to be concentrating on what Corious had said. The rest of them waited in hopeful silence.

"Can weapons kill beast?" Shrie asked cautiously.

"How large is this…beast?" questioned Ree.

"Much bigger than a Mali-Mali?" asked Tar, fearing Shrie's response.

"Oh, much bigger than Mali-Mali. Mali-Malis tell me beast is hungry and…"

"Let's not go there; let us try this again. How big is the beast?" questioned Corious.

"Maybe around fifty Shrie heights high and thirty Ree heights wide."

"It's fat," commented Tar, surprised.

"Can weapon spear through beast?"

"Probably not through it, but maybe a few feet in," answered Tar, who did not really know the answer but wished to keep the peace.

"Will it go in a few Shrie feet or a few Ree feet? Because a Ree foot is much bigger than a Shrie foot." Shrie thought that to be a very intelligent question.

Corious tried to delineate the usual measurements which the rebels used to no avail. He finally sighed. "Shrie, you see Mali-Mali head?"

"No, and you should be quiet so as not to alert beast to our presence."

"I mean imagine one," Corious insisted.

"What imagine mean? Officials never use that word."

"They probably didn't," mumbled Corious, "but try to picture one in your mind."

"Ok, Shrie can do that."

"Now a foot is as long as a baby Mali-Mali head is wide."

"Oh! Imagination," Shrie prided herself on the neologism. With everyone satisfied, they walked circumspectly forward.

"You know, I don't know why we have to kill this beast." Corious's foot sunk into a muddy hole; he pulled it out with difficulty. "Why can't we turn around and climb out the hole we fell down?"

Shrie glared at him. "Beast is angry now; he will follow us out of hole and destroy us. Is better to fight him here in the cavern."

Whispering to Ree, Corious advocated, "I say we rush Shrie and drag her kicking and screaming through the hole from whence we came."

Ree seemed to consider this for a moment but then answered, "If Shrie is right—"

"Shrie is right," she answered.

"How did she hear that?" Corious asked in genuine amazement as the brackish water surrounded his ankles. She glowered at him.

"Right, well, because if she is, and if the beast comes after us—"

"We will not be able to outrun it, and we will drown in the river," Shrie finished. "Beast is a menace to forest; we destroy him now."

An unsettling silence descended upon the four companions. Defeated, Corious threw his sword up and down. Shrie hummed softly, and Ree and Tar kicked at stones. Corious assumed Tar could hear the stones splashing in the muck and would kick at one when he heard it. *Ingenious, really.* Shrie began scanning the horizon line, waking small fears in the centers of their guts. Corious began to gnaw tirelessly on his lip. Ree unsheathed his sword, and Tar kept walking.

"Psst, Tar," Shrie hissed, "I see something." Tar stopped in his tracks.

"I hear it," he moaned, the color draining from his face.

Corious looked around wildly. He did not see or hear anything. The silence discomfited him, but then a shrill scream screeched and echoed off the cavernous walls.

Bats, previously undetected, shrieked in cacophony and fluttered away. Shrie whimpered a prayer-like chant before screaming a return challenge. By the look on Tar's face, Corious thought Tar was going to kill her. Ree grimaced as he shook his head. Any other time it would have been humorous.

Shaking with the pounding of the creature's arrival, stalactites fell ominously close to the foursome. In the seconds it takes for a wave to roll over the sand, it happened. The beast, a terrifying demon, exploded into view. There it stood, like a hideous vision straight from the nightmares which haunt all minds. Ghastly, yellow fangs hung from its foaming mouth, and its mad eyes searched the cavern ravenously. Scales rained down its sides and back, and powerful arms and legs propelled it forward. From its nostrils, thin trails of smoke snaked sharply into the air. Its whip-like tail remained coiled.

"A leviathan," Ree said, awestruck.

Corious almost threw up but caught himself. Instead, he whipped out his sword and pretended to be brave. Shrie hollered, her back bent and her arms flung from her sides. Her vulnerable pose flirted with death; Ree feared she was suicidal. If there had been any chances of avoiding confrontation with the beast, she had just ruined them. With another cry, she reprimanded their wavering spirits, and the three men yelled, running right behind her. Shrie danced in and out of the beast's legs and angry claws while attempting to spear at the soft underbelly.

The hair on Corious's neck prickled as he moved closer to the dragon-like creature. He slashed at the beast violently, only to be rewarded with a solid blow to his leg. Luckily, the beast was unable to move as swiftly or as fluidly in the cavern as it would have in the open. Corious knew he would have to exploit even the smallest weakness if he wanted to see the outside world once more.

Tar burned with hot anger. He hated the weakness that restricted him so much. In a fury, he thrust his spear and heard it bounce off the beast. He also heard it shriek in anger. The scream inspired Tar to fight. It let him know he could conquer, even if the victory was pyrrhic.

Corious gagged once more as the monster charged; it was hideous. Its small beady eyes darted to and from the four warriors who had finally broken from their paralyzed states of fear. Its eyes searched their souls. It clawed at the air and threw its bulk at Ree who had dashed forward to attack. Its claws harmlessly pounded the ground behind him as Ree avoided the blow. Corious sidestepped cautiously to escape the monster's line of sight, but its ever watchful gaze caught Corious inching behind it. The leviathan bellowed in rage as Tar's spear glanced off its body and raked several, brilliant scales from its shoulder.

Rolling behind a boulder, Corious's body jerked awkwardly as the creature's monstrous footsteps sent waves of energy surging through the ground. When he peeked warily above the rock, the monster had turned. Stepping lightly over the unfavorable ground, Corious neared the leviathan's tail. He waited a split second and then dug his sword into the creature's fatty flesh. Yanking his sword from the monster's bloodied tail, Corious began to scale the extension. He forced his mind to concentrate as the monster thrashed violently. Digging his fingers beneath the monster's scales, he shinnied onto its back.

Luring the creature after her, Shrie preoccupied the leviathan from the small pestilence scaling its tail. Meanwhile, Corious looked intently for any flaw or break in the monster's hide, but its scales were bonded together like solid shields. Dense wafts of smoke from the monster's nostrils momentarily obscured Corious's vision. Even so, he knew the small, wooden shaft flying through the air was Tar's. Like his first hit, the shaft disappeared into the monster's bulk, and the creature bellowed instantly. Seizing the chance to execute his plan, Corious called down to Ree who shuffled around the monster's leg. He imitated a spear throw, and Ree eagerly sprinted to Tar's fallen spear. He heaved it through the air, and Corious bent slightly backwards to catch it.

Sheathing his sword, Corious put both hands on the shaft. He lifted it over his head, and while he still held his precarious balance, he plunged the spear head through a knot of scales loosened by Tar's previous attack. Corious pushed heavily against the spear, penetrating the soft skin that lay beneath the creature's rigid casing of scales. The monster convulsed horridly in pain and flailed uncontrollably. The leviathan's spasms provided an open shot to the three rebels below but sent Corious rolling down its sharp, scaly back. He groped for something to stop his fall, but the curved tail slid him to the ground. Stumbling, Corious regained his footing. Wisps of smoke began to flicker from the monster's steaming nostrils as it lurched after Ree.

"No!" Corious sprinted ahead; Ree was trapped in a corner of the cavern. Running fearlessly between the pillars of moving muscles and sinew, Corious's eyes burned from sweat and focus.

Throbbing in pain, Ree slashed the monster's lip with his sword. Fire exploded and bore into the cavernous walls. Halting in horror, Corious felt himself being shoved from behind.

"Move!" Ree shouted as an infuriated claw struck the ground next to Corious. Diving, the two hit the ground. Droplets of sweat and blood flew into the air upon impact, and the warriors quickly disentangled their limbs, crawling forward under the ceiling of monstrous scales. In retaliation, the leviathan slouched to the ground so that its weight rested on their backs. Shouting in pain, they plunged their swords upwards; Ree and Corious fought the sinking force that pushed them into the ground. The leviathan's blood rained upon their heads, and Corious labored for air. Falling to the ground, Corious found that the darkness shielded his eyes, and then the weight was gone. He was free. Forcing himself to stand, Corious wiped the blood from his face.

The black eye was before him, bleeding and pierced with an arrow. It was deceivingly still, contrasting the writhing body of the beast. Grabbing the eyelid, Ree pulled himself onto the head, and his sword dug into the skull. Corious held onto a falling scale and jabbed his sword into the lower jaw before the scale ripped off and he fell to the ground. Shrie managed to heave him to his feet while shooting. A long slash rode along the jaunt of her cheekbone. She seemed not to notice it.

"Fight, Corious!" she cried. "You still strong."

The minutes passed, and eventually everything moved and lived in slow motion. Shrie's arrows tirelessly besieged the leviathan. Tar wearily hacked up and down in jerky but consistently timed strokes. Ree recklessly hurled himself from the mangled head with sword in hand, and the monster swatted at them in burgeoning agitation. The leviathan's anger would peak viciously but latently. The exhausted, aggravating rhythm broke when Corious lunged forward in resentment and Tar tripped violently over a stone.

Throwing Ree from its back, the fiend lunged at Tar and swung at him with its razor claws. Tar let out an abrupt cry and did not move.

Shrie screamed, "Go Corious! Go, go back!"

Corious panicked and shouted random curses; the attack was failing. With the entirety of his remaining strength, he ran. Out of the corner of his eye, he saw the monster's claw come down upon Tar again. This time, Corious swung mightily and cleaved the creature's fingers from its forearm, inviting a rain of blood upon his head. He grabbed Tar, threw him over his shoulder, and proceeded to fling his sword in the creature's general direction. Then he sprinted off with Tar, spitting the monster's blood from his mouth.

Ree was blinded by anger. He was weakening, and Tar had become a casualty. He could not and would not let his friends down. He swore to not let the monster defeat them. With yet another war cry, he evaded a blow and shielded his head briefly with his arms. After a rushed recovery, he pretended to swing his sword to the right but then stabbed left, hitting his target. The monster bellowed in an ululation of rage. Ree somersaulted through the air, preparing to launch his sword. Crunch. His sword never left his hand. Instead, his arm ground against his shoulder socket as it was pushed perpendicularly into his back. Breathing was impossible, and colors swarmed before his eyes in a kaleidoscope of colors. It seemed as if his shoulder had left his body. For a moment, he lay motionless; Shrie would have to fight by herself.

Ree waited for the darkness to take him as he bravely withstood the sheer pain. A deafening moan exploded in his ears after a series of slurred and muffled sounds met his distorted senses.

He forced open his eyes to see the monster stumble and then fall into the dank swamp water. For some reason, the leviathan's scales had turned black and were now waving over its body like a rippling flag. The leviathan's feeble movements, its last attempts to heave its hulk from the cavern floor, sent ripples through the water. Many wounds graced its scaly flesh, and fire leapt from the creature's mouth only to consume its own flesh. A rank smell filled the cave; Ree felt his stomach heave, but nothing left his mouth. Rolling, he painfully tried to rise but could not. *Where is Shrie?* Something pulled at the corners of his mind. He would not like to lose her. *Tar, where is Tar? With Corious...the body...* The sequence of events rolled through his mind.

"I must find them," he said aloud before losing consciousness.

Shrie stabbed ferociously at the monster.

"Dance with me," she cried jeeringly, sliding from under its massive limbs. She ran yards ahead; it followed in a sulking rage. Good—it was where she wanted it, away from the others. Her spear point was slightly dulled, but the creature's movements were inhibited by the small space. Shrie remembered in the forest when she had once seen many ants eating a grasshopper. She hoped she could bring the creature down as easily; for if not, the grasshopper could always obliterate the lone ant. Shrie retained her composure until Ree collapsed. Then, the fear seized her. Without thinking, she cried for help.

"Mali-Mali! Shan we ha! Mali! Come Mali-Malis, come! Shrie needs help!" The call of the Mali-Malis left her lips between thrusts at the repulsive beast. "Mali-Mali! Shan we ha Mali!" A movement, slow and small, caught Shrie's eye. It came from the opening in the cavern. "Why Shrie not think of this before?" She lowered her sword, and within seconds, a mass of black spiders had crawled over the creature. The Mali-Malis had come. Slowly, painfully slowly, the monster collapsed. Shrie yelled with joy and relief before the effects of the sudden battle gripped her. Hauling her weary body onto the back of a nearby Mali-Mali, she let one of its legs stroke her back before urging it to scramble into one of the cavern's recesses.

"Corious and Ree—must find them, Mali, must find them!"

Corious's feet pounded the ground in the frantic, unrelenting rhythm of panic. Sweat and shame streaked his face. He should not have run. He knew himself to be unyielding and needed in battle. *What am I talking about?* Tar's body slumped over his shoulder grew heavier with every passing moment. No, Tar needed him more. He had done the right thing.

"You're getting too used to hitching rides on my back, boy," Corious told the wilted body as a tear streamed down his face. His legs ached. How long had he been running? His knees buckled, and he toppled to the ground exhaustedly. Groaning, he tried to disentangle himself from Tar when something touched his leg. Corious let out an enraged cry.

"Go away!" Corious reached for a sword that was not there and then realized nothing had happened. Looking down at his feet, he saw the shadow of the Mali-Mali covering him. It was silent, staring at him. Corious sighed with relief and stared back.

"Why, I think I recognize you," Corious commented deliriously. "Aren't you the one who lifted me to safety in the trees?" Corious asked weakly. The giant spider seemed to smile before rocking back and forth and rumbling in a language he could not understand. Abruptly, the Mali-Mali pulled both Corious and Tar onto its back before trotting away to the front of the cavern.

Ree gritted his teeth and propped himself up with his good arm. His one shoulder felt wrenched out of place, and his ankle was swollen to the severe size of a Kwallo fruit. Even so, there were no bone breaks and therefore nothing to stop him. By pure determination, he achieved a kind of standing, hunched position and hobbled in a circle. Everything smelled horrid, and a rancid aroma streamed into his nostrils. He called for each of his friends, but the water dripping from the ceiling of the cavern was his only answer. His voice sounded hoarse and tired, even to himself, yet he called again. After an hour of prodding and searching, he found a small opening in a rock ledge. He tugged at the loose rocks until bright light flooded the cavern. An anemic cry of joy left his lips as he hurriedly scrambled through the hole. Raising his arm to shield his eyes from the light, he was surprised how rapidly they had become accustomed to the dark. Ree moved into the shade of a lone tree.

When he awoke, the light had been replaced by a rumbling noise, as if a cavalry were charging in front of the sun. He tensed and listened as the din ceased, seemingly at his feet.

"There he is!" shouted Corious as he ran to greet Ree. "You're all right! The Mali-Malis found me and must have picked up your scent!" Corious remarked thoughtfully.

"Corious!" Ree attempted to stand, but his ankle failed him. "Have you seen Shrie or Tar?" Ree's face hardened in the sad expectation of tragedy. Corious looked around and pointed past Ree's head with a smile. Ree turned slowly, and as he did, Shrie hopped wearily off a Mali-Mali.

"Ree," she laughed weakly and gave him a bear hug. "Shrie happy to see you. Is a great victory, killing the beast." She paused and then jogged lightly to Corious and squeezed him hard. "I still had more hits than you," she said impishly.

Corious smiled feebly and released her from his arms as the Mali-Mali carrying Tar approached them. Shrie hurried to it and lifted its passenger with Corious's assistance. Laying Tar next to Ree, she ran her hands over the young boy's wounds. It seemed like yesterday she had done the same thing in the jungle with the sound of the falls behind them.

Filled with worry, Ree's eyes betrayed the depth of his concern. Shrie assured him Tar would be fine. Ree relaxed; Tar had avoided death once more. Leaving a hand to rest on Tar's arm, Shrie jadedly whispered something into one of the spider's ears. It purred gently and crawled into the misty twilight. All of the spiders departed with the exception of one which decided it wanted to treat Ree's wounds. Ree became uncomfortable when it started to lick his face with its diminutive tongue, but Shrie insisted it should be done.

"Ree, don't squirm. The Mali-Mali gives love licks. Mali heals wounds. Tar and Corious already getting better from it." She curled up in the grass a little ways away from him.

"She's telling the truth, Ree," Corious chirped as he lay down, letting the lethargy he had held off so long finally seep into his muscles.

"Hhmm...yeah," Ree responded, watching as the others dropped off into sleep. Their three dark shapes blended peacefully into the landscape. *What a strange day it has been...*Ree's eyelids drooped, and the giant spider let Ree's head fall back and rest against the tree as he drifted into a calm slumber.

Tar groaned. The thrill of victory eluded him; he was no Theseus though he had slain a Minotaur. He groped for the ground; grass spread beneath his fingers. He was no longer in the cavern; Corious, or maybe Ree, had carried him, and that was as much as his memory brought back to him. Three sets of soft breathing met his ears. Despite what had happened, they had made it out alive. Tar noticed his eyes were swollen shut, as if it mattered. He absentmindedly moved his hands over his body, checking for broken bones. Though he cringed as probing fingers detected bruises and contusions, nothing hurt more than his vacuous stomach. As if to prove its hunger, his stomach rumbled loudly. Tar considered his injuries, and then he smiled. He would look forward to Shrie's fussing. Corious and Ree would sulk as Tar became the object of her attention. He sighed as the cool morning breeze swept through the trees. *Wait, is it morning?* Tar painfully twisted and patted the ground near him. Fresh dew rested in beady drops, seeping into the cracks of his dry skin. Yes, it was morning.

Birds chirped, and the last coals of the fire crackled; no one else stirred. *How are they?* Worry and concern shot through his body. He hurriedly tried to stand but found he could not. He let his body sink into the ground hopelessly and transferred his efforts into forming a wordless prayer—an expression of the bond which entwined them. His anxiety dissipated. *At least Shrie cannot die,* Tar thought dreamily. *The wild spirit of the wood lives in a sphere beyond ours, and no one, not even Ree or Corious, can catch or tame her.*

Tar attempted to sit but found again he could not. *That's funny*, he thought nervously. He tried again and succeeded, but a burning pain ripped through his back. Tar cursed the ugly beast that had rendered him so useless. Lying back down, he let the pain engulf him.

Horror paralyzed him. The scream would not leave his lips, and no one responded to his frozen prayer. The leviathan bore down upon him, incapacitating his will to live and breath. The beast was in him; it was him.

Ree awoke with a start, bolting upright. *Bad nightmare.* He shook his head and wiped the sweat from his forehead. *I do not give into dreams.* Ree rolled his shoulders but closed his eyes, sucking the clean air into his nostrils and building the courage needed to examine his injuries. Opening a slanted and swollen eye, Ree watched as the shredded skin of his left leg bloomed before him. The monster's claws had left deep gashes. Dried blood matted his pants, and newly formed scabs covered his itching legs. His right ankle throbbed beneath a gargantuan knob of purple and yellow.

"Monster coming to get you, Ree?" Tar asked grimly. He had not moved from his prostrate position on the ground. The dying fire sent ghostly shadows crawling up and down Tar's features.

Ree looked at him, startled until the shame of his terror transformed into fury. Tar had recognized his fear. "I thought for sure you had died." The thought of Corious carrying Tar's limp body subdued Ree's anger. "About the beast," Ree started slowly, "he's dead."

"Because of you." Tar had revealed Ree's weakness but complimented his strength. Ree did not respond. Tar cleared his throat.

"How are the others?" Ree inquired gruffly.

"They're fine. Shrie's worn out, but well, we're all fine."

Ree's eyes involuntarily shifted to his own wounds; they were clean but fresh, threatening to spill the blood which moved warily beneath the tattered skin. "How's your back?" Ree asked, ignoring the escalating desire to scratch at his raw legs.

"It will hurt my pride to admit the truth."

"Can you stand?"

"No, I don't think so. At least not yet," Tar ventured timidly. "Can you?"

Pausing, Ree finally answered, "No. No, I don't think I can either." He leaned his head back against the tree before adding, "You know, Tar, it would have scared me once, not being able to stand."

"You're not afraid with Shrie and Corious here."

"And you, and something else I can't explain."

Tar paused before saying with certainty, "I feel it also." He smiled knowingly. "I knew something was different about Shrie. I remember a man who used to roam from village to village; nice guy, so in love with the Almighty that he loved everyone.

I didn't understand then, but maybe I do now. One thing I know: the Almighty's presence is powerful here."

"So you believe in Him too?" Corious's weak voice entered the conversation. "Shrie talked of this Almighty. Maybe there is some credit to it after all. But more importantly, Ree, Tar, how are you?"

"Fine," Ree and Tar answered in relative unison.

"Just fine," Ree echoed softly. "Tell me more, Tar, about this Almighty."

Tar shrugged tiredly. "I know just as much or as little as everyone else. I have heard some whispers of such a being in my village, but it was never totally embraced. No one knew if there were many gods, one, or none at all. I myself do not believe there can be more than one God, and I have sustainable peace; the idea of many gods does not work for me, though both do not make complete sense to be sure."

Ree stared at Tar intently, folding his arms. He was interested in Tar's beliefs, but skeptical. He found it hard to decipher the false explanations from truthful ones. Ree merely fought, lived, and breathed battle; that had always been his life. Yet after the exacting fight with the monster, he began to hope that war would not be his sole purpose in life. For if there were no gods, then there was no purpose because humanity was therefore accidental. In which case, he really had no duty, no duty to fight for good. Performance and appearance would be the only two things of potential value, and where did that leave the ugly or the disabled? The goals of people would change; he may as well sell his life for thrills. His head spun as old values set in stone began to crumble. Ree, beginning to feel uncomfortable from probing too deeply into his set ways, thrust aside such matters. For now, he decided firmly to live in the present and not trouble himself greatly with spiritual matters. The nagging feeling that pressed him to continue his search was pushed aside. The rock wall of dependable nothingness filled the void. He felt awful after the draining ordeal he had suffered in the dankness of the underground swamp, and his weariness surfaced to the top of his mind.

"The fact that we are all alive proves there is some greater force to reckon with than what meets our eyes here on Kurak," Tar continued, half-joking about their fighting skills while trying to prove his point to Ree.

Corious yawned before scooting himself next to Tar, rubbing his bloodshot eyes.

"You look horrible," Tar joked, knowing very well he could not see how Corious looked.

Corious frowned. "Do I really?"

Ree smiled slightly before gesturing to the headband pulled over Tar's eyes and forehead.

Corious growled, perturbed he had fallen for the gag. "Well, if I don't look awful..."

"Oh, but you do, my good friend, you do," Ree started.

"Yes, your present state could have killed the monster if he set eyes on you, I am afraid." Tar interrupted humorously.

Corious muttered something at Ree in another language but continued, "If I don't look awful, I certainly feel it. My back has never been this knotted."

Tar shifted his weight from one side to the other. "I did not know you spoke Kairnian, Corious."

Corious nodded, though stopped when his shoulder muscles could only move so far. "The rebels had a fortress on Kairn in the Sea of White Pearls. That is until the Shalkans swept down the coast and found us there very ill-equipped. There were, at most, two units securing the stone compound."

Tar said nothing more, but pursed his lips in thought. He stretched his legs past the fern bed and dug his boot into some old moss clinging to a piece of slate.

After a couple of minutes of thinking, Tar threw out another question. "Where are we in relation to our old position, Corious? Ree?"

Ree peered beyond the wispy vines and saw the glint of sunshine on a body of water maybe one or two hundred yards off to the south.

"We are northeast of the cave near the river, I am pretty sure, and right now we are in the thick of the jungle. We've heard nothing from the Shalkans or anything about their positions in awhile, so we should have time to recover."

"And we should eat some real hunks of meat to replenish ourselves," Corious added emphatically, rubbing his concave stomach.

"I know," Ree agreed, "but Shrie almost speared me and roasted me over the fire the last time I suggested hunting for mere sport."

Tar remained silent, and by the time Corious and Ree looked back at him, he had rolled over on his side, breathing softly through his nose.

The next day came and went in the grogginess which often accompanies sleep. Every color faded into a different shade of the constant gray that filled the day. Tired muscles hurt only when awake, so most of their time was spent in slumber. Shrie had left once to retrieve fruit, and the small expedition had tired her so much that she slept straight through the rest of the afternoon and night. Worries of officials seldom crossed their minds, for they felt safe amongst company and under the aegis of the great trees.

Little was said about the battle or their wounds. The four were never awake at the same time, or, if they were, they kept their eyes closed. No one wished to interrupt the serenity of rest. The days passed too quickly, and the nights draped darkness over their quiescent bodies. The patient humming of bugs and the stealthy steps of nocturnal hunters filled the sleeping woods. No one stirred in his or her sleep, and morning rays crept into the sky slowly, fearing to wake its worn defenders. But even the earth with all its might cannot stop turning for the bravest of heroes, and life moves on even if one ceases to take part in its pattern.

Light gray swam next to the dark blue cloud and soon pushed the night away from the blazing chariot of the sun. The nightly prowlers retreated into their hidden abodes, and morning creatures replaced their darker brothers. Birds filled the air with their music, and Ree's eyes opened to receive the morning.

Twinkling lights played upon the faces of leaves basking in the sun. Ree straightened his back and stretched his arms, freeing them from the tight grip of sleep. Rolling his shoulders, he eyed the fruit in the center of the sleeping bodies and reached for a piece. His arms were not long enough, and he glanced at his healing legs, wondering if they would move for him. Underneath the hard muscle, his stomach growled, and Ree decided to satisfy his stomach at the expense of his legs. Stiffly, he rose like a newborn deer. His legs wobbled at first, and then he locked his knees and forced them to bend. The skin stretched and pulled, but the threat was hollow.

Ree forgot the fruit as the awe of a simple movement filled him. So easily he had taken for granted his physical ability. Only when it was taken from him did the profoundness of the working, human body instill wonder. Ree's stomach prodded him once again to eat, and he complied placidly, selecting an orange, squishy sphere from the multicolored pile. Sweet juice slid merrily down his throat. Ree could see why Shrie liked it so much. Within seconds, only the pit was left in his hand, and he stood triumphantly to throw it into the jungle. As he swung his legs back and forth to loosen them, the muscles relinquished their tight holds and adjusted themselves to use. He heard a wistful sigh and turned to see Tar's form slowly rise to the standing level. Tar's face looked haggard, and Ree, using his newly working legs, approached him.

"You look tired," he remarked.

Tar gazed at his feet but gave Ree the okay sign while brushing his hair from his eyes.

"It's good to see you up again."

Tar stretched his arms, and Ree could sense his pleasure at the pull and strain of the muscles.

"Feels good to move again, doesn't it?" Ree slapped a thick hand on Tar's shoulder as the light gray sky rose above them. "Want breakfast?"

Tar sleepily readjusted his head band over his eyes. "Breakfast—that sounds nice," he murmured, and the two walked laboriously from the small clearing into the waking jungle.

A warm, inviting aroma wandered into Corious's nose, causing him to start from his sleep. Corious rose excitedly at the thought of breakfast, but the enthusiasm was dampened when his head connected with the rock ledge above. He swiftly sat, tenderly rubbing his head.

"Stupid, stupid, stupid!" Corious muttered angrily as the pain of his injuries throbbed dully. Groggy from sleep, he yawned and rubbed his eyes; dried dirt fell from his face.

"Corious, I can always tell when you're awake," Tar said as he stirred something over a fire.

"Glad you're feeling better, Tar." Corious grimaced as he straightened his back, perching himself on a stone near the food. "Ummm, eggs!" Corious said in a droll, deep voice.

"Thought I'd put something new on the menu." Ree glanced into the pot as the eggs sizzled hysterically.

"I think it's done guys!" Tar cried, leaning over to scoop some of the mush into his hand.

"Won't Shrie be surprised," Corious remarked, "the boys getting breakfast for once!" Corious stuffed an egg into his mouth. "This is good!"

The three men began to talk, and expressive hand motions once again entered the conversation as the second language. Able to move freely, an inexpressible joy worked slowly through them.

Halfway into their meal, Shrie awoke.

"Hello Shrie," Ree said plainly, "have an egg."

Shrie sat down, still not fully awake, and combed a hand through her long hair. Ree came over and handed her two eggs.

Shrie sniffed the food, paused, and then cried out, "Ah! You boys stupid!" Standing promptly, she threw the eggs into the woods. The event had made her very much awake.

Corious, Tar and Ree exchanged befuddled glances.

"These not eggs! These Gwaka mushrooms," Shrie continued, "not safe to eat, not at all!" Shrie shook her head in disgust.

Corious reacted first, coughing and spitting out what he could of the mushrooms. He appeared positively sick. Ree and Tar did much the same, choking up what remained halfway down their throats. Tar especially looked distressed, wincing every time he coughed; the motion aggravated his back.

"You boys, you never learn!" Shrie complained as she threw up her hands. "Shrie go find good breakfast. Boys stay here, not eat mushrooms!" With difficulty, Shrie moved her rigid body forward to get her bow and came back a moment later rambling empty complaints.

"Well, one thing is for sure, the battle did not dampen her tongue," Tar observed. As she faded into the forest, Ree spoke.

"I'm going with her." He got up painfully and grabbed his dented sword. "The officials are probably swarming the forest by now," he mentioned unnecessarily. He took a fleeting look back and then bounded carefully after Shrie. Corious and Tar avoided mentioning the obvious fact: in their conditions, fighting was out of the question. Feeling good and rushing towards death were not immediately compatible; nevertheless, they knew Ree's unyielding nature and let him go, trusting the forest and Shrie to guide him.

After watching the two go, Corious and Tar were left to clean the remains of the failed meal. As Corious attempted to assemble the mess, Tar snickered quietly from his cross-legged position a few yards away. It was obvious by Corious's suppressed moans that he had by far eaten the most. Tar convulsed in hushed laughter as Corious's stomach gurgled and burped stridently. Corious turned, agitated by the sound of his friend's mirth.

"What," Corious remarked sourly, "you think it's funny?" His face turned a deep shade of red; his stomach seemed a pot of boiling slop ready to explode.

Tar's only response consisted of pointing innocently to his covered eyes.

"So maybe you're blind and didn't know," he stopped, and his face bent in a hideous cringe, "but you still didn't have to feed me poisonous mushrooms. Though, in reality, I trusted Ree to determine their edibility; you only carried them back." He groaned as his stomach threw itself violently to one side and then to the other.

Sympathetic, Tar finished tidying camp as Corious directed him between clenched teeth and stomach spasms. When everything finally had a semblance of unity, they waited, during which time Tar managed to contain his amusement and avoid offending Corious. Though Corious's stomach problems had lessened by the time Ree and Shrie returned, they still rendered him unable to eat the breakfast Shrie cooked from her findings an hour later. Meat, herbs, and fruit comprised their celebration breakfast, and despite the earlier happenings and persisting injuries, it was a blissful reunion of strength and spirit.

Lazily, the foursome ate and lounged until Corious put out the last of the fire and involved them in a trenchant battle analysis. Talk of the leviathan's size and origin was tossed back and forth and then dismissed after each had told a separate tale of both. As Tar had been unconscious for the second half of the battle and as Shrie was not one to brag about such serious matters, the conversation fell apart into a long-winded, vapid tête-à-tête. The next hours passed in a dull monotony.

Tired of the insipid state, Corious could no longer restrain his roguish impulses. Smirking, he leaned over to whisper in Shrie's ear. Shrie curled back her lips and reached for something next to her. When he had turned triumphantly to the other three men, Shrie smashed a huge, and luckily rotting, stick over his head. Corious chuckled to himself while rubbing his head. He had a knack for annoying Shrie. Without warning, a ball of mud splattered over his face. Corious leapt, releasing a small grunt and launching a fistful of mud back at her. Reaction times and ingenuity on both sides were slow and lacking, but Ree and Tar enjoyed the evening show nonetheless.

Later that evening, the companions lounged indolently around a suitable campfire with the sole purpose of relieving the tedium of blank time. They spoke about anything which presently came to mind. Corious began by leaning back on his elbows and wiggling his toes by the leaping flames.

"So, Tar, back in your village out west, did you ever get yourself a jungle girl that won your heart?" Corious asked, simply to perturb Shrie but also to unpeel the layers shrouding his aspiring protégé in typical rebel mystery.

Tar laughed spontaneously. "I had a whole group of admirers running me crazy around our village square." His lips curved in a mischievous smirk. "In fact, the High Councilman's wife took quite a liking to me!"

Ree and Corious got a kick out of his ensuing and facetiously exaggerated yarn, but Shrie knew nothing of what they spoke.

"What you three laughing at? Shrie have many friends and admirers—more than even Tar!" Shrie smiled smugly.

Corious slapped Ree on the back as they lost control of their mirth.

"Yes, Shrie," Corious exclaimed, "we couldn't even begin to charm those who adore you! Your social life is most impressive."

Tar's smile broke into open, light laughter. "Yes," he added, "I would never be able to win the attraction of those Mali-Malis."

Shrie's imperious grin turned into a horrible, contorted expression of consternation. "That because Shrie is ruler of forest!" As if that explained everything, Shrie ignored their esoteric humor and waited for their laughter to lapse, which it did as soon as their stomach muscles cramped and their breathing turned into wheezing.

"Did you have an admirer, Corious?" Ree asked, unable to relinquish the joke. But the majority of giddiness had filtered from their minds like helium leaving a rotund balloon.

Corious's eyes clouded over. "Sure—you could call her that I guess, although I was the one doing the admiring."

"What was her name?" Tar pressed.

"I'm tired guys. We should call it a night," Corious stated mysteriously.

"That's a beautiful name," Ree said sarcastically. "Your admirer had creative parents."

Tar let out an obnoxious snort which was the prelude to laughter, but he smothered it when no one joined in his hysterics.

"What does it matter now? I was a child back then with a child's dreams."

"You would have made her proud, my friend," Tar said to compensate for his unwelcome humor. "I am sure of that much."

In the brief aura of gravity, Shrie hummed a boisterous tune, attempting to free her friends from the gloomy mood in which they were suddenly trapped. Guided by her singing, Tar faced Shrie.

"I see," Tar said thoughtfully, "so that's how she gets the Mali-Malis' attention."

Shrie did not realize Tar had attempted another joke, so she smiled, thinking he appreciated her humming. "Yes, Mali-Malis love Shrie's songs. Sometimes they give her ideas for songs as well. Malis try humming too, but they not very good, not very good at all."

The companions gave up the conversation, but they did not forget it.

Days passed in recovery, and at Ree's insistence, they ate meat every night with dinner. Hunting soon claimed first place as the favored activity once their limbs were rejuvenated. Mentally, their minds conquered the pain, and they focused their energies on curing their bodies. Like the weeks of their first times spent together, they hardly bothered themselves with thoughts of officials, and no troubled sightings invaded the perimeter of the camp.

The next morning brought a glowing sun and promising skies, but as the day progressed, heavy clouds rolled wearily across the sky. Corious surveyed the scene above him as a wind blew his hair into a tangled mess. Tar stood next to him, holding a longbow loosely in his long fingers. As Corious's eyes bent from their upward search, Tar began hesitantly nocking an arrow.

"Ok," Corious began, pointing to the wavy lines of red and purple stripes he had painted on a gnarled tree. "I have created a target on the tree in front of you," Corious told the teenager. "I wish you could appreciate my masterpiece," he joked and then hastily cleared his throat when Tar did not respond. "Anyway, I'm going to throw a stick at the target. As soon as you hear the stick hit, to the best of your ability, shoot where you hear the sound."

Tar lifted the bow. As he pulled the string taut, his back, neck, and shoulder muscles stretched like a lion awaking from a long slumber. Corious knelt to pick up a sharp, fairly straight stick.

"Ready?"

Tar pulled back the bowstring a tad farther. Corious hurled the stick at the bulls-eye. Without waiting for the stick to strike the target, Tar quickly readjusted his aim before letting go. Crack! Tar's arrow hit Corious's stick, splintering it into pieces as the arrow nailed the remaining section of the stick to the tree. The shards fell to the ground, and Corious's jaw dropped.

"Not bad," Corious stated blandly after a few moments of silence. "You're half-dead from," Corious could not remember the number of days that had passed since their battle. "You're tired from last week," he improvised, "you're blind, you ate those repulsive mushrooms, and you get a bulls-eye your very first time. As I said, not bad."

In good spirits, Tar retrieved his arrow, and simply said, "Yeah, not that bad."

"Okay," Corious began, still amazed. "You did it once, but can you do it again?"

Tar shrugged but nocked his arrow as if to say yes.

"Here we go," Corious exclaimed. He threw the second stick with less force. It hit the center but barely made a sound.

Tar frowned, puzzled. He pulled the arrow back slowly, turned right and down, and then reluctantly released. Corious watched approvingly as Tar's arrow hit two rings outside the bulls-eye.

"Nice shot!" Corious said approvingly.

"How did I do?" Tar's voice sounded worried, as if Corious's approbation had not been genuine.

"You hit two lines outside the bulls-eye, where my stick struck," Corious replied.

Tar kicked the dirt in front of him and sighed. "Blindness is my only weakness. If I could only see!"

"Tar, you did fine, and you're doing fine. Your blindness has forced your other senses to sharpen, to make up for what your eyes cannot do. Besides, you have us," he added pointing to himself, though Tar would not see the gesture.

"Yeah," Tar admitted, "there's no use complaining."

"That's enough for today," Corious said suddenly, glancing at the sky which was now darker than its morning palette. "Let's head back to camp. Maybe the others are back."

Tar accepted the verdict, and they retrieved the arrow before trekking back to camp. The day steamed with a palpable heat under the stormy sky, and both wiped sweat from their faces and brows. After struggling through the forest, they came upon the camp, but the camp was not as they had left it hours before. Nature's noises seemed to have retreated behind an imposing stillness. Tar's foot crunched down upon a shard of Corious's old pottery; they were still ten feet from camp. Someone had paid them a visit, and they had not bothered to conceal it.

Blankets were strewn about in sad, rumpled piles, mourning Corious's cracked clay bowl and Ree's ripped protective gear. Leftover food from the morning had disappeared. Anxiety racked Corious's body. He bunched his muscles into coiled springs, ready to release their potential force upon whatever might lurk beyond his sight. He took a step back into Tar.

"What's the holdup?"

"I wish I knew. Either Ree and Shrie became real slobs or someone ransacked the camp."

The gray clouds swelled above them menacingly. Bewilderment rampaged across Corious's face until he regained logical thought and drew a concealed knife from a fold in his boot. Tar pursed his lips as he heard the knife leave the sheath.

"A little late for that, don't you think? If the culprit had wanted to fight us, he or she would have already welcomed us."

Nothing stirred except the wind and fat droplets of rain. Tar wandered about the clearing. Corious cautiously advanced despite Tar's reason.

"Officials?" Tar asked skeptically, guessing Corious's train of thought.

"We haven't had sightings of them for weeks," Corious replied, trying to forget the image of their shadowed faces. He squinted into the woodlands. "It was most likely animals or tribesmen. Shrie should know."

Tar shook his head. "Not animals. They wouldn't have stolen things."

"I don't know who they were, but I don't think they'll be back again." Corious put his weapon away with a touch of finality. "Let's gather everything we have left and prepare for the storm. One rests heavy on the horizon, and if I'm correct, we don't have much time before it strikes."

Proving his prediction accurate, an overweight drop of rain splattered to the ground, displacing dampened bits of dirt. The clouds billowed like smoke as Corious and Tar gathered the remains of the camp and piled them under a rock ledge. Tar proceeded to locate two blankets and some sticks which he would use to erect an overhang.

Corious conveniently found and sliced a hollow Naballo branch in half to create a gutter apparatus. Subsequently, using the sticky, inside sap as glue, he placed the branches on the perimeter of the overhang to redirect the flow of water away from their campground. Sifting through their small inventory, Tar noticed their only whole water bowl had been overturned. It was a good time, if any, to lack water. He placed Shrie's basin under the end of the gutter to replenish the starved supply.

Tar's actions halted as Corious's footsteps broke dry brush. The young boy listened intently, and after a frozen minute, Tar satisfied himself with the knowledge that Corious was not going far and that no enemy approached. True to Tar's acumen, moments later, Corious returned with an armload of sizable branches. Tar walked to where Corious had dropped the branches in a disordered heap.

"We'll use the smaller limbs to start a fire," Corious instructed, "and the larger ones to construct a wall which will shield us against the wind and the rain." Brandishing a stick in his hands, Corious tossed it to Tar who started his work despite the increasing drizzle. After completing their tasks, Tar and Corious collapsed by a fire to dry the clothes which clung to them as a frightened child hugs its mother. Their shelter successfully held off the rain tapping rhythmically against the taut, cloth roof.

"The other supplies will have to be replenished," Tar stated, yawning.

Corious shrugged dolefully, positioning himself on a ledge. The filched supplies could not be easily refashioned. "We can always raid the officials." He began to sharpen his knife against a smooth rock.

Tar wished for a superior alternative. "Say, where you think Ree and Shrie are?" he asked fretfully.

Once again, Corious shrugged. This time he was uninterested.

"Come on, Corious," Tar pleaded. "They've been out since…since our second breakfast. Should we not find them?"

"No. They're capable people. They're probably just hunting." Corious's voice trailed off as he focused on whetting his knife in the ensuing silence.

Tar sat compliantly but worriedly. He turned his back to Corious and exhaled noisily. The crackling of the fire and the continual pitter-patter of the rain were the only audible sounds. Minutes ticked by as the two idly wasted time. Tar eventually fell asleep as another hour came and went. Finally, during late afternoon, a noise at the entranceway announced Shrie's arrival.

"Shrie, you're back!" Corious tripped from the ledge into a kneeling position.

"Shh!" Shrie hissed. "Many officials marching this way; must keep quiet!"

Corious nodded his head as if he had suspected it the entire time. Shrie squeezed her way through the narrow entrance. Ree and the dead animal slung over his back entered next. The creature's blood trickled down his back, and rain water matted his hair flat against his head. As he deposited his quarry at Corious's feet, his dark eyes shone perilously behind the wave of straight, dripping locks. Beneath her black tangle of hair, Shrie's eyes revealed an unspoken misery. Grime had worked itself beneath her fingernails, and cakes of wet mud settled into the cracked skin around her knuckles. Corious hung his cape to let Ree change in relative privacy from his soaked clothes. Shrie had no extra garments, and so she stripped the outer layers of animal fur from her shoulders while Corious skinned Ree's catch. Slicing off pieces of meat, he pierced them with a stick and let them dangle over the fire.

Tar, who had awoken from his fitful rest, spoke. "What happened? Where were you?" he asked casually.

An unhappy Shrie gave no reply.

Ree glanced at her and then answered, "Officials." He shared her somber mien. "We were hunting when we stumbled upon their masses. They didn't see us. Shrie yanked me down into a ditch. We went unnoticed. I slew the last one when he caught my eye. We managed to return." Corious continued sharpening his array of knives, as if preparing to fight the officials Ree had mentioned and continued to discuss at pitched fervor. "In this time of danger, our behavior demands discreet measures. We must subjugate the officials or fall into darkness."

Shrie did understand the majority of Ree's impassioned speech, but she knew it was a statement meant to rally their spirits. She decided to lend him her aid.

"They cut down trees! They make ugliness itself appear in my forest! Their faces ugly! They defy my rule! We must usurp them of their power!"

Corious and Tar sat addled by her dialogue. Spoken in such a forceful will, her words had slurred together in a fiery, impassioned speech of inarticulated sound.

"Is she speaking in another language?" Corious whispered to Tar.

Tar shook his head, baffled. Silence prevailed, and Shrie waited first for an excited war cry and then for any sort of response. No one returned her call for quite some time, so she continued.

"I heard an animal. It was small and helpless and in the officials' path. It cried

JULIE AND RYAN DICKERSON

for help, but I could do nothing. They try to steal my power, but I will fight. That why you boys here; you help defeat officials—the dark warriors of doom. They not win against Shrie, no, they not." Shrie let her anger settle. "I not like officials!" She ended quietly but fervently.

Tar came over to her. "Soon," he said, his voice tinted with certainty, "soon we will strike, then the officials will know that Khaltharnga is not their own."

Ree shook his head, as if regretting his impassioned speech spoken but moments earlier. "There are too many. We'll be outnumbered," he commented practically, "any attack now would be folly, and our small shelter would be untenable against their numbers."

"When did being outnumbered ever stop us, Ree? We made a vow, all of us. I do not hold that vow lightly. In fact, I bind the rest of my life to it," Corious exclaimed, his blood boiling with the renewed mention of their seemingly forgotten foe. Corious started to stand but only made it halfway before hitting his head on the ceiling. "By the—"

"Shut your yapper, Corious! If Ree is right, officials might be anywhere near our camp and will hear us," Tar hissed crossly. "They can probably smell our meat cooking even now!"

Ree promptly distinguished the fire. "Yes, you better keep your tongue in check, Corious. No one wants to hear your vile curses."

Corious rubbed his bruised head crossly.

"We move camp tomorrow, above officials to keep our eye on their maneuvers."

"I agree, we must keep moving, Shrie," Corious pointed out, but then realized Shrie had just said maneuver. "Where did you learn all these words?" Corious asked incredulously.

"From Ree, and sometimes Tar," Shrie added.

"What!" Corious exclaimed.

Ree offered no explanation. Corious could understand Tar being smart, but Ree? He was supposed to be all brawn and no brain. Corious liked to think of himself as being the mind of the group. Apparently his vocabulary was lacking.

"Reconnaissance, that's my specialty," Corious said reminding the group of their quest, while thumping his fist on his chest theatrically. Ree guffawed at him, and Corious growled, enticing Ree to anger.

"Well, you'll have some fun tomorrow, Ree," Corious remarked, "trying to climb trees!" At this, Corious cracked himself up but was then subsequently shut up when voices from above filtered to him through the shelter's cloth roof. In a moment of utter astonishment, the companions' mouths froze as thousands of thoughts careened through their heads. Corious and Ree immediately drew their swords and suppressed their terror. Shrie and Tar place their cheeks against the ground, listening carefully.

"Demon bugs, I swear I'll kill them all! You'd think there's no food in the forest the way they eat at you!" cried a despondent, sadistic voice.

"Perhaps we should kill Roken and feed his remains to the bugs and thus be rid of his stupidity, eh?" chimed in another harsh voice. A chorus of discordant laughter broke loose.

"That would be an auspicious move," one of the men agreed.

As the officials trucked through the mire, Corious could see two dozen uniformed men dragging a cumbersome burden behind them. A strange contraption made of wood was held high in the air. Chains, attached to the top in pairs, ran down along the sides. Two men hung from it in shackles, and the extra slack in the chain made a monotonous slapping noise against the wood. The device did not consider comfort a priority. Corious strained to see the dangling men; they appeared to be unconscious, beaten, and without uniform. He knew the look well.

Corious crawled back. "There are officials, but not too many. They're scouts by their looks. They have two rebel prisoners. What do you say to jumping them?"

Shrie looked down as if to say no but then grabbed her spear and slipped out the back as stealthily as an invisible breeze blows across the water. Corious briefed the others before fading behind Shrie into the shadows. He jogged to the nearest tree, agilely pulling himself up with his arms. Ahead, the rattling lanterns of Shalkan scouts sent rays of dull light scattering about the forest. Flipping himself to the next branch with renewed vigor, Corious inched his way up the trunk. Shrie glided fluidly through the trees. When the branches of his tree extended and intertwined with another, Corious stopped his climb. He and Shrie were almost at the same height in adjacent trees. They had made good time.

Squinting to find the positions of the officials, Corious then glanced to Shrie who was making a series of rapid, general gestures. After she had repeated them a few times, Corious deciphered her plan: he was to be the decoy, again. It seemed his glorious battles would have to wait. He leapt crazily to another tree to procure a better position and thanked the Almighty as the branch he grasped stayed in one piece. He used his momentum to swing himself closer to the trunk, and he peered down at the ungainly force creeping through the jungle. He did not have much with which to fashion tantalizing bait, but he scraped up a crude idea.

Implementing his plan, he snapped a branch in half. The Shalkans stopped and shouted amongst themselves.

"Roken! Can you ever be quiet?"

"It wasn't me, Commander. I swear on the bugs eating me alive!"

"Shut up! I heard it again. Who's out there?"

Silence pervaded the forest. Corious tossed the broken branch at the official's head. It bounced off the gnarled helm, and the official stared at it, stupefied. The commander let out a long line of curses before trying to actually pinpoint the spot from where the stick had been thrown.

"Come on out, you condemned galoot!" The commander roared in his fury, "You can't hide from me! If you would like a fight, my soldiers are hungry for blood!"

Corious fixed their positions and his surroundings in his mind before throwing yet another stick at the enemy. He descended from his tree. The official could not see him, and Corious could see the official; Corious liked the odds.

"I don't have time for games with hidden idiots in trees! If you want to fight, fight like a man. We have two of your friends here, and we'll kill them if you don't answer our challenge!"

Corious hesitated; he had not wanted to start a dialogue with the enemy. When the commander held a gun to the head of one of the rebel prisoners, Corious attempted a casual, commanding voice.

"Archers, hold. Commander, I wouldn't kill those rebels unless you desire an arrow through your head. Face it. You're surrounded."

"I don't believe your lying rebel lips, and I don't have time for these games!"

Corious detected the commander's nervousness. His color had drained, and Corious took note of the trembling hand and the bead of sweat balancing on the Shalkan's upper lip.

"Fortunately," Corious said as he crept from behind, "for you, I make time. If you walk five paces ahead and drop the gun, my archers will hold."

"How do I know you have any archers?"

Shrie's arrow whistled past his face and buried itself into the official behind him.

The commander dropped his gun and dropped face first on the ground. The others followed his example. A glint of metal shone from the commander's side. Corious snuck forward cautiously. He knew the officials to be sly, and he did not intend to battle all thirty of them tonight; he only wanted to rescue the prisoners. Before he could make a decision, Shrie hopped from her tree. She was too early. With uncommon rapidity, the commander rose with an estranged look on his face, pulled the gun from his belt, and shot.

Shrie's body crumpled.

Corious found himself yelling and throwing himself at random officials in a panic as he tried to get to the commander. Out of the shadows, Ree and Tar joined him, fighting with no other purpose than to avenge and gain revenge. Fists replaced guns as the bullets went wide and provided the rebels with open shots. Ree and Tar used the shafts of their spears to knock officials in the gut; they did not have enough weapons to waste spearing an official through. Ducking as a Shalkan swung heartily at his head, Corious somersaulted across the ground. Black boots rose before him, and he kicked. His foot connected with the underside of an official's knee. Knocking him to the ground, Tar gave the official a finishing whack on the head before engaging another. Ree had three on him but spun about with ease, luring the officials one way and then another.

"Stop playing with them and start fighting," Corious shouted heatedly. Ripping a helmet from a head, his knuckles burned with a hot, searing pain as he brought his fist across the face of an attacker. The skin rippled in the wake of his hand and tore.

Without waiting to see how long the injured enemy would last, Corious moved onto the next opponent, elbowing him from behind. A familiar snarl met his ears, and he recognized the commander. In a rage, Corious struck high and missed; the commander butted him in the stomach. Corious groaned but swung again, smashing the commander's clavicle into pieces. The commander stumbled.

Even after the commander had fallen under the vicious jolts, Corious hit the man until he knew he was dead. Ripping his eyes from his kill, he saw the officials scatter before the wrath of Ree and Tar. Tar used Corious's short bow to pick off the closest officials as they retreated into the consuming darkness. It had taken longer than usual, but the rebels, outnumbered and out of practice, had claimed the advantage of surprise. They had bested their enemies, but not thoroughly.

Corious snarled as he spat maliciously into the face of a wounded official, kicking him weakly in the ribs. "Where did you come from, filth?" Corious sneered, tears welling in his eyes. "You're not even a good fighter! I bet all the women and children you tried to kill could have bested you with a cooking spoon!" Corious's voice rose to an unearthly volume as he kicked the man in the helmet twice, sending him into a saturnine unconsciousness. He turned to Ree and Tar who stared weakly at Corious. "We're fighting cowards," Corious murmured as he dropped to his knees, "a whole world of priggish cowards! Philistines!" He wiped away the tears that had begun to stream down his dirty face. He hated the officials and the tears that reminded him of why he fought.

Ree came to Corious, his hand closed in a tremulous fist. "What…what do you suggest we do now?"

Corious's eyes narrowed. "You trust the one who led Shrie to her death?" Fatigue marked Ree's face, threatening to swallow his features in long lines. "It's over, Ree. Go home. Go find a girl to take with you or scamper off to the remains of our pitiful rebel unit. That is what I suggest we do now."

Ree unclenched his fist and stared at Corious coldly. "I don't have a home, and for once, think before you speak, Corious. Shrie's body does not lie where it fell."

"I will not search for it tonight," Corious said tiredly. "I do want to see where she died; I do not want to know how." He held off sobs of anger.

Ree and Tar did not counter Corious's words as he slumped exhaustedly against a tree.

A gray, humid morning rose after the encounter with the official scouts. Corious had fallen asleep in the middle of the clearing, dreaming of his village and of his past to escape the harrowing present. Ree and Tar had done much the same. Not one of them had returned to camp, and they had completely forgotten about the prisoners who remained strung above them in the wooden apparatus.

Desperately stymieing the waves of emotion that threatened to crash over him, Corious concentrated on freeing the rebels who were still alive. He climbed the framework of the looming, wooden contraption to study its mechanics. He called a greeting but received no response. Working different levers, he watched as levels of wood shifted and changed shape. When nothing worked, he went to the opposite side and jerked on a rope that ran through a pulley. Releasing the rope, he grimaced as the two bodies dropped and thudded heavily on the ground.

"How are they?" A breathless voice met his ears.

"Carry them back to camp?"

Ree saw Corious gazing to where Shrie had fallen. He acquiesced so Corious and Tar could jog sadly to the pool of blood. Ree lifted the first body over his shoulder and tromped back to camp.

"She left her weapons," Tar noticed sadly, running his hands over her arched bow. "She would have wanted those with her."

A small trickle blood led away from the maroon puddle and into the emerald woods.

"Are you sure you want to see this, Tar?" Corious asked. Tar waited a moment, and suddenly, Corious felt foolish.

"Are you sure you want to see it?" Tar questioned solemnly in turn.

"No," Corious whispered. "No, I'm not sure." Shakily, Corious held Shrie's bow and arrows close to his chest, and he followed the rust red trail, stumbling through the trees, weary from battle and emotion. Tears slid down his face; he could not stop the flow. Jumping feebly over fallen trees and crawling under boughs, he knew not where he went, and the ruby trail sped onward. A thump sounded dully. Corious turned to see Tar drop one of the official's guns.

"It's the battle scene," Tar exclaimed. Corious spun and through blurry eyes recognized the place. His heart jumped wildly, but he saw no Shrie. The blood trail had stopped, but the outlines of small, graceful footprints led away from the battle. Corious sprinted after them.

Shrie whimpered as she wrapped her wound in strips of what used to be Corious's extra shirt. She had felt paralyzed, and then the pain had consumed her entire body. Shrie blinked, trying to get the uncomfortable dizzy feeling to leave. Someone was in the doorway, calling her name? She did not recognize him. Or did she?

"Ree?" she questioned.

"Shrie! You're alive!"

"Yes, yes. Shrie alive. We win battle and free rebels?"

"Of course," Ree responded as he sat next to her and examined at her arm. "Did you get hit badly?" He reached out to gently touch the arm as he lay down his burden on a blanket.

"It not hurt," Shrie lied before crying out from the sting of his touch. She faded into an unfamiliar darkness, but her descent was halted by Ree's ready arm.

"Shrie?" Ree asked, shaking her slightly. Nothing happened. She breathed, but shallowly and rapidly. He leaned her against the wall and rechecked her pulse. She would live. He hurried to get the other rebel.

Running into the tent, Corious and Tar let their eyes adjust and then saw the two slumped bodies, one much smaller than the other.

"Shrie?" Corious whispered, fearing the worst.

"She's fine," Ree's voice came from behind them outside the shelter. "If you wouldn't mind moving, I would like to set this poor soul down."

Tar moved aside. Corious's weary countenance had dissipated. Watching as Ree set the other rebel next to his companion, Corious wished he knew how to help them, and then from joy, or maybe from exhaustion, he fainted.

Tar heard Corious's plummet to the ground and reached down in concern. Ree chuckled softly.

"Corious took the good news pretty well. Set him next to Shrie so maybe when he wakes he'll actually believe me."

Tar smiled as a soft peace traveled through him. After dragging Corious next to Shrie, Tar sat. Ree surveyed their encampment and the rebels' wounds. They would have to wait until Shrie awoke to fix them. Ree had no knowledge in the vocation of medicine. There were six of them now, two more to hunt for and two more to fight for them. Sighing, Ree decided to take watch before the stars broke fully upon the horizon.

Ree saw darkness, the jungle trees, and then darkness again as his eyelids persisted on closing. He could barely keep them open. He heard someone stirring.

Shrie had offered to take Ree's watch earlier when the night had grown old and when morning had warmed the edge of the horizon. He had told her she was being ridiculous and sent her back. Quiet footsteps sounded behind him. It appeared she was back again.

"I take watch now, Ree. You tired from battle and need rest."

"Shrie, you were shot." Ree examined her arm. "You need to go back and rest."

"Arm feels good, much better today." To prove this she lifted it in the air and then made a terrible grimace.

"Yeah, that's what I thought."

"No, no, no, no, no!" she insisted. "I take watch. I not help in battle. Shrie at least help by taking watch." Shrie gulped down a cry as a feverish dizziness crept through her.

"You said I!"

"What? What you say, Ree?"

"Never mind." Ree's eyes began to close again.

"You take break. Shrie take watch. Later, Shrie teach you how to use bow and arrow, in case Shrie's arm not fully healed for some time. Anyhow, you tired and not listening. I take watch for you."

Ree finally consented and let her lead him back into the shelter. Her hands supported his defined forearm; he leaned towards her. The fine hairs on her arms tickled his side, and when she put a hand against his back to steady him, the tips of her black eyelashes briefly batted against his skin. She smelled of the woods, tangy and saccharine. He breathed deeply, and her scent quieted his restless mind. Ree lowered himself to the floor in an ineffable combination of exhaustion and peace. Shrie's hand left him to pull a thin blanket over his quiescent body. The skin she had touched buzzed happily until fatigue frosted his eyes with sleep.

Shrie observed the verdant woods between the spurts of pain which racked her arm. All of the time, she pondered the battle and the identity of the new rebels. Often she would glance in the tent to study their faces and injuries. A mental list of herbs popped immediately into her head. At midday, when she was sure the serendipity of safety would shield her, she ventured into the jungle to gather the healing plants. Grinding the leaves, stalks, and berries in specific quantities, she then spread the liniment over the sleeping rebels' injuries. The turbid concoction filled concave, torn bits of tissue and bridged ragged stretches of skin, leaving the rebels stippled with bright, purple patches of medicine. With two additional men for whom to care, Shrie had to return several times to retrieve more ingredients for her panacea. When she had finished the grisly work of painting over their wounds, Shrie squatted outside and used some leftover herbs to make dinner. She stirred the fresh meat and vegetables, setting the mixture over a fire. Even with a wounded arm, she managed to make a soup so enticing that it woke everyone from a deep slumber.

Ree's stomach gave a terrible turn. He was hungry, and something smelled ambrosial. He lifted his head to see Shrie cooking over a large, fiery pot, stirring with her uninjured arm. Immediately, he made his way to the fire, careful not to step on the others.

Corious fought; a truculent official bore down upon him. The official smelt of delectable venison cooked in vegetables. *What?* Corious awoke groggily from the dream. The Shalkan was nowhere to be seen, but the smell remained. He closed his eyes and breathed in the aroma. His stomach churned violently. When was the last time he had eaten? The many hours before the morning had gone by in a painful, regretful whirlwind. Their old lives waited to be reclaimed. Rising from his spot on the ground, his obsequious body trailed his authoritative nose out of the empty fort and over to where the others already ate.

"What are your names?" Ree asked as Corious joined them, handing the rebels enough water to wash down dinner. The one was too wounded to speak, but the other was capable enough, if unsure of his words.

"Uhh," he began, as he gulped down his water, "I'm Marcelus; I am a rebel. Well, I guess that's pretty obvious," he chuckled nervously. "I was born in Valjancar, but now I reside in Quantus Plain."

"Who is your shorter friend?" Shrie asked as she emptied water over a wound on his leg.

"He's Perry."

"Ah, well Perry quite hurt; wounds very deep."

"Those are bullet wounds, but only on his leg. All the others are from being dragged, and whipped."

"A whip?" asked Corious. "He was tortured?"

"Yes, we were captured, but Perry killed five officials and their captain. He was shot and whipped with fifteen lashes. His face has suffered the effects." Marcelus scowled and sipped at his soup. It was true; beneath Shrie's violet liquid, a line of caked blood decorated Perry's forehead and ear.

"He's a brave rebel," Ree said admiringly.

"How did you survive unharmed?" Corious asked curiously.

Marcelus's face flushed, and he cleared his throat as though Corious had impugned his dignity. "An official knocked my arm with his gun and dislodged my club."

Corious shifted himself nearer to Marcelus and pulled back the rebel's sleeve. "Whew! That's a nice welt!"

"Believe me, it hurt too."

"One might guess," Tar said shrewdly, provoking the blotches of red to grace Marcelus's cheeks once again.

"We should rest," Corious mentioned to save Marcelus from additional embarrassment. "We'll move camp tomorrow." His full stomach encouraged his eyelids to waver. Shrie continued to dish out soup and to apply herbal salves to Perry's whip wounds. Corious said appreciatively, "Thanks for the soup. Come on, Marcelus. It's late already." The two vanished behind the cloak still hanging from earlier that day.

Ree fed the flames. "It's serious," he remarked to anyone who cared to listen.

"Even more serious, you mean," Tar commented, feeling his way to Ree's side.

"The officials gather. They recognize our presence. We started out more as thieves, Corious and I. We looted the officials; they were the only ones who had much. Even so, their lucrative plots of land never satisfied them. Five years ago, they did not have a skilled army, but that has changed. With this change, the identity of the rebels has changed from the subservient to the defenders of freedom, from protesters to revolutionaries."

"Thanks for your intriguing story, Ree, but what are you getting at?"

Ree continued as if nothing had been said. "We met Shrie soon after. We made a deal; we made bonds as fellow rebels fighting a greater evil." Ree addressed Tar. "We're friends, but the officials are bigger than they seem, Tar. This won't be a one shot battle if the rebels even last that long. You saw those two."

"Ree, it's simply a cumbersome burden to worry about such things at this point. You have us and possibly a couple new allies."

"Tar," Shrie said into her soup, "he blind, but he always look on bright side of things."

"Ahh, it's just the good dinner tonight. I'm in high spirits," Tar replied, and at that they treated themselves to a quiet laugh, whether it was funny or not.

"Well, I have had enough of these deep, philosophical matters. Good night, Ree," Tar yawned as he curled upon the unwelcoming ground.

"Yes, I suppose it is good night then," Ree replied as he did the same. Shrie, though hushed throughout the whole conversation, was still awake and remained so most of the night.

Chapter 8

Marcelus woke unhappily; he was having that dream again, the good one in which he was back in the village with the native girls. *Ah, no use*, he thought. *It'll just get me wishing for what I do not have.* He opened his eyes, staring at the rough stone above him. Rays of light squeezed their way between the branches propped against the ledge. He shielded his eyes from the glow as his mind flashed back to their ordeal with the officials and the two rebels he now recognized as Ree and Shrie. Shrie he had heard of—a mysterious jungle maiden with long flowing hair and dark bronze skin. The other three were either henchmen or mercenaries, but either way, they were dedicated rebels, exactly what Lain's army could use back at camp. Lain! He would be worried about them. *Perry and I must go back.* He could bring the other four rebels with him; they would make a fine addition to the ill-trained group at Quantus Plain. Marcelus yawned noisily before tossing a threadbare blanket aside. His stomach gurgled happily as it chewed on last night's dinner. Marcelus moved his lanky body awkwardly in the cramped area. He managed to slip under the draped cloak without waking a snoring Corious. As he passed, he saw Perry shiver under his blanket. His friend's torn shirt lay uselessly beside him. Marcelus dropped to his knees.

"Psst, Perry. Perry, are you awake?" he hissed hopefully. To Marcelus's surprise, Perry lifted his head and opened an eye. The other, a distended glob, stayed shut.

"Where are we?" Perry asked in his husky voice.

"We're with some rebels under an overhang of rock."

"Where is Lain?"

"He's not here. We're not with his rebels," Marcelus replied.

"Oh," Perry said sadly. "Who dressed my wounds?"

"That would be Shrie. She does a fine job," Marcelus said, motioning to Perry's receding welts.

"Yes," Perry commented, "I feel much better. How is your arm, Marcelus?"

Marcelus shrugged and pulled back his sleeve.

"Nice welt," Perry said admiring the yellow bruising that had occurred overnight. "It hurts?"

"One would expect it to," Marcelus said sheepishly, remembering the previous night's conversation. "Perry, how should we transport you to Quantus Plain? We can't stay here."

"I don't know," Perry replied, "but we were quite a distance when we fought the officials, and who knows how far they brought us."

Marcelus added thoughtfully, "We'll have to make a stretcher of some sort to carry you."

Perry seemed to like that idea, so Marcelus raised Corious, and they both began to plan the design for the stretcher.

As the sun shed itself upon the waking earth, the jungle trees swayed in an unusually stiff breeze. Tranquility settled upon the early jungle, and life woke reluctantly from its slumber. Corious had not appreciated being woken by the taller rebel Marcelus, and Corious regarded him with a biting, crusty stare. Marcelus seemed lost in his thoughts, and he did not notice Corious's absence from his side until a banana whistled from a tree above and split open upon impact with his head. Marcelus swallowed hard and wound his hand into a fist.

"You wouldn't try and beat up a mischievous ape simply because he scared the wits out of you, would you? I thought better of you, Marcelus of Quantus Plain." Corious grinned puckishly while dropping from the tree. "Oh yeah," he added, "That's breakfast." Corious pointed to the back of Marcelus's head where the smashed banana had begun to attract flies.

Marcelus sniffed irritably. "Jungle hooligans."

Corious unpeeled a banana. "The same jungle hooligans who keep the officials from your doorstep. Are we the same ones, or am I mistaken?" Corious tilted his head sideways as he took a large bite from his banana.

Marcelus wiped the back of his neck in disgust and eyed Corious strangely.

Corious straightened his head and tossed his banana peel behind him. "I think we might become friends, Marcelus of Quantus Plain."

Marcelus shrugged. The mood lightened, and they initiated the tedious construction. Gathering smooth and lengthy branches, Corious and Marcelus laid them side by side. After estimating Perry's height, they rid the branches of their excess extensions with Ree's ax. The end branches they left longer, for handles. After assembling the logs, Corious wound vines through them and threw a blanket on top. Marcelus considerately cut a square of moss to place under Perry's head. It appeared neither comfortable nor uncomfortable.

At some point during its construction, Shrie had restarted the fire to keep the bugs at bay. She now pushed away Corious's cloak which divided the two halves of the tent and wrapped it around her.

"How you feel?" she asked the injured rebel.

"Not bad," Perry replied tersely, disturbed from his concentration. Shrie removed his old bandages and reapplied the salve.

"Is good you talk today. So your name Perry?" she asked, adjusting his bandages with sure fingers.

"Yes," he labored to sit up, "and you?"

"Shrie, ruler of forest," she replied, handing him some water.

"Ah, so you're the one Lain told us about." Perry said knowingly.

Shrie cocked her head. She tried to ignore the fact that Perry had said his name, but Lain's face came into view anyway. His shaved head in front met a full ponytail in the back; it proved he would never run from battle. A strapping, handsome chin line and sparkling, dark eyes floated before her...*He delicately traced her collarbone and smiled before kissing the hollow below her neck. His arm encircled her and brought her gently to the ground. His hand was in her hair, loosening it from its braid. Their hearts beating at the same time, the sound of a hawk flying through the sky, his lips parting as he spoke the jungle language to her, the arabesque detailing in his armor, their trysts...He was named Azazel in her tongue, Lain in his*—she would not, she could not mention him. A rustling noise from the back of the tent gave her the opportunity to reorganize her thoughts.

"Ah, Tar is up. He blind but adept at many tasks," she said. *His fingers laced through hers, the way he touched her...*

"Who else is with you?" Perry questioned, unable to see much from his position on the floor.

"Hmmm, well, there Tar," Shrie began, pointing to Tar. *It is not the end.* "Then there Corious and Ree." Perry swallowed a mouthful of water, and Shrie's heart began to pound.

"All rebels, eh?" he asked, though the question was more of a statement.

Shrie wound the last of the bandages around his arm. *Do not forget.* "Tell me about Lain," Shrie said suddenly and forcefully, unable to feign indifference any longer. She wanted to know how he was, if the years had altered him, if he was the same man who had come to her when the rain had drenched through his armor. It had been night, and he and his men had needed a place to stay. They had been running from Turock, fleeing a fight they knew they would not win unless they waited. He had stayed with her, showed her a way she had not known existed, and then he had left her so that he could wait with his men and prepare for the day when they would meet again. Her tribe had gone, and he had gone. Both times she could have left with them; both times she knew she had to stay.

"You do not know?" Perry's bewildered query made Shrie jump from her past. He regarded her inquisitively. "Ah, Lain." Perry cleared his throat. "Lain was a knight by the age of fifteen and a general warlord of the Shalkan Lord's Imperial army by twenty. This was when they, the officials, weren't conquerors, mind you. As soon as things got shady, Lain confronted them. A fracas erupted over power, and they exiled him. A band of his most loyal men followed him into the jungles and to Quantus Plain where they became the rebels. At Quantus Plain, men like me and Marcelus rallied to him." Shrie did not stop him, so he continued. "Meanwhile, Turock led the Shalkan war machine to the north. A ruthless man, he would no sooner slit the throat of an enemy than one of his own men. We plan to stop him," Perry finished with determination.

"With a handful of men?" Tar asked skeptically.

"Perhaps you'd join our forces."

Shrie's head popped up; the idea appealed to her.

"Otherwise, what do you suggest?" Perry countered defensively. "Running like mice until we are all slaughtered, caught in his trap, and baited with the stinking cheese of ambition?"

Tar thought a moment and then spoke. "No," he started slowly, "but I believe it sagacious to avoid an offensive stance. We should stay quiet and master the art of aggressive defense. Then, once properly trained and armed, we should ambush, breaking into splinter groups to pick off the officials one by one."

Perry raised his eyebrows. The cut on his temple broke open slightly. "You know a lot about warfare?"

Tar replied nonchalantly, "It was just an idea."

Perry gnawed on his lower lip. "Yes, I'm sure we had something like that in mind. Don't feel cheated though; your skills would be valued at Quantus Plain. Consider coming back with us. You would be ranked highly from the start. And the fortress itself—you jungle rebels would never believe what I'm going to tell you." Perry dragged on with elaborated descriptions, and Shrie let each detail linger in her mind. Long ago she had imagined it the same way, during a time when Quantus Plain had not existed. No, then, it had been just a dream.

"You know the way back to your grand fort?" Corious interrupted Perry.

Perry looked guiltily at Marcelus, and they both looked at Corious expectantly.

"How do you expect us to escort you if you do not know the way?"

"Is fine. Shrie know the way."

"You've never been there before," Corious protested.

"I know where it is," Shrie insisted. Closing her eyes, she remembered. Trees rushed before her as she flew over the swamp and beyond the great river. The scout towers rose before her along with Lain's face, and then the vision faded. "Across the Halfast." Her eyes popped open. "We cross the Halfast."

The next morning, Corious filled a cup with water and watched the meniscus rise above the rim in a spherical dome. He went to where Ree loitered in sleep, said his hello to Shrie, Perry, and Tar, and then lifted the cup high above Ree's head. Water splattered from the tipped cup. Immediately, in one graceful motion, Ree leapt to his feet, his hand shaking and ready to tackle his aggressor. Corious tossed the cup to Shrie and disappeared out the entrance. Ree rubbed his eyes and wet face.

"Who did that?" He opened his eyes to see Shrie holding the cup. "Shrie? I could have sworn that's something Corious would've done."

The circle of events perplexed Tar. "What happened, Ree?"

"Ah, Shrie poured water on my face to wake me up!" Ree said wiping his face on his sleeve.

"That's funny. I didn't hear her get up." Tar remarked. Ree stepped through the entranceway. Instead of telling Ree the truth, a baffled Shrie clasped the guilty cup in her hand.

"I better help them pack outside. I'll call you when we're ready to leave." Tar grabbed their few belongings from the ground while Shrie went to work weaving a blanket of plant fibers.

"What should I do?" Perry asked beginning to feel restless as the others toiled like ants.

"You drink, eat, rest," Shrie said, her eyes never leaving her blanket.

Outside, Ree removed the sheet they had used for an overhang, and streams of light flooded the shelter. Perry grumbled and hid his eyes under his arm.

"Shrie," Ree bypassed an apology, "I will teach you to fight with knives and swords. Your arm is too stiff for the bow."

"But we need another archer," Shrie protested.

"I can shoot decently," Corious offered.

"No, we need another one besides you." Shrie insisted, "I teach Ree."

Corious snickered at the idea of Ree with a bow and watched disbelievingly as the two gabbed excitedly about technique and tactics. Corious, left alone with the new rebels and a grumpy Tar, felt decidedly snubbed. He examined the fort wall.

"Hey," Corious said as the idea hit him, "we should disassemble our stick wall and use it to create a bonfire. It would mislead the officials while we hightail ourselves to Quantus Plain. What do you say?"

"And then we can pop some corn and have a festival and yeah, that's the first good idea you've had since we've met," Tar responded sardonically.

Corious easily slung the dissenting teen over his shoulder. In tight spins, he whirled while Tar protested loudly and flailed his limbs erratically. Staggering from dizziness and laughter, Corious gratefully placed his human burden on a low lying tree branch.

"Now," Corious said, "what did you say again?"

Marcelus made a bizarre noise behind them. Corious spun around.

"Who's next?" he joked.

"Ha," Marcelus scoffed, "you'd get crushed if you tried to pick me up!"

Lightning fast, Corious hoisted Marcelus over his shoulder. He attempted to take a step, but his knees buckled, and the two men fell backwards laughing.

"You were right. Your extreme bulk is too oppressive for me."

Marcelus returned Corious's sarcastic remarks with a playful shove.

"My shoulder bone is broken due to your morbid obesity," Corious continued, "They must feed their rebels boulders at Quantus Plain."

"I felt like I was flying," Marcelus said dreamily. "Let's do it again!" he added with vigor, throwing himself on Corious's back. Corious jostled him off, and both were soon wrestling on the ground. Perry cheered for whoever was winning at the moment while Tar tried unsuccessfully to get down from his branch. Corious and Marcelus tackled and clawed at each other until a loud thump arrested their movements.

"Tar?" Corious asked. Beneath the empty branch, Tar groaned and cradled his knee.

"Ah blast it, Shrie's going to kill me!" Corious exclaimed while Marcelus examined the boy's knee.

"It's only bruised; it will be fine."

Relieved, Tar gingerly brushed the dirt from his knee before limping under the overhang. Corious returned to disassembling the wall of sticks before engaging Marcelus in another wrestling match. Shrie and Ree would not be back for a while.

"No, you do it all wrong," Shrie lectured Ree. "First, you holding bow upside down, and second, you not using stronger arm to pull back arrow. Hold the bow straight and pull the arrow back to your eye."

Ree did as he was told, flipping the bow and switching hands. When he was ready, he waited for her next command.

"Okay, that better. Now raise bow and keep arrow steady on string. Keep arm straight. No, steady, Ree!"

Ree aimed precariously and let the arrow fly. It landed a few feet below the target.

"Shrie, let's face it. I'll never get this. We have been out here how long? And I still can't tell the right side of the bow from the other."

"Like this," Shrie said taking the bow from him. She had trouble keeping the bow steady with her hurt arm, but she hit the target squarely anyhow.

"You try again," Shrie said. "You aimed right for the target, not above and to the left."

"Why would I do that?" Ree questioned.

"Because arrow goes lower as it advances, and there a breeze coming from the left and pushing right that you need to counter."

Ree sighed and retrieved the arrow, taking another try. This time, he watched in amazement as the arrow whistled right into the center of the knot. Shrie smiled and clapped happily.

"You do much better. You think you can do that in battle?"

Ree nodded, handing her the bow. "Now I shall teach you some sword and knife fighting."

"Okay, you teach. Shrie learn quickly; we need to move camp soon." Taking the dagger and twirling it in her hand, she watched Ree anxiously.

When time had depleted their combined vats of patience, Corious and Marcelus scoured the woods for Ree and Shrie. When they heard voices, they crept closer to see Shrie feigning a battle with Ree, a dagger in hand. Ree beat her, of course, tapping her face with the blunt end. Shrie threw the dagger angrily.

"Shrie bad with dagger. Shrie want sword."

"Don't give it to her," Corious said jumping from the brush. "Shrie with a sword will give me nightmares."

Shrie grinned and handed the knife to Ree.

"It time to move camp anyway," she commented after noting the sun's position in the sky.

Corious and Marcelus led the way back and were soon making preparations to leave. Corious lit a torch with his flint and steel and gathered his gear.

"You help Shrie get Perry on stretcher and then give this extra bow to Ree," Shrie said. Marcelus dragged the stretcher to where Shrie and Perry were. Ree joined them and slid his arms under Perry's shoulders, lifting him as gently and firmly as a wolf carries her pups. Once Perry was settled, Shrie proudly presented him with the blanket she had finished.

"My deepest gratitude," Perry said while Ree trotted off to get his belongings and to help Tar get his bearings.

"Come help with stretcher, Corious," Shrie called. It was time to go.

"Ready? Up in one, two, and three!" Ree counted as he and Corious hoisted Perry from the ground. "Ready to go to Quantus Plain?" he asked as the rebels organized themselves into a wobbly line.

Tar cut in front of Ree and Corious to trail Shrie as Marcelus brought up the rear. The new rebel took the burning torch that Corious had left and threw it onto the pile of sticks left outside the abandoned fort. Then he sprinted into the dense jungle, nodding vigorously in response to Ree's question. The jungle with its bugs and animals made him nervous; he was more than ready to go home. Ahead, Shrie assumed the lead, partly because she claimed to know where Quantus Plain was and partly because no one else knew another alternative. They had to trust her. Besides, the three rebels had no concrete plan of action; and it seemed an admirable goal to bring the two captives back to their base. They had nowhere else to go and barely anything to lose.

The official commander stopped in his tracks. He sniffed the air, the hot, smoky breeze searing his face. Shading his eyes, he peered over the precipice.

"Sir," a small voice said, breaking his concentration. "Sir," it repeated.

The commander spun to face one of his soldiers.

"A pillar of thick smoke has been spotted southeast of here, not more than a thousand paces from our current location."

The commander murmured, "As I suspected. Official, go tell the others that we're changing plans and heading southeast."

The soldier returned hastily to his position in the rear of the group. The commander studied the black pillar rising rapidly into the blue, morning sky. Upon his command, dozens of booted feet marched in unison through the jungle.

Marcelus trudged wearily behind the others, dragging a fan shaped branch laden with leaves to cover their tracks. His legs rotated mechanically, and the leafy burden tugged his arm back from his shoulder like a hound pulling away from its master. The monotony of walking sent twinges of searing, mental agony through his mind. If the sun, the oil which sustained his weary engine, had not been shining, Marcelus did not think he could have continued.

Progressively, the jungle crammed its trees closer together, squishing plants into vertical turrets which scattered the sun's dimming light. The rebels grappled with the consuming underbrush which attempted to gorge itself on the lower halves of their bodies. From afar, it would appear as if five torsos and one stretcher floated atop a turbulent, green sea. Only in intervals when they paused to rest could Marcelus appreciate the jungle's breathtaking beauty. Huge flowers blossomed into fluorescent blues, pinks, yellows, and purples. They twisted around trees, and ferns and mosses padded every slope in myriads of shapes, sizes, and shades of green, red, and orange. Marcelus tried to focus on these things to relieve his mind of the trip's oppressive boredom.

Eventually, Marcelus had to know if he was alone in feeling the troubles of the journey. He examined Corious ahead of him. As a bead of sweat dripped off the tip of his nose, Marcelus tapped Corious on the shoulder. Corious turned, shifting the weight of the stretcher. It wobbled slightly, and Perry lifted his head before dropping back off into sleep.

Marcelus whispered, "Hey, Corious," as he half tripped over an overlooked root, "are you feeling as tired as I am?"

Before Corious could answer, Ree shushed Marcelus, but Shrie's sharp ears had caught it all.

"You complain about walk?" Shrie asked with a fiendish smile. "You right, we go too slowly. We run now."

Ree and Corious accepted her verdict without protest, but this was too much for Marcelus. He was good with a sword and an excellent soldier, but long distance running did not rank among his top skills. After ten minutes, he collapsed. Shrie ran back, helped him up, and kept going.

Even Tar, who was normally one of the fastest, fell behind when the pace exceeded normality and roots rudely interrupted his stride. Every so often, he heard someone's pounding footsteps and strained breathing pass him. After awhile, even Marcelus had passed him. Tar frowned in frustration, grappling with the weeds blocking his path; he was far behind.

After stealing a glance back, Ree noticed Tar's predicament. "Hold up!" he called to Shrie. "I'm going to get Tar." He handed the stretcher to Marcelus, and Shrie readied her bow and arrows. She should have had them out in the first place.

"Tar!" Ree hissed. "We got ahead of you, but we need to get Perry back as soon as possible," he explained apologetically.

"I can keep up," Tar protested.

"Ride on my back," Ree said roughly. Tar sighed but reluctantly agreed, climbing onto Ree's broad back. Ree trudged back to Shrie, Corious, Marcelus, and Perry. Marcelus was prepared to substitute for Ree by holding the stretcher when a loud crash sounded in the brush behind them. Shrie drew an arrow and put it to her bow, silencing the official before he could reload his gun. The Shalkan stumbled and then slumped to the ground, lifeless. Corious stared at Shrie, his sword drawn and glinting.

"Waste of good arrow," she said sadly, reloading her bow, not bothering to seek the other buried in official flesh. No one moved in the frozen moments of careful silence that followed. When Shrie tentatively lowered her bow, they knew it was safe to continue. Precious time would not be wasted lingering. Perry began groaning.

"How long until we reach Quantus Plain, Shrie?" Tar asked worriedly. The injured rebel, a sitting target, would be destroyed easily if officials swarmed them.

"Two, maybe three more suns," came Shrie's grave reply.

"That's a long time," Ree said gruffly.

"Will Perry make it?" Corious asked quietly. He did not want Perry to hear.

"If boys drop him, no."

Corious felt his fingers slipping, and in alarm, he gripped tighter. He prayed to Shrie's Almighty he could hold on for two more days. Shrie set the pace faster than before; the officials were on their tail.

The Shalkan commander was enraged by his own folly; he should have known. The rebels had outsmarted him. The fire had been a decoy, a distraction to get his attention as the rebels fled undetected into the jungle. The rebels, sly as they would be, had covered their tracks well. Only their footprints in the clearing remained. He had sent two scouts in every direction and kept the rest of the soldiers with him. None of his men had yet returned. Turock would be irate even if the commander did find and capture the rebels who had been pestering him day and night. Sometimes the jungle fiends struck with a single arrow and then disappeared into the fog laden jungle, leaving the commander with nothing to shoot at but the inexplicable unseen.

Revenge would be sweet. He was so close to destroying this elite rebel cell, but he had let them slip from his hands. Bellowing in an anguished rage, he sent his blood-thirsty men ahead.

After the rebels' encounter with the lone official, they ran at a full sprint, ignoring exhaustion and tossing aside fear. Their entire bodies were poised for attack. The officials must have found the fire and then dispersed in multiple directions, which explained the lone scout the rebels had encountered and killed. Officials did not often travel alone, and though they hated each other, they were useless without their brutal companions. They would hunt for the body of their missing soldier, and when they found him, they would start gaining. Shrie's bow was loaded.

Tar bent his head in shame. Ree supported the burden of both the stretcher and Tar. Wishing he could be running as his stomach churned with spurts of premonition, Tar anchored himself to Ree's shoulders and hips. He listened for any sounds which could signal an attack, but Ree's heavy breathing and footsteps were the only noises to be heard. He would have to hold on and wait.

Corious could not handle the excruciating pace much longer. In these conditions, he was bound to make a mistake. Switching his grip, he hardly noticed the bugs that swarmed about his face and the streams of sweat flowing from his forehead. Letting his sore arms bear the weight of the stretcher, his mind wandered down dead-end paths.

Why must we go to this Quantus Plain camp? Skeptical of any organization bigger than their foursome, especially if it put them on a run, he began to question their decision. Corious valued their previous lifestyle without any regime, leader, or ranks. He wanted so badly to fight the enemy, not to run away. Running ruined his approach, and they had been running since this morning. His legs, however, did not hurt as much as his arms. He would never admit this to Shrie. No, his pride would not allow it. Eyes burning with the sweat that dripped into them, he squinted and blinked. He could not spare a hand to wipe the salty liquid away. Complaining did no good. He tried forcing himself to think of other things, but he knew it to be futile. Eventually, he surrendered to the mindless pounding of Ree's footsteps or concentrated on memorizing the forest floor before him to avoid tripping. To add to his mushrooming list of anxieties, the officials were near. He had once wondered how Shrie had detected their presence. He now knew that too many days in the jungle gave a rebel that ability—a feeling of unshakeable, suffocating darkness. It climbed up his back and coiled itself neatly around his throat. A shiver flew up his spine. The ground blurred together in browns and greens; his head spun. Corious cleared his head just in time to catch a branch full in the face.

Desperately trying to hold onto the stretcher as he lost his balance, he inevitably swiveled sideways. He put his hand out and caught his balance as he veered. Snapping, the sapling he had clutched bent backwards. For a moment, everything seemed stationary, and then a whishing noise whipped by his ear as a rope uncoiled rapidly. As if he had touched a burning bowl, Corious let go of the tree and watched it spring back and trigger a rope in the branches above. The rope's descent stopped after a dull ringing reverberated through the forest, over and over, and over again. Corious grimaced and slowly bent his head back to watch as a large stone hit directly and soundly into a metal breast plate placed in the upper reaches of the trees. Like a pendulum, the rope swung, and the stone connected with the armor.

"Smooth, Corious," Ree snapped disgustedly. "How quickly do you want the officials to kill us?"

The feeling of darkness squirmed beneath his collar bone. "Go," he shouted fervently. No one moved. "You must run, Ree," he commanded imperiously. "Marcelus can take my place." Everyone but Corious and Shrie darted away.

"What devilry is here presented?" The ringing noise bounced off leaves and trees.

Shrie's scarred hand and arm lusted for revenge. "It old tribal warning signal—many hunters and nomads use it as well. But now, it used to attract officials." Shrie squinted into the jungle stoically. "Very close, they very close now," she murmured.

Corious unsheathed his sword. A light feeling fluttered over his body, depositing weakness in its wake. He heard a bowstring being drawn, and he whipped around as Shrie let go of an arrow. An official Corious had not seen stumbled forward out of a bush, reddened and dying. Like ghosts, a dozen officials emerged from the dim light. A second row stepped from behind them. The fluttering feeling solidified into a rock that settled and burned in his stomach. He leaned over to Shrie.

"Don't say anything." Shrie seemed perplexed, but Corious faced the rows of blue and black fighters that had formed a semi-circle around them.

"I surrender," he cried. "I give up." Corious walked forward and then sunk pathetically to his knees. "We're outnumbered," he directed his comment to Shrie but let his voice carry to the officials. He lowered his weapon, and Shrie watched in confusion. Surrender was not a word in her lexicon. "It's done, finished," Corious continued, his head hanging. No expression but hunger for flesh was indented upon the officials' faces. "You win." Shrie was about to protest but resisted.

One of the enemy spoke. "A fainthearted rebel and a coward, as they all are. Grab his arms, men!" the commander shouted jubilantly, caressing his worn musket with a calloused hand.

The two Shalkans were close. Corious smelled the stink of their breath as the heavy vibrations of their steps rattled in his chest. He fingered the daggers within his shirt. Rough cloth swept against his face and then left his peripheral vision. With a roar, his hands exploded from his shirt and the knives buried themselves into their victims. Blood spilt in waterfalls down his hands. The bodies slumped forward, and Shrie kicked them back. Disorder wrecked the official lines. For once, the Shalkans had been beat at their own game. Brandishing his stained knives with

JULIE AND RYAN DICKERSON

a grin, Corious jumped into the attack. Bending his knees for balance, he threw the crimson weapons at two charging soldiers who, overtaken by the yearning to kill, had left formation.

Loading and shooting her arrows, Shrie eliminated men in the front line as Corious's daggers flew true. Corious charged at the commander who hurriedly tried to load his gun.

"Not fainthearted," Corious knocked away the gun, "just smarter." He beheaded the groveling official.

Turning to face his next attacker, Corious saw only trees. His eyes rocketed to the ground of wilting, arrow-stuck bodies. Starting at one end of the clearing, Shrie moved from casualty to casualty, placing her foot on a back and then yanking out the embedded arrow. One Shalkan crackled hideously. It was still alive. Corious rubbed the heel of his boot into its spine as he held the smooth shaft of the arrow in his hands.

"Tell Turock to send us more officials." The official convulsed, and Corious gagged in repulsion. "I enjoy the practice." Wrenching the arrow from the Shalkan's arm, Corious heard the official scream and then kicked it forward on its knees. The official scuttled into the jungle, snarling like an injured animal.

Shrie's quiver was full again. "Nice work," Corious told her, tossing her the last arrow. "The backup support came in handy."

Shrie barely listened while she massaged her sore arm. "Come, Corious, we catch up to others."

Racing through the jungle with the stretcher, Marcelus, Ree, and Tar let the sharp branches snag on their skin. Sounds of a small battle chased them. Tar's drawn face paled.

"Ree, I hear them." Gritting his teeth, Ree pushed forward. Boots hit the ground far away. Softer footsteps more accustomed to jungle ground followed.

"It's Shrie and Corious," Tar stated firmly when he felt Ree's back muscles strain. Ree kept his vision straight ahead. A breeze wafted by them as Shrie went to the front of their stumbling line. Sniffing, Ree smelled the foul rank of official blood on her arrows and on Corious's clothes.

"It's a good thing you won or else I would have your blood on my head," Ree stated harshly.

"More are coming, so hold your oath," Corious snapped petulantly.

Ree's foot sunk into the sloppy ground, and his movement hesitated as he struggled to free his foot. The dark green of fertility decayed into a tan ground. Shrie dashed nimbly over the ground, but the men left deep footprints. The blaring noise of a foreboding trumpet grated on their ears.

Marcelus halted and sunk into the muck behind Shrie. She stopped, and the four men behind her breathed deeply, thankful for the respite. They laid down Perry and waited for an explanation from Shrie as to why they had stopped with the officials on their heels; they assumed she had a plan, and indeed she did. Directing their movements, she pried Tar's bow from his hand, handed it to Corious, and distributed an extra one to Ree; Marcelus and Tar began to dig. From the trees, she felled stringy vines and attached one to the end of an arrow. Corious copied her. Tying the other end to the base of a smaller tree, Shrie situated herself opposite Corious about fifty strides away. Ree and Marcelus fought the mud sucking at their feet and began to burrow through the slop. Joined by Corious and Shrie, the work went quickly, but the trench had to be long.

The work continued into the falling dusk, and the trumpets blared, calling the officials to trace the uncovered tracks of the rebels. Cries of astonishment and anger were heard as the old battle site was uncovered. Commanders yelled in harsh voices and pushed the massing officials together. The columns converged, and they trampled the footprints left by the rebels.

Like a shadow, Shrie and Corious knelt beside their trees. Ree, Tar, and Marcelus hid in the woods to watch. Darkness crept into the land, but Corious did not notice. Shrie memorized the angle of her bow. Pounding footsteps hit the ground. They were coming.

Officials packed together in order to fit through the small trail created by the rebels. Stringent orders to annihilate encouraged the butts of guns to ram into the backs of officials who could not maintain the excruciating pace. Though their feet and legs moved with the same rapidity, their running slowed. Something beneath sucked at the bottoms of their boots.

Shrie concentrated. Twenty strides, now ten. Wait until one stride. Five strides. Releasing an arrow, she saw Corious's coming at her. Rolling to the side, she watched it hit directly where she had been. He had worse aim than she had thought, but at least he had hit a tree. The vines held taut, and the officials tripped helplessly. Fingers triggered guns as hands reached out to stop descents, but an open hole engulfed them, and sand covered them as their weights combined with their collective momentum buried them. The Shalkans fought to swim to the surface, but others landed atop them. Corious shot another rope at ankle level when one vine broke from overuse. Ree drew his sword and attacked the back of the official lines. He would make sure they appreciated the work his sore arms and careful steps had created.

Tar and Marcelus slinked through the forest after Ree. Tearing silently into the battle, they slew the officials. The sudden dead at the back of their lines instilled fear into the enemy, and ones at the back pushed harder and yelled curses to the ones ahead.

When the onslaught of men overwhelmed the trench, Shrie leapt from her spot on the ground, and waking the shadows, she slipped into the night. Shooting vines into the black blobs that were trees, she and Corious enclosed the officials, trapping them and clumping them into a mass of thrashing bodies. When the Shalkan bullets issued forth with a sense of timing and were no longer so randomly spurted from guns, Shrie shot back arrows, but sparingly. Any she shot here would be lost. Straining against the vines, the officials roared and cursed, but the hungry sand swallowed the feet of those in front. Gliding behind enemy lines, the rebels disappeared.

The night enveloped the ghastly jungle as the five fleeting figures hurried back through the trees under the cover of night. The trees reached down to trip and block their way. As the gloom swept around the companions, they slowed the pace and crept, keeping their sword hilts not far from their thoughts or fingertips. Shrie's plan had worked magnificently, but without scouts, the band of rebels could not tell if more Shalkans would come or if the units they had confronted would break through the vines and quicksand. Corious and Ree again held Perry's stretcher. Throughout the whole ordeal, Perry had awoken only once to hit his head against a branch as Ree had stepped clumsily over a root. Perry had not spoken since.

Tar trailed the line of rebels near Marcelus, listening for pursuers. Faint cries of anguish echoed in his ears from the earlier hours of the night, and a frigid wind swept his hair across his red headband. Although he could not see it, a full moon had risen above the tree line, bathing them in a gray light and illuminating their surroundings. Tar rubbed the hilt of his short sword with his gloved hand, sensing an ecumenical presence which he could not decipher to be either good or bad.

"Good lord!" he heard Marcelus murmur. "Is this where you slaughtered the skirmishing line of officials earlier?"

Corious stared at the gruesome scene. At night it appeared even more sinister. Earlier, fresh blood had run from the officials' wounds. Now the corpses were crumpled heaps anticipating decomposition. At the front of the line, Shrie nonchalantly walked by her previous victims, muttering something about bad food. She turned over one official with her foot, squinting.

"Shrie," Corious wearily groused, "what are you looking for? They're dead. Just leave 'em and let's head to Quantus Plain." He was surprised by his own vigor to go to the fort he had previously resented.

Shrie looked at Corious irritably and continued rummaging through the bodies, searching through the officials' packs.

"Is she a cannibal?" Marcelus asked disgustedly, as if he believed his own fantasy. "It explains why she wants to stick around this graveyard."

Tar shrugged and made a face, envisioning Shrie as a head hunter.

Shrie heard Marcelus, finally threw down an empty canvas sack, and stalked over to the men. "Shrie and boys low on supplies and arrows." She put her hands on her hips. "Shrie trying to find extra supplies from officials to last journey to Quantus Plain, or else Perry might not make it." Perry's deteriorating health was a viable threat.

Corious sighed tiredly. "We cannot risk standing around here." He pointed out,

"We've obviously made it on the officials' most-prized rebel list. There will be many Shalkans pursuing us."

Shrie shook her head. "I staying."

Ree cleared his throat. "Shrie and I can stay while the rest of you head east. We'll catch up to you later with the supplies."

Corious rubbed his eyes; he was too exhausted to say otherwise, but he did have an objection. "I'll stay with Shrie. I need to replenish my arrow supply, and that stretcher is not getting along with me," Corious added sarcastically.

Ree acquiesced. "Okay, Marcelus and Tar, you're coming with me."

Shrie and Corious stood in the clearing as they had done hours before and watched as the three men and the stretcher vanished into the jungle. Ree noted the two frames outlined in black as they receded: one small, with ripples of black cascading from the top, and another tall if slightly gangly. Determination defined Shrie's face, and Corious idly scratched his chin where whiskers were aspiring to grow into a thin beard. She noticed his interest in the wispy hairs and promptly told him his beard was ugly. He folded his arms and then loosed them in order to rummage through bloody sacks as Shrie began filling their near empty packs with the leftover goods from the officials' backpacks.

When Shrie and Corious did not presently appear and when the moon descended in the cloudy, night sky, the rebels had settled neatly behind two large boulders. They had made no attempt to hide their whereabouts; Shrie would be able track them easily. Hours later, Tar woke from a restless sleep and cringed as he heard the five faint but desperate gunshots. Some officials still lived in the vine cage despite the suffocating quagmire. They would not live much longer. The four rebels, far to the east of the trench, could rest without worry. It would not be long until dawn.

Water tickled the smooth, concave arches of Tar's feet. The river was wide but not rough. He could hear it lapping subtly against the rocky shoreline. Here, the jungle rapidly dwindled into emaciated trees and stubby shrubs as it closed the gap to the river's edge. In the absence of the massive trunks, every breeze found the freedom to knock against the rebels' faces. Turning his back against a particularly humid draft, Tar knelt beside a mossy boulder. A rustling next to him signaled Ree's effort to summit the boulder and take watch. Marcelus fussed with their supplies on the other side. Shrie had been right; they were diminishing. Perry's condition had similarly continued in a downward spiral, though peaceful dreams of the noble stone walls and ceilings which he called home currently occupied his mind.

Tar's mind was not so calm, and his limbs nearly shook with residual adrenaline. After leaving Shrie and Corious, he, Ree, and the two rebels from Quantus Plain had set a hard pace away from the battlefield. They had hoped to put some distance between themselves and their pursuers. Their efforts, though noble, had not entitled them to make the trek alone. A lone official, crazed by the heat and by a substantial loss of blood, had crashed madly behind them. Corious's and Ree's hands, confined to carrying the stretcher, were unable to gird their weapons. The responsibility of annihilating the enemy had fallen on Tar and Marcelus, but before Marcelus could even draw his sword, Tar had expertly rendered the Shalkan unconscious with its own gun. Proudly, Tar had taken the sword, gun, and knife from the official's belt. The knife and sword he had kept; the gun he had offered to Ree.

"Still loaded," Tar had added, handing it to Ree.

Ree had closed Tar's hand over the handle and pushed it back. "I have no use for such weapons. Keep it."

Leaping from his flashback as the sun climbed into the sky, Tar shoved the archaic gun under his belt and unsheathed the sword. Unlike the crude sticks of steel he was used to handling, the saber's gilded hilt boasted a metallic arc designed to protect the swordsman's knuckles. To complete the hilt, a fanciful sphere evolved gradually from the handle. Thin but sharp, it would serve him well. *It was not used much*, Tar noted astutely as he compared it to Marcelus's grand sword—the one which the soldier always had by his side or tucked under his arm as he slept. Tar had never wielded a weapon of such caliber before.

The soldier from Quantus Plain noticed Tar admiring his sword by touch and smiled. "I think it's a whit too big for you."

Tar's hand retreated instantly from the sword. "You would help me sword train?" Tar asked guardedly, as if he expected Marcelus's answer to be no. Time and fortune, however, were stacked in Tar's favor. Shrie had not yet arrived, which meant no one would be energetic enough to get their own breakfast, and Marcelus, though tired, was a natural teacher.

Enthusiastically, the Quantus Plain rebel leapt from the boulder and stretched his muscles. "Sword fighting? I can teach you anything you want to know: offensive thrusts, defensive blocks, and the more complicated combinations. I've mastered them all." Red rays from the sun penetrated the sky as he continued, "You have to have a warrior's mind and perfect control to be a swordsman."

Tar confidently unsheathed his sword.

"You're asking for it." Marcelus charged Tar, jumped high above the ground, and executed a downward slash. Tar thrust his sword upward in a parry. Marcelus knocked Tar's saber from his hand with an ease that bordered casualness.

"Not bad, Tar, but when I'm on top of you like that, a simple parry won't work. Instead, try attacking."

Tar bent down to pick up his sword. Marcelus trotted away and took out Ree's sword; his own was too noble to be used in simple training. Besides, he did not want to hurt the boy.

"Ready?"

"When you are," Tar responded. He could hear Marcelus's feet pounding in his direction. Springing in the air, Marcelus repeated the same slash. This time,

Tar swung so hard that he sent the older rebel and his borrowed sword sprawling. Stunned, Marcelus coughed then rapped a fist roughly on his chest.

"My advice is too good for you," Marcelus said from the ground. "It appears you learn straight off. I'm going to save my strength for the officials though. Let's call it a day."

"Okay," Tar answered as he swung his sword at imaginary foes.

"So you're blind," Marcelus asked fatuously in an attempt to make conversation. "Yeah," Tar responded dispassionately.

"It's okay," Marcelus said, "I know many fine warriors who were blind. In fact, my father is blind in one eye. He was struck on the side of his face."

"Who did it?"

"It was a Torg—a big, hairy ogre thing. They never leave their caves."

"I do not think I've ever encountered one before."

"You probably haven't, and you probably never will. They live north where it's cooler. My father hunted them for their fur."

"What did he hunt them with?"

"Spears. Actually, they were more like pikes. Arrows cannot pierce the Torg's tough, leathery skin and bristly coat of fur." The conversation lapsed into silence. Tar wondered if Marcelus had concocted the story about his father just to make him feel better. Leaning against the rock, Tar waited for something to happen.

Across the river and above the trees, a falcon circled.

"I wonder how close Shrie and Corious are," Tar commented. The boulder seemed to harden beneath his back. He stood up and rolled his shoulders. Leaves crunched behind him.

"Who's that?" Tar asked in slight alarm.

"An official!" Ree cried his first words of the day. Marcelus woke from his drowsy state as the Shalkan aimed two, brandished pistols at their heads. In a frenzy, Tar whisked out his knife.

The official laughed. "You do not recognize me?"

"Corious!" Ree shouted, lowering his weapons. "By the vanished gods! Do you have to torment us daily?"

"Yes," Corious replied as he pulled off his metal helmet and chest plate. Shrie popped from behind him. Unfortunately, no matter how hard she had tried to get a uniform which would fit her, the Shalkan garb hung in unnaturally loose folds from her body, and her stubborn hair refused to be contained in the helmet.

"Corious, I win again," she was saying. "I counted the officials in the clearing. You get five officials. I get eighteen. You need to practice your fight. This helmet stinks," she said to no one in particular as she took it off. Able to see more clearly, she acknowledged the others before her, weapons still in hand. "Hello, Ree, Marcelus, and Tar!"

Corious held up four more uniforms.

"You lugged those things all the way here?" Marcelus asked in astonishment.

Corious inclined his head, and Marcelus saw the trip had been painful. With her bow and arrows, Shrie had only managed to carry one of the extra uniforms; Corious had been left with the other three.

"From now on, you are going to have to wear one of these hideous things." He took the uniform from Shrie.

"What is this madness?" Ree questioned. "Since when did we have to hide our identities? There are a couple days left before we reach Quantus Plain; it will drag longer with these uniforms. It will waste time. Besides, no one will believe we are officials if we're carrying the injured. Shalkans never tend to their wounded."

"Ree right," Shrie noted, directing her attention downriver. "But Corious find this in the commander's pocket." Shrie loosened a sepia scroll from her hand. Black arrows outlined a small section of her jungle.

"Several hours after dawn, an official frigate will sail on this river," Corious explained smugly, handing Ree the dirty, bloodstained uniform. "We, Ree, Perry, Marcelus, and I will pose as officials and board the ship claiming Shrie and Tar as our prisoners."

"Shrie not—"

"Shrie, face it, you'd never pass as an official. The idea is preposterous. Once we are down the river, we'll disembark under the pretense of taking the prisoners to an inland camp for interrogation. We will save ourselves time by traveling on the river. Time is something we can't afford to waste." Corious pointed a finger significantly at Perry. "Time might save Perry."

"Shrie not—"

"Agreed?"

"No, Shrie not—"

"Good!" Corious said drowning out Shrie's strident protest. Ree and Marcelus pulled the uniforms over their heads. The sun strode fully into the sky.

"Hey," Marcelus exclaimed, "why am I a regular soldier and you a commander?"

Corious smiled. "It would only be accurate that way."

Marcelus grunted unhappily as he fastened his chest plate. Tar began to pace.

"What if we are caught?"

Corious sighed, "We won't get caught."

Tar shook his head in disbelief. "What if we do? You can't ignore the possibility, Corious."

"Fine. We'll sink the ship," Corious offered sarcastically. "A dead official has no secrets."

"I guess I do not have a choice."

Shrie said nothing and sat glumly on the ground, fiddling with the feather of an arrow.

"Marcelus," Ree called, "help me get this on Perry!"

"Sure." Marcelus jammed his wrist protectors onto his forearms. At the mention of Perry, Shrie rose and bade Ree to stop.

"You boys not work until Shrie put new bandages on his wounds." Ree backed away respectfully from the stretcher.

"Sure. Tell us when you're done."

Corious felt powerful in his new armor. "Time for sword training, in case things get foul," he said as his sweaty hands almost dropped his sword.

"One never knows who the officials might have on board," Ree added as he blocked Corious's swing.

"If God is for us, then who can be against us?"
Romans 8:31

Chapter 9

A man narrowed his eyes to slits, sweeping the eastern shoreline. The sun danced in and out of the trees set against a dark shade of orange. Above him, slaves tied down sails and scurried up the rope ladders leading to the crow's nest. Towering above them, a triangular flag whipped violently in the morning wind.

The water below slipped past the hulking ship with little more than a splash. The man, without taking his eyes from the hummocky banks of the river, slid his hand off the rough, wooden railing of the ship and unbuckled his ammunition pouch. He extracted a smooth, cylindrical bullet and loaded it into the pistol perched in his opposite hand. Mechanically, he began walking towards the Captain's chamber. The Captain found him first.

"What is it, watchman? Did you see anything?"

The watchman stuck a finger at a tiny flickering object far down the river.

"Fire. I doubt they are officials."

The Captain leered. "I'll be the one telling you who's who. Do not so easily forget your position." In his guttural tone, the Captain ordered the sailors to load the cannons nonetheless, cackling as he climbed to the crow's nest.

"Corious, if they don't come…"

"They will come!" Corious exclaimed for the third time that evening. "They'll come," he said yet again. "We have to be patient."

"To say the least," Marcelus muttered.

"We've been patient for the last two and a half hours," Tar remarked offhandedly.

Corious pressed his lips together tightly. "If they don't come, then all we lose is a few hours!"

"A few hours are important to—" Marcelus stopped when he apprehended Corious's drawn sword. "Never mind," he said as he sat down.

A roaring fire flickered against their ashen faces covered in a viscous mixture of gunk and soot. Shrie hummed the chorus of a foreign song. Corious treaded back and forth across the beach until he knew every inch of it, watching for his prophesied ship. Ree gazed grimly into the forest while Tar dozed beside Shrie. From the motionless forest, Ree thought he heard human voices singing. So surreal was the harmony that he shook his head, as if to clear it from his mind, but the wafts of music sounded clearly through the trees.

"Shrie!" Ree called in a wary whisper, "Come up here!"

Shrie leapt to his side. "What happening?"

"I heard voices," he replied. One of the chimerical notes still hung shrilly in the air; she had to have heard it. He glanced expectantly at her. When he received a blank stare in return, Ree pointed upward as if the music lay bare and visible before them. Shrie barely blinked.

"Well," he prompted, "explain, Jungle Ruler of great knowledge."

"Oh, you go crazy from heat and bugs, Ree." Shrie clearly did not consider the music's origin worthy of discussion.

"Be serious. Listen, there it is again!" Surely enough, the ethereal tune filtered into the rebels' ears. Marcelus climbed the rock in order to join them.

"What is that?" He strained to catch the notes of the unfamiliar music.

"They the Kalulukian's," Shrie shrugged. "They not my tribe. They river folk of mountains. I wonder why they here." She lazily flicked a piece of hair from her face, indifferent or only mildly curious.

Ree considered her askew. "Should we talk to them? Perhaps they know something of this ship." Ree directed his statement to Corious.

Shrie shook her head. "They doing burial ceremony. Their Leirmayn must have died."

"What's that?"

"Leirmayn mean leader in Kalulukian tongue."

"Why can't we talk to them?" Ree persisted.

"They in time of mourning; also, I not speak their tongue well. I know few words."

The group listened in fascination to a loud, fast, and fluid series of drum beats. A circle of light flashed briefly in the distance.

Shrie narrated, "They believe Leirmayn leave this land for another. That end of ceremony."

In accordance with Shrie's analysis, the music grew softer and softer until it was heard no more.

"There!" Ree exclaimed. "They left something glowing." He hopped from the rock and trotted a small distance. The Kalulukians had come surprisingly close to their rock; even Shrie had not spotted them. It was as if the tribe had remained as transient and as fleeting as their dead. Shrie and Marcelus peered over Ree's shoulder as he returned with a scroll and a small, golden fruit.

"Ree," Marcelus warned, "they are probably burial offerings. We better leave them."

Ree turned to Marcelus. "You believe in superstition? Take a look at that Leirmayn." Ree said the word with careful concentration. "He's not going anywhere, and he can't use these. We may as well keep them." Ree stuck the two objects in his pack and tied it securely. "What do you think, Shrie?"

"You right, Ree. Kalulukians not very bright tribe anyway; we use their burial gifts."

Marcelus drifted over to the Leirmayn's resting place: a light blue platform adorned with gold and silver decorations. In his hands, the Kalulukian leader held four short spears, indicating his status as a great hunter. His large, webbed hands and feet indicated long years of living by the river.

"See any other gifts, Marcelus?" Ree asked hopefully.

"Even if I did, I wouldn't take them. It would be disrespectful."

"Oh, come on! You heard what Shrie said."

Shrie popped up from behind the platform. "Shrie find another scroll!"

"What does it say? Is it in Kalulukian?"

Shrie roughly translated it:

Blue and gold of Leirmayn legends,
Of reeds swaying and river bends.
He rests his head upon this mount,
And leaves it for rushing, rich fount.
The golden fruit leads him to land,
To the halls of his fathers and
The temple of the...

"And that's where it leaves off." Shrie forlornly touched the burned scroll that she had snatched from the fire burning atop the pier. "I wonder why Kalulukians here," Shrie mumbled again. A black spot advanced in the corner of her vision.

"I see it!" Corious shouted. "Hurry! Get ready!" he warned.

Shrie rolled the scroll into a tight cylinder and handed it to Ree before sprinting to the beach. Ree knelt and jostled Tar awake while Marcelus fed the fire more tree limbs. Corious ran to the fire where the others had assembled.

"Remember, Shrie, I'm not Corious when we get on that ship. I'm Commander."

"I know, Corious." She held out her hands submissively as Corious looped a rope about them. He smiled.

"Good. And Shrie, you're going to leave your bow here. No Shalkan carries a bow. It will stay here safe and sound with mine. We can pick them up on the return journey." Shrie seethed, but Corious ignored her. "How are we doing, Tar?"

Tar finished smearing the ashes over his body. "Not bad. I feel like a prisoner already!"

"You look like one too! Good job. I doubt Shrie will cooperate as well." Corious gave him a pat on the shoulder and began to walk away when Tar spoke.

"Hey, wait!"

Corious turned.

"I won't need these," Tar realized as he threw his weapons to Corious.

Ree and Marcelus approached Corious.

"We're ready, Captain." Marcelus topped the statement with an exaggerated salute.

"Marcelus, you are taking Tar aboard, and I'll take Shrie to make sure she doesn't get herself into trouble. Got it?"

Curtailing their answers, airborne boulders burst unexpectedly into shards of flying rock. Dirt rained down upon them, and the choleric land hiccupped smoke in every direction. Waves of pressure knocked the men from their feet, forcing their breastplates to dig mercilessly into their chests. Then all was still. The cannonball had wrecked havoc thoroughly but briefly. Ree stumbled from the destruction to find himself alone.

"Hey!" he called. "Shrie! Can you hear me?"

Tar crawled out from beside the boulder, his arms, hair, and ear singed.

"What was that?" he questioned weakly.

"A cannonball; the ship is just offshore," Corious responded as he emerged from the brush in which he had dove. Marcelus left the jungle's shelter moments later.

"They think we are rebels!" he cried despondently.

"Well, we are, aren't we?" Ree grinned inwardly.

"Where's Shrie?" Corious yelled in the sudden awareness of her absence.

"Shrie over here! Ugh! Perry heavy! You carry him?"

Corious laughed in relief. "Of course we'll help you carry him." After they placed Perry safely on the sand, Corious situated himself on the bank of the river where he began waving a burning branch. Once he had the officials' attention, he addressed them.

"You idiots," Corious said impersonating the deep, scratching voice of an officer. "It's a shame you fired upon your own commander! We have two prisoners and an injured soldier. We request to load this frigate." Corious pushed the air past his vocal cords in rough syllables.

The officials' pistols, previously pointed at the rebels' heads, were grudgingly lowered. After scrutinizing Corious from the deck, the Shalkans argued vociferously amongst themselves. At the commotion, the Captain appeared on deck.

"Who's this? There's no necessity to stop for a lost lot of dense soldiers."

Opening the scroll decorated with thick, black arrows, Corious snarled back, "I suggest you stop sneering at a commander. It's a bad habit that can sooner or later get your head removed. I believe you have explicit orders to pick up a battalion. I wouldn't let it get back to headquarters that you disobeyed them." Corious cackled in a convincingly evil flight of laughter. "You know what happens when commands are disobeyed."

The captain stuttered raucously for a moment at the coterie on land before yelling at the slaves to let down the rope ladders. The rebels wadded into the depths. Perry floated awkwardly along the surface of the water with Ree supporting him. Corious pretended to shove the prisoners forward before girding the ropes. As he scaled the ship's side, sea water dripped from his clothes and fell into the churning water below.

The vessel set sail prematurely. Corious ground his teeth together as the movement sent the ladder swinging erratically. With one hand, he pulled himself up, and with the other, he held the slim rope that bound Shrie's compliant wrists together. Between Corious dragging her and the use of her athletic legs, Shrie managed to force her way up to the deck. When she got close enough behind him, Corious gave her a boost over the ledge.

"No messing with the prisoners," the captain yelled, noticing Corious's movement. "Share the goods."

Shrie's eyes burned angrily as she pulled away from Corious, but she said nothing. Corious clung to the edge of the ship, and lifted his gaze from the ladder to the Captain who proceeded to turn on his heel and leave them without a single acerbic word. Inwardly, Corious sighed in relief; their identities had not been discovered.

Once aboard, Corious admired the sleek contour of the ship and its master build. The workmanship was admirable if one could imagine it without the grime left in the official's trail like mucus left by moribund slugs. Corious marveled at the sure line of the mast which jutted high into the sky where it met the graceful lines of ropes and black sails swinging in the breeze.

Meanwhile, Ree let his senses absorb and contemplate the resentment harbored by the Shalkan sailors and slaves. They were clad without shoes and wore pants tied at the knee for convenient climbing. A few wore the Shalkan insignia, a black fist, stitched into their shirts. From months at sea, their hair, as a rule, was shaggy, unkempt, and long. Metal rings pierced the tops of their ears, and many slaves displayed dark green and blue tattoos. They appeared unruly, oppressed, but yeomanly, and—

Something in the corner of Ree's eye bade him to turn.

The watchman ogled the officials from behind the mast; half of his jagged face and the entirety of his pointed nose showed. The identities of the new passengers did not completely satisfy him. As if one of the new officials had read his mind, the biggest turned, and their eyes met. With guile, he retreated into the crow's nest above. The watchman did not want to be seen.

Ree watched the beady-eyed man go before matching Corious's stride, leaving Shrie and Tar to be taken by the slaves into the brig. Corious made a move to follow his companions, but Ree arrested him.

"Don't. The slaves can be trusted."

Corious hesitantly slowed. He felt two burning holes on the back of his neck.

"The watchman," Ree murmured.

Corious ducked as they went below deck. A slave scurried in front of them, leading them to their cabins. Ree noted the stagnant air and dank smell as they entered the belly of the ship and strode by rows of identical hallways and rooms piled with cots, clothes, and supplies. Finally, next to the slaves' quarters, the boy led them into a decently sized cabin with several portholes resting just above the waterline.

"I must go now," the slave said simply.

"Hey, wait!" Marcelus cried to the slave's turned back. The slave spun, trying to hide his alarm under the standard, vacant stare.

"Where are we? Well, actually—"

Marcelus made a terrible official. Corious jabbed him, and the rebel deepened the lilt of his voice.

"We are planning an attack on a certain area." Another jab. "Moron," he added, "do you know where we are in relation to Quantus Plain? Is it close by?"

The boy stopped in his tracks, his eyes widened, and he slammed the door. Corious bolted out the door after him; the boy had to be apprehended.

The boy's heart thumped loudly; the men were rebels. No officials talked to a slave unless to rebuke or beat. The rebel had been asking for a home, not a target of battle. Who else would ask for the location of Quantus Plain? That was a hidden rebel base of which only whispers were spoken by scared sailors seeking refuge. Yes, the slaves knew approximately where it was; they knew more about it than most rebels. A curious envy settled in his stomach. He skidded around a corner but got no farther. A sinewy hand threw him to the ground.

Corious dragged the slave back to his cabin, his hand clamped firmly over the boy's mouth. As he shoved him into the room, he heard light footsteps rounding the corner. He smashed the door shut and dove into his bunk.

The watchman was not the least bit surprised to see the newcomer's door slamming as he rounded the corner. *Secrecy.* They were quite peculiar, these officials, perhaps even mendacious. As often as he could spare it, he would keep an eye trained on them. From this mission, the watchman would exclude the Captain. He smiled. He was quite capable of disposing unwanted passengers alone.

The slave curled in a corner, horrified. The man in the commander outfit spoke.

"We're not going to kill you. In fact, if we can get off this ship and across the river, we'll free you. How does that sound?"

The boy relaxed but stayed inert. "Good," he said genuinely, but softly; it was a servant's voice, a quiet wisp of wind.

Corious glanced at Ree. Ree spoke.

"We will try and save some of the other slaves too. We know you are not here by choice. You need, however, to tell us the way to Quantus Plain." Shrie knew the way by land, but Ree did not want to assume she knew the way by water. "The positions of official encampments, if you know them, will be necessary." He paused dramatically. "Otherwise, we will never escape," he finished grimly.

The boy stood promptly. Holding his hand stiffly to his forehead, he succinctly revealed the coordinates of the hidden fort. "Travel north to a brook that spreads apart in many directions. One of these tributaries is wider than the rest. That is the one you will follow into an open field. That field is Quantus Plain."

The slave rolled his tongue when he spoke.

"Where are you from," Ree asked suddenly, "and how would you know where Quantus Plain was, unless the officials on this ship know? And how would they know?"

Corious glared at Ree for harassing the boy, but the slave regurgitated the requested information.

"I was born near the river. I know the location of Quantus Plain because a rebel guard was tortured until he told the Captain. I heard his screams."

Before anyone could respond, two officials carried in Perry on his stretcher. "Captain said to put him here."

Corious bade them out the door and took Tar's dagger from his belt. "Use this when the time comes," he said gravely. "Be sure, it will come."

The boy took the dagger and devoured it with his eyes.

"What's your name?" Marcelus asked.

"Aban."

"Aban," Marcelus started, "this is your chance to become a true rebel."

The boy shifted nervously as the Captain's voice rung throughout the cabins. "They'll be needing me above," he told them as he concealed the knife under his shirt.

"Goodbye, Aban," Marcelus said a bit too cheerfully as Aban closed the door behind him. Corious ran a hand through his hair.

"He better be loyal," Corious said distraughtly.

Ree lifted a slumberous, pallid Perry from the stretcher and onto an empty cot. Perry mumbled something before promptly rolling over with a groan. Corious unsnapped his breastplate, set it down, and stared out their porthole window. Splashes of water occasionally found their way to the glass, blocking what small view they had. Ree opened the porthole, letting the fresh air filter inside. A breeze had soon cleaned out the clammy smell of sweat and gunpowder.

"When do we attack?" Ree wondered aloud.

He's right, Corious thought. The watchman knew. Battle was inevitable.

"We'll use tonight and tomorrow to prepare. Before dusk, we'll hit our marks. We should be several miles from our destination at that point."

"That is our course of action then," Ree said.

Corious laughed nervously. "You look forward to it?"

"Any fight for the rebels is where I belong," Ree said, killing any joke waiting to spew from Corious's ready mouth.

"True," Corious said, echoing the solemn mood.

Marcelus complained suddenly of abdominal cramps.

"Maybe you should get to the nearest window," Corious suggested.

Ree frowned at Marcelus. "Up and out," he said simply.

"I hate boats," Marcelus crawled onto his new cot by the porthole. Ree opened the cabin door.

"A tour of the ship is crucial," Ree said to Corious, "and Marcelus, don't let anybody in."

Tar pulled his fingers along the cool bars of his dank jail cell. *Corious better know what he is doing.* Positioned at the back of the ship, the cell was sordid. Its floorboards were soggy, soiled, and in serious need of cleaning. The dreary air deadened his mind, and every time Tar moved, the tightly shackled metal tore into the skin around his ankles. He twisted toward Shrie, but as he did, the gray in front of his unseeing eyes bended before a shade of lighter color.

"Shrie!" Tar hissed excitedly. "Is there a window in here?"

Shrie noticed the porthole. "How you know, Tar?"

"So I'm right?"

A horrid clanking noise delayed Shrie's answer. Until the harsh voices sailed away, her gaunt face revealed fear. A ray of clouded light hit her hand, and she squished her nose in thought.

"Yes, there a window."

Tar tested the length of his shackles without letting them clang upon the floor.

"This could be our way out," he paused, listening. An unexpected fear leapt up his back in constant shivers whenever the shadows changed shapes. Yet he knew that no boots would hit the ground nor would any rifles level unless he let his mind believe it. Shaking, as if to dispel his anxiety, he continued. "A knife." His voice trailed off in thought.

Shrie accepted the silence to listen.

Tar shrugged his shoulders uncomfortably. "Let's hope Corious pays us a visit soon."

"What you mean Tar," Shrie probed as she uselessly pulled at her shackles, "about the knife?"

Tar placed his hands against the slimy floor. "If we had one, we might pry open the window. That is," he mused, "we'd have to use the proper force and weight distribution."

"But Tar," Shrie protested, though she had only understood half of his words, "window is high up!"

"I'll stand on your shoulders. If you don't mind, that is."

"Is okay. You not as fat as Corious or Ree."

Tar smiled lightly, but the fear remained simmering in a broiling panic. "We still need to get a knife, unless someone brings us a key. Corious better come."

Tar moved as far away from the cell bars as he could and slumped; he had forgotten about the shackles. Even if they opened the window, they were stuck in their metal encasements.

"So what are we going to do after we get off this ship?" Tar asked for the sake of conversation, forcing himself to counter the burdensome, stygian thoughts that pressed upon his mind. Shrie shared his worries.

"Shrie thinks we should return Perry and Marcelus to Quantus Plain and maybe stay there awhile before returning to jungle. Here, officials stand at our doorstep, but there we would be safe."

"Oh," Tar said laconically, not knowing what to say next. The two suffered in silence for the afternoon and night. Neither friend nor enemy paid them a visit.

Aban worked at the front of the ship, pondering. Could he trust the rebels? He knew he despised the officials, and if the rebels could give him freedom, he would side with them. He took out the dagger the rebel had lent him and twirled it in the air, catching it by the handle. The freedoms the slaves could reap by allying themselves with the rebels posed either as a great reward or as a great punishment. Footsteps sounded behind him, and he adroitly slipped the dagger back into hiding.

"I'd think it's time for you to be back in your quarters."

When Aban did not move, the official grabbed Aban's shirt and threw him to the floor of the ship. Aban's lip split, cut upon a sharp splinter of wood. Red liquid seeped and stained the grain.

"You've dirtied the ship," the Shalkan raged, seeing Aban's blood on the ground. "Get out of here." He shoved Aban forward by the back of his neck. Aban stumbled through the hallways to his quarters, blinded by his anger. He used his frayed shirt to wipe his bloody lip and chin before opening the door. He lit a candle in the slaves' quarters and roused everyone from sleep.

"I have a way we can gain our freedom," he announced.

Hazy light streamed from dull candles hanging on the walls. Muffled voices could be heard now and then, and the squeaking of a floorboard pierced the air under the rebels' feet. When Ree and Corious reached the door of their room, they could hear the usually taciturn slaves talking excitedly several doors down. Ree stepped into their room inconspicuously. Inside, Marcelus kneeled on his cot with his head out the window.

"Oh man," Ree whispered in disgust.

A shade of pale yellow had conquered Marcelus's face. "Hi," he croaked. Before one of them could respond, a great gurgle from Marcelus's stomach disrupted the brief dialogue.

Corious grimaced. "Ree, how about you show Marcelus where he can take care of that." Before Ree could protest, Corious directed him and Marcelus out of the room. *This isn't good.* Marcelus would be a fundamental element in the battle tomorrow. Dourly, Corious reviewed their plan. They would free Shrie and Tar early in the morning, and the two would track the ship by land to escape the notice of the Shalkans. Then he would gather the rebels: Marcelus and Ree, and hopefully Aban and the other slaves. They would somehow get Perry off the vessel before lighting a fire in the ammunition room of the cargo bay. Next, they would fight through the officials and get off the ship before it exploded. *It's a shame to destroy such a good ship*, Corious reflected. But there was nothing he could do about it; it would be a close battle, especially if the slaves did not offer their arms. As if Aban had heard Corious's thoughts, the boy's form appeared in the doorway. Corious motioned him in and scouted the hallway for any signs of Ree and Marcelus before closing the door inaudibly.

"The slaves have agreed to help."

"Not so loud."

Aban frowned; he thought the rebels would have been more thankful.

"Your mission depends on us now," Aban said softly. "Now that we know your secret, we can easily trade it. I suggest you give us your respect."

"I do not question this, but let you also not forget that your freedom depends on us, and we must give each other our firm loyalty. There is no need to argue."

Aban licked his fingers and snuffed the candle's flame. "It's past the curfew on the ship; we now talk in darkness."

"You have a curfew?" Corious asked, surprised. Just then, the sound of people stumbling could be heard outside.

"Hide!" Aban cried as he dove under a cot.

Corious shook his head and opened the door. "It's just Ree and Marcelus."

A nauseated Marcelus entered, hanging on Ree's arm.

"How are you feeling, Marcelus?" Corious asked hopefully. Marcelus laid himself down on his cot and said something incoherent before shutting his eyes.

"Hello, Aban," Ree said, somehow recognizing the boy in the murky room.

"We've chosen to help you," Aban told Ree. "We only need weapons."

Ree's excitement plummeted. "We only have but a few weapons."

"There are fifteen slaves."

"Besides keeping one weapon for each of us, we only have an ax, a saber, a pistol, and two knives."

One by one, Ree dropped the weapons in Aban's arms.

"Give them to the most skillful fighters. We'll need two of your men to carry Perry off the ship."

"It will be taken care of," Aban ensured him, extending his free hand.

"Good luck tomorrow." Ree smiled and put his hand in Aban's.

"We fight as rebels."

The ship swayed back and forth in a constant rhythm. The last twinkling stars hung in the creamy blue vat which was the eastern sky. The two prisoners languished in their cell as sleep evaded them. Their expected visitor had not visited, and escape on their own seemed futile. Conversation would start only to taper off minutes later. Tar's emotions oscillated between fuming anger and dread. Had they fallen into a trap? Footsteps rattled the bleak chamber, and a familiar official entered through the hatch.

"Tar, Shrie?" Corious glanced around worriedly. "I don't have much time."

"I just need a knife," Tar interjected.

Corious bit his lip. "I gave the extra weapons to the slaves."

"The slaves?"

"Forget it; take one of mine." Corious gave the knife to Tar. "Remember, follow the ship from land. I'll meet you at the brook that leads to Quantus Plain."

Tar nodded affirmatively; he knew Shrie would be able to find the brook. Corious returned through the hatch without another word. Tar rotated to face the window.

"Shrie, I've got a knife."

"We get out of here. Shrie not like this place, but first we get out of shackles. Give Shrie knife."

In a couple hours, Shrie managed to pick the aging locks. Tar stretched his feet, happy to be free of the chain.

"Now for the window," Tar decided.

Shrie kneeled; Tar planted his heel on her back and then on her shoulders as she rose shakily under the weight. She held his thin ankles firmly and felt as his Achilles tendon strained under her grasp. Balancing precariously, he began cutting, prying, and jamming. By early dawn, the window had loosened from its frame and collided with the floor during the slaves' roll call. Tar stuck his head and shoulders through the opening while Shrie straightened her arms to push his legs higher into the air. He jumped through the window and landed in the water with a loud splash, but the bark of appellations permitted his escape to go unnoticed. Shrie leapt crazily for the rim, catching it with her fingertips. Thrusting her legs between her arms, she settled her back on the rim before propelling herself into the river.

Once Shrie had joined Tar, they dove under the cold waves of rolling water, surfacing a safe distance from the ship. Spray from whitecaps flicked beads of frothy water onto their faces as they sucked in the jungle air. As Shrie clasped his hands to lead him, Tar realized she swam almost as quickly in the water as she ran in the trees. Soon, their feet connected with the soft mud deposited on the river's banks.

"You good swimmer, Tar," Shrie complimented while patting his bedraggled head.

Tar smiled and attempted to dry his hair and face. Shrie pulled him into the cover of the forest; the ship was still close.

"We rest for a moment and then go follow the ship," Shrie decided as she rummaged through the brush to reveal her and Corious's bows. She clutched her arrows to her chest in a joyous reunion.

Tar agreed, thankful for the brief respite. It was a foggy day, and even if Tar had sight, he would not have been able to see more than thirty feet in front of himself. After Tar grabbed the bottom of his shirt and wrung it out; Shrie reversed her decision.

"We going to lose the ship if we don't go soon."

Shrie's hand slipped into his, and they crept inside the forest's edge.

Corious hurried. He had dismantled the cots and given the poles to the remaining unarmed slaves to use as quarter staffs. The sailors not on duty were in their cabins, save the two who were going to evacuate Perry. Aban had organized them and now nervously checked the hallway for the officials. It was still early, but the officers had already finished roll call and would expect the slaves on deck soon. Nevertheless, the Shalkans were not concerned with the slaves; they suspected the newcomers. The watchman had sniffed out their designs.

The door shook with a sudden pounding. Corious opened it calmly. Outside the watchman stood at the vanguard of a Shalkan unit.

"Rebels!" he announced haughtily. "Attack!"

"As you command," Corious grinned. Corious's and Ree's swords clinked against their sheaths. Seasickness still assailed Marcelus, but he wielded a staff from his cot with a stern expression etched into his face. They were three in number. In grim determination, they met the officials.

The groups clashed murderously, and Corious propelled his sword into the watchman's gut. Ree spun out of the reach of a saber and slew two officials in one blow. In no time, they had destroyed the officials. Speeding into the hallway, the rebels joined with the slaves and flew down the hall. Their feet slid across the wooden planks noiselessly; they were ghosts ready to haunt the living. The anticipation of battle strangled their hearts. They suppressed the rebel war cries that rose within them.

Slipping from the group, Corious hid himself in the shadows. Marcelus approached, and Corious motioned him aside. Concealing the lit match with the curve of his hand, he carefully handed it to Marcelus. Marcelus's eyes glistened in expectation; he knew where to carry the flame. Corious and Marcelus split ways, and Corious hurried after the rebels.

The rebels huddled at the hatch, waiting for his command. Corious let his hands encircle the rope ladder. Mist swirled down from above. Stepping soundlessly from the hatch, he saw two official forms stride towards them through the dense fog. The slaves crawled behind him, plastering their bodies against the ship's side. Corious climbed onto a beam supporting the upper deck. The officials had not seen him. As the clicking of their boots grew near, Corious delivered a swift, sickening kick to each man. One crinkled in pain. The other's chin bone crunched under Corious's punch, his equipment rattling across the deck. Corious tossed the dead men's weapons into the crowd behind him. Still, the rebels held their tongue. Ree now led them onto the main deck. Large formations of vague shapes awaited their arrival. The slaves slunk forward, closing the distance between themselves and the enemy. They wanted hand to hand combat.

Unable to stand the wait, Ree roared and charged the Shalkans. The cries of slaves and officials rang cacophonously as fist met face and sword challenged gun. Mayhem broke loose as the officials abandoned rank. The onslaught continued in ebbing and flowing waves of bodies.

Men took to the upper decks as the battle spilled across the boat. Corious hurdled over a puddle of blood mixed with brackish water and dove away from an official's stained saber. Springing up a rope ladder, Corious heard his boots squeak and slip against wet wood. Sparing a moment to glance at the material beneath his feet, he watched his platform swing riotously. Directing his sword down upon the enraged, sputtering official, Corious balanced unsteadily on the boat. The official fell, and Corious scanned the ship. His eyes and ears focused on a spot overburdened by silver armor. A single rebel fought a horde of Shalkans; they drove him continuously backwards.

Corious tapped his sword against the rope straining to keep the lifeboat in the air. Without a second thought, he flipped the boat upside down and cut the thick braiding with a swooshing arc of his sword. Corious tumbled off the wooden structure as it crashed into the group of advancing officials. The rebel, who Corious now recognized as Ree, gave him an appreciating glance.

Water battered the ship's sides as it slowed to a standstill. The Captain, or at least the steersman, had been taken from his post. The boat pitched dangerously, and an official came hurtling through the mist. Seconds before the official was upon him, Corious struck with his sword but found the official already slumped in death with an arrow through his back. Dumbfounded, Corious observed as two familiar, wet shapes came up beside him.

"How you doing Corious? Tar and I got bored. We see smoke and join battle."

Marcelus careened up the stairs, his stomach gurgling painfully. His trifling flame had ignited the cord that would soon engage the black, dry powder. As he rounded the final corner to the main hallway, he was dismayed to see it packed with armed officials. His mind raced, and an official, hearing his steps, turned. Obeying a whim, Marcelus weaved his staff through a rafter parallel to the long corridor and grabbed the other end of it. Bullets rang around him.

"Only once in four chances will they hit a moving object," Marcelus muttered, "only one in four."

The enemy cursed and reloaded. Pushing off, Marcelus was pleasantly surprised as his apparatus acted perfectly. Legs circling in rapid revolutions, Marcelus hollered in a mixture of childish enjoyment and fear. The officials fired as he slid over their heads. Almost at the door, he concentrated on landing when a loud creak signaled the strength of the wood had failed. Marcelus screeched as the rafter broke into pieces. He unsuccessfully fought for control before landing squarely on his hindquarters and diving out the entrance. Slamming the door shut, he jammed his weight against it. Bullets dug into the dense wood behind him, and a fiery explosion rocked the ship from bow to stern, knocking him away from the door. Corious ran by without offering any congratulations but tossed him what had obviously been a dead man's sword.

Corious staggered as the ship groaned. He struggled to remain standing as his ears rang from the volume of the explosion. Bright dots of fire raced about his eyes. The officials fell like raindrops under his sword, but each slaughtered Shalkan, like a head of Hydra, was replaced by more. Corious let the officials swarm him.

The irritating noise of a gun being loaded bade Ree's eyes to widen. An official aimed the barrel at Ree's head. Ree immediately rammed the butt of his sword hilt into the official's wrist, sending the gun flying. Burying his fist into the side of the official, Ree saw him hit the ground. The slaughter continued, and the conflagration stuffed itself with the sides of the ship; its appetite, unsated, would hasten their escape. Ducking under a stair, Ree avoided another official's ireful fist. He was prepared to dive off the ledge when an awkward movement took his attention from the water. An injured official clumsily, but resolutely, climbed a rope ladder; a glint of metal sparkled egregiously from the bottom of the crow's nest he was approaching. The outline of a brass horn painted in a crumbling, black paint formed before Ree's eyes.

Ree muttered heatedly under his breath as he sprinted across the deck littered with bodies. The smell of smoke clouded his nostrils as the ship continued to burn. The horn would compromise their tenuous victory. Extracting a gun from the tangle of bodies, Ree aimed and pulled back the trigger. The gun seemed to explode in his hand as it recoiled. After dropping the gun disgustedly and cursing the officials' weapon of choice, Ree leapt onto the mast, digging his nails into the rotting wood. The maimed official, though alert with adrenaline, could not surpass Ree's inborn athleticism. The inside of the official's palm caressed the horn. Instinctively, Ree seized the official's foot and yanked. Only the boot stayed in Ree's hand. The official clutched the horn and kicked viciously at his contender. Ree fended off the kicks with simple blocks; his sword was wedged uselessly between his body and the mast. In desperation, Ree climbed up and over the besieged official, reaching the crow's nest and wrestling away the horn. As he did so, Ree felt himself slide. The boat rocked brutally.

He attempted to stabilize himself to no avail. As he fell, Ree reached frantically for a dangling rope and managed to halt momentarily his descent. The foaming official inched towards Ree with the nefarious gun. With a sweep of his sword, Ree reached the official's arm as the released bullet skimmed his cheek. In horror, the official clutched at his elbow, sacrificing his hold on the mast. He plummeted to the deck, screaming in agony.

Though the slaves were strong in number and fought with a ferocious will, they were callow and accustomed to submission; revolt suited their desires if not their skills. Shrie's and Tar's presence on the ship assuaged an otherwise worried Corious. *So predictable*, Corious thought as he shoved a belligerent Shalkan over the side railing. The slaves around him hailed his ability. Marcelus appeared in a state of disarray.

"The aft end of this ship is swarming with officials! They'll be coming up any minute." Marcelus whaled an official on the head. "If you could fire cannon—"

A testy Shalkan cut Marcelus's sentence short, knocking the rebel with the butt of his gun. Corious ducked behind a cannon as he heard the official's bullet ping threateningly against the metal. Swinging the cannon on its rotating foundation, Corious, in a display of temerity, upended an official by the knees and speared him onto the deck; the official's face contorted into a horrible expression of suffering. Clutching Marcelus by the shirt, Corious dragged his friend to the safety of the cannon. Fresh officials filtered into the battle. Corious checked the cannon; it was still loaded. Grabbing a match leftover from Marcelus's mission, Corious lit the fuse.

As the cannonball found its mark in the incoming officials, Corious was flung backwards. Smoke piled in the air, and a loud boom temporarily overrode the sounds of battle. Using the cannon to its full potential, Corious forced a third official retreat. The rebels now owned the outside deck. Inexplicably, a second shudder of fire coursed through the ship. The officials in the hallway had no escape and neither did the valiant slaves who would die as free men. Without mercy or premeditation, the flames engulfed them. *Marcelus must have lit two fuses.* Wood splintered as the ship began to slide into its watery grave. No trace of the previous bloodshed would remain.

Ripping off his breastplate and letting the metal plates sink beneath him, Corious inhaled deeply as his body floated easily to the surface of the chilly water. His body, numb to all pain, stroked relentlessly through the water. Though the water cut before his hands and broke at the pressure of his kicking feet, it refused to relinquish him without ramifications. Water seeped into his nostrils and crawled into his unwilling mouth. Corious swallowed the rush of water. His limbs flailed frantically as he began to sink under the combined weight of Marcelus and himself. He was no longer in his body; he watched himself contend with nature until the ground solidified beneath him. His senses returned to him as the muck rose between his toes and as he finished pulling Marcelus through the water. In elated relief, Corious laid his friend upon the soft sand.

Wiping water and blood from his face, Corious coughed weakly before carefully putting his cheek next to his friend's blue lips. Warm breath rushed to meet Corious's face, and he knew Marcelus was alive. In a bellicose manner, Corious ripped the drenched shirts from Marcelus's limp body and permitted them to desiccate beside their owner. He did the same for himself, and his skin soaked in whatever jungle sun escaped the encompassing fog.

Ree sloshed ashore with Shrie, Tar, two slaves, and Perry. A particularly triumphant look graced Shrie's face. Sitting exhaustedly on the riverbank, the rebels warmed their hands in the welcome sand. The current washed ashore five more slaves who had trusted their fate to serrated pieces of planking. The first former slave fell to his knees on the sand; a bullet had punctured his shoulder, and a knife lay plunged in his leg. Shrie lurched towards him, and with Ree's help, she tended to him. Aban staggered onto the beach with a pool of blood trailing from his side. The next three slaves came in; all had sustained casualties. The last was a girl.

As Shrie began issuing commands to the uninjured, the skies opened. Everyone fumbled with their resisting bodies to move under the cover of the trees. Shrie prayed in thanksgiving as the rain washed away the gory remnants of battle.

"Be strong and courageous. Do not be terrified; do not be discouraged,
for the Lord your God will be with you wherever you go."
Joshua 1:9

Chapter 10

A halcyon layer of dew glazed the camp like varnish. Cooking smells covered the rank odors of illness, and under Shrie's vigilance, none of the remaining slaves died. Those who were able learned to find herbs and grind them into concentrated mixtures. They now watched as bits of leaves fluttered from Shrie's hands into a clay bowl. Ree's attentive eyes followed her every movement. Tar never would have guessed that Ree possessed a hand for healing; but Shrie had trusted him completely with the medicines once he had insisted on receiving an education. Dishing a handful of the finished cream into Ree's hand, Shrie showed him how to spread it on gaping wounds. Days later, the treated lesions shriveled like plants wilting in the desert sun, and the broken skin stitched itself together. After bodies healed, minds seized their chances to mend. It was satisfying work.

Corious, though considered one of the healthy, had not escaped unscathed. A broken thumb and pointer finger on one hand made his formerly supple hands as sore and as stiff as a board. Using the full measure of her weight, Shrie had managed to snap and reset the wayward bones back into their places. Not a tear had escaped his eyes. To ensure his full recovery, Ree had expertly constructed a wooden splint and forced Corious to complete strengthening exercises. Wrapped in dried animal skin, the hand hung uselessly at his side as he walked about to check on the slaves. He avoided the sight of a particularly bloodied stump from which an arm had once protruded. The man missing the arm had felt nothing after coming ashore—of that Corious had been sure. He had been present when Shrie tipped the foul sleeping concoction between the slave's lips before stripping the area of dead, flapping skin.

The group spent three weeks on the craggy beach. Perry recovered with rest, and before Aban was eventually able to stand, Tar, thrilled to have found someone his own age, spent his hours conversing with him. Though no Shalkans threatened their present security, Ree, Shrie, and Corious were confident in the potential abilities of their own rebel league.

Ree considered his responsibility to the group with the utmost gravity. As soon as Aban could wield metal, Ree began to teach him the nuances of sword and knife fighting. Shrie would join them occasionally, and the others watched with curious eyes, unable to participate fully. When health returned to them, they were required to memorize every move, mastering the basics of both the bow and the sword. Vying for students, Shrie and Corious instructed the rebels in the use of the longbow until they could shoot accurately and swiftly. After rigorous weeks of training, the foursome had produced thirteen proficient members of the league: six archers and seven swordsmen. The formerly handicapped now possessed the power that comes with learning the duplicitous art of war.

By the nightly campfire, Corious introduced the uneducated rebels to the systems of reading and writing; captivity had kept them from learning, and Ree had insisted an academic education was as necessary as perfecting their skills with arms. Shrie attended these meetings regularly. With his knife, Corious scrawled a word into the tree behind him and held an illuminating torch next to it. He then pointed to it with his sword's glinting, metal tip.

"Oh," Aban cried with an exulted smile. "Sword! That's the word."

"That's how it's written." Corious scrawled it again slowly, cutting into the bark and revealing the white insides of the tree. "Try sounding out the letters next time. And hey, Tar, come and feel the word so you can learn too," Corious suggested as gooey clumps of amber and saffron sap stuck his fingers together.

Tar walked to the tree, pressing his finger against the rough bark. He gingerly traced each letter.

"Okay," Corious began, "here's another one."

Aban scratched his chin before blurting out the answer. "Bow! Bow and...arrow! Bow and arrow!"

Corious smiled. "Very good."

Each night, Perry, Ree, and Corious would rotate lessons and complete vigorous training routines, ending their day with a swim in the river. One evening, minutes before the beginning of such a class, the members of the hunting party, for it took more than three to hunt for the group now, returned, carrying nothing in their sacks and fear on their faces.

"What wrong?" Shrie asked, immediately dropping the item on which she had been working.

One of the rebels forced the words from his mouth; his eyes were creepily blank, staring at things the others could not see. "There's been a slaughter. Rebels I'm sure. There must have been an ambush," he replied shakily. Heads turned, and the man repeated the lines. Hastily, Shrie divided the group. Half of the camp would stay stationary and watch for Shalkans; the other half would investigate.

Perry gripped his hatchet tightly as his hunting spear counted the time. It rapped ominously against his back with every step. While some men closed their eyes to hide their anxiety, Perry stretched his shoulders expectantly. He would take the acute thrill of danger over the rotting calm of a sedentary existence any day. *Yes, it is good to be free of the stretcher and thriving on suspense once again.* With six other men, he walked deeper into the lush jungle. They were looking for the remains of a battle—a rebel defeat. Half an hour later, at the front of the line, Ree instructed the others to spread along the perimeter of the grassy clearing littered with weapons and bodies. They had discovered the sought site. Perry knelt on one knee next to Ree. Official bodies intermingled with the grass, but next to each official lay four to five rebels. Ree narrowed his eyes and hunkered in the dim light. Taking a stick, he snapped it over one knee.

Perry's eyes nearly burst from his head, horrified as a waterfall of officials streamed from the trees. Others sprung from tall weeds in the clearing. Ree had drawn them out of hiding. After a few moments, the Shalkans deemed the noise a false alarm, sheathed their swords, and shouldered their guns before reclaiming their spots in the trees.

Ree gathered his men, and at first, the rebels retreated slowly and wearily. Then, unable to restrain their legs, they careened recklessly through the woods. When they arrived breathlessly at camp, Shrie and the others watched them expectantly. Ree spoke dispassionately.

"It was an ambush of maybe eighty officials. The rebels must have walked right into it. They paid for their mistake with their lives. We are not safe here. It is time to leave; we have lingered here too long."

Marcelus stepped to the fore of the group. "If there are wounded soldiers out there, they deserve our help." He remembered when he and Perry had once been left behind. "The officials will probably leave at nightfall to get reinforcements after today's alarm. I noticed their ammunition was low."

Ree rejected the idea. "Who says more officials won't come with reinforcements? It's too much of a risk. It is not worth dying to find rebels who are already dead."

Marcelus searched the rebels' eyes, ignoring Ree's comment. "One person," he begged, "all I need is one brave man to help me carry Perry's old stretcher. That's all I ask." Men hung their heads or folded their arms.

Ree glared at Marcelus. "If that is what you decide, we'll have to leave without you. It is not ideal."

"He's right, Marcelus. It's not worth it," Corious pressured, hoping to dissuade his friend from executing the Sisyphean proposal.

Perry groaned as he humbly approached his friend. "I'm his best friend, maybe for the worst, but it's my responsibility to get his back. I'll go."

Ree's eyes enveloped them in an impersonal stare. "So we part," he said vapidly.

"We'll meet you at Quantus Plain," Perry returned warmly. He did not want to leave in bitterness. "We know the way from here; this is our territory now. Don't wait for us."

"I hadn't planned to," Ree responded. Corious glanced at the two apologetically while patting them on the back.

"Good luck, you two," Corious said genuinely, "your mission is noble. We will meet you at Quantus Plain. We promise to see you at the Great Hall." Corious grasped his friends' hands. "On my word, we shall."

Ree shouted for Corious.

"I need to go," Corious finished, "but, don't worry about Ree. He doesn't mean half of what he says anyway." Corious slapped Perry on the arm. "Be safe." And then Corious enjoined his men, "Carry all your weapons men. We have a decent chance of meeting with those officials at any time. I want you to be prepared."

Perry and Marcelus briefly said their farewells and packed lightly. After they finished, Corious approached them one last time.

"We'll be following the Quantus Plain brook. It's a bit north of here."

Perry mentioned he had a fair idea of where it was before shaking hands and heading off. As they trekked away from the group, the two soldiers from Quantus Plain could hear Corious organizing the rebels. The friends conversed in hushed tones, unable to separate themselves from the camp and the people they had grown to know so well. Shrie had not bothered to say goodbye; she trusted she would see them again. That gave them hope, but even as the camp packed, the caliginous woods loomed overhead.

"What have I got myself into?" Marcelus muttered. "Maybe I was wrong."

"No, you did the right thing." Perry sighed, watching the eleven rebels fade into the forest. "Imagine if you were one of those rebels and still alive. No, you were right."

"I hope so," Marcelus replied grimly. They walked swiftly, expecting danger to lurk in every nook. A strange feeling seized them, and they began running through the undergrowth; they did not want to arrive too late.

Trees and brush blurred together in the darkness. Their steps pounded heavily. A thumping seemed to accompany them. Perry assumed it was Marcelus running, and Marcelus assumed it was Perry. A rustling of leaves spiked fear in their nerves; it came closer. Spinning around with swords ready, the rebels faced the black, staring eyes.

"Mali-Malis!" Marcelus cried exultantly, breaking from his phantasm of disbelief.

At the utterance of their names, the two spiders began to purr and encircle Perry. Perry stood uncomfortably. He did not enjoy their greeting ceremony. Marcelus laughed.

"They can take us to the clearing and back to the rebels much faster than we could have ever run," Marcelus said practically, bending down to pet the creatures.

He had spent some of his childhood near the jungle and could speak a modicum of their tongue.

He whispered to them, "Mali, ha chu ban a tak shi Can. Fu chu Mali ban cho chi la mak." The Mali-Malis gurgled something back and scurried back up the tree from which they had come. "They will be back soon," Marcelus informed Perry.

"If you say so."

Opting to avoid the trail until the Mali-Malis returned, they hid in the brush and lashed together the gear they had dropped. Stroking to life a small fire, Perry boiled water while Marcelus rubbed crushed oi berries on their bread rations.

"This doesn't seem like enough for dinner," Marcelus remarked sourly.

"We must save the rest until we have time to hunt," Perry stated softly. The thought of the official ambush was at the forefront of his mind. "You never know how long we may be out here."

Marcelus scrutinized his unappetizing dinner. He frowned. "Forget it, I'm not hungry anymore." He put the piece of bread back in the sack.

Roth flexed his arm under the staggering load. Sweat soaked the itchy bandage that reached from the side of his abdomen, around his back, and up to his shoulder. Aban, in front of him, at least had the freedom of shifting his burden from one arm to another. Yet the struggle was paradise compared to the back-breaking jobs he had performed on the Shalkan battle ship. Here, the labor was now voluntary, and his comrades were of his own choice. Unfortunately, in the absence of impending death, he found the time to miss his family and his village. Both had long been buried in ashes. There would be nothing to return to even if he did return, and so there was no point in pining.

At thirty-seven, Roth was shorter than most men his age but weathered and hardy from years at sea. He had dark eyes and light skin and walked with the rolling gait that betrays all seamen. A light beard and mustache covered his face, marking his days as a slave and as a rebel. His mane of blond hair hung past his ears, reminding him of a time when he had been clean-shaven and young.

The officials had impressed him into their service seventeen years ago. Before thirty days ago, he had understood life as a sailor and a slave. Now, he served as the rebels' cook when Shrie did not have the time. Variably, he had adjusted to the jump in lifestyle; the transition from tying knots with two hands to carving meat and cutting vegetables with one was not an easy one to make. A dagger, the sole instrument he could wield effectively with one hand, rested against his hip, ready to either mince herbs or attack the enemy. Compared to the others laden with weapons, he felt somewhat foolish. *What I would give to experience a free life and a whole body!* For several hours during the ship battle, he had experienced the power of wielding a decent weapon, a quarterstaff, only to be caught in first hallway by the second explosion. He had seen and felt the conflagration too late, meekly throwing out his arm as the flames engulfed him. The ship had sunk, drowning the flames; but his torso had sustained serious burns. His skin had been burnt to a crisp, and his one arm had been mutilated to the point of needing amputation. But he was alive, and the fact that he had survived mitigated his insecurities and gave him an odd sense of pride.

"Hey, Roth!" Corious stared at him. Corious continued to speak though his next words were far from necessary. As a cook, Roth had come to know a famished face. "You have any extra food on you?"

Roth shook his head sadly. "I gave it all to Perry and Marcelus. They had nothing."

Corious growled unhappily. "I'll guess you'll have to do."

Roth's mouth arched up in a small grin. "No, I'm too tough. Aban's tender; I'd try him."

"Don't get me involved in your problems, Roth," Aban admonished, "or I'll have to beat you in another archery tournament."

"Fine," Roth acquiesced, "I'll use my teeth to pull back the arrow. You liked that last time, eh?"

Corious grimaced. "Do you know how many teeth you could lose doing that?"

"It's not like they're pretty anyway," Roth shrugged.

As the evening drew to a close, the three talked less, and eventually Ree had them on a constant watch with their weapons ready. Roth would be glad when the safety of the Quantus Plain camp surrounded them.

It seemed an eternity of drudgery before the Mali-Malis scurried down the tree. In a sign of friendship and thanks, Marcelus gave the spiders some of their berries, much to Perry's dislike. Perry did not approve of handing spare food to jungle creatures.

"I'm ready to go. How about you, Perry?"

Perry observed Marcelus petting one of the spiders. "As ready as I'll ever be."

"Great," Marcelus said as he slung his pack over the spider's back, "just keep an eye out for officials."

"I would have never thought of that, thank you," Perry said sarcastically.

Annoyed, Marcelus grabbed his spear.

"Hup chu, hup chu." At Marcelus's command, the Mali-Malis trotted towards the clearing with a speed that astounded Perry. His cape streamed gracefully behind him.

The moon had risen, and its half circle shape cast a faint light below the canopy. Marcelus leaned over but left his head erect. His outline faded into that of the spider, making him appear almost invisible. Imitating his friend's position, Perry hunched over the spider, digging his hands into its bristly fur.

Marcelus thought carefully about their mission. Lain, the leader of Quantus Plain, had always stressed rescue missions. They created a potent sense of loyalty, trust, and even compassion for the fight among the men. They were times to mourn the lost, collect abandoned weapons, and redistribute hope. No one was left behind without an affray. For practical necessity, the rebels, who had few able bodies, needed to save as many as possible.

They approached the day-old battlefield; hidden in its tangled grasses would be the injured, dying, and dead. To check for an ambush, Perry broke a stick as Ree had done. Nothing moved. He did it again. They were alone.

As they entered the field, Marcelus could see where the outer skirmishes had taken place. The trampled grass and the blood-soaked earth were as injured as the torn flesh of the battle's victims. Weapons were flung uselessly aside in the grass, sometimes inches away from their owners. The dead appeared illusory in the moonlight. Ghastly and dreamlike, they lay crumpled like pale, pieces of refuse paper. Their eyes were open and blank, staring at their fleeing souls. The body count grew as Perry and Marcelus moved closer to where the heat of combat had claimed the most human life. Perry checked the vital signs of every rebel they passed; there was no response. Marcelus collected weapons.

On a sudden impulse, Marcelus whispered to the bodies, "Is anyone here? Can you hear me?"

Both men waited for something—anything. From the aphotic plain, a pained grunt distinguished itself, and a white hand groped in the air from under a pile of bodies. Perry rushed over and firmly grasped the hand. It tightened its hold, and Perry pulled the man out from under the dead and into the light.

"Kill me," the man gasped weakly, his dry lips cracking and bleeding.

Perry hurriedly ripped the canteen from his belt and held the bottle to the man's parched lips. At first the man turned his head, but Perry forced the canteen to his mouth and forced down the water. The clear liquid dripped from the man's mouth and down his chin, splattering over his chest and a tattered shirt. Perry glanced over the man, searching for wounds when suddenly a familiar insignia stitched into the man's shirt arrested him. His eyes widened, and he dropped the canteen.

"He's an official!" Perry cried in alarm.

Marcelus rode to his friend, sweat beading on his brow and upper lip.

"What do you mean he's an official?" Marcelus's eyes flickered to the enigma. "Almighty, reserve us," he whispered. "What do we do?"

The official had slumped back, his eyes only half open.

"Kill him?" Perry offered weakly.

Marcelus lightly kicked the official in the ribs, jolting him awake.

"You will come as our prisoner."

The proposition astounded the flummoxed official. "Why give me a chance?" he sputtered, blood dripping from the corner of his mouth. "You have given me a sip of water. That is more than my commander would have done. Just leave me or spear me through."

"Shush." Misgiving and disgust gripped Perry's chest.

Marcelus watched helplessly as Perry dragged the official onto the Mali-Mali and threw the stretcher to the ground; there would not be room or need for it. No one said a word, but the rebels' thoughts mixed in mutual terror.

They were rescuing a Shalkan, and they did not know if such evil could be forgiven. Perry nervously hopped onto the Mali-Mali. He would rejoin the group at Quantus Plain. Marcelus would finish the search here. The grass crunched under the Mali-Mali's footsteps, and the sound of the official's heavy breathing echoed in Perry's ears as they headed away from Marcelus. The moonlight gave off an ethereal glow, and Perry urged the Mali-Malis onward to Quantus Plain.

"So we fix our eyes not on what is seen,
but on what is unseen. For what is seen
is temporary, but what is unseen
is eternal."
2 Corinthians 4:18

Chapter 11

It was the original foursome now: Ree, Shrie, Tar, and Corious. The liberated slaves were there of course, but they followed at a respectful distance, far enough away so the leaders could talk privately but close enough to hear a shouted order. Shrie walked at the head of the formation with her arrow notched, and Aban brought up the rear as an appointed guard of the rebel force. The title was an honorary award for banding together the slaves.

Having recently said their farewells to Perry and Marcelus, they traveled along the brook which led to Quantus Plain. Shrie had not condoned Perry's search of the battlefield. He was not fully healed yet, but she would not stop him. She had just nodded her head, half in motherly concern and half in wonder. People were funny beings, rarely logical or predictable.

"What are you thinking, Shrie?" Corious asked musingly.

Ree turned to hear her response though his eyes remained focused on the forest.

"What do think will happen?" Tar's philosophical side asked.

"Shrie is unsure," she sighed. "Shrie not used to not being in control," she admitted. "Shrie just hope that good meant to conquer evil, and Shrie must trust in One who creates all."

"One who creates all?" Ree asked dubiously, "Your Almighty again?"

"Yes. One who make this earth and Shrie's jungle and Shrie. He will come back one day to save His people from evil that turns against Him."

"Now would be a good time for Him to show up," Ree sneered.

Corious pondered Shrie's statement. He remembered that when he had first met Shrie, he had scoffed at her talk of evil and the Almighty. Now that he had seen so much, he was more apt to consider such a possibility. It was the one hope the rebels had, and it gave him a purpose beyond himself.

For once, Shrie did not offer a rebuttal but instead returned to inspecting the woods. The murmuring of the rebels combined with the rustling of the brush as they passed. The birds fell silent.

"We approaching swamp," Shrie mentioned casually. "Get ready for many mosquitoes, wet feet, and much mud," she added as an afterthought.

Tar grimaced.

"How deep are these swamps, Shrie?" Ree asked in blatant annoyance.

"Only about three feet," Shrie said quickly, "but very sticky and hard to walk through."

Tar frowned again as Shrie continued.

"But Shrie has not been there in many a year, as it difficult to live near swamp. No good hunting. Plus, it across from river—far from where Shrie lives."

Tar steadied himself as he tripped clumsily through the already thickening mud. "The air is stagnant," he commented as the mire refused to relinquish his shoe. He plunged his walking stick into the viscous soup before him. "Shrie, do you have any recollection of this place?" He questioned her memory.

"It the swamp labyrinth," Shrie replied defiantly.

"It is where Turock first centered his realm before he succumbed to the Shalkan influence," one of the slaves added from behind. The swamp sucked his leg lower into the mud. "I can see why it's such an infernal place."

"Shrie lead group through swamp," she assured them. "Otherwise, other rebels fall into sinking mud. But no worries—swamp not very wide or long."

"Let's hope not," Corious grumbled. "Should we bring the others up with us? The fog settles."

As they spoke, a heavy mist inhibited their vision. Ree studied the low, bare branches an arm's length above his head.

"Yes, it would be unfortunate to lose the bulk of our group simply because of the fog."

"Up to the front, men! Aban, get them organized into some sort of decent formation!" Corious told the teenager as he heard several sizable splashes.

"I can barely see in front of me," Ree stated.

"That's another dire property to be sure," Tar remarked, "although it hardly makes a difference to me."

"But this will," Aban told them as he strode behind them. "Ree, there are snakes in the water. They've accosted us once. What do you suggest we do?"

"Snakes?"

"If you need proof, we've got it, but I shouldn't like to make a museum of it. Their numbers increase by the moment."

"Tell everyone to stay together."

Aban trudged back to the other rebels and took his place in the rear.

"You never told us about snakes, Shrie!" Corious grumbled.

"Shrie not travel on ground when she comes here last; Shrie travel through trees."

"Hey, Ree, we could do that," Corious suggested hopefully.

"We could, but it would slow our pace drastically. I'd rather kill some snakes and be out of here by nightfall."

Nightfall came, and the eleven rebels remained in the swamp.

None were alive except for the official, if the Shalkan counted as a human body. Still in the battlefield, Marcelus knew he was a good hour behind Perry, and he had nothing to show for his efforts. Stalking to an ultramarine flag, Marcelus ripped it from its pike. Tearing the cloth through the center, he ripped a black fist in two. On one of the halves, he scrawled a bloody note before mounting his Mali-Mali and disappearing into the night:

You've just won a victory; enjoy it.
It will be your last.

Perry tried desperately to stabilize the official on the spider's rotund back. The man was alive but had the strength of one who was dead. The Mali brought them into a humid valley, and they crossed a shallow creek. Perry wanted to stop and fill his canteen, but his memory of the Mali tongue failed him.

"Whoa…hold up." The Mali continued to plunge ahead. "Stop by the Almighty!" he yelled anxiously.

The Mali reversed its direction and then lay down.

"That works." He slid off the spider's back and knelt by the stream bank, refilling his canteen. He drained the water into his mouth and refilled it once more. Trudging up the grassy hill to the giant spider, he jumped on its back and gave the command to go. Nothing happened. *That's odd*, he thought. He kicked its side like a horse. A loud rumbling noise, like rocks tumbling down a mountain side issued from the spider as its chest cavity rose and fell. The Mali was sleeping; the rumbling was its snore. Perry sat hopelessly in the grass and waited; he had somehow told the spider to fall asleep, and he did not know the words to wake it.

Ternoc slipped into the marshy waters, catching himself before he fell but not before he had made general commotion.

"You have to be careful about stuff like that," Aban reprimanded. "You'll attract snakes, and who knows what else."

Ternoc snarled. "When last I checked, you were obeying my commands. Just because you're a free man doesn't mean you can chastise your elders."

Aban stood aloof at this comment and then proceeded to use Ternoc as the paradigm of how not to travel through the swamps. Ternoc scowled. He was a large man, rippling with muscle. If not for the hideous scars that ran down his face, he would have been a perfect specimen of human strength and profile. He was used to taking care of those who annoyed him, and right now Aban was annoying him. As Aban's voice carried one tone too loudly over the swamp land, he knew it was time to teach the boy a lesson. Turning swiftly, Ternoc lifted Aban from the swamp and above his head.

"We are a group," Ternoc said harshly. "We act as a group and work as a group. You are provoking your group members to possible violence and rash action. I would help your fellow freeman instead of chastising him."

Aban's face paled. "I didn't mean anything like that," his voice slurred as his eyes bulged.

"No one ever means for anything bad to happen," Ternoc said soberly, and placed Aban back into the water. "But let's face it, bad things happen, kid."

The marsh water, a conglomeration of mud and silt, moved torpidly. Radosh and Malov sloshed through the filth apart from the others. Radosh could barely decipher their shadowy forms from the fog. In case of an attack, they would act as flankers, though the officials were the least of their worries. Radosh stroked a hand worriedly through his hair, attempting to penetrate the water with his stare. He could not see any of the creatures rumored to dwell in the depths. Hardy reeds supplied the only apparent motion, occasionally moving in the fetid vapor. Even the trees were dark and damp, ominous masses with outstretched arms, vines hanging mysteriously from their branches.

"Malov," he spoke softly. A ripple spread across the surface.

"Don't move," she responded suddenly.

Radosh halted in his tracks. "What is it?"

"I think I—" The girl pulled back an arrow and aimed at the water. Whish. The arrow sailed cleanly into the water by his knee. Malov thrust her arm into the water and pulled, by the arrow in its back, a wriggling snake from the muck. Struggling to keep it from her, she averted her face. Radosh unsheathed his sword as her shriek bounced over the water.

Corious had finally economized his walk to the most efficient form of movement. It went something like: lift leg, push leg through thick, stagnant water, and force it down. Then he would attempt to do the same with the other leg. It was a process that tried the body and numbed the mind, and Corious was pleased to arrest the procedure when he heard something splash. He faced the others in his group, but none were wet above the waist; they returned his look blankly.

"Radosh and Malov," he said suddenly.

Shrie watched as Corious staggered back through the swamp.

"We wait here for now," she told the others. "If he needs help, he calls. Otherwise, we all be lost running and searching."

"That's wise. Most likely someone tripped. It happens easily," Tar added. The rebels listened to the occasional splash and watched the ripples from Corious's wake glide over the surface of the water.

Malov grappled wildly with the snake. How could she have been so stupid as to snatch it before it died? If she could reach the head, she would be able to control it. As it brought its tail around to whip her face, Corious raced to the scene with his sword unsheathed, but the snake was too close to Malov's face for effective use of the weapon. Stretching out his hand to grab the snake, Corious yelped in surprise as the reptile bit him. Recoiling, Corious clutched his hand and yelled warning as the snake buried its fangs into Malov's face.

Shrie heard Corious's howl, and alarm found its way onto her normally composed face. She motioned for the others to help when a scaly skin surfaced and hissed loudly through ivory fangs.

"Snakes! Cut off head, cut off head!" she instructed. Ree unsheathed his sword and went to work.

"Aim for the ripples in the water," he called to the petrified rebels, "and if you can, save the heads. They will make excellent poison to tip our arrows with."

The fangs dug into her face, and Malov seized the opportunity to wrench the head from the snake's body. She resolved to not scream again; she was a rebel and planned to take the hit like one. Radosh chopped the body into pieces, leaving the snake head in her hand. Both Corious and Malov sported two red dots—compliments from their underwater attacker. The venom's power worked swiftly, and they fell into a trance. Supporting both their weights, Radosh hauled them in the direction of the others.

Ree actively whacked at any movement in the water. They had killed five snakes, and it seemed that the others were either dead or scared away. By some miracle, none of the rebels, other than Corious and Malov, had been bitten.

Marcelus longed to be with his comrades. He knew the necessity of bringing the official as quickly as possible to Quantus Plain, but he wished for human company. The Mali-Malis were wonderful of course, but they were, well, spiders. Devastated that no rebels had been found, Marcelus focused on his motto: trials create perseverance, perseverance character, and character hope. Marcelus's hope insinuated the eternal destruction of the officials—for peace to return. He would fight with hope, but before he could, he would have to return to Quantus Plain. Crossing a small creek, he noticed tracks in the ground and a sleeping Mali-Mali on the next hill over. His heart leapt.

Perry had long abandoned the sleeping spider after half a day of stationary nothingness. Surprisingly, another spider had replaced the sleeping one, as if it had understood Perry's urgency. With the spider's aid, Perry sped through another uneventful, lonely day.

The sour poison stung Shrie's tongue. She sucked the venom from Malov's wounds first, forcing her to kneel in the water. The girl had received the worst of the snake's wrath and had four distinctive wounds where the snake had struck. Shrie took a gulp from her canteen, swished the water about her mouth, and then let the contaminated liquid spew from her lips before leaning over and slurping more blood from the girl's right cheek.

Shrie was thankful that Malov had taken the bite without hysteria. When the sour taste had left the blood, she patted the girl's cheek, helped her stand, and handed her over to Ree. Turning, she attended to Corious. Shrie was reassured to see his bite was not terrible, but she took the time to care for it before his condition deteriorated. When she was done, all but Ree had surrounded her in nervous circle, shifting their weight from foot to foot. It would be a couple hours before they would know if help had come too late, but Shrie assured the rebels otherwise.

"Corious and Malov be fine," Shrie affirmed. "We keep going."

No one moved.

"Let's get to higher ground. These snakes are relentless." Ree suggested, hacking at any ripple that slithered past him.

"We make for temple ruins," Shrie told them sensibly. "That good place to go. It away from snakes."

"You'll have to lead us there, Shrie." Ree stated glumly, "Between the swamp's mist and my hazy knowledge of the area, I don't have the slightest idea of where I am."

"Someone must care for Malov and Corious too."

"I'm fine, Shrie. The sooner we get to higher ground, the sooner you'll have time to help Malov," Corious assured her.

She slogged to the front of the group. "Temple ruins actually the other way; they in the center of swamp."

Despondently, the group headed back into the swamp.

Perry rode swiftly on his new Mali-Mali. He had already begun tracking the rebels' footsteps imprinted in the mud. He knew they could not be more than a day old. As he scoured the scene ahead of him, the stagnant smell of bog seeped into his nostrils in repugnant, pulsing waves. A gray, solid fog engulfed the forest before him. The airborne water particles played with Perry's vision. With the few feet ahead of him shielded from view, it felt as though he were tottering on the edge of a cliff. Leaning forward, Perry tried to no avail to penetrate the white mist that flew by his face in tendrils and then in blankets.

Without warning, the spider's movement ceased beneath him. Perry's body lurched from its perch. Hurtling through the air, he had little time to fear the landing. Wetness touched the edge of his foot and then crept up his leg. At first, he thought he had landed in water, but the wetness presented itself as a gooey mud. Almost instantly, he began to sink beneath the surface. Without a second thought, he grasped hold of the reeds which grew prolifically on the bank and heaved himself from the mire. Breathing heavily, Perry wiped his hands clean on the grass and then cleared his face with a forefinger. He studied momentarily the mud that gurgled and popped on his hand. Disgusted, he threw it to the ground and stared at where his steed had been to find its place empty. His water canteen and the official lay neatly on the ground.

"By the Almighty! Those spiders are sneaky!" Something slithered about his leg; he closed his eyes. It was the wet mist, nothing more. It came again. Grimacing, Perry hurled his hatchet into the ground. He opened his eyes to see a dead reptile coiled about his feet. He picked up the snake, fingering the large body in his hand.

A grayish yellow, the snake boasted a triangular head and a compacted, scaly body. The snake had not come alone. There were more, smaller than the last but more agile. They showed themselves above the water, writhing like a woman in childbirth. Perry swung with his hatchet and cleaved one in two. The other shot at him, and Perry dove backwards as it brushed against his arm. Rolling over, he clutched his weapon. As the snake attempted another attack, Perry held the ax horizontally in defense. The snake hissed and coiled itself around the handle, snapping it with its body. Perry released the halves, stunned. The top half of the hatchet fell inches from him; Perry grabbed it and waited. The snake had disappeared. Perry relaxed his tense body and took a deep breath, but like a flash of lightning, the snake emerged, its ready mouth opened wide. Perry had all of a moment to lift his cleaver in defense. The teeth grew before him, dripping in venom. He launched the spear into the snake's cavernous mouth.

Collapsing onto the wet ground, Perry slowly pushed himself upright and forced himself to look at the scales and bodies littering the ground. Securing the canteen to his belt, he questioned the Mali-Mali's sense of direction. As he crawled back into the forest, he gazed back to see the water stir, but if more snakes had come, they were hidden in the filth once more. Examining the two broken shards of his hatchet's handle engendered a new sense of respect for the creatures of Shrie's forest.

He approached the official laying a few feet from where the Mali-Mali had abandoned them. Dripping the last drop of water into his own mouth, Perry tossed the canteen aside and searched his sack. The contents were slim: berries, more fruit, and a slice of dried meat. Perry laid his cloak on the moist forest floor. Roughly, he took the prisoner by his shoulders and shook him; the official stirred, nothing more. Mashing half of the berries in his canteen, Perry held the concoction under the official's nose and let the sweet scent drift. The Shalkan opened his eyes with difficulty.

"Drink this. I'm not poisoning you; it's oi juice."

The man said something in his scratchy voice before taking the canteen and finishing the draught in gulps.

"Want some more?"

Shaking his head, the official hesitantly released the canteen.

"What's your name?" Perry questioned as the man started to gnaw on the piece of meat.

"Roken Tharnshald." The man's voice was more recognizable with his thirst quenched. His eyes were not completely dark, and his face was not fully shadowed. He must have been a new convert, slave, or mercenary for the shadow to have not yet taken him. The official's name echoed in Perry's mind. He jolted in surprise.

"What did you say your name is?"

"Roken," the man stammered.

Perry was dumbfounded. "Funny how people cross paths," he exclaimed after a long, awkward pause. The man swallowed the last bit of meat, and Perry continued. "I know you. I fought you and your group of officials at Faxlong Crossing! Do you remember me?"

"I do remember," Roken said weakly, the cool water had washed the rasping from his voice. "You fought and killed many officials."

"Are you a mercenary?" Perry controlled himself. "Or better yet, tell me you were a slave."

"Neither," Roken cackled hopelessly, "but don't worry. If you had the chance, you would've killed me along with others."

"How many rebels have you killed?" The question came out like a shout.

There was no answer but for sadness. Perry shifted uncomfortably and brought the hatchet to the man's throat. "What do you fight for?" he demanded.

Roken's eyes went blank; he did not know.

Sighing, Perry lowered the sword. "How long an official?"

"Two years."

"Why?"

Roken could not answer and then sputtered angrily, "To save my mother, brother, and my own life. I told them to take me and not them. By such a way, I chose the life of an official over the death of my family."

"What did they do to you?" Perry asked softly, his weapon point dropping completely.

Roken avoided the inquiry. "I knew the life of an official was death. I think that is all you need to know."

The officials could have been, could be anyone. I could have been one. This knowledge frightened Perry. "How many of them are villagers like you?"

The bleak eyes turned to him; they did not have an answer. A few moments of silence invaded the camp.

"You may not be like all rebels," Roken said suddenly. "Leave me here; you have done enough. The others will not believe me as you have. Even I do not trust myself, for the darkness has taken part of me."

Perry sympathized. "I now know we are the same people, though we have met by traversing opposite paths. The darkness will be vanquished as you come to the light. I will not leave you now."

"There it is!" Corious cried as he ran forward. "The temple ruins!"

Numerous cries of joy broke out among the voyagers. The ruins, from afar, appeared as a treeless island peeking above the thrusting, prickly reeds; its blue, haggard face seemed to struggle above the strangling grip of the overbearing swamp. Scrambling onto its shores, they soaked in its allure of mystic protection. The vanguard of the group had already reached the sloping, towering mass of the temple. At the front of the marble structure, remains of a previously elegant entrance slumped against the ground. On all sides, ancient columns, some submerged in the swamp water, stood beside statues whose condition mirrored that of their vertical, faceless brothers. The warrior gods and goddesses brandished their swords and bows in the nude. Time had eroded the detailing of their faces, and their eyes without pupils stared at the rebels. One wall, on the eastern side, had not budged from its foundations, and its ribbed ceiling flew high into the swamp trees, a backdrop for the structures sheltered under its roof.

Corious's curious hand stroked the fuzzy emerald and sapphire patches of moss growing atop the fallen statues and cracked columns. He scrutinized the anxious, glowing torches leaping from their settings secured to thirty-foot-high stone pillars. Below, bowls cupped oil of pressed olives, and the ever-present liquid sated the hunger of the flames from morning to night. Rising with the pink smoke, a sweet scent of incense hid the putrid smell of the swamp. The fragrance of myrrh, cinnamon, cane, cassia, and olive oil wound like a sinuous creature around the skeleton of the temple and the flesh of the rebels. Whatever it touched, it claimed.

The rebels wove between the twenty upright frames and projections which marked the south and north sides of the temple. Sixteen silver bases, the architectural remains of the eight frame structure of the west, or far end, supported the crumpled remains of pillars.

"Nice job, Shrie!" Aban exclaimed, his eyes absorbing the wonder and mystery of the temple and his body prepared to genuflect.

"This place is cursed," Ternoc grumbled behind them. "Look at the torches. We are not alone here."

"That's right, Ternoc," Ree said coming up beside him. "The ghost of the temple ruins is here to get you," he said dryly. Ternoc scowled.

"Maybe it's suspicious," Corious reasoned, "but would you prefer to walk in circles trying to find your way out of the swamp before starving to death or being poisoned by snakes?"

"Forget it. Either way it's bad, but I fear the temple may bring worse consequences."

Ree shrugged and moved ahead through the mist toward the first torch.

Aban turned toward Ternoc. "This place looks safe enough to me. I'm not scared."

"I'm not scared either, but I have the sense to know when to be wary. You're a careless boy. I wouldn't expect you to understand," Ternoc fumed.

"There's a spring!" an elated voice broke the tension. "There is a working fountain standing at the center of the ruins."

A path led through strangled gardens to a fountain singing at the heart of the aging structure.

"The water is still good!"

"This place is amazing!" Tar croaked. Shrie eyed him strangely. Tar's hand caressed the arm of a milky statue positioned in front of the fountain. He could see the temple with his hands, and never before had the rebels seen such grandeur. The temple spoke of glory, and the rebels basked in the overwhelming power of its suggestion. They lingered here or there as though in a stupor, fading into aphotic overhangs or drinking in the dignity of a straight pillar. Ree fought the trance that worked at the corners of his mouth. Despite poking fun at Ternoc's comments, he did not trust the place either.

"Stick together," Ree demanded tightly and abruptly. "We'll explore later. Right now—"

"We need to find a good area for camp," Corious finished for him. Letting the floating sounds of their leaders' voices direct them towards the fountain, the rebels gathered. Ree counted them as they meandered to the center of the temple. Roth was not present, but his voice allayed Ree's unfounded fear.

"What do you think of this place?" the muffled voice asked proudly.

The group moved automatically to the sound, and crossing over the threshold, they tripped lightly down a staircase and into a flat, mossy courtyard. A small, rectangular pool in the back of the courtyard caught runoff water from the fountain as it jumped into the air. An overgrown archway guarded the courtyard's rear but acted as neither an entrance nor an exit. As if to rope off the area, large posts supported the tattered remains of curtains strung together with expertly looped rings. The bits of finely twisted blue, purple, and scarlet linen waved at them. Corious did not return their morbid greeting. Patting the ground, he noticed with pleasure that his hand did not come up wet; they had found dry ground. Gratefully, Corious lay down. Ternoc scowled.

"And what if we are attacked? There is no way to escape, and the Almighty knows there is no protection here. Despite their fearsome mien, these gods and goddesses cannot help us," Ternoc pointed out sarcastically to Corious's exasperation.

Ree started to agree, but Corious cut him off.

"The officials won't come here," Corious scorned. He did not want to give up an anhydrous place to sleep. "Even if they did, the snakes would find them first. They have no reason to come and every reason to stay out."

Ree's body sagged as he relented. "We'll camp here tonight." Ternoc rolled his eyes as though trying to see something on the top of his head. Ree ignored his companion's perspicuous display of displeasure and instead scanned the courtyard, and nearly swore. A sculpture had smiled at him; he was sure of it. He studied the face of the goddess with an unnecessary vigor, willing whatever he had seen to leave his memory. Though she did not repeat the gesture, she taunted him with her secrets.

Recruitment and force had thrown Roken into war. As the days spent in travel passed, the person he had once been emerged and the person he had become peeled away in rotting strips. Today, with a chuckle, Perry wondered if Roken would ever stop talking. As an introvert, Perry enjoyed listening to Roken's unreciprocated tales. Roken's deep voice perfected a good story, and Perry imagined himself not in the swamps, but around a fire at Quantus Plain with the sound of Roken's voice lifting over the leaping flames.

"I grew up in the northern flatlands of Fal-Nunein." Roken waved his hand through the air, making a clean palette on which he would paint the details of his life. "It's a really beautiful place. You've never seen mountains so noble or so white. They protected us from the outside world. Though I had always known a war grappled with our borders, we had basically accepted the ways of the Shalkans since the effects of their leadership barely touched us. We never thought they would."

White mountains and savage dark men consumed Perry's vision. Behind the mountains lay a large, flat rolling expanse of snow dotted with the brown spots which were Roken's people. Perry zoomed in to see the details.

"The war had been endless, our elders said." Roken continued, "They gave up the hope we could ever fight them. Eventually, the Shalkans officially claimed northern Fal-Nunein as their land and constructed fortresses and training facilities. My parents knew there was no future for me there, so they sent me, on the threat of death, into the mainland of the Shalkan Empire to be trained as a squire. I did not excel at sword fighting or shooting a pistol. As you can see by my rank, I'm still an infantry recruit."

Perry smiled, his vision fading into the lines of Roken's face. "That's the problem with officials," Perry grinned. "They use inexperienced men." Folding his arms, he continued jokingly, "The rebels use only the best warriors. This reduces the risk of a high death rate in battle."

Roken took off his boots. No laughter issued from his mouth.

"I'm still tired," Roken added with a forlorn sigh foreign to his happy state minutes before. "If you don't mind, I might take a nap."

"Of course." Perry rushed his words. "I have things to attend to also. We'll be leaving first thing tomorrow."

As Roken dozed, Perry carved a short spear from his broken ax handle. Chopping off the jagged edge, he attempted to make it usable. He imprinted a comfortable indent where his hand would rest. Hefting it, he practiced the motion of throwing it. His hand nestled against the wood; with one minor adjustment, he knew it would fly smoothly. Inside the indent, he cut a small cup for each finger and then put his ax down. Again, Perry hoisted the spear, placed his hand on the grip, and inspected it. *Not bad*, he thought as he honed the point of the spear on a whetting stone. He proceeded to bring his ax head to the same caliber of sharpness. Intently focused on his work, no other outside movement caught his attention.

Marcelus whispered for the Mali-Mali to slow as it approached the swamp. He could barely discern the shadowy forms of two people sitting at the base of a small tree. The Mali-Mali dawdled.

"Hup chang!" Marcelus hissed. The spider did not move. Marcelus slid off its back, patted it on the head, and walked stealthily behind the figures. The dim lighting and impending night shadowed the figures' identities. He would be cautious in his approach. A leaf crunched beneath his foot, ruining his cover.

"Marcelus, stop hiding," Perry's voice reprimanded.

From shock and delight, Marcelus did not move.

"It's Perry you confounded idiot!"

Marcelus turned red in embarrassment.

"Perry!" Marcelus exclaimed casually, "I'm glad I finally caught up with you. Has our friend come around?"

"Yes, he's awoken. We talked."

"What did he say?" Marcelus slipped next to Perry by the fire.

"His name is Roken."

Marcelus gaped at the official once more. It was not only an official, but also one with which he had exchanged blows and lost. Under Roken's commander, the Shalkans had beaten and captured them, and Roken himself had tightened the rope and shackles around their wrists.

"I don't believe this," he uttered in complete amazement.

"It's ironic. Think how Roken's commander abused him just as he did us. He's not like the others, Marcelus. It's hard to believe. I know, trust me, even I am not so sure, but wait until you talk with him."

Marcelus closed his open mouth. Watching Roken's sleeping body recalled to his mind the latent Mali-Mali on the hill and prompted him to ask, "How was your journey with the spiders?"

The sword came down on Roken's right arm. He screamed as blood spurted from his arm. The dead were falling on him and burying him. Dull faces mashed against his in frightful numbers. Rotting skin suffocated him.

Roken woke in a sweat. It was a dream, but one which stemmed from reality. The rebels had not punished him, but the dream would haunt him forever in vengeance. Rubbing his eyes, he woke to see Perry and the other rebel talking quietly over a low fire. When he sat, they hushed.

Marcelus introduced himself frostily. "You would know me as Marcelus."

Roken swallowed. "I'm sure you remember me."

Marcelus said nothing.

Roken understood. He turned to Perry. "Do we have any food? I'm famished."

Perry broke a piece of bread and handed it to him apologetically. As the three sat nibbling on spare rations, the almost unnatural cry of a hawk pierced the silence.

Perry jumped to a standing position and scanned the sky.

"Is it her?" Marcelus asked with hope.

"I don't know. I can't see."

"Pack camp; we follow the hawk."

Roken blinked. They were following a hawk? To Quantus Plain? It seemed rather absurd, but everything he had experienced in the past few days seemed out of place. Without arguing, he helped gather their sparse belongings. Within minutes, they were trekking into the swamp. The coming night would not stop them.

In the corner of the courtyard, Malov rested on a fallen pillar. She gripped a stick in her hand and squeezed it whenever the pain of the bite worked its way through her face. Ree sat next to her, gently rubbing an ointment onto the broken skin. Shrie was somewhere on the island doing a dozen things at once; she had asked him to assist with the snake bites. Ree had graciously agreed. It was his chance to speak with Malov. He had noticed her when they were camped at the beach. She was adept with the bow but never bragged or griped. Even now, she held her head steady. A breeze sent a stray piece of her dark hair waving in the wind.

"Do you mind?" Ree asked gruffly but quietly as he tucked it behind her ear.

Malov smiled. She could only be a few years younger than him.

"Where do you come from?" he asked as the light breeze brushed their faces.

"A small island in the Sea of White Pearls," she reminisced.

"You miss it," Ree commented.

She turned her face away, not answering. Her mysterious, gray eyes reflected the temple and the mist. The cream slipped in his hand. Before she could comment, he averted his gaze.

Twenty yards away from Ree and Malov, Corious rendezvoused with Roth. Corious watched enviously as the two talked softly. Roth seemed amused.

"So you've noticed Malov, eh?"

"Hard to miss her."

"Why don't you go over and interrupt Ree. You can't let him have all the fun."

"Shut up," Corious snapped in response to Roth's coltish suggestion. "I could care less who Ree likes and doesn't like."

"Liar," Roth teased lightly. "Come on, admit it, you've taken a liking to her."

"I don't even know her!" Corious protested. "But she is the only girl I've seen in awhile."

"How about Shrie?" Roth said innocently.

"Oh, you have no idea what you just said," Corious laughed. "Shrie is…well…"

"Well what?"

"I don't know…not romantic."

"Who cares? She's not bad looking, kind of funny, and I could see you with her." Roth's face erupted into a wolfish smile.

"You're sober, right?" Corious asked dubiously.

"Sure," Roth offered.

A mud ball hit Corious in the head. Shrie laughed at him from six yards away.

"Still think it'd work?" Corious grumbled to Roth. "Because I don't."

Roth tried to hide a snicker under his arm as Corious began chasing Shrie with a mud ball readily available in his hand.

Malov touched her cheek where the snake had bit her. The cream had taken away the heat and stopped the pounding rush of blood to her face. Her cheeks tingled as she brushed the smooth skin with her finger. She placed her hand dismally on the rock where Ree had sat beside her before being commanded by Shrie to go hunting. Shrie's rush had been explained later when Corious had come running through the clearing with mud on his face and more of it in his hand. Sprinting off and leaving Malov's offer to help in the air, Shrie had scurried away from the flying mud.

Malov grinned. Shrie had an unequaled passion and capacity for the enjoyment of life. It was as if a spirit inside of her kept trying to leap out and lavish itself on others. Malov never had a companion quite like Shrie before. On a Shalkan ship, names had no faces. The workers on the ship had not known she was woman; she had hid her identity well, for women did not last long being subservient to the Shalkans. After taking the men and boys as slaves, Shalkan officers left the women of the villages behind to labor at agricultural estates or sold them for a Shalkan's pleasure. The officials' appetite claimed their spirits and their wills to continue living.

When the black ship had arrived at her port, Malov's mother had dressed her only child as a boy, hoping that her daughter's life could be better. A tear slid down Malov's face. She had never known a father. But her mother had been everything to her, and she had been everything to her mother. Parting from each other in the fiery blaze of their pathetic hut had left a wound in Malov's heart that would never heal. An official had roughly dragged her away, and another had beaten her mother as Malov watched in helpless anguish. On the ship, the work had been harsh, but doable. She had gained bodily strength, losing her past in the exacting labor. With her hair chopped short and a lissome, muscular figure, Malov had escaped suspicion. Her attitude and effort had even earned her an honored place among the men. Towards the end, however, in the weeks before the ship battle, her body had begun to betray her, and hiding it had become tougher. The rebels had arrived just in time, leaving the officials no time to notice her.

During the weeks away from the sea, her hair had seized the opportunity to descend slightly past her shoulders, and Malov's mind had returned to thinking about things she had not considered for many years. She understood for the first time that her mother was not alive—that she was dead and that there would be no going back. Burying her face in her consoling hands, she realized how much her life had changed. Her new companions came to the forefront of her thoughts. She tried to go through them one by one, but against her will and to her pleasure, Ree's face, rugged and handsome, kept reappearing. Flutters in her stomach rubbed against her sides. She fantasized for a moment about her future but then anchored herself in reality. *Who else?* There was Corious, also tall and muscular, but he had increasingly ignored her or stayed his distance. His protégé, Tar, being young and blind, immediately tugged at her sympathetic heart. Despite Tar's redoubtable vigor, his weakness could not be overlooked, and it made her resolution to fight even stronger. Everyone, in some form or another, was a victim.

Roth chatted with a mud covered Corious in the middle of the courtyard. Whenever Roth caught sight of Corious's slightly pouting face, he had to restrain his rambunctious laughter. Shrie had definitely won the mud fight. That much was clear. She had strutted back triumphantly without a single splat of mud on her. Roth chuckled, and Corious scowled.

"It's not funny," he snapped irritably.

"Sorry," Roth said, immediately somber. "But, hey, I have to know. Why do you constantly evade Malov?"

"I do not," Corious protested weakly.

"But you do," Roth said firmly. Corious's specious objection could not halt

Roth's next string of advice. "Hey, if you notice a woman, you've got to let her know before she falls for someone else. Let Ree know there's a jot of competition."

"Roth, I'm not that kind of guy. When I have feelings for someone, I pretty much avoid them to prevent myself from saying something dumb."

"Hmm," Roth mused, "exactly like me. You know Corious, you and I have a lot more in common than we would have originally thought."

Shrie scampered about the island like a mad woman, scouting out escape routes, discovering good places to hunt game, collecting essential cooking and healing herbs, avoiding Corious's attempts to muddy her, doing general organization, building the shelter, and determining the direction of Quantus Plain. Despite these time consuming and tiring activities, she did not miss Malov's attraction to Ree or his to her. She smiled.

"Ree fancies you," she exclaimed to Malov as quietly and calmly as she could. She had finally figured out the meaning of the words to fancy.

Malov's eyes sparkled.

"Shrie love bonding ceremonies," the jungle maiden continued gleefully, "lots of food and dancing." She suddenly paused and shook her head as if she regretted what she had said. "But Shrie must warn you, Ree rather—"

"I'm rather what?"

Shrie grimaced as Ree crossed his arms behind her. "Ree really great?" Shrie offered lamely.

"Uh-huh."

"Oh, go away Ree! You too nosy."

"Ree!" Corious called from a distance.

"You're lucky," Ree finished glancing at Malov who grinned weakly at him. "Corious called me away. Next time, Shrie," his voice trailed off, and he walked away.

"Next time, Shrie," Shrie imitated before continuing. "If Shrie remember right," though she remembered next to nothing of her tribe, "in our tribe, man meet girl and girl meet man and both marry." The trees had told her of these bonding ceremonies. "But Shrie decide to warn Malov not to have bonding ceremony. Ree not ready yet."

Ternoc laid the meat in front of Roth after skinning the snakes and small mammals. Both prepared to chop the meat into neat squares. Shrie had observed their activities with a shiver.

"I not eat snakes if I were you," she had shuddered. "Make sure you take out poison glands and rinse all meat," she had instructed.

Ternoc and Roth had heeded her warning, carefully extricating the glands and disposing of the neighboring meat. Throwing the quality chunks into a boiling pot of water, Ternoc added the vegetables and herbs. It was starting to smell good.

Radosh joined Aban and Tar in their walk around the island. Aban's descriptions of the pastoral landscape, which he prepared for Tar, halted as soon as they smelled the soup cooking.

"Dinner time," Radosh said, licking his lips like a ravenous wolf. "Smells good. I can't believe that Ternoc and Roth are really making that."

"It sort of makes you wonder, doesn't it?" Aban stated good naturedly. The three headed toward the court yard, their stomachs growling ominously.

Radosh chuckled. *Somehow we are safe here. It is as if we have reached an asylum, and the words of anyone who says otherwise are mendacious. It must have been eons ago that we crawled onto this island from the muck. I hope we do not return to the senseless mud so quickly. Though we speak of battle at the councils after dinner and during Ree's training sessions, I do not wish to return to that way of life. I was once conscripted by the Shalkans. Must I be conscripted by their enemies?*

Chapter 12

Logan and Hitachi pored over the wrinkled map spread smoothly over an old, stone platform. Ree strode in their direction. Dinner would be served soon, but the two brothers delighted in any chance to discuss war strategy with Ree. Little blue pieces stamped on the map represented rebel forces or strongholds, and red ones represented the officials. Of course, red pieces outnumbered the blue ones, and the information was old. Who knew if the officials had moved while they were in the swamp or if other forces had issued from Turock's tower? To make things worse, rebels elsewhere did not have the same archaic information and were divided without knowledge or foresight of coming danger.

From Ree's detailed log of Shalkan attacks, Logan had deciphered a faint pattern, assuming a large number of things. Hitachi had first scoffed at his idea, but the more they scrutinized the map and log, the more they could not ignore Logan's hypothesis. And now that they were at the temple ruins, everything seemed to have more meaning than perhaps it should. Logan would hash his ideas out with Ree, and the conclusions of that discussion would be shared with the group after dinner.

Shrie, the last link of the circle, arrived late; no one started eating until she made the circle whole with her presence. Occasionally, she rubbed her thighs which were sore from pushing through the swamp waters. Unlike her gregarious self, she observed the conversation or added an occasional thought in hushed tones. Ree talked intensely with Hitachi and Logan, arguing and listening in his turn. Ternoc strained to hear their words, and his expression would change with every sentence. Roth simply enjoyed his soup while bandying words with Corious who glanced every so often at Malov.

With a sad grimace, Shrie stroked her hair with a fidgety hand. Both Corious and Ree were captivated, but they did not know the true sacrifice of love. When they fought, they fought not because they loved what was good, but because they, like the officials, had learned to hate. She did not know if they comprehended the necessity of love's denial. The forest had taught her something of love, for everything made by the Almighty had been made in love and made with the ability to love. Love was not the shape of a face or the slant of eyes; no, it went much deeper than that. It could learn to wait, contradict, and understand. Love could stop time, allowing souls and hearts to mingle together longer than the occasion permitted. This was the love they sought in faces and in things they could not find. Shrie sighed despondently; she would have to teach them.

Shrie's attention turned to Aban and Tar. They now confided in each other like brothers. Next to them, Radosh and Malov spoke urgently. Shrie could not tell what they were talking about, but she could guess with a fair amount of certainty that the subject was a matter of importance to both of them. Shrie wondered where Perry and Marcelus were and how they would ever find them.

Lain paced back and forth, going from one end of the small room to another. It was his personal room, with a small antechamber in the front for receiving visitors. A coarse, wooden desk piled high with papers and maps furnished the otherwise plain room. If not for the clutter of swords and spears, it might have been mistaken for a scholar's room. An impressive wall hanging, depicting the great legend, the Truth, and the story of the world acted as the only decor. He glanced at it whenever hope had fled, whenever victory was near, or whenever the dead were more numerous than the living.

Stroking his short goatee with one hand, he fingered his sword with the other. In the traditional ways, he had shaved the front of his head, but a thick mane of dark hair, pulled back into a pony tail, covered the back of his head. He stood at a medium height, with no arresting feature except for a slight, hawkish nose. Lain was neither the most solid nor the best fighter; rather, he was a leader of men, and a tangible air of authority rested upon him. Perhaps it lived in his stride, confident and sure, in his broad, straight shoulders, or in his head held proudly.

Black leather boots and pants constructed from a hardy material comprised his humble attire. During battle, leather leg pads would strap onto his calf and metal spikes could be added onto his forearm guards. A loose, linen shirt covered a set of chain mail devoid of imperfections; it was heavy but worth its weight. He had a several swords: his best, a ceremonial, and an extra to throw to a fellow soldier. An old helmet sat among the items on the desk, reminding him of his purpose.

After years of evolution and development, he had created Quantus Plain. In his original vision, Quantus Plain had been a hidden, underground base, a safe house for rebels, and a place to refuel, rebuild, and train. Right now, it was half of every one of those things. It was safe enough, but there was not enough room to house too many more. One could refuel, if one found the necessary items. A rebel could be trained, but only after the battles were fought and a trainer was found. Hardy folk with high ideals, the rebels of Quantus Plain lacked the experience of the elite cells which roamed the land. Most of the time, his men enjoyed a hearty drink and dinner after battles which were only sometimes won and only presently successful in keeping the Shalkan forces from overwhelming the fort.

Some valiant women accompanied the troops into battle, but often they became nurses or cooks. Lain gave these women the respect of a warrior, for they were warriors in their own way. There were the children to think of as well, and many under the age of fifteen roamed the camp. Most of the time, by some miracle, food was abundant, but after every battle, there were always men that did not come home. That was the reality that Lain hated. At heart, he was not a warrior. For every man or woman who died, he scratched a notch on the wall of his underground conference room. He tentatively thought of adding two more.

Perry and Marcelus had not been found after the battle near the Tashorn River nor had their bodies been accounted for. As warriors and as men, they had been unsurpassed. He did not want to think he had lost them forever. As his sword tip scratched the wall, he pulled it away. He could not believe they had died. If his people were to be optimistic, he must also breathe life onto hope's dying flames. A knock sounded on his door. Sighing, he went to open it.

After everyone devoured dinner, Aban started a fire and the rebels huddled to hear Ree's words. Ree cleared his throat. Hitachi and Logan held the map before the rebels' upturned eyes and eager faces.

"As you can see, the rebels are clearly outnumbered in size but not in strength. We hold some pretty strategic locations which we should be able to hold. Here," he said pointing with his sword, "the Mali-Malis have informed us," he glanced at Shrie, "with Shrie's translation, that a large rebel group is situated in the Valley of Solitude. Their identity is currently unknown, and they have yet to present themselves. However, there is another group on the border of the Shalkan Empire and another in the Borderlands outside Shrie's forest that could use our aid. Lastly, there are wandering cells like ours, and then there is Quantus Plain, our destination."

Ree broke to take a sip of water and then continued, "We have several options for uniting the rebels if we choose to do so. We can either start missions to recruit slaves or rally small cells like our own. I will now hand this session over to Logan who will brief you on official movements."

Logan handed his side of the map to Ree and took charge.

"It appears from Ree's log book that the officials have moved increasingly eastward in their attempt to conquer Kurak. From Turock's tower, they are sent in every conceivable direction. At first, their attacks appeared desultory, but it now seems they have attacked every town or village they encounter as they head like a spreading river across the land. They plan to annihilate every single one of us. There is no town they skip and no bastion do they leave untouched. Their attacks will force us to fight them somewhere here in the east. All of their movements seem to be converging on these swamps."

Hitachi fervently continued, "It is indeed how it seems. Which brings us to wonder, what about these swamps elicits Turock's desire to rule them? The only thing of significance seems to be this temple ruin. I am hoping our enemy does not realize Quantus Plain exists, but I doubt that is our luck. There is something here he wants to find."

Hitachi quieted. "That is all we have come up with aside from questions which have no answers."

"Such as, who are the Kalulukians?" Ree offered.

"And where did Shrie's tribe go?" Shrie added.

"Also, to whom do these ruins belong?" Tar pondered.

There were many things to contemplate and not enough resources to answer the questions roiling the minds of the rebels and rippling into the silent night.

A young man with his eyes to the sky watched in wonder as the hawk circled the area. She dove into the trees and then caught a thermal which bore her high into the clouds and over the setting sun. Whistling, he stuck his fingers in his mouth to make the sound carry. She flew from the sky in moments, landing on his arm.

Stroking her head with a finger, he complimented her skill. "Good girl, Faylene. It's time to go." With two fingers, he coaxed her into a doze before throwing the tiny hood over her head. Acquainted with the routine, she did not resist his touch. The man rotated on his heel and walked a calculated number of steps before sliding on his stomach through the grass and disappearing from view.

The knock shook the entirety of the room. Lain stopped pacing and walked to the door, opening it without thought.

"Hello, Jashor. I see you have Faylene. Come in." Lain stepped backwards to receive his visitor.

"Do you have any news?"

"Not much," Jashor commented ruefully. "She cried once or twice over the swamp lands and three times at its center."

Lain pursed his lips. "That will be all. Thank you, Jashor. If you will, leave Faylene with me. I'll be taking her out later."

Jashor smiled, handing the hawk to her master. "Will I be seeing you at sword training today? You promised to teach me that one move."

"Oh, yes," Lain replied absentmindedly. His mind had already moved to other matters. "I should be seeing you there."

With a grin, Jashor waved his farewell and ran up the stairs in the direction of the ale house. Lain shook his head, this time with fatherly concern. He tenderly pulled the hood off the falcon's head.

"Once or twice around the swamp lands and three times in the middle," he mused, repeating Jashor's memorized report. Jashor had no idea what Faylene's calls meant, but to Lain, they held an ineffable significance. After a moment, he sheathed an extra sword and strode out of the room with the falcon on his arm.

"What do you see out there? I do sometimes wonder," Lain said, addressing the falcon. "I must be sure of this."

Lain took the stairs two at a time, his mail clanking against his chest with every step. At the top, he turned left and grabbed a torch haphazardly off the wall; drops of turbulent, hot oil spilled onto his hand. They did not bother him. Arriving at the end of the hallway, he hollered a swift command to a guard who immediately stepped aside. After taking a sharp turn, Lain slipped into the darkness of the underground caverns. Four miles later, he would reach the entrance of Quantus Plain by the edge of the swamp. If he kept going, the tunnel would lead him under the marshy lands. Choosing his route, he unleashed Faylene and liberated her in flight. He quieted his breathing as she called twice over the edge of the swamp and thrice in the middle, exactly as Jashor had said. Lain took a deep breath and whistled her back. Two groups of people traversed the outermost boundaries of Quantus Plain, and by Faylene's call, she was unsure whether they were friend or foe.

Towards the middle of the night, the rebels retired. The council had conjured innumerable mysteries, ones which Shrie attempted for the rest of the night to solve. It was as if they were missing an essential link—something that would connect the otherwise isolated events. With this thought in mind, Shrie decided to take a midnight tour of the island. She considered waking Malov to accompany her; but after a moment, she woke Tar and Corious instead.

"We find Ree," she stated. "Tell him to bring Kalulukian burial items, and then we search ruins for what Shrie think we will find."

Ree rested apart from the others, boring holes into the night sky with his eyes. He heard Shrie approach him; her footsteps were uniquely silent until one's ears were sharpened enough to know the slight tip taps they made on the cobble. She had brought Tar and Corious as well. So it was just them: Ree, Shrie, Tar, and Corious. That was how it had all begun. Would it be how it ended?

"We search temple ruins."

Ree faced her and asked brusquely, "And for what are we looking?"

Shrie shrugged. "Temple altar. Sometimes the Kalulukians hide treasures there," she suggested.

"Shrie, we don't want treasure," Ree chided, "but rather something on the island the officials would want."

"That why we search altar," she insisted. "Most valuable thing to island folk is hid there."

Corious peered at Ree's face in the dark. The torches sent flickers of light over his skeptical features. In this lighting, Ree could easily be mistaken for one of the many stone gods adorning the courtyard.

"We have nothing to lose," Corious said hurriedly. His blunt comment loosened Ree's stubbornness, and the human god shed his stone casing as he rose from the ground. They would search the temple ruins.

Wrought with anticipation, Shrie did not wait any longer. She knew the altar would be nearby, and it would face the rising sun. A superstitious people enveloped in rituals, the Kalulukians would have wanted everything, including the altar, to be wrapped in complicated, cryptic significance. According to their myths, if the altar were ever destroyed, then they, too, would burn. They thus guarded the altar with the will of their minds, and this will preserved the acacia wood, keeping it from harm.

Holding Tar's hand, Shrie guided him over the tumble of rocks. Corious and Ree trailed closely behind. Their eyes jumped from rock to wall, and they probed with fervor any construction which reached Shrie's chest in height and was just as wide. Each turned out to be no more than a pedestal erected in the honor of a forgotten god. Pausing in frustration, Shrie studied the broken bulwarks as they sloped protectively inwards. Several inner walls of lesser heights protruded in rough angles, protesting their entrance.

"We approach most probable place of altar," she said, her voice skidding over the night and landing in pockets of obscurity.

Corious halted in his tracks. To his left, the globular roots of a tree, half hidden by the crumbling walls, fought the stone floor slabs for space. Evidence to the long absence of the temple's inhabitants, the tree upturned the stones once set so surely. Its bark, smooth and dark, decorated the open branches and called to him. He could not resist the urge to climb it.

Shrie circumspectly stepped on certain stones and counted under her breath. Corious did not fear offending the dead gods of the Kalulukians. He hurdled over the walls as he would the dead and scurried up the tree as Shrie finally made her way through the inner walls. The chanting under her breath did not cease, and her skittish eyes did not stop wandering. Her breath came in short gasps. Once inside the walls, her stride eased into a normal one, and then from her inquisitive fingers, no inlet was protected.

Ree waited until Corious made his way up the tree before restarting the futile search. Shrie and Tar overturned even the smallest pebbles in every hall and archway. They found nothing. Ree rubbed his hand over the course surface of an angular rock. *Life is like this.* He hunted down and speared the mawkish thought, but he could not ignore the feeling that the bumps and irregularities had an express purpose in their beings.

Bending, he took the Kalulukian scroll from his pouch and compared it with the writing which he now saw was engraved into the stone. They were identical.

Here in stone was a solid link between the Kalulukians they had seen by the ship and those who had inhabited the temple long ago. Ree considered the connection. The scroll had gone with the dead, as the tribe believed the person's spirit could use it after the body died. What would a dead person need? Ree's head spun. He took out the golden fruit; it was without blemish, spot, or writing. Holding the fruit before him, he crouched by the script. The fruit's shiny surface reflected the letters. *Quid est veritas?* The writing on the stone asked him boldly. *What is truth?* Gently twirling the pear between his fingers, he watched as the words spun about the surface. At a certain angle, the moon caught the exterior of the fruit, and a ray of light shone on a previously unnoticed block of wood. Red horns rose from either side of the altar, and poles inserted into rings at four corners meant the altar was mobile. It could be moved from place to place. *Its meaning can be altered with every person who carries it away on his or her shoulders. Even the gods have no resting place.*

The altar sat five paces to his right. Dust particles swirled in the ethereal air, and Shrie's fantasy came to life: a mystery and a riddle wrapped together in one wimpled cloth. Ree instructed Corious to stay in the tree. Corious readily agreed; his eyes were glued to the light splayed on the wood.

Shrie stared in anticipation as Ree traced with his feet the path from the rock to the wood. The flawless surface of the altar beheld no inscriptions. On a whim, Ree read the scroll.

"Mala gubu, frata."

Shrie slapped her hands over her ears theatrically and groaned loudly. "Spare Shrie the agony. You read it all wrong, Ree."

Defeated and speechless, Ree handed the scroll to Shrie. The thrill of the hunt expanded into the crevices of his being.

"Malagu bufreita ga, malagu shuarta bomtrey a ilee." *Open the closed eye; open the unhearing ears unto me.*

Corious trembled. They were on the verge of finding a great power. Shrie's incantation dithered as the stone began to shift. When she stopped, it stopped. The white beam of nature waited, poised and frozen outside the prism of the temple, ready to break into a nacreous array at Shrie's command.

Corious emerged from his reverie. "Keep reading," he shouted.

Shrie continued in a shaky voice, and the stone grated and screamed. "Trayunga floreita galya; mismita floreita izchaonger." *To give up is to gain; to surrender is to win.* "Ouh julangu a miwer buan." *Bear the burden of Truth.*

An opening, through which a person could slip, had appeared in the wall. Corious slid from the tree and approached.

"It leads underground. We go."

Ree stooped to fit inside. Shrie pulled Tar behind her, wishing they had brought more than swords to guard them.

Malov woke as morning swept across her face. She rubbed the sleep from her eyes and noticed she was the first one awake, or rather the fifth as proclaimed by the four unoccupied spots to her right. Yawning, she slipped down to the small spring in the middle of the island and sprayed the sweet, clear water over her face. It seemed to laugh and chat with the birds in its bubbling melody. Malov gazed at the sparkling water. The rising sun hit the spray in a dazzling display of rainbows. After taking the time to admire its beauty, she returned to the main camp. Her stomach grumbled, and the leftovers from last night's dinner summoned her.

"From what I remember about these swamps, the snakes never used to like the night. They were generally nocturnal, but these are different creatures indeed. Worse things must have come to these marshes since when we were here last."

Roken listened as Marcelus talked and talked; he was in no mood to partake in the rebels' conversations today.

"Is the hawk still around?" Marcelus asked Perry.

"I hope so. Keep your eyes peeled for her. You too, Roken," Perry told him as he tiptoed his way through the swamp on surfaced tree roots.

"I haven't seen Faylene since a month ago at least, Perry. Do you think Lain sent search parties for us?"

"Whether he has or not, we may as well follow the hawk. We'll at least get out of the forsaken mess we're in now."

"What do you mean?" Marcelus asked, perplexed.

"That hawk circled over the swamp and went east; that must be exactly where Quantus Plain is. And if it isn't, we'll end up wherever Lain is. We must focus on each step at a time."

"Can't be soon enough for me," Marcelus grumbled as his foot slipped off a root and into the water.

"I smell smoke!" Perry exclaimed, steadying Roken who barely managed walking with his injured leg. "Who lights a fire at this time of night?"

Marcelus, ahead of them, unsheathed his two, long knives. "I don't know, but that isn't smoke. It's incense."

"It won't be Shrie's and Ree's group." Perry eliminated them from the possibilities. "They should be freed from swamp by now. They might even be at Quantus Plain as we speak."

Finally, Roken spoke. "It must be tribesman or officials; both of which I'd be wary."

As they spoke, a high-pitched cry pierced the sky.

"It's the hawk!"

"It's hopeless! I can't see it!" The hawk sounded again.

"Our course is too southeast," Perry directed. "Marcelus, we must turn northwest." After adjusting their course, the three trekked onward.

When Corious first slipped into the cavern, steep steps led him deep into the earth. The middle of each sagged from use, and it seemed as though the stairs would take them to the very depths of the earth. As they descended, wall writings increased in appearance, and strange depictions of people and animals danced across the stone. Though ancient, some colors lingered, and as the group went along, the drawings depicted a conspicuous account.

The style of the first pictures was in sync as a Great Being created the earth and heavens. Humans and animals appeared, and soon, stories of pervasive wars, famine, peace, and love filled the walls. As Corious continued, the arabesque style started to change. The artists, the Kalulukians, had strayed from the traditional ways in order to believe in the idol worship and death rituals of other tribes. War spread and captured villages in the flames of aggression. They shrouded the sacrifice and the ceremony of the dead in fantastic rituals. During this time, they had constructed the temple and had killed sacrificial animals to its marble composition. The awe which Shrie had felt upon entering the temple ebbed.

She stared at the depiction of a painted, golden blob atop a scroll and at a scene of a dead Leirmayn running towards them. Supposedly, the dead man's spirit was to use the fruit and scroll to find his way into these caverns. Once here, he would face many trials. Pits and traps opened before the tinted man's steps. If his spirit passed, he would ascend into the sky; if not, he would be thrown into the great, underground lake never to return. The drawings ended in a scrawl.

"Shrie see now. Kalulukians were led astray by other tribes. Now their temple is in ruins, and their people roam the lands without a home."

"So there is only one way," Tar mused.

"Yes," Shrie said sadly, "only one God, one Way. But One Way offers true freedom, and Almighty wants everyone to come to Him. He knows every one of you!"

"That's kind of creepy—I'm not going to lie," Ree muttered.

"No," Corious stated boldly in conviction, and then more quietly, "no, it's good. Don't you see? The Almighty's grace is the only way we can be saved. Nothing good we can do will bring us to the Almighty; the Almighty comes to us. We must accept it and live the best we can." Corious looked to Shrie for assistance. She smiled knowingly.

"Yes, Almighty offer salvation and joy in hardship."

"How do you know He even exists?"

"How do you know wind exists?" Tar asked philosophically.

"You see its effects," Ree answered bitterly.

"And you see work of Almighty; the air does not answer Shrie's prayers, and the world did not come from nothing. What else gives hope or purpose? Everything wanes and waxes on this earth, but the Almighty and His love remain to the end."

"So what happens to us?"

"If we remain in Him, He will remain in us. Our body will pass, but the spirit will live. None of us is an accident. Even if we don't know why things happen, every-thing is woven into the tapestry of life. The story does not end here." Corious trailed his fingers along the dwindling paint.

"What of the Shalkans then? Explain them."

"Even the Almighty has enemies."

"Shrie wonder if Shrie's tribe fled these wars," Shrie said, "or fell like the Kalulukians. Shrie see no pictures of officials, but she sees drawings of warriors who come and convert tribes to their ways of war and then leave. Maybe officials are those warriors come back."

"Whatever they are, and no matter what happened here," Ree started, "we know these things for sure. The Shalkans are our enemies, and we must stop them before we end like the Kalulukians—in ruin."

Corious gave his approval. "Yes, I agree with that. However, these trials for the dead may not be entirely spiritual. The Kalulukians may have set physical traps too. We should be careful."

Corious's eyes burned with an intensity Shrie had never seen before.

"Yes, we are careful," she reiterated.

As they descended the pitch black stairway into the cavern, Shrie finally knew what it felt like to be Tar. She shuddered. Already, the exhaustion of monotony dulled her senses. At last, a turn in the passageway revealed an opening in the rock; the sun had risen to welcome a gray morning. The stairs had finally terminated, and with its end, the manmade comfort of smooth walls and high ceilings were gone. They had entered the realm of the dead.

Faylene returned to her master, repeating her call. Hawk and sword in one hand, and torch in the other, Lain stood noiselessly, legs spread and eyes glued to the swamp. He stared into the darkness, wondering if it would determine his fate.

Jashor frowned as he walked through the main halls. The burning torches lit the cathedral ceilings and sent flickering patches of light to the floor. More people than usual paced the halls. Women balanced laundry and soup pots on their hips, shoul-ders, and heads, but their presence was common. Even when the men had slumped, worn out from training, in their beds, the women never rested. Today, Jashor noticed an increase in the number of stoic guards who defended each post. In time, he hoped to join their ranks. Everything about being a rebel guard appealed to him: the armor, the elite training, the glory, and the satisfaction of knowing you were protecting everything that was precious to you. Someone bumped against his shoulder as men strode purposefully down the hall, swords in hand.

There must have been an alert.

Pressing his hand against the reassuring stone walls, he reworked the day in his mind focusing especially on the sword training. His footwork had been particularly good. Lain had not been there as he had promised. Jashor wished Lain could have seen him. After the battlefield had claimed Jashor's father, he had clung to Lain in tears and had trailed his every footstep. Lain had willingly offered himself as Jashor's guardian, but Lain was also Jashor's leader. The fact that only the most important matters kept Lain from coming to see Jashor exonerated Quantus Plain's leader from the hurt caused by his absence. Running down the stairs to his bunk, Jashor hesitated at Lain's door. Finally, deciding not to be a bother, he went down the hall without a knock. He would check back tomorrow.

The rigid guard would not budge from his station at the bottom of the falls. Occasionally, a droplet would find its way onto his shoulder blade armor. Only then was he allowed to move and wipe the water from the armor to prevent it from rusting. The sleek metal of his silver armor reflected the small rays of sun that drifted through the rock crevices on an occasional sunny day. He would sound the alarm if the enemy approached, but otherwise, he questioned guests or traders about their businesses, names, and homelands.

To most, it would seem a boring, needless job, but to him, holding a spear and wearing heavy, hot armor for hours could compare to no other profession. For better or for worse, Lain had managed to make the glamour of the Royal Rebel Guard transcend all other occupations. The guard anticipated the end of his six hour shift when training in his airy linen would replace the tedium of stillness. He had to prepare. Prolific rumors of the enemy rampaged through Quantus Plain; the Shalkans had reached the Khaltharngan Wood. Would they breach the secrecy of Quantus Plain? A vicious string of battles had been predicted, and the guard had to be ready to join Quantus Plain and the last resistance of rebels.

Malov had searched the entire island but could find no trace of the four leaders. She thought of waking the others, but by the time she returned, Logan and Hitachi were already up and poring over a map like professional cartographers. When she mentioned Ree's, Shrie's, Tar's, and Corious's absence, they shrugged it off nonchalantly. Malov could not do the same.

Roth was making breakfast, cursing the captious vegetables which slipped from his fingers in malicious objection to the approach of his sharp knife. Radosh and Aban spoke with Ternoc. Malov considered joining their conversation when Shrie's pitter-patter of feet drew near.

"Shrie!" Malov cried happily. "Where were you? Where are the others?"

"You come and help," Shrie answered. "Corious stuck in pit!"

Malov regarded Shrie incredulously and then sprinted after the Jungle Maiden. Questions spilt from Malov's mouth as she ran, and Shrie surprisingly shot back answers as rapidly as Malov could think of them. When Malov could no longer talk and breathe at the same time, she simply followed, wondering if she should have grabbed more than a bow and arrow.

Logan and Hitachi scrutinized Shrie and Malov dashing into the distance, but a second of time was all they gave to consider them. *The women lose all sense of focus when together. It's too bad,* Hitachi reflected, *they are so talented alone.* Though in war Hitachi's perspicacity could not be matched, his realistic understanding of other people lacked clarity.

A short man with dark hair and squinty eyes, Hitachi resembled his brother. Both were capable of using not only their minds but also their bodies to wage war. Under Corious's and Ree's instruction, they had learned to wield a quarterstaff with deadly accuracy. *Yet physical prowess will not save us. What we really need is some new intelligence,* Hitachi pondered. Then he could prove his point.

Concentrating on the map, Hitachi made hypothetical moves with the rebel pieces to which Logan responded. They would play out the battle to its end, deciding which combination of moves would give the rebels the best advantage. Roth came over with breakfast, and he joined the two still arguing over who would have won the last battle.

Perry and Marcelus changed their course as they had several times that day. Luckily, the falcon had visited the swamps frequently, as if to notify them when they chose an aberrant course. The more the falcon came, the more Perry was convinced it was Faylene. The thought of Quantus Plain, Lain, and the reception they would receive carried him through the stinking marshes. Around midday, his pleasant daydreams snagged on a rough doubt. *Will the others accept Roken? Do Marcelus and I even trust Roken enough to pass him off as a rebel?*

Corious lay in the deep hole, in shock from his painful plummet. The mat had wilted so smoothly into the granite floor. *Why couldn't I have seen it? Why did I have to be the one to fall into a pit? Even Tar has not walked into a single wall today. Unlike Tar, I do not have a worthy excuse for my clumsiness. I hope no one finds out about this,* he groaned. His head pounded, and his eyes saw blurry spots dancing.

"Corious," Tar's voice traveled to him from above, "how deeply did you fall?"

"I'd say twenty feet, at least," Corious called back morosely.

"Hold on," Ree said authoritatively.

"What's to hold on to?" Corious shouted sarcastically as his last few words bounced off the walls of the cavern. A layer of slimy water covering the pit's floor soaked his pants.

"Shrie is coming back with Malov."

Corious cursed under his breath. He lied through clenched teeth, "Sounds great!"

Two sets of steps ran towards him.

"Shrie, Malov, down here!" Tar directed.

Corious, in a desperate, rescue attempt, leapt and slammed his back against one wall. Swinging his legs and positioning them against the parallel wall, he wedged himself in the shaft. Inching his back up, he then took a miniature, vertical step with his feet. Carefully, he rocked back and forth, proceeding with tentative steps.

Keep going, he coaxed himself, *keep going*. Halfway to the top, the distance between the walls widened a half inch. Raising his foot, he stretched his legs to their extremes, but they could not reach. He slid, landing squarely on his hindquarters and lower back.

"He fell again!" Tar cried, "He was almost to the top!"

Shrie let out a gasp as she heard a splash and a cry of pain. Ree peered over the edge.

"Corious! We've got a vine! Corious?"

Roth scratched his goatee. Corious was trapped in a hole, and Shrie had solicited the aid of Malov. As he strode into the courtyard where Logan and Hitachi ferociously slammed red and blue pieces on their map, he hoped his friend would not attempt any rash action. Roth shook his head and made his way over to Radosh.

"Radosh," Roth called, "I know you're out of arrows, and I think we both need something to do." The two men entered the smaller part of the ruins. "My father and two brothers were craftsmen; I learned their trade. I figured I could try and put it to some use," Roth stated as he gestured to Radosh's empty quiver.

"Are we going to carve them out of wood?"

"No," Roth grinned, "we'll try something different: bones."

"Human bones?"

"Don't be sick! We'll use that."

Roth's finger indicated a huge skeleton rising imperiously above several snake carcasses.

"What was that?" Radosh inquired, morbidly fascinated. "You've already gone hunting?"

"Nope. I found it last night."

"Dead?"

"Yes, it was dead. Why do you care?" Roth snapped.

Radosh stared sickly at the carcass.

"Anyway," Roth clapped his hand against his thigh, "let's get to work. You've got first dibs on this thing."

"Nobody else knows about this?"

Roth did not answer but pulled out his knife and started roughly hacking at the creature's rib cage. After a moment's hesitation, Radosh followed suit, carving notches off the creature's spine with his sword. After they had retrieved twenty arrow shafts from the butchered skeleton, they shaped the pallid arrowheads.

"Here," Roth said, "I found feathers to add to the back of the arrows."

"Why didn't you show someone else?" Radosh asked, still perturbed.

"They weren't out of arrows," Roth replied plainly.

Satisfied with Roth's answer, Radosh tied an arrowhead to his shaft with thin strips of cartilage stripped from the animal's face. When they finished, Radosh examined the slender arrows.

"Try one," he suggested.

Radosh plucked an arrow from his quiver, spun, aimed, and nailed a ripe fruit dangling from a tree. The fruit toppled to the ground and split cleanly in half.

Ree tugged at the rope. Corious had responded, but his answers did not assuage Ree's worries. After several of Ree's mighty heaves on the twine, Corious's head finally poked above the opening's rim. When Shrie yanked on the excess rope, his shoulders and torso escaped the domain of darkness, and eventually, he was sprawled on the ground.

"Are you all right?" Tar and Malov asked concurrently, bending over him.

"I didn't even pass the first test," Corious murmured as he attempted to stand.

"You stay down, Corious. Shrie must check you for broken bones."

Corious resisted Shrie's tugs on his arm. "Thank you, Ree, Tar, Malov. You, too, Shrie. But really, I'm fine, and there's a whole tunnel to explore."

"Corious," Malov said, "you would prove your wisdom if you went back."

Corious stared at Malov blankly. *She probably thinks I'm a total idiot.* He stalked back up the stairs and disappeared.

"Well, we got him out. Should we continue to explore or wait for more light?" Ree asked.

"We go a little later. Shrie need torches and maybe bow and arrow." Shrie's half truth rang in Corious's ears, and he was thankful that some of his honor would be left intact.

Marcelus strode through the shallow muck. The three knew they neared Quantus Plain, and the knowledge drove Perry and Marcelus onward. Roken lingered a dozen feet behind; he did not anticipate their arrival. Marcelus's eyes began to burn, and he wiped them as he searched for an explanation.

"Smoke," Perry mentioned when he saw his friend rubbing agitated eyes. "We are not alone."

Woodchips sprayed under the force of Jashor's knife as he pulled it along the shaft of a wooden spear. He had situated himself outside one of the three main buildings. The wild grasses and vines which adorned the buildings' facades hid him well.

A setting sun tinted the sky gold. Everything seemed stationary in the crisp air. Reaching for a smaller knife, his eyes lifted. Something stirred in the grasses behind him. *Probably one of those persistent Moasks. They are always begging food from a soft-hearted worker,* he thought, visualizing the feisty rodents. He returned to his work, his concentration unaltered until the smell of sulfur smoldered inside his nostrils. Hearing the crunch of footsteps behind him, he swiveled. A smiling official hovered over him, torch in hand.

In a panicked spree, Jashor flung the unfinished spear, striking the official under the chin. The Shalkan fell, and the torch toppled to the ground. The dry grasses burst into flames. Several similar fires spread rapidly across the fields, providing a smoke screen for the hundreds of officials sneaking through the grasses. Darting to the first building, Jashor threw open the door.

"Attack!" His cry propelled the inhabitants of Quantus Plain towards the secret entrances which fed into the underground fort. Squaring his jaw, Jashor grabbed a nearby spear. He was prepared to defend the doorway while the others escaped. *You can do this, Jashor. Just stay on the defensive. That's it—nothing complicated and no intricate techniques. It's only a matter of time; if I can hold them, we go freely with our lives.* A piece of cloth brushed against his rigid arm as another presence asserted itself at his side. Jashor turned to see an elderly man staring complacently at the flames, as though the official threat could not harm him. In his steely grasp, a bow rested, and in his quiver, arrows bristled.

"Go," Jashor said, "you have seen enough battles in your time; this is my time. I can hold the door."

The older gentleman grinned. "You are stout of heart, but at Quantus Plain, the old must join the young. I'll be your assistant and will take none of the glory; for glory I do not desire. They are coming now, and together we will defend our people."

"You are wise and brave, old man. Perhaps if we survive this battle, you would mentor me." Jashor girded the spear firmly.

The old man smirked. "Call me Hilsburn, and let us make it through the battle first."

With this, both turned to meet the blows of the enemy. Protected by Jashor's and Hilsburn's barrier of action, the innocent huddled fearfully in the corner of the building, waiting as the others before them dropped through the hatch and into the safety of the underground halls. The battle had begun, and they did not know if their turn to escape would ever come.

The commander urged his men to attack. *So this is Quantus Plain,* he thought imperiously. *Some fortress! It is merely a vulnerable set of buildings! Why Master sees this as threat I cannot tell, but we shall destroy it with the same amount of effort it takes to flick our wrists.* Like a wolf shredding its prey, a haggard laugh ripped from the back of his parched throat.

"Leave none alive!" he cried elatedly as the two pitiful men guarding one of the compounds began to stagger under the onslaught. "Spears and bows have no power against that of flame!" he crackled to them. *The people trapped in the building will be burned alive, and the guards' futile attempt will go without notice or account.* The sadistic thought elicited the commander's smirk. He gloriously watched his men slink through the grass and encircle the burning plain. They would annihilate anyone who managed to flee. The Master would be pleased.

"Hilsburn," Jashor called, "an official, over there, with the torch."

One of Hilsburn's fatal arrows immediately nailed the targeted man in the chest. "That was the commander—good sighting."

"How could you tell?" Jashor asked while repeating the battle movements he had learned in class; they did more than he had expected to fend off the officials. Fretfully, he glanced behind him. Though they were blocking the officials, they still had to beat time in its perilous race. Five people stood patiently by the hatch as the roof, weakened by fire, groaned.

"The ones with the black muskets," Hilsburn answered. "The Shalkans are so dimwitted they do not even know a commander unless he has a black musket."

Jashor could not believe Hilsburn was actually joking in battle. *This is not sword training,* he yearned to say. *We cannot afford mistakes.* Here, the enemies were real, and the fight was not for a grade but rather, for his life.

The faint, but penetrating, smell of smoke imbued Lain's room with a strange, primitive feel. Lain stirred fitfully in his sleep. *It is not the usual smell from the torches.* The realization woke him instantly. Without thinking, he hastened to the hall with his sword unsheathed. To his horror, guards tottered through the nearest hatch, carrying scorched people and blackened weapons.

"Fire," Lain whispered before pounding up the stairs. He undid the hatch and surfaced inside the smoke-inundated smithy shop—the third building. No one was inside. From the walls, he blindly, for the bitter fumes scratched at his eyes, took as many weapons as he could fit in his grip. Stumbling through the door, he stared in momentary disbelief as the infernal conflagration tore towards him. Hastily, he recovered his wits and forced his legs into motion. He had to make sure the other buildings were empty.

The heavy burden of heat pulled persistently at Hilsburn's eyelids, and his watering eyes longed to blink. Hilsburn denied them even a short respite, shooting arrows mechanically through the flame-licked doorframe. Most of the fiery shafts landed in the hearts of Shalkans, though some pierced the already scorched land. His body seemed to shrivel, and he found it difficult to believe that the excruciatingly hot floor beneath his feet had not yet melted the soles of his boots. To add to his worries, a deafening shriek resounded over his head.

"Hilsburn, the roof!" Jashor warned as a burning timber collapsed onto the floor in a shower of sparks. "We have to leave!"

Hilsburn released his last, precisely aimed arrow before sprinting towards the hatch. Without warning, the roof and floor spun before him. His vision went gray. Panicking as the smoke and fire billowed around him, Hilsburn covered his face with his shirt. His breathing came more easily, and rational thought returned to him along with the filtered air. After several seconds of searching for the lip of the hatch in the smoggy room, his inquisitive hands finally located the square entrance. He lowered his relieved body halfway down before realizing Jashor was not with him. Curses spewed from his mouth as the roof began its dive to the floor. *Where is that boy?* After a frantic scan of the building, Hilsburn nearly clapped for joy when he distinguished a slumped shape crumpling to the floor. Crawling on all fours, Hilsburn desperately grabbed Jashor's hand and heaved. Another creak drove Hilsburn to near insanity.

"Agghh, curse it!" he screamed as a timber crashed upon his left leg. Flinging it off with an arm powered by pure adrenaline, he shoved himself and Jashor through the vague outlines of the hatch. The roof tumbled behind them, sealing the entrance shut like the top of casket.

Chapter 13

As he ran, Lain heaved the spears and axes into the encroaching enemy. Once his hands were free of all but his sword, he peered into the second building. No one remained, but propitiously, weapons graced the walls. Stuffing his hands with the steel instruments, Lain once again proceeded to hurl them at the officials until he approached the third building where a Shalkan materialized feet from him. Lain guided his sword through a swift swing, cleaving his opponent's head from his shoulders. With a disgusted choke, Lain arrived at the last building as the roof collapsed. He was left with no choice but to make it back to the second building.

Two guards caught Jashor and Hilsburn as they plummeted from the hatch of the first building. The people they had defended cheered boisterously.

"Move out of the way," a guard commanded forcefully.

"Give them some air!" another cried, pushing aside the concerned onlookers. "Clear the hallways! We have to get them to the medical ward!"

People scattered as the guards rushed the two men down the hall. They had suddenly realized that heroes could die.

Lain barely reached the second building, dropping through the open floorboards as Shalkan warriors streamed through the door. Gasping for breath, he barricaded the opening just in time. As he stood recovering in the hall below, the officials pounded furiously against the hatch, but the distinct hammering of their fists turned into the horrid sounds of nails scratching hysterically. Within the span of a minute, the sound of the building's walls giving way drowned out the ululations of the dying. Lain's heart thumped feverishly against the cage of his chest. *So the officials have found Quantus Plain, have they? They will soon have to meet the fighters they have offended.*

Perry sniffed the air in revulsion. "That can't be a normal fire," he choked, holding his nose delicately between two fingers.

"Stop acting like a little kid," Marcelus chided. "It's just a campfire belonging to some outlandish tribe."

"That's not correct in any manner of mind or tongue," Perry said distastefully.

"Shut up," Marcelus and Roken said at the same time.

Satisfied that he had received the expected reaction, Perry changed the subject. "I can't wait to get to Quantus Plain."

"I as well," Marcelus agreed heartily.

"I'm not too sure."

"Don't worry about it," Perry assured Roken. "We were some of Lain's best men. He will welcome us and any of our friends."

"I hope so," Roken commented dourly, "because I think we'll be there in the near future. You said it was right outside this swamp, right?"

"Yeah, why is it that you ask?" Marcelus wondered aloud.

"The fog fades, and the water clears as it reaches its shallows."

"You're right," Perry said admiringly. "We have a tracker on our hands."

"Not a tracker, you fool, a good observer," Marcelus grumbled. Something did not feel right.

"However you would have it." Perry rolled his eyes and parted the final bushes separating them from Quantus Plain. The unfolding scene paralyzed him, and he stood as though encased in ice. *It cannot be!*

"Let's go. What's the hold up?" Marcelus impatiently shoved the immobile Perry but then wisely decided to walk around him, stepping gingerly over the swamp plants. "Come on," he demanded.

"No," Perry's voice sounded distant. "No," he repeated hopelessly in solemn shock. "Quantus Plain burns."

"What?" Marcelus whispered in consternation. When he pushed his way completely past Perry, the sight enveloped his vision. "Those dirty, filthy," Marcelus began as he unsheathed his sword, inchoate.

Perry stilled his friend's arm, suddenly composed. "Don't let the Shalkans see us. The officials need not know there are three warriors of Quantus Plain still living."

Roth stopped cutting into the carcass as the others arrived. No one had said anything against his doings, but he felt like a criminal being caught red-handed. He hid his knife behind his back, leading them away from the dead animal.

"What's going on? You guys were gone all morning."

"We find a way out of swamp," Shrie said decisively. "Through underground cave."

"We're not positive about that," Corious belied.

"Shrie is. Breeze passes through cave; it must have come from another opening at end."

Ree thought her words sounded hauntingly familiar. "Let's get moving," he said, shrugging off the presentiment.

"I'll get extra rations," Roth offered, collecting his cooking supplies while the others packed blankets and weapons.

"Can we get a briefing?" Hitachi asked professionally.

"Oh, that," Shrie said. "Well, cave is ancient realm of Kalulukian dead."

"Okay, I'm not going," Radosh said seriously.

Shrie stamped her foot. "Shrie mean dead people in there, but they not really there—only their bodies are. Anyway, there many traps, but we avoid them."

"There are no other choices?" Aban asked, coiling a long vine and placing it in his pack.

"Icky swamp with snakes and icky weather," Shrie offered, giving everyone an unpleasant reminder of their trek through the mire. "Plus, Shrie forget way out of swamp," she admitted sheepishly.

Logan groaned exaggeratedly. "That really doesn't leave us a choice, does it?"

"Nope," Shrie said happily. "Okay, we go now. Come with Shrie."

Ree slipped into the entrance first with Shrie right behind him; Corious and Tar comprised the rear. The rest of the group traveled in a single file with torches for every three people. They were the torches from the island, the ones that never went out. Quietly, the group descended the long flight of stairs. The newcomers glanced wonderingly at the lifelike pictures of animals and people on the wall; those who had seen them before did not look twice. They had a mission, and on it their minds were fully focused.

Ashes filled the air. Fire and sword had victimized Quantus Plain. The broken bodies of officials lay scattered across the fields. It was impossible to tell who had emerged the victor.

Roken gaped at the horrendous scene. "I'm so sorry," he uttered over and over again, "I'm so sorry. You have talked about nothing other than Quantus Plain, the closest thing which the rebels had to a home…Now it's gone."

"It's not gone," Perry said. "It can't be! By the Almighty, it can't! There must be that entrance somewhere around here." Perry started to kick at the ground. Marcelus, in simulation, began to shuffle the dirt under his feet.

"Entrance to what?" Roken said staring at the empty plain. "There's nothing here."

"The fort is underground," Perry commented like a tour guide. "The fire didn't necessarily reach there. Everything but the entrance doors is made of stone."

Roken immediately shed his shirt and threw it to the ground, rubbing it into the dirt. He would rather go without a shirt than wear the signature of an official

before the rebel forces. Perry and Marcelus stared at him momentarily before returning to their methodical work. As soon as they had directed their eyes to the terrain,
Roken took a step forward and plunged into the earth with a strident yell.

"Marcelus, Roken found it!" Perry cried exuberantly. "The hatch must have been
weak from the fire," he continued joyously, "and his weight was probably enough to
break it!"

Marcelus did not answer but ran to the hole and jumped in after Roken. He
landed squarely on his feet and took a deep breath of the familiar scent. He opened
his eyes as Perry dropped in behind him and as three burly guards hoisted Roken
promptly from the floor.

"Halt," he yelled, "by the order of your Captain Marcelus."

Roken's jaw hung open as the guards willingly dropped him and turned with
a happy cry to greet their captains. The open display of passion embarrassed Perry,
invited spectators, and confounded an already very bewildered Roken.

Lain witnessed the guards jumping the two people. Worriedly, he touched his
sword. As he sped to the scene, he could not believe his eyes. Perry and Marcelus
had returned.

Roken sat adjacent to Perry and across from Marcelus and Lain.

"You said the officials have frigates on the Halfast and Tashorn Rivers?"

"Yes," Marcelus answered readily. "We sunk one in a battle with Ree, Shrie, Tar,
and Corious whom I have already told you about."

"Then the officials must own the southern ports in Armendor and Bacl. We will
now have a war on two fronts: north and south."

Roken raised his hand meekly. "If I may sir," he began, "the officials talked of
forming an elite fleet of ships to conquer all ports: north, which they already control;
west, which they will attack next; south, which is in their grasp; and east, which they
will attack last."

Lain glared but then reset his face to mirror neutrality. "So Roken, you say they
are more interested in war at sea than on land?"

"For the time being, that is what I have heard."

"How many rebels have you slain?"

Roken, taken back by this question, stuttered before supplying an answer.
"Maybe five or six."

"With your agreement, Perry, we'll punish him with six days in the mines, a
small punishment for his crime. If you've truly turned as Perry insists, then after your
time is finished in the quarries, you'll be inducted as a citizen of Quantus Plain."

"Thank you," Roken replied quietly.

Lain gave a hint of a smile. "Now go find a guard and ask him to show you to
the weaving room's inventory. Tell him you have my approval."

Roken saluted and walked promptly from the room. He could afford to make no mistakes.

Lain returned to his chair. "Shrie and her group were ahead of you last time you saw them?"

"Yes, they should have already been here."

"There have been no visitors here for three days. I'm sorry. They must have gotten lost or were slain by officials."

Perry glowered. "It is not like you to condemn them when you know nothing of them or of their skills. They have more of a chance to survive out there than any soldier of Quantus Plain."

"I do not believe in giving people false hope."

"The enemy may have taken the fields," Perry countered defiantly, "but they will not take my hope."

With Ternoc's one step onto the cavern's uneven floor, he joined the unending staircase with a puddle of sewage. He shook his boot ruefully but then jogged ahead so as not to lose sight of the torch holder. Inexorably, the great wall paintings captured his attention until they tapered off into the insignificant stories of battle losses and Leirmayn deaths. At this point, Ternoc directed his eyes back to the unpredictable stone floor which was beginning to rise sharply. Above him, the ceiling sagged like the skin on an old woman's face. To his right and left, the walls of the tunnel strained towards themselves in a forever thwarted embrace. Ternoc gulped; he was a big man, but it only took a small space to make him feel uncomfortable. He ducked as the ceiling jutted lower.

"Hey guys, how does it look ahead?" he asked in a polite tone rare to him.

"Looks okay for a little while, but then the ascent gets pretty much vertical in about thirty feet," Logan called back, his voice reverberating through the cave.

"Oh," Ternoc replied. He did relish the thought of climbing.

"Hold up!" Logan called not moments later.

"Time for the dead man's test," Ternoc muttered irritably as he groped for a foothold. He did not know how the torchbearers managed the incline. Encouraging him onward was the huge opening ahead. *A room, I presume.* In a couple of minutes, he discovered how vastly he had underestimated the space beyond. Crouched atop a small ledge that had plateaued after the steep climb, he overlooked a cavernous area of pure blackness. His feet grew unsteady.

"Is there a bottom?" Corious asked behind him, his head peeking over the top of the rock shelf.

"Who knows?" Hitachi offered as an answer. "You know as well as any of us."

Corious countered, "You're not quite right about that, Logan."

Hitachi shook his head.

"Maybe we should drop a torch down there and see where it lands," Malov suggested in an attempt to ease the tension. Across from Ternoc, she huddled near Ree who placed an arm around her shoulder.

Ternoc smiled. "Well, why don't you peel yourself off Ree and try?"

Malov snatched Corious's torch from his hand, fumbled, and dropped it in her anger. Instead of picking it up, she kicked it off the ridge. The eleven rebels watched in anticipation as the torch sailed and splashed. She stalked back to her former position at Ree's side and moved closer to him, glaring at Ternoc.

Shrie sighed, "Torch only fall twenty, thirty Ree feets, so we could go for swim. But Shrie find this narrow ledge leading to another entrance." Shrie scampered on her newly found path while beckoning everyone after her. Ree and Malov went next, relieved to avoid the gloom of the mysterious unknown. Corious watched his robbed torch disappear underwater. The torch that could never go out was gone.

Roken roamed the halls of Quantus Plain in awe. The place had an elegance which no Shalkan structure could match. High stone ceilings arched above his head. Fiery sticks hung on the walls every five feet, and a veil of smoke scurried to the ceiling, chasing away the damp coolness of the earth. Coats of arms hung over red, wooden doors spaced every twenty feet apart, identifying the rooms' occupants or purposes. As he walked, the click and clack of his boots echoed off the smooth, gray walls and ceiling. *Third hall, first corridor, eighth door on the right,* he repeated. *This place is a maze,* he thought as he stopped to determine the location of the third hall. A chorus of painful moans broke his train of thought. He spun around to see an elaborate sign set above one of the red doors. He walked over slowly, afraid of what he might see through the door's window but inevitably drawn forward by his curiosity. Glancing tentatively through the glass, he saw many beds supporting the sick, the injured, and the dying. He noticed someone being taken out a back door. He shuddered.

Despite the dead and dying, the room was beyond his imagination. The officials had always left their injured to die; but here, healers scurried from bed to bed with droughts, bandages, and encouraging words. Someone had even bunched vibrant, cheerful flowers into bulbous vases; one bouquet stood by every bedside. The sheets were spotless, and the walls were without marks or stains. Numerous torches lit the room, and a faint aroma of sweet incense pervaded the room. One healer caught his attention. She held a metal tool that stood out egregiously in the otherwise pleasant room. She walked farther into the room, and he decided to enter. As he passed through the door, a wounded soldier instinctively reached towards him.

"Just a touch of water," he asked, mistaking Roken for a healer.

"Sure." Roken walked to a small fountain playing in the corner of the room and filled a cup. The man gulped its contents before placing it on the table next to him and falling into a fitful slumber. Aside from the soldier, no one else noticed Roken, for which he was thankful. He did not want to answer any awkward questions.

Left alone to examine the herbs hanging from the ceiling, Roken was surprised when he recognized most of them. He hovered nearby as people cut, chopped, or ground the substances from their natural states and formed them into pills, sprinkled them on food, or placed them in water. Afterwards, they handed their creations to the healers for systematic distribution. Fascinated, Roken lingered to observe the process.

Hilsburn rested in a bed next to Jashor. They were not injured really, just tired and graced with minor burns. Lain had been in earlier to thank them for their bravery and service. Since then, rumors had spread that the famed Perry and Marcelus had returned and that another cell of elite rebels was on its way. The news had wrought Hilsburn into an excited state. On the opposite end of the spectrum, Jashor slept soundly; his loud snores testified to this fact, but Hilsburn did not mind. The man with whom he had otherwise shared a bunk had snored much louder and had slept with more violent dreams. As he stretched comfortably, Hilsburn noticed an ill-groomed young man walking through the room with a stride that was neither aimless nor purposeful.

He tapped a passing healer. "Who is that?"

"I'm not sure," she said, slightly puzzled. "Would you like me to inquire?"

Hilsburn thought about this. "No, leave him be. I'll find out later. Just tell him he needs a haircut and a new shirt."

Roken's fingers tightly gripped the bedpost as two healers performed a rebuilding. The spectacle astounded him; what the healers were capable of nearly blew his mind. With a noxious potion, they put the injured person to sleep and then opened his or her body to fix it. Their composed, practiced motions clipped blood vessels, sewed muscles together, and removed foreign shards. Never before had he seen metal tools be used for such constructive purposes, and the only other time he had seen a body lie so still and so open had been on the battlefield. Though the comparison made him slightly queasy, Roken could not peel his eyes from the procedure. He finally refocused his vision when someone tapped him authoritatively on the shoulder. *I've been caught.* Roken's heart sank but then worked on overtime when the healer he had noticed earlier spoke.

"I'm sorry, sir, but we really can't let you in until you have taken a shower and washed your hands."

The blood rushed to his face, and he was positive his cheeks matched the brilliant, red flowers on the adjacent table. "Right," he tried to recover his dignity, "I was just on my way to the weaving room."

Surprisingly, the healer smiled warmly. Roken's mind slipped into a happy daze as she said, "It's okay. I'll show you where it is. Also, the man in the bed over there," the healer pointed to Hilsburn, "would like me to tell you that you need a haircut."

Roken stroked his beard fondly. "Where can I take care of that?" he asked dumbly. *When was the last time I saw a pretty woman?*

"At the barber's room, of course," the healer said, catching his gaze. "But I could do it for you sometime," she added mischievously.

"I'll take you up on that." The complicated rebuilding behind him immediately took second place to his current conversation.

The healer flashed him a smile. "I'm glad. Now, let's see about getting you a shirt."

As the two departed from the room together, Hilsburn smiled and turned over on his back; yes, life was agreeable, even in the midst of war.

Shrie scrambled through the narrow passage. *Had they made the right choice?* Like Corious, she had seen the torch putter lugubriously once hurtled over the rock ledge. Fire represented life to the Kalulukians, and if the cavern's lake, for she was sure that a noteworthy body of water filled the depths beyond the rock ledge, swallowed fire, it probably would not have provided them with a pleasant swim. No, Shrie would not go into the underground lake even if it was her last choice.

To counter the oppressive darkness, Ree carried one of the two remaining torches, and from its glow Hitachi and Malov did not stray far. Shrie was glad the threesome had gone ahead of her; it allowed her to watch Hitachi whose antics increasingly intrigued her. Something in him continually fought the necessity of crawling and encouraged him to stand. After hitting his head for what must have been the sixth time, he bent down, singing about stone fortresses and hidden beams of light. Shrie tried not to laugh. Hitachi was not a good singer.

Ree's torch snuffed out. Shrie froze.

"Ree?"

No answer.

"Malov?"

A tiny grunt.

Shrie crawled rapidly to the end of the passageway. The path dropped sharply into a precipice. She gulped. The tips of Malov's fingers gripped the edge of the path, imperceptibly sliding backwards as friction lost its battle against gravity. Placing an iron grip around one of Malov's thin wrists, Shrie pulled. Malov's body resisted, as though it were made of stone. Without letting go, Shrie squatted, adjusting her position to gain more leverage. With all of the weight on her thighs, she strained backwards and felt as Malov's body rose slightly into the air. Encouraged by the result, Shrie jerked backwards in a full attempt to save her friend when an elbow buried itself into her back. She rose on her tiptoes in lost balance and then tumbled head over heels into the vacuous space. As she plummeted, she screamed, and her limbs flailed wildly as she groped for anything onto which she could hold.

Seconds later, Shrie's hand closed around an ankle—Ree's. He in turn clutched

Malov's ankle. No wonder Malov had been so heavy. *How is she holding on? Ah.* One of Ree's feet had discovered a small indent by which he could support, at least partially, his weight. He tried to say something, but Shrie could not hear him.

On a whim, she threw a rock into the darkness below. She saw the splash but did not hear it. So their circuitous route had brought them to the lake after all. *The lake is the last trial,* Shrie thought, recalling the pictures. *It is the trial of silence and darkness—one only the deaf and blind can pass.* At least their path had saved them some trouble, bringing them beyond the middle of the lake. They had thus bypassed the worst of the potential traps, though now they would suffer a much longer drop. Shrie grimaced, and then let go.

A stick of dismay detonated in Ree's stomach as Shrie's hand slipped from his ankle. *She let go on purpose.* Taking a deep breath, he followed her lead.

Shrie plunged in a dizzy descent. Her foot touched water, and then she slammed forcefully into the lake. She had physically violated the realm of the dead. As she treaded water, ten bodies fell towards her. She spent her time avoiding being hit and watching as the lights of the last two torches entered their eternal rest. Oddly, the rebels did not need the torches; a weak light emanated from the bottom of the lake. It distinguished one shadow from another. Shrie ran her fingers loosely over the face of the form next to her. It was Corious. She grabbed his arm and swam to the next person until they were linked and swimming for the lake's shore. It would only be a matter of time until the next trial. They had trespassed onto Kalulukian holy ground, and they were not about to be welcomed.

In a tight fist, Tar clenched Roth's shirt as Ternoc grabbed Roth's only arm. *We must look ridiculous,* Ree reflected as they passed through the clear water. Still, the group reached the rocky shore without hindrance, and it took the first presented path into the darkness—the path that would bring them to the outside world.

Lights sputtered ahead. Excited, Shrie quickened her step. As the hallway widened, the group tingled with anticipation. Stepping through an impressive archway, they found themselves not outside as they had expected, but in a spacious, underground chamber with mysteries written on every wall.

Ree admired the workmanship of the statue. In the likeness of a muscled Kalulukian man, the statue's back faced them, and with a spear in its hand, it sat upon a gigantic lizard. Earrings pierced the statue's ears, and a gold circlet was clasped around its forearm. Tattoos covered its bare arms and back in such detail that Ree very nearly questioned its reality. Stealing a torch from the wall, he chucked it at the sculpture. It abruptly turned, catching the fiery missile.

Shrie gasped audibly as the man's skin moved over his sinewy muscles and as the flesh on his face resonated with the power known only to an avatar. No one moved.

Dread and awe had taken control of their limbs. Shrie cringed when the sound of Tar unsheathing his sword grated in the air. The Kalulukian whipped his spear point under the boy's chin, but Shrie spoke before blood was shed, throwing herself to her knees.

"Forgive us, Leirmayn," she blabbered. "We had no knowledge; we come in innocence. We have passed the tests of your gods. Please do not harm us," she importuned.

The man let the spear rest inches from Tar's Adam's apple. "Our gods have died long ago, Maiden. They were always dead. Even our faith did not bring them to life."

"You are right in this," Shrie said to the ground. The others, except Tar, knelt like Shrie, facing anywhere but the Leirmayn's face.

"You are the last of your kind who knows this Truth?"

"I am." The man took the spear from Tar's throat like a cat retracting its claws. "Do not bow to me. I am but a servant with you in your fight."

The party stood, relieved.

"You also, Jungle Maiden," his eyes flickered to look deeply into hers, "are considered to be the last of your kind, are you not?"

Shrie composed herself before answering. "You know of my tribe."

"I can take you to them."

At this, Roth studied the Kalulukian. He could have been Shrie's father but for the bluish tint to his skin. His steed was the living form of the carcass he had cut— and had eaten. His eyes widened. Serious trouble awaited him. As if his thoughts had been read, the Kalulukian bore into him with brown, knowing eyes. Everything was silent, waiting for the inevitable explosion of anger, and then the Kalulukian turned back to Shrie. Roth released a thankful breath.

"Is that your wish, Maiden," the Kalulukian probed, "to see your tribe?"

Shrie inspected her friends. Sadness and fatigue defined their features.

"Must Shrie leave her group?" she asked tentatively.

"You are to make the trip alone." There would be no negotiating.

"Go, Shrie," Corious's voice held an unmistakable sorrow. "We'll miss you, but you have to go. You've waited your entire life to have this chance," he added gravely. "Take it."

Her body and mouth involuntarily obeyed his voice. "Leirmayn," she asked as she stepped towards him, "what about the fare of my friends?"

"You had allies that were to meet you at Quantus Plain?"

"Yes." The extent of his knowledge shocked her. "You know of their location?"

"They have arrived safely at their destination."

"You have any other news?"

"Perhaps you should know Quantus Plain has been burned."

"But you said they arrived safely," Ree protested.

The Kalulukian raised his eyebrows. "The buildings above ground, yes, have succumbed to fire, but the heart of Quantus Plain lies underground. That is where I shall take you, if you consent to my leadership."

Ree folded his arms but gave his assent grudgingly. "Lead on then."

Shrie nervously glanced at Ree; the Leirmayn appeared in a terrifying rage. "I give the commands."

Ree reached for his sword in a motion of aggression, but Shrie's hand timidly pulled back on his arm. He could not afford to jeopardize their mission.

"As you wish," Ree acquiesced with clenched teeth.

"We will go to your tribe after your companions are safely pointed on the right route. Say any farewells you must. Our trail is no easy one."

They had come so far together. Shrie rushed to embrace Corious in a tight hug. His arms encircled her, and she hid her face in his chest. Tears welled in her eyes and stained his shirt as he let her go. He averted his face to her gaze. Running next to Tar, she squeezed him hard, and then she went to Ree. Surprisingly, Ree held her the longest.

Finally, he said gruffly, "The Almighty be with you."

"And with you," she said happily through a tear-stained face.

To each of the others, she gave one of her arrows and the advice to seek the Almighty and to trust in His love. Each nodded. To Malov she added one more request.

"You must keep boys in order, yes?'

"I'll do that," her voice quivered.

"I am ready, Leirmayn."

The Kalulukian pushed open a door at the end of the chamber. He addressed her friends.

"Follow this passageway for two miles until you reach the inner chamber of Quantus Plain."

Ree strode stiffly through the doors, leading the others away. Shrie felt her heart leave with them. When Ternoc, the last to go, had shut the door, it felt as though the strings that had carried her heart had snapped. Shrie sighed emptily. What was she doing? Her true tribe was her friends. Memories of Ree making pottery, Tar climbing, and Corious flinging mud at her made her want to laugh and cry all at once. She let her emotions reign wildly; and then, with a sympathetic yet virile will, she caught her memories and passions, winding them carefully into a tight ball; she would appear unbreakable before the Leirmayn. The test of her faith would be the hardest: letting go of the ones she loved and trusting them to the Almighty. His presence felt almost palpable, as though He were next to her, comforting her. A voice spoke softly to her. *Is it you, Almighty?* But the voice was too loud and distant; it belonged to the Leirmayn.

"It is your destiny," the Kalulukian reminded her dispassionately, "to suffer for the Great One. You will do wondrous things," he assured her, "and by leaving your friends now, I promise you that you will see them alive again one day."

Shrie memorized his words and blinked away the tears. She would share in his hope. Alone, she waited for him to take her to her tribe, but instead of embarking on the journey, he opened a chest at the end of the room. From it, he delicately lifted an ancient bow and its quiver of arrows. Gravely, he handed them to her. His hand did not touch hers in the exchange.

"These belonged to the leader of your tribe," he said in his steely voice, as though he was unused to speaking with others. "They are yours now. Use the arrows sparingly and wisely. Even a glance will kill, and they will fly far. But once they strike, they cannot be retrieved."

The ancient weapon simultaneously elicited her apprehension and admiration. Taking the bow and arrows from the Leirmayn's hand, she strapped them to her body. The quiver fell perfectly into the curve of her back, and the bow seemed to shape itself to her hand. In amazement, she examined the workmanship.

"How you get these?"

"We will get you a steed to ride, one like mine," the Leirmayn continued, ignoring her question.

Shrie eyed the giant lizard. "Mali-Mali not work?"

"The spiders would not be able to handle the nasty climates we will encounter or the arduous trail will we take on the way to the Valley of Solitude."

Shrie briefly shut her burning eyes. "Valley of Solitude," she repeated; what an apt name for the occasion.

Roken tagged after the healer as she entered a room that smelled like fresh laundry. After eyeing him, she estimated his size and then decidedly selected a shirt from one of the many stacks lining the perimeter. *This place is fantastic*, Roken thought wildly as she handed him the bundle of clean cloth. He slid the garment easily over his head; it was light and comfortable.

"Looks good," she complimented, "but now for that haircut."

Roken could not help but grin nervously. "Don't cut it too short," he joked. "What do you plan on doing to it anyway?"

"Depends," the healer said seriously. "Do you plan to be a fighter or a healer?"

The bloody battlefield and his mangled victims lay strewn before his mind's eye. *I will not kill when I can save.* The white beds of the healers washed away the gruesome vision.

"A healer." He would atone for the blood he had spilt.

She smiled. "Not many men are healers, but I think it is a wise choice for you. I will cut your hair accordingly."

Her response pleased Roken, but pleasing him more was the healer's hand in his as she pulled him down the hall to another room—a room dedicated to the sole purpose of cutting hair.

Lain practically jumped when the former official, called Roken, appeared before him with a healer's haircut.

"After I am finished in the mines," Roken announced, "I would like to become a healer."

Roken's desire astonished him. "If that is your wish."

"It is."

"In that case, we'll have to shorten your time in the mines to four days. Salene tells me they are in need of healers, and the captains tell me they are short on healthy men."

"No, I will do all six," Roken insisted. "I will not shirk the punishment I deserve."

The commitment to justice satisfied Lain. *Roken may earn a place here after all.* "Then six it is," Lain affirmed.

Stunned, Tar's mind whirled in confused circles. His trembling hand rested on Corious's shoulder under the pretense of needing physical guidance, but its true purpose was to glean a small comfort—the knowledge that someone was there for him. Within the past year, his parents had died, and his brother had sacrificed himself. Now one of his best friends, possibly his best, had left him. *I am glad Shrie will find her tribe,* he tried to convince himself. *No, you're not happy,* he admitted to himself. *But it's okay, because you could still go back,* another voice reasoned. *Shrie has been gone for less than three minutes and is probably still in the chamber behind you. You could go with her.* He shoved the maudlin thought behind him. *Still,* he confessed to himself, *the closeness makes the inevitable distance seem greater.* He had to divert his attention. "Has the hall changed any?" he questioned. "Is Quantus Plain near?"

Corious smiled sadly at Tar. "Everything is pretty much the same; the air seems a bit lighter though. Quantus Plain must not be too far off."

"Yes, I smelled something different. Besides, there's a bit more moisture in the air, and I hear muffled voices."

"Yes, I hear them too!" Corious exclaimed, but as they continued, Tar realized the voices were, in actuality, the resonance of hammers and axes chipping away at the rock under their feet.

A padded mat and a feather pillow supported Lain's head and body. The leader of the rebels did not live in luxury. He rubbed his eyes. Ideas and memories streamed incessantly through his head; he could never stop thinking. Maps and past battles relived filled even his dreams. No one had died today, but the Shalkans had burned the blacksmith's workshop, weaponry storage room, the watchman's lookout, and the traders' building. Nothing but black ashes and tilted wooden beams interrupted the scarred plain. No one could use the main entrance now except at night, and that would inhibit the flow of supply wagons. On the other hand, Captain Marcelus and Lord Perry had returned safely; they were thinner and grungier than when he had last seen them, but they were safe and well. Lain would be relieved of their duties which he had taken upon himself when they were presumed captured. Lastly, and perhaps most importantly, a group of trained rebels were supposedly making their way to Quantus Plain. Though skeptical of the rebels' existences, he hoped for their arrival. A knocking came at his door, and he rose to answer it. The guard practically tumbled into the room, the words spilling from his mouth.

Scooping a cup of ground fish meat into a bowl, the Leirmayn placed it before his ravenous lizard, Magog. Watching the creature gobble the food greedily, the Leirmayn balanced his spear against the wall solemnly.

"We will stay here tonight. In the morning, we will exit through a staircase at the end of my quarters," he said, attempting to soften his gruff voice.

"Shrie do what you think is best."

The Kalulukian opened the door to his quarters and stepped inside. Shrie inquisitively eyed the spacious room. Sparkling, green fish swam lazily in the pool of water that serenely occupied one corner. A mat resided in the opposite corner while a stone table upheld an open scroll. Stone statues lingered in the room's recesses, cradling large torches. In the center of the back wall, the Kalulukian opened a small hatch and brought out another mat.

"Set this wherever you please," he told her, handing it to Shrie. "If you get hungry, spear one of the fish in the pond."

"Thank you, Leirmayn."

The man sighed in sympathy. The girl seemed upset. The ice that surrounded his nature cracked, melted, and rushed into a puddle at his feet. "I suspect since we are going to be riding together for a long time, you might wish to know my real name." His voice grew warmer, as though it had finally adjusted to talking.

Shrie beamed brightly. He smiled back weakly.

"Shrie would like to be your friend! What your name?"

"In my tongue, they call me Desarmujct, but in yours, it would be Dashjmar."

"Dashjmar," Shrie repeated, eyeing the lizard, "you say I receive a steed like yours?"

"Of course," he motioned with his hand, "right this way Shrie. Gog is a kind, gentle lizard. I'm sure he will behave for you."

Shrie trailed behind Dashjmar, her doubts vanishing. She would soon see her people again.

Chapter 14

The guard rapped hastily on Lain's door. It opened, and Lain appeared.

"What, Sir Ferowl of the guard, brings you to my door at this hour of the night?"

"We've got ten men, er, nine men and a woman. They were captured above the mine. Roken spotted them and claimed them to be no officials, but I am not about to trust his word."

"Sir Ferowl, I welcomed Roken here, completely trusting his character. I suggest you do the same. Where are these men being kept?"

"They are being brought from the upper level to your room. I thought I should alert you before they arrived."

"Did they resist the capture?"

"They did at first, but when it came to actually unsheathing swords, they left theirs in their belts and let us lead them away. Some have bows as well. They appear healthy and muscular."

"Go awaken Lord Perry and Captain Marcelus," Lain commanded the guard. "I will need their judgment in this matter."

A guard roughly shook him awake.

"I'm up," Perry complained agitatedly, throwing armor atop his bare skin.

"Try putting on some normal clothes first," Marcelus suggested. "We're going to see Lain. And leave the armor."

Perry yawned. "Sounds good," he said before falling back in bed.

"You leave me no choice," Marcelus sighed, sprinkling pepper under Perry's nose. With a yell, Perry shot out of bed like a bullet from the mouth of a gun. Soon, both were walking sprightly down the hall to Lain's room.

"I wonder what he wants from us this early. Or maybe it's late. I can't really tell."

"I don't know," Perry answered. "Maybe he missed us so much that he had to see our faces again."

Marcelus interrupted his friend's bad attempt at a joke with a swift knock on Lain's slightly opened door. He peered inside.

"Rebels!" Perry exclaimed, tripping. His system had not been fully drained of sleep. The others tried not to laugh.

"Where's Shrie?" Marcelus asked curiously after scanning the room.

Lain's head swiveled, and memories reeled in the back of his mind...*The rain was soaking through his armor. They were forced to huddle together under the small overhang, but then her hand had pressed itself into his, leading him and his men away from the Shalkans...*

"What happened to her?" Perry asked the laconic group.

"She has gone back to find her tribe," Ree supplied.

The pictures would not fade.

"Ah," Marcelus said, a little saddened. "Well, that's good I guess."

The others shrugged morosely.

Lain tried to think clearly as he addressed Marcelus. "You will testify these are rebels?"

"I will."

"So be it," Lain vowed. "It is late, and you have not yet rested from your journeys. If Perry and Marcelus will so kindly show you the way to the kitchen and to some bunks, we will talk tomorrow."

Perry and Marcelus eagerly led their companions down the hall. They talked gregariously of their journey until they arrived at the kitchen, for good food always muzzles a hungry man. Instantly upon entering the kitchen, Perry sprinted to the pantries like a child discovering freshly baked cookies on the counter. Marcelus shook his head.

"The food was for them, not for us," he reminded Perry.

"I always love a midnight snack," Perry said gleefully, intentionally ignoring Marcelus.

Marcelus thought for a moment. "It's only fair if you share," he rhymed before taking his share of the bread and meat.

The others laughed and ate. Ree, Corious, Tar, and Malov convened apart from the others. For better or for worse, they were at Quantus Plain.

In the small, circular room, she placed the lizards' breakfasts before them. Rubbing Gog's head, she watched as he devoured a fish. Her steed had big, dull green eyes and a grayish blue layer of smooth skin. In the corner next to him, Dashjmar's lizard, Magog, slept fitfully on his stomach. The room was dark.

"I will be sitting on you a long time Gog, but do not worry, Shrie is light," she whispered to the lizard in an attempt to alleviate his fears. "We will be going to the Valley of Solitude where my tribe and some of yours live. You will probably see lizards like you, Gog!"

The lizard moaned a low, gurgling, response while munching on the fish.

"You are happy too, Gog?" she asked cheerfully. The lizard finished his meal and lay down. "Yes, Shrie tired too, but we have to leave soon."

When the lizard closed his eyes and flopped on his side, Shrie entered Dashjmar's room. He was rolling his mat and stuffing it into a leather pack.

"You are up early; you should have saved your energy and rested like the lizards." He took several fish and tied them in a smaller bag.

"I heard Gog calling; he hungry, I think."

"No, Gog calls for his former master who perished long ago. Gog's master was also my companion."

Shrie did not know how to respond to the revival of a dismal past, so she mentioned the prospects of the present. "Gog eat big fish Shrie brought him!"

"Gog is always hungry, and nothing seems to fill his bottomless stomach."

At the stone table, the two consumed a meager meal of fish and snake seasoned with herbs from the world above. Dashjmar spread an archaic map on the table by which they pinpointed their route.

"Shrie think we should take southern route through forest, south of the mountains into Gashneirn and then Borderlands. That way, we avoid Fal-Nunien."

Dashjmar traced Shrie's route with his finger. "It would be scenic, but it would be painfully long. We should travel by your river in Kaltharnga."

"No," Shrie argued, "that take us much too near officials."

Her statement took him aback. "The Shalkans' reach spreads like a pestilence. If not my route, and not yours, what route then shall we take?"

"There no other way, Dashjmar."

"We could go through the mountains," he suggested. "Magog and Gog could do it."

"If we take southern route, there are many rebels and villages to help us."

Dashjmar rolled the map. "I can see there is no swaying you. You have inherited your tribe's pervicacious nature."

Shrie gave no reply but was thankful she had persuaded the Kalulukian.

"Shrie," Dashjmar called as he secured his supplies to Magog, "saddle Gog and gather your provisions." Now that their route had been finalized, Dashjmar rushed to leave. Shrie left her unfinished breakfast to retrieve her belongings. As she slung her last few possessions onto Gog and mounted his big back, Dashjmar handed her a small paper.

"These are Kalulukian words which will help you control Gog. You should have no problem learning them, and Gog will listen."

Shrie thanked him while Gog lumbered about the room. He had not received sufficient exercise in the caverns, and his stiff muscles resisted the sudden work.

He opened his mouth in what seemed like an eternal yawn before Dashjmar came beside Shrie and took the reigns. Leading them out the door and through his chamber, Dashjmar carefully guided the creatures around his scattered belongings. *For a Leirmayn*, Shrie thought, *he not terribly organized.* She squinted at the Kalulukian letters on the aged paper.

"Ogsheloam," Shrie said, and the lizard continued at a slow crawl. As they went higher up the staircase, the smell of burning grass and smoke infiltrated the sluggish air. Shrie sniffed; oil torches had started the fire at Quantus Plain. Closing her eyes sadly, Shrie leaned forward to prevent herself from tumbling off Gog's back as the stairway's incline increased. *I wonder how he is taking the hit; I wonder how he is*...Forcing herself to open her eyes, she ignored the temptation to imagine his face juxtaposed with the burnt buildings. Instead, she studied the mesmerizing paintings which frolicked across the walls in harsh, rhythmic patterns. Their lines and colors were painted with less finesse than the ones she had seen earlier, but they were imbued with more energy.

"Dashjmar," Shrie questioned, "you draw all these?"

Dashjmar examined the paintings. "Yes, I painted some. They represent the temple and my tribe."

The temple torches, the snakes, and even the fountain out of which Corious had drunk decorated the stairway. According to Dashjmar's drawings, the mystical water of the fountain, if consumed by a worthy being, would enhance the consumer's physical potency. The muscles, however, of one deemed mediocre would flatten into flimsy strings of sinew. Shrie imagined a wizened Corious shriveling and shrinking; she hoped he had been worthy.

Although Shrie and Dashjmar neared the top of the stairs, no welcoming light made itself visible. Shrie's optimistic expectancy dimmed. They had been in the musty darkness for too long; her mind longed to be in the open, and her face yearned to feel the fresh air blowing against it. The constraining, cramped staircase stroked her desire until she thought she would burst. Shrie strained to see the paper. When she tried to decipher the letters to no avail, she presented her query to Dashjmar.

"What word for faster, Dashjmar?" Shrie called to the obscure shape in front of her.

"Oashgh." The hulking animals perked up and crawled at a medium pace. "Why are you so anxious to leave this place, Shrie, daughter of the forest?"

Shrie considered, choosing her words cautiously. "I not anxious to leave this place; I anxious to get to Shrie's people."

"Ah, so that is your reason. Do not be impatient; these are not healthy animals. They cannot breathe well due to the torch smoke, nor can I for that matter. From years spent in these caverns, their vision, also, is corrupted, and contrary to their appearences, they are not nearly fed well enough."

"Oh, Shrie is sorry. She not realize lizards sick."

"Ujdkalkan," Dashjmar commanded the lizards. "That means stop. I must open the latch," he informed her.

Shrie waited excitedly as he fiddled with a key and a lock. Moments later, he lifted the hatch, and sunlight lit the stairwell. Shrie blinked though the day was overcast; she had already become accustomed to the darkness. Dashjmar climbed back upon Magog and snapped the reins. "Ogsheloam!" he ordered.

The lizards climbed up the last steps and paused, unused to the flat, soft ground beneath their feet. Situated in the southern portion of the swamp, on the border of Quantus Plain and Kaltharnga, they were close enough to see a small wisp of gray smoke lingering above the trees.

"We must make haste for the Halfast," Dashjmar said in a crisp, military voice. "We are vulnerable in the open. We will go around the swamp until we reach the River." With their route settled, they enjoyed the peace and quiet which rarely was awarded them.

Roken lifted the pickax above his head, his muscles burning. Grunting while exhaling, he let the ax come down with a force that he had not known he possessed. Sweat and grime poured down his dirtied face. Just an hour ago, he had spotted the group of armed men and a lone woman venturing onto the grounds in their jungle garb. The brief respite he had received while notifying a guard seemed days old, for in return for his conscientious efforts, he had been roughly shoved back to his section of the quarry.

Shifting the position of his pickax, he struck the rock again, this time splitting the slab away from the wall. Small shards of rock picked at his face, cutting his cheek and forehead. *I'm supposed to be the one breaking the rock, not the other way around.* He squatted low to the ground and in one motion slid his arms around the stone, heaving it off the ground. He bit his lip; he could not let his burden slip. Roken took small steps, zigzagging his way to a huge cart across the pathway. He was about to place the stone in the cart when someone pushed him purposely from behind. Inwardly, he groaned as his momentum and weight forced him forward; he dropped the stone as he toppled into the cart. Three fellow miners laughed at his expense.

"We thought you needed a little help," one said innocently enough.

"We just wanted you to move a little faster, that's all," another added.

Roken smiled tightly as he gathered his wayward limbs and hopped out of the cart. "Thanks, but I can manage on my own." Roken was surprised to see them gasp and scatter to their stations. Roken sighed; his stone lay in three pieces, none of which were large enough to put in the cart. He had spent two hours on that slab, for nothing. A hand dug into his shoulder, and he spun around, his hands ready in defense. His heart sank when he saw a uniformed guard with a whip in hand.

"Five lashes," he said in a monotonous voice.

Roken clenched his teeth and bent down to receive the unjust punishment. He bit his lip as the first lash came down, then the second, and then the third. By the fourth, his lip and back bled. As the guard delivered the fifth and final blow, he sank to his knees. When the guard left, he opened his eyes, let go of his lip, and stood shakily. Already he had forgotten his whipped back. He had to keep going; he had to prove his worth. Giving his offenders a courteous nod, he clutched his pickax. Each time he swung, he let out a yell, splitting the rock. He hacked away, pulling muscle after muscle trying to meet his quota of five stone blocks per day. In an hour, he had carved out two, and despite his raspy cough and the dust laden air, he was determined to get his work done before the curfew.

He bathed in his own perspiration, exerting himself until he heard the ninth bell ring. It could have been the signal to set him free, but Roken had not completed his fourth stone. A guard paced the wooden walkway, overseeing his efforts. Roken watched the penultimate slab slide from the wall and leave an almost perfect, square indent in the rockface. He staggered to the crate and unloaded his burden before trudging back to his pickax.

He was tired. The soot was so thick on his face he could barely see, and his muscles cramped. He labored uselessly on the fifth stone before collapsing; his muscles would no longer support his weight. His attempt to rise ended in the dust. He lay there, breathing heavily, when a guard stuck a spear point under his chin.

"I don't have time for your antics. I have a family waiting at home that desperately needs my daily income, and I don't get that until every worker is out of the mine. Also, by request of Lord Perry, I am to let no worker go home until he meets his quota."

"Lord Perry," Roken rasped.

"Do not beg for mercy." The guard added quietly, "You had that chance before." Roken could not move. The guard prodded him angrily. "Get off the ground!" When Roken did not move, the guard lifted the spear, jerking Roken's head back and kicking him against the wall. Satisfied with Roken's incapacity to move, the guard walked out the door of their section and closed it definitively behind him. Roken dabbed at the blood under his chin before picking up the ax. After several heavy strokes, he fell again, coughing violently. As he did, three guards opened the door and bade him to rise to his feet. Roken stood on wobbly legs, and then he fainted.

Salene sat on Roken's bunk, holding a healer's uniform in her hand. She had been planning to begin his basic training in medicine after his return from the mines, but he was already late. His tardiness made her uneasy. She had never been to the mines, but she had heard stories of official prisoners being driven for days until they could work no longer. She knew that before that point they were told the truth, and that they were given mercy and a choice: become a rebel and receive a second chance, or die an official. Until Roken, not one had chosen the life of a rebel.

Salene smoothed her uniform and brushed the hair out of her eyes; she did not know why she was doing this. She was tired; for in her line of work, it was compulsory to wake early. Salene considered leaving, but she did not. She liked this man Roken; he was kind, and he cared for people. She refolded his uniform as she heard booted feet stomping outside. She hoped it was Roken, but the man the three guards dragged in was unrecognizable. Bloodied contusions covered a body adorned in grime. Salene gasped and backed away. The guards unceremoniously deposited the man on the floor and stalked away.

"Wait!" Salene received no reply from the solemn guards walking down the hallway. "Roken?" she whispered tentatively to the man on the floor, taking his trembling hand in hers. Roken weakly grasped her hand and rolled onto his back.

"Leave me," he gasped, "I would rather not be seen like this." He turned over again; his raspy cough jarred her.

"No," Salene said quietly, "come with me. I can help you."

"No! I am the way I am because I deserve it! Can you not see? I am not strong enough to be a rebel."

Salene shook her head sadly. "Other things in life matter more than physical strength, Roken." She paused and rubbed his hand. "You possess valor and virture," Salene told him as she aided him to his feet. "Come, you can get a shower in the waterfall."

Roken leaned on her unsteadily and took her other hand. "This is embarrassing."

"I am a healer," Salene reminded him unnecessarily. "Even the most valiant in battle require my aid."

Roken released her hand and started down the hallway. "How horrifying do I look?"

Salene laughed, "I've seen worse."

Roken hesitated but refrained from expressing his next thought. They made it to the waterfall where Roken took off his shirt and boots to wade in the water.

"You coming in?" Roken asked as he splashed water on his arms and face. Salene shook her head ruefully.

"No, I really should be getting back to my room; it's late you know."

Roken dunked his head under the surface. Soot dripped off his nose in gray droplets. "I understand. Thanks, you know, for everything."

Salene smiled. Roken watched her as she waved goodbye and walked briskly down the hallway. Rubbing the adhesive muck off his chest and shoulders, his eyes flickered to the guards near the waterfall. Surprisingly, nothing but a throbbing pain rose within him. He fought back the dizziness and the tears which threatened to flood his eyes. Hurriedly collecting his things, he ran to his bedroom down the corridor. With quivering hands, he opened the door and dropped his boots and shirt in the doorway. Staggering over to his low bunk, he sank into it, not bothering to close the door.

In the room he shared with Ree and Corious, Tar leaned against the chilled wall. Until this respite, the three had stuck together the entire night, talking, unpacking, and visiting the other rebels in their group. Now, to entertain himself in their absences, Tar recalled the location of the others' rooms. Malov, Radosh, and Aban were in the adjacent room on the right, and he was almost positive Ternoc, Logan, and Hitachi were in the room directly across from them. In his mind's eye, Tar walked to the end of the hallway where Roth now slept in a single room on the left side. If he crossed several hallway junctions and counted five steps beyond the aperture of Lain's room, Tar would find Perry and Marcelus sharing a common room with the other lords and captains of the fortress.

Tar did not know what to think of Lain. The famed leader of Quantus Plain had only briefly made introductions and thanked them when a soldier had pulled him away to address a matter of greater concern. Lain had promised the rebels a formal reception tomorrow night in the Great Hall, as though by doing so he could curry their favor. Despite his doubts, Tar had to grudgingly admit that the others had proclaimed the Hall to be a skookum sight. He, on the other hand, would have to be content with the feel of the stone against his back and with the sound of water quietly trickling behind the rock. As far as he could tell, the water sprang forth from someplace in the Hall, and from his chamber, he could hear it flowing in its guided path. The constant hum bade his eyes to close and encouraged his body to relax. A settled feeling of contentment washed over him, and no warning signals drummed in the back of his mind. They would be safe in Quantus Plain.

Interrupting his pleasant state of drowsiness, the clanking of three guards' heavy footsteps outside Tar's door conjured the image of Perry and Marcelus in their brilliant sets of mail. The military glory of a Quantus Plain soldier inspired Tar's veneration. *Tomorrow,* he decided, *I will partake in a sword training class and prepare to join the ranks of soldiers or archers.* In such a profession, he could finally protect those he loved. If he was indeed skilled enough to follow his dream, it meant he would experience battle, but this did not bother him. Every confrontation with the Shalkans stimulated his drive, and to die for a friend was the greatest honor for which Tar could ask.

Corious's snores distracted Tar from his dreams of valor and persuaded him to attempt sleep. Though Tar's eyes would close, the gears in his mind initially scorned rest and instead directed his thoughts towards Shrie. *I wonder where she is?* After exhausting all possible answers to his question, Tar squirmed restlessly. *I miss her,* he admitted, his sightless eyes burning. *But she would not want me to pine for her. She would want me to be happy...* Yawning, he placed his head on the astonishingly comfortable pillow. *Yes, she would want me to find rest.* With that reassuring reflection, Tar finally drifted off into a light sleep.

Slipping into the swamp with an inherent grace unusual to creatures his size, Gog glided through the murky water.

"You good lizard, Gog," Shrie complimented. Gog released a loud moan. Shrie patted his scaly head. He groaned again, and though ruffled, she continued to pet him soothingly. "What I do wrong?" she asked Dashjmar, upset.

"Nothing. That was just something his old master used to tell him. Perhaps he laments him; I know not."

Shrie tried to understand Gog's mentality. How he missed his master might equivocate to how Shrie missed her tribe. Gog let out another terrible whimper. He began flailing his legs and swimming in the wrong direction. Sticking his head violently into the water, he came up with a large snake dangling from his mouth. Snapping off its head, Gog swallowed the rest of the body whole. Shrie laughed in delight.

"Gog was hungry! Those his warning cries for snakes!" Shrie exclaimed, thumping Gog on the head playfully. Gog turned back to her with what could have passed for a lizard smile. Relief slipped into Dashjmar's mind as Gog and Shrie continued their banter. If a lizard could not trust his master, or the master his steed…well, Dashjmar had seen too many disastrous endings. Inhaling, the Leirmayn detected an unfamiliar scent.

"Shrie, do you smell that?"

"Not anything abnormal. When you last leave dark realm, Dashjmar?"

"Maybe ten years ago," he commented.

"Ah, you smell scent of the Mali-Mali."

"Mali-Mali?"

"Yes. Giant spiders populate greatly in last years, but no worry, Mali-Mali our friend. Yes, they destroy officials and aid Shrie. They not as fast as temple lizards, but they hard working and almost as big."

"A Mali-Mali?" he mused suddenly. "Is that your own name for the legendary spiders?"

"Shrie like to name things."

"I can tell," Dashjmar acknowledged. "Do you know, though, the history of the spiders you call Mali-Mali?"

"No. You tell story, Dashjmar. Shrie listen."

"If you wish." Dashjmar adjusted his bags and cleared his throat. "The giant spiders were called Merseegens in our language. First of all, I must ask, as it is essential to the story, do you know about the nestings?"

"Oh yes," Shrie said gravely. "Malis lay eggs all in one group. One Mali does not know her egg from another. As they hatch, communities of Malis teach the young ones."

"Good. So you realize the eggs and hatchlings are in one spot; they are vulnerable."

"No, not vulnerable," Shrie protested. "There many Malis that guard nesting area."

"That is new," Dashjmar mulled over the information. "They have learned then."

"You go on with story?"

"Of course. I shall start from the beginning. As with all creations, the Mali-Malis were made by the Almighty. They were sent to earth with the express purpose of being helpers of humankind, as we are easily swayed by power and greed. In the first of the Great Wars, they would carry us into battle and fight fearlessly. During one of the last battles, they realized that their population had decreased drastically; for nearly one-half of their race was slain. They laid many eggs in one nesting but were then unable to lay any the next year. They were at their weakest, and so the enemy burned the nesting. The catastrophe devastated their race."

Shrie's face turned ashen. "How can men be so evil?" she whispered. She could see the hatchlings screaming as they burned...the unborn demolished before they had a chance to live. "How Malis survive?"

"Barely. They rounded the last of their forces, and in a last battle, they conquered their enemies before retreating deep into the forests. There, they gradually regained their former strength."

"Evil men killed, but not evil," Shrie mused.

"The only one who can destroy the evil is the Almighty."

"Why He not do it now?"

"The Harvest is the only time He can do it. The evil men mingle with the good, and even the good are led astray by the evil. The Almighty will not yet separate the two, for fear that while uprooting the evil, He will uproot the good. He must wait until the perfect time when all have heard of His name. When all have made their choices, He will perform His miracles."

"Shrie have known this, but now it has been made clear. Shrie go to her tribe to gather them for the last battle—for the Harvest. She prays that the Almighty will carry us there with speed."

"But do not pray for speed, for our mission may entail other quests which we have been sent to complete. Pray rather for guidance."

"Guidance," Shrie said firmly, "is always useful."

Malov sprinted from her room to the bathing house. Ree would be coming soon; she should at least smell decent for the occasion. After all, when they were in a place that provided soap, she had no excuses.

Ree knocked softly on Malov's door. Presently, he heard someone inside flipping the latches. To his disappointment, a sleepy Aban opened the door.

"Hey, come on in. Malov should be back any second."

Gratefully, Ree entered. "Get a good night's rest?" he asked quietly to avoid waking Radosh.

"It was good to be in a bed again, that's for sure."

"I am used to the ground," Ree responded dryly.

"I might take one of the classes," Aban continued, "just to see how well they train their soldiers."

"That's an interesting thought."

"I might go in the next couple of hours, though I want time to get ready for the welcoming ceremony tonight."

Ree sat silently. He liked Aban, but conversation troubled him. Aban, who knew Ree had put forth his best effort at dialogue, applauded his comrade's attempt.

"Well," he said, to lessen the awkwardness and to disencumber Ree from the burden of pointless chatter, "I'm going to explore the place, but I'll see you tonight. We're all going to meet outside this room and go together. The ceremony starts at sundown."

Aban left the room. Relieved to be alone, Ree reflected upon the small group of people to whom he had grown attached and for whom he felt responsible. As a rebel, he promoted brotherhood, not the fatal close relationships which would only end in pain. *Though I suppose the purpose of my being here, waiting in this room for a woman, goes against my unwritten creed.* Before this could trouble him, the light darkened in the room, and Malov's body stood silhouetted in the doorway. He rose to meet her.

"How do you like Quantus Plain?" he asked, enjoying the feel of her hand resting on his offered forearm.

"It is wonderful, but I fear for its safety. It will be hard to protect."

Ree nodded understandingly as they entered the great cavern. "The leader of this realm is wise. He knows how and when to defend its residence, and stone hems us in safely on all sides. Even so, I share your premonition. I do not know why."

Guards began marching toward them in two lines of six, leaving their posts. Concerned, Ree glanced around him before stopping. Nothing about his person seemed out of place, but one guard stepped forward sternly.

"Good morning," Ree said nonchalantly.

"Good morning," the guard echoed. "Due to past occurrences, we are not permitted to let anyone leave this fort until the given time. We do not know when this may be. Good day, Sir and Madam," the guard said, returning to his post.

"Now that our plans have been ruined, it looks like we'll have to keep occupied with something indoors."

"That's okay. Don't they have an ale house around here? We could go there for breakfast," Malov suggested.

Ree's stomach grinned. "Sounds good. I thought I saw one in the second hall. Shall we taste its fare?"

Corious lingered next to Lain. The leader of Quantus Plain was almost a menacing figure, with his goatee gracing a heavy chin, his shaved head scintillating in the torch light, and his black armor and boots scolding anyone who dared to approach too hastily. Corious's original plan had been to visit Marcelus, but he had found his friend deep in conversation. Huddled near the three sets of steep staircases by the officers' room, Lain's and Marcelus's heads had been bent together, their words flying in whispered rushes. The halting footsteps of Corious's boots had echoed across the room, and Marcelus, with his usual vigor, had invited Corious to join the discussion. Hesitantly, he had approached and listened, but he was a newcomer and was able to glean little from their hushed words.

As the flow of their talk began to ebb, Corious used a rare silence to intercede. "May I inquire," Corious cleared his voice respectfully, "as to what exactly has happened here?" His question was tentative and humble. He prayed wordlessly he was not about to sacrifice his honor with a belittling question.

Lain's penetrating eyes greeted him. "The Shalkans, or officials as they have come to be called, razed the outer buildings and surrounding fields in their sudden attack. The floor hatches in the buildings were damaged. We must repair them without detection. Above us, the miners extract stone blocks for the new outer buildings; these will not burn."

"You risk much here," Corious contemplated, "staying so concentrated in one place."

"We all risk much." Lain's attention flittered from Corious to a man bounding up the stairs and apparently trying to go unnoticed. "Hanor," Lain reprimanded him, "bring those blocks up immediately. We've almost finished the new hatches; let's get moving." Lain shook his head. "That man is always trying to avoid me. His department is lagging behind as usual. Marcelus, I would like you to oversee the building of the hatches and make sure everyone stays on schedule."

Wasting no time, Marcelus rushed up the stairs with a salute but then whirled around; he always had to add in a last word. "Lain," he called. "You know, Corious is excellent with the blade," Marcelus's arm demonstrated a complicated sword movement in the air, "and an excellent archer, as are his companions." He cut his eyes slyly at Corious. "We should give them some sort of honorable position in our army," he insisted.

Lain's face lacked expression, but he studied the taller rebel. Corious did not flinch under the scrutinizing eyes. His intrinsic, warrior bearing could not be dismissed. "Marcelus," Lain remarked, "I am grateful for their deeds of valor, and over time I will see their skills. Be patient," he stated simply.

"I am very much willing to work my way to a ranking I desire," Corious hurriedly inserted. "Your army will provide a nice challenge for me."

Marcelus snorted. "Well, aren't you putting on the noble air, Corious! You would be one of our best commanders, and you know it. Lain will see it in time, but he is not one to be rash."

Corious gave his friend a thankful smile and then stepped away from Lain, feeling jittery under the man's intense stare. After momentarily standing uselessly in the corner, Corious spoke. "Master," he fumbled for the right title, "Lain, I should like to help outside, if you need another hand or two."

Lain looked at him oddly but gave his consent. "Good, we're behind," he mentioned, as though Corious had not been listening earlier. "Ask for Tollis upstairs. He'll tell you where to go."

Corious, happy to be free, sprung up the middle staircase and lifted himself through the opening. The fresh air hit him squarely. It felt good to be outside, though the solid smell of some exotic paste lingered in the air. Corious found himself surrounded by a bunch of scraggly men. They chiseled stone, placed rocks on a wall, and nailed wooden supports together. His head snapped sideways when he heard someone shout.

"Ey, Tolly! Tell ye're workers to lug those stones ova' ere. 'E almos done!"

Corious meandered in the right direction, observing two laborers lifting a stone block with a pulley system. Extra archers lazily patrolled the outskirts of the construction area. Deciding Tollis probably was simply too busy for him, Corious got in a line of workers creating a foundation for the third building.

He slid in behind a particularly portly gentleman and waited his turn. Poking his head around the man's bulk, he tried to see how everyone else went about his or her task. From his location, he watched a man take a stone and place it on a wide strip of mortar that had been applied to the previous layer. The man then applied some mortar to his own stone. Guards roamed in and out of the structures with whips in their hands. Corious noticed the first building. *The workers must have been up since dawn to finish.* It had five levels of stone, and the interior columns and rooms were now taking shape. His building remained in the beginning stages of its assembly, and he doubted it would be complete by sundown. When the generously proportioned man in front of him had finished his task, Corious eagerly scooped a stone block with his arms and lowered it into an opening. Then, he grabbed a brush and slapped a hearty layer of mortar on top.

He wiped his hands clean and moved to the back of the line. Only a few more turns were allotted to Corious before a guard switched him with a frailer man to work the pulley system. After working with the coarse rope, calluses and blisters sprouted on his hands like flowers. He continued his work until a horn was blown, and then another shift of workers emerged from the hatches below. *Guess it's break time already,* he thought, gladly lowering himself down into the third hatch with his abused hands.

Once underground, Corious washed in the waterfall and decided to stroll. Last night they had barely been given a glimpse of the place, and he did not wish to get lost on other, more important errands. After departing from the waterfall room, he arbitrarily took a right. An attractive aroma subsequently guided his steps down residential corridors and past a row of windows. Corious peered in each one, curious to see what lay beyond the casements. Some looked into storage areas while others revealed training rooms. Behind the panes of the last window, he blissfully discovered his destination. The entry next to the glass portal swayed under his eager hands. He glanced around expectantly, but soon closed the door abruptly. *I wish I hadn't been hungry.* He had walked into the pub just in time to witness Ree and Malov at a remote table kissing each other fondly. Corious pushed the scene to the back of his mind. He badly needed something to do. His stomach rumbled angrily, but he stalked unwaveringly back to the work area.

Aban pushed the headband higher on his forehead as sweat mercilessly drowned his eyes. He held his short sword in perspiring hands and yelped in surprise as an older teen rocketed after him. He felt foolish as he ran like a madman in the tiny training room littered with old hay bales from the last archery class. At least the several inches of straw covering the floor cushioned his body as he dove behind a hay bale. The whoosh of his opponents practice sword met his ears. He tried to move but only managed to slip. The hulking form of his enemy bore down upon him. Before Aban could wet his pants, his reflexes took over, and he violently kicked upwards. The older boy hollered in pain. Victoriously, Aban pointed his sword at the teen's chin; his opponent raised his hands in defeat. Aban grinned as a single round of applause, which came solely from Tar, broke out in the musty room. Like a true gentleman, Aban shook hands with his incensed opponent.

The instructor, a skinny man burdened by bronze armor, wispy top hair, and a thick beard, interjected his thoughts. "I would say you did an excellent job—if, my boy," he critiqued, "you had used your sword and not your foot."

Aban turned red and shrugged. "Do I advance in the tournament?"

"Yes, my boy," he coughed, "yes you do. Remember men; use your surroundings like the boy, yes?"

The group of young adults fidgeted.

The instructor mumbled to himself while he eyed the group thoughtfully. "You," he said pointing to Tar, "and you, Davory, you will compete against each other."

As Aban undid the clasps on his coat of light mail and helped Tar into it, he whispered, "Davory will be slow."

"Gentlemen, settle down. You have five seconds until the match begins. Step back, yes?" the instructor shouted over the class's raucous talking.

Tar swung his sword as Ree, Corious, and Marcelus had taught him. The instructor clapped his hands, giving the signal to begin. The onlookers were silent, waiting for something to happen. Tar smiled; he heard Davory slinking towards him. The straw floor basically invited Tar to hear his opponent's every move. Tar shrewdly delayed one more second before blasting into action. He let go of his hilt mid stroke. The airborne sword hit Davory squarely in the stomach, knocking the wind and his sword from him. The two swords clattered to the ground, and Tar lunged for and retrieved both. He situated them centimeters away from the older teen's neck. Although Tar could not see it, a gasping Davory had lifted his arms and begun to pout miserably.

The instructor threw up his hands. "One uses his feet, the other his hands! This is not martial arts? This is sword training, yes?"

Tar turned. "Actually sir, it is a highly effective way of defeating your adversary. I've been in battle; so has my friend. We know what it takes."

The odd instructor stood in the center of the room with his fists clenched at his side. His lower lip trembled as his mind raced for something intelligent to say, but when he found the catalogues of his brain empty, he merely dismissed class. "Class will be held tomorrow in training room number five. That's three doors down from here. We will finish the tournament tomorrow."

Chatting, the teenagers filtered out of the room. Tar and Aban shook hands.

"That was incredible, Tar!" Aban congratulated him proudly. "My victory wasn't so elegant or so swift."

"Yes, well, to be honest, I wasn't sure who was going to win."

Upon leaving, the two boys found themselves accosted by a majority of the class. The men and older boys gave their names respectfully. The two boys were at a loss; they had not considered their successes worthy of earning the adults' admiration. It seemed strange that people here deemed their feats great. In the jungle, Ree and Shrie probably would have been critical of their performances.

"I guess the better swordsman you are, the more revered you are. This place revolves around knighthood!" Aban mused as the two wound their way through the damp halls.

"I almost forgot about the ceremony tonight," Tar told Aban. "I'm not sure if I'm excited or scared out of my mind. I'll probably trip over a table or something stupid like that."

They broke into nervous laughter as they came to their hallway.

"I say we go exploring, Tar. I've heard people talking about fountain rooms and all different types of places."

Tar acquiesced readily.

Roken dragged the four, massive stones across the dead grass and closer to the buildings. The muscles in his thighs strained against the weight. Fatigue ailed him, but after being exposed to the cooler, outside air, his raucous cough had dissipated. Unfortunately, such relief from the heat had only lasted in the earliest hours. Though the midday sun had just risen to its peak, he had long since abandoned his shirt.

Embarrassingly enough, it had taken two guards to haul him from bed that morning. It had been before sunrise, a time to which his body was not accustomed. He usually slept late because during the night, his eyes refused to close—for night was when his Shalkan memories would leave him no peace.

Roken toiled under the Chief of Labor and Development, as the man had dubbed himself during the morning briefing. His real name was Captain Tollis, though the tall, pudgy man hardly could pass as a Sir in Roken's mind. With a smirk, Roken bent down and stacked the clasts in a cube near the first building. The structure was almost finished; Roken felt certain that the building and its stone walls could be penetrated by nothing other than the Almighty himself. Two rows of broad blocks served as its width, and its height rose twenty blocks high—the equivalent of two floors. Enclosing the perimeter of the roof, a wall surrounded a lookout deck and protected a lone bench and warning horn. Another support column would complete the basic structure. Meanwhile, construction on the second building neared closure. From a set of stairs cleverly built into the inside wall, workers climbed easily to the top of the building where they started their work on the roof. With three planned rooms on each floor and an expansive sentry area, the third building seemed monstrous when compared with the first two. Due to its size, three-quarters of the structure lacked finality. Under normal conditions, such a cyclopean project would have taken years for a single village to finish, but Lain had recruited hundreds of men, positioning them at the construction site from dawn to dusk.

Roken returned to the staircase, ready to provide more blocks to the workers toiling under the scorching sun. He knelt down and took a sip of water from the waterfall, but not before a guard tossed him abrasively from the falls.

"I'm sorry, slave. You are not permitted to drink from the falls during labor hours. Come back at nine o'clock," the guard informed him.

The straight, blue line of the waterfall tempted his dry mouth, but Roken pushed away his desire before entering the doorway to the mines. Traveling down vertical shafts, narrow walkways, and wooden pathways, Roken reached the quarries. He uncoiled his rope and began to tie it around four stones at the top of a wide pile when he saw a tall, tan man working beside him.

"Are you new?" Roken asked politely.

"I guess so. Came in a few nights ago; my name's Corious."

Roken almost dropped his stone. "Corious?"

"Yep."

"You're not a slave! Perry and Marcelus talked about you."

Corious lifted a stone, not taking his eyes off Roken.

"Yeah," Roken's voice trailed, "so I'm Roken. Perry and Marcelus rescued me from the battlefield."

"Oh, really?" Corious asked. "Then why do you have the brand of a slave?"

Roken grimaced; he longed to forget his past. "I am making up for past wrongs," he said finally.

"You have suffered much; that I can see. It is noble of you to sacrifice your time and muscle, but to be treated as a mere slave, that is true service."

Roken shrugged. "I have four more days left, and then I can work as a freeman and a true rebel. That is what I set my eyes to; it eases the pain of the work."

"How long have you been here?"

"This is my second day. The work is hard but the construction goes quickly which is gratifying. Why are you here? Quantus Plain is known for the sword classes, the ale, and the women. There is no reason for a man like you to be here in the mines."

Corious laughed. "Life is short, and I resolve to spend every minute adding to the resistance that is the last hope for our kind."

"That is true. But I must know, is there a girl involved here?" The healer flashed in Roken's mind. "Behind every good man is the love of a woman. Besides, work yourself too hard and you won't be able to work in the future." Roken searched the rebel's eyes. Corious was robust, of able body, and surely a fantastic warrior; they would need him more inside training troops than outside laying stones. Yes, there had to be another motive.

Corious finally admitted, "Perhaps there is a girl, but that is of no matter to me anymore. Her love belongs to my blood brother, Ree. He deserves her love more than I."

"Do you truly love her?" Roken asked.

"I thought so."

Roken sympathized. "Perhaps it is that you always compare yourself to Ree, and in this aspect of love you feel you do not measure up? You do not need a girl, Corious. Be content in your independence. The right person will come at the right time. Let go of this girl. What is her name?"

"Malov."

"Let go of Malov and open your eyes to new possibilities, eh?"

"You think you know much, Roken," Corious said dropping his pile of stones. "Normally I would resent advice that was not asked for, but I respect a man who speaks openly. When did you develop an expertise in these matters?"

"I have found myself attached to a beautiful healer. Her name is Salene. I plan to become a healer and work alongside her when I am done here."

Corious rubbed his arm thoughtfully; and the two conversed as they traversed towards the back of the building, carrying their heavy bundles. With time, conversation grew animated, and their excited gestures disturbed the rhythm of the work. A guard pulled them back by the shoulders.

"Five lashings for arguing, gentlemen," he said apologetically but sternly. Corious began to protest, but Roken silenced him.

"I will take our punishment. I spoke out of place."

The guard smiled weakly. "Sorry, Roken, but it is the custom that both deserving their respective punishments receive their dues."

"No one will be getting a lashing," a firm voice commanded. The guard froze and stepped aside as Lain and three other guards stepped forward.

"Lashings shall be saved for the true enemies of Quantus Plain. Those men, yes, must learn their place. As for these, they are summoned to my war council."

Corious and Roken dropped to their knees before Lain. Lain's falcon, Faylene, was perched menacingly on his arm.

"You may stand; you are rebels fighting the same battle as I. Commence to my room as you are. The council will begin shortly."

Lain abruptly saluted the guard and headed toward the council room with his cape swirling majestically behind him. Guards fell in his wake like ducklings lining up behind their mother.

"Wait!" Roken shouted. "I still have time to serve."

"That is in the past. You have served wholeheartedly, and we need you more as a healer than as a laborer. Your prior wrongs are forgotten and your deeds forgiven. You are a rebel now, Roken of Quantus Plain, and shall be dubbed so tonight along with the rebels from the wood."

The honor of the invitation was incogitable and dumbfounding. Corious nudged Roken forward. A guard saluted them stiffly. Lifting the recently repaired hatch, the two slid exultantly through the entrance.

"Congratulations, Roken," Corious said joyously. "Let's wash and get to this meeting."

Roken's heart swelled as they stopped momentarily at the waterfall. He had been accepted as true rebel. Entering Lain's room, which was overwhelmed with voices, Roken let himself belong.

Tar and Aban ate a late lunch contentedly in the pub as Perry walked in searching for someone in the dim lights. When the captain saw their heads bent together over bread and soup, he directed himself accordingly. Despite the clamor, Tar distinctly heard Perry's footsteps tapping the cold, hard floor.

"Captain Perry, why would you be seeking the company of two humble rebels?"

"Knock it off, Tar. The sword instructor already told me about you and Aban; he was impressed."

Aban nearly choked on his soup. "You're kidding, right?"

"No. You were taught by the best. I'm not surprised by your skills—skills which will be called upon. Lain is reorganizing the army and needs you to attend the latter half of a significant meeting. The details of the earlier matters will be relayed to you at a later time."

Tar bit down lightly on his lower lip. "The situation is serious then."

"It always is. Enjoy your short time of rest here; it won't last. The ceremony tonight will be a fantastic occasion, but this meeting is simply the reality. The dancing, music, and food tonight will be a reminder of the freedom and future we fight for. Remember that." Perry stopped suddenly. "Do you happen to know where Ree is? Or Malov?"

Aban chuckled slightly. "Find one and you'll find the other."

"You're funny, Aban," Perry said sarcastically, "but I'll keep that in mind. Eat up. I'll see you later."

"Good luck, Perry," Aban said as Perry waved his goodbye. "You know, today I feel somewhat important," he said to Tar.

"As you should," Tar replied, thumping his friend on the back.

The pub had been a pleasant time for Ree and Malov to talk and eat. Additional food had been requested to keep them together at the table. By the end, Malov's stomach was filled to bursting, but their options on the menu of conversation were dwindling. At this point, Ree mentioned casually that he wished to take a class, so Malov gave him a warm kiss and then slid from the table gracefully. She smiled as he walked down the hall ahead of her, swinging his sword and walking with the unmistakable swagger of a warrior. Watching him go, she knew there must something she was supposed to do. Her mind pondered this absently, and when Ree's figure disappeared around a corner, she remembered.

She was due at the medical ward; Lain had told her many of the women could be found there. As for the rest of the females, Lain could not be sure of their every doing; he was a busy man. Malov laughed. She wanted to teach the women to at least use a bow and arrow. Apparently they were capable of wielding weapons but had no real training. Wondering how inept they truly were, Malov suddenly wished for Shrie's presence. *She would have been able to teach them so well.* Malov sighed; no matter how bad she would be at teaching, she knew she had to give it a shot.

For the time being, she would be the one to receive instruction. One of the women would teach Malov dancing, or at least how people danced at Quantus Plain. Shrie had instructed her in the ways of jungle dancing, but jungle dancing consisted more of a hop and plop. Snickering at the thought of herself doing this on the dance floor of Quantus Plain, she firmly decided to not make a fool of herself. With this resolve in mind, she sought the healing room. On the way, she passed Logan and Hitachi. Arguing vehemently over some trivial matter of strategy, they headed towards the map room. Malov said a quick hello to them before continuing through the hallways.

Ree entered the elite sword class. In the back of the room, he commenced with the motions through which the instructor led them. *The man has the basics right*, Ree noticed, *but that's about it.* As a warrior who had seen much conflict, he knew the instructor's more complicated positions to be incorrect, awkward, and exposing. If the instructor were to attempt one of his moves in battle, he would probably impale himself before the enemy. Ree scrutinized the trainer. The sword mentor was young and had probably only seen a few battles. Ree could not believe it. Lowering his sword, he crossed the straw covered floor. Others eyed him strangely, but they lowered their weapons. Ree signaled for them to continue while he pulled aside the slim, young man.

"What are you doing?" the trainer expostulated.

Ree held up his sword. "Do you see this blade? It was forged in the ancient days by the great Lords of Renland. It has been handed down to the warrior who will use it to protect peace. I am familiar with battle and need to correct your methods. My name is Ree, and if you need reassurance of my credibility, I can get it," Ree said in a cavalier manner. The instructor seemed frazzled and annoyed, even defensive, but Ree had expected the reaction.

"This is my class," the man sputtered angrily. "I am the best swordsmen here, and aside from Lain, Perry, Marcelus, and Hilsburn, I have seen the most battle."

"I understand I am new here, but Lain has permitted me to instruct as I wish. I am to be a new member of this army, and I will not let my fellow knights hurt themselves because of a mere mistake in stance."

The instructor's proud chin sunk sadly. "I am placed here, and I do my best. I wish to be a great captain, but I see my dreams are dashed. We are living here in a false hope anyway; our days are numbered, Ree."

Ree put a hand on his shoulder. "Hardly. You are skilled, to be sure. You only need to be taught. What is your name?"

"I am called Rohash."

"Well, Rohash, do you admit that it is time to switch places?"

The young man pursed his lips in a half smile. "Go ahead," he motioned, while joining the first line of students. Ree faced the class.

"I will now be teaching you to fight like men and like rebels—skillfully and aggressively to strike terror into the hearts of your opponents. Battle requires superior mental strength, but if your moves are not perfected, any flaw will have ramifications."

Confidently, he swirled his sword through the air. The men copied hesitantly at first and then more comfortably as they lent him their trust. Abruptly, he swung the sword stiffly to the right.

"A thrust," he instructed. "Its goal is to defend oneself from a hard blow while obscuring your opponent's view and toppling his stance. If used effectively, it should, for a split second, push the sword away from your enemy's body. A split second is all you need to bring your sword in for the kill. It may sound harsh, but do not waver in this matter. The officials are merciless; they will spare no one. Many times we have ignored them and offered them our hospitality, but they have refused. Now they have the power to kill and to dominate Kurak if we let them. We must not let them take it."

With each enunciated word, Ree exaggerated the movements of his sword, whirling the class through footwork and technique. After an hour of intense concentration, the perfection of movement, and the sweat of labor, Ree let his students break.

"Rest and get some water, but otherwise do not wash. This class is not over. We will begin tournaments for thorough training and for my personal amusement. I will also partake in this tournament. The more people you fight, the better you will become. Let your weaknesses and losses be known here. They will make you resilient and resolute in the battles to come—battles in which there will be no second chances."

An older man wanted to say something. Ree gave his consent.

"You are young, Ree, but wise. I am Hilsburn. I have seen many battles and have barely survived most of them. I am much more used to the bow and arrow, but through your instruction, I feel strength returning to my muscles."

It had been an odd speech with mingled feelings and an assortment of statements, but Ree recognized it as the first speech of loyalty.

"Thank you, Hilsburn," Ree acknowledged. "I am here to fight for the rebels and train future knights. I do my best and expect you to do yours. Let the tournaments begin. Rohash, I want you to fight...him," Ree said pointing to someone around his same size and ability.

"What's your name?"

"I am Tripeto, Captain of the Eleventh guard. I accept this challenge."

"And you, Rohash?"

"I accept."

The two stepped to the middle of the room, and the remaining men formed a circle around them. Ree snapped them to attention.

"I want you to observe the battle and make mental notes of the faults and strengths of each man. Rohash, Tripeto, put down your swords and use these practice ones. Do not hurt each another. Use your technique and footwork to trap your opponent, placing the tip of your sword to either the throat or the heart. That will constitute a win."

Rohash bowed solemnly to his opponent, and Tripeto did likewise. Ree shouted the command to start and watched satisfactorily as the two began to dance in and out of each other's swords. They had already improved, and the battle took much longer than he had hoped.

The guard finally cornered Rohash and was about to put his sword to his neck when Perry stalked into the room and beckoned to Ree. Ree bade the two to stop and assigned two other men to begin.

Perry folded his arms and watched the two men spar. "I see you've taken over the class."

"Do you mind?"

"No, but there are things I must talk to you about: training and battle. You are requested and required to come to a meeting in Lain's room in a mere two hours' time. We expect you to be there."

"You can count on me, Lord Perry. It will be done before the ceremony begins, I hope?"

"If things go as planned, it should be so."

"I will see you there. I will be spending the remainder of my time here."

"So it shall be. Two hours, Ree."

"Two hours."

Malov stuck her head through the door of the medical ward. Lain had been right: most of the healers were women. She did not want to interrupt their schedules, but as one healer exited on her break, Malov decided to catch her. The healer washed her hands and fixed her blonde hair before noticing Malov waiting pensively.

"Can I help you?" she asked courteously with a slight interest. There were not many women at Quantus Plain she did not know, but this woman was one of them.

Malov smiled at the greeting. "Yes, actually, I was hoping to get to know some fellow ladies here. I'm a new rebel here."

"A rebel?"

"Yes, are not women here rebels?"

"Well, yes, I suppose so. We fight when we have to, but…"

"Lack experience and training?"

"Exactly. There are not enough classes even for the men. The women do their best, pick up the slack, and do the background work. Sorry, I'm rambling. What's your name?"

"I'm Malov, and you?"

"Salene. Nice to meet you, Malov. So what can I help you with?"

Malov blushed. "Well, I can fight. And I would like to teach the women to do the same. All able bodies will be needed soon, so I've heard, but I have a favor to ask of you first."

"What is it?"

"Well, this may seem rather blunt, but I need to learn how to dance before the ceremony."

"Well, I can do that." She wiped her wet hands on her white cloak and then speedily changed into regular clothes. Taking Malov's hand, she led her through a hall and up a stairwell.

"I am going to take you to the dance floor, and if I can work a little magic, I'll pull in the musicians. It's hard to dance without music," she added unnecessarily.

"Don't get too many people," Malov said nervously. "I haven't tried, but I think I'm pretty bad at this."

"Oh, don't worry about it. Everyone can dance. I can tell you'll be good. We need to find you a dress too. Do you have one?"

"Not really."

"Not a problem; we can get you one."

Salene stopped to get a full view of Malov. "What do you think of blue?"

"If you think that would be the best color on me."

"I do. I'm thinking tight at the top, but with frills at the bottom. That's the style, now, very western and sophisticated. It's sure to attract any man you want."

Malov blushed, thinking of Ree. Salene understood; she too was anxious about the ceremony. She hoped Lain would let Roken attend. Knocking on a nearby door, she called to the musicians practicing in their rooms. They graciously agreed to play for them, and the group headed to the dance floor.

Malov blinked when they entered the large room. The floor spanned evenly across the space, tiled in radiant mosaics of dancers and woodlands. The walls were of the usual stone, but the ceiling arched higher than was common, and numerous torches mounted the wall, most of which had yet to be lit. Women arranged meager decorations, draping ribbons from torch holder to torch holder in simple, elegant arcs. Long tables outfitted with utensils for the feast beset the front of the room. A larger, heavier table commanded the front and center attention of the room; Lain and his top officers would sit behind it. The back of the room had been cleared for dancing along with a corner for the musicians.

"Ready?" Salene asked.

"Ready as I'll ever be."

"I shall begin. By far, the most important dance to learn is the waltz which is in a three-four tempo."

Malov stared at Salene, pretending to understand. She could not fool the quick healer.

"Don't worry, it just means that the first of every three beats is emphasized, so you simply move your feet to the beat, moving in a square fashion, placing one foot," Salene said moving her foot to demonstrate, "and having the other follow. Now for the sake of practice, I'll do the man's part, and you will synchronize your movements with mine. Place one hand on my shoulder, that's right, and hold my hand. Good. Musicians?"

The musicians swayed as they played the classical beat, and soon Malov was swirling about the room. After she had mastered the dance, Salene motioned for the music to stop.

"Very impressive for your first time," she congratulated. "You have it down great!"

"Thanks." Malov smiled exuberantly. "What's next?"

"A fast one. Place your feet like so." Salene's voice faded as a hand rested on her shoulder. She whirled around to see Roken.

"Roken!" she exclaimed. "I didn't think you'd be done yet."

Roken's expression seemed a bizarre combination of joy and severity. "Don't rush, but Lain has called us, and you also. Malov should be your name? Lain has summoned us to a meeting. I am exempt from any other job I might otherwise have had to complete." Roken paused with a significance Malov could not place. "You have enough time to finish your dance lessons, but the meeting will carry us right until tonight's ceremony, so do anything you need to do before you arrive." He glanced quickly at Salene, shook Malov's hand gently, and then left the room.

Salene watched him go.

"You will dance with him tonight?" Malov asked, already knowing the answer.

Salene smiled furtively. "Perhaps, but let's get back to you. After two more dances, you'll be perfectly set for tonight, except for the dress of course."

Malov obediently learned the next two dances. They were fast and proved difficult to remember. By the end, her breath came in rushed flows. When the musicians retired, she and Salene headed down the hall to check on the possibility of finding a dress. Malov caught her breath on the stairs.

"Thank you for helping me, Salene," she said genuinely. "I appreciate everything."

"No problem. Besides, you will soon return the favor by instructing us in the ways of battle. You will be our very own Ares."

"While that may be true, I wish no one needed my knowledge."

"That is why I chose to become a healer, to heal wounds and not inflict them, but the times have changed. I must fight because if I do not, everything I know will be destroyed beyond my healing ability. The course of life is never in one's hands."

"True," Malov said simply.

A couple more paces and a turn brought the women into the seamstress's room. A beautifully flowing dress spilled from a nearby table, and the older woman who held it beamed.

"I was expecting you. Hurry up now! Stop gawking and try it on. I am told I have but five minutes before the council, and last minute adjustments have to be made. Come, come, there is a room in the back."

Malov and Salene followed the short, elderly lady to the back of the room. Halfway there, her bobbing gray bun halted while she picked out a green dress for Salene and then continued. At the back of the room, one makeshift wall separated an enclosed area from the outside. The seamstress handed Salene the green dress and tossed another to Malov. Numerous layers of diaphanous tulle shone as the women hurriedly slipped the garments over their heads. Malov admired the excellent workmanship. It wasted no fabric. Letting her hair down and brushing it hastily with her fingers, Malov examined herself in a dull mirror hanging from the wall. The dress's bottom slanted, ending mid calf on one leg and mid thigh on the other. Pretty straps and several flawlessly placed flowers perfected the gown. She twirled.

"This is so beautiful." Malov could not help but whirl around again. "You know, this is the only dress I remember wearing."

"Isn't it fun?"

"Oh yes! I hope I remember those dances you taught me. It would be horrible if I forgot."

"You'll remember when you hear the music, don't worry."

At this sentence, the seamstress returned and praised the girls' beauty, smiling and admiring her own work as she pinned a small, fabric flower in each one's hair and smoothed any residual wrinkles from the dresses.

"Now you need these," she commented, holding out supple dancing shoes made of cloth. *This must be a really big occasion if a special set of shoes are required*, Malov thought as she slipped the pair on her feet. The only shoes Malov owned were a coarse pair of leather boots. Most rebels would consider her lucky.

"Does everyone get these?" she wondered in amazement.

"Yes. After each event, some dresses and shoes are kept for next time, but most of the material is recycled to make cots or shirts for the soldiers."

Malov approved. Quantus Plain seemed outside the realm of reality, and she decided that for tonight, she would forget what would soon be her fate. Her chimerical thought shattered as a rebel guard, dressed cap-a-pie in his ceremonial uniform, entered to escort them to the meeting. Chances dictated they would be the only women there. Salene and Malov gave each other a quick hug and then headed to the library, fully dressed for the occasion.

Lain settled into the enormous, wooden chair. Concave from use and age, the chair's back seemed to bend to Lain's back. Polished wooden carvings scurried up and down the arms of the chair. Lain lifted his sword and sheath carefully from his side to sit more comfortably. His eyes could barely adjust to the insufficient lighting of the somber library.

"Tollis!" he called to a man across the long room, "light candles in here, would you? We might want to see the people we are addressing tonight."

A man waddled over to Lain from one of the many, narrow bookshelves filled with numerous manuscripts. Most of the texts belonged to Lain. "Master Lain, we only have five candles!" the man announced solemnly.

"Then five is all we shall use, Tollis; now go fetch them before our knights arrive."

Unraveling the large map from his room, Lain traced the Halfast River from

Bacl to the Quantus Plain brook and to his own camp in Quantus Plain. He thought of Roken's words. *"They will try to take all four ports."* It *would take nothing more than a flick of Turock's wrist to capture the ports,* Lain reflected. *They will pervert the port's beauty, transforming prospering villages into barracks. There is nothing I can do; the port will fall whether or not I send men. It is too late.*

Lain put his head in his hands. He would not prevent the massacre because he could not. If all the peoples of the land mobilized their forces or wills, perhaps then Lain could conjure an army worthy of battle. He knew the Lords in Renland were a formidable foe, and that the people of Meneas prospered on their foundations of trade. Combined, their forces had a chance against the massive, Shalkan army, yet both nations preferred to lock themselves in their own wealth and riches; they would do nothing to tarnish their empires of gold and silver. Kurak was truly a divided continent. There remained nowhere else for Lain to turn but the willpower of Quantus Plain, but willpower alone would not save them from the reality. *To what does this all come?*

In the eyes of man, it was an answerless question.

At the end of an hour, Ree dismissed his class and relaxed on a bale of hay, watching each man leave the room.

"Good job today, Jashor. I hope I shall be seeing you tomorrow."

"I intend to be here. I wouldn't pass up a match with Hilsburn for anything, no matter how nervous I am," Jashor commented, seeking Ree's approbation.

"Good," Ree said tersely. "Until tomorrow."

"Goodbye, Ree."

After the last man left, Ree studied his sword. Turning a finger over its noble blade, he twirled it in a rapid combination of moves before sheathing it once more. Standing, he walked from the room, almost directly into Corious.

"Hello, Corious."

"Good to see you, Ree," Corious stated. Without saying a word, they came to the end of the hall and turned together into the wash house. As they changed into new clothes, the silence weighed upon Ree like a burden. He broached the forbidden topic.

"Do you love Malov, Corious?"

In surprise, Corious dropped the pants he had started to pull to his waist. With a deft movement, he quickly hoisted the pants to their former level. Corious guided a belt around his waist while oscillating between embarrassment and disclosure. The question had been brought upon him suddenly. He shrugged.

"I've often wondered that myself," he said almost mechanically. "I have, however, come to the conclusion that I do not. Perhaps I envied you for awhile. Such childish emotion was nothing that would tear us apart, but enough to make me think I had feelings for her. I know now that I do not."

Ree exhaled in relief as Corious combed his hair idly. Corious had not lied to him. "Come; let's get this meeting over with."

Satisfied, the rebels walked down the hall.

Lain took note of every person who entered: their expressions, their stances, their body language, where they sat, who came first, and who would come last. Everything would be of paramount importance. He needed to know how his men felt, what they thought was going to happen at this council, and what they planned to do. The first two to arrive, besides Perry to his right and Marcelus to his left, were members of the recently arrived rebel group. They were brothers, and they introduced themselves as Logan and Hitachi. They had come sufficiently early, and they spent their time talking to each other fervently. Lain could not place their distinct nationalities.

Tar and Aban arrived next. Though young, they represented the strongest and brightest of those their age. They would learn to lead their generation if war demanded. Their demeanor betrayed their excitement, but their words revealed their concern. They did not wish to speak rashly or in a callow manner. Their mannerisms pleased Lain.

It was not surprising to see everyone's head turn when Salene and Malov entered. Lain led them to a seat, complimenting them on their dresses. They flashed him radiant smiles. At Lain's invitation, they stroked his falcon Faylene, who, if she had been a cat, would have been purring in delight. Roken entered, wearing his new rebel garb proudly. He bowed, and Lain returned his act of respect with a salute. Roken walked directly to the women. Lain smiled. *How predictable.*

Hilsburn and seven other captains entered in a single file, each kneeling on one knee in front of Lain before uniformly taking a seat. Lastly, Ree and Corious sauntered in, taking their time to greet everyone and to salute Perry, Marcelus, and Lain. They took seats next to their comrades. After their entrance, the room could not accommodate more people, but several wandered in anyway and plodded towards the back of the room. Lain addressed the assembly.

"Thank you for responding to my call in such haste."

As if to demonstrate how swiftly they had arrived, Faylene flew across the room to Lain and perched on his gloved hand. He continued as if he had not noticed Faylene's flight. "As you realize, tonight's ceremony will be a celebration of life. This meeting, hours before, has been convoked to deliberate a plan to protect this life and the last alliance of men." His words sunk deeply into the minds of those present.

"I am not one for bombastic words, but tonight we have much to review and many matters to discuss. I will begin with something with which we are all familiar: Quantus Plain." With this, he unfurled the map containing a bird's eye view of the underground fortress. Labels identified extensively detailed rooms.

"I could use one of those to get around," Corious murmured to Ree in jest. He had not meant for others to hear, but the shoulders of those near him either shook in laughter or turned from him contemptuously. Lain found the comment slightly amusing but did not pause to give it attention.

"You can see," Lain noted, "the various locations of the weapon storages, guard posts, supply stocks, and healing wards. Each is relatively close to one of the entrances, providing easy access to weapons. The entire setup depends upon the entrances evading enemy notice. While various escape routes lead into the caverns, they constitute a dangerous option. If we are to go to battle, we must first ensure our front is fortified."

Malov spoke, "Forgive my ignorance. May I ask a few questions?"

"You may."

"How well are the entrances hidden? Do we plan to engage in battles nearby, and what is your opinion on women in battle?"

"One thing at a time. As for the entrances, they were once secluded, hidden by the fields and heavy brush. We have recently covered the ones situated near the outside edges with dirt to blend them into the landscape. Otherwise, they are fully functional. From now on, the three entrances in the repaired stone buildings are to be utilized. Moments ago, a messenger informed me of these structures' completions. We have guards posted inside."

"How do we plan to issue troops from these?" Malov asked incredulously.

"By night and by single file, and that is if we plan to march from Quantus Plain, or if the enemy discovers the entrances. They are designed to accommodate heavy battle and are strategically located to give us the advantage. It will allow only one foe to enter at a time, and thus he is easily defeated before the next enters."

"And the women?"

"What are you suggesting?"

"I am wondering what your take on women in battle is."

"Very well. I hope that war does not demand as much. We need the women as healers as many have chosen this profession. However, I do not condemn the teaching of swordsmanship or bow and arrow to any of them. They may very well have to fight. Will you take the responsibility of training them?"

"I will."

"Good. We have concluded that affair. Are there any more questions or suggestions?" Lain did not ask this because he had nothing left to say or because he deemed the matter finished; he asked it because he knew a leader did not lay down ideas and then demand their completion. Rather, a leader organized his men and made their priorities his.

"Yes, I do have a concern," Roth said from the back.

"Go ahead."

"As a cook, I would like to know where our pantry or storage of food is, how we keep it fresh, and how we get more. Additionally, how do we keep heat and fresh water coming through here?"

"I will tackle the issues of heat and water first. All of our warmth is emitted from the torches. As for the water, we have a natural spring that bubbles in the nearby cavern, part of which contributes to the waterfall and fountain room. That is our sole source of water."

"About the food?" he reiterated.

"Right. This is one of our more recent concerns. We have a season's worth of dried meat and fruit in the pantry, and we use the deep recesses of the caverns to keep items cool. As for procuring the food, supply trains used to deliver it to us. With the fields gone, the trains commence by night for fear of being spotted, and recent official skirmishes have depleted incoming shipments. Our chances of having a reliable source of sustenance dwindle with every passing day. It is my wish to find an alternative source of food."

Lain had thrown the gauntlet; Roth retrieved it. "I would suggest cultivating the nearby land; the soil is rich, and I could lead this project. We must also assign hunters to attain meat. Jungle plants should be planted alongside the crop to make the whole procedure less suspicious."

"Where are you to find the seed?"

"Leave that to me, and if you will, may I be excused to begin the rather daunting task I have accepted?"

"You are dismissed. The council officially allots this to you as your task," Lain promulgated. Roth left the room. "Anything else?"

When no one responded, he moved on. "War is upon us, and we must find a way to defend the place that has become our home and a refuge. We cannot, however, stop there. We must form ranks; we must unify. We will fight to the last man or woman."

The man next to Corious, Hitachi, was practically bursting with something to say.

"Yes, Hitachi?"

"Lately, we have seen a significant decrease in the number of active troops around the Halfast River area," Hitachi presented a small map to the group, "and an increase in official warships."

"Yes, Hitachi. I'm not sure how you discovered that information, but that would be so. The Shalkans organize their last sea campaign, directing their forces against the last, unoccupied ports."

A husky guard supplied a proposition. "Master Lain, it would be a wise to destroy the scanty official regiments who remain on land. They would be at their weakest without backup."

"You're right, except for one thing," Hitachi's brother stated. He did not bother to stand. "The Shalkans own the south port. Once they get word of our attack, they'd have their whole navy swarming the Halfast River, placing us in a most uncomfortable situation."

Lain raised his hands to silence the ensuing chatter. "You are correct, Logan. What I have not shared with most of you is that the officials have already launched that campaign. They are sending reinforcements to the southern port, invading the eastern port, and gathering their troops to regroup again. So now, gentlemen, what do you propose we do?"

Not a single mouth opened, and no words or ideas spilled onto the table. Lain had not expected such a sparse response. Finally, the tall warrior, Ree, spoke.

"We can do nothing about the ports. We have no navy; we all know that. Our battles must be fought as they have been in the past—on land. Unification of the troops will be paramount if we wish to corner the officials in a trap."

"Which brings us back to the officials' navy."

"Logan, this does not come down to strategy, my friend. Strategy is for armies that have the freedom to move where they wish. We are stuck underground, with every official spy, commander, and scout in quest of us. Any possibility of triumph lies with our armies. We must march against the Shalkans and take them by surprise. That is my suggestion," Ree finished, placing his hands on the table.

"Ree, I do believe you have given us a fresh point of view. Does anyone have an alternative? Or things to add?"

Logan shook his head miserably. His subterfuge had come to a bitter end: dismissal. He could not argue with Ree; any superior ideas had abandoned him.

"When do you suggest we leave?" a woman's voice asked.

"Well Malov, it depends on how rapidly we can mobilize and train our men. It could take a matter of weeks or months. Even so, a schedule shall be issued," Lain assured her. "Now," Lain suppressed the crowd's rising voices, "to pinpoint the details of our plan. Before the fighting commences, I will appoint leaders over set groups of men formally divided and enlisted. Tonight I plan to induct the new rebel group as soldiers and will invite any others to do the same. Anyone under the age of sixteen shall remain as a squire, with the exception of Aban and Tar. As for captains, I would normally have a test of skills, a duel of some sort, but our time runs short. Are you Ree, and you, Corious, willing to become a part of the Quantus Plain Guard? You do not have to answer me now, but tonight you shall. Think on it. As for Malov, I shall give you military permission to train the women; you shall be their captain. My top commanders will be Perry, Marcelus, Ree, and Corious if they so choose. Logan and Hitachi, you are welcome to join as specialized strategists."

At this, the brothers gleamed in pride.

"All shall be inaugurated tonight. A list of commanders and troops shall be given to each man tomorrow. I expect training to begin immediately. As is the obvious, my command expects to be obeyed, though you will find I rarely act on my own wisdom. Is this clear to everyone?"

Everyone saluted Lain in various manners.

"Thank you. My strength will win not the war and neither will our collective strength. If He chooses to empower us, then empowered by the Almighty we may yet conquer. We shall monitor official movements and wait for the opportune moment to strike."

"What about supplies, Master Lain?" a guard interjected. "We need more uniforms and weapons, especially since the old workshops were burned."

"Expediency, my friend. The seamstresses and shoe makers should convert to producing war supplies by tomorrow morning. Is there anything else?"

"Yes," Tar commented. "I assume the motivation behind our attacks will be clarified tonight, so all may know exactly why we fight."

"Of course."

"Also," Hitachi stated, "new weapons are called for. I have plans for long-range projectiles." He unrolled a set of blueprints.

"Take that up with our engineers."

"I shall, but one more thing."

"What is it?"

"I wish to keep track of potential allies and threats. We do not know who or what we face."

"That task is assigned to you."

"As I had hoped."

"If no one else has anything to add, then I shall give closure to this meeting. Know now, however, that this is not the last of its kind. I must be updated on your tasks with a formal report every three days." Lain scanned the room; solemn faces gazed back. "Everyone is dismissed, with the exception of Ree, Corious, and Roken."

The company filtered out of the library; the seriousness of contemplating war washed from their faces as they dwelled upon the ceremonies about to begin. Malov and Salene practically danced down the hallway, and the guards marched hastily up the stairs. Corious, Ree, and Roken remained plastered to their seats. Ree drummed his fingers on the table. For minutes, Lain said nothing, seating himself at the head of the table and stroking Faylene. When at last he spoke, his voice echoed from the dearth of people.

"You are men of Quantus Plain if you so wish it." Roken fidgeted; he could not conceal his mounting ebullience. "Roken, do you wish to be a healer?"

"I do."

"Then go and leave us. I trust you. Your duties in the mines shall be transferred to the medical ward."

Roken bowed, and left with a jump in his step. Things could not be better.

Corious spoke, "I, for one, will be a captain."

"And you, Ree?"

Ree paused. He loved the independence of his nomadic rebel group. As a vagrant he could drift in the wind, roam beside rivers, and migrate with the seasons. Things had changed since his Bedouin days. Shrie had left them, and there was Malov and the others to think about. No, he would stay. To be inaugurated as a captain entailed a certain amount of honor. He brushed a thin layer of dust from the table. Besides, they needed him here, especially in the sword classes. If he did not accept, he would return alone to the wilderness. But was he completely ready to give up his old way of life, the one he had known so long? Lain would not detain him if he chose to go. He thought of Shrie and then of the small children he had seen running through the halls. They deserved his best, so did their leader, and so did the people who had accepted him with so much hope.

"I accept."

Corious let out a breath of relief, and Lain saluted them both.

"I thank you on behalf of Quantus Plain. You realize there is no payment for your service except for glory, trust, and love."

"We would not have accepted without knowing these things."

"Well said. I believe we are late for the ceremony."

Lain, Corious, and Ree hurried from the room and bounded up the stairs, joining the throngs of people on their way to the festivities.

"I was afraid you weren't going to accept," Corious said over the mounting brouhaha.

"Me too," Ree commented.

"Well, that's all done."

"It's done."

As they arrived at the landing, the voices of thousands of people brought the previous racket to a crashing crescendo. The sight beyond the doorway shocked Corious and Ree to a standstill.

"I have never seen so many people," Corious gasped.

Ree chuckled. "Let's go find a table."

"And some food," Corious managed to say as Ree shoved him into the crowd. People mingled and chatted excitedly. Afterwards they would eat and dance, and the entire place vibrated with their expectant energy. As Ree and Corious found a table with two empty seats, an attendant hushed the crowd with a command.

"We have many inaugurations to make, but it is late. Lain thinks it best to feed our stomachs simultaneously. Then the dancing can begin."

Waiters poured from the doorways, dressed in black and white and carrying steaming trays of ambrosial food. The people cheered appreciatively as the servers dispersed and dished out enticing varieties of meats, breads, and cheeses. Even the luxury of ice was available for those who preferred water.

Corious took a sip of water and started to eat like a glutton. He had never seen such fine and abundant food. Scanning the gigantic reception room while chewing mechanically, he found himself not looking for anyone or anything in particular. He recognized Ternoc and Radosh coming into the room, their eyes wide with amazement. Corious waved his arms in the air and caught Radosh's eye. The other rebel pulled Ternoc swiftly away from the crowd.

"Well, don't you look dapper?" Ternoc commented, frowning at his own simple tunic and plain sword.

Corious grinned. "They only let me wear this stuff because I'm Captain Corious now."

Ternoc's frown deepened. "I hadn't heard. Will Lain be announcing anything about us?"

Ree separated himself from his cup. "Yes, he's going to formally inaugurate us. I suppose he'll knight you, Ternoc."

Ternoc said nothing at this, but an obvious touch of happiness worked its way onto his face.

"What an honor!" Radosh exclaimed.

"It's a big responsibility." Ree promptly returned to his cup which Corious soon conjectured to be filled with ale.

Radosh shrugged nonchalantly. "I'll learn."

Corious silenced his friends as a euphoric applause cascaded through the crowd. Lain, escorted by five captains and two dozen guards, entered the room, his guards marching in precise unison. As the thousands of guests quieted, Lain, dressed in a shiny black tunic and breastplate, with a dark red cape flowing behind him, made his way to the rock platform which tonight served as a stage and podium.

"Welcome to the Great Hall of Quantus Plain! Thank you, honorable guests, gentlemen, and ladies of Quantus Plain. Thank you for celebrating our freedom, our new members, and our mission!"

The ecstatic plaudits ceased as Lain's gloved hand rose into the air.

"I appreciate your enthusiasm, but like you, I am anxious to move on. So without further interruption or adieu, I will begin the induction of the rebel group, which has and will be a great blessing to our community. They are solely responsible for rescuing and returning our highly respected leaders: Perry and Marcelus." More applause. Lain gave up trying to silence them and simply spoke over the constant hubbub. "To reach us, they have fought the fury of both the Shalkans and nature. We owe them our deepest gratitude and sincerest thanks."

At this time, the guards stepped apart in a set of parallel lines, making a narrow walkway leading to the front of the room. Extending their spears at sixty degree angles, they formed a triangular archway under which the rebels could walk. A bugle rang, whistling its melodic tune and summoning the rebels to the fore. Ree and Radosh pulled themselves out of their chairs hastily as Aban and Tar crossed the room. All eyes were on them. Corious's hands grew clammy. He tried to maintain a straight face and a normal, even stride. The massive form of Ternoc blocked his sight, so Corious peered around his friend to see ahead. Four steep, long steps led to the platform where Lain and two guards awaited them.

Corious noticed a little boy gaping wondrously at him and winked. He watched as the boy giggled and put all ten fingers in his mouth at once. Corious furrowed his brows in consternation. The four bugle players continued to play from their positions on each corner of the platform. Crimson and gold flags hung from the instruments, declaring the colors of Quantus Plain. Saluting Marcelus with a smile, he proceeded through the ranks of gold armored guards. Marcelus mouthed good luck as he passed. Under the ceiling of spear shafts, Corious could hear Malov behind him. He guessed Ree followed. As he reached the end of the guards' formation, he gave Perry a friendly smile as he slowly made his way past him. Lain's sword was unsheathed and ready to knight them.

Corious stepped aside in a sudden realization of manners, whispering to Malov, "Ladies first!" He let her and Ree pass. Slipping in line after Ree, Corious made his way up the stairs carefully. The majority of the group waited on the stage for their final members to join them. A loud pounding of boots and armor startled Corious as the guards marched back to their assigned positions. Corious's heart settled.

"You will be formally knighted if it is your wish. There are other occupations which need additional men and women. Do those here desire to obtain the ranking of a knight?"

All shook their heads, some vigorously, some tentatively.

"Then I knight you in the name of the Rebel Cause. Ree, come forward; you shall be the first." Ree strode forward, and Lain placed both hands on his sword hilt and gently tapped Ree on each shoulder. "I hereby announce that Ree of Kaltharnga will leave this place as a captain of Quantus Plain. Go from this place with honor and pride." Corious silently chuckled; Ree did not need more of the latter.

Ree trotted down the stairs and into the row of guards with his head held high. The crowd clapped enthusiastically for their new captain. Corious wondered if he would be welcomed so joyfully.

"Corious, come forward."

Corious shuffled hastily to salute the guards and Lain before kneeling, his hands resting on his lifted knee. Corious brushed his hair from his forehead and bowed his head slightly. Lain touched Corious's shoulders. The motions seemed endless. Though the knighting could have constituted one of the best moments of his life, Corious wanted it behind him.

"I hereby announce that Corious of Kaltharnga is now a captain of Quantus Plain, and so shall remain one until he passes from this earth. Be proud of your responsibility."

Corious rigidly saluted Lain and bowed, releasing a deep breath. He lurched down the stairs on weak, almost doddering legs. If the crowd was clapping, he did not hear them.

Tar listened as Corious hustled by him and Aban on the edge of the stage. The crowd continued their effectual display of enthusiasm. *They are lucky to receive warriors like Corious and Ree.* A bugle player was near him, and each time Lain knighted someone, the bugle would emit a shrill note. Tar's eardrums practically burst. Between the loud bugle and the crowd's incessant roar, he could barely hear or understand the procedures of the knighting. *All I know of such matters remains in my past.* In the small village in which he had lived, there had been a simple feast and ceremony in which the boys from ages fifteen to nineteen participated in various competitions. Whoever won a competition was announced an honorable man and warrior. If they never passed a test by the age of nineteen, the townsmen and villagers would shun them. Tar's brother had won the tournament at the mere age of sixteen. His mind drifted to his brother before the bugle sounded routinely. He jumped; he had not been prepared.

"Now, Tar, my young rebel, will you come forward?"

Aban put a hand on Tar's shoulder and shoved him into the correct position before Tar could embarrass himself. Tar kneeled, hoping he did so in front of Lain. Lain did not say anything, and no ripple of laughter traveled through the room. Tar sighed; he must have done it correctly.

"We at Quantus Plain acknowledge you, Tar, as a devoted knight of our realm. Do not be frightened; be joyful that you fight for justice." With the blunt side of his blade, Lain touched Tar's shoulders. The cold metal sent a shiver down Tar's spine. He was about to stand, but Lain firmly held him in his current kneeling position. Tar could feel the blood rising to his face. *What is he doing?*

"To you, Tar, I give a special gift which represents my respect and thanks. By receiving your knighthood, you inevitably devote your youth to the protection of mankind and of our home. I give you a small token of my thanks." Lain pulled out a small package and placed it in Tar's hand.

Awestruck, Tar was unable to hold back a wide smile. Lain had honored him. If Tar died fighting for this man and for the rebels, he knew he would die proudly. Tar saluted Lain energetically and walked from the stage, clutching the leather pouch. At the bottom of the stairs, he heard someone fall in step with him.

"Congratulations, Tar!" a voice which he recognized as Marcelus's whispered. "I'll be your escort until everyone finishes."

"Thanks," Tar said simply. "Will you open the package for me once we get to the table?"

"Of course, I am curious to see what it is. Lain has never given such a parcel to any of us before."

At his table, Tar placed his package delicately on his lap before reaching for his mug. It was not where he had left it. He groped about the adjacent areas, and his hand squished into someone's food. Hurriedly pulling his hand back, he located a napkin and wiped the food from his hands, trying to hide his embarrassment. He could hear the conversation around him, and luckily it appeared his mistake had not been noticed. Deciding to forget the drink, he simply asked for someone to pass the meat and soup. Someone slid it to him from across the table, and Tar successfully placed a hunk of meat on his plate. When it came to the soup, judging the distance became tricky. Soup spilled onto his meat. Frustrated, he pushed the soup away and slurped at whatever he had managed to get into his bowl.

As he began searching for his utensils, a girl's voice reached his ears. "Are you okay? I often hear of men going wild from drink, but you appear sober."

Tar blushed at the pleasant voice. "Yes, I am fine. Um, can you pass me a drink?"

The girl grabbed a nearby mug and passed it to him. The effervescent liquid sloshed as he took a swig. None of it missed his mouth.

"I don't mean to sound cruel, but are you…well…blind?"

"I am." He had hoped to avoid this. No one would ever respect him if he or she knew, and one of the few girls he had ever talked to would now eschew him.

"I can't imagine what you must go through. You are so brave."

"Brave?"

"Of course. You were just knighted, which means your skill in battle is tremendous. To fight without sight—that's incredible!"

Tar could not believe what he was hearing. He would not let this chance slip. The package could wait. He handed it to Marcelus to hold and began to talk with the girl who thought he was so brave.

Lain allowed the commencement of the festivities as he finally knighted the last man. There had been so many men to add to his force, for which he was thankful, but the induction ceremony had been long.

"Hilsburn, pass me a sip of something?"

Hilsburn, at his right, put his spear into a resting position and poured him a small cup. Lain took it gratefully. He released the guards to eat and motioned for Hilsburn to make a final announcement.

Hilsburn grinned and called out loudly, "Enjoy your fill. The dessert should be coming out soon, and then I'll call for the musicians and the jesters."

Joyous cries of laughter erupted from the younger audience; they loved the jesters who could juggle or tastefully poke fun at members of the audience. Lain had often been the subject of such humorous attacks, but tonight he hoped to thwart the extra attention. Adjusting the broach that secured the ends of his cape together, he clattered down the stairs to greet the elderly gentlemen and women awaiting him. Although Lain held the position and responsibility of an elder, his age was far from theirs. He acted as an elder and thought as one because the times demanded it. *Perhaps one day it will no longer be necessary.* In the middle of his gracious salutations, a horde of boys ran loutishly towards him. Their arms waved wooden swords like windmills spinning in the winds of a hurricane.

"Mafta Lain!" one cried with a lisp, due to the absence of several important teeth. "Cwen I becomfe a wawior wike you?"

Lain knew the boy; he was Jashor's sibling and only five. Lain smiled and bent down, staying the rampaging arm with his calloused hand. "I don't know, Jammil. We'll have to see that strong sword arm of yours."

Jammil pulled back his sleeve and showed off a puny, stick arm. His peers gathered around him enthusiastically.

Lain whistled loudly, feeding into their antics. "You'll be a knight soon enough."

Jammil drew an excited breath, and immediately he and his friends sprinted to their mothers with animated screeches and exultant gestures.

Lain chuckled. The horror of the war had not infected the children yet. Lain dropped the searing thought; it was irrelevant to tonight's festivities. He made a point of chatting with Corious and Ree but could not avoid the teenagers and young women crowding about him. Like a true gentleman, Lain kissed each lady on the cheek, and like a true rogue he exchanged with the boys a quip or two. With each, he was careful to never share more than a moment.

Stealthily, he slipped from one group and over to the tables of food. He relaxed once there and began heaping his plate with tender meat, crispy fruits and vegetables, and some spicy bread and soup. He saw Tar talking eagerly with a young girl who he did not recognize and decided not to intrude upon him despite his desire to see the boy's reaction to his small gift. Even so, Lain's growling stomach distracted him from Tar, commanding his full attention.

Malov found herself amongst women her age. Salene had introduced her to them before flitting off with Roken, grabbing his hand and strolling leisurely through the crowd. This night would be the greatest of her life, and so Malov did not mind much Salene's disappearance. She understood that one had to seize an opportunity when it came. Besides, the women were pleasant, making it easy for Malov to hold her own. Though they lived in a home built with war in mind, they did not complain. No, they enjoyed life fully while never losing sight of their goal. For this, Malov admired them. Their smiles and friendly ways made her feel at ease, but she soon found herself scanning the crowd for Ree.

Roth came late to the ceremony which made everyone cringe. What was he to do? He had had to formulate his ideas for a self-sufficient farm, one that could feed a few thousand. Besides, he had arrived at the best part: after the knighting, during the eating, and right before the dancing. Finding Radosh and Ternoc, he proceeded to enjoy himself thoroughly.

Corious winced when the buglers announced the dance. A fanfare of twirls and toots on their shiny, brass instruments ensued. He watched as Ree went off with Malov and as his other companions swept a girl off her feet. Corious liked to dance. He flinched inwardly as even Tar led a girl into the multitudes of dancing couples. After clearing the tables to make more room, he situated himself in a corner. The waiters had already tidied the place with an inhumane efficiency and were currently stealing partners to join them in a lively dance. Colors and laughing faces passed him in a swirling, jovial mass. Corious pretended to enjoy tapping his foot by himself. As he watched, someone tugged at his pants. He worriedly grasped at the waist of his clothing; he had forgotten to wear a belt. Seeking out the culprit, Corious attempted to look down angrily at a little girl of six years admiring him with large, blue eyes. She was obviously proud of her frilly little dress, and Corious could not help but smile encouragingly.

"Now what can I do for you, Miss?"

"Well," the little girl said shyly, "my name is Lily, and I was just wondering, if um, if um, you will dance with me?"

Corious laughed. "You want to dance with me, Lily?"

"Uh huh," she said sweetly. "My mama always tells me that I'm gonna have a tall husband one day. You're really tall, so I thought I'd ask you."

Her innocent speech baffled Corious. He started to say no, but when she looked at him with such hope, he shrugged, bent down, took her hands, and led her into the horde of dancing people. He could not believe himself. Of course several guys cracked jokes, but most assumed that he was the older brother bending to the whims of a younger sister. He certainly did not contradict them. By the time the second song came around, he noticed a woman squeezing through the crowd to get to them. He paused and crouched next to the girl.

"Do you know that woman?" he asked.

"Uh huh. That's my older sister, Jenny. Jenny," she called, pulling Corious along behind her. "Jenny, this is my friend."

The young woman humorously indulged her younger sister. "Oh, really now. What is the name of your handsome prisoner?"

The little girl turned around. "What's your name?" she asked Corious amiably.

"Corious."

"Well, Corious," the older sister said, "I can relieve you of Lily now. You've been a good sport."

"My pleasure. We had fun dancing, right, Lily?"

"Uh huh," she said smiling.

Jenny took her little sister's hand, glanced at Corious, and said, "Stay right there. I'll be back in a second."

Jenny led Lily to a lady who Corious guessed to be their mother. He had not failed to notice Jenny's sparkling brown eyes and her irresistible smile. She was tall and very graceful. Corious suppressed the hope that she would want to dance with him; he would not excite himself. He liked women, but he was not the stoic hero like Ree. In spite of his fears, she hurried back.

"So Corious, would you grant me the same honor you granted my younger sister?"

"A dance it is!" he said while taking her hands and stepping in time to the beat. She followed his lead and they flowed over the dance floor. Corious sent Ree a significant look, and Ree returned it with a subtle smile. Corious grinned and dreamed vainly that the night would never end. Laughing as he and Jenny completed an exerting dance, he wiped the sweat from his nose with his shoulder. He took Jenny's hand and waited for the next song to begin. As the musicians opened the song with a slower beat, Corious decided to give conversation a try.

"Is Lily your only sister?" Corious asked.

Jenny laughed though her eyes seemed sad. "No, I come from a family of eleven. Sometimes my parents leave me with all my younger siblings, and I am confined to our room for weeks. They have so many of us that they sometimes treat us like pets: providing meager meals and a comforting pat."

Jenny's candor took Corious by surprise; he had expected a simple yes or no. "I suppose I took for granted the freedom of being an only child," he responded. Jenny stared at him, and for some reason he did not have the courage to return her gaze. He felt himself blushing. He could kill men, but he could not look a woman in the eye.

"When did you leave your village, Corious?" she questioned, envying his freedom.

Corious racked his brain for an answer, but the years spent in the wilderness had skewed his sense of time. "I don't know," he answered simply. "The jungle has its own sense of time independent from that of civilization's." Jenny shook her head ruefully. "What?" he asked, nervous he had said something stupid.

"What I would give to have a life devoid of schedule and monotony," she sighed openly. "I wish a lifestyle like yours was to be mine."

"Well it is now, is it not?"

"You're here to stay?"

"I suppose so. Lain set up this whole ceremonial service for us, right? It would be rude, I believe, to leave so abruptly."

"Unless my ears lie and your words are disingenuous, you're a man of gentry. So my swain, you're not leaving then? I thought your group was simply passing by, but I see it's not so," Jenny stated happily.

"I plan to stay here for as long as I can, Jenny, but a captain's job takes him many places, sometimes beyond the battlefield."

"Oh, stop," she joked, hitting him playfully on the shoulder. "You're trying to sound all serious and grave!" She did not know battle as he did. "Besides, you're just as old as I am," She added, as if that explained everything.

Corious raised his eyebrows. "Where I came from, you could get married at fifteen if you wanted."

"Hmm," Jenny remarked, making a face, "That's—different."

"Why?" Corious laughed, "Are boys still nasty little varmints at that age?"

"No, but my sister is fourteen and hasn't worked a blessed day of her life!" Jenny mused.

"You don't have to work to get married."

Jenny seemed perturbed by his comment. "Marriage, my friend, is the definition of work."

Corious feigned gravity. "Yes, I wouldn't want a wife that couldn't make good soup. Though that's not my first priority, because you know, I'm not a bad cook. Actually, I'm the unofficial connoisseur of jungle delights. You ought to taste my snake soup."

Jenny made another face. "Snake soup? I personally would go for some hot bread with honey and faszilwhet."

Corious snorted. "Vegetarians! I never could choke down that sticky faszilwhet stuff. It would always get stuck in my esophagus and give me—stomach problems." Corious whacked himself inwardly. Could he have possibly embarrassed himself anymore? He gave an estranged smile, and the responding expression on Jenny's face reverberated between a smile and a frown. She could not decide if he was funny, disgusting, or just plain blunt. Corious cleared his throat timidly.

"I'm sorry, Jenny. You see, without a woman, man is nothing." Corious hastened to explain himself. "During this lifestyle of mine that you envy, I've been stuck with eleven men in the woods for a long time," he shrugged, "and this is the lame excuse for a man it has made me."

Jenny laughed this time.

"It wasn't meant to be funny," Corious muttered, confused.

"No, it's fine, Corious, believe me. I get stuck with my sisters all the time, and their personalities rub off on me too. So don't worry," Jenny assured him.

Corious smiled at her for about the tenth time that night. "Your sisters must have great personalities, because there isn't one thing about you that I find fault with."

Jenny blushed, unused to the flattery. "You say this with truthfulness?" she asked softly.

"Undoubtedly, to dance with a guy like me, one has to be sympathetic and kind," Corious kidded.

"No, seriously, you really mean it?" she asked earnestly. "Too many people have taken advantage of me in the past; I'm not eager to have that happen again."

"Of course I do, Jenny," Corious answered seriously as the lighthearted jokes of the previous moments fell away. "I mean it very much. I'm a man of my word. I would never treat anyone like that."

Jenny smiled. "Well, aren't you romantic, Captain Corious, but hold your breath. They're playing *The Sal'sasinno*, and I've never seen one pair of dancers dance the entire song yet."

"Is that a challenge you pose?" Corious asked playfully. "Because if it is, I accept." After living with Shrie, Corious did not consider challenging and competing with a woman lightly. Shrie had given him the toughest workout of his life; but he was positive he could handle a mere dance.

Two drums sent the music's beat rapidly into a frenzy of carefully placed notes. Corious strained to keep his feet off Jenny's and to keep from tripping into an unnecessary upsurge of flailing limbs. His cape swirled over his shoulder as the two spun in a circle, planted their feet, and began twirling the other way. Jenny seemed untouched by and unconcerned with the dance's crazy tempo or trying steps as she moved with a harmonious fluidity. Corious, meanwhile, strove to maintain vitality and a standing position until the song ended. Out of the corner of his eye, he noticed a young man bending down, swiftly and gracefully somersaulting under his partner's legs as she twirled over him. Corious thought hard about whether he should try this. It could end either with him and Jenny sprawled on the ground, mortified, or with an extraordinary, showy move that would enthrall his dance partner. He waited until the rhythm was at the proper time, and then he launched into action. Diving to the ground, he landed on his upper shoulders and back. He meanwhile lifted and turned his arm upward to send Jenny into an airborne spin. His momentum carried him through the summersault and into a straight stance in time to take Jenny's hand and provide her with a graceful landing. Jenny laughed with enjoyment, and a few impressed onlookers clapped.

"This song isn't so bad!" Corious exclaimed softly as he pulled Jenny closer to him. "Is this the hardest they've got?"

As if the musicians heard him, the melody flew into a racing pace. Corious bit his lip and stepped here and there with the concentration of a blacksmith forging a needle. Without warning, he stumbled clumsily over a foot gone astray. Corious tipped precariously, watching in his mind the disastrous plummet. In a split-second reflexive decision, Corious threw himself into the air as high as he possibly could go. He brought his chin back and tucked his knees close to his chest. More than enough air between his body and the floor provided for an easy back flip, though he landed five yards away from Jenny. The dance was over for the pair; once they stopped holding hands they were disqualified. Other couples circled about him, sweeping him toward the outside of the dancers. He shuffled disappointedly off the dance floor. He had let Jenny down, and he feared some other dashing lad would sweep her away. A bead of sweat dripped from the tip of his nose, and he hurried to the side wall where he found a water basin waiting. Like a dog, he stuck his entire head in and let the water trickle off the ends of his shaggy hair. He grabbed a towel from the rack next to it and dried himself, feeling restored. He saw Ree fly by, and he smiled as

Malov gave him a quick wave. Corious turned momentarily around, but someone hastily tapped him on the back.

Jenny appeared, smiling from ear to ear. "You can't hide from me that easily."

"Sorry, I stumbled. Some guy behind me must have fallen, and I tripped over him."

"That's okay—you should've heard all the compliments which I received about us being the best dancers on the floor!" Jenny exclaimed.

"Really? Of course they must have been referring to you, my lady, not the lucky, but clumsy knight with whom you have chosen to dance."

Jenny arched an eyebrow. "You must be thinking of someone else then, because the man I was dancing with was strong and swift, not clumsy at all."

Corious chuckled. "Should I dare give the song another try?"

"Only if you promise to dance the entire song through with me."

"You present me the honor?"

"I do."

"Let us go then," Corious said, smoothing his wet hair and adjusting his limbs to the movement of sound. Jenny spun around and placed her hand in his, and they made their presences known on the dance floor, making jealous the incompetent. During one particularly difficult part, Corious's elbow accidentally knocked into someone. He did not stop to offer an apology, and a struggling Ree glared at him. Ree's muscled bulk was tiring from all of the jumping and constant motion.

"Getting tired, Ree?" Corious taunted.

"To the contrary. I am barely exerting myself."

"We'll see about that," Corious said with a smirk, flipping Jenny in the air and catching her. She screamed in delight as he set her back on the floor. Ree grumbled something incomprehensible. Licking his lip, Ree did a back flip before picking up Malov and spinning her in the air.

Corious frowned. He had not thought Ree was capable. *Oh, well*, he thought, complicating his steps. He was a better dancer and would prove it. At the perfect moment, he completed a front flip over Jenny and landed on the exact beat. Ree grinned.

"That's your whole show?"

"You can do better?"

Couples had stopped dancing and began to clear the floor to watch the emerging competition. Judges wandered the floor, tapping shoulders to inform several couples that they were out of the competition. Five couples remained. The audience took sides and began cheering for their favorite dancers. Corious doubled his efforts. The battle would come between him and Ree. *An interesting prospect*. It took eight more songs to narrow down the last couples. As Corious predicted, he and Jenny, and Ree and Malov, were the last two couples.

Tar listened as the music's volume and tempo increased. He wondered if the musicians ever got tired. They had to be out of air or arm strength by now. He tapped his foot to the beat and enjoyed the warm atmosphere. Ryeane, the girl who thought he was so brave, described to him the events in intoxicating detail. He grinned as he thought of Ree and Corious dancing. Tar knew them for guerilla war tactics, rolling in mud, fighting in trees, hunting—the typical strength for which every man wished. To imagine them dancing in their ceremonial uniforms was almost hysterical. Nonetheless, he held onto every word of Ryeane's account. Supposedly, there were three couples left, and the song continued in its intensity.

"Oh Tar, the judges are coming out again!" Ryeane exclaimed dramatically. "They're heading toward…no! Both of your friends are still in!"

"Yea, Corious! Come on Ree! Show them your stuff!" Tar laughed and encouraged his friends at the same time. As if hearing him, Corious did an impressive move, one which Ryeane tried to describe unsuccessfully. Tar did not need to know exactly what he had done; the exclamations from the crowd were enough.

By this time, Corious was sweating more than he had in any battle, and his legs were so sore. He could not stop now, though it took all he had to fight the lassitude that threatened to overwhelm him. He hoped that he could hold out. Still, every time the music started, Jenny shot him a smile, and his energy returned with vigor. He feared her smile and her footwork would never cease.

Ree took in air rapidly and exhaled as slowly as possible. Trying to smile at Malov and do a half twist, Ree lost where he was in the song and stumbled.

Corious saw his friend fall; he would not let Ree make a fool of himself in front of all these people. Corious dove to the floor. Everyone laughed, and the song ended. Ree gratefully slapped Corious on the back.

"Good dancing."

"You too."

"I can still beat you though."

"No, you can't."

Both tried to maintain serious faces but failed. Shaking hands and eyeing the ravishing desserts, they headed off the floor with their partners. Salene enfolded Malov in a giant hug.

"You were great!" she said, full of admiration.

"Me? I just danced the way you taught me. Besides, Ree's capability came out of nowhere. I had no idea he could dance like that!"

"Roken surprised me too. He lasted through the first ten songs, more than I imagined!"

The two women laughed. "Want to try some dessert?"

"What kind is it?" Malov questioned hesitantly.

"I don't know; let's try it."

"If you say so."

They waited in the long queue to grab the small bowls as the last hour of the ceremony came to a close. The musicians began to pack their instruments. Only a few of their counterparts continued to play a soothing melody—a far cry from the loud, boisterous music rampaging the hall moments before. It lulled the crowd into a quiet daze. Sitting with Jenny, Malov, and Ree, Corious wolfed down his bowl's contents in a happy stupor. Everyone seemed to be in a similar state, and Ree wondered if the dessert had been drugged. For the last time that night, Lain, with his soldiers behind him, stood before his humble, brave congregation. He rested his hands upon the sturdy table's polished surface and spoke, his courage pulsing through his strong chin line and bright green eyes. He was the epitome of a man who people would follow.

"I trust you enjoyed yourselves tonight," he said, his deep voice reverberating through the hall.

A sleepy cheer rose from the crowd milling about his table.

"I realize it is late, so I will dismiss you. Thank you for a wonderful night. All of the hardworking people behind it receive my praise." Even as he spoke, the waiters and waitresses cleared the bowls and tables. "Tomorrow is a new day with many tasks, so I encourage everyone to get a good night's rest. The day will begin three hours after sunrise, a later start, but start then it will with the necessary preparations required of a fortress. You are dismissed."

The people chatted and gradually rose from their tables, parting with a hug or cheerful adieu. Lain watched sadly, and only after everyone had made it to their chambers did he retire. He had not mentioned war; he had not wanted to dampen the happy thoughts of the night. He had, however, mentioned in a quiet reminder that Quantus Plain was a fortress, and a fortress, no matter how much a home, was built for war.

He witnessed the changing of the guard and entered into the privacy of his room. He had barely taken off his ceremonial tunic, revealing his mail, when he spotted a small figure hunched in the far corner of the room. Cautiously he placed his hand upon his sword.

"Who goes there?"

A small woman gasped in fear, put her hands behind her head, and crawled forward on her knees. Lain stepped back in alarm but then noticed that Faylene sat comfortably on the intruder's shoulder. Gently, he knelt down. The woman trembled.

"There is no need to fear. I am Lain, protector of this land. What brings you here? Have you traveled far?"

The woman seemed familiar. Clothed in vines and animal skin, she was a petite figure with dark skin and long hair. She had slightly pointed ears, a sharp chin, and oval eyes; she was a jungle woman. Shrie's face flashed in his mind.

"I am friend and messenger. I come far from my native land. The elders send me; they anticipate the arrival of the Jungle Maiden. We count on your help against officials."

"Shrie is alive then?" His voice wobbled against his will.

The maiden's eyes opened slightly, and a smile spread tenderly over her face.

"And her tribe, has she found them?" He searched her eyes, but the brown eyes closed, and the jungle woman lowered her head. "Tribe lost long ago and only now thinks to return."

The past brought faint traces of meaning to the uttered riddle. He had heard of the jungle people and had met them—if meeting one means that he had met the entire race. *Allies.* Quantus Plain could not win the fight alone. He attempted to speak simply but clearly.

"Stay the night; I will send troops with you. If you are an enemy to the Shalkans, then we are your sworn allies." The woman seemed confused. He tried again. "Take this ring," he said, pulling it from his finger and pressing it into her hand, "as my sign that I will fight alongside your people, no matter how many or how few. I have a debt and a friendship to return." She firmly grasped the ring, and he closed her fist around it. "I will call one of the women to find you a bed," he said. "Stay here until I return."

She crouched obediently back in her corner. Lain could not help but study her face once again. His eyes reaffirmed her jungle origins. *I swear I know her. It's been many years since then, but could it be possible?* A dark shadow flickered on the edge of his mind, and by instinct Lain did not probe his memory further. If he knew her, she was lost to the sinister, unexplored regions of his past. He exited briskly but could not shake the ominous portent. Biting his lip in rumination, he then doubled back and ordered the guard at his door to secure the room. He did not want anyone leaving or entering. If something was amiss, he wanted it contained.

With these worries in mind, he headed toward the women's quarters. Traversing the halls, he fortuitously found Salene almost at once and called to her. Small groups of women suddenly stopped their conversations and edged closer, as if they had heard the urgency in his voice and wanted to catch every word that passed between them. To their disgruntlement, Lain suavely offered Salene an arm. Taking it, she walked beside him unquestioningly.

As the halls emptied, he told her of the strange occurrence, concluding, "I am unsure of how to provide for her needs. You will aid me in this?"

"Of course."

They entered an empty room.

"Where is she?"

"I don't know."

Lain circled the perimeter of the room. "There's no one here," he repeated in disbelief. "I don't know what to make of it." Never before had his guards failed.

"I will speak with my friend Malov. The name Shrie sounds familiar," she said pensively.

"No matter," Lain said a little too quickly, pressing his lips together. "Perhaps the situation is more pressing than I had anticipated."

"I hope she is no quisling."

"I am positive she is not a traitor," Lain mused confidently.

"Then let us hope she does not fall into enemy hands," the healer said grimly. "For willingly or not, she would lead them to us."

Skytrue dashed through the hallway and into the underground cavern. She heard the shouts of guards behind her but ignored them. She had his ring and his alliance. That was enough. She had to get to her people and give them hope. She would not delay. The rebels had to gather before it was too late, for late already the time had become.

"Therefore, strengthen your feeble arms and weak knees. 'Make level paths for your feet,' so that the lame may not be disabled, but rather healed."
Hebrews 12:12–13

Chapter 15

Roken lumbered out of the Great Hall; the sound of clanging plates and chatting waiters faded behind him. His stomach was in knots from eating, dancing, and eating again—not an agreeable mix.

"Well I ate five nights' worth tonight. I will sleep pretty well even if it is only for four hours!" Roken exclaimed, rubbing his gorged stomach amorously.

"Healers sleep in the medical ward. You never know when injured scouts or spies might return from unsuccessful quests. Besides, the nighttime is everyone's favorite time to fall ill or trip and break a bone," Salene informed him comically.

"Oh," Roken mocked extreme interest. "Is that why the healers are so short? You never get enough sleep. Lack of sleep stunts your growth, you know."

"Sir Roken, I am a mere inch shorter than you, and yes, I did know that lack of sleep stunts your growth."

Roken released a huge yawn. "I must be stunting my growth right now; I should be asleep."

Salene rolled her eyes. "You're falling asleep before the toddlers, Roken."

"Well," Roken stated, "it would be very ladylike of you to let me go to bed on time, Salene."

"It's not my fault we were having fun."

"Okay, you—" Roken was interrupted by Lain's heavy steps and the calling of Salene's name.

Salene frowned. "Roken, you'll have to walk without me; the ward is down the hall on your left. You'll see it." She waved goodbye to him as she trotted down the hall to meet Lain.

"Bye," Roken muttered to himself as he yawned obnoxiously and groggily made his way to the medical ward. He swung the doors open and was astonished to see an active room. Rubbing his eyes to block out the unpropitious situation, he determined to slip unnoticed into the back room. As he was not in his robes, he managed to evade the other healers' notice and thus avoid an assignment. Feeling rather pleased with himself, Roken slunk into a small room with five bunks and sunk into a vacant, lower bunk.

Corious lingered outside the hall, chatting with Jenny, her brother, Ree, and Malov. Everyone had either settled into a pleasant food coma or raged about in a busy furor. Both Corious and Ree fell into the latter category. The women had never seen the men's mouths open and close so quickly. Malov was convinced Ree had spoken more words than he had in a year, and Corious was working towards becoming the worst story-teller ever.

"So I thought, amazing! This place is awesome! We went in thinking we'd be in and out in a few minutes. Well, turns out I fell in this hole that was about what, Ree? Maybe twenty feet deep?"

"Yes," Ree agreed readily, "maybe more. You took a pretty good fall."

"Then I decided to try and do this maneuver to get myself out of there and save myself some embarrassment. Well, I did what I usually always do: embarrass myself more! I ended up at the very top only to slip and fall the twenty feet all over again. Believe me, twice was more than enough."

Ree laughed as Corious lowered his head and pretended to punch his shoulder. "We had to drag you out of there. I didn't know you were so heavy, Corious."

"Well I'm sure Malov has noticed your overhanging gut," Corious fibbed.

After Corious and Ree had regained a semblance of self-control, Jenny asked curiously, "So how did you reach the end of the swamp?"

"Well," Corious started, "we went under it, actually."

"Nasty! You swam through that stuff?"

Malov supplied an unembellished answer. "No, we went through the underground caves, the same ones Corious fell in."

Corious cleared his throat loudly when Malov mentioned his name. "That place was creepy. I never knew I needed to talk that much until I found out I couldn't for those few minutes."

"Trust me, Corious, we know you like to talk," Ree chided. "I don't think Malov, Jenny, or I have gotten in more than four words at one time!"

"Ree, it is called social skills. Something you need training in," Corious suggested, patting Ree empathetically on the shoulder.

"If that's my only problem, I'm doing pretty well." Ree stated, "But back to our story, which we probably won't finish due to Corious's choleric nature."

"Yes," Corious said loudly. "We went through these passages and halls until we came to one where this huge Kalulukian on a lizard gave this little talk. At the end, Shrie left for her tribe, and we continued to Quantus Plain."

"Wow!" Jonas, Jenny's brother, marveled. He was eleven. "Did you slay any officials on the ship battle?"

JULIE AND RYAN DICKERSON

Ree and Corious exchanged glances. "We fought only the ones that endangered us personally, and they attacked first mind you," Ree answered diplomatically.

"Wouldn't all officials be endangering you personally?" Jonas pointed out.

"Yes, Jonas, you're right. Ree fries his brain when he thinks too much."

Ree caught Corious in a headlock. "Well, Jonas, ladies, I think it's time we wrap up the evening. We'll hopefully see you both tomorrow. Good night!"

Jenny and Jonas said their farewells while Ree let go of Corious's head.

"Well, I must say," Malov stated, hiding a subdued grin, "for being captains, you have not matured. You are a sight to see, still teasing each other."

Ree and Corious shamefully stopped bickering.

"Oh, you're hopeless. You didn't even catch that was a joke?" Malov exclaimed.

"I knew," Corious assured her, "but you know, you had Ree thinking too hard again, and he just couldn't handle all that pressure."

Ree reached to grab Corious, but Corious dashed away. "I'll leave you two alone for a moment. I am going to get washed up for bed; goodbye!"

The two waved as Corious rounded the corner with his cape flowing behind him.

Corious sauntered down the hall at a leisurely pace. He passed a flight of stairs and saluted two guards at the bottom. "Did you men come to the ceremony?" Corious asked, figuring he may as well be friendly.

The guards did not know what to do.

"Well," Corious said in a hush, "they have all the leftovers in the pantry. If you did not go, you should grab some. It's delicious. If anyone asks, tell them Captain Corious sent you. Trust me, I know Captain Marcelus; he'll understand."

The guards stared at each other. They only took orders from Lain or a sober captain.

Corious failed to realize he was neither and laughed. "What a man wants most is what a man can't have," he stated softly. He stepped down from the last step and surveyed the halls spanning to his left and right; he had no idea where the wash-room was. After a moment's deliberation, he trusted his intuition and continued going straight. Nearby, a group of girls chatted in front of an open doorway. As he approached, they eyed him with coquettish smiles and began to whisper. It was the perfect opportunity to request directions.

Corious tossed aside his cape and flashed them a dazzling grin. "Would any of you ladies happen to know the location of the washroom? I'm terribly unfamiliar with this place," he stated politely.

The girls broke out in a chorus of answers.

"Well, I received more than I asked for! A direction is just fine though, thanks."

Several shy girls blushed or giggled, but an assertive girl with blonde hair cut them off. She pointed a definitive finger into the distance. "It is one corridor down; there will be a stone entrance with no door except for a piece of leather hanging from the top. Would you like me to show you there?" She batted her eyelashes. She was extremely pretty and seemed to know it.

"I believe your excellent description will be more than adequate, my lady, but I do appreciate your offer. Night to you all!"

Corious turned on the heel of his boot and departed at a comfortable pace. *And I think I trip over my tongue,* he thought as he shook his head. He found the desired room and showered with the cool water spurting from a hole in the wall. *Almost like the waterfalls of the jungle.* Other holes lined either side of the room like soldiers at attention. Drying his damp body with a fresh towel, he considered himself lucky to have showered alone; the idea of a communal washroom had never appealed to him. *Privacy is luxury!* He rung out his hair, dressed, and then proceeded to victoriously grace the nocturnal halls one last time. The girls had disappeared. *They probably tired of waiting for me,* he thought smugly; but the reliable guards remained in their places.

"Hello!" he called informally. "How was the food?" he asked, forgetting that they had not gone to get any.

"Great!" one exclaimed humoring him. "I am glad I took your advice, Captain. My stomach and I thank you for it!" His friend rubbed his stomach with wide eyes. Both seemed to be laughing at him; he did not understand why.

Corious walked faster, suddenly feeling the overwhelming need to lie down and sleep. In front of their room, Ree was talking with Malov but stopped and said a normal hello to Corious who hurriedly reciprocated the salutation. As he jumped inside, the new captain undid his cape broach and untied his boots. With another, quick brush of his hand, he removed his ceremonial garments before dropping into bed and dreaming of dancing, food, and Jenny.

Roth blinked. Propping himself up with an arm, he shut his eyes and opened them again. They burned, bloodshot from several days of continuous smoke. Lain had requested a final layout of the crop fields and farms, severely limiting the amount of time which Roth could afford to spend at the ceremony. After dancing to a couple of songs and eating a hearty meal, he had subsequently left without bothering to say his proper goodbyes. The rest of his time had been spent sketching myriads of ideas for the tree farm. To his utmost frustration and disappointment, his work had been futile. To be completely accurate in his design, he would need to scout the land methodically.

Roth yawned and slid off his comfortable bed. Time was impossible to tell, but when he heard people outside, he concluded it was early morning. Painstakingly, he extricated himself from his twisted shirt and lumbered to the washbasin where he removed his pants. To his delight, the water was still warm. After eagerly scrubbing all evidence of grime and sweat from his body, Roth used his cape to towel down and then squeezed the water from the red cloth. He would later send his other clothes to the washroom to be dried and ironed, but for now he was too much in a hurry and too paranoid to relinquish his only spare pair of pants to strangers. Instead, he grabbed a writing board, an ink pen, and a dagger, placing them in a satchel secured to his cloak by a broach. With his one arm now free to open the door, he slipped out and managed to avoid awakening his friends in the adjacent room.

Down the hall, guards paraded through what would have been the commons if Quantus Plain were outdoors. Others drilled in the Great Hall, and there Roth recognized Marcelus instructing soldiers in an intricate technique. Roth clung cautiously to the perimeter of the room. Roiling the revered guards would be the last thing he wanted to do, though the temptation to request an escort did assail him. In an attempt to blend suavely into his surroundings, he pretended that he too existed in a state of perpetual occupation. He nodded to a few passersbyers, scanned the lines of guards, and then walked to the officers' room with what he hoped looked like an authoritative swagger. The door to his destination, the political fulcrum of Quantus Plain, was open, revealing the small luxury of bunks with carved shelves for the officers' belongings. Stairs at the opposite end of the room led to a second story. Roth excitedly took a step forward but was abruptly stopped as two spears shot from both sides of the doorway. His way was barred. Two guards pivoted on their heels, expertly aiming their spears at his chest.

"What is your business here and with whom do you wish to speak?" a guard spat forcefully.

"I was hoping to reach Lord Perry. I have a request," Roth said icily.

The guards did not reply, but one left, presumably to find Perry. Roth expectantly tapped his foot, but the remaining sentinel did not move his spear to permit an entrance. Roth sighed impatiently. Beyond the guard he could see numerous side rooms with several guards patrolling the area. Several captains discussed tactics and battles while they donned their boots or capes. The room felt comparably warmer to his own which was always surprisingly cool. Minutes later, Roth heard the clatter of metal and heavy boots signaling Perry's arrival. The captain came down the stairs two at a time, grabbing a torch from the wall as he went.

"No," he was saying, "I fought with him; he's a darn good cook too. Learn to recognize friend from foe. What has Marcelus told you about our new policy towards visitors?"

The guard said nothing but pointed in Roth's direction and saluted Perry before disappearing.

"Ah, hello, Roth! Miss me, did you?" Perry greeted him warmly.

"To the contrary. I actually need some of your men and possibly your advice," Roth declared, shaking Perry's hand vigorously.

"Yes, you're in charge of starting that farm."

"I'm glad you've skipped to the point. Shall we discuss this over breakfast?" Roth suggested.

"You're a man after my own heart, Roth." Perry dismissed the guards who would otherwise tail him once he left the room.

On their way out, they passed through the Great Hall where Marcelus had mustered his soldiers. Infantry, pike men, archers, and even some cavalry riding Mali-Malis had assembled dutifully for inspection. All soldiers wore the same simple but regal uniform with body armor or leather leg protectors strapped to their shins and thighs. Some carried large quarterstaffs, and at different commands, they twirled their weapons in unison. Most wore black, leather boots and a simple tunic made of rough cloth to protect their skin from the sharp grasses of the plains outside. The color was noncommittal; it appeared tan at one angle and green at the next, camouflaging its respective soldier with the undergrowth. Men riding the Mali-Malis wore helmets, and several foot soldiers were privileged enough to bear mail. The quality of weapons ranged from new to ancient, but each soldier held his proudly. Roth marveled as the neatly arrayed rows moved swiftly under Lain's command.

"Impressive, eh?" Perry commented. In awe of the army that he would soon join, Roth had stopped walking entirely.

"Indeed."

The proud smile melted from Perry's face. "But they still need much more training, much more. They're fearsome here, but on the battlefield I fear the worst."

"At least you know their courage will not fail."

"What allows you to say that so confidently?"

"If I know the men and women of Quantus Plain correctly, then I can promise you they shall not run, not even when the merciless fist of the enemy pounds them."

"You are so sure," Perry sighed. "Even so, their courage will not save them. But come now, one thing at a time. Breakfast—and then talk of our food supply." They swiftly passed the assembly. The clanking of their boots' heels chased their elongated shadows.

Roth pushed open the door to the pub, welcoming the smoky smell which had become so familiar; it smelled of warmth on a winter day and of meat cooking over a roaring fire. Finding a small, isolated table in the corner, the men waited for a server. One came shortly.

"Sausage and eggs," Roth said. "And a bitter brew of coffee," he added as an afterthought.

"Sorry, no sausage today," the waiter apologized politely. "The supply trains are a little late."

Perry eyed Roth, as if to point out how necessary a farm would be.

"Just eggs then." He would have his work cut out for him.

"And you, Master Perry?"

"Same."

"It will be several minutes."

Perry cleared his throat. "You see what I mean when I say we need an alternate food source? How am I to keep my men healthy without meat?"

"You keep adding to my responsibility," Roth grumbled, "first a farm and now livestock."

"You know hunting isn't an option. It would busy men needed for the army. Plus," Perry continued matter-of-factly, "all too soon we would deplete the population of animals in the surrounding area and would be forced to search territories beyond what safety allows. Not to mention the damage done to the ecosystem by destroying so many animals."

"I will find a way."

"Good, I was hoping you would say that. I already canceled our supply train, and the men who formerly worked the carts will join the army. But don't rush," Perry reassured Roth, "our stores should last us awhile." Perry stalled as the waiter brought them their food.

"Thank you," Roth said absentmindedly as the food was put in front of him.

The waiter hurried away and Perry continued, "Yes, as I was saying, you have a rough plan. Let's hear it." He picked up a fork and took a bite of eggs, washing it down with the steaming coffee.

Roth pushed his eggs to the side of his plate. "I have made a list of the produce stored in the pantry and of the fresh things we will need daily. There is a dearth of the plants and herbs needed for the healers. I don't want to dig into the stores we have if possible."

He handed Perry the list.

"It's quite long," Roth pointed out needlessly. "Providing the constricting space I have to work with, I would deem it untenable to satisfy the requirements. As it is, the menu will be limited, and food distributions, or rations, will have to start being issued."

"People won't like that."

"People will have to like it, and this is war not a restaurant. People will be happy to eat three times a day."

"Continue."

"The food supply cannot be placed anywhere the officials might stumble upon. It cannot be in the open fields, as would be optimal, and as I formerly mentioned at the council meetings."

"Why not?"

"It would entail putting too many men in the open to protect it. It would be easy to spot and easy to burn. If our food burns, no matter how protected we are in here, we will die."

"So where do you plan on growing these things?"

"A few places. For the low lying herbs and plants, I want to build a room off the medical ward near the hot spring. The temperature will be constant, and the water underground will be readily available to make the plants self-sufficient. Seeds can be obtained from the drying plants the medical ward already has."

"What about light? The plants will need light."

"That is the tricky part, and the main reason why only a small room for the medical needs will be underground."

"Will they grow by torch light?"

"Even if they did, it would be too risky to have torches in a garden. I am proposing skylights."

"Any one could see in."

"Wrong. Right over that area is the new scout tower, made of stone which will not burn. This tower will be well fortified. We will construct minute hatches which can be opened during the day. These small hatches will let in light but not people."

"Could arrows fit through these hatches?" Perry asked worriedly

"They would."

"So these hatches would also provide a way, if the tower was taken, to shoot up at the enemy."

"Precisely."

"I shall ensure their construction at once. But how do you propose to build the inserts with stone?"

"That I will show you later. They are already completed. Logan does excellent work."

"Wonderful. Have you also then initiated the building of the other room?"

"For that, I have awaited your consent."

"Wait no more."

Roth drained half of the coffee from his cracked mug. He had never talked so much in his life. "So that is taken care of."

"It is. What about the main food supply and the livestock?"

"The main food supply shall be farmed in the trees."

"The trees!" Perry choked on his drink and tried to smother it with a cough. Perry's reaction pleased Roth.

"Not in just any tree, Perry, but in the tallest, sturdiest trees. If the officials are stupid enough to clear the surrounding area of trees and put themselves in the open, very unlikely for cowards to do, then we simply would have the advantage in battle, kill them, and start over."

Perry remained confused. "How do we build farms in the trees?"

"I have experimented. We burrow under the tree and hollow the trunk so men can climb inside. When the workers emerge from the main trunk and reach the high branches, the canopy will cover most of their activity, and the plants should blend with the surrounding foliage."

"But where do we plant these plants?"

"For the vines bearing fruit, we shall simply plant them at the base of the tree, and the plants will wind themselves among the others. For the more conspicuous plants, we will dig troughs in the tree branches, fill the troughs with dirt, and plant."

"And this will not weaken the tree?"

"I had Hitachi examine my plan. He is an engineer and has drawn rough blueprints examining the amount of weight per square inch the tree can bear et cetera. We can only plant so much in each tree, but we have a profusion of trees."

"Interesting, I will believe it when I see it. But I have faith in you, even if I do not understand it all."

"Do I have permission to begin?"

"Yes, but you can only farm a couple of trees to start, you understand, just to make sure the idea works."

"We will need to begin farming as many trees as possible if we wish to yield a crop by the time our stocks diminish. It is a risk we have to take."

Perry calculated the jeopardy. The fate of Quantus Plain bore heavily in his hand.

"I will think on this," Perry mumbled, disturbed. "Now for the livestock," he said curiously as he finished his eggs. "How will you devise a way to solve this dilemma?"

Roth beamed. "Livestock is the simpler plan."

"Good, I'm glad to here it."

"I was being sarcastic."

"Oh," Perry said as the waiter came back to clear his plate.

"Are you finished?" the waiter asked, seeing Roth's food strewn on the plate.

"Ah, not yet."

"Take your time; I'll be back when you're done. More coffee?"

"Yes please and thanks," Roth said as the waiter managed to balance three dishes on one arm. Poised like a tightrope walker in a balancing act, the waiter did not drop a single item.

"The livestock?" Perry prompted.

"The livestock," Roth repeated. "The livestock will also be in three expansive rooms under the scout towers for the same purpose as the medicine herbs. Similar hatches will be constructed. Our animals must be able-bodied. No weak ones shall be bred."

"What types of animals? And do we know anyone who can breed them?"

"I would volunteer myself to that job, but with one arm..."

"Right, um..."

"No matter, I will supervise. Do you have any younger men not needed for military service?"

"Plenty."

"Good. I shall teach them. You will recruit one for me?"

"Besides a boy to help with the livestock and workers to build your rooms, what else will you need? You have blueprints from Hitachi, I assume."

"You assume correctly. I will need straw and animals."

"Animals?"

"Animals."

"Where do you expect me to get you animals?"

"The forest of course."

"How many and what type?"

"We'll need at least seven of each type: five female and two male. Don't get them until the rooms are finished. We'll need moracs, clukokians, and pigs."

"I am unfamiliar with these names. From what region do you originate?"

"West," Roth said vaguely.

"Ah," Perry said. "Shall you explain to me then, the appearances of such creatures?"

"Moracs," Roth began as if reciting a memorized piece, "are bulky creatures, perhaps the size of an oversized dog. They are known for their milk and methodical ways. They should not be hard to capture."

"I know of what you speak. We call them corionas. Will they not need exercise?"

"They are lazy creatures that will not run unless forced. No, they need not exercise."

"Clarify, for me, the other two."

"The second type, clukokians, is a small bird creature, rather feisty in disposition and peevish. They seldom fly, but are able to flap ten feet in an awkward fashion. Males are brightly colored; the females are duller. They produce funny clucking noises, hence their name, and—"

"Of course! They live in abundance in the surrounding area. While moracs, as you call them, chew the cud, what do clukokians eat?"

Roth paused. "Actually...I'm not...maybe they...oh, right," Roth said remembering, "they eat seeds."

"Seeds are sparse and precious."

"Well, I think they'll actually eat anything you throw to them as long as it looks like a seed."

Perry laughed lightly. "Whatever you say."

"Their eggs are also numerous but need to be stored in the colder caverns if we plan to save them."

"That is understood. The last animal, you called it a pig?"

"Perhaps you call them quogs?"

"Quogs! Those are messy little creatures."

"But delicious nevertheless."

"Right again, Roth. Does this conclude our discussion?"

"I believe it does."

"Excellent, I shall dispatch men right away," Perry stated loudly, getting up from his chair and pushing it back under the table with a scraping noise.

"I'll check on the progress they have made with the first tree after I finish my eggs."

"By the time you finish, it will be lunch."

Roth just began eating, and with a full mouth he said goodbye as Perry departed from the pub. Roth chewed, swallowed, and slumped backward as his eyelids drooped. It had been a long night, drilling through stone to make the hatches with the dust in his eyes. He inspected the fuzzy blueprints with overworked eyes, and the overwhelming lassitude of sacrificing a badly needed night's rest assaulted his system. Roth could not give in to sleep; the progress of the farm as well as its efficiency rested solely on his shoulders, and the beginning stages were the most crucial. He had yet to designate other trees for farming, and he needed to discover a way to transport the food safely underground to the stores. There was so much to do, and he was so tired. Maybe if he rested his eyes for a minute...His hope for a quick nap was dashed as the waiter returned.

"Done?"

"Sure," Roth said, jerking up from his sitting position, knocking the entire table over as he stood. "By the gods of the nine moons," he exclaimed under his breath.

"Excuse me?" the waiter asked courteously.

"Nothing. Sorry about the mess," he said gloomily as he attempted to fix the fallen table with one arm. The waiter efficiently cleared the mess. Thankfully, a scattering of people filled the pub; not many had seen Roth's accident.

"Don't worry; I got the rest," the waiter said picking the last plate off the ground.

"Thanks."

"No problem," the young boy said. Halfway to the kitchen, the waiter paused and retraced his steps, as if searching for something he had lost. As Roth swung open the pub door, the boy strode gracefully towards him. Roth let the pub door bang shut.

The boy shrunk back from the noise but then said meekly, "Please do not be angry with me, but I could not help but overhear what you and Lord Perry discussed as I bused the other tables. I really like animals, and when you said you would need people to help care for and breed them, well, I thought I might just, well, you know."

"Help?"

"Yes," he said with a gleam of hope.

"Are there many waiters on this shift?"

"More than enough."

"Talk to the head of the pub; report back to me."

"Now?"

"I won't wait all day."

Precariously balancing the last evidence of Roth's disaster, the boy bustled through the crowded room and kitchen door. After several minutes, the waiter hurried back.

"It's fine if I join you," he announced breathlessly.

"Come then."

"Where are we going?"

"Do not fear, you will have your time with the animals, I promise. First, I need your help finding Lord Perry. I wish to tell him that we no longer need extra men to capture the animals. I think we can handle that task between the two of us."

The boy started to run, but Roth caught him by the back of the shirt.

"I'm not done. Before that, you'll have to help me investigate the progress of the tree farms. Can you read and write?"

"I can."

"Then you will take notes on the progress. This will be your responsibility. Lastly, I want you exempt from all other responsibilities with the exception of training for battle. Do you still wish to do this?"

The boy's eyes shone. "Definitely."

"Good. Call me Roth. Your name would be?"

"Bill."

"Bill it is. Now go find Lord Perry and meet me at the stairwell that leads to the outside, and bring a knife with you."

Obediently, the boy burst from the room. Roth strode after him. He would have to secure some rope and a sturdy cloth bag. His heart pumped with adrenaline. It would be wild catching twenty-one untamed animals, but he was sure Perry would have the rooms ready by sunset. Hitachi had laid out the plans plainly and concisely. With the outside buildings completed, there would be plenty of workers to build him four rooms. Roth began to hum an old sailing tune as he proceeded to raid the storage room.

Perry found Lain in the same spot as he had before; he approached Lain's chiseled form.

"My, aren't you happy today, Lord Perry."

Perry stopped in his tracks. He had barely reached Lain's turned back. "Should I be scared, worried, or amazed, Lain, by your mind-reading abilities?"

"Neither. I know when you're happy because your stride is looser and the heel of your boot makes a distinct clicking noise."

"You've known me too long."

"What news?"

"We should have a running farm shortly."

"That is good. This is a crucial stage for Quantus Plain, Perry."

"I know, my Lord."

"We have to prepare."

"I know this."

"We have to become greater than our opponent in mind, spirit, and body."

"We do."

"We have to fight."

"We have to fight," Perry repeated.

Both men stared at each other grimly. It was during this eternal moment when Bill erupted onto the scene.

"Roth and I are going to check the tree farms and capture the animals we need," he said in one, rapid sentence.

"Tell him I'll have the rooms ready."

"The farms are already in progress?" Lain seemed pleased.

"Yes, the process has begun."

"Excellent. What is this talk of rooms being readied?"

"I am to finish four underground rooms in the six hours given to me this day."

"Four rooms," Lain said blankly, "was I informed?"

"The blueprints should be getting to your desk right about now. I am sorry I did not report back to you sooner."

Lain did not answer immediately. "I trust all is according to my plan."

"It is."

"Then I shall review these ideas. Where are these rooms to go?"

"Under the scout towers."

"They will not weaken the support?"

"We need to clean up, square off, and add on. I believe the area is already cavernous, but its structure is sound. Hitachi's plans include complicated formulas to prove its stability. I do not understand them myself, but the concept appears systematic."

"Take whatever resources you need to do this. If you need me, I will probably be in one of the training rooms."

Tar woke with a start. He had overslept. The festivities had gone so long, and he had stayed up even later. Thinking about the ceremony, he remembered Lain's gift and decided to finally open it. Tossing aside his sheets, he swung his legs over the edge of his cot and stretched. Reaching over to a small, adjacent table, his hands fumbled along its surface. When they connected with a parcel, he tested its weight; the object was substantially heavy. As he traced its outline, his fingers slipped into an indent where the pieces of folded cloth met. Carefully, Tar unwrapped the gift: a sword and a leather glove. Curious and amazed, Tar felt the hilt's intricate engravings come to life. Exotic animals, warriors, and battles leapt under his fingertips until the handle ended in a swinging, silk tassel. He replaced his old sword with the new. Sitting on his bed, he fit the glove onto his hand. It was soft on the inside but coarse on the outside. He searched the cloth for its mate but found none. *That's strange,* he thought. Had he somehow lost it? At this moment, Aban chose to stick his head in the door.

"Just wake up, Tar?" he asked.

"Pretty much. How about you, Aban?" Tar asked, recognizing his friend's familiar voice.

"Not too long ago. Why are you wearing a falconer's glove?" he questioned as he got closer.

"Is that what it is? I was looking for the other one—"

"You only need one to be a falconer."

"A falcon, you say. Why would Lain give me a falconer's glove?"

"Well, it protects your forearm from the talons of the bird when it sits on your arm."

"But I don't have a falcon," Tar said, still lost.

"Lain does," Aban said quietly. "I hear her name is Faylene, and she is the Queen of all birds in the air. She obeys only Lain and is more intelligent and beautiful than many a woman."

"Do you think Lain means for me to care for Faylene?"

"I don't know," Aban shrugged. "Anyway," he continued, as if the matter was done and over, "let's do something. A sword class begins in ten minutes."

"Sure," Tar said as he pulled off the glove. Tar's mind, however, was far from the sword class. It was trenchantly reviewing the smells, tastes, and sounds of the ceremony. Placing the glove under his pillow, he wondered why Lain had chosen him. Neither gift was cheap, and Tar was blind; he probably could never appreciate the beauty of the sword or the sight of a falcon in flight. *Why then, of all the things Lain could have given me, did he give me these?*

What Tar did not know, was that more than any, he could appreciate the whish of a perfectly honed blade through the air, a secure hilt that melted the sword into his hand, the whoosh of a falcon's wings as it returned to its master, and the grip of its talons on a waiting arm. These two things, such small gifts given with an open heart, would change him, showing him a world he had never before imagined.

Roth blinked the dirt from his eyes. He could not spare a hand to rub the perspiration from his brow. Halfway up the trunk of the tree, his one calloused hand gripped the rope ladder. Behind him, Bill carried a canvas bag over his shoulder. So far, all appeared sound and well-built. When he finally came to the round opening in the vertical tunnel, Roth took a few deep breaths to settle his pulse. He wanted to appear at ease and in control when he surveyed his newest idea and its workers. Roth hauled himself over the top, and an incredible scene mushroomed before his eyes.

Sunlight streamed through the canopy of leaves. Workers squatted unnaturally in the branches. Occasionally, they consulted their plans as they busily dug troughs, filled them with dirt, and planted seeds. They did not notice at first as Roth wandered through the giant limbs with relative ease. Bill made quick sketches of bean troughs, marking the locations of the tomatoes and jotting down progress reports. Garbed in camouflage, the workers blended in perfectly with the tree. Roth marveled at the workers' diligence. He had just reported the plan to the Captain of Agriculture, Lord Valitus, late last night, but already the work was in full swing. He made his way over to the center of the tree where a small platform of wood had been built to support a sentry. Right now, it supported the booted feet of Valitus.

"This is inimitable work," Roth told himself out loud, proud his rough plan had turned into the brilliant invention before his eyes.

"Indeed," Bill commented, "these men sure work more cooperatively than the mess boys in the pub kitchen."

"Bill, let me see those notes."

Bill scribbled some other report he had forgotten to add and then handed it to Roth.

"Let's see," Roth mumbled, rifling through the notes Bill made. "Bean plants: done and given water. Repairs completed on irrigation troughs, and the rest of the plants under progress. Looks like everything is well under way; but we'll have a chat with Lord Valitus to make sure."

They trudged forward.

"Hello, Lord Valitus," Roth greeted the stern man. "My name is Roth, and this is Bill; we're here to supervise."

Pretentiously, Valitus raised an eyebrow as he surveyed Roth and Bill. "What rank do you possess to check up on me, may I ask?"

Roth smiled tightly. "Sir, these plans were designed by me for you and for the others; these plants will go into your stomach. So I tell you with all the civility I can muster, to the ditches with your rank. I'm a regular peasant yet I'm about to feed over a thousand people."

Offended, Valitus refused to answer.

In exasperation, Roth threw his hand in the air. "I'm sorry you caught my rude side. If you could kindly tell me how things are turning out here, I'd appreciate it a lot," Roth said, the brusque edge worked out of his voice.

"Well, Roth, feeder of thousands," he started mockingly, "we are doing very well, and we should be on our way to the next tree by mid-day."

"Splendid!" Roth stated, slapping his thigh. "Now, Bill, we'll let Lord Valitus be, and we'll get on our way." Roth hastily stalked off with Bill on his heels. When they were out Lord Valitus's hearing, Roth shook his head sourly.

"Of all the prigs I've met, he's got to be one the worst!" Roth told Bill. "Well Roth, feeder of thousands," he mimicked.

Bill snickered. "Where did you learn to stand up for yourself like that?"

Roth snorted obnoxiously. "It's not something you learn how to do, kid; it just happens. After weeks of living with one arm, you inevitably contrive every snide comment known to man."

Glancing at the stump of an arm protruding from Roth's shoulder, Bill felt the horrid question rising from his lips. "How did you?"

"Lose an arm?" Roth finished loudly. Workers in the boughs turned toward the sound of his voice before returning to their labor. The boy seemed embarrassed. Roth continued unabashedly, "One third was broken, another third was shot, and the last third was burned to a crisp."

With wide eyes, Bill demanded, "Really?"

"No," Roth sneered sarcastically, "I felt like randomly chopping off my arm one day, so I did." Roth's cynical nature quieted Bill, and the boy tilted his head toward the ground in shame. The boy's display made Roth feel uneasy. He shifted his weight awkwardly. "Sorry, kid, I barely slept last night, and anger comes easily in sleep's absence. Don't take my ranting too seriously." Bill lifted his eyes cautiously.

"Hey," Roth slapped Bill on the back good naturedly, "let's get some quogs, huh? They're the closest little devils around here."

Showing his approval, Bill rocketed down the tree trunk and motioned eagerly for Roth to do the same. Roth did as he was bid as promptly as his disability would let him, but his pace remained painstakingly slow for Bill's impatience. Once the two were on the ground, they set off at a fast walk, hugging the tree line.

A bell clanged harshly in the next room, throwing the blanket of sleep from the bed of Roken's mind. He tried desperately to remember where he was. He retraced his steps from last night's party and determined his location in the medical ward. Roken listened as his slightly protruded stomach gurgled distractedly, digesting the food of the previous night. Rubbing the final touch of sleepiness from his eyes, Roken blinked dramatically before studying the tiny room surrounding him.

Each corner hosted four bunks and their corresponding water basins, tables, and cabinets. Bandages and herbs lay scattered on shelves. Otherwise, the room remained bare. The bell echoed vaguely in Roken's mind, and he pondered absently its significance. As he pitched his legs over the side of the bed, flocculent fabric brushed against his leg. He still wore his cape and formal robes. Groggily, he unclipped his cape and robe before lifting his arms over his head in a lazy stretch. With a yawn, he swaggered to the water basin in which he proceeded to dunk his head. In a shower of droplets, Roken whipped his head from the basin, patting his face dry with the sleeve of his robe.

Feeling significantly refreshed, Roken returned to his bunk where it dawned upon him that he knew not a blessed thing about healing; he had merely chosen the profession as the fear of returning to battle overwhelmed him and as Salene had saluted his choice. Thinking of her, he vowed solemnly to become competent at the profession he had chosen. Loosening his belt and smoothing the wrinkles from his beige uniform, he strode outside.

Roken froze. Several female healers rushed by him and were swept into the madness of the room. A cacophonous roar of groans and screams spilt into the hall. A dozen uniformed men, bloody and dirty, lay on beds, and several more were carried in on stretchers. Their previously brown and green scout tunics hung from their shoulders, tattered and red. As another healer flew by him, he gently grasped her arm.

"What happened here?" he questioned, aghast.

"Some scouts encountered officials and were caught in a violent skirmish. These are the rescued ones. Mostly bullet and saber wounds," the lady spat out the report briskly. "Are you new?" she inquired abruptly but not unkindly.

Roken began to feel sick as memories of the battlefield threatened to engulf him. The healer either did not notice his paling skin or she chose to conveniently ignore it.

"Follow me," she said, grabbing his arm and leading him to the bedside of a particularly gruesome scene. At the sight of the man's torn side and mutilated hand, Roken repressed the bile that rose in his throat. The man held his mouth closed tightly, and he stared straight ahead, channeling his energy into maintaining his stolid front.

"It's all right," the healer was saying. "Stay calm. We have two healers on you. There's no way you can fall into a worse condition. We'll fix you up."

"You're lying to him," Roken hissed in surprise.

The healer glared at him, took the man's hand, and grabbed a canteen next to her. "While my friend here is getting your medicine, you drink this." She turned to Roken. "Go get Fursolc; it's in the white chest over near the doorway."

Roken hesitated; he could not read well. She gave him a violent shove, and he set off at an accelerated pace. He wound through the cluttered room until he saw the white chest. Hurriedly lifting the lid, he began sifting through the bags of herbs; and to his dread, they all looked alike. He began to sweat nervously. A hand moved him aside. Salene crouched down and pulled out a bag; surely enough the letters came together: Fursolc.

"Thank you, Salene," Roken whispered before running off with the bag clutched tightly in his hand. He found the bed, and shoved the bag into the healer's hands. She ripped the bag open. In her hand, she crumbled the leaves, letting the light green juice run through her fingers before opening the man's shirt. Roken peered over her shoulder, but recoiled from the grisly site. Mixing the ground leaves with some water, the healer then smeared the gooey concoction onto the man's wound. When the healer poured the mixture onto his side, he did not make a sound, but his rigid hand curled into a fist. Minutes later, he began to drift in and out of consciousness.

"Go get a towel. They're hanging in the back of the room."

"Sure." Roken rocketed to the towels, selected a clean one, and hurried back. He handed the towel to the healer, but she shook her head.

"Dampen the towel with water, fold it, and hold it to his head—that should bring his temperature down." Roken did as he was told and vigilantly placed the cool towel on the scout's head. The man's eyes fluttered open. Roken's heart beat dangerously fast, betraying his edginess.

"Now what?" Roken asked the healer quietly so as not to alarm the scout.

"Wait," the healer told him, working on another mixture.

Roken tensed in anticipation. Due to his lack of experience, he did not feel comfortable being alone with the patient. A healer's duty required more stress tolerance than he had realized. He jerked his head sideways as the door flew open. Two guards entered, carrying another scout on a stretcher. Straightening his lax posture, Roken tapped the healer on the shoulder.

"Is this man stable?" he asked her.

"Yes, thank you for your assistance. If you like, you can take a break."

"Thank you, though I plan to help the man that just came in," Roken told her.

"Another one? That makes fourteen for the day!" she said, exasperated.

Roken repositioned the towel on the man's head and swiftly made his way to the other side of the room near the doorway where the scout was being placed on a bed. There were no other available healers to come to the man's aid. The man writhed in pain and groaned loudly. Roken firmly took the man's shoulders and laid him flat on the cot.

"Keep still," Roken instructed the man. "You'll be fine, don't worry." Roken slid off the man's tunic and cape and unbuttoned his shirt. A lesion similar to the other scout's wound met his eyes, but this laceration was shorter, deeper, and closer to the man's heart. Roken knew he had to slow the bleeding by applying a clean dressing and wrapping the wound. When he finished applying the bandages, he felt the man's head. It seemed to burn through Roken's palm. Immediately, he snatched his hand away to grab a towel. Dampening the cloth with water, he wiped away the sweat and applied the towel slowly, trying not to exacerbate the man's injuries. The man squirmed in agony, and Roken asked a healer for the name of a cogent pain killer.

"Get Aquilonz, and find a good disinfectant if it's a saber wound," the healer answered while hurrying to another bedside. Roken thanked her and ran to find the needed herbs. He could not let this man's life slip away.

Ree crouched in the tall grasses. He and his men approached the banks of the Halfast River in a training exercise. It was time to assert his authority. Corious and his men were somewhere to his right, and Lain was with a larger group to the left.

The idea was to be as invisible as possible. If one team spotted another, they had to tag a member of the opposite group with the white rag signifying a loss. The goal was to reach the river first, slip into its waters, slither up the opposite bank, and find a flag hidden in the forest without losing any men. Ree had lost none of his men so far; he was tied with Lain. Corious had only lost one. Letting his hand down to indicate forward movement, Ree let his men advanced cautiously. As he pushed aside a bushy clump of grass, he came face to face with Lain who not only tagged him with a white cloth but also clamped a hand over his mouth to stop any grunt of regret. Ree frowned. Lain looked too serious.

"Ree," he said in perfect confidence, "there are more than fifty officials crossing the River. This was unexpected, but we must not retreat. We're too close to Quantus Plain; we'd lead them right to it. If you lose more than five men, disperse. Wait for my command and ready the troops." As soon as he whispered these words, Lain vanished into the brush in the direction of Corious's troops. Ree glanced at his ten men.

"Officials ahead. Let's show them the power we possess. I have complete confidence in each of you. Load your bows and await Lain's command. We have the element of surprise on our side."

Sudden fear passed over the men's faces. They were not ready. They were callow recruits who had signed last month. Crouching, ready to assail the enemy, Ree heard the cry of a falcon. At the thought of the ensuing ambush, his heart thudded in his chest.

The falcon circled high in the air before diving four hundred paces from their location. Ree watched intently as the falcon pulled up at the last minute. She had stolen an official's pistol before swooping towards the safety of Lain's arm. The officials were dangerously close, and the situation favored them: open fields, an outnumbered enemy, and a strategically sound location. Ree licked his lips as his men grew antsy behind him.

"Load your bows," he said in a hushed tone. He inspected the men and squinted at the spot Faylene had just been.

"Take aim." He waited for Lain's command. A knife took flight from the hand of one of Lain's men and dug itself into the neck of the commander who toppled from his horse with a short gasp. "Shoot."

Three sets of ten arrows shot into the air. In graceful arcs, they soared into the air and plunged. Bodies falling and yells of pain issued from thirty yards away. Wiping the sweat from his face, Ree readied his hand on his sword and motioned for the next two rounds of shots to be fired. The Shalkans were close.

"Away arrows, out swords," he said low enough to avoid detection. He heard someone fidget in the brush. The men slung their bows over their shoulders and took out the weapon issued to them. A hand planted itself on his shoulder, and the face of his second in command officer, Captain Davory, appeared next to his.

"This is dire," he commented blandly. "We've always had the upper hand in our other operations."

"Hold," he said sternly. The men kept still. The sound of marching boots reached their ears, and the vibrations undulated through the heels of rebels' boots. All crouched, perfectly motionless. Some held their breath. When the enemy was seconds from stumbling upon them, Ree exploded from hiding with an earsplitting war cry and rushed at the closest official.

The last arrows were loosed, and several found their marks before the two sides converged. Ree attacked ferociously, driving back the astonished officials in a trail of blood. A nearby Shalkan soldier prepared to load his musket. Ree pushed aside the final weeds separating him from the man. The official shouldered his musket and took aim. Ree stopped and staggered. He lunged backwards and tried to take cover, but the official had locked in on him. Ree gasped for air, expecting the loud explosion. It did not come. Lain's sturdy form had shot from the brush and nailed the man in the ribs with a violent jab. The official cried out as he crumpled to the ground with a broken ribcage. Lain turned gracefully, and in one fluid movement, cut an official from his horse while reaching for the reins. He gripped Ree firmly by the shoulder and flung him onto the horse.

"Get the wounded out of here!" he shouted. Ree sat straight in the saddle and directed the horse towards the injured. He dismounted, noticing two men limping desperately from the battle.

"Ride, and get Marcelus and his men. Tell them to come to the Halfast River!" The men saluted and rode hastily; even with their injuries, they were excellent riders. Ree rallied his men. Two more from his group were injured—one seriously. His group now numbered six in all, including himself. There had been five casualties. According to Lain's order, he was supposed to pull back. Ree had little time to think.

"Davory!"

Davory came over to Ree; a gash cut across his side. "Yes?" he asked breathlessly.

"I want you to assist Lain on the field. I'm going to lead a sortie of men to the rear," Ree explained.

Davory slid through the grass.

"Load your bows," Ree instructed the remaining men. "We'll pick off the Shalkans from the rear." Ree vigilantly wound his way through the meandering field until he reached the optimal location. "Let's take aim, men."

The rebels, arrayed in their forest tunics, blended into their surroundings. Invisible to the world, they felt invincible for the first time. They could see the officials' torsos above the swaying grass.

"Fire."

At Ree's behest, arrows whizzed by his cheek, tossing a stray strand of his hair into his eyes. Officials fell to their knees.

"Fire!" Two more officials clutched at their chests and stumbled to the ground. Their deaths alarmed the official with the horn. "Flank attack!" he screamed. "Flank attack! Cavalry to the rear—" his warning was cut off as an arrow plugged itself deep into the man's neck. He gurgled, coughed, and then fell with the rest of his men. The rebels shot one last round of arrows before the officials were upon them.

"Retreat," Ree told his men. "Join Corious! I'll keep them at bay."

"But Captain!" one man protested.

"Go!" Ree shouted as he slew the first cavalry rider and dove out of a charging horse's and rider's way. The horse sped past, but the rider was not fooled. Swinging his steed around, he came full speed at Ree. Ree groped wildly to achieve a standing position, but the horse collided with him. He was floating, it seemed, in the air for an eternity, sailing away. The air swirled around him, and then he landed squarely on his head in the water. The wetness brought him to his senses, and he began coughing up the cold, clear water of the Halfast River. His armor felt like an anchor as his weighted arms slowly struggled to break the water's surface.

After a vicious struggle, he surfaced under an overhang. There, he inspected his weapons. He had released his sword upon impact. Poison darts and a hunting knife were his only weapons now. Dragging himself onto the bank, he favored the arm that had been jammed by the horse's chest. Severely dizzy and in shock from the intense impact of his fall, his head swam, his vision blurred, and everything seemed to run into and over each other. He hoped his men had retreated safely. If spotted, they would easily be overrun. As he began to regain full control over his body's functions, a cadaver tumbled from the ledge above.

Leaning forward, Ree strained to identify the corpse. He recognized the dreaded blue coat. He sighed in relief; it was not one of his men. The officials had been pushed to the Halfast River; Lain must have driven them back. In sickening thuds and splashes, entire masses of bodies tumbled from the ledge. Some were still alive, and their hideous screams echoed throughout the plain. Ree knew the ones who survived the fall would be ruthless, and they would be upon him in seconds. He was terribly disoriented, but in a merciful answer to his worries, a line of arrows plunged into the river. Most found their marks. Ree watched as the water diluted the thick, red blood streaming into the current. He had to move. Ree hauled himself out of the water. His fingers dug into the muddy bank, ramming the glop under his fingernails. Eventually, he dragged himself back onto the grassy fields. A hand grabbed his shoulder. Immediately, Ree's reflexes kicked in, and he unsheathed his long knife. He swung it wildly until the hand pulled him straighter. Ree's eyes met Lain's.

He placed his hand in Lain's and whispered, "Thank you," before passing out on the ground. Lain had saved him twice too many times.

Mounted rebel soldiers graced the once primarily blue battlefield. A small number of injured officials were clumped together in the center. Restless, Corious paced the battle ground. He knew the officials would be back with their warships, and he wanted to return to the fort before dusk. Overall, the unexpected operation had been an unarguable victory, and his men had responded spectacularly. He had joined forces with Lain's men early in the battle while Ree had led a flank attack. Twelve men had been injured—three severely. From Ree's group, two men had been trampled while retreating from the cavalry charge. They had suffered broken bones and were in critical condition. It was amazing that they had not died. Lain's group had suffered four casualties while heading the frontal assault. The rest of men had been regrouped and accounted for.

In the end, the rebels had slain thirty-four officials and captured seventeen. The result of the battle and Lain's command had earned Corious's respect. Even now, after toiling for four hours under a sun reigning fiercely in a blue sky, Lain remained passive, untouched by battle or by elements.

"Men, we return home. You fought well and nobly, and for that I will formally address you and the people later today when we hold council. Let the injured mount the Mali-Malis before the healthy. I will leave last."

The men sauntered to the spiders, tired from their long, violent morning.

"My stomach's full of killing. I'm done." A soldier wiped a bloody hand on his uniform.

The men nodded their heads in agreement, riding morosely towards Quantus Plain.

Ree awoke to the familiar rhythm of a Mali-Mali. A sweet scent filled his nose, and for a moment, he thought he was back in the jungle smelling the sugary fruit Shrie always ate. *Where is Shrie?* He speculated in a dreamy trance, *she must be getting some reeds to weave a new basket.* His body, unusually light, floated, and he felt a small smile creep onto his face. Corious would be getting up soon, and then they would teach Tar to use a bow and arrow. Without warning, his body jolted forward, and his eyelids jerked open to soak in the body-drenched battlefield. The sun's fiery radiance outlined the silhouettes of Quantus Plain's outer buildings. The pain sent sharp, throbbing prongs throughout his body. Someone slapped him on the back.

"Stay with me, Ree. Thought I lost you there. It's a good thing Lain picked you up." Ree thought he detected a hint of authentic concern beneath the lighthearted tone.

"I'm with you," he said as a trickle of blood traveled down his lip. "I'm still here."

"Don't worry," Corious assured him, "we'll have you in the medical ward in no time."

"No medical ward."

"Don't squabble with me."

"I've been rescued twice today. That is enough to humble anyone."

"You saved the operation with your flanking maneuver. You are still the formidable, heroic Ree I know. Besides, you always let Shrie tend to you."

"Yeah, but Shrie was different. She didn't pity me; she had that way," he said weakly. "How did my men fare?"

Corious responded grimly, "None have departed from this life yet, but three are in critical condition with wounds greater than your own."

"I failed," Ree said miserably.

"No one failed, Ree. One group could not have won without the other. We're protecting a society here, not just ourselves."

"No medical ward."

"That means I'll have to tend to you."

Ree nodded weakly but happily. "There are few in whom I would trust to do so."

"Why?"

"You are the extension of me."

It was silent for a little while, and then Corious said, "Yeah I guess so."

Marcelus approached. "Ree."

"Marcelus."

"You up to hear something kind of funny?"

"Sure."

"Malov wanted to come."

"Come where?"

"Into battle. She and twenty or so other women had armed themselves."

"You didn't let them come?"

"No. It was too late anyway. I will allow the women to train, but I will not let them enter battle until it's absolutely necessary. Their other jobs are too vital to completely abandon."

"Sounds fair to me."

"They didn't like it. Can you talk to Malov for me?"

"Sure."

"Don't forget. Those women will have my head."

"They looked impressive?"

"Thought they were guards at first."

"That's what I love about Malov; she's remarkable."

"You like your women wild, eh?"

"To a certain extent."

Marcelus shook his head. "It's your life. Anyway, we're almost there. Can you get off the Mali-Mali?"

Ree grunted his approval as he painfully dismounted and limped through the door of the first building. Dust-filled air blasted him in the face.

"They're drilling hatches."

"What for?"

"Council meeting tonight will explain much. I suspect it's about the farms."

"Ah," Ree said as he slipped through the discreetly placed hatch, shielding his eyes from the truculent dust. "I assume the women will be there?"

"Maybe. That's another detail to discuss along with our army."

"Any news?" Corious pressed eagerly, cleaning his sword on his cloak.

"I know no more than you, brother." Marcelus supported Ree on one side, ensuring his friend would not slip down the stairs. "Most of the injured have been transported to the medical ward. Roken has apparently taken charge." Marcelus did not tell them that the medical ward was severely short staffed, and that the staff was hardly more than a little inexperienced.

Roken knelt at the man's bedside, numbing the wound that severed the man's skin as a fault line would the earth. He had already diagnosed a steady set of herbs to combat infection, bleeding, and pain. Since then, the man had fallen into a fitful slumber. Threading the thin needle, Roken prepared to close the spacious slash. The patients nearby averted their eyes as Roken mended the skin as he would a shirt. The last men came through the door with minor wounds and abrasions. Roken tied a knot, washed his hands, and attended to their needs. None of the healers had received a break since the morning. His bladder was packed, but his stomach was empty. As he slid a chair up to his penultimate patient, Roken's legs sighed in relief before cramping relentlessly. Despite the tense situation, Roken opened his mouth in an embarrassingly loud yawn. There were seven empty beds in the medical ward, and Roken thought he might be the next person to fill one.

Roth slipped through the tall grass, often chastising Bill for tripping in an ungainly fashion. He dragged two quogs behind him, annoyed by the fact that their small, rotund bodies could pack both weight and power. Ducking under a scraggly tree branch, he glanced back to ensure Bill was at his heels. The young boy bounced along, unburdened by animals or gear. Roth grimaced as the morning sun bore down upon his back.

"Billy," he began, using Bill's nickname, "we are going to those gnarly trees to start searching for the mating grounds." Bill agreed solemnly as they trekked to the stand of unappealing trees.

Within a dozen minutes, they reached the hilltop. Roth plopped his squealing quogs on the ground and unsheathed his hunting knife. He motioned for Bill to hurry, and the two slunk deeper into the foliage. Roth smacked his lips together obnoxiously when they came upon a bedded area of pine needles and fine dirt. Two moracs snuggled together peacefully, making shrill sounds within their throats.

"Good," Roth muttered, "we'll pick up a male and a female." Bill looked at him curiously, but received no explanation from Roth who tightened the loop on his rope.

"Circle around to the back. If they run, stop them," Roth instructed, though he hardly believed the boy could hold his ground against disturbed, charging moracs. A quog snorted loudly. The moracs stirred.

"Go," Roth told the boy.

He watched in dismay as Bill fervently crashed through the forest, snapping twigs as he went. Roth, with a snarl, dashed from his hiding place. He threw himself into the air and landed squarely on the male's back. Wrestling it to the ground with one arm, he straddled it. The morac thrashed its oblong head wildly. Roth, from his squatting position, cracked his rope like a whip and bound the female's hind legs together with his crude lasso. The morac's seizure-like movements gradually abated. Roth brushed the dirt off his tunic arrogantly as he and Billy subdued the animals. After a painfully long wait, the animals calmed, allowing Roth and Bill to lead them to where Roth had left the spastic quogs which now rolled delightfully in the morac's old dung.

Roth swore quietly, sincerely antagonized by the quogs' antics. He considered roasting them for breakfast.

"Hey, Roth," Bill asked excitedly, "how did I fare?"

"Not terribly," Roth admitted.

Bill gleamed in obvious pride. "According to the plan you told Master Perry, we still need five more quogs, five more moracs, and seven clukokians."

"Good memory. Here, tie up these moracs. Then, we'll find the rest."

Bill happily completed two half hitches and a square knot, securing the sedated moracs to the tree. Stroking their noses, Bill arbitrarily tore up some grass by the roots and presented it to the moracs in the flat of his hand. The moracs sniffed lazily and then licked the greens from his hand.

"Where to next?" Bill asked as the moracs lost interest in his emptied hand.

"Think you can handle catching some quogs by yourself?"

"If you think I can. Males?"

"Get three males and two females. Remember, females have curly tails. I saw a herd down in one of the grass fields. After you catch two, tie them to a tree a few yards from the others."

"What are you going to do?"

"I'll get the rest of the moracs." At this statement, Bill's face fell. "Don't worry," Roth rapidly added, "I would have had you help me, but you did such a great job with these. Plus, our time is running out. Lain mentioned we might have a council later, and I want the animals to be situated in the rooms soon." Roth swallowed.

With any luck, Bill would not see through his extensive lie. Billy nodded leisurely, as if untroubled by Roth's statements, and then saluted Roth in his funny way. Without another word, he headed for the field.

"The other way, Billy," Roth called. Billy stopped and darted the other way like an escaping fugitive. It was time for him to catch the quogs.

Several hours passed before they captured all of the animals. The clukokians had proved irascible and frustratingly fast. Their eggs, which had glistened like little moons in the brush, had been ever so delicately placed in a bucket by Billy while Roth had tried unsuccessfully to ensnare the adults with one arm. More often than not, a hulking Roth had bent forward and tackled the birds, crushing many. Billy had been extremely upset over this, so Roth retired to the frustrating job of quog watching: halting them from becoming dirtier than they already were. If anyone had later seen the two dragging the seven crazy quogs, several drugged moracs, and the caged clukokians in wooden boxes, they would have been treated to an amusing sight.

Fitting the motley herd down the entrances required even more talent.

"Billy, shove him down the stairs," Roth said agitatedly for the fourth time. The clukokians were safely underground, but the quogs and moracs remained upstairs. One morac was halfway through the entrance, making piercing noises of excitement.

"I don't want to hurt him!" Billy exclaimed from upstairs.

"Shove him! He's a big one; he won't feel a thing." The shrilling noise increased to a deafening pitch. "For goodness sakes, Billy, shove him down. You know when they get excited—"

Billy hissed as the morac tried to back out into him. The morac turned and sped for the doorway, knocking Billy over. Uttering curses, Roth jumped the stairs two at a time and threw himself onto the animal. Bill stood sheepishly as Roth thrust the animal firmly down the stairs. Glancing at the older man, Bill waited for a scolding.

Roth simply sighed, "Send the next one down, okay?"

"Okay," Bill called back. As they rolled the quogs down, Corious met Roth with a grim expression on his face.

"What's wrong?"

Corious said confidentially, "Battle at the Halfast River today. It was unexpected. We suspect the Shalkans wait for us. Hurry up here and then head to Lain's."

Bill watched as the captain approached Roth and whispered something in his ear. When he left, he noticed the carefree look had vanished from Roth's face.

"Can I send the next one down?" he asked tentatively.

"That's fine," Roth said distractedly. "How many are left?"

"Two."

"Let's go then."

One of the quogs Bill had set on the stairs snorted. The boy suppressed his laughter. If one of the captains had approached Roth with something serious, he did not want to break the solemn atmosphere. As the last of the quogs entered, Roth sent Bill to check on the progress of the rooms. Bill was happy to report their completion. Perry had even included coops for the clukokians and padded the rooms with straw. Roth and Bill settled the animals in their new environment.

"Billy, you are free to go. Meet me here tomorrow at six. The moracs will have to be milked. I'll get pails from the kitchen."

"What about food and water?"

"Good point."

"I'll get some now," Bill volunteered.

"No, I don't want you going outside without an escort anymore."

"Okay," Bill said, slightly perplexed.

"Go to the kitchen and get the leftover scraps of vegetables and seeds. Feed them that and put water in these buckets. That should work until we find a trough."

"I'll do that. See you tomorrow at six."

"You got it. Bye, Billy."

"Bye, Roth."

After Bill skipped down the hallway, Roth headed directly to Lain's room. He did not bother to wash thoroughly. If the council was as urgent as Corious had insinuated, then the council members would graciously overlook his stench.

As he pushed open Lain's door, the talking behind it halted. Inside, a select group of people represented the population of Quantus Plain. Salene and Malov would speak for the women, and Logan and Hitachi attended with several other engineers; but most of the chairs were reserved for the men of war. Of the numerous officers lining the table's sides, Marcelus, Perry, Corious, and a bandage-swathed Ree were the only ones rewarded with positions alongside Lain at the head of the table.

"Now that everyone is present," Lain began hastily, "we'll begin. I regret waiting so long to call this council, but fortuitously all have arrived. For time's sake, I will be straightforward. Today we were conducting training exercises on the bank of the Halfast when several columns of heavily armed Shalkans proceeded north along the riverbank. Threatened by their proximity to Quantus Plain, we launched an assault. Our cavalry saved us."

A small murmur swept through the crowd.

"How did we muster cavalry soldiers, my Lord?" a stout, burly officer questioned.

"A relevant question, Hans. We summoned average men and bade them to ride. Though callow and hardly able to fight, their mere presence was enough to frighten the enemy. It was a risk we were forced to take. None of our reinforcement troops were injured."

Worry strangled the listeners. Their army had resorted to tricks in order to defeat a minute group of fifty officials. What would happen when the enemy's numbers increased?

Lain cleared his throat. "Since I've briefed you on the military matters, assuming there are no questions, we shall move on. I do not know the medical status on our injured. Salene, would be so kind as to bring us up to date?"

Salene smoothed her stained healer's robe. "There were initially fifteen wounded men, but some have already recovered. Others will leave shortly, no longer in need of our care. Three will be long in recuperating. This morning there were twenty-one healers on duty, including five recent recruits."

As Salene finished, Lain unraveled a worn map of Kurak. It stretched from the southern port of Bacl, to the western Kairn Island, and to the northeastern, arctic Shalku Icefall. Lain brushed his hand over the sepia map, planting a finger on the western port.

"Here," he claimed, "are the ports of Osc and Danresh. They are better known as the western ports. Their scouts have confirmed that ten official warships have set sail from the Shalkan Empire. As of yesterday, the lead ships had reached Valjancar in Fal-Evein and plundered it. They are now leagues past the northern city. On the brighter side, Fal-Evein Separatists have engaged the Shalkan warships from land and have succeeded in sinking one ship. It appears, however, that they are waging a losing war. They have no resources, hardly any men, and few hopes of improving their situation. Meanwhile, the Wathien people own the strategic port of Osc, but they have foolishly rendered themselves useless by declaring neutrality. Shalkans do not respect the boundaries or desires of other nations; it is highly unlikely that they will spare Osc. As we are the best supplied rebel base known to exist," Lain declared, "the burdens of supporting, maintaining, and coordinating a continent-wide, rebel front fall on us. We are therefore planning to send a supply train tonight to the rebels on the edge of the Borderlands. The contents of our carts would include barrels of wine, barrels of fresh water, boxes of salted meat and vegetables, swords, pikes, and shields. We will send about thirty scouts and twenty infantry soldiers as escorts. The trip should last about a month or two at the most. I need your vote to assemble and approve the notion," Lain said in hopeful summation.

The men and two women shuffled in their seats.

"And what, my Lord, will happen when the official scouts annihilate our sluggish supply train?" a man asked bitterly. "Nay, I vote we should keep our men and supplies for ourselves. It is not selfish; no, it would be smart if we kept the fruits of our labor."

"But you will let fellow rebels fall helplessly like grain under the officials' sickles?" Lain asked. A fiery light gleamed dangerously in his dark eyes. "Let us vote. All in favor."

The council chewed on lips and nails in thought, and then gradually, the men and women supporting Lain raised their hands high.

"All against," Lain called.

Again, men raised their hands, and Lain counted them.

"The council has voted, nineteen to twelve, to aid the rebels of the Borderlands." Though his voice was composed, Lain was dismayed. The severe split in votes had rattled his normally unanimous council. Men sighed while others pounded their fists against the table in displeasure.

"I thank you for your opinions. This council is to be dismissed."

"Do we really have enough supplies to be giving away so much so freely?" one of the losing voters cried despondently.

"We have plenty of grain," Lain replied evenly. "With the blacksmith grinding out weapons, the main problem assailing us is the lack of men to fight with them."

"We'll draft men then!"

"I will never allow unwilling men to fight for our army," Lain remarked.

"Well, we can promote marriage," an advisor suggested.

"I will not breed soldiers!" Lain roared. "Do you know that is exactly what the Shalkans do? They treat their women as they do their livestock! Never will I use humans in such a way." Lain forced himself to regain equanimity. "There is no simple answer. We will simply fight and live as we have."

At his last word, Faylene rocketed from the shadows and swooped onto his shoulder, shrieking loudly. Lain scowled but stroked her head lovingly.

"I see you've been hunting."

Faylene began ripping her odd prey to pieces on his shoulder. Lain rolled the map and tied it with string. Roth approached and saluted Lain with his one hand.

"I couldn't help but notice that your hawk had some kind of bird in its mouth." Roth glared at Faylene before continuing. "I was wondering…since she did not come in through the doorway—" Faylene let a feather drop from her yellow beak, and Roth caught it. After inspecting it closely, he exclaimed, "Oh!"

"What?" Lain asked patiently.

"She's gotten into our stables. This is a clukokian feather!"

Lain did not understood Roth's troubles in order to sympathize, but he said in a consoling tone, "She must've been hungry. I'll keep an eye on her."

Nettled, Roth shoved the feather into his tunic.

Tar paced the perimeter of the room, brooding. They had gone training without bothering to summon him. *What do they take me for, a child? Perhaps in years I am, yet in skills and strength, I am twice my age. Has Lain not given me the glove and sword?* Tar unsheathed his sword and twirled it elegantly with subtle flicks of his wrist. The air beside him swirled as the sword completed the movements. Then Tar went to work, tirelessly chopping down imaginary officials as they opposed him with their sabers and guns. What he would give to be out on the battlefield feeling true air slide by his face! Sheathing the sword furiously, Tar did not notice the blade threatening to protrude through the bottom of his white sheath.

Slumping onto his bunk, Tar let the self-pity spew from his center and wash over him. He thought of Shrie riding through the jungle on a Mali-Mali. Her hair would be blown away from her smiling face, her bow slung over her back, and her jagged spear in hand. *She's free. She is free while I am trapped and deemed useless.* He opened his eyes, not realizing he had closed them, though either way it did not matter. It was useless to waste time in rumination. Whether he recognized it or not, Quantus Plain would need him more than the forest would.

Anything resembling life had deserted Corious after the battle. Devoid of energy, he glanced languidly about the hallway and noticed Roth stalking angrily from the council room.

"Roth, did the vote not turn in your favor?" he called.

Roth noted Corious's presence blankly. "No, I voted to send the supply train. I wish I could go and help. I know the forest well enough."

"Why don't you go?"

Roth held up his one arm.

"That's no good reason, and you know it," Corious rebuked him. "Did Ree, Shrie, Tar, and I teach you nothing in the jungle?"

"These days, a one armed man is limited to tree farms and breeding animals."

"Providing the food for the people is a noble job. Besides, you will see battle sooner than you think. Trust me, the glory you think you will find in war is not worth the horror. You have fought enough to know this."

In disgust, Roth replied, "Don't fill me with false hope. The officials are coming too fast. You know it is over for us."

"Don't say that, Roth," Corious warned.

"You know it though," Roth's voice escalated. He was slowly losing it, and he did not know why. Something about the way Faylene had torn apart the clukokian disturbed him. "They are coming, Corious, and we aren't prepared." Sliding a hand in his tunic, he toyed with the feather now maroon with blood. "The officials will slaughter us!"

"Shut up, Roth!" Rage replaced lethargy as Corious gripped Roth's shirt and hauled him close, his body trembling with anger. "If you won't be quiet, I won't hear you out." Corious's voice climbed to a dangerous pitch.

"You don't want to hear it, do you? You were free in the forest, and now you are confined to a building destined to fall."

"Shut up! Right now, Roth, right now. Do you hear me?"

At the sound of their voices, Lain calmly exited his room. Sorrowfully but firmly, he loosened Corious's grip on Roth's shirt.

"May I have a moment, Corious, Roth?"

Lain pulled Corious aside but did not speak until enough distance prevented his words from reaching Roth. "You are one of my captains, Corious," he said disappointedly. "I trust you to protect the people of Quantus Plain." Lain stared Corious in the eyes. "I will not question your actions, but I will remind you of your purpose."

Corious returned Lain's gaze. "I know this, Lain. Forgive me," he said stiffly. "I forgot myself in my anger. The people already stand on edge. I do not ask that you excuse my behavior, but I quote, 'the officials will slaughter us.' Do you think those words inspire confidence?"

"Using force against your friend does not inspire him either."

"It might silence him for the greater good."

"Enough has happened today to bring anyone to desperation."

"Lain," Corious pleaded in disbelief, "he wasn't even there!"

"I know," Lain replied.

"What was I to do? Tell me, honestly."

Lain's face seemed pained. "Roth has expressed our deepest fears, Corious. As captains, we are willing to lay down our lives, but we aren't willing to watch those we protect die. We don't want to see the potential validity of his statement. What Roth says, if it comes true, will be our gravest nightmare. But now that you have heard your fears verbalized, remember that our only success will come from the Almighty. Only He can save us, and even if He doesn't, we must still fight."

"And what of Roth?"

"I will extract from him his seed of fear and plant instead, hope."

"How much time do we have before they come upon us?" Corious asked suddenly.

Lain kept his gaze steady. "Two weeks, two months maybe. It depends on the success of the resistance they encounter in the woods and from the ports. You know more of the independent rebel groups than I."

"There aren't many, but they fight the hardest."

"So I figured."

"We are left with little time to prepare," he noted bitterly.

"It will have to be time enough."

"How do you suppose they will attack?" Corious wet his lip with an anxious tongue.

"Do not worry about what you cannot control. It shall be discussed in due time. As for now, how does Ree fare?"

"He grows restless."

"As do I. Tell him to be patient. Tell him our time will come."

"That is all?"

"It is." In the corner of his eye, Lain saw Roth take a cautious step forward. "Roth, you wish to speak with me?"

Corious slowed as he reached the door. His heart beat loudly. Pausing in front of Ree's door, he noticed a familiar figure down the hall. Squinting, he recognized Jenny. Ree could be told later. Corious's feet lost control as he danced down the hall; his previous worries went into hibernation.

"Jenny!"

"Corious?"

"Hey!" Corious caught up with her. "I have not seen you lately."

"Have you been missing me?" she joked.

He cut to the point. "What would you say to meeting with Ree, Malov and I tomorrow for breakfast at eight?"

"I'd love to," she said earnestly, but her eyes did not twinkle in delight. "Corious, I heard about the battle today." Corious quieted and let her continue. "I was worried about you." She shrugged. "I like you a lot, but don't ever let me love you, okay?"

Corious stepped back, as if her words had literally hit him. *What is this?*

Jenny shook her head. "Sorry about that. Forget it, okay?"

"Okay..."

"I just, I began to think about this war. It's coming closer to home."

Corious deepened his voice comically and said, "Don't worry, I'll save you." He lifted her off the ground.

"In all seriousness, be careful."

"I will if I can see your lovely face tomorrow," Corious teased.

"I'll be there. I better go though; my family is expecting me to make dinner."

"Is it that late? Well, until tomorrow!" He jetted down the hall.

"Bye, Corious."

Corious skipped the rest of the way back to Ree's room and let himself in. Ree was writing something furiously on a piece of paper. At Corious's unannounced entrance, he hastily rolled the scroll and then set it back on the table, letting it unfurl.

"What's that?"

"Nothing much."

"Lain wanted me to tell you to be patient," Corious repeated the enigmatic statement.

Ree closed his eyes. His face looked jagged, as it always was, but something about it seemed different, wrong somehow. Corious studied the face as the revelation dawned upon him. *It's tired.* His comprehension scared him.

"Ree, are you okay?" he asked tentatively.

"I'm fine."

"You're writing."

"Was writing."

"I did not know you wrote."

"Where do you think Shrie learned her vocabulary?"

Corious grinned. "You are very tricky, Ree. What are you writing?" he probed.

"What have I been writing? Nothing much. A few notes on our travels."

Corious did not wait for Ree's permission. He grabbed the scroll.

Corious, my new companion, and I met an odd yet intriguing jungle girl by the name of Shrie. She has long, dark hair and is tiny, but strong. I have not known her long, but it is obvious she is just beginning to learn our language. When she concentrates on saying something perfectly, her eyebrows knit in a funny arch that reminds me of a bird in flight, and if I say something disagreeable, she squishes her nose at me and praises Corious.

Ree ripped the page from his hand. "We can read these once our job here is done. No flashbacks, brother. Focus straight ahead and reach the end of the tunnel. Then we can glance back.

Corious sighed; tonight seemed to be a night of lectures. "Sure, Ree," he said, "by the way, I like that description of Shrie. You know, I never noticed that thing about her nose." Corious continued, "Oh yeah, I volunteered you and Malov to have breakfast with Jenny and me tomorrow."

"Sounds good."

"Shouldn't you tell Malov?"

"I'll get her tomorrow."

"Okay, she's your girl."

"So she is."

Corious did not like Ree's sense of ownership. "If I were your girl, I wouldn't put up with that last minute nonsense."

"It's a good thing you are not my girl then, eh?" Ree laughed abruptly at the thought of Corious as a girl. "You know Corious, as much as you may hate to hear this, if you were a girl, you would be more like Shrie than Malov."

"Oh yeah?" Corious replied as his mouth gaped in a shocked rictus. "I'll take that as a compliment, because we both know we love Shrie. Besides, if you were a girl, my friend, you would be dreadfully putrid!"

Ree gawked. He shook his fist in mock anger. "As a girl, you'd actually have to wash your undergarments!"

Corious grinned and jumped on Ree, tackling him to the floor.

Tar walked in as Corious shouted something incomprehensible at a prostrate Ree.

Tar squealed foppishly in pretend fright, "Oh, should I leave now? I don't want to interrupt you two. Ree, you look lovely. Don't worry about a thing Corious says."

Tar's effeminate squeal secured the attention of Marcelus who ran into the room, looked at Ree and Corious in a tangled heap on the floor, and then ignored them as he held a glass box in front of him and announced, "I am breeding ants on an ant farm to contribute to the new farms Roth is engineering."

Everyone froze, sat in silence, and rubbed their eyes. Marcelus was building an ant farm.

"And what," Corious asked, "propelled you to do this?"

Marcelus glared at him. "You think it a waste of time."

"Well, it's just slightly irrelevant, that's all."

Marcelus laughed hysterically. "You simpleminded humans, you think like children!"

Ree and Corious exchanged puzzled glances.

"Why do we need an ant farm?" Tar asked rather bluntly.

Marcelus hesitated. "I'm working on that aspect of…things."

The group laughed until they toppled exhaustedly onto the bunks.

"Ah, this smoky air must be getting to our heads," Ree said, recovering first.

"Stop being so intellectual," Marcelus admonished as if upbraided. "I myself might have stayed at the pub a bit too long."

Corious's face hardened. It seemed everyone was getting away from their worries some way or another.

"But don't worry! I'm sober enough," Marcelus assured them as he yawned.

Tar rolled off his bunk. "Why did you leave without me this morning?" Tar addressed them, ruining the brief moment of tranquility inspired by Marcelus's humor.

"Tar, we only went to train. We practiced stuff you would have been bored doing. We had no intention of encountering and fighting the officials. As Lain had said, they had never been on the eastern banks of the Halfast before. We couldn't have expected them there."

"It would have been better than staying down here," Tar grumbled.

"You were sleeping," Corious reasoned.

"Aye!" Marcelus called out, "as was I!"

"I saw your afternoon cavalry class wandering aimlessly around the halls. I thought something was unusual," Corious reflected.

Marcelus blinked. "Cavalry class?" he blurted. "Curse the ants!" He bent over his box. "You made me miss my cavalry class!" he told the scurrying insects before trudging down the hall and heading towards the training rooms.

"Marcelus, you—" Corious started to call. But it was too late; he had left his ant farm on Corious's bunk.

"Crazy captain," Tar muttered. "Should we report him for drinking?"

"Don't bother." Ree tapped his scroll thoughtfully. "He's a good leader, if a nut job."

Corious carefully picked up the glass cube and set it down next to the water basin. "I think we better put this here until Marcelus comes back. As for me, I am probably going to an archery class. Anybody else interested?"

Ree shook his head. "I'm going to keep writing."

"And you, Tar?"

"I might practice with my new sword," Tar said, swinging the weapon around in the air and narrowly missing Ree's bent head.

Corious suppressed a laugh, but Ree did not bother to react. "Well, in that case, I'll be seeing both of you," Corious called as he swung his longbow onto his back and shut the door behind him. He was tired, but he needed something to do.

Hurrying down one set of stairs and going up another, Corious arrived in the training room and was amazed by its emptiness. A couple of boys hacked at each other with blunt, wooden shafts in the corner, and four men parried against a wooden dummy to his right. Randomly stacked hay bales and wooden dummies were scattered on the opposite side. He was again surprised, and rather disappointed that sparring soldiers did not pack the room. *Every man should be here.* Soon, the war would come close to Quantus Plain. Corious shook his head in dismay.

Taking the bow off his back, Corious crunched under his feet the dead straw littering the floor. He aimed at a far from menacing straw figure. Some humorous man had taken the time to position a dented official's helmet on the figure's head while another person had painted on a dopey face. Corious nocked his bow and let the bowstring snap with an echoing twang. The arrow flew from Corious's bow in a startling whoosh. His entire arm vibrated from the release, but he did not notice. A resounding whumph sounded as the arrow connected with the straw man below the belt line. Corious smiled in satisfaction and nocked two arrows to his bow. He released with poise. Though his perception was not as accurate as he would have preferred, he wielded his bow with as much confidence as he did his sword. His first arrow deviated from its course but landed snuggly in the dummy's lower left torso. The second arrow was too high, and the helmet deflected it with a loud ping.

Corious retrieved his three arrows, placed his quiver and bow next to a nearby wall, and unsheathed his sword. He studied it momentarily. The sword had a thin, leather handle and a silver plane of metal which served for a crossbar. The metal was especially wide and curved, covering most of his knuckles. Perfectly straight, the honed blade came to a needle-thin point. A short, scarlet ribbon adorning the bottom of the hilt, the sign of a rebel warrior, traced the sword's movements gracefully through the air.

Corious threw the sword, sidestepped, and caught it by the sphere on the bottom of the hilt. He examined his target. The dummy had two inches on Corious and an abnormally wide trunk. Arms of wood protruded from its splintery torso, and a rough, round head rested upon a metal rod. The rod ran down the remaining height of the dummy, serving as a rather crude spinal cord. The strange opponent had no legs but was instead graced with a hollow base and a flat wooden wheel. Cuspate shafts girded the dummy's waist.

Corious tapped his target on the arm to turn it. Creaking as the wheel below turned, the dummy leisurely completed a half circle. As it moved, the wooden shafts lining its base struck at his legs. The dummy was no toy. Planting his foot to avoid a nasty blow, Corious watched helplessly as an arm swung at him. He meekly thrust his sword forward to stave off the merciless shaft. Blocking it, he sent his manmade opponent lurching in the other direction. Before he had time to collect his thoughts, the dummy smacked him roughly across the face. Stunned, Corious collapsed. As if this beating was not enough, a lower, jagged stick cut him across the arm as the dummy's momentum carried it through a plethora of nauseating revolutions.

Blinking in shock, Corious scrambled from the dummy's path and fell against the soft straw into which he expectorated blood. He rubbed a hand delicately over his face but pulled it back instantly when the splinters in his face threatened to attack his palms. He berated himself for his foolishness. He had not been careful. Although loath to restart his battle, Corious warily stepped forward. He twirled his sword and attacked. This time, he swung low and cracked the dummy's left arm with his blade. The torso shuddered and groaned, but refused to release his sword. Corious's arms were jerked forward. He groped madly for stability as his left cuff caught and snagged on the dummy's appendages. Attached to the revolving monster, Corious spun in sickening circles until his lower sleeve tore. Gasping for breath, Corious slid across the stone floor. He stumbled into a standing position and leaned heavily against the doorway.

"Not fair," he coughed, mourning his tattered tunic. Staggering back to the dummy, he found his sword vibrating in its chest. Regaining his composure, Corious seized the hilt tenaciously. To his displeasure, the sword slid easily from its prison, sending him sailing into the haystacks. The top hay bales teetered and then crashed down atop his head. Corious grumbled a string of foul words before brushing the hay from his body and gathering his equipment. Walking from the room, Corious did not notice the other men watching him. If he had turned back even for a moment, he would have learned some interesting things about himself.

The man in the ragged shirt watched dourly as Corious left the room. He turned to his companion. "That's one of the new captains coroneted at the ceremony some nights ago?"

"It is," his companion replied. "I heard he came from the jungle and lived his whole life there with a jungle maiden named Queen of the woodland people. Supposedly his best friend and battle mate is Captain Ree."

"Aye. Well, Corious is the one who fought the Dummy and won."

"He received his bruises for it."

"I will follow him, eh boys? What do you think?" the man in the ripped shirt asked. One of the younger ones stepped forward.

"He gains my respect. Did you see how tirelessly he fought?" The man eyed the dummy. "I believe I'll try it myself."

"Not going to let the newcomer beat you?" one of his friends prodded waggishly.

"No, it's not that. See, he is my specific captain. I want to live up to his expectations. They are high."

"I was told he makes you train for hours each day."

"He trains us enough to better us but not enough to drain us."

His friend picked up a sword. "Well then. Try the Dummy if you wish. If you beat it, then I will know, truly, how good a captain this Corious is."

The man in the frayed shirt scowled. "That isn't fair. It is rumored only Lain can beat the Dummy."

"Obviously this Captain Corious can as well. Let's see how well he trains his men," the friend responded. "Besides, you know what we must face, later."

"In battle, yes. We have time though."

"Not as much as you would think. Go on now, fight the Dummy."

Lain overheard the discussion; he too was curious to see how Corious trained his men. The rumor had otherwise been true. Lain was no longer the sole conqueror of the dummy, for which he was relieved. His army had to be strong. He held in a breath as the man approached the dummy and found a comfortable grip on his sword.

One of his friends taunted, "No time to eye up the enemy in battle! Just go!"

Wetting his lip, the man struck and then jumped away as the dummy circled, creaking with use. Protecting himself with the sword outstretched before him, the man nailed the dummy's other arm, retarding its momentum. As it slowed, he hit the chest of the dummy, but one of the lower projections hit him in the leg. Landing on his back, the man lost his breath. One of his friends cheered.

"Figuratively you may have died, but you stuck the Dummy!"

"I guess Captain Corious isn't a bad teacher. When does he hold a class tomorrow?"

The man drew a protracted breath and eyed dreamily his sword in the dummy.

"Hey, you, hear me?"

The man shook his head. "Classes? One tomorrow before brunch."

"I'm going."

"Yeah, me too," cried the other, swishing his sword in the air a few, safe feet away from the dummy.

Lain furrowed his brow. He would not fight the dummy tonight. No, he would call on his new captain. Striding from the room, he headed purposefully to Corious's room. He knocked, and Corious opened the door.

"Lain! I didn't expect you."

"Corious. Care to duel?"

"I can't say I was expecting that either. What is this about?"

"I need a challenge."

"What if I beat you?"

"I'll fight you until I win."

"I don't know if I want that sort of commitment." Ree shoved Corious out the door.

"Beat him for me, brother," Ree said, "and try not to hurt yourself."

"You're not coming to watch?" Corious asked, ruffled and baffled by Ree's response. Ree kept writing, so Corious addressed Lain. "Where are we to fight? Surely not in the common practice room!"

Lain considered this. "No, we will fight in the common arena, so everyone can watch me reestablish my authority."

"Is this so?"

"Yes. It will be an inspiration to the men."

"To watch us clobber each other?"

"The fight will not be with swords. I have decided on hand-to-hand combat."

"You're picking my specialty."

"The men need to learn. They will begin by watching. You know Tar is especially good at this."

"Tar doesn't watch; he's blind."

"I meant he has had to learn by experience. Bring him too. I need to speak with him."

"As you say. Give me fifteen minutes."

"No, now."

"Ree, send Tar down for us. This should be interesting."

Crowds gathered in the training room.

"I hear that Lain will battle one of the new captains!" someone whispered.

"Who?" someone else asked in anticipation.

"One of the new recruits," another answered, enjoying the rounds of gossip.

Milling around the center arena, soldiers maintained order. Excitement and tension escalated as people entered with surprised exclamations issuing from their lips. Corious and Lain observed the action from behind the curtain that separated the training room from their audience. Corious noticed Jenny had joined the crowd. *So this is Lain's idea of inspiration. Should I let him win and allow him to restore his control over Quantus Plain?* The thought settled in his mind but was then discarded. Lain wanted a fair fight, which meant Corious had to give his all. As he pondered this, he remembered something from the council meeting. The supply train was supposed to be sent off tonight. Perhaps this was Lain's way of sending them off—with a show and a warning that things will not be easy. Corious wondered who would accompany the supply train and if Roth had reconsidered his vantage point.

When the crowd began to call for Lain and Corious, Lain addressed him, "Dramatize it."

"Is this an act or a fight?"

"Show off all your skills and every trick of the trade."

"How do we want to end this?"

"I suppose you will think I want you to surrender after an amazing performance by myself. I decline, but thank you. No, we will fight until one of us wins, or until it is time to send off the train. For either outcome, I have a speech that should cover us from shame and stir the people."

Corious shrugged. "If you say so. Should I enter now?"

Lain nodded.

Corious ran from behind the curtain, ripping off his shirt as he completed a front flip. He landed perfectly and solidly. The crowd cheered in admiration. Corious stepped to the side, waiting for Lain to enter. Lain did so by walking sensationally from behind the curtain, pushing it behind him. He threw his mail aside and bowed formally to Corious. Corious returned the gesture, positioning his body into a perfect right angle. At the sound of a gong, the crowd hushed. In unison, the two jolted upright.

Uptight, those accompanying the supply train watched anxiously. They knew some meaning abided in the fight, but they could not place it. The gong sounded in the moted air.

Corious sprung from his spot and shot a fist at Lain. Lain evaded the blow, edging closer to the center of the arena. Corious assaulted Lain with a fury of fists. With simple blocks and nimble pivots, Lain kept away Corious's pugnacious hands. *When will he tire from the modesty of defense?* Corious wondered as he engaged in a series of flashy offensive maneuvers. Corious did not have to wait long. In a switch of tactics, Lain flaunted a complicated kick. Bending backwards, Corious narrowly avoided Lain's jaunty boot shooting over his head.

As Lain stalked threateningly towards him, Corious racked his mind. Barely a foot separated Lain from Corious when Lain lifted his arm, aiming to end the fight with one, crushing blow. Abruptly, Corious did a back handspring and landed trippingly on his heels near a dummy. Lunging backwards with an accelerating velocity, he snagged the dummy's arm before almost colliding into the ground. Gasps popped out from the crowd. Corious swung himself around the dummy, regaining his balance. Lain rushed the faltering Corious, and they tumbled into a hay stack. They saw the crowd's edge a yard away.

Corious lunged at Lain, ramming his head into Lain's shoulder blade. The sound of bone grating against bone rang through the room. Corious cringed as pain bubbled in his jaw. Lain swayed but recovered first. He leveled Corious with a single punch. The room rang with a roar of cheering and shouts. Corious writhed momentarily in anguish, trying to mentally block the pain. Stoically, he wiped the blood from his face and sprung upwards with a great heave of his legs. With a renewed fury, Corious's blows found their way to Lain's chest and face. Lain's vision blurred. In a panic, he threw Corious from him, antagonized. Bloodied and bruised, they stumbled, shaking off the wooziness which accompanied each mind numbing blow. They circled the other, loathe to restart the fight.

Corious crept closer, and Lain likewise began his own advance with his hands drawn below his chin in fists. Corious spun and drove forward, but the exertion drained him. Lain struck, driving Corious back with curving swings. Corious's and Lain's arms entangled. Planting his legs on Lain's chest, Corious extricated his body from the mess and forced Lain into a backwards somersault. In an effort to override the disgrace of his fall, Lain exhibited a series of fast, impressive, but harmless maneuvers during which Corious caught him under the jaw with a hook. As Corious admired his punch, Lain delivered a straight blow to the gut. Laboring for breath, Corious forced himself to straighten his torso when the gong rung mercifully in his ears. It was time to end.

Sweat dripped from Lain's brow and splattered to the floor. Corious had fought better than Lain had expected. The people would want a speech. *What if I told them I fought to prepare myself? What if I told them I had wished to test myself, and that the fight was more to confirm my own abilities than to help them?*

He examined the eager, confused faces in the crowd. They wanted an explanation—a sliver of hope to sustain them as the soldiers were sent into the unknown. Would he lie and tell them everything would end well? Would he tell them the harsh truth—that official forts paraded along the Halfast River? Would he tell them that the Shalkans had massed in numbers beyond Quantus Plain's ability to fight? He felt Corious shake his shoulder.

Squaring his shoulders, Lain closed his eyes, took a deep breath, and began. "Our supply train leaves tonight, and along with it, our soldiers." Lain saluted the crowd. "They carry our honor, our pride, and our spirit from Quantus Plain to rebels in great need of our aid. Let us support them, and may they fight the fight for which they were born. Like the action you saw here tonight, their journey will be tough and long. Their reward is, however, much greater: the perseverance of good against evil." Lain paused as hands touched foreheads and eyes flickered to the stalwart, unmoving soldiers standing in the front row.

"It is in the Almighty's holy name I send them to uproot evil and uphold justice. The Harvest has come, my people. It is up to us to trust in the Almighty and continue in the path of Truth set before us. Every thread of our lives shall be woven into the great tapestry of life. Let our colors be bright and never fade though we walk into darkness." Lain removed his hand from his forehead, terminating his salute to the soldiers. "My soul goes with you," Lain addressed the soldiers directly, "for my body itself cannot. Follow the route that takes you far from the Halfast River. Go. The time has come."

The gong rang for the third and final time that night, sending the soldiers on their measured cavalcade through the crowd. The young girls draped their necklaces around the soldiers' necks, and the young boys tossed their caps into the carts. Women scattered petals before the steady march of the soldiers. The guards gave their salutes and held their weapons loosely at their sides. Between the columns of soldiers rode the carts and supplies to be transported. The last cart supported the volunteers who would help cook, clean, and care for the soldiers and supplies. Corious recognized one head as Logan's and another as Hitachi's. His heart sank. He jumped from the stage and pushed his way through the crowd.

Reaching the cart, he jogged alongside it and caught the brothers' attention. He started to say something, but his throat clogged. Instead, he tossed them the twin set of knives on his belt. Logan caught them and handed one to Hitachi. A glistening tear slid from the man's eye.

"I did not tell you we were leaving because I did not want you to become upset. We owe you, brother Corious. We will not forget you or what you did for us."

Corious nodded lamely as the cart rounded the corner. A guard politely held him back.

"No more people beyond this point."

Corious raised his hand in a salute. The brothers returned it until the cart disappeared from view and traveled into the gloom of the caverns.

The two struggled from the powerful tug of the river and fell onto the beach. Grabbing one under the armpits, Corious turned him belly up and brought him into the cover of the trees. Ree took the other. Corious stared from one to the other. They were twins...

Logan stared at the map as if tomorrow would never come. Hitachi sat next to him, picking at the heavy, dark hair of his eyebrow. Logan started to say something about western movements when Hitachi slammed his hand violently on the table to protest.

Corious showing Logan how to twirl the knife correctly and teaching Hitachi the bow...the firelight bouncing off Logan's face as he enthusiastically helped Corious and Ree teach the others to read...Corious wondering vaguely when and how they had learned...

Corious snapped from the memories. The supply line would probably stay in the caverns, avoiding the open plains and the swamp. *What do I have to worry about anyway? I have taught them everything I know. I can only entrust them to the Almighty.* As the small speck which had once been the neatly arrayed formation of soldiers vanished, the guard dropped his arm, and Corious released his salute. He shivered in the hiemal caverns; he had left his shirt in the practice room. Without it, goose bumps rose from his flesh. On his way back through the halls, he bumped into Ree.

"So you came."

Ree shuffled his feet. "I wrote for a while but then stopped because the thought of you fighting Lain distracted me."

"What did you think?"

"Not bad, but there are some things we need to work on."

"Yeah," Corious admitted. "Did you know Logan and Hitachi left with the supply train?"

"Did they?" A faraway look entered Ree's eyes. "That is well. Their skills will be needed there." Then he added angrily, "Battle changes things, changes people."

"I know, Ree. I just thought you would like to know." Corious could not help but think of Ree and Malov. He knew his friend must be getting worried. "It's fine, Ree. I'll see you at breakfast tomorrow, right?"

"I'll be there."

"Good. It's late. Let's head to bed," Corious said tenderly, as if he were a mother attempting to comfort a distressed child.

"Got to say my congratulations to Lain, first," Ree protested. "Besides, I brought Tar like Lain asked."

"I also need to give him my support," Corious admitted. "He's probably in his office."

Two sets of feet were admitted into Lain's room.

"Corious and Ree, I was hoping you would show."

"Good job tonight, Lain." Corious offered.

"Don't be ridiculous. I need to discuss something with you if you aren't too tired."

"What foul news?" Ree asked, reading Lain's thoughts.

"Sit."

Ree and Corious picked chairs and sat down close to Lain.

"The scouts came to me before Corious and I practiced."

"I'd hardly call that practice," Ree volunteered, but then quieted when Lain waited for his attention.

"There are officials massing on the Halfast River. They fortify the entire bank of the Halfast in a semi-circle around Quantus Plain."

"They know we're here?"

"I do not know how much intelligence they have gathered or how. Believe me when I say that nothing has slipped from a tongue, unless an official escaped the small skirmish today and reported our location."

"When do we attack?" Ree asked solemnly.

"I want to do it soon, before they bunker. The attack would necessitate intricate planning. I will want fresh information on their progress in the morning. Security will be tripled around the hatches and doubled elsewhere if possible."

Corious suddenly felt drained. Lain must have noticed his wan face for he stopped the briefing.

"We will talk in the morning. Do not brood over this or let it trouble you. It will be dealt with tomorrow."

Corious wished he could let it go completely and not remember until morning, but he did not know if he was physically and psychologically able. Ree sat up as if he remembered something important.

"You said you wanted to see Tar."

"That I did," Lain answered, pleased that Ree had not forgotten. "Did you bring him with you? I should have met with him weeks ago," Lain reprimanded himself aloud.

"Do not show him any sympathy," Corious advised. "Tar does not want your pity. Do not let his weakness fool you into underestimating his strength. Do you want me to leave?"

"When Tar comes."

Corious played with his sword strap until Ree returned with Tar.

"Lain, you wanted to see me?" Tar seemed nervous and excited.

"I did."

Corious and Ree left Lain and Tar alone. The two, though so opposite in appearances, did not seem odd together as they leaned over the table in conversation. Lain's medium height, athletic body, and shaven forehead somehow fit alongside Tar's far from fierce demeanor. Tar stood a hand's length shorter than Lain, was peculiarly slim, and had ruffled, cropped hair while a goatee and set of mail made the leader of Quantus Plain almost formidable. Tar's build, like a young tree's, was easy to bend but strapping and flexible. When the boy moved, his strength was apparent in his well knit sinew and muscle. Tar turned his head to the sound of Lain's deep voice.

"I suppose you wondered about the glove and sword."

"I did, Master Lain. Aban told me the glove was for a falcon. I have no falcon."

"Did your friend Aban tell you I have a falcon?"

"Yes, he did. He said her name was Faylene."

Lain lifted Faylene from her perch in the corner. She emitted a small squeak.

"How old do you think I am?" Lain asked suddenly.

"That is hard for me to judge," Tar answered honestly. "You must be at least twenty but not as old as forty."

"You are correct. I am not old, though I feel the burden of responsibility that comes with age. I must pass my skill and knowledge to the next generation so that Quantus Plain may be ruled with more skill than mine. My falcon, Faylene, is one of my most trusted advisors. Her words are never fallacious, and she always returns to my hand. She's feisty, but she's well worth the strife. With your consent, I will teach you the commands of a falconer. One day, Faylene may be yours."

Tar thought his jaw would drop like an anchor, but he managed to regain a semblance of dignified control. "That would be an honor, more than an honor," he answered hurriedly. "May I ask, Master Lain, why you have chosen me for so noble a task? And why have you presented me with such a valuable sword?"

"I chose you, Tar, for several reasons." Lain stroked Faylene's head in thought. "I have lived with and observed many types of people. Certain ones have the gifts of patience, kindness, and a willingness to learn. These are the people capable of becoming a falconer. You are one of them."

"The sword?"

"The sword was to replace your old one, something I would have done for any of my soldiers."

"Thank you."

"You're welcome," Lain said simply. "Perhaps you would like to hold Faylene before you head back?"

Lain transferred the falcon onto Tar's gloved forearm. Tar clenched his hand as the vices, which were her talons, encircled his arm. Hesitantly, he traced the contour of her beak. She squawked, unused to his touch. Tar timidly rubbed her head and then moved his arm towards Lain. The unexpected movement scared Faylene, and she whipped her wings up and down in a flurry of motion. The wind whistled past Tar's face in cool reassurance. Lain soothed Faylene and returned her to her perch.

"Will I see you tomorrow?"

"Anytime you want," Tar answered readily.

Lain smiled. *At least one thing has gone well this day.* "Excellent. I wish you a good night."

"Thank you…for everything."

"It was nothing. Now go."

After a heartfelt salute, Tar exited the room, and with an unmatched excitement, he allowed himself to run recklessly to his room.

Alone at his desk, Lain knew there was no more he could do. They had been discovered, but he would not rush into battle's murderous embrace. He had to play the deadly game right and make the officials play it at his pace and by his rules. There was much to do before the war enveloped them. There were people with whom he must correspond and last minute things to teach, but there was nothing he could do tonight. Though the unfinished tasks hung over his head, it was almost a relief to know he could delay them. For one night, he would escape from his overwhelmingly packed schedule and from the foreseeable outcome to which his actions would lead his people. True escape, however, would always elude him; for though Lain fell asleep peacefully, he slept burdened by the mail and uniform he still wore. Only the morning sun that no longer shone would somehow awaken Lain the next morning.

Corious could not and would not open his eyelids. *I never should have woken.* His muscles felt wrenched out of place. They were rigid, feeble, and barely moveable. His back was in a tight knot, and every time he moved, it reminded him of his troubles. Corious released an inaudible groan and flopped over on his side, ignoring the flaring pain. He lazily opened one eye and eventually the other. Indifferent to those in the room, Corious rolled over and hoisted himself to the ground noisily.

Corious bent low over the washbasin; the black outline of his head in the clean water stared at him. Swishing his hand back and forth along the surface of the basin, he watched as his dim reflection stretched, broke apart, and turned red. The crimson water stupefied him. *What happened?* He pulled his hand from the bowl and observed drops of blood seeping from a partially closed gash on his wrist. They plopped into the once sanitary bowl. Corious remained aghast and immediately removed the washbowl from its stand. He set it over to the side and then stood immobile, drinking in the silence. Darkness built cinereous siege ramps about him. Corious snuck towards the heavy, wooden door and was about to open it when a monotone voice halted his movements.

"Go back to bed, Corious. There's no attack."

"What?" Corious questioned. His brain was working in low gear.

"Go back to bed," Ree told him, even though he knew Corious would not.

"What time is it, Ree?"

"It is night, considering the single level-headed person in this room still sleeps." Ree gestured to Tar.

"You couldn't sleep either?"

"I chose to evade it," Ree said simply.

Corious twisted his face questioningly. "Common sense has seemed to evade you as well."

Ree huffed. Corious plopped onto Ree's bunk.

"There are heavy and troublesome things on my mind," Ree remarked, running his hand along the wall. Corious did not respond. "I believe Lain has held back information from us, and even from Marcelus and Perry. Yet if we cease to hope, we accept failure. I fear we will meet both in the path the future holds for these people. Corious?"

There was no response.

"Corious?"

Corious lay still, breathing deeply with eyes closed peacefully. Ree was glad. If sleep had eluded his grasp, at least Corious had found it. During his last sleepless night, Ree had vowed to finish the chronicles of Shrie, Tar, Corious, and himself; it was the tale of their revelation and insurrection. If he did not live to tell it, it would live in writing. Slipping stealthily to the stolid floor, he flipped open his parchment and lit a small candle. He must finish.

Corious woke for the second time that morning. His numb cheek rested against the algid stone. His sore back reminded him of its limited capabilities. It had been a broken night. Corious squinted through his crusted eyelashes. Perplexed, he pondered why he was on a top bunk. The memory of the past night came back to him gradually. It was probably morning, and he did not care to be late for his and Jenny's first appointment. *An appointment. How romantic. Let's not get ahead of yourself, Corious,* he coached himself. *It is merely a breakfast rendezvous.* Corious stretched and yawned. Falling back into his sheets with a careless plop, he wondered if he had inadvertently stolen Ree's bunk.

Drifting from any relevant concerns, his mind momentarily concentrated on nothing in particular. The darkness of the room comforted him; it was a blanket that muffled all noise, a barrier that protected him from the warring outside world and from the Shalkan warriors who otherwise would grant him no rest. The scratching of a pen scribbling across old parchment penetrated the night's silent fortifications, but then the noise stopped, and he passed it off as nothing. Minutes later, a hand roughly shook him awake.

"Is it time to go to breakfast?" Corious mumbled sleepily.

"No, but it's time to get up."

"What?"

"Get up."

"Is it time for breakfast?"

"No. I already told you that."

"Ree?" Corious listened as Ree threw on his mail and a tunic. The wheels in Corious's mind began to turn. They were heading outside. Grumbling, he got up and dressed. "Is this a training exercise? A caveat against the might of the officials?"

"Keep quiet and obey."

"I am a captain now. I follow no orders except those demanded by my instincts."

"What?"

"I don't know. What did I say?"

Ree shrugged. Corious always acted oddly when he first awoke. Ree was not concerned; he knew the brumal, night air would wake his friend. Besides, Ree needed him. Corious was the one he trusted the most, with the exceptions of Tar and Shrie. As it was, Corious would go wherever Ree wanted him. It was as simple as that. Ree ensured that Corious put the correct clothes on the proper body parts before handing him his sword and heading to Tar's bunk.

"Need we hasten his battle days?"

"Better to prepare him while we can," Ree replied severely, slapping Tar lightly on the face. The boy groaned, but with an astonishing alertness, he swung himself into a sitting position and rubbed his eyes vigorously.

"Tar, we're going on a scouting mission; you're coming with us."

Tar flipped his mop of hair away from his face and hurried to the washbasin without a word. Corious gathered knives as one would pluck flowers, shoved them in his belt, and met Ree at the room door.

"I'm not sure I understand, Ree. Has Lain asked us to do this?"

"Lain is a busy man, Corious. We are civilized men and are certainly capable of making our own decisions. Lain would not object," Ree explained.

Corious seemed upset. "It's not like that anymore. We are part of a government, a systematical distribution of authority."

"We are that government!" Ree stressed.

Tar approached the debating men, snaking his new sword through the air in elaborate twists. "Are we ready?" he asked, hiding his impatience.

"Let's go," Corious said blandly, taking hold of Tar's shoulder and steering him to the Great Hall where torches illuminated the guards on their night shifts.

"Shoot!" Corious mumbled, "They won't let three heavily armed men out of Quantus Plain!"

Ree shoved himself past Corious and whispered, "We're captains; they're guards."

They proceeded onward. Corious clenched his teeth in disapproval as Ree's theory worked. The guards waved them towards the hatches without a single query.

"I told you," Ree said smugly to Corious.

They continued up the stairs and waited while Ree fumbled with the confusing latch. Small wisps of crisp air floated through the wooden hatches, making them freezing to the touch. Ree finally opened the lock, and the three anxiously awaited their turn to burst into the fresh, clean world above them. Corious was the last to hoist himself into the domain of the first building. *It's the one I helped construct*, he remembered proudly.

"Fire!" Tar exclaimed, sniffing the night air.

Sure enough, in the middle of the compound, a dozen men in tunics and battered gloves lounged about a small fire. All of the men bore longbows and knives, and at Tar's exclamation, one man stalked menacingly towards them. The others tended the fire absentmindedly.

"Get back inside, sentries," he spat.

Ree glared at him. "We are captains."

"I thought the likes of you never left your luxurious holes down in the cavern."

"Have you never been inside?" Corious asked, bewildered.

"Hardly. Smoke doesn't agree with my lungs; I am the head scout. I station my men outside."

"I have never seen you before," Ree said, sauntering around him warily, surveying his appearance.

"Well, I am certainly not an official," he chuckled hoarsely, "and you wouldn't have seen me because I'm a scout; I'm not supposed to be seen."

Stepping in, Corious said hastily, "Our apologies. You understand it is our duty to question. I do not doubt your identity. Your weapon has the Quantus Plain emblem and is of our metalworker's hand."

"What if it is a stolen sword?" the scout challenged. He had never seen the captains before. Now it was his turn to question.

"No man of Quantus Plain would surrender his sword in battle," Tar supplied.

The scout sneered, "Good observation, young one, but I don't suppose you've seen our opposition across the river."

"That's where we—"

"We're completing the standard, routine checkup," Corious interrupted Tar. He did not doubt the man's identity, but there was no need to explain their mission.

"You can watch for us in the coming hours. If we aren't back by daylight, perhaps you will send some scouts looking for us, no?"

Corious laughed heartily, disguising Ree's snide comment with humor. The head scout wore a troubled grin. The two parties had reached a mutual consensus.

Ree stormed from the building. He wanted so badly to hold onto every freedom he had had in the jungle, including the ability to say whatever he wanted whenever he wanted. Government and authority had never molded him before, and the terms of serving at Quantus Plain did not mesh well with his free spirit. Still, he had made a vow, and to fulfill it, he would temporarily sacrifice his sovereignty. As the one skilled in politics, Corious would have to speak on Ree's behalf. For Corious, their social contract was not so much of a burden.

Once away from the building, the three hunched to hide their profile. The darkness enveloped them, but the moon's light pierced the night and spilled onto the ravaged plain. The rebels would be able to see the forts, but they would be at equal risk for detection. A subtle thought scurried across the perimeters of Corious's consciousness. They had embarked on a scouting mission, and Tar could not see. He would not be able to decipher fort from forest. Why had they brought him? *To give him practice.* The answer came to him with vigor. Even now, without any guiding, Tar kept close to Ree. Tar had once told Corious that he saw with his feet—through the shaking of the ground.

Ree sunk to the ground on his hands and knees, picking his way to the forts in a roundabout manner. On the opposite bank of the Halfast, two structures spiraled ominously towards the heavens. Danger radiated from their pointed tips, and cannon barrels peered from thin slits like malevolent eyes. Bulky, broad stones comprised the polished walls and made the forts practically impossible to scale. Corious wondered grimly where they had harvested the rock. Either it had been looted from the ports or carried from quarries by ship.

Straining his eyes, he focused on the river line. No ships towered from the flat river's surface, but he did not dismiss their potential existence. As they crawled, Corious held his sword firmly against his thigh. He did not want the metal to chink against the charred, rocky ground. They crept closer, and moon's light revealed a jagged half of another fort rising behind the other two. Laying the groundwork while Quantus Plain slept, the Shalkans had wasted no time.

Unable to see the fine details of the structures, Corious nudged Tar who in turn pushed Ree. The rebels parted. With an unobstructed view, Corious squatted to take full advantage of the moon's light and his uncanny sense of sight. At his strange angle, the inner structure of the unfinished fort bloomed before him. Vertical wood beams enforced a layer of stone. Wood would burn. It also explained the fallen trees in the adjacent area. Corious hoped that Roth's tree farms had been spared. The underground tunnels led directly from Quantus Plain to the hollowed trunks of the trees. No matter what the cost, they had to dislodge the Shalkans to avoid infiltration. Quantus Plain could not afford to wait until the Shalkans discovered it.

Returning to his trenchant study of the forts, Corious dismissed no fact as irrelevant. The officials had built the structures proficiently. *The Shalkans must have used tons of soldiers to construct these monstrosities.* Corious estimated the number of necessary laborers and then hurriedly discarded it. Tar pushed Corious, and Corious received the signal to head back. As they reached the safety of the first building, Corious looked back into the night sky. His eyes may have been deceived, but he thought he spotted the small shape of a distant bird circling the forts. Ree shoved him inside before Corious could protest.

As they slipped into the first building, they found the head scout gone and the fires doused. Without the scouts, the place seemed eerily deserted. Opening the hidden hatch and heading down the stairs, no one uttered a noise until they had entered their room and shut the door. Hastily retrieving an old match, Ree lit a candle and grabbed a thin sheet of parchment from his pile on the table. Tar pulled up two chairs for himself and for Corious. Corious watched and Tar listened as a hasty drawing of the forts appeared on Ree's paper. Ree passed the visual to Corious who added notes and made minor adjustments. Silently they agreed on their final map. Tar felt strangely useless.

"How did we fare?" His hushed voice sought reassurance. "I know I wasn't much help."

"You were fine." Corious shared a knowing glance with Ree. "There wasn't much to see anyways. We'll tell you about it when Lain holds council tomorrow; for the most part I think we want to keep our little quest strictly between ourselves."

"Of course. Did you hear the hammers?"

"No."

"It was soft-like," Tar continued, "but continual. Though muffled, it was always on beat."

"They are still working through the night then," Ree replied in alarm.

"Are you sure of this, Tar?" Corious pressed.

"I am. It was a very distinct sound. I do not think I could have mistaken it."

"We were mistaken, Tar. You were of more use than we could have imagined though you bear ill news for Quantus Plain," Ree commented dourly.

"This ill tiding shall be used to our advantage," Corious stressed.

"I will not allow myself to become overconfident."

"Do not allow yourself to become pessimistic either."

The three hung their swords and mail on the posts driven into the frames of their bunks. Dawn hovered on the horizon, but sleep beckoned to them, tugging at the corners of their eyes and blurring the edges of their minds.

Breakfast dragged. To any commoner, a breakfast with two women would have been happily enjoyed and prolonged. Yet as the morning wore on, breakfast seemed terribly extraneous. Ree's glazed eyes randomly stared at unimportant details on the dark, wooden table. Corious drummed his fingers furiously while earnestly straining to seem interested in their chat. The last thing he intended to do was insult Jenny or Malov by seeming preoccupied. Resting his chin in the palm of a hand, he tried to put himself at ease. At least Jenny and Malov's garrulous natures saved him from the pressure of contributing to the conversation.

"This is the finest food I've ever tasted," Malov remarked, expressing her obvious pleasure. She finished a mouthful of roasted potatoes soaked in melted cheese and seasonings. "So Jenny," she began, dabbing her mouth with a plain cloth napkin, "I hear you do a fair share of cooking for the family?"

Jenny set down her utensils. "Yes, I usually do the cooking. To no avail, I've been trying to impart my skills onto my younger sisters. I am convinced that the only thing they can create is havoc."

"I can cook a bit," Corious lied, trying to impress Jenny.

Malov raised a skeptical eyebrow.

"Really? That's wonderful! You can take my place anytime," Jenny exclaimed genuinely. She paused before asking, "What can you cook?"

Corious was stumped. "Tons of things!" he lied again, flipping his utensils in the air for added affect.

"Unfortunately, the only thing I've cooked is poisonous mushrooms. By accident," Ree added quickly, "by accident, I assure you."

Corious laughed fondly. "I remember that. You and Tar fed me that stuff. It tasted fine, but good lord did it give me digestion troubles."

Jenny and Malov grimaced.

"So Corious," Jenny inquired, "you seem to be a resourceful man. What else can you do?"

Ree muffled an amused grunt.

"Well," he started with a smug voice. "Well," he repeated, at a sudden loss for words, "I can sing."

Ree's food spewed from his mouth and into his napkin.

"Really?" Jenny asked; a hint of doubt tinted her voice.

"I can demonstrate," Corious remarked confidently.

"Please, go ahead," Malov told him, smirking. She had known him long enough to know he could not sing.

Corious stared at Malov, his face burning red. "I don't know many songs," he mumbled weakly. Ree's head bent to conceal his disbelief.

"Do you know *The Sovereigns Overture?*" Malov challenged.

"I do know that one," Corious admitted hesitantly.

"I always love a good performer." Jenny clapped her hands to start the beat.

Corious cackled nervously before clearing his throat and standing at the front of their table. He began.

"Oh, the grand king of old,
Sat on his throne of gold,
Living life of power and strife,
He sat beside his beloved wife.
He drank, and he ate,
Downing the victuals on his plate.
Oh, the grand king of old,
With his silver and his gold,
His tale is quite sad, but yet it's still told!
He slept, and he wept,
Until he set out with a sack
And gave out all his gold!
Oh, the grand king of old,
Now his story's told,
He lives blissfully…evermore!"

As the last notes rang in the air, the entire pub erupted in a loud roar. Across the room and at adjoining tables, others restarted the song. One burly man brought Corious a quart of ale and slapped him on the back, laughing heartily. Corious slumped onto the table bench, relieved and smiling. The room vibrated with the sound of at least forty voices. After several minutes, Jenny pulled him off his seat. Filled with a new vigor, Corious danced the silly jig for the remainder of breakfast.

"Well, you outdid yourself, my friend," Ree sighed. "I never knew you could sing!"

"Neither did I, Ree. I suppose the Almighty was pleased with me, for surely, that's what it must've taken for me to sing decently."

Ree and Corious tottered back to their room; their hefty breakfast and ale rested like rocks in their stomachs. Ree began humming a verse from the very song Corious had sung earlier that morning.

"I suppose we'll train with our men today as usual," Corious murmured, thinking beyond their previous pleasure.

"Yes, we must. Will you give them the dire news?"

Corious smacked his lips together thoughtfully. "No, we are not in the position to relate that news yet. Lain will announce it when the time is right."

"Neither rules nor people have ever held me back."

"Do as you will, Ree, though I advise you to shed your stubbornness. I am going to hand over our sketches of the Shalkan forts to Lain. It might be beneficial for him to have them at the council." Ree turned down the hall which led to the training rooms. He would prepare his men until dusk.

Corious skipped ahead into their room; it was empty. Grabbing his belt and sword, he hastily fastened both to his waist. After securing his belt, he snatched the tied parchment from the small desk and hurried out of the room. With every step, the sound of running water guided him. He passed few people: a guard and several gaping children. Each he acknowledged as he made his way toward Lain's quarters. A sense of authority rested on his shoulders, but chilly drops of water sprayed him within a dozen yards of Lain's stark door, as if to douse his confidence. Oddly, there were no guards. He knocked respectfully once or twice. No one answered.

"Lain?" Corious called.

No answer.

Corious shrugged and pressed against the creaking door. It opened easily, revealing the items strewn about Lain's room. Lain's bed was tucked away in a desolate corner, but maps and contracts hung everywhere. Numerous sets of leather body armor hung on one wall while a worn map was secured to the parallel wall. A lone table and chair were placed near antiquated sconces. Books, weapons, and parchment littered the top of both the chair and table.

Cloying incense burned, biting at Corious's nostrils. *Where would Lain expect me to put a drawing?* He scanned the room and found a large crate labeled "parcels." Corious placed the drawing on top of the pile.

"Though Quantus Plain is not far from the jungle, it is amazing how a slightly higher altitude can cool things off," Tar commented to himself.

Tar jumped when someone replied, "Cold for the jungle maybe, but a great deal warmer than elsewhere."

"Lain?" Tar asked with a hesitant salute.

"It is I. Faylene was wondering if you would like to take her for a flight."

In response, Tar pulled the leather glove from his pocket and fit it onto his left hand. Having received instructions that morning from a guard, Tar had approached the first building before breakfast. Unbeknownst to him, Lain had planned to meet him there. As Tar secured the glove, a small rush of excitement filled him as the talons of Faylene gripped his forearm. Lain gave him no guidelines. Tar familiarized the bird with his touch and voice, stroking the falcon with his two forefingers.

Lain's voice pierced the morning air. "Last night, what did you observe?"

Tar stiffened, and Faylene tightened her grip.

Rolling his shoulders to relax himself and to keep Faylene from taking flight, he responded calmly, "I was with Ree and Corious."

"Scouting? Do not fear to answer me. It was an unauthorized mission and a dangerous one, but I shall deal with its consequences later. I was there too, not far from you."

Tar absorbed the information. Finally he answered. "I heard the sound of hammers. They did not cease. They sounded muffled, as though deep within the earth."

"So I feared." Lain gazed into the distance. "Enough of this," he said bitterly. "A council will be held shortly. For now, I want you to send Faylene over the forts. Let her be your eyes, but do not abandon your other senses."

Tar thrust his arm from his body, providing Faylene with the momentum needed to take off. The breeze from her liftoff tousled his hair. The sound of her wings pumping through the sky seemed to him the paradigm of freedom. Faylene soared above the earth doomed for war. "That was good," Lain said, summoning Tar from his daydream. "But you realize she will return shortly."

"What did I do wrong?" Tar asked, detecting an amused note in Lain's voice.

"You did not give her a command."

"Right," Tar replied, trying to cover up his embarrassment.

"Keep your arm out so she has room to land," Lain continued, "otherwise, her wings will hit you." Tar did as he was instructed. "Also," Lain advised, "next time you send her off, say Numinlor. That will let her know you want her to scout ahead. Then say Enheminon, so she knows to inform you whether or not a friend or foe stands before us."

"How does she know?" Tar asked as the falcon came soaring down onto his arm.

"I will let you discover that for yourself. If you want to get to know someone, you don't go to the person who introduced you. You go to the person you wish to know. It's the same way with Faylene. I will teach you the commands; you must learn her personality."

Tar nodded solemnly. This could be difficult. Deciding to attempt a command, he whispered, "Numinlor. Enheminon," and thrust his arm into the air. The same rush of air met his face as she took off in graceful flight.

"One call signifies a friend. Two signifies the enemy. If she makes no call, there is nothing."

Tar listened intently. The two shrill calls whistled over the plain followed by a series of complicated notes. Grabbing his arm roughly, Lain shoved Tar to the ground. Hitting the earth with a surprised thud, Tar heard as something whistled through the air above him.

"It appears the enemy is tightening the noose," Lain's voice came rasping to his ears. "They are testing their reach by determining the range of their guns," he explained.

"Faylene said that?"

"No, but I got the gist of it. Hurry, the cannons could be next. We're going to crawl through the door of the first building, jump through the entrance, and bolt it. It's to your right."

"What about Faylene?"

"She'll return."

As they crawled, several shots burst from the forts and then stopped. There would be no more the rest of the day. As the two hurried through the hatch, Faylene flew in behind them. Lain was pleased to see her land on Tar's arm.

"Take care of her for a few hours? You can fly her in the waterfall room if you want. I'm calling a council and will summon you before it starts."

Running down the hall, Lain's mail chinked agitatedly against his sword, and his footsteps pounded against the floor. Reaching his office, he flung open the door and noticed a roll lying on top of his crate. Unfurling it hastily, a layout of the official forts sprawled before him in immaculate detail. Without bothering to close the door, he rushed to the council room. Crashing into the next room, he appeared to find it already full of people.

Corious approached him solemnly. "We heard the gunshots. We took the initiative to get things started."

Lain resisted the urge to grind his teeth. It was not yet time for battle and already his officers were taking matters into their own hands. Taking a moment to send a guard after Tar, Lain took a deep breath to settle his roiling mind.

"Gentlemen, ladies," he greeted the concerned faces and hardened soldiers. "I thank you for being here though I did not call this assembly. You are able, responsible men and women, but you must not forget who your leader is and who he is not," he said gravely. "But since we are gathered here, your actions will not go in vain." Lain stifled a sigh as he shuffled through a coarse folder. "Today, we discuss military matters." He paused as he whipped out Corious's sketches. "Whether we will it or not, the Shalkans have found our relative location in the vicinity of this plain." Lain pointed to the map he so often used as a reference. "They have two fort complexes across the Halfast River. They can easily transport food, slaves, and supplies to their troops garrisoned there." He tapped a long, wooden ruler against the edge of the table. "Our choices are these: wait or conduct a full-scale attack. If we choose the former, we risk a siege. If we choose the latter, and defeat comes upon us," Lain did not bother to complete his sentence. "And our last choice is to blockade the river and thus cut off their only supply route."

Lain's proposals seemed irrational, even to himself, but he had no choice. These were rash days. Although fleeing was a feasible option, Lain did not consider it as a choice, and his consultants knew better than to suggest it as such. He waited momentarily and then said, "If no one has any questions or ideas, then we will vote to decide."

"Can a vote simply determine the final fate of this stronghold?" Corious interrupted doubtfully. The controversial supply train popped to the front of his mind. "We have voted on everything else, but today we will determine the fate of thousands of lives, Lain."

"I understand your fear, but what then, shall we do? Shall we ponder our dwindling options until the officials are at our doorstep? I think not. Or, should we have the entirety of the people vote, counting hundreds upon hundreds of hands? Although I wish it were otherwise, I find no better solution than the ones presented before you today."

"Give us until tomorrow. Then tomorrow, we shall vote."

"Agreed?" The majority of the representatives shouted their accord.

"Meeting dismissed."

The men and two women scraped their chairs against the floor, placing an inordinate amount of pressure into their movements. It was as if the psychological burden of war rested physically on their sagging shoulders. Though the pending vote would decide the fate of both sides, Lain knew the delegates would not choose an overt attack. An open assault would spell an end to the rebels. *We are not rebels. We are fighting for the homes and land which are rightfully ours. The Shalkans were and are the invaders. They are the rebels,* Lain mused. *By the end of this harvest, I pray we will lose that infamous title.* For better or for worse, he would see the end of the war. That much he knew. So long as his people lived, then so would he.

Abruptly, the siege walls loomed in his mind. Tucked in a wide crevice on the left side of each hall entrance, huge brass handles adorned their sides. In the wall, wooden hatches flipped up and open from which archers would shoot. About a year ago, when whispered words of war had come too close, the walls had been installed. They had been Perry's idea. Perry's pessimism made him a great tactician, constantly attuning him to potential dangers. The siege walls were sliding stone walls, thick enough to provide cover but thin enough to pull out of the walls. In a sense, they were not siege walls; they were a defense against a siege. If ever Quantus Plain became surrounded and the rebels failed to hold the Great Hall, they could retreat and seal off the surrounding hallways. By dragging the walls across the hall entrance, which would not be an easy task as the distance was not small, they would cut themselves off from the enemy. War was coming, and Lain prayed Quantus Plain would be ready.

Malov stretched uncomfortably under her metal armor. As scraps from the armory, the pieces felt and looked archaic. She wore no helmet upon her head, but an arrowbrimmed quiver was slung over her back. Shrie had crafted the arrows and quiver. A sword hung from the belt girding her waist. Her equipment, Malov surmised, had seen battle many times. A pair of feet made their way towards Malov; Salene was ready.

"Another unauthorized meeting. Will Lain be happy?" she asked anxiously. She had nothing but respect for her friend and leader.

"When we are finished," Malov added, "Lain will have another two hundred, able soldiers." She emphasized the last word as she unsheathed her sword. "I do not believe Lain to be discriminative towards women, and we will be a much-needed addition to his army."

"Lain believes a healer's job is just as important as being a warrior."

"It is." Malov did not dispute.

"He might not like us abandoning those jobs for soldiering," Salene pointed out.

"Not when we are fighting for our existence."

Salene paled. "Do not share those words with the others. Their souls are not as resilient as ours."

"If they have the courage to fight, they can deal with words."

"Some of them cannot fight."

"That's why we're here."

Salene shook her head. "Let's get going before Lain finds out about this whole ordeal."

Malov eyed her agitatedly before addressing the masses milling around the old arena. She attempted the rallying commands. "Attention!" she cried out in a loud, domineering voice. "To the fore!" A number of startled faces gazed at her. Some women shuffled over into position and instructed the others to do the same. "Direct, contour," Malov cried hopefully. The command puzzled everyone, including Salene. "How many of you can draw a sword?" Malov asked after a painfully long silence.

Several women stepped forward and raised their hands tentatively.

"Come here." As the women came onto the stage, Malov turned back to the other women. "Please attempt to form two columns with your weapons presented in front of you."

The women coached each other before shaping themselves into a messy, though somewhat organized group.

"So," Malov started, addressing the five women before her, "since you claimed you can draw a sword, you're about three steps ahead of the others. I want you to grab about twenty-five women each and teach them everything you know. At the end of the session, you will form them into rows and have them draw and present their weapons. Thank you, ladies, for helping."

The women saluted their unknown leaders and extracted their peers from the messy conglomeration in order to form smaller groups.

"And now?"

"Now," Malov started, "we start our own groups."

Malov saluted Salene before leaping down the seven steps to the stone floor. Salene knitted her eyebrows; she knew why she had become a healer five years ago. A warrior was noble, but he or she did everything on impulse, without logic or reason. Reluctantly, she shuffled down the steps, unused to the awkward weight on her hips and shoulders.

Malov brushed her hair from her face as she strode toward the remaining fifty women. They were still obediently in the dictated form, and they were almost positioned right. Malov noticed the anxiety on their faces. With the exception of kitchen knives, they had never held anything like a weapon before. Malov had learned so much from Shrie, Ree, Corious, and even Marcelus and Tar. *If only I could teach these women the same way,* she mused hopefully. The women stiffened when she passed. Some dropped their weapons or fumbled to adjust their armor straps.

Now I know how Lain feels. She was unsure of how to address them. "You are not warriors."

The women tensed once more. One girl who had arrived late stepped forward.

"You are wrong, teacher," she stated. Her words were reinforced as she spun with two shanshir daggers. "I am quite the able warrior, and I believe with practice these women will learn or even surpass us in skill."

Malov's face brightened. "Wonderful! We shall give these ladies an instructional demonstration on how to use the awkward steel and wood tools which they are so loath to carry."

The two stepped onto the center of the dais.

"Let's begin," Malov remarked as she drew her sword.

The two melted into a rush of parries and blows. They knew each other's moves before the other attacked; they were perfectly matched. On Malov's command, they eventually stopped.

"Women, we've shown how you will be able to fight after some months. Your training, I'm afraid, will be mere weeks due to military impediments."

"And why will this be?" questioned Malov's competitor.

Malov took a deep breath as she sifted through her list of ready excuses. A boy saved her when he brought them the true answer.

"Masta' Lain says everyone should go to the Great Hall! I hear that they've seen riders on the horizon," his voice trailed off as he relayed the message to the next room.

What is this?

The women rushed from the room, and Salene hurried towards Malov.

"What do you think happened?"

"I don't know. Maybe the supply train came back," she said distractedly. "Let's go." The two women bounded down the stairs and joined the stream of people spilling into the hallways.

Corious filled the doorway of the stone building. Scouts wedged their heads eagerly over his shoulder like puppies fighting for their mother's milk.

"Couldn't be rebels," he reasoned under his breath. "There's too many of them." The overpowering vibrations rattled the compound. Armor rubbed against his shoulder as Lain stalked past him.

"Shalkans?" he asked in a stoic manner, his sword catching and reflecting the remaining sunlight in the sky.

"They're not rebels; that's for sure. Cavalry is my guess."

"Go summon the troops," Lain directed the man behind him in an icy manner. "Corious, you stay." An inevitable dread hung over him.

"Shall I call for Marcelus or Perry?"

"No, we should get back inside the watchtower. If we summon the troops above ground, we will invite outright war," he explained as he withdrew to the safety of the stone building.

Corious had never been in the second story of the watchtower before, and even in the midst of a possible attack, he bounded up the stairs like a giddy child. He could see to the edge of the swamp, to the Halfast River on the horizon, and to their deserted tree farms to the right of the small bastions.

"The troops will mass below. The rumbling is far off yet. I can't tell if it's a large or a small number," Lain admitted, his face twisted in thought.

Corious tensed as he saw the cloud of dust and dirt appear and disappear on the horizon. "There are definitely horses."

"Probably about three or four hundred," Lain estimated.

Corious shuttered. "If they're Shalkans, I do not understand their plan. If it were a siege, they'd bring ships and unload infantry from the Halfast."

"And they'd be quite dull to conduct a three hundred man scouting mission."

"It seems we are not in immediate danger."

Lain neither refuted the statement nor agreed with it.

"Could they be allies?"

"What allies of ours have cavalry that large and come from the northeast?"

Corious raised his eyebrows. "My knowledge of Quantus Plain's history and their allies is little, but if they're not Shalkans, I'd like to assume they're rebels."

"Optimism is nice, but realism is needed. I doubt these are any known rebel allies."

Corious opened his mouth.

Bang. A single shot.

"Get down to the Great Hall. Address the people and tell them to arm themselves adequately and remain in a state of crisis. Have our men in battle formation." Lain was urgent. Corious stole a last glance at the dust cloud before slipping underground, unnoticeable to the world.

Lain stayed in the watch tower. His body was submerged in adrenaline, fear, and a sudden willpower. He did not know what awaited them. It had happened so fast: the vibrations, the scouts, and now the shot. Whose was it? The thunderous noise neared. Lain paced, restlessly listening to the cavalry before rushing downstairs through the hatch. He had to attend to his people.

"Uhm. Attention!" Corious stammered after clearing his throat. "By the order of Lain, our commander, I have been sent to address everyone. As you might know, there's a group of unidentified riders coming towards Quantus Plain." He took a shaky breath. "They are not necessarily Shalkans, though Lain has taken precautions in the case of an attack. There is no expected siege. Let me assure you, Lain and the captains shall repress any raid." As he finished, Lain burst through the hatch and onto the platform. Corious saluted Lain and retreated from the podium.

"Ladies, men, warriors of Quantus Plain! The time has come to put your bravery and swords to the test. Stay calm but arm yourselves appropriately. If you are a soldier or an archer, you must be in uniform and formation with your regiment and captain. Any men or women who desire to serve our army may also report to this hall as quickly as they can to find a weapon and armor. This gathering is dismissed to fulfill its duties," Lain completed his address within a minute and gave no time for objections or questions.

Corious stopped Lain by the shoulder. "Should I prepare my men?"

"You are a captain, Corious. I do believe I have told my men to go to their captains."

Corious saluted Lain rigidly. He guessed their visitors would arrive before sunset. Ree appeared at Corious's shoulder.

"Touching speech you made, Captain Corious."

Corious half laughed and half sighed which resulted in a unique snort. Ree eyed him curiously as he led him down the stairs.

"Our men have had very little battle experience," he stated. "If open war comes upon us, I fear the worst."

"As do I," Corious confessed. "Personally, I no longer believe these riders to be those of the Shalkans. Lain would have taken more drastic measures if he had thought so."

Ree adjusted his mail underneath his crimson and butternut tunic. "Nevertheless, we must get our regiments in formation."

They were working to align their men when Lain reappeared.

"All captains outside! They've crossed the Halfast!"

Corious tore up the steps and unlatched a second hatch. In his eagerness, he lost his balance but caught himself on the lip of the opening. He scrambled up and out of the building. The rumbling made his ears throb, and he could now decipher small figures on horses thundering their way towards the compounds.

"Lain," Corious asked, "do we know who they are yet?"

"They are too far to tell. Maybe knights from Renland, yet in that case, they would have come from the east."

"Oh," Corious said, watching the group of horsemen approach. He knew nothing of Renland. Ree and Marcelus tailed Corious, anxious to see the riders that had Quantus Plain in an uproar.

Marcelus seemed out of breath, and his words were heavy and far between. "Lain, who are these riders? I was training my cavalry troop when a kid ran in and said we were under attack. That little rogue!"

The rest of the captains gathered in the dim light.

"If these men are friends, I would dearly wish to know why they see it relevant to send no notice of their arrival and create such a panic on our behalf."

"They could be Shalkan mercenaries," Perry mentioned casually.

Lain rested his arm on his sword hilt. "That is a very dangerous possibility."

"They've stopped," Ree stated, pointing beyond Lain's head.

Lain whirled around. The rows of horsemen had halted in perfected form. They bore pikes.

"Go and have counsel with them," Ree suggested.

"And if they kill me?" Lain asked.

"Then we slay every last one of their dirty hides," suggested Marcelus.

Corious interjected, "I will go meet them."

Lain dismissed their ideas. "I do not fear them or my fate even if they interlock. I will be back. If I whistle twice, they are allies." Lain strode through the swaying grass of the plain.

"I don't necessarily like this idea," Perry stated.

Marcelus snorted. "You are the biggest worrier I have ever known, Perry."

Corious was antsy, and the anticipation of what was to come filled his veins. He unsheathed his sword and began twirling it absentmindedly in his left hand.

Lain neared the horsemen. Fifty yards separated him from the unfamiliar banner they bore. As he walked, a knot of riders pulled to the front, and one rider galloped in his direction. His heart thumped once for every two hoofbeats he heard coming his way. On a whim, he whistled a quivering note; it was the call that would send Faylene swooping down onto his gloved arm. As the horse neared, Lain began to see the details of the rider's uniform amidst the swirling dust from the plain. The muscular rider leapt from his horse.

"Greetings, horse master. What quest of yours would bring you into the realm of Quantus Plain?"

The hulking beast of a man scratched his thin beard but said nothing.

Lain stepped forward. "I asked, what is your quest?"

The man straightened to his full height. He towered over Lain. "My name is Boragheld, Chieftain of the guardians of the wall."

"Where might this wall be that you guard, Chieftain?"

"I am a knight of Meneas. My men and I have come to assist you in your undertaking to kill the Shalkans. We seek the warrior Lain."

Lain knelt on one knee in a sign of gratitude and presented his sword as he would a platter of food. "I am he. I thank you, Boragheld, chieftain of Meneas. Your assistance will hardly be in vain."

Boragheld pulled Lain to his feet. "I have not told you our whole tale, my friend."

"Come, we shall give you a grand welcoming here at Quantus Plain. We need not stay here in darkness with evil brimming across the river."

Boragheld looked at Lain from under thick eyebrows. "We were attacked more than once by the evil of which you speak."

Lain's eyebrows twitched beneath a furrowed brow. "You live in Meneas, Chieftain. How would the Shalkans assail you there? Has there been a revolution in your country?"

"That is part of the story I wish to tell you."

"Come then and relate to me this tale. I am afraid your horses will have to be left outside. We have no stables for them underground."

The chieftain grunted but did not complain. He waved to his troops and clicked his tongue harshly at his squire. "Kojan, bring Farl's horse to me. The Master needs a horse. Farl was slain by Shalkan riflemen," he explicated. "His horse, Bajhidia, needs a new master. Would you take him?"

The burly chieftain's offer honored Lain, and he felt obligated to accept. "If that is your wish, I certainly have no objections."

The knight nodded approvingly. "You would make a grand horse master, Master Lain. I believe you will be as competent a master to Bajhidia as Farl was."

Boragheld's squire brought the raven stallion to Lain who eagerly swung himself onto the scarlet, leather saddle of the sleek war horse. The horse whinnied, adjusted to the weight, and flicked its silky tail, brushing Lain across the shoulder. Faylene swooped jealously from the darkening sky, giving a startling cry as she plummeted to Lain's forearm. The horses neighed furiously and stamped the ground.

"You carry a hawk," the chieftain commented.

"Her name is Faylene. She is my eyes and ears past Quantus Plain. She is an excellent scout and friend."

Boragheld held out his meaty hand and briefly touched Faylene on her head. She squeaked but did not recoil. Boragheld said in admiration, "She is disciplined."

"Aye. That she is. Now you must let Quantus Plain welcome you." Lain galloped from the mass of riders, whistling twice to signal their friendship.

A single torch lit the atramentous building. Inside, Lain could barely distinguish the tired faces of Ree and Perry from their somber background. Lain dismounted Bajhidia.

"Is she yours?" Perry questioned.

"She is indeed," Lain said proudly before addressing the riders outside. "Fit as many of your horses as you can inside these three buildings. The rest of you may lead your steeds behind the buildings. There is grain in the underground silo."

Some riders grumbled irritably at having to leave their horses outside, but most seemed too weary to notice. Every warrior had jet black hair, and most had light skin. They wore heavy armor and mail complemented by swords at their hips and pikes in their hands. Their appearance remained unexplained. Historically, Meneas had never supported the rebels. Boragheld must have mustered his own men to assist them.

"We are ready to enter, Master Lain," Boragheld stated. "My men also thank you for your ready acceptance."

"Boragheld," Lain began, "you should not thank me. You are the one coming to help me and my cause."

"We must hold council after the initiation," Boragheld suggested somberly.

I don't understand. "Perry, are the people gathered?"

"Somewhat," Perry admitted as he opened the hatch.

Lain entered surrounded by his captains. Behind them strode Boragheld, and behind him came his redoubtable men. The stately procession passed through the hushed, sepulchral halls. As the men passed, the people shrank to the wall. The uniforms of the Protectors of the Wall were worn and stained with recent splotches of blood. Drawn faces revealed no emotions, and their steps were precise and mechanical. Lain did not notice their gravity; his heart was too full of joy. The men who fell in step behind him were grim, experienced warriors. Each wore a cape that rippled from his shoulders and swept across the stone floors. Power emanated strongly from their athletic bodies, but their dark eyes shone sadly with the horror of war and the determination of desperate men. In their mien, they were the epitome of perfect warriors—a seemly and timely gift from the Almighty.

"Boragheld, your men may rest from your journey here. Food and drink will be brought shortly." Boragheld tapped his foot impatiently. Lain's eyes flickered to the foot and then to the face. "Or do you wish to hold council immediately?"

The Horse Rider scratched at his beard knowingly. "Now is best, I should think. Turethelm and Ghuendar, come. We shall hold council with Master Lain and his warriors."

The men strode gracefully to their leader. They bowed elaborately and then turned respectfully to Boragheld.

"May we first sharpen our swords, Boragheld?"

"If Master Lain consents." Boragheld turned to Lain expectantly.

Furrows formed on Lain's brow. "Sharpen your swords? I understand we are in danger, but I assure you, no harm shall befall you before nightfall."

"Sharpening our swords is a custom in our country to prepare for council and talk of war. It symbolizes that when war comes, we will be prepared."

"Then sharpen your swords, mighty Riders. Sharpen, and sharpen well."

The council room felt small and cramped. A single torch cast ghastly shadows on nearby objects. Though ravaged by hunger, Boragheld and his men refused to touch food until the meeting ended. Their tough, craggy faces held an eerie resemblance to Ree's. Assimilating to the Riders' customs, Lain had dressed in full battle attire. Their eyes now scrutinized every detail of his armor and being.

"I will be brief and honest with you, Master Lain. We have not been dispatched as soldiers coming to your rescue. My Riders, and I, Protectors of the Wall, have fled." At this statement, a gloom passed over the men's faces. "We fled from our positions like pusillanimous boys," he grieved, "and when we heard of Quantus Plain, we hoped you would be sympathetic to our needs. We were right in our surmise. We have failed once, but we hope to redeem ourselves by dying side by side with your men if you grant us the honor."

Lain was dumbstruck.

Ree spoke in his place. "Riders and Protectors of the Wall of Meneas, we do not doubt your ability or your loyalty, yet I must know what pushed men of your valor from your home when the enemy was near."

One of Boragheld's men answered, "The Shalkans have developed a weapon which hurls boulders and fouler missiles at great speeds. After five months of battering and many lives lost, there was no wall to protect us. The enemy rushed and overwhelmed us. We fled."

"And what of the people of Meneas?"

The Rider bowed his head. "Once the wall was breached, we retreated into the towns, thinking to warn the people. When we arrived, we found ourselves too late. The cannons had found them first."

The mournful council fell silent.

"This evil does not rest," Lain whispered bitterly. "We must stay its blood thirst. Across the river, the officials huddle on our borders. Our fortress is not impregnable. It can be breached. Do we fight?"

Corious answered vehemently, "We have waited far too long for this moment. At present, we have the men and the reinforcements. We need to attack the officials while they have not fully mustered. We fight."

Boragheld slammed his fist on the table. With a terrible roar, he jumped from his seat. "For Quantus Plain and for the Border Wall!"

His men echoed, "For Quantus Plain and the Border Wall!"

"For freedom," Corious added.

"So this is what the last alliance of men looks like," Lain commented sadly. "May the Almighty fight with us."

"May we fight with the Almighty." The men unsheathed their swords and lay the naked steel upon the table.

Outside the scout tower, the night air swirled about Tar's face as he awaited his regiment. A lump rose in his throat. For once in his perilous life, Tar was scared. His eyes did not dart, and his hand did not tremble; but the uneasiness in the pit of his stomach twisted his insides into complicated knots. The tramping of dozens of boots went by him as envoys crisply delivered directions. Tar's regiment, led by Lord Perry, would be the second infantry regiment to head southwest to blockade the river. Another five infantry regiments, led by Lain, Ree, Corious, Malov, and another captain by the name of Hans would complete a straight journey west towards the closest Shalkan fortress. After Tar's regiment blockaded the Halfast River, they would join with Lain to conduct an assault on the fort. The Meneas Riders along with Marcelus and his cavalry would head north, curve southwest, and then attack the second Shalkan compound. By the time the cavalry had begun their attack, Lain's and Perry's regiments would arrive to aid them. Lain's voice interrupted his troubled thoughts.

"Tar, Faylene would not be as of much use to me as she would to you. I believe she wanted to go with you anyway."

Tar lifted his arm. In a moment, he heard the wings smoothly cutting the air and Faylene's shriek as she transferred her weight onto his leather arm guard.

"You don't have to go, Tar. Aban and Radosh have decided to enter a guard unit."

Tar understood the implication of Lain's statement. As a guard, Aban and Radosh would avoid most of the harsh fighting. Tar had joined the infantry. "No," Tar answered, "My purpose is set. I must protect Quantus Plain and avenge my village. I will go."

"Then I wish you good fortune and safety. May the Almighty protect us all."

The Almighty? There was no Almighty when my village needed Him.

Where were you when the Almighty needed you? Shrie's voice shot back. *When we thrust the Almighty from our lives, evil replaces Him. Do not let the darkness take you.*

In a surge of emotion, Tar returned the support. "May the Almighty protect you. And let the Shalkans be defeated." Tar listened as Lain's footsteps faded away. Another gust of wind pushed through the blustery night. He unsheathed the beautiful sword Lain had given him and wished dearly to use it worthily. Lain was a good man and leader; Tar hoped they would meet again after the assault on the Shalkan fortifications. The hawk on his arm repositioned her talons as she ruffled her feathers.

"Well, it is time, Faylene," he sighed, gripping his sword tightly as he heard his regiment called to formation. The weapon gave him little comfort, but the quiet, fearless hawk on his arm reassured him of his mission.

Forlorn, sickly mist shrouded the base of the Tower. The ghosts of murdered men howled and, like the mist, they twisted their mutilated, ephemeral bodies. Sooty turrets like ghastly knives pierced the sky. No light distinguished between night and day. It was a desolate, forsaken land in which he had chosen to establish his reign. Here, he had learned to forget his past. His name was Turock—a harsh, guttural, and much feared name. It fit him well.

Massive metal plates covered his body, and etched into each was his insignia: a black fist rising. Three heads taller than most men, he towered above his henchmen. Men strangled by contempt and bitterness were drawn to his presence. Like flies to dung, they massed at his Tower, awaiting his commands.

The official ran harder; he was getting closer. The message he carried seemed a heavy burden. The sole survivor of a skirmish near Quantus Plain, he came to tell the Ruler of the last resistance. Quantus Plain was not defeated. He could feel the minatory darkness thickening about him. He hated it and loved it; for he was confined to it forever. The Tower grew before his eyes. Rushing through the doors, he sprinted past the guards and up the stairs which wound through the heart of the Tower. They would lead him to the Ruler.

Turock listened to the monotonous footsteps. They faltered, as they should. His forces waited. He would not address them until the footsteps ceased.

Hours later, the official collapsed at his door.

"Tired?" The question darted from his mouth in biting pleasure.

The official scrambled to his feet. "No, Ruler," he rasped, "I have a message." His breath came heavily and stunk of the swamps. "Quantus Plain is persistent in its resistance."

"So they remain alive." Emotion was void from the words, but a rage filled him. It surged uncontrollably through his body, consuming him, fueling his wrath. Picking the official up by the back of the neck, Turock flung open the windows. At the sight of their Ruler, the Shalkans below roared and bashed their guns against the ground. The Tower shook with the energy. Standing on the sill, Turock's voice reverberated hoarsely.

"There is a messenger with an undesirable message. He says Quantus Plain still thrives."

The officials bellowed loudly.

"So take your messenger back," he said hurtling the man through the air, "and change the message. I once promised you that the Shalkans would one day establish their reign. That time has come."

The officials cheered once more before marching swiftly away. Their procession could be heard from miles away, and the vibrations were felt from even greater distances. With an effortless, unnatural speed, Turock descended the stairs and slipped into the tunnel which ran below the Tower and under the swamps.

Perry stealthily worked his way to the river. The mist which often haunted the river rose like a drove of humming insects. Perry's ears rang with the constant droning, but he was thankful that the noise covered his steps. Behind him, his men fell perfectly into line. They reached the bank of the Halfast without trouble, engraving their muddy boot prints into the sloppy bank. The night was calm, and a false sense of security invaded their consciousness.

Perry pursued the gurgling water downstream to where it would open and meet the ocean. The rebels had been sent to blockade its width. If anymore forces rendezvoused with the Shalkan's heavily armored infantry in the forts, it would spell disaster for rebels. Perry shivered. He detested the prolonged wait before battle. Sweat rolled down his face, though the night was not warm. Uneasily he shifted the pack on his back. Identical to his were the bulky bundles strapped to his companions.

With sore backs, the rebels arrived at their destination. A layer of sweat and mist covered their faces and arms. As gently as a mother places her baby in a crib, the men removed their packs and set them on the ground. Perry fingered the rough sketch of the barricade. Worriedly, he surveyed their materials. The plan seemed far-fetched and unrealistic. They were to stretch a long chain across the river, securing it to posts on either side of the bank. He had seen the posts before; the broken columns had long rested as the reminders of a forlorn and otherwise forgotten civilization. No one had ever tried to move them.

Perry reviewed the plan. The chain's width was the size of his fist and hundreds of paces long. Dense spikes, meant for the piercing of hulls, jutted from its exterior. Every man wrenched a coiled piece of the chain from his pack and as hastily as possible connected his sections with the others. Holding one end, Perry placed the flat of the metal over his shoulder and waded into the shallows.

Tar fumbled the chain. Its coarse surface scraped his hands, and even his calluses did not protect him. He looped one end around the old pillar and then twisted the other end through the loop and back out again. The men next to him took the other end and heaved as the stone gave a horrendous groan. Tar heard a chink as the spiked chain grew taut and rigid. Perry's behest arrested them. The men waited for another section of the chain to be attached.

The inky night hid their movements, and a soldier unwittingly hit Tar in the head as he grabbed for a piece of the chain. Tar grimaced but said nothing. Hurriedly, he motioned for someone to tighten the slack. As the opposite end became taut, a piece of discarded chain jammed into Tar's foot. He groaned inwardly.

"Dam up the bottom. Make haste! Lain will not want his reinforcements unfashionably late." Only Perry would link fashion and war. With the mention of battle, the soldiers became more attentive, and they completed the work before any shots were heard.

Tar shifted his weight impatiently as Perry conferred routes with the other captain; his mind had too much time to contemplate the inevitable battle. Tar called for Faylene. As she landed swiftly, voices carried the argument to him through the night air. Faylene shrieked agitatedly. Tar had to speak.

"If we don't go now, routes will serve us no purpose. We cannot arrive too late, Lord Perry," Tar called, rousing some agreeing murmurs.

Perry faced his troops. "The young lad is right. Forget formation, soldiers. We make for Halfast's crossing with headlong speed. Stick together."

The furtive soldiers melted into the terrain which had birthed them. The fort was not far.

Marcelus bounced in the saddle. Not even the heavy armor he wore could hold him down. Though an adept horseman, today he could not find the rhythm of the run. The overwhelming sound of hundreds of horses thundered in his ears. Betwixt the men of Meneas, he and his unit rode north to the Shalkans' second fort. Moving swiftly over the barren plain, Marcelus strained to see past the head riders. For better or for worse, they had decided to attack during the night. Marcelus had not been prepared for the rushed attack. He hoped the officials would share his dismay. After several minutes of hard riding with the fort looming ahead of them, they slowed to a walk.

Marcelus grinned; this was his cue. Slipping off his horse, he took a solid, wooden rod from the saddle. Using some flint and steel from his saddlebag, he created a spark and set the tip on fire. He could sense everyone's eyes upon him. As he snuck towards the fort, he searched the wall for any lips or crevices which could serve as foot holds. Scanning the vertical surface, he noticed discretely placed archer holes lining the wall. With a snap of his fingers, he called his horse to him. Climbing onto the saddle, he stuck the rapidly burning rod in his mouth. He choked on the smoke but leapt crazily at the wall.

Boragheld barely resisted verbalizing the steady stream of curses running through his head. *The stupid captain!* Lain had told him this Marcelus was brave and reliable, not insane. The chieftain almost did not believe it as Marcelus's hands gripped the edge of the hole. The rod burned dangerously close to Marcelus's face as he swung his leg in the air and as his foot caught in the adjacent hold. Using one hand, he precariously removed the rod from his mouth and peered into the rectangular opening. An eye stared back.

Marcelus stuffed the rod into the aperture. Riding beneath a precariously balanced Marcelus, Boragheld tossed him another burning stick. Methodically, Marcelus worked his way around the fort, throwing the burning poles into the center of the fort or lodging them in the wooden frame wedged between the stonework.

As Boragheld threw the last torch to him, Marcelus heard strange noises issuing from the fort. The amount of smoke gushing forth was enough to make him lightheaded. A glint caught his eye, and he noticed a shiny barrel poking from the last hole. With the rod, Marcelus bashed the gun, and it hurtled to the ground. Boragheld called indistinguishable words to him. *The lure must be working.* With this alarming notion, he gave a loud war cry, dropped from the wall, and landed on his horse. Far from pleased with Marcelus's maneuver, his horse reared, throwing its front legs into the air. Reaching crazily for the mane, Marcelus managed to hold on and direct the incensed creature back into formation. He saluted Boragheld and rode to his men as shapes spilled from the compound.

Beyond the sight of officials but in the immediate view of their rebel captains, Lain had massed his troops in no particular configuration. Heading the irregular mass behind him, Lain could already hear the trickle of water forty, if not thirty, yards away. He could find Halfast's Crossing in the dead of the night, which was fortunate, because night it was. The fort stood no more than forty or fifty paces from the shallows. Lain adjusted a metal plate on his shoulder before crawling on his hands and knees.

Momentarily, there was a break in the underbrush, and he saw the fort. Lain signaled the men to draw their bows. No sooner had he voiced the command when an arrow whizzed over his head, arcing silently in the clear night and dropping behind the stone ramparts of the fort. Lain ground his teeth.

"Assail the invaders!" Lain charged forward blindly, crashing through the last of the underbrush and diving into the river crossing.

Corious heard the twang of the bowstring next to him and watched horrified as it fell into the official compound. He cursed the dimwitted man next to him before fitting an arrow to his bow. Lain would not waste time after their position had been compromised. Bounding through the reeds, the sea of rebels converged on the fort. Corious broke through the last of the undergrowth and let his arrow fly over the fort's stone walls.

"Hold your fire!" Lain cried. The chilly water rose above his head as he tumbled into it. As he hurriedly regained his balance, the first gunshots exploded around him and plunged into the river beside him.

Someone knocked into Corious from behind; he turned to yell at the offender before realizing the man had been shot twice in the head. Corious felt his stomach heave violently as the dead rebel slid beneath the water. In the midst of the bullets, he loaded his bow. Sighting the arrow's path down the shaft, he chose his target. The arrow struck the intended man in the upper thigh. Oblivious to the charge around him, Corious witnessed in satisfaction as the man hit the ground and as the partially exposed arrow shaft snapped beneath his weight. A man's legs collided awkwardly with Corious's chest. Someone grabbed Corious, and he narrowly avoided a bullet threatening to slice his tunic.

"What in the Almighty's name are you doing Corious? This is a battle!"

Corious could not find the words to reply as Ree tossed him ashore. He slogged ashamedly out of the mud as the sounds of the battle swept around him. Rebels dove for cover behind a grove of trees near the fort. Corious copied their movements.

"Where is Lain?" he asked another rebel.

The rebel pointed into the trees and loaded his bow. Corious trod towards Lain and the knot of captains which had formed around him. Before he could reach them, he heard a familiar creaking and rumbling. Corious's heart skipped a beat. Bullets shredded trees. His clammy hands retained a tenuous grip on his bow.

"Cannons," he murmured as he whipped out his bow and crept closer. He aimed at the closest man. "That's interesting."

Thump. The first man fell.

"Yet they are useless."

Thump. The second man died.

"If there is no one to man them."

Thump. The third man died with his lips to his horn.

Corious shot the fourth and final man as he fled down the stairs. He did not linger to admire his shots this time but rather whistled the assault call to Lain. The answer was staggering. Lain and Ree, along with their men, tore from the trees and broke their former silence with calls of vengeance. From behind their ramparts, the officials fired steadily. Corious answered the officials' bullets with his arrows.

"Steady yourselves, and fire!" Corious positioned his bow at an obtuse angle. "Aim for the cauldron bearers!" Corious shrieked as several Shalkans brought immense cauldrons of hot oil to the top of the wall. Arrows pierced the tenebrous night. Several officials prepared to free the cauldrons of their contents. Corious released an arrow hastily, and it glanced harmlessly off the top of the cauldron. He loaded another frenzied arrow, but a well-aimed arrow of his fellow soldier hit one man in the neck first. "Bless you!" Corious gasped. He aimed his second arrow with the deliberation time now allowed him. After Corious's arrow embedded itself in flesh, another rebel nailed an official in the head. The Shalkan jerked erratically and knocked the cauldron of oil inside the fort; hideous, tangled screams scratched at the night sky.

"Men, we must load our bows with lighted arrows!" Corious rushed into the mangled grove of trees and found what he sought. On a carefully hidden stump, smoldering ashes covered a cache of extra bows, knives, swords, and spears; small tongues of fire warmed the coals.

In anticipation, the men gathered beside him. Corious took a moment to admire

Lain's ingenuity before lighting his arrow. In a second, the flame caught, and with the fiery tip of his arrow, Corious aimed for the fort's courtyard. As a tongue of fire licked at his face, he released the string. The tiny fireball diminished as it dived over the wall. Seconds later, a poof of flame erupted from the compound.

Lain watched as the pinpricks of inferno sailed through the sky. Calling his men away from the flames, he arranged them in a hastily organized ambush as the officials emerged from the fort. He waited uncomplainingly. The Shalkans on fire rewarded his patience by springing the trap and running frantically for the river. Lain's men loaded and released their arrows at the sound of his sharp whistle. Their positions were compromised with the carnage, and at another call, his men drew their swords and danced through the enemy's raining bullets.

Lain rushed into battle. He slew the nearest official and disarmed another in one stroke. Evading a gun barrel, Lain then bashed its owner mercilessly in the head before confronting a tall Shalkan and delivering a shattering blow to his knee. The Shalkan soldier groaned deeply as he staggered on the severed leg. Lain advanced, faking a slash to his right. The Shalkan began to defend himself from the feigned blow as Lain drove his sword through the man's useless resistance. The man choked on his own blood and clawed at the blade jutting from his neck, scraping off his finger nails. Lain ripped his sword swiftly from the official's throat, and to end the man's misery, he beheaded him. Reuniting with his men, Lain cleared a path through the remaining Shalkan defenses.

The remaining officials fled into the woods, and the stone of the fortress radiated heat. Lain and the rebels crept forward. Acrid fumes introduced their eyes to a macabre scene. Flames devoured the ground, and the remains of buildings and soldiers tormented the forsaken ground. The rebels kicked aside corpses spread evenly throughout the complex. A creeping movement caught Lain's attention.

"Shalkans!" Lain pushed the word from his lungs forcefully. Lain and his troops backed away the skulking forms. Behind him, a pike speared a rebel. "If they do not have the sense to surrender, slay them!"

In their fervent desire for victory, the rebels trampled, slew, or threw the last defenders of the garrison into the fire. Malov approached Lain.

"Master Lain? I'm afraid some of the women ran away."

"Did you not think some of my men did not run as well? Don't be worried, Lady Malov; they always are found back at Quantus Plain."

"Some of these women do not know their way back as easily as your men do."

"That is a risk they took. What does your company number, my lady?"

"I do not know. Some women are back in the forest, some are in the fort fighting, and the others I have mustered at the eastern wall."

"We shall extinguish the fire and regroup. If you and your women wish, you have my permission to wash your faces and weapons in the river."

Malov vanished into the receding chaos to relate his message to her troops. Lain had suspected a female regiment would be awkward and inefficient by virtue of their inexperience, yet Malov had done well leading them. The first rebels emerged from the burning fort.

"Well done men," he addressed them informally. "Let us count the dead and wounded."

Smudged with soot and dirt, Corious and Ree walked side by side out of the burning garrison. Though Ree had been nailed in the chest with the butt of a gun and could hardly take a deep breath without coughing up blood, his injuries and worries were soon forgotten as he strode victoriously under the raised portcullis of the fort. The rebels, for once, had outnumbered their foes and had won an outright victory. As for the Shalkans, Lain's men had left none alive.

Corious slapped his knee. "Your prowess in battle has claimed more lives than mine."

"Shrie would've beaten us both." Ree slipped into a reverie. "She missed out didn't she?"

A sharp whistle broke their reminiscing.

"We are the victors today!" Lain announced. "Yet there are bodies to recover, a fire to douse, and men to reinforce. Let us work swiftly and be on our way." The rebels swarmed the fort, either carrying buckets of water, bodies, or unpacked supplies. Ree and Corious recovered the bodies of their comrades. Corious went to the river to find the man who had fallen in behind him. A number of bodies claimed the same spot as their temporary residence.

Corious yanked a bloated body from the water by its wrists but rinsed his hands vigorously in the water before pulling out the others. One man's chest lifted.

"By the Almighty," Corious gasped. "You there, hello?" Corious poked him, but he did not stir. Corious cut the leather bindings that held the man's shattered breastplate to his chest. As he discarded the bits and pieces of jagged metal, the man's torso shuddered, and water dropped from his mouth as he sat momentarily in a contorted cough. The man shut his eyes as fresh blood squeezed out from between his fingers. A bullet had pierced the skin beside his heart.

"Can you talk? Are you okay?"

"I am in pain," he murmured.

Corious held the man's flaccid hand and reassured him, "We'll get you back to Quantus Plain."

Marcelus spurred his horse onward. He rode a grey stallion with a silver, pointed patch of hair on her head; he rubbed it superstitiously. She neighed agitatedly as a Shalkan began to fire into the riders. Marcelus reached down with his sword and beheaded the offender. Swinging back in his saddle, he cried out as a single Shalkan bore down upon him. Before Marcelus could react, the stallion reared and battered the man with her powerful hooves. Marcelus laughed in relief.

"That one counts as yours, lassie," he told her as he swung his sword above his head like a lasso. There were plenty of Shalkan soldiers to keep him busy, and it seemed like more issued from the compound with every passing moment. Marcelus cut down a fleeing official, galloping to the head of the riders.

"Assault the compound!" The cavalry galloped towards the door, driving the Shalkans back into the buildings. Those of the enemy who could not run as fast melted under the rolling waves of horsemen. Marcelus brandished his sword in front of him.

The blast of a deep horn resounded through the air, and the rallied officials burst from the compound doors. Their guns were loaded and aimed. Marcelus gaped as the commander waved his gloved hand and as dozens of cracks boomed in the night. Marcelus tightly squeezed his eyes shut. He waited for his horse to crumble beneath him, but she did not. He smashed through the official lines before they could reload. Tearing apart any man who unsheathed his saber, his horse eliminated any man who otherwise obstructed her path. He stampeded the enemy front. The Shalkan commander awaited him.

"Feast upon your own devilry!" Marcelus cried as he fired the pistol into the Shalkan's face. The commander's face warped in pain, and his body crumpled.

The remaining rebels collided with the battered Shalkan lines. In impassioned clashes of flesh and steel, mayhem flung riders into the air. Empowered by destruction, chaos governed.

"Regroup, men!" Marcelus sheathed his sword, devoting both of his hands to his horse's reins.

Boragheld rode towards him, smoldering in anger. "They shoot down our horses like dogs! Curse them!"

Marcelus narrowed his eyes. "What do you say we chase them into the river, eh?"

Boragheld gave a gruff cry as he entered the compound. "Follow us men! Avenge your horses, avenge your brothers!"

The rebels' valiant war cries pained the ears. Marcelus and Boragheld searched intently for the remaining Shalkans. The men crowded in among them, and the riders filled the static compound.

"Where are they?"

Strange shadows frolicked on the wall.

"They're outside burning the compound!"

"Out the door! Go! Go! Go!" A burning timber collapsed against the doorway. At the bifurcation of the structure, an avalanche of stone showered from the wall. Marcelus's armor grew dangerously hot, and sweat poured profusely from his body.

"Hold your nerves!"

But the fire had startled the horses which whinnied maniacally within the fiery compound. One horse ruptured a back wall and tumbled into the river dozens of feet below. Marcelus threw off his helmet and gloves and desperately tried to find his way through the maze of burning wood. He called for his men to pursue him as he narrowly avoided a falling torch. A back door came into view, but it was locked and barred. Spurring his horse on nonetheless, Marcelus and his stallion exploded through the wood weakened by fire.

Marcelus sucked the fresh air into his lungs, but he was not free. The Shalkans waiting outside had noticed his escape. He fled. Galloping along the field's edge, he prayed his horse's speed would surpass that of Shalkan bullets.

Marcelus's face hit the ground as he lost control of his horse. Stumbling back onto his feet in a rush of momentum, Marcelus felt his head spin. His entire body vibrated like a ringing gong. He stepped towards his horse but swooned in dizziness. He crawled to the river. Arrows whizzed past his ear. Hundreds of hooves thundered past him, and his body sagged. Changing his direction from the river to his whimpering horse, Marcelus coughed. The smoke invaded his lungs, and he stroked his horse mournfully. He did not know if she had been shot or if she had fallen, but before the world turned black, he curled against her, burying his head in her mane.

Boragheld left the compound behind his men. He vowed on behalf of those dead to squash the last resistance. Rallying his men, he hunted the remaining splinter groups of officials. Bullets shrieked by his face, thrilling him. The battle was vicious and bloody but barely lasted two minutes. After an intense show of strength and spirit, Boragheld and his men inundated the enemy.

"Round them up and tie them at the wrists." He would not give them the pleasure of a quick death.

Scurrying to obey his commands, the men checked their knots. Boragheld watched the proceedings closely. Marcelus was missing.

"Rider Numinrare, have you seen the Captain?" Remorse filled him as his rider sadly shook his head. "Gather the officials into a small group and await my command. Have any extra men you can spare help me find the bod—"

The bestial detonation rattled the ground and sent Boragheld from his mount with an unnatural speed. Fire ravaged the spot where his men and the officials had once been. The ships had reached the blockade.

"Retreat! Back to Quantus Plain!"

His remaining men stooped and headed for the buildings. The echoing sounds of firing cannons traveled through the air. As the vibrations pitched the ground up and down, Boragheld struggled to keep his horse under control. He urged it into a canter. Beside him, he noticed another horse carrying a limp man. Sidling beside the mad creature, Boragheld grabbed the man and thrust his slumped form over his lap. Taking the reins of the other horse, he tossed them to a limping man below. The man gratefully took them and managed to mount the horse.

For as long as was humanly possible, Boragheld bore the heat of the flames and located his lost men. The soot was overbearing, and he caved in the saddle. This was not how he wanted die. He had a responsibility, a duty, to the man he carried and to the people of Quantus Plain who had welcomed him…His vision blurred, but with a strangled cry, he kicked his horse and headed blindly towards Quantus Plain.

Lain dragged the last, bleeding man to a makeshift cot. With hardened hands, he bound the wound with a strip of his shirt before relinquishing his patient to several of his soldiers. They would carry the injured to the overflowing medical ward. Wiping his hands on his tunic, Lain surveyed his fighting forces. Less than half of his men would be able to join in the next battle. Filing everyone into place, he congratulated his soldiers proudly. Malov jerkily reached for his arm.

"Lain, do you hear it?"

A falcon's cry coursed through the air. Lain froze. Four calls lingered on the wind.

"What does it mean, Lain?" a soldier cried out, half in alarm, half in hope.

Lain clenched his jaw. "The enemy draws near. Unsheathe your swords."

Swords scraped against sheaths. Thuchuck. Masses of metal recoiled forcefully. Lain's body tensed. The success of the entire battle depended on where it would land. A blast throttled the ground. His eyes closed involuntarily, and the breath rushed in and out of his lungs.

"Cannons! The ships have reached the river."

"We may yet make it. Corious, set the pace back. Soldiers, if you cannot keep up, abandon your armor."

As Corious rushed to the front, Lain gripped his arm. The words would not leave Lain's mouth, but Corious understood Lain's unvoiced command. Hacking up something caught in his throat, Corious ran. Another cannonball flew through the air. This time it landed closer. Corious stumbled. His legs felt like jelly. There was another presence beside him. He knew the grimy face to be Ree's.

"Corious," he shouted over the commotion, "if they're going to win, make them work for it!" His breathing quickened. He saw Malov stagger.

"Ree!" she cried.

Ree hoisted Malov in his arms. Her hair trailed behind Ree like a flag whipping in the wind. The others were close behind as they approached the outside buildings of Quantus Plain. So close. Thuchuck.

"Someone's got to sabotage the ship."

"Corious, you have an order. You cannot abandon your position. Take Malov."

Slowing, Corious shifted her weak body onto his back. "What are you doing?"

"I'm going to the ship."

"My spirit is with you."

Ree blended into the masses of men running behind him. Some attempted to turn him around, but the man's decision would not be altered. As they distanced themselves from the ship, hoofbeats filled the air. The Riders of Meneas had returned; their assigned fort was in flames. *How ironic*, Corious mourned. *They usurped the official's power only to run from them.* They had won, and they had lost. Corious labored for fresh oxygen. Malov's body sagged against his shoulders. Searching with his hands, he located the straps that secured her armor. With his knife, he cut them loose and listened as they clattered to the ground and were trampled. The smoke began to clear. The officials would see them.

And then they were there—entering the building, ushering in the Riders and the survivors. *Why are there so few?* Another cannonball connected with the ground, but it was too far away to wreak havoc. Smoke billowed in all directions. Everyone was in. He had completed his job. *Where is Lain?* Small flickers of light erupted from the ship; gunfire spattered into the late night. A bleeding figure rushed towards them. Passing Malov into the arms of another soldier, Corious recognized Ree.

"What happened?"

Ree shook his head. "I couldn't get close, but at least the chain was holding."

"Let's hope the spikes sink the ships."

The group from the river arrived; Lain had gone back for them.

"Is everyone in?" Lain gasped.

"Everyone! Now hurry!" Corious encouraged. Tar strode confidently behind Lain. Faylene was perched on his shoulder. "Tar!"

Tar halted at the sound of his name. The units spilled into the buildings. He was a rock around which flowed the river of people. "Is that you, Corious?"

"Over here!"

Tar directed himself towards Corious's voice. "I slew two officials on the ship with river rocks."

"Sink the boat too?" Corious joked. Tar shrugged. They were the last to enter the building and slide down the dusty hatch. Lain closed, locked, and barricaded it.

"Get the injured to the medical ward, officers to the council room, and Roth! Where the hell is Roth?" Lain seemed furious.

A sturdy man stood at attention. Lain greeted him brusquely. "The tree farms, how do they fare?"

"As well as they can surrounded by smoke and fire."

"Good. Bring in all the food you can."

Corious found himself behind Lain. "You expect a siege."

Lain met his eyes. "I expect nothing but the worst."

Pandemonium filled the halls as people's voices bounced stridently off the walls. Soldiers haphazardly carrying the injured on stretchers barely avoided crashing into bystanders. Healers frantically attended to patients, and wives virtually ransacked the crowd in search of their husbands while hushing crying children. Boragheld joined Corious, Ree, Lain, and the other captains in the procession to the council room. Corious thumped Boragheld on the back.

"I've never lost a battle before."

"All is not yet lost."

Corious's eyes were downcast. "How was your battle?"

"We had won. You?"

"Same."

"Curse the ship and the forsaken that sail it."

Swords clattered against chairs as the men sat. Lain ripped a map from the wall.

"If the officials break the chain, more ships will come. More ships bring more officials and more death. They will surround us. We have to keep them out by attacking from the outside. Who agrees?"

Silence, at first, pervaded the room, and then a slight, high pitched noise grew in immensity and volume until the men covered their ears and slid to their knees. The sound of metal being strained to its ultimate breaking point grated on and on as the Shalkan ship bashed its hull against the chain. Wood cracked, and metal grinded. Thump, thump, thump. The hearts of men waited. Abruptly the noise ceased.

Men kept still, their hearts elated for a moment's hope only to be dashed in resounding fear. Snapped under the immense pressure, the chain sank. In their suicidal mission, the officials had destroyed their first warship but breached the rebel's last defense. Involuntarily, everyone turned to Lain, and what they saw terrified them. Standing before them was a man whose eyes shone with the inevitable fate he would face. The grim set of his jaw, his pinched lips, and his white fist encompassing a sword spoke of death. His cape swirled around him as he neared the stone wall engraved with tiny marks. For every man that had died, he carved a new mark on the wall and on his heart.

The thundering of footsteps and the creaking of innumerable ships making their way through the river made the hearts of men falter. The ground pulsated, and stones showered from the ceiling as Lain carved his last mark. Quantus Plain was under siege.

So ends the first book of the Chronicles of the Insurrection

The Second Book

Chapter 1

"We also rejoice in our sufferings, because we know that suffering produces perseverance; perseverance, character; and character, hope."
Romans 5: 3–4

Fires flickering in ancient wonder,
Ambiguous shapes and thrashing thunder
Premonition, petition, fruition.
The jungle people of this wood
Valorous, cavalier they stood,
Justifying their existence.
Against the darkness bearers—foes,
They fought as the great River flows:
Coursing, boiling energy.
A rising fist from a fiery hole,
Extinguish the light of living souls;
Horrendous victor, come and destroy.
Resistance, prevail and conquer my heart!
I hear Almighty's voice, a piercing dart.
Leave me a promise.
Of an eternal world spurned.
Throw chaff, enemy to burn,
Take your loyal, faithful home.
Good does not always prevail; times come closed,
Though time has not yet, we can suppose
That it will, and we wait patiently.
In the final clash to determine
War—immortal powers seeped in sin,

Almighty, return in clouds of might
Rest thee, you in an eternal spite.

Dashjmar sang over the fire, his eyes closed in solemn ceremony. Shrie regarded him intently. It was night, and they had bivouacked at the old island. She was alone with Dashjmar.

"Of what you sing, Dashjmar?"

He did not seem perturbed by her interruption. "Of the old ways and of the ways to come," he answered fluidly.

"Hhean," Shrie grunted. "Dashjmar, how you think Corious, Ree, and Tar do?"

The humming stopped abruptly. Dashjmar answered her without opening his eyes. "I cannot tell."

"Dashjmar speaks vaguely," Shrie said, distressed. "Maybe is a bad idea Shrie goes to find tribe."

"No," Dashjmar said firmly. His gold armband twinkled in the firelight. "No, you are to go. That much I can tell." The humming heightened into a chant. The fire danced, but the island, without thirteen bustling figures training, laughing, and talking, seemed dead. Her former companions were dreams escaping from a waking sleeper's mind. Shrie could not envision them amongst armored soldiers defending a civilization she had never seen.

A zephyr coaxed her hair from her shoulders and lifted it in twitching strands. Distractedly, she brushed a floating tress away from her face and patted Gog. The scenes of the past, tucked in the corner of her mind, threatened to melt away before the tides of the present. She held unrelentingly to the last memories of her friends and her tribe.

She missed being surrounded by them; in comparison, Dashjmar seemed like ersatz company. While he admonished her or taught her about the ancient realms of Kurak, layers of seclusion shrouded his past and identity. He had bestowed upon her one of his tribe's battle staves though her skills with the tribe's bow could easily challenge his. And even when Dashjmar occasionally gave her his approbation, he never failed to give her his disapproval. His voice echoed in her mind.

"Whether you choose to believe it or not, you are part of the weaving of this age, of its battles and of its future. It is a time of insurrection for this land. Aid it well."

Twirling the staff, she rose from the fire, leaving Dashjmar to meditate on the past. She would take his advice and act in the present. She did not notice him watching her as she strode away. Her bare feet made slight imprints in the soft ground until broken cobblestones vanquished the wilting grass. Reaching the middle of the yard, she bowed to her imaginary foe. With her staff, she worked through the motions: jumping, swinging, and kicking. She handled the weapon with less and less awkwardness until it melted into her hand and became an extension of her arm.

"What say you now, Dashjmar?" she whispered to herself smugly. She jabbed at the air vigorously. In the heat of her zealous ambition, she faltered in her step. A small, cracked pebble scrambled from her misplaced foot. The temple towered over her in disappointment. The wraiths of the dead floated from their coffins and wrapped their sodden bodies around her chest.

You are not worthy.

Eerie screeches tore through her mind, and the abyss of the night encompassed her, pinning her feet to the crumbling ground. She knelt, sputtering. And then, as quickly as they had come, the voices of the dead disappeared and took with them the light of the ever-burning torches. Shrie gasped in the eternal, melanoid night. *More than spirits fill this place.*

Her mind groped for something, anything to explain her strained breath and the solitary sound of her blood pulsing tirelessly through her veins. The noises of the nocturnal creatures had been silenced, drowned in the harbinger of spiritual tempests. Shrie gripped her staff uneasily as the noose of premonition tightened around her stomach.

Rustling brush met her ears. The proximity of the movement arrested her breath. Shadows wove between the tree trunks, casting supernatural silhouettes upon the forest floor. They were the shapes of deformed men: twisted and unearthly. Wrestling with the despised vision, Shrie closed her eyes and pulled her staff closer to her body. As she willed the hallucinations to leave her, the ethereal shadows vanished. Wind whispered through the trees, and she listened as the hissing leaves finally grew still.

She forced her weakened knees into a jog. Nothing accosted her. Tensely, she traveled the trail that led to Dashjmar. When she arrived, Shrie let the radiating heat of the fire soak into her chilled skin. Calmly, she strained to open her stiff hand and demanded the muscles to loosen. Her gaze shifted to Dashjmar. His eyes remained closed in the tranquility that had escaped her. She sank to the ground; his eyes snapped open.

"What did you see?"

"Shrie see nothing."

"Tell me." He looked positively terrible in the iridescent glow of the fire.

She scowled. "Shrie see shadows in the wood, no more."

"What did the trees tell you, Maiden of the Wood? They tell me nothing, but they were moving; they were speaking. Do not deny me. What did they say?"

A small smile crept onto her face, the fear vanishing with the turn in conversation. Dashjmar had given her a title. She was capable of a talent he was not: listening to the trees. *Is this what I had been hoping for?* She had resisted listening to Dashjmar, fighting his authority and every suggestion. For so long she had been the sole ruler, and now here was one with a greater power. Shrie hung her head; she had been prideful. Dashjmar was not like Ree or Corious. He was here to guide her. He was a guide sent from the Almighty. She should respect him. Staring into the fire, she spoke.

"Shrie was practicing with staff, so as to do it honor in battle. Then, Shrie hear a noise, and Shrie stops and looks up to see shapes moving in the trees. Shrie hear the trees saying to her, 'like clouds on a summer day they come and cover light.' The trees repeat this message to Shrie, though Shrie does not know what it means."

Dashjmar's forehead formed a single furrow of concentration. He repeated the message with mute lips.

"Dashjmar know what it means?" she questioned after some time had passed. He shook his head as if coming from a daze.

"It is though I cannot defend us from it, or know when it shall strike." A small shiver passed down his spine, an instinctual horror gripping his body. "Come, we must keep the fire heaped high with fuel."

"Shrie will get kindling."

"Can you say I?" Dashjmar asked the question in a faint voice, as if calling to her from the inside of a cave.

"Eye?" Shrie threw a piece of wood into the flames.

Dashjmar did not reply, and Shrie did not delve into the Kalulukian's thoughts. Instead, she began, with charcoal from the fire, to sketch. Random lines appeared on the white rock before her, and she soon recognized it as the map Ree had completed long ago. It included much of the western half of Kurak, with the port cities which Corious had added, as well as the vastly uncharted regions of the north. She began to color it in lightly until she hit the land from which the dark men poured. She hastily colored in the region darkly. Dashjmar must have heard the scribbling, for his hand found its way to her arm.

"May I see it?" His face was earnest.

Shrie hesitated and then handed the rock to him. He turned it over in his hands, and Shrie placed the piece of charcoal in his palm. Carefully, he touched the charcoal's tip to the level surface of the stone. The line he drew on the map was clear and strong. It ran out of the swamps, along the river, through what Corious called the Borderlands, and across the mountains before stopping. After a brief thought, Dashjmar lifted the makeshift writing utensil and created a faintly dotted line heading north and then trickling back towards Quantus Plain, as if questioning the validity of its dashed, serpentine course. Handing the map back to Shrie and wiping the residual ash from his fingers, he tossed the charcoal back into the fire. He would not need it to make changes; the route was final.

"That is where Shrie and Dashjmar will travel? The line leads to Shrie's tribe?" she asked, studying the course, inculcating it into her memory.

"Hush, yes. Now throw it into the fire; none must know our route."

"What about dotted line, Dashjmar?"

Nothing.

"Dashjmar, what about dotted line? Where we go after finding Shrie's tribe?" He would not answer. She studied the faint course once more before feeding it to the hungry flames. In the sparkling light, she waited for a response. His head lifted in her direction.

"Shrie, do you realize a battle will soon take place—one that will destroy many people? Evil and its servants will be pitted against the last strength remaining in Khaltharnga. As the Ruler in his Tower gathers evil to him by his presence, so we must summon the good. Do you know of what I speak?" Dashjmar looked intently into the girl's eyes.

"I know of what you speak." Dashjmar jerked. The voice was not the same. It amassed fervor and passion. "You speak of the old wars that have forever devoured Kurak. You speak of the Last Battle, the Harvest, when the Almighty will come and save the seeds He once planted. You speak of the time when the dark men will fall and when the soldiers and servants of the Almighty will live in peace, and of the time when all will be as it was in the beginning—the very beginning before there was time. You say that we must, with the ever-gracious help of the Almighty, make this come true. I tell you now," Shrie spun, and her green eyes, sparkling with the reflection of the fire met his, "that we will."

Dashjmar resisted from shrinking back. Mustering his authority, he enjoined her, "Shrie, sit." Noiselessly she followed his command, and the light went from her face, making her seem almost smaller than normal. "So we shall." After a moment he added, "We leave tomorrow for our destination. There is a strange heaviness in the air that displeases me. I suggest you pack your things."

Shrie did not have anything to pack; neither did Dashjmar, so both simply tucked their weapons close. On an afterthought, Shrie wrapped some dried meats and fruits in a cloth and placed it on Gog's back. After throwing more wood on the fire, Shrie fell asleep on her ferns.

Dashjmar stayed awake for some time afterwards. Shrie contained more secrets than the old forest and was more unlikely to surrender them. He sighed. Roads of peace and chaos lay before them. They would travel both despite the caveat of the trees: like clouds on a summer day they come and cover light. What light was left in these days? Dashjmar's eyes drooped. The elements of the outside world were trying to him. His underground tunnels had protected him from affliction and beauty. Abandoning his tribe to help the Jungle Maiden return to hers, he had run from the spears of his people. They had sought his blood. The ruined temples of the swamps had provided him with a refuge, but the caves had transformed him, preparing him for his task and submerging him in power and knowledge.

Shrie stirred in her sleep, and Dashjmar considered her sleeping body. A small pouch apart from her arrows was slung across her shoulder, and her hand rested atop its leather flap. The markings on the bag were unusually familiar. A corner of a paper stuck from the pack's mouth. That too seemed to call to him. Lifting her hand from the pouch, he opened the tie that kept the bag's contents shut inside. His fingers found a piece of crumpled paper and a small, golden fruit. His brow furrowed for the second time that night. He unfurled the paper to find the Kalulukian burial writing. Astonished, he keenly read the symbols which he had not seen in so long. The words would open the altar and lead to the tunnels. It was how Shrie had found him. Shrie's eyes popped open, blinking away the few hours of restless sleep.

"Where did you get these?"

The invaded pack had not awoken her. There had been a noise—something in the woods which had alarmed her. As Dashjmar shifted his attention from her back to the items, she rose with a ready staff. The presentiment dissipated. Shrie could not see anything; her senses went dull.

Suddenly, her body convulsed as grotesque arms clasped her own and as a contorted hand clamped her lips flat against her teeth. Her misshapen captor pulled her head roughly to one side. She found herself looking into the pale blue eyes of the dead. Her stomach exploded in fear, and Shrie bit the scarred hand. Its grip tightened, and she squirmed against the encompassing body. His disfigured kin lifted stained swords and marched ceremonially towards her. He pushed her chest forward to meet the sword.

The rusting metal nicked her breastbone when the ground crashed into her face. Her subjugator had dropped her, and Dashjmar's staff had sunk into his skull. The others wildly stabbed at her fallen body. Rolling frantically, Shrie stretched for her staff. Dashjmar slammed his head into the stomach of an oncoming attacker. She indulged a quick breath of relief before Dashjmar grabbed her and they sprinted away. Bursting into the courtyard of the temple grounds, Dashjmar unleashed Gog and Magog. Arrows showered them.

"They were Zabyn warriors," Dashjmar explained hastily. "They come for the burial treasures."

Scrambling shakily onto Gog's scaly back, Shrie urged him through the trees. Revolting sounds stalked them. The trees twisted into moaning, repugnant creatures, and the moon hid itself behind the night clouds.

Their eyes burned as the lizards carried them through the thick of the swamps. Shrie struggled to relate the incident with reality. Diverging rays of pale light illuminated the fog that fell in front of them like sheets. The moon shone brightly enough for Shrie to see and duck under moss-covered branches swaying in the nonexistent breeze.

A freakish heat increasingly consumed her body, and her mind wandered aimlessly. Her body sagged. An aberrant voice eroded her resistance; the power of the pursuers surged.

So their last leader has died? I wonder who they chose after I left. Perhaps they will follow me again, redeeming themselves before it is too late. Ha! Why do I tease myself? I know they will not.

They must have formed an alliance with the Ruler. No, not the Ruler. Turock, I must call him Turock; he isn't the Ruler. An alliance…he must have discovered Quantus Plain's existence. Without the burial treasures it would be possible, but terribly difficult to penetrate the underground fortress. The Zabyn warriors would be the perfect choice to serve him: they loathe the Kalulukians.

Shunned years ago for some reason lost to all but vanished archives, the eschewed warriors make their abode in the southern Nialsnem Valley. It is a dead place. Any spirit they once had must have had died in that forsaken place. If the shadow has taken them, they are to be doubly feared. They have grown bold to attempt to capture the Maiden of the Wood. But Truth and Light are on our side. Both of these things terrify them. Shrie and I will have to bypass Bacl. The mountains will take more time to cross; we don't have any time to spare. We'll have to push hard where we can and travel on the river. Falls will be the only danger. Besides, if we can cross water, the Zabyn will lose our scent, unless daylight no longer hinders them…

Syrupy, swamp mud sprayed Dashjmar's face. The water seemed to coagulate. The labyrinth of trees and the fog characteristic of the swamps obscured his view. Any conspicuous movement in the water would compromise their safety. Nothing moved in the swamps but snakes, and even they did not move unless chasing prey. He would have to be alert. Magog jostled him in the saddle as he moved around some unseen object in the water. Dashjmar's hand went immediately to the pocket in his pants where the treasures lay. *A decoy!* As they reached an area heavily strewn with fog, he ripped material from the bottom of his pants to write the cursory letter.

> *Brothers, I write to you in sincerity. The Almighty can yet redeem you as He has me. He has taken my old name, Relliknem, and replaced it with Dashjmar, or servant of the Most High. I have since that time, like you, been shunned and hunted by my own tribe. I was abhorred because I recognized the Almighty. The time has come when the Almighty will return not with peace but with chaos. Perhaps we may not fall dead in vain if we have brought others to the Truth. The Almighty will take you back if you accept Him, but you have only one chance to do so. Take it, and end your foul ways as I have ended mine.*
> *Dashjmar.*

With a rushed deprecation, Dashjmar abandoned the leather to the water. It floated away, but he had no doubt they would find it. He would either ignite their anger or assuage it, but either way, the Zabyn would hunt them harder. It was a consequence he would have to accept. Even the Zabyn deserved to know that salvation would greet them if they chose it.

The moon was rising, or setting. The swamp escaped the confinements of time. Mangled trees hunched in the swamp water; they were tangled tombstones guarding the freshly churned earth of a graveyard. The water, saturated with silt and mud, held the trees' shadows as though they had not moved in a very long time. One more day would pass before they would be able to spring free from the swamps and launch into the river.

Running her hand up and down over Gog's scaly head, Shrie fought to retain lucid thought.

"Shrie very tired, Gog," she told him. "But Shrie must stay awake so Zabyn warriors do not make a fool of her again. She must prove herself to Dashjmar." Gog simply murmured a gurgled response. Shrie could not comprehend his every expression, but she thought he approved. Another throaty response from the giant lizard was issued as Dashjmar pulled up beside her.

"Keep Gog quiet."

"Shrie cannot control Gog completely, but she will try. Shrie was talking to Gog, and he was being polite and answering. Do not be mad at Gog, great Kalulukian Chieftain," Shrie defended her steed. Surprise shone on Dashjmar's face.

"Do not apologize to me, Jungle Maiden, simply heed my word. You talk to Gog?"

"Sometimes."

"You understand what he says?"

"Sometimes."

Dashjmar grunted in response. "Can you speak Lizard to him?"

Shrie disapproved. "I could, but Gog might become confused and think I am another lizard."

"Even if you tell him you aren't?"

"Yes. Gog smart lizard, but he tells me it happened once to another."

"Really? What lizard was that?"

Shrie blushed, and Gog made a faint gurgling noise. "Magog."

"Magog!"

"Keep your voice down, Dashjmar!" Shrie admonished.

"Tell me about Magog's confusion."

Again Shrie blushed. "You talk Lizard, Dashjmar?"

"At one time, I did. Perhaps I still do, though the syllables have left me." The lilt of his voice was doleful.

"That very sad, to lose a language. Well, no need to tell story. Must keep on watch for Zabyn warriors."

Dashjmar gave her a most terrifying look. Shrie sunk back and averted her glance but then proceeded to answer his question.

"Once you spoke Lizard to Magog." Shrie hesitated, but Dashjmar's fervent face encouraged her. She continued, "You tried to tell him to go faster, but you told him you loved him. Magog is confused and thinks you a lizard."

Dashjmar stared at Magog. "I think we better clear that up. Will you tell him?"

"Then Magog think I am a lizard."

"Well how do you talk to Gog?"

Shrie was suddenly baffled, but then remembered. "I speak to Gog in language of forest. I talk to Magog that way and see what happens."

"I would be much obliged."

Shrie cleared her throat and addressed Magog in the clear, flowing tongue of the wood. Magog replied in a series of guttural noises. Shrie listened intently and then sat quietly for some time after he stopped.

Dashjmar did not want to press Shrie, but he finally asked, "What does Magog say?"

"Magog say Gog was telling me a joke, and that he was never confused."

Dashjmar raised his eyebrows in disbelief. He left Shrie with a funny grin on her face. Gog appeared to be laughing as Dashjmar swam ahead on Magog. He shook his head up and down vigorously.

"You laughing or dying, Gog?"

Gog did not stop. Concerned, Shrie began stroking the spot between his eyes. He became so loud that Dashjmar sent them a chastising glare. Shrie shrugged and urged Gog forward. He did so readily and literally flew through the water. Dashjmar's memory, like Pandora's box, opened …

April had come, in everyone's mind much too early, and with its arrival it brought many unexpected events. The glistening lake had become cold and brown. A smell of rotting left it in the form of mysterious vapors. Battle had desecrated it, and to that battle I was headed. As we, I on Magog and Desselb beside me on Gog, approached the scene, shapes shifted in the penumbra of the lake's banks. They had been there too long.

I shifted slightly on Magog. The archers were further back to be sure, with their arrows staunch on their strings. Clad in mail, our host of riders from the mountains stood stalwart and intrepid under the weight of the shadows which clung to their shoulders and pressed upon their souls. Their banners of silver, blue, and white did not move under the gray sky; their adumbration of a soaring hawk lay tranquil in the unwavering cloth. As my eyes wandered over the swamp, a plume of smoke, black as the deepest shade of night, rose into the air.

Our challenge had been accepted, and as written, the Dark One stirring on his throne would meet us in three days. The riders were solemnly silent. Battle would not come to us this day. As we turned, Magog began to grunt and swing his head wildly. He would not cease despite my measures. We were not far from the mountain pass. Whatever bothered

Magog would have to wait. Then Desselb yelled to me; and as I turned, the fighter was upon me...

Gog began to mercilessly fling Shrie in the saddle. Flitting shadows flew in and out of the trees.

"Fly, Magog! Fly, Gog!" Dashjmar cried as he and Shrie fled.

Shrie endeavored to stay on the giant lizard as he thrust himself through the swamp. Her eyes alight with potential battle, she loaded an arrow to her bow. Dashjmar motioned for her to crouch over Gog. Arrows rained down upon them, but Gog raced beyond their reach. Gaining speed, the lizards nearly skimmed the surface of the water. The dark shapes continued to track them.

"I assume they didn't like my letter," Dashjmar whispered to himself. He had not thought they would.

The wind blew fiercely as the lizards bolted from the swamps. Their trackers had been lost. Shrie thought it bizarre that she had not recognized the Zabyn's presence in her forest.

"They are a formidable enemy," Dashjmar warned as if he had heard her thoughts, "relentless warriors forever seeking revenge."

"Dashjmar? Why Zabyn banished? Once they good Kalulukians."

Dashjmar's facial features gathered together in anger. "Do not be so eager to associate the Kalulukians with the Zabyn. Your tribe as well shares in their misery and hatred. All tribes once used to be and live as one."

He had still not answered her question.

Dashjmar twisted his body to face her. "The Zabyn were banished long before I became chieftain of my tribe, Shrie. The reason remains hidden from me. The only thing we need to be aware of is the danger they pose to us. These men are wells without water, humid air driven before a storm."

Shrie glanced behind her worriedly. An unnatural glow illuminated the outline of the gnarled, swamp trees. She clutched her staff tightly in her protective hand.

The lizards swiftly crossed the stretch of plain covering the eastern border of Khaltharnga. She bounced rhythmically in her saddle as her meager supplies swung near her feet. Shrie had not eaten since their time on the island, and her stomach seemed drained and dried. During their exodus, Gog had yanked a fruit tree from the ground, causing the fruit to fall on the moist ground where he could eat it with ease. Shrie had watched in a strange mix of misery and satisfaction as Gog consumed the fruit. Although her stomach was painfully empty, Shrie's eyelids felt like a chopped tree on the verge of crashing. She dozed in and out of sleep as they entered bristling vegetation. Putting her small hand around Gog's smooth, scaly neck, she bent over and fell asleep.

Her parched mouth woke her. The top of her tongue stuck painfully to the roof of her arid mouth. As she forced her eyes open, she found her thirst unbearable. Her insensate brain then registered the sound of water hastening over a river bottom and the sight of it rushing about her ankles. They were crossing the river. She sat up, her head spinning as the blood plummeted to her feet. She flipped her hair back over her shoulder from where it had cascaded into her face. She closed her eyes again, and with a slight sigh she leaned forward.

"Shrie," Dashjmar interrupted, "I have speared some fish if you would like one."

Shrie raised her head. As she took the fish sleepily and put it to her mouth, the Kalulukian stopped her.

"I meant if you would like one to give to Gog. They're uncooked, and I believe they are unfit for eating."

A devilish grin spread across Dashjmar's face as he flipped another fish from his spear into Magog's mouth. Shrie's face darkened into a shade of red as she lowered the fish from her mouth. She reluctantly tapped Gog on the head and slid the fish towards his big snout. With his massive jaws, he snapped the measly meal in half. Cupping a handful of river water in her hands, Shrie splashed it into her lips. The refreshing water slid down her dry throat and made her stomach feel somewhat cavernous. Shrie knew she could not take the fruit from their pack; it was not ripe enough and as hard as a rock.

"Dashjmar, we make camp soon?" Shrie asked in the hope of assuaging her stomach's vociferous demands. Gog's powerful legs pushed through the deep water.

"When the Zabyn are far behind."

Shrie frowned thoughtfully and then said in complete seriousness, "But Shrie's stomach may alert Zabyn to where Shrie and Dashjmar are."

"We will stop for food in due time."

Calling into use her last dregs of self-control, Shrie resisted asking when due time would be and instead grunted in dissatisfaction.

"Stop pouting. You need to be alert. The minute you let your guard down, they will strike."

"You be attacked by Zabyn before, Dashjmar?" Shrie asked, excited by the prospect of an intriguing conversation—one which did not revolve around responsibility and duty. Though the Kalulukian leader did not know, she knew more of responsibility than most. She had been entrusted with her tribe's last claim for the old ways: the Forest of Khaltharnga. She had had to care for herself for a long time. "Dashjmar?"

"Yes, I have fought Zabyn before."

"Teach Shrie of their battle tactics, so she can be prepared for battle," she goaded.

"You are a good fighter. You do not need a story to know this."

"Not story, Dashjmar, battle tactics!" Shrie remonstrated. He waved a hand at her as if to brush off an annoying fly.

Shrie flared her nostrils in displeasure but watched for the warriors that were supposedly tracking them. It still bothered her she had not sensed them enter her forest as she had sensed the dark men. A sputter of softly glowing radiance emanated briefly from the otherwise lightless forest. She halted Gog to investigate.

When Dashjmar did not stop, Shrie asked, "Dashjmar, you see light?"

No answer came from the silhouetted figure on Magog, but Dashjmar's body tensed visibly. Without meeting her inquisitive gaze, he inquired, "A light? From where does it shine?"

Shrie rotated to get a better view, positioning Gog lengthways across the river. "No more light now, Dashjmar, but it came from within the depths of the swamps. Not firelight, Shrie would like to add; it white light, soft—"

"The very antithesis of the swamps?"

"Antithesis...antithesis mean...opposite!" Shrie coached herself under her breath before answering Dashjmar. "Yes, light very much the antithesis of swamp."

A mysterious smile found its way to Dashjmar's face. "You have seen the first of its kind. The light is good news, but there is no need to delay." Brow knitted in consternation, Shrie skillfully guided Gog next to Magog. As she approached, Dashjmar's voice lowered. "When we left the island," he paused and started over, "you realize we left the swamps at an unheard of rate?"

Shrie remembered how long it had taken her, Corious, Ree, Tar, and the others to find the island. Yes, to make it across the swamps in less than two days time was amazing, but then again, so were the lizards they rode.

"Yes. We traveled very fast through swamp."

"The Zabyn, to track us this far, also then are very fast." Dashjmar let his logic sink in before continuing, "They are more dead than alive. They are a people moribund in spirit but increasing in number. They sought the burial treasures to desecrate the Kalulukian graves, uncover the entrance to Quantus Plain, and honor Turock whom the tribes detested from the start."

"Explain Turock. Ree, Corious, and Tar speak of him sometimes." Lain had also spoken of him to her; but while the rebels shouted Turock's name with loathing and the Shalkans whispered his name in fear, Lain had said the name in sadness. Shrie did not say the name at all. He was called Turock in their language, Taberah in hers. It was a name saved for profligates and destroyers: people not worthy of mention. "Who is he? How old?"

Dashjmar did not look at her with the surprise he felt, but a slight twitch of his lip indicated that something had perturbed him. "Turock is the leader of the dark men, the Lover of Death, and the Companion of Violence. His henchmen forget why they fight and who they are. Turock's danger is not swords or guns but rather apathy. When men are ignorant, he thrives. When men put their faith in abstracts without reasons, his power ripens. When men refuse to open their eyes, he lives glorified. Turock transforms his enemy into a subordinate image of himself, and he in turn serves another. We are mere pieces on a gameboard, Shrie, but we have some say in where we move. Let us pray to the Almighty we move according to His plan."

"What does this have to do with the light?"

"I will begin with why you did not sense the Zabyn; Turock's presence is the atrocity you suffer in his dark men. He has not fully consumed the Zabyn though he has baited them with the allure of revenge. With this in mind, I left a fake scroll for them. I knew their greedy hands would snatch it. I had little hopes of deterring them from their present course, but with news of the light, I deem it was worth-while." Shrie contemplated Dashjmar's words. "It was once rumored that if a Zabyn eschewed his evil ways, he would return to the Kalulukian traditions though he would die in a brilliant shimmer of light."

"How," Shrie began.

Dashjmar interrupted, "I must be quick in telling you this, and you must dwell upon it in the little time we have, for I feel time expiring as we speak. When we left the swamps, I left the fake scroll, and upon it, I wrote the words of Truth."

Shrie gasped, and then said proudly, "Dashjmar, you very, very wise."

He did not accept her praise. "Give the Almighty the glory. I do not know for certain, but I believe the light you saw indicates the transformation of a Zabyn. Perhaps one has died a good man."

"What will the others do?"

"Hunt us viciously. We now know some are in the swamp, which means some-thing has delayed them. I do not know what. Pull to this side of the bank."

"We make camp?"

"We will find something to eat and then be on our way."

The sun graced the sky with its glory. Faint yellow and pink streaks chased away the night sky and hastened the jungle morn. Birds chirped, and animals scurried along the forest floor. From Gog's back, Shrie unleashed an arrow. There was no need to wait. Gog moved obediently towards the bank without direction, and Shrie contin-ued to shoot arrows, most of which found their targets. Dashjmar did not bother to take out his bow.

"I hope you know what you're shooting."

Shrie shrugged. "If Shrie shoot bad animals, we eat the berries and mushrooms." After three more shots, Dashjmar insisted that she cease. Shrie regretfully slung her bow over her arm.

Gog sloshed onto the bank and bent his head forward so she could slip off his neck easily. She did so and found her quarry. Dashjmar also dismounted and began to dig the deep hole which would conceal the cooking fire. After skinning some of the small, edible rodents and birds, Shrie foraged and located a miniature bush of bright red berries the size of her thumbnail. She sniffed them, determined their edibility, and popped them in her mouth. The juice spurted merrily from the berry, and Shrie gratefully swallowed it. Amassing an armful of the delicious spheres, Shrie fought away some envious birds and made her way back to Dashjmar, using her nose as a guide.

Smoke curled lazily from the small flame sparkling above the rim of the pit. Dashjmar tucked plants and herbs into the meat as it cooked. The smell tantalized her.

"Go get some water from the river," Dashjmar said to rid himself momentarily of her hovering presence. Shrie snatched one of their waterproof pouches and sped to the river, the thought of a warm meal spurring her forward. Filling the pouch to the top, she then returned and placed it by Gog. She knew the water would be saved for when they passed through less fertile lands.

It was morning when Shrie contentedly slurped the last of Dashjmar's brown soup. The bright, golden rays of sun trickled onto the forest floor, giving vibrancy and shape to what had been indiscernible lumps hours before. They had moved their camp inland from the open trees by the river to a shallow dip behind denser brush. Shrie watched sleepily as Dashjmar untied the lizards from their trees.

"We leaving, Dashjmar?"

He gave her his typical blank glance before positioning the lizards. Twirling his staff, Dashjmar approached Gog and Magog. They did nothing.

"Dashjmar, Gog and Magog no fight you."

Dashjmar spat. "You are not the only one that knows these lizards, Shrie."

Though she was nettled by his comment, Shrie tried not to be offended. Standing, she stretched the wish for sleep from her limbs and observed Dashjmar from the corner of her eye. He was still now, hand under his chin in deep thought, his lips moving silently. Letting her arms down to her side, Shrie crept closer. As she proceeded, her brow deepened. *What is he trying to do?* His demeanor appeared altered.

After waiting in her spot for many minutes hushed and unmoving, Shrie continued forward, legs bowed in a half squat, distributing her weight evenly on the forest floor. She was so close to Dashjmar's body that she felt the heat radiating from him. A swift blur fled the corner of her eye. Reflexes sprung her knees from their bent stance. Dashjmar's staff landed in an alarming thud inches from where she had landed. Gog stirred uneasily at the commotion. Dashjmar took a slow step forward, raising his staff; his gaze focused steadily on her. Her first reaction was to reach for her bow, but it was beyond her reach.

Her only available weapons consisted of her fists. Dashjmar's eyes were utterly blank and unyielding. Shrie tried not to panic.

"What you doing, Dashjmar?"

He approached her again. She stepped away and saw a bulky stick lying not too far from her. Carefully, she backed up while keeping her eyes frozen on Dashjmar. In one fluid motion, her hand encompassed the stick. Grasping it firmly, she rolled away in a somersault. Rushing her, Dashjmar swung his staff aggressively. She parried and side stepped. Dashjmar ran at her. Gog, uneasy, roared deafeningly into Magog's ear. Magog shifted uncomfortably. Both began to eye the skirmish closely.

"You crazy, Dashjmar!" Shrie cried as they battled furiously.

Dashjmar lifted his staff, leaving a fair portion of his body vulnerable. Shrie did not wish to hurt one of whom she thought so highly, so instead she kicked him in the chest as hard as she could. It forced him to take a faltering step. Shrie did not sympathize; she thought her foot hurt more than any injury Dashjmar had received. A bellow from Magog ripped through the air. No one had ever touched his master. Shrie had trained with him, yes, but never attacked him. Fiercely loyal, the lizard charged Shrie. Gog stirred, confused as to where his loyalties lay. They had always been with Dashjmar, but Shrie had been so kind.

Magog was unsuccessful in attack. Shrie simply ducked under his massive bulk and grabbed onto his saddle straps. She was so light compared to Dashjmar that poor Magog did not realize Shrie's location in the saddle. He searched incessantly for her, and Gog was so utterly confused that he just hissed at Dashjmar and then started to charge Magog. Abruptly, everyone stopped, halted by the most unusual sound they had ever heard and perhaps would ever hear. It was deep, resonating, and struck the bones in such a funny way that not one of them knew what to do except turn to the origin of the sound. All three saw Dashjmar but immediately dismissed him; the din could not possibly come from such a stern man.

But after finding nothing that could satisfactorily produce the sound, Shrie asked in disbelief, "Dashjmar, you laughing?"

He was. He was kneeling with his staff at his side, laughing. His chest heaved, and his face contorted into a cheery sort of shape. Shrie slipped off Magog and warily crept to him. Again he was up and slashing his staff at her. At her immediate recoil, he erupted into laughter. Shrie threw down her staff, frustrated to the point of rage.

"Dashjmar, what you doing?" The question marched off her tongue with a staccato precision.

The laughing intensified into spasms of convulsing coughs as Dashjmar rolled to the ground in exhaustion, befuddling the lizards. No one, not even the all-knowing gods, had heard Dashjmar laugh. Shrie sullenly watched his erratic display of mirth until he hurriedly rose. Shrie panicked and grabbed for her staff, preparing for the inevitable attack. With a careless swing of his arm, Dashjmar reached for his staff. Bracing herself, Shrie narrowed her eyes in suspicion, but when his hand grasped firmly the ancient wood, it was as though the touch had soothed him. The Kalulukian composed himself.

"Dashjmar?" she questioned faintly.

"Maiden of the Wood, if you had seen what I just saw!"

"What you see?" she asked in consternation.

"I saw a future legend running eccentrically in circles, confusing two gigantic animals, and attempting to beat the guts out of a man twice her size."

Dashjmar sucked in his stomach as if to restrain the oncoming fit of laughter. Shrie studied him fiercely, searching for physical causes of his insanity.

"No, Dashjmar. Shrie correct you. You confuse Magog and Gog and make me run."

Dashjmar chuckled. "You did not see the plan, did you?" Shrie's eyebrows rose skeptically. Dashjmar clarified, "I wanted to retrain Gog and Magog to fight. I suppose confused loyalties got in the way."

Shrie did not understand Dashjmar's sense of humor. "Okay, Dashjmar. Why not we go, now?"

"You are right. Mount your pitiable Gog. He is over there, rummaging through those bushes for something to eat, I suppose," Dashjmar smiled. "Whenever he is distraught, he eats. He does not understand a life without food." He shoved her in Gog's direction while he headed for Magog.

Extricating Gog from the berry bush, Shrie soothed him. Dashjmar was already atop Magog and heading towards the river. The morning was refreshing and peaceful. Fish wriggled through the water as the sun shed leaping spots of light onto their scales. The river skipped gaily downstream, and the lizards plunged into its depths. The river itself was not terribly deep, rising barely to the animals' leathery, green knees. Slithering furtively through the water, as stealthily as porcine animals can, the lizards swam abreast. They swung their stout tails back and forth to keep their balance against the flow of the widening, jocund river. Dashjmar scanned the horizon and eyed it as critically as a connoisseur of art would a painting. Shrie did not mention the oddity of the morning's events and instead enjoyed the relative, mutual placidity in which they traveled.

Two days passed in pristine stillness. They did not stop for meals, but Shrie and Dashjmar speared fish for the lizards. If the great animals were forced to hunt by themselves, they would sporadically dive into the water, soaking their riders to the core. Shrie discovered this predicament after frankly refusing to spear fish for Gog as part of her futile attempt to teach him independence. As for the riders, river plants ranging from edible reeds to appetizing underwater plants comprised their diet.

During those days, Shrie and Dashjmar worked hard to maintain the thin facades of sangfroid with which they gilded their anxiety. To distract himself from his core of inner turmoil, Dashjmar related to Shrie the history of various kingdoms. The Kalulukian taught her of other worlds and peoples not her own, losing himself in the prose of fluidly memorized lines. Shrie listened intently, storing in her memory the verses which intrigued her. The third day came and went, and on the night of the fourth day, the lizards began to fidget.

"Gog no like the river anymore?" Resting her head on Gog's powerful neck, Shrie strained to discover the cause of his apprehension. Though the sky still contained a hint of daylight, she closed her eyes and let her head remain nestled in the tough, lizard skin. The days of travel had fatigued her.

Dashjmar glanced at Shrie with a paternal smile and opted to answer the question previously directed to Gog. "These lizards ache to be on land where they can move freely. They were never meant to traverse deep water as we have made them do. Nevertheless, they do so uncomplaining," Dashjmar commented. He affectionately bumped the potbellied Magog on the head before swiveling his head sharply. Keeping his gaze on Shrie, he flipped his staff and plunged it ferociously into the water.

Something like a knotted piece of tree floated to the top of the river. As Dashjmar disgustedly lifted it from the water, Shrie's breath caught in her throat. It was the body of a Zabyn warrior. Small ripples fanned across the water's surface. With a sickening thud, Dashjmar disposed of the body. Bubbles began to rise to the surface and pop at regulated intervals. Shrie's stomach convulsed as deformed shapes burst from the water with honed swords. Like snakes dancing to the tune of a charmer, the Zabyn rose from the river. Gog's eyes rolled back into his head. A frenetic Shrie gripped his sides tightly with her legs, chafing her inner thighs. She reeled with the memory of the near dead. Her heart palpitated, and worries like pain seized her chest.

Her fear made her impatient. With an earsplitting war cry, she loosed her arrows. Though several Zabyn stumbled, the enemy's solid phalanx streamed ahead. Shrie jammed her trembling knee into Gog's side. Gog whisked his colossal tail through the water, and Magog followed suit. As though disturbed by Poseidon, the water rolled in forceful waves. Shrie struggled to stay on Gog's back.

"Ogsheloam! Slow down!" she cried. As Gog's mighty bulk crushed the enemy, she reversed her logic and shouted from her dizzy post, "Faster, Gog, faster!"

Bodies sank under Gog's weight, but the enemy jabbed their swords at Gog's hide. One Zabyn dug into Gog's skin with his nails. Shrie shrieked in terror and brought her staff down wrathfully upon the Zabyn's head. Her attempt did not deter Gog's attacker, the Zabyn began to scale his tail. Screaming wildly, Shrie fought frantically. Enemy arrows streaked by her face, and one skimmed her skin. Infuriated, she hacked the Zabyn off a bleeding Gog. She tried desperately to keep her enmity in check. *I must not hate.* But Shrie's entire frame shook with anger as she endlessly raised the staff and brought it down as hard and in as many places as she could.

Minutes passed, and her muscles ached. Her heavy staff grew slippery. In her weakened state, she could not fight them. She urged Gog forward. Perhaps if they were lucky they could outrun their enemies

The Zabyn cackled and raced across the water, cutting him off from Gog and Shrie. Magog pivoted sharply, but Dashjmar expertly adjusted to the movement. Calmly, he engaged the first Zabyn, breaking its neck in a single stroke. Assailing his swarming attackers, Magog opened his mouth and easily snapped off an enemy's limb. Dashjmar gutted another opponent in the stomach, sending the offender flying back into the sea of oncoming Zabyn. During the commotion, a hand reached Dashjmar's throat and dug its hardened fingers deep into his shoulder joint. Raw pain exploded in Dashjmar's shoulder as the Zabyn tore the shoulder from its socket. He collapsed in pain as the Zabyn piled on top of him. Dashjmar weakly poked the berserker with his staff before it was splintered into tiny pieces by a shamshir. The sword point narrowly missed Dashjmar's face but scratched Magog. The lizard jolted. Agonizingly retrieving a dagger from his belt, Dashjmar cut off the hand that had wrenched his shoulder out of place. Stabbing upwards, he killed the body and rid himself of the zealous warrior.

A club connected with Dashjmar's foot. His step faltered, but he managed to regain his balance and snap the wrist of the oncoming soldier's hand. The Zabyn howled in pain as Dashjmar buried the dagger in its chest. As it fell, Dashjmar sacrificed his balance in order to snatch the warrior's club. Swinging it like a cutlass, he defended himself on the western bank. Downstream, Shrie fought desperately. Dashjmar knew they could not hold for long.

Shrie's fury had cost her. She had made careless mistakes, and as a result, Zabyn arrows incised her skin. Shrie planted her foot on the face of particularly hideous warrior, pushing him underwater. She held him there as Gog plowed through a morbid crowd of combatants, momentarily freeing herself from the Zabyn's grasp.

Dashjmar and Shrie retreated downstream. Bruises covered their bodies as evidence of the Zabyn's clumsy, ungraceful strokes. Avenging her throbbing body, Shrie administered mortal blows to the enemy. In the middle of clearing a path through the river, she abruptly stopped.

"Dashjmar!" she cried in warning.

A lone warrior leapt from the shadows to accost Dashjmar. With his club, the Kalulukian countered the blitzing blow of the foaming Zabyn. Gog tore towards Dashjmar as Shrie brought the trusty string of her bow back to a flashing eye. Her hand quavered, and the arrow went wide. A hot tear trickled down her face. She loaded two arrows and shot into the gruesome scene. Blood squirted from the tangled bodies atop Magog, but the gashes hardly discouraged the enraged Zabyn warrior. It did not relinquish its harsh attack.

A shiver pulsated down Shrie's spine, and she threw her staff as she would a spear. As it collided with the enemy, Dashjmar's fist crashed into the Zabyn's face. Despite the shattering blow, the unearthly Zabyn struck Dashjmar and seized Shrie's staff—the one Dashjmar had entrusted solely to her. Clenching her teeth, Shrie jumped from Gog into the freezing water. She opened her eyes underwater and saw the bucking object on which the Zabyn had been standing: a wooden platform floating just below the water's surface. From her perspective, it appeared as a shaking outline from which two black pillars rose. Her lungs ached for air. Denying their request, she swam frog-like to the platform which bounced under the movement of the fierce fight.

Shrie reached the board with enough strength to pull it out from under the Zabyn's feet. The two pillars collapsed upon her. She flailed in the water, kicking to the surface. The bestial man grabbed hold of her forearm, yanking her back underwater. Shrie gasped for air inches below the surface. Frantically, she clutched the wrist that held both her arm and the staff hostage. Burying her teeth into the gruesome flesh, she rejoiced as the staff fell free. Her arm remained imprisoned. She managed to grab the sinking staff with her free arm just before Dashjmar heaved her and the struggling Zabyn above the water. River water spewed from her mouth. She kicked at the Zabyn while it drew its wet sword. Swiftly, Dashjmar hacked the fighter's arm in half. With a sharp scream of agony, the warrior crumpled into the water. Dashjmar lugged Shrie onto Magog. Gog was too far ahead, and the water was too cold to reach him otherwise.

The tides of the battle had turned, and Shrie and Dashjmar attacked from Magog's back in relief; they would survive the battle. As the ghoulish warriors diminished, a weary Shrie and Dashjmar let the current whisk them away from the scourged Zabyn and their death trap. They had neither the desire nor the energy to pursue their attackers beyond the riverbank. Shrie strove to sit straight despite an accosting, overpowering lassitude. Her wounds belched blood, and the last thing she felt before the dizziness consumed her was Dashjmar's hands supporting her swooning back.

It was agonizing to wake. Shrie's neck had cramped into tight knots of muscle, and she could have sworn the slash on her cheek burned with fire. Her legs stung, and the matted hair which alighted atop her throbbing head seemed wild enough to grow wings and fly away. Her eyelids were the only parts of her body capable of immediate movement, and so she moved them up and down warily as if to test their abilities. Though she could not see him, she knew Dashjmar was nearby. She shakily extracted her hand from under her head. Propping herself on one elbow, she saw Dashjmar sprawled under a tree still holding Gog's and Magog's reins. Slumping irregularly from his back, his one shoulder seemed departed from his neck. She shuddered at the damage.

Contrasting their physical appearances, a beautiful, crisp morning welcomed them. The pounding of a waterfall stirred the forest around her, and wisps of white clouds hung in the breezy, blue sky. She stumbled to where Magog stamped impatiently and tugged the reins away from his master's hand. Gog, who had taken a cruel beating in the battle, slept peacefully behind Dashjmar. Shrie approached the sleeping beast. She rubbed his shiny, worn coat of scales fondly, careful not to aggravate his wounds. His tail flicked ever so slightly. Humming one of her tribe's soothing melodies, she caressed his back.

A profound splat rang in the air, and a gelatinous drop of sweet liquid bounced off her head. Shrie's mind raced to find the source and quickly found it. Gog huddled beneath a fruit tree. Shrie licked the juice that drizzled down her face. Supporting her weak body by holding onto a low branch, she examined the tree. She was in no condition to climb it, but a stick would suffice to shake the fruit from its limbs. With a renewed vigor, Shrie set to work, and not too long thereafter, Gog woke to a sizable pile of fruit. On his long, greenish tongue, Gog balanced several fruits before devouring them skin and all.

"You hungry Gog, aren't you!" Shrie exclaimed as she spryly tossed him another. Gog caught it in his powerful jaws. He rolled his head in delight when Shrie began sorting and skinning the outer layers of the small citruses. Shrie always allowed him to eat the ripe, mushy, or bruised pieces. As she threw the colorful spheres in the air, and as Gog reached to swallow them whole, Shrie resisted the temptation to clean and bandage Gog's wounds. Dashjmar would know more about healing the lizards than she did. Eventually, Gog returned to his slumber, curled in a warm sand bank with his rotund stomach protruding abnormally.

Since Gog had finished his food, and since Dashjmar and Magog were both sleeping, no responsibility constrained her. Through the leafy branches, she caught a glimpse of the river. After parting the brush, she dove into the water without hesitation. The wet sand and mud slipped between her stiff toes, rejuvenating her as the chilly water rose to her stomach. The invigorating current swept her off her feet. Her hair floated back from her face, and a slight breeze pushed her downstream. On either side of her floating tresses, the riverside jungle remained a dense, overgrown, and luscious explosion of green. From these verdant forests, neon parrots rocketed across the river while other animals cavorted in the branches. Beneath her, schools of sparkling fish swam upstream. Shrie studied the river through which the fish had already traversed.

Towering pillars of spray and steam rose lazily downstream, accenting the gallons of water which plummeted over the lip of the falls. Beside the falls, piles of smooth, worn stones glistened surreally. The jumping fish had to climb the falls yearly in order to reach their breeding waters. She admired their fearless determination. In encouragement, she began to swim alongside the daring fish before resting on a glossy stone. The thunderous falls echoed in her ears, and the mist sprayed her face as it bounced through air.

Yes, she thought, *a gorgeous day indeed has come to congratulate us on the success of last night's battle.* The terror incited by the Zabyn specters melted in the fires of her current bliss. When the sun moved past the middle of the sky, she forced herself from the water. Shaking the river from her hair, Shrie started to lie out in the sand when Dashjmar stepped from behind a tree. Water from her hair dripped down his bare upper body. Dashjmar did not comment. Shrie did.

"We rest today, Dashjmar," she called from behind a shady tree.

Dashjmar leaned against a tree. "If you are in any condition to swim, then we will be leaving."

Shrie poked her head out from behind the tree. "You are in no condition to travel, Dashjmar. I would be too fast for you. We stay."

For once, Dashjmar capitulated with no additional argument, and they decided to stay not one day in the secluded grove, but two. Over breakfast, they discussed yesterday's battle, or what Shrie thought had been yesterday's battle.

"You slept, or were unconscious, for one day and two nights. This is the second morning since we fought the Zabyn."

"How you know Dashjmar? You were probably sleeping most that time too."

"I'm afraid not, Daughter of the Wood. I scouted for the Zabyn while moving out of their reach."

Shrie wiped fruit juice from her lower lip and pondered his words. "You have separated shoulder Dashjmar? It looks grievous."

Dashjmar shifted it gingerly. "It can be fixed with the use of a sling. How do your wounds fare?" Shrie tentatively rubbed her hand over her cheekbone. Dashjmar took note of the motion. "That should leave a scar. You are fortunate a Zabyn arrow did not pierce your face."

"They have bad aim," she commented simply.

Removing the rations they had been saving since leaving the underground caverns, Dashjmar announced, "In honor of the valiant battle we so courageously won."

In the tranquil light, Shrie could almost imagine her tribe: the men spearing fish and the children riding Mali-Malis as the women cooked and talked. The scene shattered as a huge, warm tongue clobbered her in the head. She fell over from the force as Gog sniffed the dried meat in her hand. He bent down and nudged her, grunting softly.

Shrie laughed, and even Dashjmar grinned. "Gog wants food too, Dashjmar! Here," Shrie said, "I give him mine."

Like gluttons, the three ate more than they had their entire trek. Even though his left shoulder drooped unusually low, Dashjmar managed to shove food into his mouth with both hands. Eventually, they slept with full stomachs on the spongy, green moss of the riverside. The sun kissed the horizon line in a brilliant panoply of colors as the moon rose to take charge of the jungle. A few hours before dawn, the pressure of Magog's nose pushing into Dashjmar's side woke him.

"Shh, we do not leave early today, Magog. We will go later," he whispered to the lizard. Magog rumbled happily and curled protectively beside his master. Dashjmar patted him on his side and proceeded to roll over. He could see Shrie's small, sleeping form several feet away. Within minutes, he had joined her, falling asleep to the quiet murmur of the jungle.

The sunlight opened Shrie's eyelids in a squint. The maiden jumped from her bed of moss and stretched; it was late. Dashjmar was gone, probably hunting, though she knew not how with his injured arm. She yawned happily and tied back her hair after combing it with her fingers. She hoisted her pack onto her back and then paused as she recognized a familiar leaf crushed beneath her foot. Remembering Gog's injuries, as well as Dashjmar's and Magog's, she dropped her pack and hurriedly picked it. If Dashjmar did not plan on attending to himself and to his lizard, Shrie would have to take the initiative. Sniffing, she got on all fours and found her way to another of the plant's kind. Filling her palm with the green fibers, she started a fire and filled a bowl with water from the river. She turned over her cupped hand and let the leaves flutter into the bowl. With Gog's help, she retrieved the other needed ingredients which were harder to reach and let them boil. After Shrie stirred the watery concoction, it solidified into a mushy salve. Removing the bowl from the fire, she let it cool and then dipped her forefinger into the mixture. Gog did not like the smell of it, but Shrie pursued him until he let her apply it. Rubbing the pulp over his injuries, Shrie was confident it would work as well on his skin as it had on hers and on the Mali-Malis' in the past. The solution would hasten the healing of the wound by cleaning it and stitching the skin together. As she finished attending to Magog, Dashjmar returned with food. He instantly smelled the curative balm and sniffed the air with disdain.

"What is that?"

"It healing potion. Gog and Magog be fixed in no time! Come Dashjmar, let Shrie see what you bring for food, and then she give you ointment too."

Dashjmar defensively held the already skinned meat between his body and Shrie like a shield. Shrie waited until he had speared the meat on a stick and hung it over the burning fire. As he knelt, he uncertainly let Shrie dab the last of the mixture onto his cuts.

"We leave soon?" Shrie asked while blending the salve into his skin. He flinched as she hit a tender spot.

When he relaxed, he answered, "After we eat."

"How your shoulder feel?"

"It is feeling better," he sighed contentedly. "You are well yourself?"

"Shrie is very hungry," she said as the smell of the meat wafted from the fire. "It good thing breakfast is almost done. Shrie will get some fruit to go with it."

Dashjmar smiled. If he predicted correctly, the next part of their journey would be relatively uneventful. Now would be the time to push the pace and conserve time by traveling during sleepless nights. A scampering Shrie brought him back to the present: a sunny, cheerful day, the sixth since the fight. Humming a lively tune, she brought back eight pieces of fruit, one for her, one for Dashjmar, and three for each of the lizards. Shrie launched the fruit in the air, and Dashjmar watched as the lizards snapped comically at the flying, circular shapes.

Shrie grinned, plopping one of the giant fruits into his hand. "Done yet?"

Dashjmar rotated the smoking meat over the flames. It appeared done. He handed it to Shrie who eagerly dug into the crisp meal. Juice dripped down her chin, and she wiped it off carelessly with the back of her hand. Dashjmar ate similarly, and they finished their meals in record time. After throwing her stick into the dying fire, Shrie rinsed her face and hands in the river. The Kalulukian leader meanwhile destroyed any evidence of their camp, covering their fire pit with dirt and placing a fresh slab of moss over it. Hopping on Gog and Magog, Shrie and Dashjmar rode from beneath the green, arched trees of their proven sanctuary.

Chapter 2

"When you pass through the waters, I will be with you; and when you pass through the rivers, they will not sweep over you. When you walk through the fire, you will not be burned; the flames will not set you ablaze."
Isaiah 43:2

For two insipid weeks the two jungle warriors traveled the plains on the border of Bacl and the Zabyn Empire. Shrie grew accustomed to Gog's loping stride, which was longer and more powerful than that of a Mali-Mali's. The first several runs were by far the most uncomfortable thing she had ever endured.

Shrie leaned over Gog with her back almost parallel to the ground. Her arms cramped as they folded beneath her and gripped the top of the saddle. Supporting her weight, her thighs pushed against the loops that hung from the blanket strapped to Gog's girth. The position reduced the drag invited by the trapped winds constantly swirling atop the sunken fields.

Shrie gritted her teeth as Dashjmar and Magog increased their speed. Dashjmar jerked ahead of her on Magog. Considering their sizes, the lizards were amazingly fast. Contrary to her previous opinion, the bulk that comprised the lizards was mostly muscle. With every stride, those muscles contracted and stretched, rippling beneath Shrie's frozen form.

"Oashgh!" she yelled as the wind hit her face and sent her hair streaming like seaweed in a fierce ocean current. With her hand, she shielded her eyes against the sand routed by Magog's feet. She could see mountains forming on the horizon.

"Oashgh!" Dashjmar did not want to be caught.

Gulping in air, Shrie pushed Gog into a fierce gait. He compliantly increased his velocity. The grasses passed in undulating waves, and the jungle disappeared behind them. *How ironic*, she thought, *that the rider should be more exhausted than the mount.*

Shrie noticed again the blue, fuzzy line rising from the plains and vanishing into the clouds. They were the first mountains Shrie had seen not blanketed by trees.

At midday, the race which began at dawn had yet to cease. Carefully reaching into her pack with one hand, she balanced precariously atop Gog as she grabbed her day's ration of dried fruit. Dashjmar kept the rest of the food in his pack; he did not trust Shrie with it. Bringing her hand to her mouth, she inhaled a handful. Slapping her pack closed, she caught up to Magog and called to Dashjmar now directly adjacent to her, "Mountains, Dashjmar! You see them?"

He met her inquisitive gaze, narrowing his eyes to clear his vision. "So we approach them at last. We will not be crossing these. We will go around," he shouted over the wind.

Shrie summoned the mental image of the route to her mind. She envisaged the dark line from Quantus Plain through the swamps, across the plains, and through the Borderlands. The mountains had not been on her stone map or Corious's. Maybe Corious had never traveled so far.

"There is a pass on the far side of the mountains. See the dip?"

Shrie followed Dashjmar's pointing finger. "I see it, Dashjmar. Be ready for mountain bandits," she warned impishly.

"Mountain bandits?" the Kalulukian called questioningly from his stead.

Shrie almost fell off Gog as she made a shrugging motion with her shoulders. "Ree tell me sometimes there people in the mountains who attack travelers."

"I doubt there will be any where we are going. There are few who go through that pass. Since the last time I have been there, your friends, the Mali-Malis, dwelt happily there. Evil cannot coexist in the presence of good."

An exulted smile broke onto Shrie's face. It did not escape Dashjmar's notice. He should have told her about the spiders long ago. He only hoped they still lived there in peace. Grimly, he shifted the weight of his staff in his hand and glanced at Shrie's quiver bouncing on her back. There were too few arrows in it. They would have to stop early.

When the sky was the strange dark blue that is not yet night but not quite day, Dashjmar halted Magog.

"Ujdkalkan." Gog broke from his run. "Why we stop so early, Dashjmar? We so close to Mali-Malis!"

"Several more days and you shall see them. Until then, we need to replenish your supply of arrows."

"But Shrie have no paint with her to put her mark on them, or at least no spare berries that she could turn into paint."

"You need not mark them, simply make them. It is better for people not to know the owner of the arrows. We do not want anyone tracking us."

Shrie slipped from Gog's back. Her taut muscles groaned as they stretched.

When she could walk normally, she set about finding the materials needed to make her arrows. Wood was less plentiful, but a stiff, circular reed egregiously placed among the flat, flaccid grasses presented itself. Gathering bushels of the reeds, she carried them to the small clearing Dashjmar had made in the grasses. Shrie noticed that he had piled bunches of undergrowth in the fire pit. It would be a long night. Shrie sighed and placed the reeds on the ground before sitting with her legs crossed. Dashjmar reached over to take a reed. He hit it against his palm and against his thigh vigorously, but it did not break. Holding it in the light of the young fire, he ran his finger over the material.

"It is a little thick to be the perfect shaft for your bow, but without an arrowhead, I believe it will work. A pliant material, the Yitiuquimba is a good choice." He handed it back to her along with a menacing dagger.

"I saw the thin knife you have. It will not be tough enough to cut the plant."

"Shrie still need feathers," she said as she took both the reed and the knife. "No birds live in this plain?"

"Hardly. There will be no meat in our diet for awhile, but I can solve the problem of feathers. I saved these from the birds I shot the last morning by the river."

"You think very far ahead, Dashjmar. It a good thing, too," Shrie complimented as she began cutting, shaving, and sharpening. After she finished the first arrow, Dashjmar tested it with her bow. It flew true.

"If you trust me to, I will help you make arrows," Dashjmar offered.

Shrie eyed him curiously and then surrendered half of the pile of reeds. Dashjmar drew his other dagger. The firelight painted strong highlights their faces which were bent studiously over their work.

"You ever make arrows before?" Shrie asked as Dashjmar measured his first cut.

"At one point, yes," the deep voice answered her.

"You hunt with them or fight?"

"Both."

"How old you, Dashjmar?"

The onslaught of questions, though intransigent in their insistence, did not bother him. "Even I do not know. I spent many years in the caverns beneath the swamps."

"Your tribe used to live there?"

Dashjmar did not answer, and Shrie did not probe. Dashjmar had a right to his own past. By the time Shrie reached for the last reed on her side, her fingers were numb and chaffed. The rough reed had cut into her hand, and Dashjmar's knife had grown cumbersome for the slight cuts she had left to make. When she completed it at last, Dashjmar had already finished. He grouped the arrows like a bouquet and stuffed them into her quiver.

"We do good work, very fast. Tomorrow I get more reeds in case Shrie use all arrows and cannot retrieve them." Dashjmar raised his eyebrows in amazement. "What so…funny?" she asked when she could not think of another word.

"Nothing, you just said I."

"I? Shrie not say I, only Dashjmar say that," Shrie protested not remembering the use of the word.

"That's fine," Dashjmar replied honestly, "I believe I've grown rather attached to the third-person narration," he teased.

Shrie eyed him. "You funny, Dashjmar, but Shrie too tired for jokes."

"You're right." The humor drained from his face. "We should rest, for we continue at dawn."

Shrie patted down an area of grass and fell asleep with her face turned towards the clear, night sky. Dashjmar stayed awake longer, twirling one of the arrows he had made; he did not put it into Shrie's quiver. On the edge of the arrow near the feathers he scribed "The Maiden of the Wood." Rubbing his finger over the letters, he tucked it safely into his pack.

Morning came, the sun lighting the grasses with a golden sheen. Dashjmar shook Shrie awake and tossed their bags atop Magog.

"We shall go easier this morning; a tired warrior is no warrior at all."

"Shrie disagree. You not a warrior until you fight through weariness or go on despite it."

"That is true, but there is no need to deplete ourselves before coming upon open battle. Reserve your strength, but do not worry, we shall be flirting with speed and swords soon enough."

Having satisfied Shrie, he prodded the lizards into a jog. Gog did not protest though munching his grass became a considerably more complex feat. Shrie patted him thankfully.

"You good lizard, Gog. You would like the Mali-Malis. They are Shrie's friends in the mountain pass and jungle. They gentle, like you. They also like fruit." Gog's head swiveled at the mention of food but dropped again when he realized Shrie had none. Shrie chuckled. "I think Malis will like your humor. You will like them, too. Only, remember, they wary of newcomers; they may take time to warm up to you, but don't be discouraged, Gog. Once you their friend, they welcome you into their home. The Malis very faithful like you, Gog." Gog gurgled something, and Magog answered with a similar gurgle.

"What are they saying, Shrie?"

"They discuss the Mali-Malis. Gog thinks he has met one before."

"He has," Dashjmar confirmed. "Both he and Magog have been through this pass before. Neither of them got a close look at your spider friends, but they have seen them."

"That good," she told him. "Now they not be afraid if we be surprised by them."

"Rarely are these lizards scared, my lady." In the misty morning, Dashjmar swung Magog around skillfully and fell into step with Shrie and Gog.

"You sense something?" Shrie said in a hushed tone, bending closer to Gog as they moved through the narrowing pass. Droplets of water from a small stream bed running along the hillside splashed him.

"I believe we must head northward; we are too close to the mountains. If I remember correctly, we should be passing through a rocky plain and then some villages." Dashjmar talked slowly, pulling at the back of his vast memory. The Kalulukian then slapped Magog's side, encouraging him up the precipitous, craggy rock face to their right. Shrie turned Gog's head in the same direction, and they were soon blazing their own path to the plains of the south pass. She ducked every so often as bits of rock, chipped away by Magog, crashed towards her head. The fog engulfed them as they went higher, and Shrie nearly lost sight of Dashjmar. When they finally reached the top of the plateau, the sun struck the sky and revealed a sloping meadow of waving grasses. The horizon boasted topless peaks which pierced the clouds.

"We very high up, Dashjmar," Shrie told him.

"No, Shrie, we are merely on an unforgiving hilltop overlooking the lowlands. But I will admit it could appear daunting to a tenderfoot."

"Tenderfoot?"

"Newcomer or beginner."

Shrie recoiled at his tacit insult. "You tenderfoot in forest, Dashjmar." Shrie bounded down the dirt slope ahead of Dashjmar. She would prove to this arrogant Leirmayn that she was certainly not a tenderfoot.

Dashjmar took the lead again as they descended into tan meadows spotted by assortments of colorful lilies. Stepping into the spongy soil, the lizards completed the last twisting and turning mile. "The villages are ahead."

"They tribe people?" Shrie asked Dashjmar eagerly.

"No, they are mostly common people: herders, craftsmen, and some warriors."

"How come we see no Mali-Mali?"

Dashjmar plucked a stalk of something near him and stuck it in the corner of his mouth. "These last days have been chilly for the Mali-Malis. They should be out soon though. Once we get to the villages in the north, they will probably reveal themselves."

Mesmerized by the dips and raises of the stick in Dashjmar's mouth, Shrie forgot her other questions. "What that in your mouth, Dashjmar?"

Dashjmar bit into the stalk and sucked the sappy liquid dripping from its hollow center. "Here," he offered, handing the rest of the stalk to Shrie.

Shrie took the offered food from Dashjmar's open hand and gingerly stuck it between her lips. She tried to bite the outside, but it was completely stiff. She frowned and moved her jaw, trying unsuccessfully to break the stalk. Confused, she brought it from her mouth and studied it.

"Suck on it," Dashjmar advised.

Shrie glared at Dashjmar, thinking his words a joke.

"I'm serious," he assured her.

She stuck it back into her mouth, wrapping her lips around it. Golden-green syrup emerged from the stalk and trickled onto her tongue and onto the inside of her cheek. She let the liquid sit pleasantly on her tongue before slurping the remaining nutrients from the hollow. She was about to throw it away when Dashjmar protested.

"Wait! You can eat the stalk now that the syrup is drained."

Shrie crunched on the stalk's shell as the morning sun passed its midday mark and began its descent. Small birds perched in the occasional tree or chattered atop flowering cacti. Shrie and Dashjmar almost constantly reached down to grab a handful of Quaga stalks, and their extra sacks were stuffed to the brim with them. Dashjmar collected cacti needles for weapons he claimed he could create. An abundance of herbs for stew could also be found in the armful of things he brought back that night to the campfire.

While Shrie masterfully climbed the tree near their camp, Dashjmar took it upon himself to conduct a census of their supplies. Shrie hung upside down from a thin branch. The leafy tree was not comparable to the broad tropical and deciduous trees which towered regally in her forest. Shrie pitied this tree with its sad, drooping branches. Red bark covered its stunted trunk, and roots unable to divide the earth radiated above the ground. Even so, Shrie was happy once the branches encircled her. She finally dropped to the ground when Dashjmar informed her that dinner awaited her.

Building a small fire, they leaned back and admired the stars in the black sky. Shrie's eyelids drooped as the warmth from the fire caressed her face and as the grasses beneath her yielded to her weary body. Gog and Magog were already asleep, and Dashjmar whittled something with his knife in contemplative silence. Leaving Dashjmar, Shrie climbed once again into the tree's receptive arms. The warm smoke trailed idly behind her. Curled in a pleasant nook, she soon fell asleep.

Dashjmar gazed steadily into the flames, listening as Shrie settled herself in the tree. Under the silvery light of a glinting star, he fretfully anticipated their trip to the village; he did not want Shrie to reveal her identity. If word of her spread, the officials would soon discover their intentions and capture them in a preemptive strike. The thought encouraged his passionate prayer. *Almighty, guide me.* Shrie was bold and daring, but he was cautious. She respected him; but he had yet to see if she would trust his guidance.

The next morning, the two rose as usual and continued their travels. Days passed drearily in the plains. The only change in the drab scenery was the gradual appearance of sickly trees sprouting more frequently among the receding grasses. Much to Shrie's chagrin, a biting chill had also entered the air. In her jungle attire, she found herself rubbing her arms vigorously. The tiny bumps which arose like bubbles on the surface of her skin fascinated her; she had never seen anything like them before. Like Shrie, Dashjmar had not changed since leaving the caverns, and his tattoos were the only coverings for his bare chest. The gold arm band which had appeared so frightening in the Kalulukian firelight now looked dull as it reflected the monotonous spans of brown grass.

Shrie might have despaired but for the slim trail of gray which rose optimistically over a knoll. It meant they were close to the villages. From the top of the small hill, Dashjmar made out a cluster of huts situated in a low valley. Layers upon layers of woven grasses from the plains comprised tight roofs, and the mud and homemade brick were the building blocks of the houses. People bustled to and from the various venders which gathered in the central square, and children and dogs roamed the streets. Shrie watched with wonder; she had not seen so many people in one place before.

As they initiated their descent, mounted soldiers on Mali-Malis rode to meet them. The soldiers' clothes were worn, having seen too many fights and too few days of washing or patching. They carried crude weapons, but their faces were grim with experience. Shrie knew them to be rebels and allies of her friends. Smiling, Shrie waved readily. When the soldiers did not return her joyous greeting, she instead called to the giant spiders which ignored their riders and scattered forward eagerly to the one who called to them in their own tongue. Dashjmar shushed her as the riders jerked forward in amazement and frustration. When they had regained control over their steeds, they drew their weapons. Shrie yelped in surprise, but Dashjmar simply knitted his brows and waited for the soldiers to speak. One did so, nervously; he had not failed to notice the imposters' impressive array of weapons.

"Who are you and why do you come here?"

Shrie answered before Dashjmar could restrain her, "I Shrie the ru—"

"We are travelers from afar," Dashjmar interrupted. "We carry weapons to protect ourselves from bandits and officials, and we come to replenish our bags. I and my handmaiden," Dashjmar paused as Shrie bristled, "are in need of supplies. We are willing to trade or pay for everything. You have no need to fear us. We will only be here an hour or two."

The soldier eyed them skeptically. "There have been far too many raids on the villages near to us; you must understand that we are required to question any whom we see as dangerous. You will have to leave the lizards with us on the outskirts of the village."

"In any case, they will hardly fit in our widest streets," the other added.

"I would not have it any other way," Dashjmar commented dryly. "They will be docile for as long as we tell them to be."

Waving Shrie and Dashjmar through, the soldiers reluctantly closed in behind them, escorting them to the village while Shrie chattered.

"Who raid villages?"

"Dark men, my lady," one replied shaking his head. "They abound in number. Our village has been fortunate to avoid them, but only time will tell if we can escape their wrath."

"You fight them?"

"Several times." As he answered, the finger of his left hand twitched involuntarily. A bulging scar popped from his forearm and impressed Shrie.

"You fight hard, then. That good to know rebel forces have spirit."

"So be it, my lady. And if I may be so bold as to inquire of your native country? I cannot help but notice you carry an accent."

"I fight for rebel cause. I come from jungle." Oddly, something inside restrained her from telling them she was the ruler of the forest.

"It is true, then? The stories of the jungle people coming to our aid?"

It killed Shrie to quash the hope in his voice, but she had to tell him the truth. "I search for them," she said with austerity. As they approached the edge of the village she added, "Have hope, soldier, in the Almighty."

"I shall."

Shrie and Dashjmar dismounted and soothed Gog and Magog as the soldiers took their reins.

"Be good, Gog," she instructed him. "We be back soon."

As they parted ways, one of the soldiers enthusiastically called, "Hurrah!"

"Hurrah!" Shrie yelled back with her hand in the air.

Dashjmar said gruffly, "You handled your first confrontation with civilization smoothly. But don't get smug about it."

Shrie ignored him and strode confidently into the village. People stopped mid stride to gawk at the sight of the two exotic visitors; apparently travelers did not come through the village often. It did not take long for the amazement to drain from their faces and for the venders to swarm them with items. Dashjmar aptly traded some of his syrup canes for shirts while the ladies surrounded Shrie. They separated her from Dashjmar, offering her earrings and dresses. Shrie reveled in the attention as she examined the different outfits. Finally deciding on two simple tunics, she paid for them in a set quantity of canes. The people readily broke them to drink the cane juice or distributed them to calm their rowdy children. Shrie hurriedly threw one of her tunics over her hand and stuffed the other in her pack. The material was soft against her skin. She wondered from what plant they had woven it.

When the people realized Shrie would not buy more items, the people dispersed with the exception of one patient haggler who pointed to Shrie's ear and presented her with a single, silver earring. Her curiosity piqued, Shrie reached for it, holding it up to the light. It was slender and light, but strong. Engraved along its sides were the tunes of an old, tribal song. *Where did she find this?*

Having already haggled for the items he needed, Dashjmar searched the crowd for Shrie. Pushing through the people who were at least a head shorter than him, he finally located her. In an instant, he comprehended the meaning of the earring poised between her fingertips and handed the haggler a more than equitable share of cactus needles and canes. Shrie stuck the purchased earring in her ear. She searched the crowd for the mysterious vender, but the woman had already spirited away with her goods. As Dashjmar directed her through the muddy streets, she could hear the people gabbing animatedly about their trades.

"Why you buy it for Shrie?"

Dashjmar pushed away a lock of Shrie's hair so he could see the ring in her ear. Like Shrie, it was sturdy, slender, and one of the last of its kind. When they were out of earshot, he said, "Keep it as a sign of the promise you made to find your tribe and to take your place in the Harvest. When times get rough, remember your word."

Shrie fingered the ring thoughtfully. "You hint so much of bad times to come. Well, Shrie will meet those with perseverance and strength when they come." After a moment's pause she added, "You see tribe writings on it?"

"Yes; but I was unable to read them from afar."

"It is the spirit in a man, the breath of the Almighty, that gives him understanding," Shrie said solemnly.

"That is what it said?"

"That is what it said."

"It is true, is it not?"

"Yes."

Entering a poorly kept inn, Dashjmar said, "We will get some food here." Shrie wiped off the dirt and dust that had settled on her legs from their rushed passage through the center square. She took her time, apprehensive about the prospect of standing beneath a covered roof. Dashjmar beckoned her inside.

Pushing on a crude piece of wood which was the poor excuse for a door, Shrie stepped into the murky hut. Her eyes watered, stinging from the smoke of the roaring fire. Spitted on a stick, a hunk of animal roasted. As Shrie's eyes adjusted, tables made of a dense, orange wood materialized. Men and women occupied benches. Before them were full mugs or plates scraped clean. Shrie and Dashjmar found a secluded, corner table and asked for bread, vegetables, and meat. After refilling their almost depleted water sacks, Shrie and Dashjmar ate and drank. For once, Shrie let Dashjmar answer any questions from curious locals. *Dashjmar tells me I will be a leader of people. This will be hard if I never interact with more than twenty people at one time.* Observing their interactions, she learned many things.

Supposedly travelers had come to the village less and less often, and communication between the villages had dwindled as each one retreated into itself. No one had arrived from the ports to the west for over a year. Rumors of Shalkan atrocities wandered closer and more frequently to the village, carrying with them more evidence of their realities. Shrie thought of the soldiers they had met and touched the ring in her ear as a local woman, who also happened to be the cook, chattered uneasily of the shadow that had begun to cover them. When Dashjmar had heard all that he had wanted to hear, they left the hut at midday, later than expected.

"The locals tell me there is a rebel fort not far north of here," Dashjmar commented as they made their way back to Gog and Magog.

Shrie grunted in reply.

The soldiers waited anxiously to be relieved of their obligations. Watching the lizards had required more effort than they had anticipated. Gog had almost freed himself from their clutches, tugging a little too hard on the reins in order to graze on the specific blades of grass he wanted. Shrie thanked the soldier while reprimanding Gog lightly. Gog looked at her sheepishly and made a gurgling noise of regret which caused the soldiers to twitch uncomfortably on the Mali-Malis.

"He says he like you and spider," she informed the soldier.

"He told you all that?" the guard asked, patting his steed thankfully on the head. After struggling to control the lizards for several hours, he could now fully appreciate the Malis' dependable and compliant natures. Wishing Shrie and Dashjmar the best of luck, he hurried to relinquish the lizards' reins.

Shrie said a rushed goodbye and nimbly mounted Gog in order to catch Dashjmar who already rode hastily from the village. Disappointment weighed upon her as she left the rebels behind. Seeing the soldiers had reminded her of Ree and Corious. *And Lain.* If events went well for these rebels, she felt that somehow everything at Quantus Plain would also be working in her friends' favor. She missed their brainless jokes, loyal companionship, the wild fights, and savage war cries. Now she was bound to a glorious but taxing duty. It was a heavy burden, but one which was nobler than the one she had left behind.

Shrie and Dashjmar made camp early that night in a shallow dip of land. No fire was made, and Shrie donned her extra tunic. She slept restlessly, waking twice to the distant crashing of muffled thunder. It was so faint that, when she woke, she passed it off as the result of her imagination or particularly potent pieces of residual dreams. Before dawn cascaded over the horizon, Dashjmar woke her with a finger to his lips and a hand to his ear. The rumbling was the sound of men marching and carts rolling.

"They have come a long way," Shrie whispered to Dashjmar, "their footsteps are heavy and weary. Hear how they drag along the ground?"

Dashjmar crawled to the top of a craggy knoll. "I cannot tell who they are," he said. The shapes coming towards them formed a disorganized, single file. Minutes passed before Dashjmar said, "They are passing to the left of us, and I believe they are singing."

"Singing?" Shrie's ears pricked up, and then she smiled as the breeze carried the tune to her. It was the song of men going off to war. It was a song of purpose and conviction. "They must be allies," Shrie said certainly.

"If so, probability demands they are headed for the base. Saddle Gog. We will follow them there."

"Why we not meet them?"

"They are prepared for war and ready to attack before asking questions. I would not want them to mistake us for our enemies."

Shrie saw the wisdom in his words, and so they waited. An eerie silence descended when the footsteps and songs of the marching men faded. Shrie was relieved when the faint, morning sun began to burn off the mist of the night.

"It should not be much longer now. Halt Gog; they have stopped ahead of us."

Holding her breath, Shrie strained to see any sign of the base, but it was useless. The train of men and carts was long. After a few moments, the train jerkily pulled into motion and disappeared into the mist. "They must be entering the base." Shrie allowed Gog to move forward. "We go now?"

"It is a good idea, Shrie," Dashjmar noted, "to follow the judgment you exercised in the village—the one that led you to conceal your identity. The time will come to show yourself for who you are, but I am convinced that time is not now. I fear that rumors of who you are already beginning to spread."

The snaking line of men had stopped on a hilltop of green grasses overlooking scattered villages and the plains of the south pass. To their north and west lay a dense forest of conifers. Dashjmar enjoined Shrie to dismount and move into the cover of the leafy shrubs. A tingling thrill permeated Shrie's dispassionate cover of control as she studied the men. They wore cloaks and tunics dyed in varying shades of red, gold, and silver. The once vibrant fabrics were torn and dirty, and their swords were dulled and tinted red. Shrie frowned.

The rebels continued to follow the irregular, circuitous path that meandered out of sight. If the trail led to the rebel compound, it did not disclose any hints of military splendor or recent use. Dashjmar gave Shrie no signal but swung his lower body up and over Gog. Slapping Magog's hindquarters, he swept down the hill after the train of men. Shrie came in his wake, and they soon saw the scout tower rising prominently from the bottom of the hill. Dashjmar fell back at the impressive sight. At once, they squatted in the brush to observe.

The sharp repetitions of drumbeats broke the crisp air as a huge mat of grasses was removed from the hill. A tunnel entrance leading through the hill appeared, and the men vanished around its bend. Stubby, hanging torches lit the way. Behind the last man, levers restored to the hillside its seamless surface. Dashjmar concealed his frustration with a blank tone. "They will never let us through there. The lizards won't fit either." Before Shrie could protest, Dashjmar had mounted Magog and headed off towards the edge of the woods.

Shrie tagged behind Dashjmar, traversing the quiet ravine behind the rocky hill through which the rebels had passed. Aimlessly wandering without knowledge of where or how to reach the rebel fort, they surreptitiously scanned the outlying area. The path dove steeply over the top of the precipice. Gog made his way steadily up the treacherous hill. At the top, Shrie and Dashjmar tied the lizards to a tree and scouted for signs of an entrance. They passed over the hilltop only to discover additional rock faces. Ennui filled their hearts, and the morning sun seemed to bore down upon them in enmity.

Shrie stripped one of the tunics from her body. She did not impugn Dashjmar's motives, but she lagged behind him as he tirelessly scaled the rough rock wall. Shrie made it to a small ledge a good eight or ten minutes after Dashjmar, but he did not mention her lassitude. It seemed he did not notice. He moved horizontally, searching incessantly for a break in the rock. When he found one, and Shrie peered over his shoulder, dismay and awe accompanied the subsequent disappointment.

The other side of the hill was still clothed in stone, but grass now accented its descent. The slope dropped off into a gorge before the obsidian landscape flattened and spread like melting butter for miles into the distance. An ocean of rocks and grass, the vast plain swirled in circular motions, as though moved by the winds of a hurricane.

"No fort," Dashjmar muttered, his eyes surveying the land in consternation.

Shrie closed her eyes; she wished she was back at the village or in the trees of her jungle. The rocks here were sharp and rough, not covered in the moss to which she was accustomed. She sucked a small scratch on her hand, her reward for climbing the sheer incline, before leaping to where the lizards shuffled about. Back on the lizards, Shrie and Dashjmar headed forlornly back the way they had come, entering the plains once again. The sun rose higher, beating pitilessly the two circling searchers. It was noon when Shrie recognized the familiar scene.

"Dashjmar," Shrie said, feeling utterly hopeless, "there the same gorge we saw from other side of the hill."

"You are right. We shall wait for night when the torches are lit."

Dashjmar's plan seemed relatively feasible, and the prospect of receiving rest readily agreed with Shrie. Any thoughts of continuing the search dissipated as she used Gog's warm belly as a pillow. Dashjmar paced back and forth; an inquisitive glance at hills above them occasionally broke his rhythm. *When do we move on?* Two steps forward, one step back. *The Valley of Solitude awaits us; the land knows we come, but her people may not. If her father dies, the people will move...* There was no question of this in Dashjmar's mind. Three steps back. *The Valley is beautiful, but it holds many secrets. The tribe people would be fools not to leave.* He sat in defeat.

As the sun threw its last beams of light over the horizon and as the nocturnal animals waited eagerly at the edges of their abodes, he worked sedulously on his blow darts. Cutting a reed adeptly and whittling it delicately, he stuck four needles around its perimeter. Hollowing a denser reed, he fit a dart inside and aimed it at a bulge in an old stump. He exhaled in a fury and watched as the dart whistled in the air before thudding into the knotty lump. The dart reverberated in the dead tree as Dashjmar waited for darkness to come.

Chapter 3

A little after midnight, a torch brightened a spot on the horizon. Under the unearthly shadow cast by the torch, nothing stirred. Dashjmar estimated five thousand lizard strides separated between them from their destination. Upon hearing him wake, Shrie had risen and sleepily woke Gog. Magog, like his master, had not slept. If times did not demand the suppression of humor, the uncanny similarities between riders and ridden might have been humorous. Even Shrie, who normally valiantly defied the suppression, succumbed to its power. Almost immediately, Dashjmar and Shrie pushed the lizards into a run, skirting the edges of the scout tower. Streaming over the slopes and rises of the ground, they often lost sight of the single flame burning in the distance. At each slight glimpse of it, they redirected their course.

By the thin light of the stars and moonlight, Shrie did her best to guide Gog around rock piles and ditches. The lizard's feet scrapped agitatedly against the ground. Occasionally, when stones and boulders could not bear the lizards' weights, Shrie and Dashjmar swung erratically in their saddles as the creatures beneath them slipped. One hand steadied them; the other supported a ready staff. A force not of themselves led them closer to the base after each wearying hour. Shadows of varying gradients of gray shifted in the darkness. *What a deadening place to live.* The venerable animals, plants, and daring rebels that endured the harsh lands received Shrie's esteem. As they summited a particularly steep coil of ground washed in an incandescent glow, Shrie blinked her eyes. The fort towered above them in formidable force.

"Not as big as Quantus Plain, but it will do," Dashjmar muttered. As he completed his sentence, silhouettes of men stepped from the gloom. Shrie retreated but held her staff high. The men were rebels. Shrie lowered her weapons as they raised theirs.

"You are hereby summoned to the Captain of the Fort under immediate charges of trespassing and suspect of being the enemy."

Shrie cried out indignantly, but Dashjmar replied quietly, "Well, there's our passage into the fort."

The commander of the group scowled in his direction and led them under an impressive, black archway lit by numerous torches. Without an audible command, the portcullis plunged shut behind them as a pulley system of chains unfastened a giant, iron gate. The rebels lowered a ramp across a deep ditch filled with refuse. Shrie clamped her nose between two fingers as they crossed the bridge. With a loud crash, the gate closed.

A ceiling of towering height loomed above them, and numerous fires danced within alcoves set back into the wall of the circular room. The basalt walls endowed the place with a foreboding, dismal feel. Though the fires burned, their warmth was lost in the high ceilings. Flickering shadows of irregular shapes frolicked across the shiny floor, and the soldier's boots clicked distinctly against it. Guards spilled dourly from the hallways.

"You will have to leave any weapons you carry here," the commander instructed. "It is a routine procedure that must be obeyed." Dashjmar consented, but the guards shifted, unnerved when the disarming process took longer than usual.

From every possible hiding spot, Dashjmar extracted his collection of knifes, blow darts, and daggers. Shrie solemnly refused to surrender her bow and arrow until Dashjmar threatened to snap it. She handed it to a guard ruefully. Three guards transported the weapons to a separate room, and three stern guardians of the fort materialized from the gloom to replace their occupied counterparts. Expression and talking were taboo, and so the guards led the two jungle warriors noiselessly through various halls and numerous turns. Approaching a steep set of stairs, the guards instructed them to dismount the lizards and to stand still while they tightened chintzy blindfolds over the intruders' eyes.

"Shrie not like this," she growled as one guard held her hands behind her back and secured the itchy blindfold. "I rebel warrior."

"It is for your safety, my lady, that we do so. In an unfortunate case of capture or interrogation by the enemy, there would be no way you could release information on the position of our headquarters," responded the guard who gripped her hands tightly with one hand and steered her with another. She tripped when they met the first stair, but the guard caught her agilely. Shrie grunted resentfully, her pride injured.

"Dashjmar, you ahead or behind me?" Shrie asked after the first set of stairs.

"I believe I'm ahead," was the only response.

"When stairs done?"

"Soon, my lady," the guard steering her replied in a tone flagrantly incongruous with the fort's atmosphere. His voice summoned the memory of training on the beaches of a forgotten shore, of being taught the letters of writing by Ree, and of discussing tactics with Logan and Hitachi.

"Men from Quantus Plain come here?" she asked in mounting expectancy.

"Why would you ask that?" The guard turned her kindly to her right and pushed her lightly. Shrie strode forward.

"You ever be a sailor before?" Shrie questioned; a strain of eagerness entered her voice.

He did not answer right away, and then he whispered in her ear, "It is best if they do not know we are acquaintances, Shrie."

Shrie's heart leapt with joy. It was Hitachi.

"Why not," she asked as softly as she could. "And why you grow beard?" she added as his face touched her cheek.

"I've been on the supply train delivering supplies to independent rebel groups. I didn't have a razor. As for your other question, it would create too many complications. They could force you into serving here, as they did with us already," he added. "That would not be how you would want it to be, if I am correct."

Shrie acquiesced. She would have to play down her fighting abilities. "How Corious, Ree, Tar, Malov, and the others?"

"What's going on over there?" a guard bellowed upon seeing Hitachi closer to Shrie than their business permitted.

"Pretend to struggle." As she obeyed, Hitachi called to the other guard, "She's putting up a fight!" As his excuse was established, Hitachi answered Shrie, "Very well, my lady. All is well. They are happy, though they miss you. If I return to Quantus Plain, would you like me to relay a message?"

"Tell them Shrie say that the Harvest is coming, and that it time to muster troops. Tell them also, that she misses them, and for them to trust in the Almighty who is with us."

"I will do that. Here we are now, so remember my advice."

Shrie's eyes fluttered open as the blindfold fell from her eyes and as she and Dashjmar were presented to the commander of the fort. The commander, tall, gray-haired, and solid, awaited them in the small, windowless room. A cape flowed from his square shoulders, and his leather boots were dried and cracked from use. The premature age which comes from battle and worry lined his face. All of the guards except for the one who had blindfolded Shrie and Dashjmar returned to their posts.

"Ah, so these are the intruders that so skillfully avoided the eyes of our watchtower. You do not appear like enemies of the people or like the spawn of dark men. Nor do you appear in normal rebel garb. Tell me, why do you ask entrance of our fort? I am most interested."

"I am Dashjmar, a Kalulukian leader of old, and this is Shrie, the last of the forest folk. We search for her tribe. Surely we are on your side, for we go to gather the armies of old and unite them at Quantus Plain in preparation for the Last Battle of the Harvest."

The commander's gray eyes held Dashjmar's gaze and then grabbed Shrie's. "So it is true: the legends will have their fulfillment in our time. I could not have hoped for a more opportune time to fight for the Almighty and express my allegiance to Him." His eyes sparkled in genuine honor. "I have waited for the day when I would muster my troops, march to reinforce our brothers, and achieve eternal peace. I will believe you because I want to, and because I have to. The validity of your message is confirmed by your titles alone: the Maiden of the Wood and the Kalulukian Elder of Old. They have come back to gather the last of the jungle people." When the surprise registered in Shrie's eyes, he added, "I see that even those called to fulfill ancient prophesies are not versed well in the legends. I will not contain you any longer, that is, unless you would be pleased to fight for us?"

Shrie answered eloquently, "We are fighting for same cause in another land."

The commander accepted this with disappointment. Shrie did not blame him. He felt it was his task to win over as many men as possible to his cause. He asked honestly, "Can my men aid you in any way?" The guards shifted their feet.

Dashjmar shook his head. "None but for your promise to help in the Last Battle. Though, if you could provide us with provisions for our journey and information concerning Shalkan positions, we would be grateful."

"That will be done. Anything you request, Maiden?"

"News of tribe?"

The commander shook his head sadly. "Only a rumor brought from the supply train of a single jungle girl coming from Quantus Plain. It was never confirmed."

Guards entered the room with a package of food. One whispered confidentially into the commander's ear before leaving. The commander's face darkened, and he directed his gaze back to Shrie and Dashjmar. "There is news of black shapes following in your tracks. My scouts have been unable to shoot them."

"The Zabyn," Shrie hissed angrily. "How could they have tracked us so far?"

"I will dispatch men to kill them if you wish."

"That would be folly. The Zabyn will destroy more of your noble men than you can sacrifice at this time. Shrie and I will deal with them if they find us. May I request use of your underground tunnels?"

"Indeed, I will appoint a guide to you; and despite what you say, I shall unleash my powers upon these Zabyn. It is of the utmost importance to eliminate them. Trackers are far worse than those who would fight outright. As for enemy positions, I am sorry that the report from last week is vague at best. Shalkans haunt the mountain passes, and more stream from the north, making their way down the shore. I would recommend taking a route through the Borderlands. I do not believe the dark men have infiltrated that troubled land yet. From there, I do not know where your course will take you." He rubbed his fingers against his chin meditatively. "I do have one question. How do you know to mass the troops at Quantus Plain?"

"Where else would the officials attack but the last, great bulwark in the east?

Read your legends more closely, and you will find that there are more than enough hints which suggest Quantus Plain is the chosen place. Take the villagers with you when you march, for it is best that they leave under the protection of an army rather than remain as an inadequate buffer against the extending reach of the black fist," Dashjmar warned.

"The black fist, indeed," the commander repeated. "Hitachi," he motioned towards Dashjmar and Shrie, "take these two through the tunnels and then return to your post. It was well you came here," he remarked to the two as they parted. "May the Almighty fight before you and be your rear guard."

"The same to you," Dashjmar replied solemnly. To Shrie, he related, "I believe he will spread the news rather quickly."

"You gave away identities."

"They will not be disclosed," Hitachi replied. "The commander supposedly has never acted in such a way before. I have just arrived, and yet it seems with your arrival we will be leaving again."

Shrie grinned as guards hurried to and fro, obeying hasty mandates to transport this or that to different parts of the tower.

"The commander seemed awfully zealous to make such a drastic move," Dashjmar commented, pleased with their work.

Hitachi supported his opinion. "Yes, I have not seen him so moved, but then again, he clearly delights in battle and honor. Here, come this way, I do not think there is any need to blindfold you this time. We will take you to get your weapons, yes?"

Shrie was grateful. Without her bow, she felt naked and isolated.

"And then I will take you to your steeds," he said, leading them down the flight of stairs they had come up moments before. "They are quite extraordinary, I might add. I have rarely seen anything like them."

"They exotic creatures of the Kalulukians," Shrie stated proudly. Her hand trailed along the wall while her feet briefly skimmed the surface of one stair before falling to another.

Shrie's statement had received the desired effect, arousing both his curiosity and awe. Scratching his beard, Hitachi brought them around a corner and into the weaponry. Shrie checked and double-checked her arrows. Nothing was out of place. After taking several minutes to place knives in secret pockets under boot flaps and to toss weapons onto their backs, they were ready. Hitachi decided not to question his friend about her journey or about the dangers that required arming herself so.

Instead, he simply watched in bemusement and commented, "The Zabyn don't stand a living chance."

With a wry smile, Shrie stepped from the doorway of the room and stated, "Zabyn already dead in Shrie's mind."

"I thought so." Hitachi grinned and waved them down one last flight of stairs, bringing them to Gog and Magog. Hitachi stopped in admiration. The lizards' bluish-green skin stretched tautly over leathery necks bunched with flexing muscles.

"You can come on Gog with Shrie," Shrie said as she hopped on Gog and pulled Hitachi up with her. She guided Gog through the door with her knees. Many a soldier stopped racing up or down stairs, delaying their individual tasks in order to watch the procession walk through the tunnel entrances.

"Take the third right," Hitachi instructed, as he gripped the blanket atop Gog. Rigid but composed, he did not let his body adjust to the movement of the lizards, as though afraid of offending the great beasts. Not fifteen minutes later, the ground began to slope downward. The air held a musty smell, one which the torches were unable to dispel, and trickles of water escaped through the stone barrier. They were in the outermost ring of the fort, descending into the tunnels which were a crude but usable series of underground halls. Some were natural, like those of Quantus Plain, but others had been dug hastily to facilitate travel without detection. The weathered stone deteriorated into dirt muddied from use, and the ceiling grew uncomfortably low for the lizards who were becoming cramped in the small space. When they could no longer ride upon the lizards without their heads brushing the top of the tunnel, the three rebels were forced to dismount.

"This tunnel does not get progressively smaller, I hope." Dashjmar casually disguised the question as a remark.

"Have no fears. This is the smallest part of the tunnel. Mind you, I have been in ones through which you have to crawl. It's a most unpleasant experience; never do it if you can avoid it. More unpleasant things than rats and worms abound in the deep places of the mountains."

Plant roots dangled from the hard, compacted dirt of the ceiling. Shrie had to speak to Gog several times, explaining to him that he could not eat the roots which, if torn from the ceiling, would weaken the tunnel structure. Hitachi watched the scene apprehensively. When they arrived at the exit, Hitachi pulled the lever which opened the hidden door. Dashjmar and Magog left first, and Dashjmar gave Hitachi a grateful nod. Leaving last, Shrie embraced Hitachi in a hearty hug.

"You be brave, Hitachi, and remember everything Shrie show you," she said, swinging her staff in demonstration.

"I will try, for your sake. I'll miss you, Shrie. May the Almighty let our paths cross once more in this life."

"Shrie will miss you too, Hitachi. She will be discontent if she cannot see you fight for cause of good and do heroic deeds."

Back on Gog, she rode out the door, and Hitachi lowered it, watching as the last of Gog's tail disappeared. Sighing, he jogged back through the tunnels to find Logan.

The moon lingered in the sky, lighting the tumble of rocks and grass spraying from the base of the door. Talus and scree littered the outline of the plains. Rubbing her eyes, Shrie struggled to concentrate. To keep herself awake, she imagined the archers of the fort hunting the Zabyn. Shrie would have liked to meet the Zabyn once more to vanquish them.

When lighter clouds floated on the horizon, and the glory of the stars had dimmed, Dashjmar led Magog into a small indent in the side of the hill. Shrie clung to her last reserves of wakefulness as she dismounted and happily sank to the ground. A few hours of sleep would refresh her greatly.

"We'll stay here for awhile," Dashjmar said unnecessarily as he unburdened Magog of his load. Gog was still saddled. Irritable from lack of sleep, Dashjmar chastised, "Shrie, go unsaddle Gog, he'll," his voice trailed off as he noticed Shrie fast asleep on the dirt. Shaking his head, he went to unsaddle Gog by himself.

"See him there?" the soldier questioned hoarsely.

His companion followed the accusing finger into the darkness. "I don't see a thing. It's so dark," he bemoaned. "Where did the rest of them go, anyway? There were only seven or so left," he paused as the shadows shifted. Something rose swiftly from the ground.

"Ah, I see him, now."

"He's been hit four times already! These things die hard," the other soldier grimaced as he loosed two arrows.

Immediately, a ghastly smoke rose from the spot of contact, and a high-pitched scream rang in the dark. A sickening smell of rotting flesh overwhelmed the men from the fort. Swooning, one lost his dinner before falling on his hands and knees. He attempted to drag himself from the fumes. The other glanced horrified over his shoulder before fleeing. The soldier's legs felt wobbly, and he began to sweat and shake. A sharp tingling radiated from the back of his neck where the Zabyn had dug its venomous fangs. With open eyes, the guard fell to the ground.

Sapping the life from the guard had taken the last of the dying Zabyn's strength, and it crumpled. Screams of dying rebels joined the Zabyn's shrieks. Stalling on the stairs, Logan and Hitachi watched the fire tipped arrows, the smoke, and the death from a window of the tower. Torches were lit and thrown onto the hideous bodies of the creatures; the smoke billowed high into the sky.

The commander charged the Zabyn. His foolishness was not repaid with death as foolishness in battle is commonly done, and the spirit of his men came from hiding. A horn sounded as the last creature was hunted and destroyed, but its sound was not jubilant. It rang as a warning, and the people in the huts of the nearby village lit their candles. They gathered in the square where estranged exclamations left their lips. They wondered from where the sedentary smoke had come, for the fumes did not dissipate in hours or even days. It rested forebodingly upon the land, spreading the terror of an impending evil.

"We have been liberated from our trackers." The sound of Dashjmar's voice vibrated against Shrie's sleeping ear. Yawning, she rubbed a forearm across her face. Dashjmar's back was to her, and the morning light revealed the strapping contour of his body. Standing, Shrie walked to where he stood. Plumes of acrid smoke rose from the fort, and her nose twitched at a trace of it.

"They incinerate the Zabyn's bodies." After a pause, he mentioned, "Just because we are not being pursued does not mean we must hold to the shimmering delusion of safety. Mount Gog. I saddled him for you."

"Breakfast?" Shrie questioned, ignoring his caveat.

Dashjmar shook his head. As usual, she was not listening to him. He simply tossed her the bag of provisions bestowed upon them at the fort and cautioned, "Don't eat too much of it."

Chapter 4

"Be wise, and keep your heart on the right path."
Proverbs 23:19

Dense fog shrouded the horizon. It was a land on the edge of many nations. Perhaps once in its mysterious history it had hosted a civilization, but if it had, no one knew about it now. It was a land without a people, and whatever its true name used to be, it had been forgotten. Its visitors were few, and a mere selection of dismal animals claimed a permanent stake in the land called the Borderlands. No romanticism should be attached to the name, for in no one's mind did it conjure even a smidgen of glory. From its name, nothing more than the obvious should be determined or deduced. The borders of other lands determined its boundary, and so its frontiers remained barren. No one wondered why peoples chose not to seek conquests in the Borderlands, for there existed little to be wanted. Covered in an ever-present mist which sedated the mind, the Borderlands wound between the mountains dividing countries of an independent and isolated nature: the Forest of Khaltharnga, Shrie's native land, Zabyn, Fal-Nunein, and Wathien.

The flat land led to the sea, and the sea was fed by a river that skirted the flat lands as though afraid of plunging into the land's murky depths. The river supported sparse, graying vegetation. Sporadically, one could find these ashen plants sprouting from the ground like dried seaweed plucked from the ocean. Though sharp angles thrust the plant waist high above the misty ground, the plant was pliable to the touch. What the ground looked like beneath the haze remained unknown, but the vapor dissipated with height and only regained its strength high in the mountains.

From the plants sprung the rumor of the poisoned mist. People living near the Borderlands claimed that the mist took the lives of those who stayed in its midst beyond their allotted time. An old tale it was to be sure, but no one ever contradicted its validity; and science refused to prove otherwise. A ghastly place, the sky always remained in a pearly gradient that was both peaceful and perilous. It was here in the Borderlands that the occasional traveler lost his way or the fleeing warrior found refuge from his enemies. A controversial place by its very essence, it was as much beautiful in its consistency as it was serene.

The plants seemed to shift though the breeze was stagnant. Of course, no one could prove that the vegetation moved, but many a traveler swore that clusters of the clawing plants would disperse or gather, leaving them without reliable landmarks.

"It is a generally known fact that where the plants prosper, water or food lay not too far below the surface. When dug into, the ground may either yield water or desiccated, small, round knobs. These edible bulbs have the texture of a nut and the taste of dried beans. Small roots spring from them, so it's necessary to crack the shell before eating the insides. Leading to either the food or water, the plants will become a salient element of traversing these lands," Dashjmar explained to Shrie as he refilled their canteens at one such plant.

Their spirits despondent since leaving the fort, Shrie and Dashjmar felt as though they had clambered from a pleasant valley into the wrath of the Almighty. Rain and sleet plagued their morale as they plowed deeper through the white fog. Shrie swore they were in the mountains, but Dashjmar insisted that people classified the area as a plain. Shrie preferred to think they were in the treacherous mountains so that her griping could find rationalization.

For living in the humid jungle climate her entire life, Shrie adapted as well as she could, but the sleet, freezing rain, and fog overwhelmed her. She had come down with a severe cold a week after leaving the fort, and even Dashjmar had shivered in the milder storms. The sun had broken through the clouds only once in those seven days, and even then, the sleet had merely turned to rain. As they plodded along with Shrie wrapped in every warm blanket and tunic they owned, they saw a circle of white covering the cloud-shrouded peak nearest them. Shrie could not comprehend its existence; she had never seen snow, and the fever forced the gears of her mind to grind torpidly.

"Dashjmar, the mountain," Shrie said sniffling, "it white."

"It is a form of rain, Maiden. In boreal regions, the rain transforms itself into white shapes. Mount Tinshagwea is a cold, unforgiving mountain."

"We go up mountains?" Shrie asked apprehensively while rubbing her arms vigorously.

"Yes, but not these, fortunately." To Magog, Dashjmar asked, "How do you fare, my lizard friend?"

Magog slipped with every step he took; the footing was treacherous.

"Poor, Gog," Shrie lamented, "carrying Shrie in terrible weather with no break. I think I walk next to him."

Dashjmar heard her say this but did not think much of it; for with her fever she rambled even more than usual. Worried, he knew he would have to find the first village out of the Borderlands to obtain more clothing and blankets; they could not afford sickness. Turning to say some encouraging words, Dashjmar blinked in confusion. Shrie was sitting sideways upon Gog and talking to him. With a plopping noise, she dismounted and began to run beside him.

"Shrie, what are you doing?" Dashjmar demanded.

"Shrie is running beside Gog," she answered in an unsteady voice backed by a resolve that was nearly comical.

"Well, Shrie better get back on Gog."

No answer.

"You might offend him," Dashjmar lied in the vain hope of persuading her from her whim. "And then he wouldn't like you anymore."

"Gog love Shrie," Shrie cried indignantly. "Besides, this activity making Shrie hot!" With that, a blanket flew off her back and onto Gog's saddle. Her legs burned. She had not been able to run freely for a long time. All the tunics that had once not been able to keep her warm were now a weighty, wet burden. Dashjmar stared in amazement, and after a moment of indecision, he threw himself from Magog with a loud cry. Four figures now, two big and two small, ran across the misty plains.

Shrie exclaimed, "Ha! Dashjmar see value in Shrie's resolution."

This was Dashjmar's turn not to respond. He had once thought Shrie a little off the edge; now he knew he was too. Delightful insanity appeared to be contagious. Through the white haze, their figures pushed deeper into the Borderlands. Their legs cycled as if gravity held no power. Breathing came easily, and the air rushed in their nostrils and out their mouths in spirals of vapor not unlike the mist curling about them. Beads of sweat rolled down their legs, pumping endlessly in time to a music that could not be heard by anyone but themselves. Filled with a vitality which rang in spite of weakness, they moved with the powerful stride that is the pride of lions and the bane of their prey. In the course of that night or day, for the mist would reveal neither, more mileage was covered than the entirety of three days before.

Rising a victorious fist into the air, Shrie stumbled, but swung herself atop Gog. Leaning forward with her legs bent and back arched, her focus demanded that her gaze be lighted solely upon the course which would spring them from the Borderlands. Grabbing hold of Magog's stirrups, Dashjmar likewise mounted his steed and sped after her.

It could have been hours or days before Shrie learned she could ride Gog standing upright. Her legs had wobbled precariously at first, but then as she adjusted to the new form of riding, her legs rose like tree trunks from the roots of the stirrup. In about another two days, they had discovered the land's dearth of food and shortage of water. Their old rations were stale and putrid smelling, but it was all they had to eat. Fortunately, they had stumbled upon a running stream where they had filled their canteens but, in their eagerness to quaff, had wasted the water on their chins and faces. They had reveled in the water's touch, for no other water flowed in the capacious void between the mountains.

As they rested, a glowing tincture painted a land empty of people. The first birds of the morning fluttered to perch upon the graying plants which substituted for trees. Shrie blinked fiercely as the sun sent its rays like envoys over the domineering mountains. The luminosity pained her eyes which were accustomed to the constant dusk that had greeted them in their past mornings. A brisk breeze whistled down from the mountaintops in violent gusts, negating any of the sun's offered warmth. As Shrie lifted a hand from her eyes, Dashjmar scanned the early morning. Shrie pulled her cloak tighter around her shoulders and put her head back down on Gog's belly. She was content to lie down and forget her responsibility. Fatigue convinced her that sleep was more important than food. Meanwhile, Dashjmar defied the deadening tiredness, packed their belongings, and aroused the lizards.

"It's a better day to travel than to rest," Dashjmar insisted. Shrie seemed unwilling to believe any logic Dashjmar presented. "If we rest," he continued, "there might be horrible weather tomorrow, in which case we would end up expending too much energy just to travel a couple dozen miles. But if we travel today, we'll travel at least fifty or sixty miles. Then, we will be that much closer to shelter, food, and water."

Persuaded, Shrie finally mounted Gog. Two days of tough traveling passed, during which they rationed their dwindling water carefully. At one point, they had stumbled upon the outlandish plants, and Shrie had jumped hurriedly from Gog in order to dig. The dry ground had revealed bulbs but no water. Fleeing from despair, she had methodically picked out the corms which would provide them with four days worth of food if distributed sparsely and carefully. Even so, the discovery was not completely helpful. The bulbs, when consumed, made the mouth ache for water, and so Shrie avoided them entirely.

Hours later, Shrie unselfishly gave the final mouthful of her water to Gog who licked up the handful eagerly. Throughout the day, Shrie's throat grew increasingly dry. Towards evening, her face twisted painfully as she struggled to swallow and moisten her throat. Even stoic Dashjmar grew uncomfortable when the top of his tongue began to stick to the top of his mouth when he spoke. Shrie found this hilarious but would immediately stop laughing when what would have been a light-hearted chuckle came out sounding like a hoarse choke.

In an attempt to assuage the tedium, they held occasional races on Gog and Magog who hardly appreciated it. Shrie would try chattering with the lizards, but that soon began to gnaw on Dashjmar's patience and composure. The single positive asset working in their favor was the sun which provided suitable traveling weather. They stopped only one night out of the two, pushing onward in the hope of finding a village somewhere on the edge of the Borderlands. That night, as always, they lay down their water flasks to catch the morning dew. The crystal droplets provided them with several mouthfuls of clear liquid, and then the flasks were as empty as before.

In a rare sense of desperation, Dashjmar steered them northward, heading into higher altitudes and snow-capped mountains. He had not told Shrie of his plan: one which included braving the frigid, inclement weather of the mountains to obtain snow and melt it into their flasks. As Dashjmar drove the lizards up a steep incline of rock, the trees surrounding them bent towards the earth, shriveled and dead. Shrie noticed the change.

"Why we going into cold, cold mountains? It windy, harsh, and no water here, Dashjmar!"

Dashjmar brought Magog to a halt on the top of the ridge, overlooking the five hundred feet of rocky slope they had covered. "Up in the clouds, Shrie," Dashjmar told her, pointing a slender finger towards the whirling mass of white at the summit, "there will be snow. When we melt the snow, it turns into water."

Shrie was about to protest that they did not have the clothes needed to survive the trip, but Dashjmar held a finger to his lips. Shrie exhaled noisily through her nose, frustrated by the rashness of Dashjmar's plan. Shrie told Gog in lizard that Dashjmar was crazy, and Gog responded with a swift shake of the head as if agreeing. By wearing the extra tunics from the town, she withstood the bitter chill until the glacial fall of night. For warmth, Dashjmar and Shrie squeezed into a nook between two rock faces where the stone overhang protected them from the elements. Dashjmar sealed the narrow entrance with the innumerable dead limbs which dangled from the mountain's abused trees, and he tied the lizards near the doorway.

"Won't lizards be cold, Dashjmar?" Shrie petted Gog.

"These lizards suffer little from hunger or thirst, heat or cold. To think otherwise would be to insult their strength of mind and body." Whether or not his statement was true, Dashjmar felt little compunction for leaving the hardy creatures outside. He started a fire and rubbed his hands together rapidly as he sat across from Shrie. Shrie shivered involuntarily as a string of frosty wind seeped into their alcove. She nibbled on a piece of bread from her pack as Dashjmar poked and prodded the coals of the fire.

"Did you know many men say these mountains are under a horrid curse?" Shrie shuddered violently upon seeing Dashjmar's expressionless face. "Hunters and explorers tell of a white, hairy ogre which sleeps when the mountains are devoid of life." Shrie was not gullible, but her eyes opened wide despite her tiredness. "A huge beast of a man, almost," Dashjmar added, getting swept away by the drama of his own story. "He prowls on all fours and has the nose of a wolf and the voice of a bear. He feasts upon his kills every night in a cave no man wishes to ever see or be near." The wind howled outside. "But he is also intelligent. Deep pits have been found with broken sticks littering the bottom. They are the deadly traps he constructs."

"It a good thing we not have to travel through snow, only up to it," Shrie said honestly, before adding hurriedly, "but it not matter anyway; snow-wolf-man not exist." She held her hands over the fire.

"Before you make such a hasty judgment, first let me give you a solid background. If I am correct, this is the first mountain of the range separating the Borderlands from the Forest of Khaltharnga and Fal-Nunein. Another range branches off this one, marching northwards to our first destination."

Shrie started at the word "first" and then remembered the dotted line leading far north and then due south to Quantus Plain. Dashjmar noticed her realization but simply continued.

"It is a great hulk of a mountain and deserves a rather frightening and imposing name to fit it, but like the Borderlands, it carries a rather bland name if analyzed; for Taerg Niatnuom is simply Great Mountain backwards. Any simpleton could have contrived such a name. Rather ironic, I suppose," Dashjmar mused, "for the man who named it was a man of much ingenuity and contemplation. Anyways, I digress. The man is only present in legends, but in the legends he is called Evitaerc. Of honorable men from the line of Niagauoytog, he was raised a warrior, and of his many righteous deeds there are many stories to tell. One of such stories concerns Taerg Niatnuom."

His introduction complete, Dashjmar paused for a breath and then launched into the tale. "Supposedly journeying to his home in what is now Wathien, he was urged by a beautiful, distraught maiden to accompany her into the mountains and save her brother. He could not refuse the young woman her request. When they ventured deep into the snowy regions, she disappeared in one of the blizzards which frequent the mountain. Evitaerc huddled under his shield and was buried under many feet of snow, but when the blizzard ended, he thrust through the piles of white powder above him and began his search.

All was white and harsh upon his eyes, confusing where the horizon began and where the ground ended. After going some ways, he slipped, and his fall thrust him forward into a hidden cave. Inside, the woman and a man of similar age sat bound and almost frozen in a strange contraption. Immediately alarmed for their safety, Evitaerc used his sword to free them. It was a long and complicated process in which he had engrossed himself, and he did not hear the quiet padding on the snow. Soon it, the creature of the snow, was behind him. Our hero turned, but stunned by the creature's repugnant appearance, Evitaerc did not strike. According to the story, the beast, for some inexplicable reason, granted them unhindered passage from his lair. Yet when Evitaerc turned to find the maiden and her brother, they had vanished."

Shrie had curled up by the fire. "That a good nighttime story to help Shrie fall asleep."

Dashjmar frowned, puzzled; the story was supposed to frighten her, or at least prepare her for what they might face. She took it as a bedtime story.

"I can probably speak language snow creature speaks anyway, Dashjmar. If we meet him, I can tell him to not harm us!"

Dashjmar smiled and wondered if Shrie would have been able to communicate with the beast. He stayed up for several more hours, stoking the fire and retracing their route in his mind. Shrie, meanwhile, had fallen asleep, and her snoring aggravated Dashjmar's ear for the remainder of the night.

In the morning, it was cold. Very cold. Sometime during the night, a heavy snow had fallen and their fire had been extinguished. The lizards stirred noisily outside, bringing Dashjmar from his sleep. After his strident curse, Shrie awoke.

"What you yell about Dashjmar? You ruin my sleep."

Dashjmar prodded the frozen ice that sealed them into their nook in the mountainside. "We're frozen in." He paced the perimeter of their confinements. "The snow must have come in last night and risen around us. Our body heat as well as the fire melted it into water, but when the temperatures dropped, it froze into ice. We're walled in."

Shrie pulled the blanket up around her neck. "I still have staff."

Dashjmar eyed the staff skeptically. "I probed the ice; it is frozen solid for at least four to six inches."

Shrie looked blankly at where the fire had been, sleepiness etched into her face. "We could start another fire and melt a hole."

Dashjmar regarded gravely the pitiful remains of their fire. "It's got to be well under freezing in here. The heat of a small flame could not persuade these icy sheets to melt. I don't think we have any wood left anyway."

Shrie stared at the ice hanging from the rock ledge above them. "Did you check ice on roof?"

"It's packed solid." The place that had once seemed a haven was now their tomb.

"Then there only one way, Dashjmar: the entrance."

Dashjmar discarded his own ideas and helped Shrie hack at the entrance. Shrie loaned her staff to Dashjmar as she used two of his longer knives. One hour passed; only three inches had been scraped from the barrier. The second hour passed, leaving them little promise of progress. The third hour came and went, and the knives as well as the two's perseverance had dulled. Angrily, Dashjmar slammed Shrie's staff into the flawless ice. He shook his head in despair until a slight crack resounded in the silent cave. Shrie and Dashjmar exchanged glances of relief before attacking the ice wall with renewed drive. Another hour passed, and the ice cracked and toppled. Snowflakes twitched as they tumbled through the tunnel of ice. Shrie and Dashjmar squeezed through the passageway, plowing through the snow until they reached the lizards. They breathed in the raw mountain air and observed the snowy landscape.

"Praise the Almighty!" Dashjmar shouted in a rare display of thanks.

Shrie repeated the phrase in a quieter tone that reflected her level of energy. After a brief respite in which they filled their canteens with snow, they abruptly made their way back down the mountain. Weighted with ice and snow, slight tree branches broke from their trunks and succumbed to the burying snow. The snapping and crashing accompanied the thunderous plodding of Gog and Magog. An escalating rumble in the background seemed an appropriate backdrop to the rupturing of the maimed trees and the lizards' strained exertions. The crashing continued and persistently grew in volume. The ground began to grumble, as if it protested their leaving. As Shrie turned, she could not decipher what she saw.

"Dashjmar, what that cloud doing?"

There were no clouds in the piercingly azure sky. Dashjmar turned in confusion but nearly jumped from Magog in terror. "Run!"

Shrie sensed Dashjmar's fear, and the amount of it caused her to pound Gog on the head as she frantically sprinted after Dashjmar and Magog. The cloud pursued them without fail. Its growing girth closed the gap between them. Shrie cried out in fear as the cloud grabbed at her hair. Her vision blurred in tears as the frigid wind bit into her face. She pounded Gog on the head even though she knew he was going his fastest. The cloud on her sides doubled its efforts to beat her to the bottom. Gog moved more ponderously in the thickening chaos. A white and brown blob careened towards her. An image of the snow creature Dashjmar had described flashed in her mind. She screamed, but she could not hear herself over the moving cloud. Curling into a fetal position, she ducked her head closer to Gog. The alteration of weight caused Gog to lose his footing. Shrie gasped for breath. The cloud pounded her into the snow. Ice pried open her throat and slid down it. She lost recognition of up and down as she was carried deeper into the swirling mass. She gagged before slipping into a wet darkness.

Dashjmar had beaten the avalanche, but shame ate at him. He had abandoned Shrie. He had not meant to; his faith in Gog and his own dread of dying had spurred him forward without any thought of braking. Veering left under an overhang of rock, Dashjmar had flattened himself against the rock, and the snow had blasted over the stony extension, washing over the landscape below him like water released from a broken dam. He had shut his eyes as a score of snow particles swept under the ledge in a backlash of wind. And then it had been over.

Dashjmar laid a hand on Magog's snow covered head. "We've been through the worst, Magog." Dashjmar took a strange pride in defying nature. Men and their weapons did little to intimidate the Kalulukian; only the Zabyn and nature's unpredictable dangers proved themselves worthy of his competition.

Mounting Magog, he plodded around the base of the mountain, waiting for Shrie and Gog to materialize from the wintry slopes. He had not given a second thought to their safety. Only when he had traversed halfway up the mountain without seeing them did he become troubled. He now called their names continuously in a hushed tone of disbelief. Through forests and gorges, he whispered their empty names. Anguish mutated into rage. *Had the Almighty granted us passage from the Zabyn to have my companion breathe her last breath in an avalanche?*

Dashjmar glared at the gray sky; darker clouds scurried above him. The halcyon moment after the deafening roar of the avalanche unsettled him. A gruff growl broke the quietness. Dashjmar calmly lowered his head, though his heart heaved.

Standing at one side of the steep pass, the beast rose to its hind legs; it towered a head and shoulders above Dashjmar. Shrie's earring shone in its white hand, or paw. The Kalulukian spoke vehemently.

"Where is she, brute?" he spat as he swung Magog closer to the one who confronted him.

The creature's light green eyes flashed angrily, and it dropped to all fours. It loped into the trees. Without a second thought, Dashjmar pursued the beast. As he trekked farther into the forest, Dashjmar could not help but notice the magnificent gleaming white coat it bore. Layer upon layer of fur kept the harsh climate of the mountains at a distance, but a brown, sinewy skin covered its face and paws. It had no tail, and its paws were a hybrid of a wolf's paws and a man's hands. Unsightly claws extended unnaturally from its appendages.

A quarter-mile later, it stopped at a small, snow-dusted clearing. Heavy evergreen trees had protected it from the storm's fury.

"Is this where you took her?"

The creature rocked its head to one side. A deep coughing resounded in its throat before it bounded into the clearing and disappeared. Dashjmar remained at the perimeter of the clearing. Soon, the creature returned on its hind legs, carrying Shrie over its muscled shoulder. A badly limping Gog trailed behind.

"Is she alive?" Dashjmar asked worriedly.

The snow beast put Shrie down and shrank back to the opposite side of the clearing.

Dashjmar took Magog forward into the clearing at a trot and swung himself off a good ten yards before Shrie and Gog. Gog hobbled up to Dashjmar, and Dashjmar put his free hand around the lizard's neck comfortingly. He dropped to the ground beside Shrie, holding her head with one hand. She did not breathe.

"Pulse, come on," Dashjmar mumbled hopefully as he slid his hand across her neck and into the groove under her chin.

Dum-dum. Nothing. Dum-dum.

It's so faint. Her limp body recalled to his mind a time long ago…

His father had not wanted him to go on the long hunting trips with the other older boys, but Dashjmar had insisted. After days of Dashjmar's complaining, his father had given in to his requests, but he was allowed to hunt all animals except the giant eel, the Great Valwakhash. Most boys his age could handle the younger eels with ease, but in his pride, he had tracked the largest adult eel through the river. He had not understood the eel's strength, and it had dragged him beneath the water. Later, as he had been pulled from the water's clutches, his father had breathed for him until the swallowed water was spewed from his mouth.

Hesitantly, he tilted back Shrie's head and breathed into her mouth. She began weakly throwing up water. Dashjmar supported her as she threw up the last mouthful of water and searched for breath; this time she found it.

"What happened?" Dashjmar asked hastily.

"It you Dashjmar?" Shrie's eyes wandered until they found him. As soon as the air returned to her, her voice came quickly in suit. "I fall in cloud. There no air there, only snow creature."

"He saved you," Dashjmar said bitterly, "though I believe he needs to return something to you."

His words baffled her. "How he save me and Gog in cloud?"

Dashjmar bypassed her question. "It was not a cloud, Shrie. It was snow descending the mountain."

Shrie stood reluctantly, as if testing the solidity of the snow beneath her. She searched for her rescuer.

"It's by that tree," Dashjmar told her.

The white mass of fur huddled under a pine tree. Steadily, she made her way toward it. Two green eyes watched her from under a shaggy coat. She dropped to all fours to be at eye level, but as she neared the snow creature, it uncurled and stood erect on its hind legs. Shrie rose, a bit embarrassed.

"I Shrie," she spoke in a clear tone.

It rumbled a reply and held out the earring. Shrie returned it to her naked ear as the creature's words rained upon her. As she began to understand its peculiar tongue, she replied. Dashjmar shook his head in bewilderment. He had never met a person who could talk to nature so freely. *Some are capable of confronting nature and its beasts, but to talk with and have peace with them is indeed a rare gift.*

As Shrie and her champion conversed, Dashjmar inspected Gog's leg and constructed a fire near the clearing. The snow beast eyed him and the fire warily. Shrie patted the creature on the shoulder and mumbled some disjointed sound that it seemed to understand.

Gog had lost the supply pack on his back, but Magog had carried most of their necessities anyhow. They would survive. Unburdening Magog of his saddle and pack, Dashjmar draped the supplies over a low tree branch near their weak fire.

Snow continued to fall throughout the day, and Dashjmar, Shrie, and the creature made an odd trio. Shrie did a copious amount of rough translating through which Dashjmar found the beast to be unusually like mankind in thought but undeniably primitive and wild in appearance. It was this primordial, exterior that had killed many of its kind. Once there had been multitudes of his brethren in the mountains, traveling and living in clans. When the men had come, they had slain them and left their bleeding bodies in the snow.

"Shrie," Dashjmar enjoined, "ask him his name. Does he or his kind have a name?"

Attempting to imitate the civilized human customs, the snow creature reclined in a fashion similar to Shrie's and Dashjmar's positions; but Dashjmar could tell the snow creature's limbs were not at ease. *He is truly a phenomena*, Dashjmar thought. *He strikes the balance between civilization and barbarianism, avoiding a return to his primeval state and yet unable to attain a status beyond "animal." His instincts and reactions will therefore be hard to judge and nearly impossible to predict.* He knew if Shrie had not approached him in a blithe manner, the white animal would have remained anonymous. Being around humans had reawakened the refined attributes of the wolf-man. Even so, he had refused their lunch of rations to hunt for his own raw meat. Shrie insisted he was being polite; Dashjmar thought otherwise.

"He says some call his kind Shalku, and he also says he return now to the forest to hunt."

"Great," Dashjmar exclaimed sarcastically, "he is not actually as primitive as I thought." He could not lie to himself; he was uncomfortable around the wolf-man.

Shrie took the flat bread from its wrapping. "He never sees people, Dashjmar. He lonely. No clan, no people that do not scream or run at the sight of him. We only kind people he see since his clan!"

Dashjmar let Shrie's words sink in. His compassionate side was left untouched. *What life does the snow creature live on a diurnal basis?* As Shrie and Dashjmar waited, they fed the fire lazily until the sky darkened. The snow creature returned; no blood stained his mouth, and no dead animal lay felled in his hands.

"You go hunting?" Shrie asked in his language.

He tentatively answered, "Yes, but I wish to appear cultivated before the bald one."

Shrie laughed. Dashjmar had been renamed the bald one. The snow creature seemed to smile broadly as Shrie laughed in a giddy flight of joy. Dashjmar did not find the exchange humorous.

That night, the snow creature dug himself a shallow cave in a snow drift nearby. Shrie and Dashjmar piled their blankets on top of each other. As Dashjmar lay his head down, he reflected dourly upon the day. It had been unfortunately unproductive. They would need to cover many miles to keep on schedule. With Gog's hurt knee, their pace would struggle to keep time. Thinking unhappily upon the days ahead, he soon grew tired and closed his eyes.

In accordance with Dashjmar's accelerated plan, they left early under a friendly morning sun. The glowing sphere timidly threw its first rays of light into the sky while the last stars tripped from the heavens. They had meant to say farewell to the wolf-man, or Shrie had, but he was nowhere to be found. After Dashjmar had hurriedly stamped out the dying fire with his foot, they had presently packed their goods and descended the final slope of the mountain. The air was thawed and warm compared to that of the night before, and an easterly wind hinted of good weather ahead.

Shrie trotted beside Gog who limped slightly. She seemed recovered from her encounter with the avalanche, though she carried her staff for reasons Dashjmar could only guess. He had offered her a ride on Magog, but Shrie felt responsible for Gog's injury and vowed to stay with him on the ground. Dashjmar complied with her wishes but remained on Magog, driving them at a continuous, rapid pace. An entire day had been lost; it could only be replaced by extra, toilsome hours on the trail.

Thankfully, they made good time that morning, traveling nineteen miles before stopping a little after midday. Shrie had run for nine of those miles, which was nine more than Dashjmar had expected. Though she had lagged behind, she had not caused any setbacks. Shrie was a good runner, but running made her hungry. Their small lunch of water, the last of their bread, and syrup stalks was not enough.

"Go hunting, Dashjmar," she complained openly. "Shrie hungry; she not able to run with no energy."

"You should have ridden Magog with me. We cannot afford time to go hunting. Today we must keep traveling. From here," Dashjmar drew the outline of Kurak in the dirt and traced their route across the map, "we will go southwest until we reach the river between Wathien and the Borderlands. At the narrowest width between the banks, we can travel down the river until we reach a village or the port. It will be easy going as the river travels into the Sea of White Pearls."

Shrie swallowed a mouthful of syrup. "That different plan than you had before, Dashjmar. You say we find village in north and go south to port before. Now you change it. Last time you have better plan," Shrie placed an emphasis on the word better, "Shrie get swallowed by snowy cloud. Shrie do not like your plans anymore, Dashjmar," she finished gravely.

"I believe that was your own fault," he stated over her protestations. Dashjmar continued, "You decided to mosey on down the mountain instead of saving yourself, which the snow beast ended up doing for you."

Shrie tilted her head and said smugly, "I can talk to snow beast and you cannot."

"I deem that to be exceedingly irrelevant to the topic we were discussing."

Shrie began to talk to Dashjmar in the snow creature's dialect, stressing certain syllables as he proceeded to repack their food bags. When they finally set off, Shrie was certain that she had thoroughly defeated Dashjmar in their war of words, despite the fact that Dashjmar had not been able to understand her polemics or defend himself. With one victory under her belt, she figured she could afford to heed his advice, and so she rode on Magog while Dashjmar jogged beside Gog who bounded unevenly with his hurt knee. Shrie would, on a notion, surge ahead, increasing the pace. Dashjmar simply forced his legs faster, and if he experienced any fatigue, he kept silent.

"We can keep traveling, Shrie. Gog seems to be doing fine; I estimate we'll have racked up a sizeable number of lizard paces by the end of the day."

Shrie faced Dashjmar. "Many lizard paces? We reach river today?"

"Probably not. As it is, it will be two days before we reach the lake."

"This long trip, Dashjmar. You might not make it."

Dashjmar bayed in frustration as she insolently spurred Magog ahead. "Can you keep up, Gog?" he asked, not really knowing why. After all, Gog had never turned down a challenge, and even now, the lizard stamped the ground restlessly as he watched Shrie's and Magog's lead increase. "Let us catch them then!" Dashjmar exclaimed, dashing through the senescent light. If Shrie intended to make this a race, he would play along, and win.

Leaving behind the fog of the Borderlands, the two stumbled into a grove of trees neck and neck. Gog limped twelve yards behind them, snorting in perseverance.

"We'll camp here," Dashjmar gasped, his heart pounding.

Shrie had cheated, swinging into the trees like a monkey and scrambling among the limbs with an unnatural speed. When a gap between trees had thwarted her arboreal travel, she had flung herself to the ground a step ahead of Dashjmar. From then on, the lead had fluctuated between the two until they had burst upon the ideal camp spot, and there Dashjmar had called the race to an abrupt end.

"My forest is better than this one," Shrie proclaimed, placing two saucy hands on her hips. "It has more trees and animals to talk to. It warmer too."

"You have much to be modest about, Maiden of the Wood," Dashjmar retorted calmly.

Shrie nearly burst at being called the Maiden of the Wood. She liked that title, but this time Dashjmar mocked her with it. Instead of lashing out at him with her limited vocabulary, she thumped him over the head with her staff.

"Ow!"

Shrie hit him a second time in rapid succession of the first. When she rapped him across the knuckles, he picked up a nearby, fallen limb.

"You challenge me, Maiden of the Wood?"

Shrie hit him in the gut. "I am winning the challenge!"

Dashjmar coughed hoarsely as she knocked the air out of him. Not to be outdone, his body melted into a swift combination of strikes and attacks. The race had ended, but the night's competitions had just begun.

A dull, throbbing pain consumed Dashjmar's head, waking him from his slumber.

What a dumb idea to fight Shrie, he thought. He made a mental note not to encourage rivalry between them again. *We are supposed to be preparing ourselves to fight against our enemies, yet here we are beating the pulp out of each other.*

"That fun last night, yes?" Shrie's happy, victorious voice reached him from the opposite side of the burnt-out fire.

"It was good training. You have much strength, but I now perceive some of your weakness. We must correct them."

Shrie did not like this response. In retaliation, she dug ravenously into the packs for breakfast. She pulled out two syrup canes and was slapped lightly on the wrist by Dashjmar.

"Until we replenish food, you'll have one."

Shrie did not complain; she knew Dashjmar was not going to eat anything this morning. She obediently put one back, chewed on one half, and attended to Gog who was bouncing up and down excitedly for no other reason than to do so.

After a few frustrated minutes of attempting to check his injuries, she declared, "Gog better."

"I'm happy to hear that," Dashjmar replied as he saddled Magog, "we're ready to go then?"

After Shrie gave the affirmative, they set off. The morning was humid but not dampening to the spirits. Every once in a while, a lone rain drop would float from the sky and land on a hand or foot, washing away bits of the dirt that had ingrained itself into their skin. For the entirety of the morning, they traveled under the wood's sagacious, drooping trees. Moss grew in increasing abundance, and small trickles of water sputtered from under arched tree roots. Shaggy vines surged from solid limbs, and canopies floated like emerald clouds in a sapphire sky. Sunlight shone through the transparent leaves, and everything was bathed in a sheer, golden light. The peace seemed an insubstantial dream that would dissipate with the quick snap of her fingers. Shrie reveled in the tranquility, and in the quiet atmosphere, she knew her mission was real.

With partially closed eyes, Dashjmar rested, letting Magog lead. The lizards were thirsty; they would find the lake much sooner than Dashjmar could. Once they reached the lake, it would be a short journey to the port. Traveling through water once more, they would be brought to the mouth of the river, to the face of the ocean, and to the first port by the sea.

Opening her palm, Skytrue studied the circular imprint in her hand. She had clenched the ring there so firmly that the open air touching her clammy skin seemed foreign. She balanced the ring perfectly on her fingertips, and the elders stared at it. The Chief of the tribe traced the surface of the ring before scooping it from her hand. With a wave, he dismissed her from his presence. Enclosing the ring in his fist, he bore deeply into the eyes of the elders. Their response was unanimous. They would wait. No ring would hasten them to battle until the one who was to be sent arrived. The ring was a sign of trust; but until the appointed time, it would hold no other meaning.

The lake was an immutable presence. Completely still, it lay like a piece of shimmering glass in the middle of the forest. Its depth and width were not known, nor had they ever been tested. Bizarre fish of varying sizes and colors swam among the seaweed and silvery water. Occasionally, the lake reflected the dark browns and rich jades of the forest above it, but mostly, it shone. A hidden power coursed through it. Here, the land was alive.

Within the time of a day, a night, and a half of another day, Magog had discovered and refused to deviate from the path that led to its shores. Gog had followed in anticipation. By nightfall of the second day, they made camp. No fire was lit, and their dinner consisted of berries from a nearby tree. After an ill sleep, the travelers were awoken by the lizards' impatient snorting. Rising, they hid any evidence of their camp and left. Only a short trail separated them from their destination. If Shrie and Dashjmar had known how close they had been the night before, perhaps they would have not stopped; but their rest was for the better, for the lake was as ominous as it was beautiful.

Standing upon the shore in veneration, Dashjmar spoke, "In ancient days, it was said that this was the place that the Almighty's soldiers chose to descend from heaven, and where they first stepped forth into this world in search of the evil one." Shrie's attention focused on him. His words painted a captivating vision. He continued, "The lake captured the light that struck it when the heavens opened and when the staircase rippled from the sky. It is considered holy ground." His eyes swept over the majestic sight.

"And some say there is no God and that everything comes from the lake. They neglect to say from where the lake came." Breaking from this thought he added, "It should take half a day to cross the lake at its smallest part. The distance is still far, but Gog and Magog are swift swimmers, and there is no calmer water than this."

Respectfully, Shrie and Dashjmar descended gracefully into the water, creating small ripples which spread across the surface. Gog and Magog peddled through the water towards a narrow opening on the opposite side. Easy to miss as it blended into the scenery, it would lead to the river which would eventually part and then cross again on its journey to the ocean.

Shrie did not mean to be disrespectful, and certainly the allure of the place had in no way left her mind. Yet, in the hours she sat upon Gog, it was inevitable that her curious mind would yearn to stare into the water. Upon obeying her desire, she was frustrated to find she could see nothing beyond her own reflection. She looked at it first with annoyance and then with a critiquing eye.

"It is your face, Shrie."

"Shrie knows this," she retorted, "but Shrie did not know she was getting ugly," she whispered honestly, still not wanting to disturb the peace of the place. "Her face is dirty and her hair is in many knots. She cannot present herself to her tribe like this! Dashjmar, hand Shrie your dagger."

He handed it to her with a shake of his head. "If you want to cut your hair, Shrie, it might be easier if I did it."

Shrie hesitated and then gave back the dagger, commanding, "Cut right above huge knot at end of hair; Shrie does not think she can comb it out." Gathering her hair into a pony tail, Dashjmar grasped the end of her tangled tresses and chopped right above the gigantic tangle. He handed the cut hair to Shrie who stuck it on top of Gog's head.

"You very pretty, Gog," Shrie complimented him before brushing it into the lake. With unforgiving fingers, she managed to rip apart most of the remaining tangles. Unraveling a piece of string from her tunic, she used the strand to tie her hair neatly away from her face. Once she was satisfied with her hair, she proceeded to remove the stubborn dirt from her body. The water splashed across her face, hitting Dashjmar quite by accident. Unable to resist, Shrie stuck a cupped hand into the lake, shooting the holy water once again at the Leirmayn when he was not looking. With an angry shout, Dashjmar twisted Magog around violently. The displaced water built into a huge wave which easily knocked Shrie off Gog. She came up sputtering in disbelief.

"You violate holy ground," Shrie said in hushed tones.

"You violated it first." When he laughed softly, she replied by gathering water in her mouth and ejecting it in a graceful parabola above her head. It was meant to hit Dashjmar, but it landed on Gog's nose instead. She rolled her shoulders and glided forward.

She imagined the soldiers stepping onto the surface of the water in which she now swam. *Shrie does not deserve this honor*, she thought to herself. Nevertheless, she made no effort to leave the warm water, and she only did so when Dashjmar offered her lunch. By midday, she felt the tug of a current. They would soon pass into the river. Eventually, the lizards no longer swam but allowed themselves to be swept by the increasing might of the flow as it jetted around a jagged curve. Almost immediately, the lake became a river. Like the lake, the river stayed tucked amongst the forest's protecting presence, but the undercurrent drew them from a still forest into one which was waking and filled with life. Deep and secluded from sight, the river allowed the lizards to swim side by side without the worry of detection.

The river swung sharply north, and it took them only four days to be carried through the geographically varied land. Even through dying lands, the river was surrounded by lush, riparian vegetation which survived on the river's numerous silt deposits. They made their journey unnoticed by all except for the fish of the river and the birds of the air. Superstitious men did not make their trade by the mystical river.

During this time, Dashjmar improved Shrie's method of fishing since he could not instruct her in the history of the land. Old stories about the river were scarce for the same reason there were no new stories. The river's general lack of civilization left only nebulous ideas and vague uncertainties to be exploited by imaginative tale tellers.

Dashjmar was unprepared for the sudden junction of the two rivers. The water sucked itself into a vortex and gushed with bubbles as the currents ran into one another and clashed. One river dipped dangerously into the other and then split again in moments. Shrie whooped lustily as Gog plunged over a small drop. They were covered in frothing water. Dashjmar and Magog bobbed in the water several feet away. The gurgling water spun them into the next river. They were so close to the port that Dashjmar detected a trace of smoke in the air.

"Shrie," he yelled excitedly to her above the noise of the current, "there is the smell of smoke from the village fires. We arrive at our first destination! Lead Gog from the river. We have but this one hill to climb, and then the port will be on the other side."

Thrilled at the prospect of reaching a landmark in their journey, Shrie exclaimed, "Out of river, Gog! Come on, we be at port soon, and then to Shrie's tribe!"

Shaking her head and spraying water, she joined Dashjmar on the shore. While the river skirted the edge of the hill and went directly to the ocean, Shrie and Dashjmar opted to simply climb the hill which rose from the bank. Shrie perused the grassy slope and imagined the village on the other side. Plumes of smoke were visibly rising over the hill and into the sky. Perhaps a celebration at the port would greet them. She had never before seen such an impressive display.

"What they burning in those bonfires, Dashjmar?" Shrie asked inquisitively.

"I don't know," Dashjmar replied truthfully, "but we shall see, will we not?" With that, he encouraged Magog to the top.

> "Some trust in chariots and some in horses,
> but we trust in the name of the Lord our God."
> Psalm 20:7

Chapter 5

Boom, thump. Boom, thump. The fort was marching; every man had been called to duty. Carts overflowing with the provisions were being pulled hastily behind the formation. The village inhabitants spilled from their houses in confusion and fear.

The commander straddled a wooden crate. He announced with pride that they were on their way to fight evil, and that he would take volunteering villagers with him. He bade them to carry a sword or a spear. Without a fort to protect them, he said, it would be best if they traveled with the army.

Men and women alike remembered the rumors of looted towns razed to the ground. Gathering children and scrambling to amass valuables and necessities, they put the elderly and the very young in carts. Farmers hitched the wooden boxes to their old mules and hoped the wheels could handle the forest terrain. Items were strewn about as people hurriedly threw things together. The procession continued in less than two hours, leaving behind a dead village of those too stubborn to leave and those unwilling to believe.

Relinquishing their Mali-Malis to weaker travelers from the village, Logan and Hitachi watched in amazement as the people rushed to procure weapons and join the ranks. Men held their hoes like swords proudly against their shoulders. Behind the carts loaded with men and supplies, the ones which had once ridden forth from Quantus Plain, the brothers were given the name and position of rear guard.

"Back to Quantus Plain! And I thought our adventuring would lead us somewhere distant."

"Then again, Logan, not many have traversed deep woods to deliver supplies to rebels."

"Shame we can't pick others up along the way too, eh?"

"Yes...a shame," Hitachi murmured. His eyes twinkled.

Two days later, select groups of elite rebels were sent into the forests of Khaltharnga. Endowed to them was the mission of gathering the independent rebel forces. To rally the free and roaming rebels would be a challenge. To convince them to abandon their refuges in the forest and fight to almost certain death would be relatively effortless. To ignite their spirits would be unnecessary. To prove to them it was time at last for open battle, well, some already believed that. It would more be a matter of finding them.

An acrid smell pervaded the area; ripping through the white clouds, it knew no bounds. Black smoke slept in the valley and exploded into the sky as sparks flew chaotically. Smoldering buildings and bodies comprised the decaying compound. No celebration graced the village. Dashjmar absorbed the sight with little comprehension until his wandering eyes darted to the ocean. There, he found the cause, and he regained his focus.

"They've leveled the village." His voice was distant. "We come too late." Dashjmar's morose voice reached Shrie's ears. "Look to the ocean." Shrie obeyed.

Fascinating shapes rose from the sea in the form of three sets of black sails. Cylinder contraptions were being pulled into the ships' bulwarks, and rows of oars replaced them, moving in a uniform motion like the wings of a bird flapping up and down, up and down. Slaves powered the motion, and the ships sailed for the horizon. The dark men had come and left, leaving their mark.

Shrie rode down the slope, her mind refusing to believe the destruction was real.

"There is nothing more we can do here," Dashjmar called to her. Shrie remained sedentary. "We'll move on to the next village," he said gently.

As though her body responded to his voice, she directed Gog back to the top of the hill. Her mind wandered with the smoke. This was a defeat she had neither anticipated nor could have prevented, but the scarred land of embers and corpses would never leave her memory. Slipping off Gog, she knelt on the ground and scooped mud into her palm, mixing it with the prevalent ash. She smeared the concoction under both cheek bones. Her action symbolized vengeance. She remounted Gog and looked at the scene once more before roughly pulling away. With knuckles white from gripping her staff, she turned with a slight smile to see similar mud smears under Dashjmar's eyes.

With a loud yell, Shrie thrust her staff into the air. Shadows from the smoke chased them across the land, and the monotonous gray they thought they had escaped after leaving the Borderlands haunted the skies. Swooping wings and shrill calls hastened the oncoming night as carnivores of the sky came to claim a meal from the obliteration. Eyes narrowed and body staunch above Gog, Shrie felt the adrenaline chase away the tiredness clinging to her in an almost tangible presence.

Threatening wisps of clouds strung helter-skelter in the sky masked the stars.

The moon barely managed to send its feeble rays to light Shrie's and Dashjmar's path. Shrie's breathing came harder with the frosty air and deepening night. Any sound of the river rushing to the ocean was gone, replaced by the irritated sound of grasses rustling against one another. The howling wind swept in and out of the meadow like the tides of a raucous ocean, refusing to abate as the warriors rode late into the night, the mud firmly sticking to their faces.

> "Defend the cause of the weak and fatherless;
> maintain the rights of the poor and oppressed.
> Rescue the weak and needy;
> Deliver them from the hand of the wicked."
> Psalm 82: 3–4

"One day life is kind, and on another it unfurls its wrath. It accepts and allows certain things, but it will not tolerate others. How is it that the evil man is rich, but the good man suffers? And who is man with all his faults to judge what is good and bad? One person deserves one thing, but another man takes it. Nothing is for certain except the continual presence of the love of the Almighty, and who can fathom His ways? Everything wrong will be made right, and good will endure. There is no more that we can do than to do our best to heed His call and play our part in the grand scheme of things," Dashjmar meditated aloud when neither Gog nor Shrie could hold their pace any longer. Early morning had come and gone, but Shrie nevertheless insisted that they must continue.

Knowing that the excruciating journey would take its toll, Dashjmar suggested avoiding the next village. To save time, they could go directly into the mountains and scrounge for food until they reached her tribe. This potential course was almost accepted; but their supplies were running low, and the miles separating them from the village were fewer than those keeping them from the mountains. It would be impractical to bypass an opportunity to restock their provisions. In the emotion of the moment, Shrie had also not contemplated the prospect that the Shalkans may not be at the next port. In her mind, she and Dashjmar had to go there in order to defeat the officials and so regain their honor. To Shrie, going to her tribe after witnessing the incineration of innocent people and doing nothing afterwards would be more than humiliating. It would be an unforgivable disgrace. With these things in mind, Dashjmar consented to delay the trek into the mountains, though foreboding thoughts were determined to deter him from that course.

They began to jog through a rather nondescript plain of varying, tanned, knee-high grasses and patches of dirt when a caustic smell pricked Shrie's nose. "Smoke, Dashjmar!" Shrie readied her bow and shielded her eyes against the sun. A column of smoke rose from a brown clump in the distance.

A vast hole gaped in the village. As the fighting escalated, Dashjmar could hear both the shuddering booms of rebel and official cannonballs. Shrie's premonition had been fulfilled. Racing through the once sleepy compound, Shrie raised the battle cry and met a Shalkan as he forced his way into a house. She did not have to loose an arrow, for Gog had trampled him. The town's people rushed to obtain weapons as officials from the first ship poured onto the dock. Shrie dodged the Shalkans' spherical bullets, using a shanty building as cover. She instructed Gog to stay where he was; combined, they were a large and easy target.

Shrie pulled back her arrow and shot skillfully. The villagers and the scanty brigade of rebel troops instantly deteriorated beneath the onslaught of unwavering Shalkan attacks. Shrie managed to shoot twice more, but the Shalkans had already broken through the ragged rebel lines. She ducked, and a Shalkan tumbled over her back. Springing up, she stabbed two officials with an arrow in each hand. Not until she had slain seven more did she grab the rebels' attention; one shouted something. Thinking it a warning, she quickly loosed an arrow at the closest enemy in his direction. The same cry echoed more clearly in the ranks of the dark men.

"The Kalulukians come back from the underworld!"

Though it was certainly not true, Shrie encouraged this belief by whopping and dancing savagely as she shot her arrows in the Kalulukian way. Dashjmar rode swiftly into the officials' midst, whacking them promptly with his staff and confirming their beliefs. Under his cover, Shrie gathered a group of men to diverge and destroy the invaders.

"Split into two groups. One group attacks from the front; the other attacks from rooftops or from behind," Shrie instructed breathlessly.

"It'll work." After this verbal expression of support from one of their leaders, the men accepted the rest of her ideas rapidly and unquestioningly. When a miracle is sent, no one questions why or how it came.

Sneaking behind several huts, Shrie located the nearest dockhouse. Two men came with her and boosted her to the top from which she leapt wildly seconds later. She barreled feet first into the Shalkans emerging from the ship, killing any formation they had once maintained. One rushed her. Shrie curled her head to her knees and let him roll off her back and into the water. As she came up, another jabbed at her with his knife. Her stiff arm deflected his wrist in time, but his brute force overpowered her hold. Digging two fingers into his forearm, she pinched the skin and watched as his knife clattered to the dock. Grabbing it, she thrust it into his leg, and he collapsed.

One of the men who had boosted her onto the roof now valiantly fought three of the helmeted horrors; Shrie shot and eliminated one. Looking around at the scattered officials, she jetted back to the hut where the other men were instituting the second part of her plan. They had lit several torches and loaded them into a homemade flinging contraption. Seeing their work was well done, Shrie rushed back into battle and found herself next to Dashjmar who had also left Magog somewhere.

With his staff, he feigned a clout to the head, flipped over the enemy, and struck the Shalkan from behind. Shrie bashed the man's legs as fire began to rain from the sky.

The first two torches landed short. The men rolled their device closer. This time, the torches landed on the ships' sails which subsequently drooped and died in the reigning fire. Shalkans rushed back to save their ships from damnation, and the villagers pressed forward. Shrie was about to join the charge when Dashjmar grabbed her arm and led her to Gog and Magog.

"Hurry, the villagers are fine now. Let us leave before we are stuck at a victory ceremony and plagued with questions. They do not know who we are yet."

"But they must know about the Almighty and the Last Battle," Shrie insisted.

"I had a feeling you would say that. I left a message with the village religious man who I fortuitously bumped into before the battle broke completely loose. The note was brief but should be affective. Now hurry. The only thing separating you from your tribe is the mountains."

As Shrie and Dashjmar left the shouts of victory behind them, the Shalkan ships retreated in plumes of smoke. One was already sinking. The other lacked its mast.

The people never clearly saw Shrie and Dashjmar leave, but a few claimed they saw two disappearing but recognizable spots on the horizon. The message Dashjmar had left with the religious man had done its trick. The people knew from where their victory had come.

"My honor is restored," Shrie stated as they rode off. "I now able to go to my tribe with confidence."

"You fought well and aggressively."

Shrie cocked her head to one side as if she could not decide whether to agree or disagree.

"You don't have to answer me."

With Dashjmar's terse statement, Shrie settled into her seat. There would be no lectures or stories today. Though they had lost time on their wavering trail from the first port back to the second, they were weary and traveled little the remainder of the day. Again, Dashjmar knew he would have to press the lizards and themselves if they were to make it to Shrie's tribe in time. *In time for what?* In truth, he did not know, but a rare compulsion consumed him. He had to get to the Valley of Solitude, and he had to get there soon.

Spptht! Hitachi spit the bug from his mouth in disgust. Thousands of the small flying creatures swarmed the rebels' heads. The bugs were kamikaze warriors crashing to their deaths. Wiping another bug from his tear duct, Hitachi held his hand above his head, and the swarm immediately flew upwards to slam incessantly against his skin. His hand was filled with the small, prickling sensations of the bugs buzzing him. Hitachi glanced at the dirty rebels under his command. With the vain hope of deterring the pesky insects, they squatted low to the ground with their hands raised above their heads like eager pupils. Covered in a thin layer of slime, which was the combination of perspiration and dirt, the rebels reeked. To make it worse, the shade gave no relief from the incessant heat as they sought their way through the jungle.

Piercing the leaves and brush with keen eyes, Hitachi recalled the words of the elderly villager. Though the man had seemed senile, his fellow villagers had insisted upon the validity of the man's stories and had vouched for the sanity of his mind. A twig snapped in Hitachi's face as the story rolled through his mind. In his younger days and in a search for excitement, the elder had joined a group of political and military radicals. During this time, Turock had risen in the ranks, but only the far-sighted had known what would become of his ascent. People then did not know the name of Turock, not because it was masked as it is now, but because to many, he did not even exist. The political radicals, who would become the rebels, never trusted Turock. His obvious ambition had repulsed them. They had preferred Lain—who ironically had been Turock's closest confidant. Their support meant nothing, however, when Turock swayed the military to his side. The land had been vast, the government shaky, and beyond that, the old man remembered little. The other villagers related pieces of what the old man could not recall...

One night, the old man, who was then young, stumbled into the village from the jungle. Suffering from a severe head wound, he blabbered urgently. From his mumblings, they learned of the inevitable split between Turock and Lain. Nothing else could be comprehended, but a vague memory of the political group's meeting place was retained by his memory. *To the left of the stream and to the right of the boulder covered in moss, take the path that passes between them.* He had directed Hitachi in this general direction after giving the rebels his blessing; he assured Hitachi that men would still be there.

Moving slowly on his hands and knees, Hitachi and his men had passed the stream and the rock, but the path they were to take was basically nonexistent. Still, Hitachi felt certain that he would find the descendants of the men who had once abided here. As another bug crashed into his face, he offered a small, heartfelt prayer to the Almighty and hoped Logan was having better luck.

The mountains towered before them. Brown fog rolled from craggy crests in whirling clouds. The copper scene elicited from Shrie a joyous reaction. To her, these mountains were a long-awaited milestone. What would happen after them mattered little to the jungle maiden. She longed for her jungle, for Corious, for Ree, for Tar, and for the people and leader of Quantus Plain. She longed to return. Yet at the same time, she longed to know what her people would look like and if her memories were about to find their future counterparts. She buried her face in her hands. *Will they recognize me?*

The stabbing query filled her with apprehension, and as they began to climb the hills which led to the foot of the mountain, she questioned Dashjmar almost mournfully, "What if tribe no recognizes Shrie?" His pause made her slightly fearful. "Dashjmar!" Shrie rode up to him and whacked him on the back. "Dashjmar, you no listen to Shrie?"

"Don't do that!" he remonstrated fiercely.

"But what will happen if tribe no recognizes Shrie?"

"Shrie, it would be hard to mistake you. Just as you knew the earring was of your tribe, how much more will your tribe know you? Hmm? Think about that for a while, and while you are at it, prepare yourself. Your tribe was once a flourishing people; I do not know what has become of them since they settled in the Valley of Solitude."

"Shrie not like that name—the Valley of Solitude. It sounds sad."

"You lived for many years in solitude."

"Yes, but Shrie had Mali-Malis, and she had human friends as well: the rebel Lain, Corious, Ree—"

"That is true," Dashjmar said, interrupting her.

Shrie did not mind. Dashjmar seemed particularly thoughtful. She restrained from interjecting and instead watched as the mist unfurled and hung about the mountain like clothes set on a line to dry.

"You know where you're going, Dashjmar?" Shrie asked without really expecting an answer. A small breeze sent a chill down her spine, and clouds rushed to assemble above them. Pulling her extra tunic over her head, she spoke to Gog. "It is going to rain soon, Gog."

In agreement, a concise rumble rolled across the sky. Shrie retreated into silence; any desire to chatter away the quiet dispersed as a raindrop fell heavily upon her nose and splashed across her face. Shrie loved the rain of the jungles which drenched the steamy air. Cool, it sent mist to ward away the rays of the scorching sun. It was peaceful in the jungle, but here, the rain was harsh. Shrie did not understand why her tribe preferred it. As if the clouds could not lose their weighty loads, they released scanty drops of rain for the next hour of travel.

Where the hills ceased to be hills, and where the mountain began, lofty, vertical trees unlike any she had ever seen before projected from the mountain. Spiky needles replaced the leaves on their sea green and cerulean branches, and instead of luscious vines, blandly colored moss adorned the trees' trunks. Navigating through the narrow passageways formed by the wall of trees was like pulling a tapestry apart one thread at a time. The irritating process grated upon their nerves, and soon, any exposed skin was red and irritated. Dashjmar assured her that the height and robustness of the jagged trees would decrease in the higher altitudes of the mountain.

It was drizzling now, the air sagging with moisture. A thunderclap preceded the loosing of the rain from the heavens. A waterfall from the sky plunged through the air, soaked their clothes, and washed away secure footing. Nevertheless, they pushed on until nightfall. Eventually, they found an overhang under which they could huddle. Any kindling was waterlogged, but Shrie collected it anyway and set it in a spot not yet violated by the rain. Dashjmar found his flint and "shiny rock" as Shrie called it. Some sparks caught the wood momentarily but soon died. Shrie refused to give up, hoping the activity would at least warm her muscles. Meanwhile, Dashjmar wrung out his shirt, the only one Shrie had ever seen him wear, and somehow managed to hang it from the ceiling. Shrie went back to her work until her eyelids would no longer stay open, and she soon fell asleep to the sound of Dashjmar humming.

The rebel sentinel watched them carefully. They were not officials, but they hid and moved warily through the jungle. *Did they not know they were moving into friendly territory?* Tracking their movements, the rebel kept his distance; there was no need to get too close. Dipping his hand into the mucky ground, he reapplied the mud to his face. It was a simple solution to ward away the bugs and probably the reason the group had not spotted him. They had halted several times to converse quietly, but they had never altered their direction. Passing the first fort entrance, they now headed towards the ground above the heart of the compound. At some point, they would have to be stopped and interrogated.

On their stomachs, Logan's group made their way through the jungle; it was the only feasible way they knew to avoid the incessantly swarming bugs. Even though the conditions could surely dissuade officials from investigating their activities, Logan wondered how the rebels could stand it. He thought they should have reached the entrance awhile ago, but no doorway was to be found. They forged ahead.

"They are more like snakes than humans," the rebel murmured to himself, "but then again, they've been perfecting their technique for awhile."

At the sound of a shrill birdcall, the rebel scouts dropped from the trees and burst out of hiding, thrusting arrows and spears inwards at the group some mere feet away.

Logan stopped mid-slither while the others froze.

The armed rebels parted as their leader spoke. "Your leader, who is he?"

Logan looked up from his prostrate position, and his voice cracked slightly from misuse as he said, "I am he, Logan."

"Ah, Logan, you may stand. What is your business here in the Khaltharngan forest?"

"We are fellow rebels who have come to tell you news and ask a favor. If you remember, a supply train passed through here a month or so ago. One of your clan received weapons from it. We are men from that train. Can we ask for your hospitality?"

"Men, put your weapons down," the leader commanded with an astonishing rapidity, readily granting Logan's request. "I believe we shall escort these men into our humble compound and talk of such matters that are imperative to discuss."

Relieved when the spear and sword points dropped to the ground, Logan's men relaxed their tense bodies before jolting in surprise. With muddied nails, the other rebels had wiped the sable mud from their faces to reveal ivory skin beneath.

"The mud is efficacious in ridding oneself of pesky insects, but we remove it to show you our friendship and our true identities," the leader explained. He still had not offered his name. "And we are very near to the fort, so you needn't think we troubled ourselves too much on your behalf," the leader said as he brushed aside tenacious vines and threw his body into the stone wall behind them. A door opened. Logan marveled at the ingenuity of the construction; there had been no visible crease in the wall. "It is time for you to enter the realm of the jungle rebels."

One by one, the rebels entered the black, rectangular opening and were lost to sight. The last man closed the door behind him, leaving them in a warm, damp blackness. Sticking out a hand so he would not fall, Logan's fingertips connected with a slimy surface. No torches hung on the wall until the stairs rounded a corner. *So Quantus Plain is not the sole rebel compound underground,* Logan noted. *Apparently many people understand the dangers of living above the surface of the earth. Even so, no guards stand at hallway corners, and not all the torches burn. Perhaps they need to conserve both men and fuel.*

Only when they entered the main hall did other signs of life appear. Talking, eating, and drinking, people occupied the long tables spread across the room. At one table set apart from the rest, several official people were engaged in serious conversation. Mugs and spears were an arm's length away from their ready hands. They passed a scroll amongst themselves, and the rebels' arrival went unnoticed until a loud, brusque introduction announced their presence.

"We found these men outside the compound. They come with news and asked for our hospitality." With these words, all of the scouts except their leader exited to their posts in the jungle. Logan watched them go before refocusing his attention on the table.

"I am Logan of Quantus Plain," he said fluidly.

"Welcome, Logan of Quantus Plain," one of the men replied formally. "Not many weather the journey to our depths. What news do you bring that is so urgent? There have been many rumors; perhaps you can validate or disprove them. This scroll you see here has not been reviewed for many years. It is a collection of ancient documents concerning the rise of the officials and the scattering of the people of the Khaltharnga. With news of great change abroad, I look to the past to discover the future."

"A wise thought. What have you deciphered from these readings?"

"We have learned of battles, of fragments detailing the evil that hopes to sway or take us, and of the evident presence of the Almighty. We are a perceptive people and have long foreseen that the time would come when one conflict would encompass the vast forces of good and of evil. Reports inform us of a colossal Shalkan gathering, one that individually we have failed to conquer. Tell me, Logan of Quantus Plain, is now that time when the forces of the Almighty must join?"

"You know that if I tell you this, many will not believe it. Many will try to run from the inevitable. You also know that if I told you anything otherwise, then I would be lying. Where I go, the chances of death outnumber the chances of life, but if we do not unite, we will be forever and unalterably torn apart. There is more hope in the protection of the Almighty and in His will than in disobeying it. I tell you, the time of the Great Harvest has come. The Jungle Maiden rides north to gather her people, and valiant men gather in the halls of Quantus Plain."

"So the horizon is not as bleak as it first appeared. Do not fret, Logan of Quantus Plain. The people shall be gathered; we know our way to Quantus Plain and will not be late. Sit and take some food. Then we shall direct you to the next rebel compound if to you that proposal sounds pleasing."

"Indeed, it does," Logan said grandly as he helped himself to the available bread and ale. He conversed comfortably with the rebels, feeling rather triumphant about his day's work. When his thoughts slid to Hitachi, he hoped his brother fared well and far from the insects. Logan did not mind bugs, but Hitachi abhorred them.

It was a very cool morning. Shrie woke with a start. Her breathing was short and raspy.

"Mountain sickness," Dashjmar stated.

"Wha…?"

"The air in these mountains is thin. There are not enough vital air supplements."

Shrie coughed up some phlegm and spat it out in disgust. "Are lizards able to go on?"

"They are." Shrie craned her neck to glance at the majestic pines and icy mist surrounding them. "According to my memory and to the last map I've seen, we're currently skirting the outside ring of the mountain range we need to cross."

Any determination Shrie once had that morning crumbled. "We not even to big mountains yet?" Her despair turned into anger. "You going too slowly, Dashjmar. We no poke around mountains all month! Get going or I set pace."

"Shrie, don't be foolish. We haven't even had—"

"Shrie eat when Shrie meet her tribe."

Dashjmar threw his hands into the air. "I don't have a say in this?"

Shrie glared at him as she packed camp. "You take too much time to travel very little mileage. I show you how things get done, Dashjmar." In a split second, she had hopped on Gog and sped into the forest.

That despicable mouth of hers! A vexed Dashjmar ground his teeth. "You're going the wrong way!"

Shrie hastily nudged Gog who trotted back to their hillside camp. "You can be Gog's and Shrie's guide," she stated imperially as she notched an arrow and aimed it at Dashjmar. Defiantly, Dashjmar set his jaw tightly. Shrie pointed the arrow dangerously close to his face. "You deserve this arrow, Dashjmar," Shrie said vehemently. "You frolic here while Ree, Corious, Tar, Perry, and Marcelus fight dangerous men!"

Dashjmar spat. Her words had left a vile taste in his mouth. He would not lose his temper. *Just because she is a Jungle Maiden brat does not mean she can turn me into one,* he thought bitterly until he realized his thought did not make sense. Recovering his wits, he retorted, "Considering I'm the only one here who knows my north, south, east, and west, I'll be giving the orders. And since you don't have a thumb's width of a clue as to where you're going, I'll be setting the pace as well!"

Shrie forced a smile. "You very funny, Dashjmar." She rode off, and this time, she was going exactly in the right direction.

Wings flapping roused excitement in her veins. Shrie perked up from her sullen silence. Wildlife usually did not emerge in this dreary weather, and their meat supply was running low. Shrie scanned the sky for several minutes and disappointedly lowered her bow.

"You hear that, Gog? Shrie not going crazy, right? It sounded like flight of a bird," Shrie mumbled to herself. "But cloud cover is low; he could be hiding in it." Sighing, she kept her bow near her side, just in case the bird should venture near.

At about midday, Dashjmar had finally caught up to Shrie. She had somehow stuck straight to the course for the Valley of Solitude but was stationary when Dashjmar finally closed the gap. She turned with a mournful look on her face.

"You right, Dashjmar. We only at hills. Look at mountains; they huge."

Dashjmar edged his way into the little clearing where Shrie stared over a narrow valley and into the face of the largest mountains in Kurak. "It's the Almighty's creation, Shrie. Don't hate it so. Look at the waterfalls."

The valley was lush and deep, full of running water and vegetation. A graceful waterfall trickled down a rock ledge to the left of them. Birds soared in and out of little holes in the hillsides, swooping back down into the warm air above the valley. Their wings flapped as they chirped joyfully. *Perhaps one bird had gotten lost in the fog earlier that morning.* Shrie put her bow away as Dashjmar exhaled noisily.

"Is there a way to cross the valley? We cannot go down it. It's too steep."

"Nothing is too steep," Dashjmar said, happy to regain the lead as he blazed a trail through the rock and underbrush. Shrie reluctantly followed. The imposing mountains spied on them from above, and a steep rockface slowed their pace to a crawl. Shrie and Dashjmar pushed the lizards up the precarious slope. When they were almost at the ledge, Shrie let out a relieved breath and broke out into a trot. She had relaxed too soon.

A warning crack echoed in the air as eroding stone folded beneath itself. Shrie felt the ground give way beneath her, and her stomach seemed to fly into her mouth. She scrambled up Gog's back and sprang agilely into the nearest tree branch, freeing Gog to scuttle his way to solid ground. Meanwhile, the landslide had jostled Dashjmar from Magog and into the sharp incline. The Kalulukian lost his footing as the rock beneath him began to roll down the mount. He sailed backwards, and with a deep cry, he tumbled over the edge.

"Dashjmar!" Shrie gasped as she dove from the tree and slid to the edge of the cliff. "Stay there!" was the strangled reply. He had not fallen more than three yards before an old root had met his groping hands.

"How you going to get up?"

Shrie watched anxiously as Dashjmar swung his dangling legs laboriously up and over the root. With a free hand, he wedged the tip of his fingers into a slight indent in the otherwise smooth stone. Delicately balancing his feet on the old root, Dashjmar used his own skill as well as a hefty amount of prayer to make it to the top of the ledge.

"That wasn't so bad," Dashjmar puffed exhaustedly.

"You pick another bad, slow route Dashjmar," Shrie exclaimed in a motherly tone, "next time it might be worse."

Dashjmar restrained from glaring at her before leaping swiftly onto Magog. "Let's get going. We should be able to cross this valley by nightfall."

Shrie nibbled on the end of a cane, twirling it aimlessly in her mouth as she struggled to see Dashjmar ahead of her. It had been unanimously decided that they would continue into the first half of the night. She spit out the cane which had lost any semblance of taste. Not eating anything that morning had made her hungry. She had not forgotten her promise to fast until finding her tribe, but Dashjmar had coaxed her into eating half a cane. She had just spat out the last piece.

"Thirsty?" Dashjmar's voice carried softly to her. Though steep and narrow, the ravine provided a safe trail. Shrie tagged behind Dashjmar obediently. "Are you thirsty?" Dashjmar asked again, this time his voice slightly above a whisper.

"Shrie is not thirsty," she replied stoically.

Dashjmar simply handed her a water flask. There was no way one could not be thirsty after eating a sugary cane. "You did not vow to abstain from water," he reminded her.

Pouring the water into her mouth, Shrie imagined the smirk that probably played on Dashjmar's lips. In reality, Dashjmar's face beheld no insolent leer. He had grown to understand Shrie—her unpredictable, demanding nature and her dexterous mind. As he returned the flask to its spot, he urged Magog to go faster. They were leaving the valley, and he wanted to cover as much ground as he could before morning. They would not stop until they reached the next mountain.

When they did reach the premises of the mountain's base, they found a sheltered alcove, slipped off their lizards, and rested their heads on patches of moss. Unusually drained, Dashjmar did not delay sleep.

The men of the tribe seemed agitated. They sneered at his decisions as a Leirmayn. He could not understand. He had led them to victory upon victory and had kept them safe. Yet they called him heartless. They scoffed at the knowledge which proclaimed their sacred practices false, condemning his every thought and belief. They were obsessed with meaningless traditions and a crazed cult. Mutiny was near.

They had tied him to the bed and had set fire to his hut. In pure anguish and in a rush of fear, he had pulled himself from the knots, but the heat...the laughing...the joyful voices of his tribe outside...They had wanted him to die.

At breakfast they determined to stay in the barren valleys between the mountains. It would be harder to navigate through the valley in which the gorges, tunnels, and cliffs were deep and treacherous, but Shrie's breathing could not handle the higher altitudes. Getting her adjusted to the northern, thin air would cost too much in the way of time.

"Are there snow beasts living in these mountains? Is not stupid question, is it?" Shrie waited impatiently for an answer.

"Hmm?" Dashjmar blinked solemnly.

"You were talking in your sleep again."

"Well if you were awake to hear me talk, I was probably saying, 'go to sleep and save your energy.'"

"No. It was not that."

Dashjmar exhaled noisily. "Can I ask you something Shrie? Can I tell you anything without you asking questions about it later?"

Shrie was confused but replied, "I will try, Dashjmar."

"You are my friend, but do not let your pride of being my equal compromise our mission. I know what is right and what is wrong. I'll let you voice your feelings, but do not endanger my authority for the sake of yours."

Shrie started to ask a question before realizing the full extent of Dashjmar's request. Instead she simply stated, "Okay, Dashjmar. I sorry about yesterday."

"No, it wasn't about yesterday. It really isn't even about you."

Shrie opened her mouth, but then shut it.

Releasing his breath, Dashjmar cleared his head. *Talking in my sleep? What have I come to?* Though Shrie had always challenged him, she had never directly impugned his authority. *Is that what I want: for her to never question me the way my conspiring tribe did?* Like the tribe that haunted him, Shrie was obstinate and would act against the desires of her own heart if pride was at stake. The Almighty had sent him to guide her, and if guiding her meant he had to exercise his power, then he would. But to subdue her personality was not ideal, and even if it had been, it never would have worked.

Shrie said nothing to him until midday when they stopped at a small stream to splash their faces. The extent of their conversation was limited to discussing food. After lunch, Shrie forced Gog forward before Dashjmar had the chance to do the same to Magog. They rode through the valley, and at night, Dashjmar let the stars determine their course.

Chapter 6

A clear day met the Shalku from Taerg Niatnuom as he bounded through the snow. Rapidly traversing the mount, his plush, white fur bounced. He was positive it had been her: the legendary Jungle Maiden. The time had come, and many risks would have to be taken. By instinct, he ran along the path which leads north and west to the coldest tips of the ice lands. Imagery of the mammoth ice mountains, ravines, caverns, and waterfalls rushed back to him. Rarely did his kind leave their sanctuary. They had once before, but most had returned to their homes in the north when Turock had usurped the government's power. Fighting the inborn instinct to return to his homeland, the Shalku had stayed behind with several others in the hope of changing the times. In the months that they remained apart from their cavernous homes, the way back had gradually been lost to them. Attempting to return while they still retained some memories of the path, numerous others had left Taerg Niatnuom. Most had wandered aimlessly, dying from hunger and leaving the Shalku to his solitary life.

He had been resigned to lonely fate, but a fortuitous one it had become. For if he had returned earlier, he never would have been able to warn his kind. He never would have met the Jungle Maiden. He was like her—the Jungle Maiden. Both were destined to find their kind at the end of an age, and to them alone was given the burden of reuniting with lost family only to lead them into battle. Increasing his speed as the scent of the trail grew poignant, the Shalku knew the way once hidden from him had been revealed.

Shrie was uneasy. They had been in the mountains, or rather the valley, for three days. The Valley of Solitude was supposedly situated in the middle of the mountain range. If her tribe was good at hiding, as she suspected they were, they could be anywhere in the extensive range of gorges and plateaus. Dashjmar insisted he knew the way, and Shrie did not doubt this. He may very well know the way to the place her tribe had been years ago. But what if they had moved? It was time to question.

"Dashjmar," Shrie asked quietly, "how you know about my tribe?"

His chin touched his shoulder as he glanced at her. From his seat on Magog he replied, "Once your tribe was not so different from my people."

"How old you, Dashjmar? My tribe not Kalulukians, are they?"

"They abandoned the Kalulukian ways before I did. Later, they gave me refuge in a time of need." Painful flashbacks of the run flooded Dashjmar's mind but soon left him in peace. His past was behind him. "Now I am simply returning the favor by leading you to them."

"They ever talk of me?" Shrie wondered aloud. "How surprised they be when they learn Shrie rules all of Khaltharnga."

Shrie had not brought up her ruler of the forest spiel in awhile. As her tribe had lost their home there, so her rule over it weakened also. She had allied herself with the rebels, but even so, the rebel forces would not be enough to stand against the unleashed wrath of Turock. She would need her tribe's aid.

It was raining. The courtyard was slippery. Everything was as it had been then. The blood stains were still ingrained in the stone where they had last fought. Trees towered over the inlaid earth, casting shadows that flickered as the rain fell. *Next time,* he vowed, *it will be Lain's blood spilt upon the rock.*

The sight nearly maddened him, and his muscles longed to yield the sword that would bring down the leader whose betrayal had caused him so much pain. Standing under the open sky, the water dripped down his face as the sweat had done...

Lain stood before him with his sword in hand. He had already won the council; this fight was no more than a child's play. To sway Lain to his side would be optimal, but Lain suspected something. He had always suspected something. Yet there was no concrete evidence that Lain could use against him. There was no reason for Lain to battle him. Lain's motives existed as mere misgivings.

As Lain's Achilles heel lay in avoiding violence, he had challenged Lain to the fight: a gentleman's sport and nothing more. No killing would be involved; the first one to touch the sword to the neck would win. Lain had only accepted on these grounds. Rushing forward in a series of blows, Turock had known he would break them; rules never meant much to him unless they were his own or adventitious to his purpose...

Lain had parried his blows; sweat had dripped down Lain's face matching the perspiration Turock knew must be on his own. The battle had dragged for hours in a deadlock for control, and then he had slipped and found himself on the ground with Lain's sword at his throat.

"It's over, Turock."

"It is over," he repeated. With the cue, the army rushed from hiding.

In Lain's momentary hesitation, Turock lunged forward, aiming for the neck but missing. The army cornered Lain; there were only twenty paces until they would be upon him. Lain did not bother to protest the breach of rules. Turock almost admired his outnumbered foe before the admiration turned to jealousy. Consumed with hate, Turock lost control of himself. In defense, Lain struck. Watching as his own blood spewed from his body and landed on the ground, Turock roared in frustration as Lain slipped from his fingers.

The scar remained. It was time to even the scales. His armies were on the move, destroying pockets of rebels and villagers. Turock did not want any surprises coming behind him. Slowly, surely, his forces would converge on Quantus Plain.

"No, Shrie. I do not plan to go hunting."

"But Shrie hear another flight of bird, and even if we don't hunt bird, that mean that berries—"

"Nor do I plan to go foraging through the entirety of this forsaken mountain looking for berries. Yes, this land is lush; but no, I do not think we will find any berries, not any of the kind you want anyway. You tried the one kind there is here, and if I remember correctly you said, 'Eeewwww, this gross, Dashjmar.' So, no, I do not plan on looking for more. Have the last piece of cane if you wish."

"Shrie does not want the last piece of cane. Shrie did not mean to complain. Shrie just wanted to bring gifts to tribe members when she comes."

"I do not think getting gifts to bring them is important."

"Shrie wants to be welcomed and help tribe."

"You will do that in other ways."

Gazing at the horizon, Shrie wondered how much farther they had left to go. "Will they help us, Dashjmar?" she asked in sudden apprehension.

Dashjmar lay in a clearing which overlooked a shallow valley; the bulk of the mountains still hulked overhead.

"That is not our decision, Shrie. We will have done our part by the time we reach them, and the Almighty will have to do the rest. We should turn east and head deeper into the mountains."

Shrie accepted Dashjmar's briefing with tranquility, but inside she was screaming. The tedium of travel cultivated ennui like stagnant water breeds mosquitoes. With the mention of her tribe, she had grown anxious for the day of the arrival. Now she realized it could be weeks until that day came. The hours crawled by with an unusual emptiness. Nothing went wrong, but the neutrality of everything shaded their minds with dullness.

"Tonight would be any hunter's dream," Dashjmar admitted, trying to lift the fog from their minds. "A full moon stands in a clear sky, and the stars shine as though it were their last night."

Shrie nodded subtly when the sound whistled like a crack in the night. Dashjmar sat up so quickly that his momentum carried him to his feet.

"Wwhoooeeeee! Whooheee! Wheeohe!"

Shrie gave an exuberant cry as she too clambered to her feet. "It hunting cry!" Dashjmar clapped his hands together.

"Maybe that the hunting cries of my tribe! Wind carries it far, but it close!"

"Are you sure?"

"Yes!"

At that, the two embraced in a joyful hug and whooped their own cries back until the voices faded behind the nearest mountain. The time had almost come. The Valley of Solitude was before them.

Pit-pat, pit-pat, pit-pat, pit-pat, pit-pat. The next morning's downpour drowned the hunting calls and soaked Shrie and Dashjmar to the bone.

"Dashjmar!" Shrie cried irritably. Dashjmar appeared from under Magog. "We should find cave or a tree or something!"

He shrugged. "I'm pretty dry under Magog over here. Why don't you give Gog a try?"

Shrie skeptically glanced at Gog. "We should travel to better spot, and in meantime cover area that way."

Dashjmar swung himself up from under Magog and into a standing position. "Our view in this driving rain will be splendid."

Shrie missed Dashjmar's sarcasm and acted upon her proposition despite the rain. As they had done the many mornings before, the solemn figures packed, saddled their lizards, and continued. As the duo left the valley, the journey seemed a passive affair, but as they steadily traversed the mountain, the steep slabs impugned their climbing capabilities. The uneven rock sliced the lizards' feet, and the biting rain inhibited their views as it morphed into an icy hail. The conditions did not lift, and the weather seemed a harbinger of cataclysms to come.

"Wonderful," Dashjmar muttered as a piece of sleet bounced off his nose. The rain slid down his face and ran across his bare torso in wet sheets.

Shrie said nothing, contemplating her tribe. A feather falling from the overcast sky unraveled the mystery of the odd, primitive whoops of the night before. Shrie caught it as it wavered in the air.

"Look at feather, Dashjmar; it fall from sky."

In contrast to Shrie's delight at discovering the bright feather, displeasure bloomed on Dashjmar's face. "Where'd you find this?" he demanded.

His annoyance concerned her. "It fell from skies."

"When?"

"I heard wings flapping throughout time in the mountains, but the feather fell on Shrie just now." She stirred uneasily under his intense stare.

A fist-sized stone buried itself into Dashjmar's cheek and knocked him violently from the saddle.

"Dashjmar!"

Magog fervidly pawed at the ground. A shrill screech ripped at the air, and a rock bashed into Shrie's leg. Shrie suppressed tears as varying tinctures of deep purple colored the indent left by the rock in her thigh. Sharp needles of pain crawled up her limb as Dashjmar reappeared from behind Magog.

Both Dashjmar and their winged attackers were yelling. One swooped in a gluttonous frenzy. Like a tree squirrel, Dashjmar bent and sprang. His leap carried him onto the back of the flapping bird. His weight toppled the creature awkwardly to the ground. Another bird, at the head of a triangular formation, ravenously circled above the man and beast locked in an unyielding struggle. Dashjmar managed to cry a warning as he rolled atop the thrashing creature.

Shrie rode fitfully into the fray, nailing one of her flying attackers with a deadly arrow. It plummeted but did not die. The injured bird lumbered towards her, its weapons an ear splitting screech and fatal talons. Gog lurched forward as the bird rapidly met his challenge. The flying creature whipped its wings in a rapid and formidable craze. Gog charged to keep the beast at bay.

The bird, burdened by the arrow, lunged awkwardly at Shrie. She laughed at its clumsy movements, underestimating its remaining strength. In her moment of humor, it seized her arm in its vicious beak and shook her from a helpless Gog. Shrie screamed and fought to free herself, but the talons ripped into her skin like vices. Frantically, she grasped and tore at the arrow protruding from the bird's belly. The bird choked in pain as Shrie cut the arrow through its body; its talons dug deeper into her satisfying flesh. Hot flashes of blinding light obscured her vision as she gasped for breath. In a last ditch effort to save herself, she arranged the released arrow in her hand like a spear and buried it into the hawk's upper neck.

The three birds outnumbered Dashjmar. He adroitly evaded the hawks' dives until one forced Shrie from Gog. Swiftly, he mounted a bird as it launched from the ground. It writhed, attempting but failing to rid itself of the extra weight. The top-heavy, disoriented hawk shrieked and fluttered among its brethren, transporting Dashjmar perilously close to another of its kin. To avoid the razor talons, Dashjmar transferred his body onto another of the mammoth hawks. He steadied himself and grasped a handful of feathers to keep from falling. Fortunately, the astonished hawk could not react before Dashjmar leapt to the next bird. He was playing stepping stones with airborne, gruesome birds.

The distance to the bird directly over Shrie was too far, yet he had no choice. Dashjmar hurled himself into the air. The sky cradled him for two and a half seconds before dropping him, as though realizing he did not belong in its expanse. Groping, Dashjmar barely dug his hands into the bird's feathery plume. The bird gave a sickening squeal and dove. Gravity aided Dashjmar in securing his position. As the bird approached the earth, Dashjmar leaned over, found the bird's neck and shoulder joints, and twisted. Snap! The bird dropped like a stone from the sky.

The bird did not relinquish her arm, though Shrie had stabbed it four times. Of happenings after that, she was not cognizant. The pain forced her into a state of delirium, and the impact of her injuries did not seem as crushing as they should have.

Dashjmar groaned inwardly as he crashed among the birds he and Shrie had killed. With two of their group dead, the other beasts hesitated to commence the assault. Dashjmar used their uncertainty to his advantage, bribing his bruised body with the prize of life to hurl rock after rock at the birds circling higher and higher above them.

As Dashjmar gently lifted Shrie from the ground, her eyelids popped open, and she managed to stand by herself though she faltered in her step.

"Pesky birds they were, Dashjmar. How you fight them all off?" she murmured as she reached out a hand to steady herself. Dashjmar grabbed it, and she held onto his arm.

"You killed one of them, you know."

Shrie proudly displayed her kill. "I can make blankets of feathers to present to tribe as a gift. Then they will know that Shrie was brave enough to deserve their allegiance."

A small smile found itself on Dashjmar's face. "That would be a good outcome from an otherwise disheartening event. I did not realize those birds still lived here."

"What they called?"

"They have an ancient name, but it has been forgotten, even by me. They are not to be trusted. I do not see them as part of nature; they have been twisted somehow, filled with an ancient power and the lust to kill. I have not encountered them before this."

"Nasty things," Shrie commented as she hoisted herself onto Gog, "not like good Gog," she said rubbing his head. "Gog almost killed one of those birds."

"I'm sure he would do anything for you, Shrie," Dashjmar commented grimly. "He is very loyal to you now. I'm afraid I won't be able to demand him back if our ways should ever part."

Shrie grinned. "Hear that Gog? That make Shrie happy, but Dashjmar will not leave Shrie's path. There no time to leave Shrie before Last Battle. You stuck with me, Dashjmar."

"And a good thing it may prove to be. The fact that those birds were nearby…I do not like it."

"My tribe and I will hunt them down."

"I hope that your speculation is right," Dashjmar turned toward Shrie with sympathy in his eyes, "but I do not wish for you to raise your hopes. If the birds live here, then your tribe may be losing the power to protect themselves."

"Shrie will restore their hope," she said fervently. "Besides, Shrie heard flapping of wings when we entered mountain; birds must have followed us. They must have been hungry to attack. They must have thought we were vulnerable."

Dashjmar paused. "Still, the event is inexplicable. It bothers me."

"Well, they not bother us again."

"No," Dashjmar mused, "perhaps not, but it does not mean they won't try to stop us in other ways."

The latter part of Dashjmar's thought was lost to Shrie as she rode on Gog, resting her curvaceous hands on his brawny neck for support. The journey had started to take a permanent toll on their bodies. Cautiously, Dashjmar girded his staff with a hand covered in small scrapes, and did not let it rest. He had become lackadaisical in the relative solitude in which they had traveled; perhaps he could have thwarted the assault. But it was too late for regrets; there was only time to plunge ahead.

A deep grunting noise issued from the jungle accompanied by heavy hooves pawing the ground. Hitachi gulped; the dirt and bugs were forgotten. Warthogs, ugly and deadly, were closer than Hitachi would have liked. There were three of them, but that meant six horns and twelve hooves.

"They're really very temperamental," Hitachi said attempting to tell a joke to his comrade beside him. "I mean, all's what we did was—"

"Stomp through their territory, ignore their boundaries, and proclaim ourselves the enemy with our actions?"

"Exactly. Well, I guess we better take care of the little brutes."

Hitachi hunkered down behind a large rock, hoping it would prove a form of protection. The small rocks Hitachi chucked landed on one the warthog's back. Roaring, it rushed forward in his direction. The other men squirmed.

"Hold, hold," Hitachi commanded. "Now!"

The beast was barely five feet from them, careening ahead as they thrust their spears in front of them. The rebels braced themselves for the impact. Mud flew in the air as the warthog charged forward. Hitachi felt his bone grate back into his shoulder socket, and he gritted his teeth in pain. Blood spurted, and many disgruntled cries erupted from both warthog and humans as the animal tried to free itself in a series of hideous contortions. It landed still and dead from its effort.

"Aah," Hitachi yelled triumphantly from behind the rock, pushing an aching arm into the air. He had just enough time to plant his foot on the odious hide and pull out his spear before the other warthogs charged. He was not a man known for his limberness, but his adrenaline pumped with the pigs' attack, and he managed to find a nearby tree branch into which he swung.

Another warthog snorted, confused. It did not strike. Hitachi vacillated for a moment as he saw the number of warthogs increase and the number of men decrease; the rebels were fleeing. He was left alone in his tree.

"Men, come back!"

Some men inched their way back, but most waved their hands for him to join them.

"They're deserting!" Hitachi muttered angrily. Just then, a low rumbling, like the sound of many light feet trampling the earth resounded in the jungle. Hitachi frowned at the thought of more warthogs.

The miserable weather tapered as Shrie and Dashjmar clambered into a welcoming and warmer valley. The mountain held the storm stationary on its one side, and here the sun instilled vibrancy into every life. Normal, pleasant birds took off in flight above them as Dashjmar's head skimmed the tops of their perches. It was as if winter's worst had receded and spring had taken its spot, displaying its full beauty. As Shrie let her head ease back, it seemed as though the mountains had disappeared.

"We out of mountains?"

Dashjmar scratched his chin. "It does look that way doesn't it? But I doubt it; we would have had to travel longer."

"We in Valley of Solitude?"

Dashjmar held up a warning hand. "I never said that."

Despite his caveat, Shrie bounded ahead and whooped like a rabid animal. She babbled to Gog excitedly and hummed incoherent tunes. Hours later, she finally slowed. The sky, a mottled mix of pinks and light blues, did not ebb in its warm consistency. Runoff water surged into waterfalls and rivers which collided at the lowest point of the ravine in the valley. Dashjmar and Shrie reached the swirling amalgam of water and reeds around sundown and stopped on a grassy ledge to eat their dinner, or to find it anyway. Dashjmar presented her with one of the remaining syrup stalks, but Shrie declined his offer, claiming the sticky syrup stuck the walls of her stomach together. Their bread from the villages had long since vanished, and their water would not satisfy their hunger for solid food.

"I go hunting, Dashjmar!" Shrie claimed after sharpening a branch into a spear.

Dashjmar fell back into a stretch of grass. "I approve," he said, "as long as I get to eat some."

Shrie grinned devilishly, "Dashjmar can hunt for himself!"

"Whoever comes back to camp last has to eat the brains of the other person's animal. What do you say?"

"Oh! Dashjmar going to have to eat rat-hog brains!"

Although Shrie had to eat a salckphrat's brain that night, her stomach was satisfied and filled.

Chapter 7

They had been watching her for some time now, enough time to know she was their own. They had witnessed the attack of the ancient falcons, but the elders would not accept it; they wanted more proof of her bravery. That is what Shrie meant in their language, bravery. The Kalulukian who traveled with her had also fought fiercely, but the tribe needed to see she was independent of him. If he fell in battle, they needed to know she could lead them. The tribe did not trust the Kalulukians though they used to be of them, or rather because they used to be of them. The Kalulukians had abandoned the Almighty. But this one, Dashjmar as she called him, if he was indeed on their side, would prove an indispensable addition to their dwindling army. The tribe had foreseen the desolation the dark men would bring, but it refused to fight until the Almighty called them. Had the long-awaited appeal come with the Jungle Maiden? Fingering the ring in his hand, Ryanous wondered what the leader of Quantus Plain looked like.

"Is she the one?" Calamer asked, his dark, oval eyes turning from the two human forms to Ryanous. Parting the branches behind which they kept cover, Ryanous peered closer at the sight. Riding atop the great lizards, one outline was significantly smaller than the other; that one held a bow. The other held a quarterstaff.

"She rides well," Calamer observed. "You are a good rider as well."

"That does not mean anything. Even if it does, I should not want to tell her."

"Don't you wonder though, what would happen if you did? Was it not your own kin they left long ago?"

"It does not mean it is her," Ryanous hissed.

"I believe it is her," Calamer observed. "How long have we known each other? I would not suggest this if I did not think it was true. Look, they grow closer. She shares your eyes. Few have eyes of brilliant green these days."

"Calamer, stop. I do not want to think of this. If she passes the test, then I will give her my sword and my word of allegiance." His hand let the branches fall back into place. "Until then, we must meet them before the pass."

Jostling his quiver into the groove of his back, Calamer led the way, running swiftly behind the brush. The way was not far.

Blood trickled down his fingers; it was not his own. Using a sweaty forearm, he wiped sweat from a heavily drenched brow. Both warthogs were dead with his spear strung through their hearts. Nevertheless, Hitachi did not take full credit for the pyrrhic victory. As he bounced along on the back of the Mali-Mali, he was grateful for the spiders' appearance at the fight. An embarrassing amount of men had remained to see the jungle reinforcement. Despite their cowardice, Hitachi was too exhausted to find within himself the anger necessary to reprimand them.

After the encounter with the warthogs, the spider had motioned for Hitachi to climb onto its back. Lost and tired, he had accepted the ride with little thought of their mission. A light drizzle now found its way through the jungle canopy and wet the dirt and blood covering his body. The water loosened the blood's sticky hold on his skin and mixed with it, running in pink rivulets down his face. Eight men rode near him in the pack of spiders; some let their eyes close and their bodies slump forward as the day began to drain from the sky. Drearily forcing his own shoulders out of a slouch, Hitachi did not notice the two stone columns discreetly placed or the men in discolored attire walking to greet them.

"Dashjmar, something smells funny."

"Smoke; I smell it too."

Shrie twisted in her saddle, gauging the direction of the wind. "Is coming from over there," Shrie said, using the reins to turn Gog. Anxiety and apprehension gnawed at their stomachs. Apprehensively, Dashjmar followed her lead.

"They are coming."

"Tell me when; the tribe waits."

"A few more seconds, Ryanous, and then we will know."

Shrie slowed Gog. Something felt amiss. *Where are the voices of my tribe? What smoke rises without people?*

"Get the Kalulukian."

"He is too close; she will notice."

"Not if you do it quietly."

Calamer waved his hand. Twenty others materialized from the rock behind him and surrounded the back of the lizard. Three jumped upon the giant tail and scaled it with such agility that even Magog did not have time to flick them away before they were atop him. One pulled a cloth from his belt and wrapped it tightly about Dashjmar's eyes, but Dashjmar struggled and knocked the tribesman from Magog. The other tribe member placed his hand over Dashjmar's mouth to prevent the Kalulukian from hollering, throwing Dashjmar from the saddle. Grabbing Magog's reins with a free arm, Calamer jerked Magog away from Shrie. The Jungle Maiden would have to face this test alone.

"Dashjmar, where you think tribe went without covering fire?" Shrie asked in consternation. "They leave fire unquenched."

Hopping from Gog, she crouched by the small fire and used a stick to excite the coals. The flames ignited nothing but wood. Throwing the twig down, she searched the ground for tracks; not a blade of grass was bent.

"How strange!" she exclaimed to Gog. "No one is here, or has been here today, Dashjmar. What you think?"

No response.

"Dashjmar?" Sometimes he needed prompting. Aggravated by the lack of response, she began to stand, and then felt the pointed tip of a spear on her back. If any more pressure were applied, the skin would break. "Dashjmar?"

"Why do you call for the Kalulukian, Jungle Maiden?"

Upon hearing the unfamiliar voice, Shrie whirled recklessly away from the spear point. She found herself looking into the eyes of a tall man with black hair and brown skin like her own. Standing across from her, he had left his chest exposed. Others encircled them. Gog and Magog were out of sight.

"I ask again. Why do you call for the Kalulukian?" the man repeated earnestly.

Shrie, initially taken back with fear, almost froze. Then she narrowed her eyes, approached the man, and circled him, examining his posture and clothes. So this is how her tribe greeted her. She would greet them likewise, suppressing all emotion. She could not afford to make a mistake.

"I call for Kalulukian..." Leaping in the air like a cat tired of lurking, Shrie kicked hard under the bent elbow of the man, grabbed his spear, and landed yards away from him. "Because Shrie needed a spear, but now—" Shrie's words died as she studied the man from whom she had taken the spear. He was very strong. "Why you let Shrie have spear?"

"It would not be right to fight a weaponless opponent." As if on cue, Calamer thrust an extra spear to Ryanous. Catching it, Ryanous lifted his eyebrows. "Shall we?"

Shrie was not ready but lifted her spear as Dashjmar had taught her. "What other men do while we fight?" she asked, keeping her eyes trained on the face of her opponent, hoping to distract his thoughts. In those precious seconds, she executed another, vain attempt to detect any weaknesses.

"They will drag away the dead body of the loser."

"I guess they drag you away soon then."

"A little bold, that statement, don't you think?" Ryanous asked as he spun the spear before him and let it whirl with perfection by her neck. Shrie avoided this strike by inches.

"You not get me," Shrie stated smugly. "You have to try harder!" she mocked as she rushed forward, her point trained at his stomach.

Smashing her spear to the ground, Ryanous watched as the momentum threw her. Gracefully, Shrie flipped and landed steadily with the broken spear in her hand. Shrie frowned at her half of a spear, dismayed by her incompetence to attack. Charging again, she loosed a blow to Ryanous's shoulder before sliding under his legs and attacking from behind. He took the blow but managed to snatch her waist and pin her to the ground. Reaching up with her legs, Shrie wrapped them around his torso and swung herself atop him, but her weight was not enough to force him to the ground. Realizing this, she spun from her position and once more found herself looking into the eyes of her opponent. Suddenly, Shrie felt very foolish. It was not that she had not fought well; she had for the brief encounter, but she now knew that they were not testing her strength in battle. She backed away and bowed respectfully.

Ryanous had not moved. Instinctively, he brushed his fingers against a braided necklace. Shrie's eyes lingered there briefly.

"I not fight a brother who is my tribesman," she paused, restraining the emotions which surged within her. "I come a long, long way to meet my people." She could not help but add with a strained voice, "You not recognize me?"

Calamer exchanged a knowing glance at Ryanous, who said solemnly, "The only people we have encountered in these lands have been intruders. We therefore test all those who pass through this Valley of Solitude. It is required by our tribe's law. We were hopeful you were one of our kind, but we could never be sure. Now that we know you are one of us, I formally greet you with relief and elation. Come, we will go to the house of the Chief in our tribe's capital settlement."

Shrie barely contained her excitement. She wanted to run and hug each and every one of them, but she knew there was a time for everything. They were not accustomed to her and her new presence. She had not developed long enough in their society and culture to really be one of them. She briefly touched her earring; its purpose had been fulfilled.

Ryanous offered her an arm which she accepted, leading her to the trail which would bring them into the heart of the tribe's community. The men formed a rigid escort around them. Shrie fiddled with the spear fragment in her hand.

"Shrie never had such an opponent before. Dashjmar maybe as good as you."

"Neither have I," Ryanous disclosed quietly. "Not one with so much spirit anyway. Shrie, is that what you call yourself, Jungle Maiden?" He peered at her intently, searching for something that would prove to him she was who he knew she was. They had called her Shrie.

"Yes, Mali-Malis name me that or tell me that my name," she said joyfully. "They faithful friends like Gog and Magog and Dashjmar. Where you hide them all anyway?"

Ryanous laughed, partly at her question and partly in shock. "They will be waiting for you at our destination. You knew none of your tribe family?" he asked, at once somber. This Jungle Maiden was his sister, yet it was too surreal to believe. He really did not know her, but he felt as though he did. The sound of her voice in his ears recaptured his attention.

"No, but Shrie had faith she would meet them one day. Perhaps you know them? What your name?"

"I am called Ryanous."

"Ah. Ryanous in language of great lizards means grand fighter. You are well named."

"Thank you, Jungle Maiden, but I fear I was not named as well as you, brave one."

Shrie grinned. "Shrie like her name, but she would like one that meant best of all fighters." She had already forgotten her question about her family; Ryanous had evaded it well.

"That was not for you to decide. We approach the center of the tribe soon. You have passed this test, but I do not know what the tribal leaders will demand of you. Know this," he said as they reached a field seemingly cut from the mountain, "I will speak for you."

Shrie gravely handed him the end of her broken spear. "I will meet them."

Admiring her determination, Ryanous and the others marched to the buildings beyond. The valley below supported trees bearing long, snaky vines. The trees did not stand upright like those of the forest but leaned against one another for shade and protection. These types of trees, formally named draping hirsutes, flourished in the moderate climate that the tribe had chosen.

Calamer led them down a hillside and deeper into the valley. The laughter of children and the grunts of livestock replaced the relative silence of nature. Settlements of farms and small villages eventually prevailed over the strangled vegetation, interlocking harmoniously with an ordered landscape. Among the concinnity of the settlements, guard towers and posts sprouted into the sky. Below one such fort complex, a guard lethargically rose from an early dinner.

"Ah, Ryanous," the guard acknowledged him, "your father is very anxious to hear of the Maiden's arrival. It is she, is it not?"

Ryanous grasped the guard's wrists in the custom of their tribe. "Yes," Ryanous affirmed, "this is Shrie of the Khaltharngan wood—from our prior dwelling."

"Of course. I remember the Khaltharngan Forest all too well; but if it releases our long-separated sister from its depths, then it receives my gratitude." The guard's eyes flickered to her face but refocused on Calamer who hurried the procession on its way.

"I want to reach the capital by nightfall. Crossing this ridge will take us there," Calamer informed the group.

"Yes," another tribesman spoke. "We have had a long day, and a nice chug of ale would do me some good."

"Don't be a fool, Farwhen. You know ale is only for the elders and chieftains."

"Am I a fool for wishing?"

"Apparently so," Ryanous muttered as he lit a torch. "Listen, everyone must stay together after sundown. Even inside our borders it is not safe."

Shrie shook her head, attempting to distract herself from the captivating allure of somnolence. The last ochre flares of daylight cascaded over the mountains, and then her eyes dropped with the sun.

Ryanous caught Shrie's fall with his hand and heaved her off her feet as he nonchalantly threw his spear to the tribesman behind him. They rounded the final bend of the ridge which overlooked the expanse of the Valley of Solitude. As the group steadily approached the stone pier of the Ghier Caviniel, Calamer pursed his lips and released a wavering, mellifluous note. After minutes of needless apprehension, a great swan and Ghier Rider soared into sight, gracefully hovering above them.

"We have the Jungle Maiden with us. You must take us to the chieftains' hall without delay."

The Ghier Rider made no effort to hide his stare as they landed. Ryanous shifted Shrie in his arms.

"Certainly, Calamer," the Rider responded, "Jahq does his best flying at night."

Jacq lifted his head and shuffled his gargantuan webbed feet on the stone dais. The tribesmen were soon mounted on the swan and gliding above the lake. The cool wind blew in their faces. As they neared the other side of the placid lake, Ryanous shook the exhausted Shrie awake. She blinked heavily.

"We ride on giant swans!" she exclaimed in immediate awe, rubbing the delicate, white feathers beneath her.

"We near our destination," the Ghier Rider called from ahead.

"Prepare to dismount," Ryanous instructed, "and clear your mind from all distractions; the council awaits you."

The courtyard bustled with people. The tribesmen escorted Shrie into the wooden building where people waited in a restless buzz. A vaulted roof topped the structure, and a dauntingly protracted walkway of parquetry led to the back of the single room. A sturdy table spanned the width of the space and hosted the figures of the tribal elders. They wore the ancestral clothing: long sweeping robes and tediously ornamented belts. Their weapons were propped in their hands. No papers lay before them, and their unrefined faces coddled their hawkish, piercing eyes.

Standing in the arched doorway, Shrie listened as Ryanous whispered his last words of advice into her ear. A bubble of nervousness threatened to burst in her gut.

"Do not feel compelled to answer their questions immediately; take time to think them through. Answer truthfully. The elders will know if you lie. You are our rightful leader. Show them this."

Ryanous gave her a small push, and she strode awkwardly down the hall. The huge expanse of the interior dwarfed her small form. Joining Calamer and the other warriors standing alongside the walls, Ryanous watched anxiously.

"You are nervous for her," Calamer said beneath his breath. He did not look at Ryanous. "Relax. If she is the one, the Almighty will see her through."

In his clandestine spot, Dashjmar held his breath as Shrie bowed before the elders. She did this three times, and then when she was three paces from them, she undid the strap that held the quiver to her back and dropped her bow and her quarterstaff. The elders scrutinized, analyzed, and interpreted her every move. She let her arms relax at her side.

"Who is this who enters the territory of the Khaltharngans?" the eldest, the father of Ryanous, asked ritually.

"It is Shrie, also of the forest of Khaltharnga."

Dashjmar released his breath. She had not introduced herself as ruler of the forest; she was holding back.

"We have watched your journey from afar." The elder rose. "You have been pursued by a persistent and haunting malevolence. Why do you bring the clouds of evil with you and trespass onto sacred land?" the Chief interrogated.

"I come with a message from the Almighty who makes this land sacred."

"You fought my son, Ryanous," the elder rapidly bypassed her reply. "I see him still. You have lost or won?"

"I have won his respect but not his spear in battle."

"A cunning answer," the tribal leader next to the Chief stated. "But can you tell me, who are you to bring a message from the Almighty to us?"

For the first time Shrie hesitated, forming her words carefully. "I not know why the Almighty picks who He does in such times. I only know that I come to do His bidding as one of your own. The Almighty did not pick a foreigner to come and lead His people."

"You have come to lead us? Lead us where?" another leader asked incredulously, penetrating her with dark, intense eyes.

"The Almighty's will be done. It is as you say. A great battle looms ahead, the last battle of this earth, one in which evil will come to blows with good. If we do not meet the enemy at the appointed time, everything we love will be lost, and we will die without honor. To and into this battle I am to lead my tribe."

"We have heard of such a battle, and we have heard of the much-anticipated messenger of the Almighty. For this time we have waited expectantly, but you bring us to certain death. Give us proof of your strength; show us the Almighty is with you. We have fought dark men before. Why do you call us from our peace to do so again? Have we not tried to fight this fight before when no one would help us?"

The crowd was gravid with anticipation.

"You will find true life in the Almighty, and thus no death can defeat your spirit. You have fought dark men, yes, but you have never been able to join in an alliance with others. The men and women of Quantus Plain gather their armies, the rebels of the woods come from their hidden dwellings, and even the last Kalulukian of his kind joins us. As for a sign from the Almighty, I do not think it wise you test Him. If He wishes to reveal His power to you, then so be it."

"You have not yet faltered in your speech or stumbled upon our questions, but would you be willing to accept a challenge to prove that what you say is true?"

"What you propose will stand."

As Shrie finished her last word, only the head of the tribe remained erect. Speaking to her in the language of the Mali-Mali, he enjoined, "Summon to us the ice creatures."

The dotted line on the stone map floated to the top of her thoughts along with the image of the ice creature. Closing her eyes, she prayed to the Almighty that He would lead her, and then she allowed the language of the snow creature to come to her lips. Urgently, she called them.

"Assist them!" the rebel commanded. "They have come a long way."

Twenty pairs of feet padded through the mud to the Mali-Malis streaming by the gate posts.

"I do not know why they come," the Commander muttered to himself. "No rebel has ventured here in many a year."

"They are covered in blood but not wounded seriously," one of the men yelled as he and another lifted Hitachi off the spider, dragging him towards the primitively built compound.

"Good. Someone who knows the tongue of the spider, tell them to stay. I have an uncomfortable feeling we will need their aid."

The entire underground fort had been evacuated. Logan, refreshed by a fresh swig of ale, rode the Mali-Mali through the jungle with the others. Fifty of the men had been sent to warn other rebel groups and were to join them later with men and supplies. Commanding this particular group was a man called Redael. He seemed wise and confident, though his appearance declared him a common rebel. At first circumspect and then accepting of Logan and his cry to gather the rebels, Redael had promised that all rebels in the Khaltharngan forest would be summoned. Logan's hopes of seeing Hitachi rose. Trampling freshly cut vegetation, Logan's Mali-Mali moved quickly, swiveling its head constantly. Logan warily simulated the motion. He saw nothing but the rebels and the gargantuan ferns which arched over him. The plants dripped with water accumulated from the constant humidity.

Like the soft prattle of rain, the chirping of tree frogs and the occasional songs of birds serenaded the party, and the footsteps of the giant spiders reverberated over the resilient forest floor. Logan watched as the colors of the day dimmed; only the silhouettes of his men and allies remained in his sight. With night, the intense heat of the jungle relented, and the velvet skies brought cool relief. Reaching for his canteen, Logan took another drink of spirits. The water, he was told, was not good for drinking until a fresh spring trickled into a small tributary where their paths would intersect.

"Give him a drink." The Commander handed the caustic-smelling cup of liquid to the healer who brought it to the man's lips.

Situated in a rather crude setting until the exhausted men could be moved, the rebels of the village worked in the sordid conditions. The healers had washed away the hogs' blood to reveal minor cuts on the men. Afraid that Shalkans had inflicted the injuries, extra sentries had been posted and scouts had been sent into the jungle. All came back with the same report: clear territory for miles. The arrival of the blood-drenched rebels remained unresolved.

"He is coming to, sir," the healer said, removing the cup as the man sat abruptly and wiped the vile drink from his lips. Blinking in his surroundings, the man came to focus on the arresting figure of the Commander.

Rough-hewn with an impressive scar on the right side of his face, the Commander looked older than his years. He had seen loyalties upheld and perfidy from close friends; his experience in war was exceptionally superior to the gangly, lean volunteers who comprised the framework of their rebel unit. Like the volunteers, the series of earthworks they called a fort had much spirit but little strength. The Commander knew it would not hold under a serious attack; he knew also that the officials' arrival was inevitable; their numbers had been rising without ceasing. It was only a matter of time. Inspecting the recently woken man, he wondered again what his presence foretold.

"What be your name, strange rebel?"

"My name is Hitachi of Quantus Plain, and I come to beckon you to our aid." In order to stand at the Commander's eye level, Hitachi threw off the scanty blanket that had been spared him.

"You come bearing news from Quantus Plain?" The rebel leader was taken aback

JULIE AND RYAN DICKERSON

by the man's sudden strength. "But that would not be the direction from which you came, unless the forest has twisted your senses?"

"I was sent from Quantus Plain on a supply train. Our goal was to arm our brother rebels in the fight against the officials. Any news I bring from Quantus Plain is old, except for this: all rebels must be present at the last battle. The officials will be closing in—"

"And what aid do you expect of us, Hitachi of Quantus Plain?" He waved his hand to the pitiful sight behind him. "There is not much to offer your mighty fort."

"Every man is of value when the enemy draws near, my friend. You will be useless in this pocket of isolated jungle. The great cloud of darkness sweeps through this land, and unless the rebels take a stand, all will be lost, and you shall perish. As for me, I will not die a coward's death."

"Nay, I plan not to. What do you wish us to do? Your men are just recovering, and from what?"

"We encountered a nasty band of warthogs. It was nothing more than a bit trying. Our recovery shall be hasty. Now, Commander, your hospitality to my men shows you are a good man. You realize the officials come by way of sea to hasten their journey. After they hit Quantus Plain, I believe they will come back by land to destroy any small pockets of resistance. We must not let things reach this point."

"We are not by the sea. How do I know I can trust you, Hitachi of Quantus Plain? Even if I thought what you said may be true, how do I know that this battle will not be useless?"

"No fight against the enemy is in vain, and I shall swear my fealty to thee in honor of my word. Would you accept this and journey to Quantus Plain with me?" Hitachi knelt expectantly. The Commander watched him do so without a word; Hitachi opened his mouth to speak when a sentry rushed into the compound.

"Commander, a messenger from Redael has arrived." Hitachi rose as the messenger continued, "He summons our people to join him at the Halfast River. He will pass through the swamps and expects us to meet him there."

Before the first sentry read from the scroll, another man rushed in from the north. After catching his breath, he gave a hurried salute to the Commander and glanced momentarily at Hitachi before he reported, "Redael is mere miles from us; he and his troops have set a hard pace for this camp. Hurry and gather your things so that we may leave with him."

"Men," the commander addressed the sentries, "I bid you to go and do as Redael's men have asked. Sentry, send these messengers back with this reply: we will come. Rebels," he addressed the motley crew, "prepare and arm yourselves well. We will leave when Redael's men arrive. Those without steeds—ask one of the spiders for assistance. Hopefully they will grant you your request." In an aside to Hitachi he admitted, "So what you say is true. You need not swear fealty to me." Then, at the sight of the unorganized soldiers he muttered to himself, "By the Almighty we could use some women to keep these men in order."

Soldiers rushed to disassemble worthless tents and claim unattended weapons for themselves. Walking into the midst of the bedlam, he left Hitachi alone in the middle of the compound to gather his thoughts and his men.

"Wake up, Master Logan. We near the rebel fort."

"I am awake, Redael."

"One would not know it. You are deep in thought perhaps?"

"I am wondering. How many other rebel groups are still out there?"

"Not many, anymore. At least not many large ones. The one we come upon is small, and yet it is one of the largest remaining. My messengers, as you have seen, bring back small clusters of men. I know not where they come from, but come they do. Four have joined the ranks this morning."

"When we combine our forces with those of the supply train, what do you surmise our number in men will be?"

"That I cannot say."

"Whatever it is, it will be a grain of sand in comparison to the boulder of the enemy!"

"Shh, do not speak so. You have not seen the enemy's forces and seem to forget that Quantus Plain has men of their own. Keep your spirit, for that is what will make one of our men drive ten of the enemy from the fortress of Quantus Plain."

"You are right Redael. My mind is satisfied, but I must admit that my stomach is not. I believe I have forgotten my rations."

"Here, have some of mine." Redael tossed Logan the crusty end of a loaf of bread. "I'm sorry; hunting has not been made a priority. Once we reach the spring, I can allot some time for that, if you say we have that time?"

"I wish I knew, but either way the men must be fed if they are to fight." Logan peered into the jungle. "I see nothing of this fort."

Redael chuckled, "As it should be. It is disguised well to evade the eyes of the intruders. Made of nothing but earth, it blends into the ground. Watch for the two pillars of stone on your left. You, I, and forty of our men shall enter to greet the Commander of the fort. My messengers say he has accepted my offer."

"So quickly! It is amazing."

"Remember, other forces are at work during times such as these."

Logan ripped away at the crust of the bread with his teeth. "Have you long had interactions with the Commander?"

Redael paused unexpectedly for a moment with his head slightly bowed. "With his father, yes. With the Commander himself, well, this is the first message that has passed between us, for his father died in a recent battle. The son of my friend is young but carries his father's authority. I wish I could say his father died in direct combat with the enemy, but I cannot. He was struck by an arrow flown off course."

"He was shot by his own men?" The horror was apparent in Logan's voice.

"It appears that way, for what official carries a bow? Yet, the jungle is dense and the owner of the arrow could not have known what lay too far ahead; the victim sanctioned the offender without malice. No one knows to this day who it was, but I talk of things not pertinent to this mission. Here are the stone columns."

Veering to the left, Logan bent his right knee gently into the side of the giant spider. Giving the pitiful remains of his breakfast back to Redael with thanks, Logan brushed the dirt from his pants.

"How do you plan to address the Commander?"

"There is not much to say since he has accepted my call. As for his name, that I do not know. The people, or his men, for his father refused women and children the right to fight, call him Commander. That is how I will plan to address him. Many say he has ties to Quantus Plain and that he was once close to Lain, your leader. You must understand how his people admire and trust him. Try not to use bombastic language; flowery words rankle his type, and his support is key not for his number in men but for his leadership."

"That is understood, Redael."

Conversation died when the once-hidden earthworks reared abruptly before them. Halting his Mali-Mali, Redael yelled to a specific spot on the wall. Logan observed the structure of the earthen wall. Running his trained eye over the heaped earth, he studied its acoustics as he listened to Redael announce his presence.

"It is I, Redael, and I have come with Logan of Quantus Plain to summon you and your people to the call—"

"Which I have already answered," the Commander replied, appearing redoubtable and fully armed from an overlooked opening. "Do not fear, Redael, wise leader and friend of my father. My men and the men of Hitachi of Quantus Plain are ready to fight. You accept our humble armies?"

"Of course, friend. Ride with us?" Redael silenced Logan whose eyes had widened at the mention of his brother's name.

"As you say." With a flourish of his hand, the men issued from the fort, most riding atop Mali-Malis. The Commander supervised the performance critically. "My men without steeds, shall they be sent with your messengers to gather the surrounding rebels? They know the area well."

"That would be wise."

Knowing this would be the answer, the assigned men slinked with a wildcat grace into the dense jungle.

"They will be back within three days. We will be at the swamps by then, if my timing is correct."

"It is."

"Good then, enough of this. Hitachi of Quantus Plain, ride with us."

Logan's Mali-Mali took a step forward. Redael sent him a glance as if to stay him. At last Hitachi came, and at his entrance, Redael exclaimed, "So it seems identical brothers have been sent to us to call us to our duty. I do not think we shall waste any more time on pleasantries. We ride?"

"We ride."

No zealous shouts echoed from the men in response, but the grim silence in which they conducted themselves was more frightening than any war cry Hitachi had ever heard. With disciplined precision, they efficiently mounted their steeds and transferred their weapons from their backs to their palms. No one stole a last, affectionate glimpse at the abandoned stronghold, for none of them had left behind anything deserving fondness. Sweeping over the ground like water after a rainstorm, the assembly flooded the forest floor. Their eyes focused ahead, and their minds prepared for war. The black fist had risen, and the men had realized the truth—they each had one possession: life. They would fight to protect this possession, but in the process of doing so, most would lose theirs. Hitachi began to question his quest. He had summoned these men to give up everything they had, and he still did not know if it would be enough. As the somber men sallied from the fort, they respectfully parted so a distressed Hitachi could ride with Logan.

"Brother," he called, "it appears as though the Almighty has deemed it well for us to see each other again. You have done your job well." His words were encouraging but hardly joyous.

"And you likewise, Hitachi. Back to Quantus Plain we go! To Lain, our liege, we go." Logan's reply spoke more of devotion than of destination, for the brothers would willingly join Quantus Plain and its intrepid leader in whatever fate the fortress and Lain chose to suffer. They were as loyal to their underground compound as a true captain is to his ship. The only death they despised and feared was one far from their beloved home.

Chapter 8

"I have fought the good fight, I have finished the race, I have kept the faith. Now there is in store for me the crown of righteousness, which the LORD, the righteous Judge, will award to me on that day—and not only to me, but also to all who have longed for his appearing."
2 Timothy 4:7

White hair, long and straight, flowed from Aissii's regal forehead. Like the ice caverns glistening about him, his skin shone. It did not radiate the heat of the sun or the warmth of love, though small beads of sweat dripped down his face. Instead, his face shone with cold worry and intense concentration. His people, the last remnants of a once-prosperous civilization, watched him apprehensively. Though small in number, the stalwart warriors who remained were physically unequalled. Their powerful arms swung loosely from broad shoulders supporting lean necks. Muscled legs permitted the ice natives to track their prey with a deadly accuracy. This acuity had never failed them, and so they had supported themselves without the company or goods of others. The exception to their isolation manifested itself in the presence of the befriended ice creatures, gigantic mammals which some might have compared to savage wolves but which the ice people deemed a holy gift from the Almighty. Of the ice people, other peoples only knew to what the legends alluded. But now the ice people had been called by one likewise mentioned in legends. One of their own had returned to them from the mountains, bringing tidings of the one who hailed them in their own language. Aisii could almost see her fading image in the icy cavern walls, but her words did not dissipate. Rather, they echoed clearly throughout the space.

"How can this be, Aisii?" one of the men whispered in wonder. "She is far from us, but her voice sounds plainly."

Aisii's eyes fluttered open. "When strange voices call your name from afar, I am wont to answer them. Who can possibly do this but one sent from the Almighty, or the Almighty himself?"

"As she returns to her tribe, so one of our own remembers the way back to us; both were things long deemed impossible. We cannot ignore the signs."

"You are right, Aisii," another man spoke. "I feel we must go to the Valley of Solitude and to wherever we are led next."

"Aye, I would feel well if this was done," a woman announced.

"This decision shall be final," Aisii said grimly. "You yourselves have declared our course of action, but the Valley of Solitude lays many leagues from here. Are you ready to carry our banner to meet the one who calls us?"

The man sitting at Aisii's right-hand side immediately pulled from the ground the banner of the ice people. "This flag has long yearned for the wind of travel to blow it straight and for the sounds of war into which it can charge. For this I am prepared." Holding the flag, he waited for Aisii to stand and lead them from the room. The sweat cleared from Aisii's face as he prayed. *Tell the Jungle Maiden I will come.* Aisii stood gracefully.

"Let us ask the ice creatures to accompany us, no? One of them is worth many of us in battle, and they too have been summoned." Walking ceremoniously to the entrance of the cavern, Aisii lifted the unused silver sword and fitted it into his belt. "How many days do you think it will take us to reach the Valley of Solitude?" he questioned abruptly.

"Six if we run, five if the ice creatures agree to take us when we tire."

"Then we best start running," Aisii stated quietly. The ice people heeded Aisii's words, running swiftly atop the snowy plains and frozen falls as the sun rose in the sky. Their white hair streamed behind them, and their legs moved easily in syncopated rhythm. Long had been the day since the ice people had left the caverns, and long would be the day until they returned.

When Shrie released her cry, she languidly let her arms drop to her side. The elders did not move. After regaining her equanimity, she stated, "Shrie has called her friends, the ice creatures. They will come. What more tests do the elders wish to give me?"

From his position in the compound, Ryanous observed the elders with a budding antipathy. *How do they expect Shrie to call the ice creatures? It is a miracle she has arrived, but now they demand the impossible. I hope they do not dally too long inventing such useless tests. They tempt fate, placing more weight on an already unbalanced scale. Soon we will have brought destruction upon our own heads. They have given her seven days, and in that time, no matter how urgent their mission, they will wait. Hopefully Shrie is as stubborn as they are.*

One of the elders addressed Shrie's concern, "No more tests will come your way until it is deemed well to do so. If and when the ice people come, leading us into battle will be your test. For now, Jungle Maiden, you are free to go."

Shrie bowed low. "I thank the Almighty for the power He has given me so that I may do as you have asked. Shrie will lead her people into battle; the test will be passed."

"She makes a bold statement," Ryanous noted to Calamer beside him, "and yet I do not doubt her. I would pledge my sword to her before the arrival of the ice creatures had it not been forbidden by the elders." Ryanous continued, "After the people leave, I believe it wise to take her to her friend Dashjmar and talk of war."

"You say it so calmly."

"Do not fear, Calamer, you are a good fighter, and the Almighty will not leave you, or us."

"I have never seen true battle with the enemy."

"You are lucky then, that your first battle will also be your last. Come; let us rescue Shrie from being swallowed by the people. The elders have not dismissed them, but they already leave their seats."

"Whether the elders like it or not, the people will listen to Shrie. They have waited too long for their Maiden to come from the jungle. Now that she is here, there will be no stopping her."

Watching inconspicuously from the back of the room, Dashjmar was pleased. Shrie had not done poorly, and her success would directly affect his status in the tribe. Until the elders officially proclaimed Shrie to be the prophesied Jungle Maiden, he would not be accepted as a fellow warrior. Already he felt brazenly out of place amongst Shrie's people. His bluish skin contrasted their dark skin and hair, and his shiny earring studs and gold armbands clashed with the simple garments of her people. His tattoos, though admired by the children, were a taboo in the community. No one here even faintly resembled him. He knew his tribe had fallen on hard times; nevertheless he had harbored the childish hope of finding other Kalulukians in the valley.

Dashjmar unfolded his arms and walked through the back halls of the building. The biting night air swept over him and brought to him a certain awareness of the serenity around him. He sauntered over to a balcony where the elegant framework of an open ceiling rose above him. The woven patterns let the moon's dull, silver rays cast its glow on the balcony's wooden deck. He leaned over the edge of the railing, ogling the vast stretch of silvery, shimmering lake water.

I've finally completed something I was meant to do. The thought crept into his stirring mind. His past, once nothing but failure, deception, and exile, had made its peace with him. A face poked into his peripheral vision, and he was abruptly awoken from his contemplation.

"Who you talking to, Dashjmar?"

Dashjmar smiled in spite of himself. "Nobody in particular. I decided to grab a breath of fresh air, Maiden of the Valley."

"Acghh!"

"What?" Dashjmar asked, confounded.

"Maiden of Jungle has a better ring to it."

"I suppose you're right, though we'll be leaving on the seventh moon for Quantus Plain and not for the jungle."

Shrie did not bother to transition her thoughts. "Snowbeast did not answer me. I think he eating."

"If he doesn't come, we'll be chased out of here like blasphemous fools."

Shrie slapped Dashjmar on the arm. "You doubt Shrie?"

Dashjmar laughed softly. "I do not know, Shrie. You seem to have your tribe wrapped firmly around your finger, but when you lead them into battle, you need to know your north, south, east, and west." While Dashjmar chuckled at his own joke, Shrie ground her teeth together as she fumbled for a suitable retort. Abruptly Dashjmar's laughter died. "Shrie, would you do me the honor of introducing me to the elders? I have certain matters I would like to resolve with them."

"How you know elders?"

"Oh, I don't. That is why I want to meet with them."

"Elders seem grumpy, Dashjmar. They judge people. They might not accept a Kalulukian in their court."

"I do not fear denial when death itself I fear not."

"You fear losing competition against me, Dashjmar; that what you fear."

"Yes, I cannot deny that reality," Dashjmar teased, "but I remind you, you have still never beaten me to this day."

Shrie growled, "Go talk to elders."

Dashjmar retraced his steps to the council room, without Shrie's escort. Traveling back through the hallways and stairs, he encountered a domed, open room in which the elders sat illuminated by an abundance of lamp light. He got no word of refusal from the sentry lethargically patrolling the courtroom's premises, so he walked to them in plain view. One rose.

"Ah," he murmured thoughtfully as he studied Dashjmar's outward appearance, "the Jungle Maiden's guide and caretaker."

Dashjmar bowed and then spoke with all of the eloquence his vocabulary allowed. "I am hardly her caretaker. I shall amend this misconception; but yes, I am Shrie's guide and friend."

Another rose and stared down at him from an old, aquiline nose. "You come here to reprimand us?"

Dashjmar did not falter. "If in such a small manner as I exercised prior, if need be."

The youngest one, tiring of the rituals which prolonged simple encounters, spoke from the other end of the stone table. "I care not for the minor imperfections the both of you stress. Time is not under our control, and there is much to be dealt with. What is it you seek from us, Kalulukian?"

Dashjmar crossed his arms, his triceps bulging under the metal armbands. He scanned the elders before carefully stringing his request in plain tongue. "I am Dashjmar, a Kalulukian chieftain of old and a warrior of the rebel cause. I share all but one similarity with most of you: I am a Kalulukian."

The youngest one replied, "That is most obvious, please clarify your intentions."

Dashjmar tightened his jaw. "If you would have the decency to let me, I would certainly like to."

The elders gestured for the young chieftain to take a seat.

"You could say our tribes have had a less-than-enchanted past. Yet you must realize that if our present clashes with our future, both will be extinct." The chieftains were deathly silent. "If we are not willing to unite, how do we expect to conquer the dark men? If not for the rebels, we would have been pushed aside like sands moved by the waves. Though my people dwindle, I implore you to resurrect the bond we once possessed. It was because of the division amongst us that the Shalkans carried their war into the Khaltharngan Forest. As we will soon march off to battle once more, let us raise the same banner."

The elders gradually exchanged glances and whispers as they discussed Dashjmar's proposition. The young one contemplated alone with his eyes fixed on a map hanging in the back of the room.

One of the elders exhaustedly waved Dashjmar forward. "Come, sit. We shall work out a state of peace between our tribes. We began together, so we shall die together."

The sound of many voices and the bustling of life roused Dashjmar. He jostled his brain from a paralyzing slumber. The fluid in his head rolled back and forth as he blinked lazily. He brushed the crust out of his eyes as the sights and sounds around him became more distinct.

What am I doing here? he wondered, shaking the last bits of drowsiness from his face. He languidly peered down at the table and at the maps and documents littering its surface. *The council meeting!* Eagerly pushing aside the multitudes of papers, he finally found the document for which he was searching. His signature alongside those of the elders stared up at him promisingly. The elders and he had worked late into the night and early into the morning, sealing a bond of union between their tribe and the Kalulukians. They had reestablished their loyalty to the Almighty. It had been a trying night, and Dashjmar had constantly been tested by the chieftains in his words, actions, and even expressions. He must have drifted off during a lull in the meeting. Taking the two documented scrolls which held the bond of the tribes in his hand, Dashjmar decided to go check on his faithful steed.

Dashjmar wandered the extensive tribal grounds until he found the stables. Dew glistened on the draping hirsute trees, and the rising sun brightened the valley in which Dashjmar was now welcomed. By the elders' solemn fealty, they knew him as a loyal warrior of the united Khaltharngan tribes.

Tribesmen and women bustled about on their morning duties. Soldiers tramped down the road toward the capital building; all tribesmen were expert soldiers or archers when the need arose. Dashjmar noticed the commander, or Leirmayn, of the men rode a Ghier swan. He let his admiring eye linger on the elegant creature but knew he would never trade Magog's unfailing companionship for the thrill of flying. When he neared the stable doors, he found them unguarded and ambled through the huge stable stalls holding unfamiliar creatures. Toward the back of the stable, he found Gog and Magog blissfully crunching on oats and gruel. He swung open the gate, and with a big grin, he met his oldest and best friends.

"Hello, Magog and Gog. They feed you well by the look of you two."

The two lizards tramped around in an unidentifiable response, but then tossed their heads gaily.

"Yes, I'm glad to see you also. It has been a long night." Gog swung his head back and forth as if looking for Shrie, while Magog pawed the plentiful hay under his feet. Dashjmar rubbed Gog's head as he got up from his crouching position. "Do not fret, Gog, Shrie will be here soon enough. She likes you just as much as you like her."

After consoling Gog, he moved to saddle Magog who, after spotting the saddle, became visibly excited. Dashjmar labored with the gear as Magog uncooperatively swayed in anticipation. Soon Dashjmar had hoisted himself onto the ecstatic lizard and directed him past the other rows of animals. Outside the stable doors, a warm day greeted him. A breeze drifted by him lazily, and a slight humidity in the air made his movements seem lethargic and surreal.

Meandering by the compound that served as the tribe's headquarters, he waved a firm salute to the elders who returned it. Riding past them through the luscious grass, Dashjmar made his way to the expansive, brown plain of the training field. The life of its previous vegetation had been pummeled by pounding feet and bodies. Dust rose in whirlwinds as men spun and twisted about each other in a flurry of attacks and parries. Hopping off Magog, Dashjmar absentmindedly patted him on the head and loosely tied him to a nearby stake. Part of the barrier that fenced off the training area, the stake resisted the lizard's thoughtless movements. Leaning against the fence displaying a wide arrangement of weapons, he observed the two fighters. Their form was foreign to him, though the warriors' footwork was quick and the blows swift and accurate. Power backed their strokes, but one blow did not overpower the other for long. They were either extremely well-matched or lackadaisical. Dashjmar would wait and watch his tribe. His tribe...he had not thought he would live to hear himself say those words.

Calamer and Ryanous carefully stepped while thrusting their swords. Both did so silently, as they had done every morning for the last seven years. Sweat dropped in tiny beads down their faces, attracting the dust and dirt which erupted into the air with each firmly planted foot. Ryanous made a small grunting noise, breaking Calamer's concentration.

"The Kalulukian watches us." Ryanous' eyes flickered involuntarily to the spot where Dashjmar rested against the fence. "The tribe has accepted him as our own. It would be rude not to greet him."

"Do you wish to test his strength, Ryanous?"

"You know me too well." A frolicsome grin bloomed on the face of the warrior as he continued the exercise.

"Well then, we shall stop? You do not want to hurt yourself before the day of battle arrives."

"It is not me you have to worry about."

"I hope not," Calamer responded as he let his sword slip into his sheath. "Shall we greet him then?"

"Of course." Striding in Dashjmar's direction, Ryanous called, "Ho! Peace! Kalulukian, you enter our tribe?"

"What you say is true," Dashjmar responded.

"Your name, it is Dashjmar?"

"Indeed, and you, Ryanous, son of the Chief?"

"You know me then." Ryanous approached the fence. "Do you come to train?'

"I do not know your method of fighting," Dashjmar answered evasively.

"Perhaps you would like me to teach you."

"If it pleases you."

"Calamer, take my sword, thank you. Hand me the practice one."

"You need not use practice swords against me. I learn quickly," Dashjmar said, controlling the annoyance elicited by the inadvertent insult.

"Of course." Ryanous handed the sword back to Calamer. "As you wish."

"Thank you. So tell me, Ryanous, is my quarterstaff to code with your line of fighting?"

"Any and all weapons are to code."

"Ah, well, that is good to know. Shall we commence?"

"Yes. Do you mind if I talk as we exercise?" Ryanous asked as he did a simple, direct strike which Dashjmar blocked easily.

"I love conversation. I'm sure you'll find me quite amiable."

"Excellent," Ryanous commented as he increased the swiftness of his footwork to match Dashjmar's. "You must know that I am interested in the Jungle Maiden; she is a legend come alive. It is a natural curiosity that prompts me to ask of her."

"Of course." Dashjmar blocked a high strike and pressed forward. "One thing I can say: she is an extraordinary warrior."

"She has beaten you then?"

"Once I thought she had that ability, I did not challenge her. If she knew her strength, she might not have valued my guidance."

"Does our Maiden have a mind of her own?"

"Does she?" Dashjmar asked sarcastically. Ryanous did not know Shrie's iron will. "That you will see soon enough. Did she not tire you in the first test and carefully sway the elders to accept her? I was not present during any of these trials."

"We have yet to see if the ice creatures come." Ryanous struck, missing his mark by inches as Dashjmar's staff stopped his sword. Ryanous had little doubt of Shrie's ability, but he needed to see if the Kalulukian would falter. He wondered if she remembered a brother, one she had had very long ago. Dashjmar's encroaching staff whiffed by his face, and Ryanous knew he had lost his focus; the Kalulukian had missed on purpose.

"You were distracted by some deep thought," Dashjmar said as he let his staff slip and rest on the ground. "I do not think it sportsmanlike to fight a man whose mind is elsewhere, no matter how skilled he may be."

"I'm sorry. I will admit my mind was…preoccupied."

"Tell me, truly, did you want to implement your strength against me to test my worthiness as a member of your tribe?"

"Only partially."

"Did I pass?"

"You did; forgive my misgivings."

"All are pardoned. What other idea encouraged you to converse with me?"

"As I said before, curiosity. Do you know where the Maiden is now?"

"I am no longer her keeper. I never was, but if you want my opinion, I would guess she visits Gog."

"Gog?" Ryanous' eyebrows knit slightly. "I do not know of this Gog."

"It is her steed—a great lizard like my own." Dashjmar's answer pleased Ryanous.

"Few of the ancient lizards remain. Their scales drain of color, for they grow old, and so we rely on the Ghier swans and Mali-Malis. Would you like to accompany Calamer and me to the stables?"

"I'm sorry to say I cannot indulge in the pleasure of your company. There are matters with the elders I must discuss."

"Understandable." Ryanous jogged towards Calamer who had been waiting patiently.

"Did he best you, Ryanous?"

"He was more than fair."

"That wasn't my question."

"I know."

"Right then," Calamer answered pursing his lips. "Where to? I figure we will not be training again until later."

"To the stables. I wish to speak with Shrie before preparing for war and for the arrival of the ice creatures."

"The elders trust the ice creatures will arrive? Have you talked to your father?"

"They do not know what will happen, but they must be ready in case they do appear, and in case they don't."

"If they do?"

"Our troops and village must leave immediately for Quantus Plain. The entire compound will be cleared of everyone except those unable to fight."

"If they don't?"

"They will exile her."

"You plan to warn her then?"

"I do not think we will have the need," Ryanous commented hastily. "Calamer, six days is a long time, and the ice people move rapidly when called. Dashjmar lingers at the training ring, and I believe that is Shrie ahead."

"She is talking to the elders," Calamer noticed as they got closer. "She is pleased, I suppose, by Dashjmar's induction." As they walked, their swords clicked against the outside of their thighs, counting the seconds. "Shall we go up to her now or wait?"

"Now is good," Shrie answered with a smile, having left the elders. "Hello, Ryanous and friend Calamer. You hear news of Dashjmar?" Registering their looks of acknowledgement, she continued, "Yes, it is good that tribes finally united. We only need ice people now, and they come soon. Shrie send message to a friend; he says they crossing the mountains. Three days at most separate us. They move faster than anticipated. Your troops ready to move?"

"They will be ready," Ryanous promised, "but I hear Gog grows antsy in the stables. Would you like to join us on a ride?"

"Shrie likes rides on Gog. Yes, that is good. Come, follow Shrie, and tell her everything she must know about leading her people."

"Precisely. We'll saddle up the Ghier swans and meet you by the capitol compound."

"Shrie will beat you there," she called as she sprinted to the stables.

"I really think she will too." Calamer shook his head and then sprinted ruefully after Ryanous who had taken the challenge seriously. "You'd think they were brother and sister or something," he began. "Funny how perceptive I am," he added to himself as he caught up with Ryanous. Hurrying to saddle the agitated, giant swan which had been woken at a time earlier than to which it was accustomed, Calamer raced after his friend.

Aisii thrust his body against the wind as it whipped his hair into a tizzy. The mountain range was in view—the one which cradled the Valley of Solitude. They had barely been gone one day, but from his vantage point on the cliff, their destination was in sight. Beyond the cliff, however, the land would dip below the mountains, and no longer would the direction be clear. He did know that a pass would open before them in a day or two, and there the air would be much warmer. Aisii studied the ridges and falls of the land; he had not been farther than this point in many years, and his memory struggled to grasp the path to the Valley. Stealing one last glance, he motioned to his people.

A dormant strength awoke in their bodies. They would forge ahead with little rest, only using the ice creatures as a last resort. The creatures needed to hunt often, and the peoples' presences on their backs would hinder the process. Jogging lightly down the snowy incline, Aisii let his senses guide him to places his mind could not recall. The vision of the Jungle Maiden and the urgency of her call thrust him into a deep concentration. His thoughts were bent on a single goal: reaching the Valley of Solitude. After that, only the Almighty knew.

Calamer rode to the left of Shrie, and Ryanous rode to the right. She had beaten them to the front of the compound, but her task had lacked the necessity of saddling and mounting a stubborn, shrieking Ghier swan. As they toured the tribal grounds, Shrie never let their conversation fall silent or drab. The tangible presence of her tribe made her soul dance, and so of the depressing war she had not spoken. She would wait for Ryanous to breach the topic she knew he wished to discuss.

Passing clouds dulled the sun's intensity and ignited his troubled thoughts. "Tell me, Shrie of the Khaltharngan forest—do you remember any of us?" Ryanous threw out the question casually, but Calamer knew Ryanous awaited the answer in suspense.

"Shrie remember a few things." Her head cocked slightly to one side. She recalled the old memories she had sought to find in the blast of a trumpet long ago. "She remembers sounds of tribe: fire crackling into starry night, people bantering in woods, and soup boiling. Shrie remember vague faces and some very clearly."

"You never ask why you were left behind."

"It is the work of the Almighty," Shrie answered confidently. "How else would Shrie survive and return to her people?"

Ryanous would leave her with that answer. The three continued to converse until a loud, musical note reverberated across the village.

"There is a meeting. We best go back," Calamer mentioned as he dug his heels into the feathery side of the Ghier swan, pulling ahead towards the compound.

"You think the ice people have arrived?" Ryanous asked.

"No, ice people not come. There several days of distance between us," Shrie said earnestly.

"Do you really know that or do you just say it?" Calamer impugned.

Shrie threw back her head in laughter. The two men were puzzled. What had she found so amusing in the sour comment?

"You funny, Calamer," Shrie said as she regained her breath. "You think Shrie tell you about things she not know! Shrie never willing to make a fool of herself."

"I am sorry to have questioned you," Calamer said dutifully, provoked by a glare from Ryanous. "But I must know how you know."

Shrie laughed again. "That's what is so funny; Shrie does not know how she knows. She does some estimating, combines it with prior knowledge, and just knows. The Almighty help with that I think."

"You never cease to speak of this Almighty either," Calamer said in exasperation. He had to understand the girl who might soon become their leader. Her plans seemed so arbitrary, her spirit too lighthearted. "Why?"

"Why Shrie speak of Almighty? Almighty is good to Shrie. Anyway, Calamer, what you think this meeting is about that they call?"

Dismounting his Ghier swan as they neared the stables, he called, "What else can it be about but the upcoming journey we make to Quantus Plain?"

Hurriedly tying Gog, Shrie followed him into the building. Her eyes scanned the crowd as Ryanous and Calamer stood at attention with the other soldiers. She saw Dashjmar in deep conversation with some elders and rejected the idea of sitting next to him. Instead, she started for an empty seat in the back when one of the elders called for Shrie to come to the front. Composing herself, Shrie strode respectfully to the front of the room where she bowed once to the elders.

"Shrie of the Khaltharngan wood, you were told that no more tests would come your way until the ice people came. This word will not be broken, but there has been a call from some of the community for a display of strength. You have been accepted as one of the tribe but not as our leader. If the ice people answer you, fine; but it is yet to be seen if the Khaltharngan people do. I therefore present you with an opportunity to prove yourself."

Out of the corner of her eye, Shrie saw Calamer nod approvingly.

The youngest elder added, "To fight and defeat one of our top warriors would be sufficient. You can choose out of our five most skilled; you have until tomorrow to decide."

"Elders," Shrie spoke rashly, "Shrie has already chosen the one which she would fight if they would be so gracious as to agree."

"Who is it you have so quickly chosen?"

"Shrie would challenge Calamer, friend of Ryanous, for she feels he, out of any other, doubts most her skill." Her eyes flashed to where Calamer stood. Her statement had startled him. "Tell me, was my volition wise?"

"It was. Tomorrow morning then, we shall battle. The first one to put the weapon point to the neck wins. No one will die. To pit tribesman against tribesman would be a grave mistake when battle approaches."

Two more days remain, Aisii. The tribe grows anxious; they seek proof that Shrie is the one. Men doubt her ability, and tomorrow she battles the most skeptical of them all. She acquiesces to their requests, but she is not a tree made to bend. Two more days, Aisii and I expect to see you at the Valley of Solitude. Two more days.

Aisii jolted from the vision. With a shaky hand he wiped the sweat from his face. He sat upright in the temporary igloo his people had shaped hours ago. They had needed rest. *Two more days, Aisii.*

Aisii rolled over and shoved his knives back haphazardly into his belt. "We leave now," he called. Sheathing his sword, he listened as the others woke and rolled their thin blankets.

"We are to catch up with the ice creatures," he enjoined, pausing as he ducked through the small entrance. "We will ride the rest of the way; tell them not to hunt for the rest of the trip," Aisii commanded, stepping into a gelid blast of air. His hair whipped about his face, and he tied it with a rough piece of leather. "The ice creatures are some miles ahead of us," he commented. "We must not let them get beyond our reach." When his people were ready behind him, he broke into the long stride which would catch the ice creatures by dawn. His people did not question his decision. *Two more days...*

Logan rode beside Hitachi, Redael, and the Commander. They were to rendezvous with the supply train outside the swamps, but if they maintained their speed, it seemed feasible to overtake them before the desired time. To relive the tedium of travel, Logan nonchalantly studied the sky. The hermetic sun had sequestered itself behind the clouds and refused to come from its hiding. Despite the golden sphere's absence, humidity abounded as though loosed from the pits of the earth. Spitting out a bug that had flown into his mouth, Logan watched as the little black spot flew from his lips and landed in the brush. As he did so, Redael stopped.

"Commander, how close do we ride to the ocean?"

The troops curved around Redael and the other three halted leaders.

"Why do you ask?"

"We were to meet with the supply train by the swamps, but if I am not ill of ear, then waves crash upon the shore. The breeze I feel does not often sweep through the deep jungles. Why have you taken us by this path?"

"You can arrive at the swamps using many paths, but the jungle by the ocean is less dense, and the fresh water spring lies along this trail. Also," the Commander glanced ahead, "if I am correct, I am taking the same route the supply train did."

"They would not head so close to the water," Logan protested. "They would have passed too close to the Zabyn."

"No, like you, they were deep in the forest but swung by my fort, which is not far from the coast. They did not see us, and I said naught to them, for other rebels had arrived. I recognized their tracks as we left, but with less foliage to break, their tracks grow faint."

"I wonder why they changed their route," Hitachi mused.

"As do I," Logan added.

Without another word, the Commander rode ahead.

"Redael, I have a presentiment I cannot place," Hitachi whispered. "It is not that I do not trust the Commander, he seems wise enough, but his words stirred something within me. We must be cautious, I think."

Redael shared Hitachi's concerned look but answered stiffly, "Cautious! We will meet the enemy one way or another, sooner or later, Hitachi of Quantus Plain. This is a battle which cannot be avoided." Spurring his steed faster, he caught up to the Commander at the front of the army. Hitachi shook his head as he heard Redael voice his concerns.

"Show me signs of the supply train," Redael commanded.

The other rebel leader laughed cynically. "I see you share your friend's anxiety. If you cannot trust me, who will you trust?"

Redael kept the heat from rising in his face. "Do not get haughty with me. I deserve the right to see the tracks you claim. I do not doubt; I only wish to know. If you are killed on the way, someone will have to take your place." Redael exhaled. "Where are they?"

The Commander searched the ground ahead of him. "Do you see those faint lines in the dirt?"

"I do."

"They traveled closer to the ocean where the dirt is no longer muddy and wet. The carts bearing supplies leave a shallow rut. Nevertheless, they dragged giant ferns behind them to cover their trail. Those lines left in the dirt are from these ferns."

"I see it now." Redael's eyes scanned the scene. "How will you know when they cross inland again?"

"The tracks have to be fresh for no animal to have disturbed them. I believe we are less than a day behind them."

"Amazing."

"Many are on foot, remember, and many are villagers who have not walked farther than their farms. It is obvious that they will be slow."

"How many days until we reach Quantus Plain?"

"That depends, of course, on how fast we go. Do you hear that?" The Commander whirled to look behind him.

Sounds of men shouting came from the back of the group. An overwhelming apprehension broke and spilled upon them. The Mali-Malis were jittery, and men spun their heads quickly, not knowing for what they sought. Logan rode hurriedly to the two leaders.

"What's going on here?" the Commander demanded.

"One of our scouts," Logan answered, "has spotted black sails on the horizon."

"Ahead or behind us?"

"Both."

"Coming towards us, or riding away?"

"Two are ahead, sailing to Quantus Plain. Some are behind us; but do not look back, for I fear the ships pounce upon us as locusts upon a crop."

"Well, they will not get a share of the crop," the Commander said gruffly. "Tell the men to ride inland. There is no use in being blasted to bits before arriving at the battle scene. If we are to die, let us at least take the enemy with us."

"I will tell them so." Logan turned and rode back, shouting the order.

Veering sharply to his left, the Commander led them inland, but his gaze did not leave the horizon.

Chapter 9

The morning seemed to shimmer in the soft sunlight. Though it was early, Calamer had already been up for hours, readying himself. He could not afford to lose this battle, but his people could not afford to see their Maiden fail. It was a precarious situation. Rumors that Shrie had finally awoken came to him. Apparently she needed little preparation. She was either very haughty or very foolish. For the sake of his integrity, Calamer badly wanted to beat her.

Studying his sword, he speculated what weapon Shrie would choose. No rules aside from the time and place of the battle had been set, but those two things were enough to bring the entire village into the fields outside the training ring. He looked dispassionately from a small window in one of the compounds outside the training ring. Masses of people cheerfully gathered their food and spread it on blankets placed on the ground. Contrasting this obvious glee, the elders sat sternly inside the ring. They would settle any disputes and declare the winner if necessary; this simple battle would determine the future fate of the tribe.

Observing the rituals of battle, the contestants would not see each other before the fight, and no one would attend to them. No time limit for the battle was set, but it was apparent the people thought it would be a protracted engagement, for most had lunch and dinner baskets set side to side. Calamer let his mind skim over the routine. The elders would blow the horn. Then they, Shrie and he, would turn and face each other wearing the oversized battle robes. Another horn would blow, and they would drop the robes which would conceal their weapons. Then, they would commence. At the end, a young boy from the tribe would retrieve the robes. It was the fight, the part between beginning and end, which he could not picture. He did not know how she fought or what moves he should use in defense. It would be complete improvising. He inhaled deeply. He whished his sword skillfully through the air and then sheathed it, reaching for the ceremonial robe. He was ready.

Burrr! The first horn rang, overriding the people's chattering and the beating of their hearts. Shrie donned the bulky ceremonial robe with her back facing the courtyard. The pleated rows of cloth piled around her feet as she walked backwards; the grainy, tan sand ran like water over her toes.

Calamer breathed deeply. The second horn blew, but it seemed distant, so far away. In a dream he pulled the sword flawlessly and swiftly from its sheath. The robe slipped from his muscular body as he threw his arms apart.

Shrie heard the horn ring in the air. She stepped from the cloth confines of the robe. Her arm pulled back the arrow on the bow. The crowd froze, and shock stampeded freely through the eyes of the elders. There had been no weapon restrictions; Shrie had honored the rules. No one moved, as though by remaining still they could hold Shrie's arrow frozen against the string.

Calamer stood forever with the tip of the arrow trained on his forehead, debating what course he should take. Finally, with a yell, he lunged forward. Shrie ducked from the blow and danced around him with her bow lowered; she wanted him to attack. Placing his feet carefully, he moved his sword adeptly, but she remained always and just beyond his reach.

Shrie toyed with Calamer, evading his blows. She forced him to press the offensive. His sword missed her by finger widths. Fingering her arrow, she reached up as he brought his sword down.

The sword cut towards Shrie's unguarded neck. The sparkling edge hovered inches above her neck when he jerked short. The tip of an arrow pierced lightly the skin on his neck. They were eye to eye. Shrie's dark green eyes locked into his brown. She held the arrow firmly in place, and he kept the sword quivering inches above her neck. Neither heard the people gasp. With her eyes, Shrie commanded him to put down his sword.

Put it down. I do not have to be stronger than you to lead you.

He resisted. *Intelligence will not win you a war.*

That's why I have you.

Calamer's will shook; his hands loosened on the sword. Ever so slowly, he sheathed it, his eyes still locked on Shrie's as he knelt. Shrie took the arrow from his neck and placed it in her quiver.

"Get up Calamer, warrior of Khaltharnga. Today you have shown yourself to be an unmatched warrior, but I have proven myself your rightful leader. Do you accept me as such?"

Calamer seemed not as a man defeated but as one who had won, one who had

JULIE AND RYAN DICKERSON

cemented the fate of his tribe and erased all doubts from his mind. "I do," he said, "and I offer you my sword and spirit in battle." The dust whipped up from their skirmish began to settle about them.

"Offer me your sword and the Almighty your spirit. With honor I accept your word."

"And I yours, Maiden of the Jungle. It is my desire to serve."

An unexpected cry of exultation rang through the crowd. Little children clapped and sang, reenacting the battle as adults let small tears of joy and relief run down their faces. Everyone exchanged hugs. Another man knelt and offered his sword.

"I also commit my sword to your service."

Recognizing the voice as Ryanous's, she smiled sadly; she did not share in her tribe's joy. Her duty lay before her. "Ryanous, I accept your sword. Stand and join Calamer in Shrie's army."

A line of men and women fanned behind him, and Dashjmar was in it. As he knelt before Shrie, tears streamed down her face. "Now Shrie knows she is able to lead her people if even Dashjmar offers her his staff." Shrie tapped him lightly on the back with her arrows. "It time for you to get up, Dashjmar, and take your place as one of the tribe."

"I have more than confidence in you, Shrie," Dashjmar said as he rose. "I have put my hope in you."

"As I have," said another as he fell on his hands and knees before her. "I am Heraldshold, a rider of the Ghier swans. Maiden, if it pleases you that I enter your service, then so be it."

The ceremonies continued into the afternoon since the tribe had had enough forethought to bring provisions lasting until dinner. Everyone but the elders, who watched critically but peaceably, had acknowledged her authority. They would wait until the ice creatures came to give their word. They would be tougher to penetrate than she had thought, but this morning had brought her a victory. She gave praise as she dubbed each man and his sword in the spirit of the Almighty.

Even after the last man had risen and gone, Calamer, Ryanous, and Dashjmar refused to leave her. With the three of them escorting her, she approached the elders, who, like her, had not eaten since the morning. Bowing three times she said, "I thank you, elders, for allowing me this opportunity to prove myself. Your wisdom is beyond understanding and your standing of great respect. When the ice creatures come, I hope we will ride together to Quantus Plain."

When the elders did not respond, she turned quietly on her heel and walked away with her companions beside her. Her feet left tranquil imprints in the dust.

"How far must we go inland until we are out of sight?" Logan questioned the Commander worriedly.

"Farther."

Instilled fear crept through Logan's veins, threatening to burst through his fingertips. Licking his lips, he peered behind him; the horizon was deceptively clear. "We must near Quantus Plain and the river, for that is surely where the ships head."

"Several miles of jungle separate us, but I do not think we will be going through the swamps. We will catch the supply train and then—do you smell smoke?" he interrupted himself suddenly.

Logan inhaled deeply. He regretted his action as he began to hack on the burning air. Apprehension pulsed in his body, spreading from his stomach in wavering gyres.

"Damn it!" the Commander cursed under his breath. "Logan, Redael, lead the men forward. I'm heading back to pick up the rear." He trampled the underbrush and disappeared into the multitudes of men. Logan doubled the pace and bounded into the woods behind Redael. The smoke thickened, and Logan brought his shirt to his nose.

His eyes wept from the smoke which refused to rise. Choking on it, Logan thought he would lose his last meal to the ungodly fumes. Lowering his head to the side of the Mali-Mali, his face drained of color. His stomach heaved its possessions onto the ground. His head hung, bouncing with the rhythm of the Mali's movements. When he opened his eyes, he gagged. Beside him and embedded in the dark mud of the jungle was a human skull. Inky eye sockets stared at him, and scraps of burnt flesh clung to the blackened bone. Jerking himself into a sitting position, Logan felt the presence of another behind him. The official grinned with empty eyes.

"God, Almighty!" As Logan rushed forward, a breeze blew through the smoke, and his sword slashed emptily in the air. The official vanished, disappearing with the smoke.

"Logan!" Logan stopped. "Do not let your senses get the better of you," Redael said sharply, though his face too was colorless. Logan's chest tightened, and his breath came sharply. "The supply train has been slaughtered," Redael continued after swallowing, "but not by official troops. The ships' cannons have done their damage. We will search for survivors."

A chill traveled down the back of Logan's spine.

"Prepare yourself, Logan of Quantus Plain," Redael enjoined. Though sweating profusely, he carried himself confidently. Shadows frolicked demonically over the jungle. "Do not look behind you," he continued, "or to the left or to the right. Look straight ahead, and for the sake of the men, don't show any emotion." Redael's voice shook. "Come, we have stalled too long."

Breaking the wall of smoke with his body, Logan rode next to Redael, and the rest of the army broke from the woods behind him. The smoke and the saturated stench sickened them as the debris forced them to maneuver slowly in the unnerving silence. From the corner of his eye, Logan could see the white, bony fingers of a hand sticking from the dirt. Tongues of fire licked the brush, and craters of desolation ravaged the ground. A broken cart littered the soil. How many had there been, four? More stinking bodies lay open upon the ground. Two men lost the contents of their stomachs behind him.

A shadow passed over them, and the air chilled. He forced himself to look. Logan's voice froze as the black sail rose from the water and loomed over the trees. The cannons protruded from the sides of the ship; his numb body began to sweat. Without asking, Logan forged ahead with an earsplitting scream. The black sail consumed his vision. It was all he saw, all he could see. He heard the boom and roll of the cannons being loaded, heard it but did not see it. He only saw the blackness.

"What in God's name is he doing?" the Commander watched in awe as Logan and the few men who trailed him raced from the cover of the trees. Hitachi let his eyes widen, and then he gritted his teeth and pulled out his sword.

"I'm following him. He's my brother, and if he rides to death, then I ride with him."

The Commander's lips pressed firmly together in regret. "So be it, Hitachi of Quantus Plain, but if you are so brave as to sacrifice yourself, at least take the ship with you."

"I swear it to you." The words came out whispered, but as Hitachi turned, he called out and raised his sword in the air. Skimming the surface of the ground, he ran to death with a willing heart. The cannon shot forward and then recoiled, fire exploding from its mouth. The shot was not aimed at the army.

"Alright men, move up, move up!" Redael shouted over the frenzy. "They threw themselves away so we can reach Quantus Plain alive." Redael's eyes moved wildly in his head. "Make your sorry rear ends move so they don't die in vain."

Allowing himself one last glance at the small triangle of men running to the ship, the Commander watched in admiration and fear. "Almighty, save them, for you are the only one who can help them now." To his men he exclaimed, "For Quantus Plain, men, for Quantus Plain! If we're not in sight of that noble fort by nightfall, God save our souls."

The day and the next was a flurry of motion and nonexistence. Preparations were in constant progress. Men had packaged their rations and clothes in small parcels which were slung purposefully over their shoulders. The women and children had armed themselves willingly. A dozen tribesmen and women wished to stay behind with the children who were too young to go. Shrie granted their requests and felt the stare of the elders on her back every time she did so. They watched her closely. Tomorrow they would decide, but until then, the village scurried.

Overseeing the myriad of ongoing tasks, Shrie supervised from the back of faithful Gog. She delegated responsibilities to men and women who she had never before seen, judging their capabilities based upon their eagerness to serve. To those with the brightest sparks in their eyes, she assigned the hardest assignments. Never did one of her invaluable people disappoint her; for as a whole, they listened to her attentively. By the end of the day, she and they had accomplished more than she had thought possible. Every volunteer had been organized efficiently into fighting units, issued extra weapons, and instructed in basic battle formations. Those accompanying the tribe had stacked a supply train with heaps of pots, weapons, clothing, and food. The entire community had emptied their huts and gardens in order to contribute to the war effort. Once unified, the tribe was unstoppable. As dusk settled, Shrie had never been more pleased, and Gog had never been more tired.

"It is time to head back, Gog," she assured him as he blinked languorously. "It has been a long day, but we ride back. And soon, we will not depart for the journey home," Shrie clarified, "but for a destination beyond. Shrie is taking you into battle. Gog likes fighting, no?"

Gog made a noncommittal grunting noise with which Shrie agreed. To Shrie's ears, the wind blew the plodding of a Ghier swan's webbed feet upon the ground. Seconds later, a voice floated into her thoughts like a bug bumping into the gossamer strings of spider's web.

"I did not realize you spoke Lizard." A familiar face entered her peripheral vision.

"Hello, Ryanous," Shrie greeted him as he rode from behind her on the Ghier swan.

"Your handle on our own tongue improves, especially when you talk to the elders. Do you practice with Gog?"

"Shrie always careful with the words she uses around the elders. Your father, does he, will he, accept Shrie's claim as Maiden?"

The grass rolled like waves in the wind, every blade of grass swaying in harmony. Several minutes passed as Ryanous thought, and then he assured her, "I think he will. When do the ice people come?"

Pleased to hear his question feature the word "when" and not "will," Shrie pensively closed her eyes. "They come early or middle of day tomorrow."

"Then early or middle day is when he will offer you his staff."

"That will be a great honor," Shrie mused, opening her eyes. "Shrie has had no time to sit with you and speak of battle. I fear there is little we can plan until we reach Quantus Plain."

"You did it again," Ryanous chuckled.

"Did what?"

"Started using I."

"Oh." Shrie responded lamely. "Ryanous, Shrie misses her friends at Quantus

Plain. She prays hard that the ice people will come quickly so she can return to them. She worries about them." With this confession, she hoped he did not think her weak hearted. "You think Shrie silly?"

"No, for I have been in such a state for many years." He slipped from the present and into the past. "Many years we have awaited our Maiden, and now she misses another people."

With a quiet, cheerless laugh Shrie responded, "You right, Ryanous, Shrie should be, and is thankful she has found her tribe! Know though, that the other people of whom you speak were Shrie's tribe when her own abandoned her. Shrie is greedy; she wants all her tribe to be one people and together. Ryanous, understand? He would like Corious, Shrie thinks, and Calamer would like Ree and Tar. But Shrie rambles. What you come to talk to Shrie about?"

Ryanous sighed and shrugged, the word "sister" suddenly not able to escape his lips. "To get away from talk of battle," he lied.

"You a warrior, no?"

"I am, but I fear it at the same time."

"Ah! Do not fear, Ryanous. With the Almighty on our side, the enemy is outnumbered! Rush to battle with bravery in your heart."

"I knew I would hear such words of encouragement from you. It was what I needed. The sun sets. Shall I escort you back?"

"Race back?"

"Anything my Maiden commands," Ryanous retorted with an elfin grin.

Running, pounding, falling, running, pounding, falling. Fire lustfully bit at his clothes in endless cycles. It wanted him alive, for corpses no longer suited its taste. Another click and clank of the cannon being loaded separated him from Logan. *Where will it land?* The heat crawled up his back and wrapped its fingers around his neck.

"No!" He choked on the dryness of his own throat. "Ride, Mali-Mali!" He dug his heels into the spider's side. "Ride!" The spider careened forward, the fire on its heels. Closing his eyes, Hitachi bowed his head, waiting for the impact to shake the ground. Vibrations sent water sloshing about his legs. Prying his eyes open, he discerned the rebels' motley figures just ahead of him. Their spiders swam decidedly through the yellow water which reflected the blazing cannon fire.

"Hitachi!" one of the men yelled to him. "Get off or lay low on your Mali! We will be in shooting range soon!"

Hitachi slid off his spider as bullets buzzed around him like a swarm of angry bees. He gripped the side of his spider, hoping it would pull him through. He approached Logan. "Logan, brother, look back!"

Logan did not look back.

"It's Hitachi, Logan!"

"He has gone crazed," one of the men called to him. "He goes without knowing what he does. Look back, the army escapes."

Carefully keeping his head near the water, he turned back. The conflagration had consumed the thicket behind the beach, concealing the fleeing rebels from sight. *If I am throwing my life away, then I am doing it for a noble purpose. No man could ask for more.* The deadly splashes of deviant bullets diving into the water reminded him of the present danger. The black sail could no longer be seen; nothing besides the wood of the steeply sloping hull came into view.

Logan treaded furiously through the water, searching for something near the ship. The men waited. Bullets continued to fall like black hail, but the hull reached over the rebels, its angle protecting them from the worst of the assault. Once the officials discovered their targets were safe, it would only be a matter of seconds before the ship left. An earsplitting splintering of wood crackled into the steamy air.

"Logan has found a soft spot in the wood!" someone cried.

Hitachi nudged his spider to the right and witnessed as Logan pried off a piece of planking and squeezed himself through the small opening.

"My God! He's found a way in." Patting his spider in wordless thanks, Hitachi pushed off its side and joined the men congregating around the ship's torn side. The others squirmed in, and the Mali-Malis swam back to shore. As they left, Hitachi felt strangely helpless.

"For Quantus Plain!" his brother called furiously.

The men echoed, "For Quantus Plain!"

With a renewed spirit, Hitachi pulled himself from the water just as the ship lurched forward. The man who had gone before him slipped his arms under Hitachi's shoulders and lugged him inside. Both fell onto the wooden floor, bedraggled and dripping.

"Come, Logan has run off this way," the rebel said, stumbling into position and pointing into the dim light. "Have you your sword?"

"I do, good sir."

"Then let us go and steal ourselves this ship."

Logan knew not where he ran; but he saw cannons, and he knew the rebels could use those. His eyes examined the structure of the ship and the mechanics of the cannon. A loose plan formulated under his heavy brow. As the other rebels stumbled in behind him, he went to work.

"Logan, brother, what plan have you devised?" Hitachi asked excitedly as Logan groaned and pushed the cannon into position. The cannon made a horrid squeaking noise as metal rubbed against metal.

"What is that?" an abrasive, throaty voice called. Though the voice stiffened the rebels, it did not deter Logan from intently pushing the cannon forward. "Gheragald, are you guarding this entrance?" Sneering, the official hackled in enmity, "Get into shape boy. We're not far from Quantus Plain now!" Whap! The official backhanded the guard across the face.

"What are you doing, you lazy bastard?" another voice yelled from above the hatch.

Hitachi's eyes opened wide. The number of enemy outside their door swelled. Eechhhh! The cannon swiveled and pivoted perilously on its side.

"What are you doing down there?" The captain was unprepared for the counterattack of the guard.

"This here asinine Shalkan is making too much noise!" With a wicked grin, the guard jumped on the official who had just smacked him. Eecchhh!

"What in the name of the nine moons is making that ghastly noise?"

"Sir, the spiders are swimming away; the riders are gone," someone else called. "What would you have us do?"

"Shoot the spiders," the captain replied without hesitation. "And tell the slaves to move faster. They're getting sluggish."

A swell of hot indignation surged through Hitachi as the other voice faded with a "yes sir." The scuffling of the guard and official had died. Only one set of footsteps was heard as the champion walked away.

"We've got our problem solved, Captain," the official cried merrily.

The footsteps neared. Hitachi ducked behind a nearby barrel labeled "water." Click, click. The thumping of the official's boots beating against the wood floorboards reverberated throughout the corridor, stopped outside the door, and then passed.

Hitachi's body tingled with elation. They had infiltrated the ship undiscovered.

Eechhh! Logan had not gone into hiding. Hitachi grimaced, and his heart sank as his hand reached for his sword. The other rebels did the same. The footsteps ran back to the door, and an ugly face peered around the rectangular frame. When the official saw his find, a lone rebel, he grinned. Then, without warning, Logan fired.

"Whoahe!" his voice shot through the air at an ungodly level, and the cannonball burst through the wall, taking the official with it in a celebration of fire.

Hitachi jumped. Grabbing the scuttlebutt, he dumped it on the spreading flames. He opened his mouth to say something when the captain's agitated voice came from above.

"What the hell do you think you're doing down there?"

With a ferocious yell, Logan fired the cannon, and this time he increased the angle of its launch. Flames enveloped the entire wall. The rebels repeated Logan's yell, and without bothering to douse the fire, they rushed out the door and to the top of the deck. No captain hindered their way. As the black sail dipped and rose above them, Hitachi lifted his sword and charged at the first official in sight. Caught by surprise, the enemy was swiftly taken.

Boom! Logan had remained in the hold, and another cannonball shot through the middle of the deck.

"Someone go down there and tell him to stop it! Next time that will be us dead on the deck," Hitachi commanded as he dashed to engage an approaching official. In a collision of movements, the officials fired at the few rebels running to stop Logan. Half the officials were shot down by their own men, and the others were slain by the rebels. They had not gotten far from the hatch when another round of bullets barely missed rebel heads and arms. Smoke from the guns overpoweringly replaced the smoke from the cannons as the battle brought the rebels too close for effective use of the bulky armaments.

"Goodbye," Hitachi whispered in the ear of an official before running him through. He would extort vengeance.

An excruciating roar announced Logan's arrival as he dove into the midst of the battle. Officials began simultaneously attacking adeptly from the rigging and higher decks. The switch of weaponry and tactics took two rebel lives and many more slaves.

"Free the slaves!"

The fervent cry redirected Hitachi's attention to helm. The official who held the key to the slaves' chains stood triumphantly untouched by combat.

"Logan," Hitachi called, "the driver!"

Like lightning, Logan left the man he had been fighting. Snarling and pounding up the steps, he hunted the driver. Hitachi saw his brother mercilessly jump the man before an opponent forced his concentration elsewhere.

With ease, Logan slew the driver and fished the keys from the official's clamped hand. On instinct, he ducked, missing the well-aimed blow of a gun at his head. *There are too many.* Running, he catapulted himself from the top step as bullets screamed towards him. One hit him solidly in the arm. Containing the scream behind gritted teeth, Logan watched the blood streak down the hand that held the keys. His feet smashed forcefully into the lower deck. After his knees absorbed the racing shock of the impact, he jetted across the deck. Tearing a piece of cloth from his shirt, Logan used his mouth and good hand to tie the rag about his wound. The slaves were not far off now, and their faces waited in hungry anticipation as the sound of the keys bouncing in his hand neared.

"I've come to set you free," Logan announced as he reached the first slave. "Can I count on you?" Logan took the keys from his lame, cramped hand.

"Yes," the slave said with conviction. "Break me free, and I shall see the ship taken," he continued vehemently.

"That's a mighty claim," Logan said softly, "but as I too was once a slave, this I do not doubt." Kneeling, he jingled the key into the lock until the shackles broke free. "Take the guns from the dead bodies and then climb the mainstay. Rid us of the officials in the crow's nest, aye?"

"Aye!" the grateful, but terrified slave responded, rubbing his sore wrists.

Logan suddenly felt lightheaded; the ship was spinning, but he could not stop it. The deck was under him. He forced himself to stand, but the deck rushed again to meet his face. *The black sail…*

When the officials pushed Hitachi into the middle of the fracas, the rebels lost ground instantly. Soon they would be back down the hatch. Warding off an official, Hitachi prayed he could hold. *Do not despair*, he told himself, but he no longer heard Logan's cries of encouragement. Without his brother's infectious zeal, the spirits of the rebels wilted. Taking advantage of Hitachi's anguish, the attacker thrust him into the side of the ship. With a mangled cry, Hitachi pushed the official from his chest, and to his dismay, the man separated from him as the skin of a snake peels from its body. The happy grin of a freed slave replaced the official's grimacing cadaver.

"Don't worry, rebel. We will win the battle now!"

In wonder, Hitachi witnessed as the slave jumped with the agility that comes from years of practice up one of the masts and into the spiraling ropes leading to the top of the ship. Almost concurrently, a black splotch hurtled from above.

"Watch out below!" another slave called. "The officials fall!"

The gunfire from above lessened as the slaves poured into the rebel ranks and as more dark men plummeted to the deck. The slaves clumped the Shalkans in the middle of the deck. By numbers alone, they were now overwhelming the enemy. Cornered, the officials grew vicious with desperation. The rebels fell back. Then, like a creature slowly awakening, the rebels pressed forward. Officials began to flee for the sides of the ship.

"Do not let them get overboard," Hitachi yelled over the noise of battle.

Several officials reached the railing of the ship, but they were picked off as they dove into the water. The Shalkans in the center were slaughtered. Once again, Hitachi noticed that Logan did not fight in the fray. His mind continued to panic. Hastily wiping his sword clean on his shirt, he scanned the ship for Logan. The body count was high, and it was impossible to tell the wounded from the dead or a rebel from an official.

"Throw the dead bodies overboard from the back of the ship," Hitachi commanded, hiding the fear he felt. "May the Almighty have mercy on their souls."

"What of our own?" one man questioned.

"A seaman's burial with honors, tears, and haste."

"Yes, sir."

As the others toiled, Hitachi reviewed his memories of the battle, and he headed to where the empty shackles hung—to where he had last seen his brother.

"Commander, smoke rises from the ship!"

"Aye, it does," the Commander answered as the smoke billowed.

"Perhaps they have taken it!"

The Commander did not respond. It was simply impossible. "The odds stacked against them were extremely high." He suppressed the tremor of his heart and the wild joy that he feared would deceive him. He rushed his men through woods wrought with the shambles of the supply train. The army maneuvered swiftly.

"Commander," a man called, riding towards him. "I carry a message from Redael. The survivors of the supply train have been found!"

"By the Almighty! In what condition are they?" He swerved from his position to meet the messenger.

"They sustained minor injuries but still carry their weapons. Redael has doubled up men on the spiders to accommodate them, but he wants to stop at a spring halfway between here and Quantus Plain to replenish our supplies. He suggests the soldiers will fight better with a bit of rest."

"Let me see the survivors, and I shall judge if this is so. I want to be at Quantus Plain as soon as possible."

"We will pass the spring anyway," the messenger offered. "Would it be of harm to refill our canteens?"

"No, but I do not plan on staying the night and sleeping while the enemy moves. Tell Redael such. I shall check on the condition of the survivors at the spring."

The messenger started off but then stopped when the Commander called to him. "Tell Redael," the Commander paused, "that one of the black ships burns."

"I shall!" The messenger sped ahead with the vigor of a hawk catching its prey.

Someone rattled her.

"Shrie, wake up! Hurry!"

"Aghh!" She blinked her eyes. The sun had not even ascended above the horizon, but Dashjmar towered above her with his arms crossed.

"Dashjmar, you come early to wake Shrie. This is an embarrassment! Shrie can wake by herself." Grumbling and still not completely awake, she staggered out of bed and grabbed her bow and arrow.

Dashjmar stepped back, watching in amusement her flurry of movement. He noticed she still wore the same clothes from yesterday. Their days of travel had obviously set a trend for her.

"You're not going to change?" he asked lightly.

Shrie stopped, and one eyebrow quirked above the other in confusion. Finally she said, "Not with big, ugly Dashjmar in room. Why should Dashjmar ask that question anyway?"

Floating somewhere between laughter and annoyance, he decided to tell her the truth. After all, it had been his choice to swear fealty to her, not hers. While he loved her jungle audacity, he hoped the coming of the ice people would bring to her the seriousness she had demonstrated before the elders. Shrie interrupted his thoughts.

"Dashjmar, why you here again? Shrie is happy to see you but is—"

"Scouts have spotted a white mass on the horizon. I can only assume it is the ice people."

Shrie smiled. "Good, they come even earlier than Shrie thought. Thank you for bringing Shrie this good news. Now hurry and leave so she can get ready."

Dashjmar shook his head and left, waiting outside the door. He remembered the time when he had been the one doing the guiding and Shrie had simply trusted. She made the demands now, but he would try to leave her with one last piece of advice before the ice people arrived. Compelled by a gnawing sense of urgency, he decided to talk through the door.

"Shrie, when the ice creatures come, I think it wise to meet them with the army behind you. You need to show them your power not your friendliness. In fact, do not even consider going to meet them without the army. When I say meet, I mean for you to wait for them; let them come to you."

"Shrie talk to them in their own tongue."

"Good, but don't translate it. The tribe and ice people must have a mutual awe for each other and for you. Both are a powerful people, and if what you offer to share between them is not something they want to share, that quarrel will be more than we can handle."

"Dashjmar, are you talking to yourself?" Calamer appeared in the hall.

"You're funny, Calamer," Dashjmar said blandly. "Remember, you are a warrior of Khaltharnga. There is nothing amusing about marching to battle."

Shrie opened the door, and Dashjmar danced out of its path. Calamar studied Shrie with an approving eye. She wore a red cloak that swept just above the ground. A woven, silver belt girded her waist, and from it hung an impressive sheath and sword. Unlike most days, a pair of close fitting, leathery brown boots covered her feet and came up to her knee. The strands of long, black hair which usually clung to her face had been pulled back. Her bow rested on her shoulder, and arrows almost burst from the full quiver. All vestiges of somnolence had vanished, and the sparkle in her eyes gleamed like a star in the sky. Resisting the urge to ask where she had obtained her attire, Dashjmar simply fell in her wake alongside Calamer. Neither said a word.

Under the leadership of their respective captain, the soldiers organized themselves by rank. Before Shrie, they parted uniformly. Only Ryanous, Calamer, and Dashjmar ascended the stairs with her to the meet the elders.

The rough grain pressed into her hands as Shrie shoved the doors ajar. She walked into the compound noiselessly, and the elders stood before her. She refrained from bowing. The elders were not fools; they knew why she had come. Ryanous stirred behind Shrie.

"Scouts have brought me the news. The ice people are on our borders," the Chief paused. "The elders have not yet broken a promise made to their people, and you Shrie, of Khaltharnga, have proven yourself to be one of us. Therefore, our word is binding. We swore that our fealty would be yours if the ice people came on the seventh day. They are here, and so I offer you my staff, Maiden of the Wood."

Kneeling, the Chief hoisted his staff in the air, and the elders likewise extended their weapons towards Shrie. Posed in perfect eloquence, their proud heads were now stooped, and their noble hearts beat true. Pleased, Shrie touched every man's staff, allowing each to rise.

"Truly I have succeeded if such honorable men offer their staffs to me. Stand, and come with me to meet our allies. Remember your old strength and recall your former days of battle. Your knowledge will be needed before the end."

"There is one more thing." The Chief uncurled one by one the fingers which comprised his fist. The ring stood out starkly against his skin. Lain's face flashed before Shrie in jagged pieces and in blinding lights. The elders stared at her frozen form. The past leapt before her, grabbing her hands and urging her to relive its colorful images. Slowly, painfully, she grasped each wisp of stray emotion and strained the tips of her fingers to touch the ring in the Chief's hand. The skin on her fingers tingled as she lifted the ring from his keeping and fitted it around her thumb; surely she would return to him.

The hearts of the ice people heaved, pumping vitality through their veins. The small, brown dot before them on the horizon grew and divided into the separate, more recognizable shapes of huts and majestically constructed compounds. Aisii slowed the pace; his hand trembled slightly in anticipation. Five days of strenuous riding had brought them from rolling lands of white, through jagged mountains, and to this knoll of green peace. *Where is the Maiden who calls us so urgently?* With keen eyes, the ice people scanned the empty buildings; and with an indescribable grace, they entered the village.

"I see her," one of the men cried suddenly. "There, in the red robe, she stands waiting."

"Dismount," Aisii commanded. "Show your respect to the one who will lead us into battle."

Obeying, the people slid from the backs of the ice creatures and marched behind Aisii. As they drew closer, they did not falter but studied in awe the one who had called them from their icy caverns. At twenty paces away, Aisii halted and shouted greeting.

"We have been summoned from our dwelling of snow and ice by the one named the Maiden of the Wood. She is backed by her tribe and by the Great Almighty.

What need is so pressing that the last armies of men are called together to fight under her?"

"Dark ages are upon us, Aisii of the ice caverns. The last garrison of the rebels, Quantus Plain, falls, and the Dark One moves with his mobilized armies. Even as I speak, they march."

"Is there no one to resist them?"

"There are some, but not enough. Do you not know the legends? There will be one last battle—one opportunity for us to destroy the foulness that has taken hold of this land."

"You speak our own language in tongue and in battle. Forgive my impudence, but will it be in victory I return, or will there be the graveyard of my people?"

"That is for you to decide, Aisii, when you reach the battlefield. The Almighty is with us; this much you have said yourself. With that thought, perhaps you will change your question."

Aisii smiled. "When do we ride?"

The pale moonlight bounced off the waters of the spring. The soldiers rode in single file, slinging the leather straps of their canteens back over their shoulders. The bottles rested comfortably against their hips. The Commander, the last in this line, accepted with a restless patience the delay and listened as his men filled their canteens. The jungle leaves rustled.

"Sir, what of the supply train survivors? Have you seen to them?"

The whisper sounded strange behind him in the silence of the night, but he answered, "I have."

"What of their spirits?"

"Redael, I recognize your voice. Trust, for once, your own judgment. Do not feel you must submit yourself to me because of my father." He paused. "Their spirits are well enough encouraged by our presence."

"Have you any plans for the attack?"

"What were you thinking?"

Redael paused and then said cautiously, "We advance if possible, but we should not risk an open attack until the end. Kill their leaders from behind and lose as few men as possible. We are clearly outnumbered, so our strategy must be superior."

"Will they not hear the shooting arrows behind them?"

"We must aim from specific heights and locations to make the attack seem like freak accidents as opposed to an organized attack. I do not think the officials will take the time to venture into the jungle to destroy a lone rebel."

"It sounds like you have everything under control, Redael. You don't need me."

"Fill your canteen. The spring is before us."

"Redael, there will be no retreat in this battle," the Commander said lightly, unscrewing the cap from his canteen. The clear, cool spring bubbled over his hand.

"I know that."

"We must dislodge the officials from their forts."

"What forts?"

"If the dark men have any sense, they'll have set up forts across the river to fortify their troops. These forts I shall overrun. You will take your men and organize them accordingly in the morning."

"I want the men situated before then; we must arrive tonight."

"Tonight then, good Redael, we shall arrive."

"Tonight it is."

With his canteen full, Redael rode to the head of the line. The Commander watched solemnly; the plunge into war gaped before them.

Chapter 10

Unnerving silence cascaded over the rebel armies and over the men of Meneas. Gathered like sheep to be slaughtered in the underground fortress of Quantus Plain, they waited as dirt and rock showered them from the weakening ceiling. Their feet shook as powerful vibrations tested the foundations of Quantus Plain. With eyes glued to the solitary, black square in the ceiling, the soldiers watched as the heavy wood creaked under the profound resistance. It was splintering now, bending under the pressure. Their faces were grim, and their stature was perfect; nothing but their eyes revealed their terror. The creak of an arrow pulled too far back on a string prompted the desperate command, "Hold," from Lain, and then with a hideous crunch, the entrance broke. Shards of wood and dust escaped the ceiling's hold in a violent explosion. No one moved, paralyzed by the phantoms of his or her fears. From the entrance appeared a black booted foot, muscular legs, and a thick torso.

"Fire!" The call rang throughout the Great Hall, bouncing rebelliously off the stone walls and back to the soldiers' ears. Even as the words were not fully off Lain's lips, hundreds of arrows pricked the official's porcupine back.

"Halt," Lain cried above the commotion around him. "Only the first column shoots."

The mass of armed men in the Great Hall stirred at the sound marching above their heads. They were caged beasts waiting for the bars of their prison to suffocate them.

"So this is what it looks like," Corious mused as his ears groaned with every reverberation from above.

Lain's stern face gazed stolidly ahead. His hands held the impressive longbow that Corious had once seen hanging on the wall of his quarters. He flinched as the crunches and creaks of artillery met their inundated ears. Lain's mind inadvertently categorized Corious's comment as a useless noise and paid it no mind.

Ree's face mirrored the knowledge of condemnation etched in Lain's. Both were taciturn despite the dark shadows creeping into their views and slipping through the decimated hatch in the first building. Corious's heart caught in his parched throat as men behind him released brief measures of strangulated cries. The menacing shadow dragged its chains upon the ground behind it. From it came a hellish shriek as its chains of bondage broke, and it swept like a ghost into the cavernous expanse of Quantus Plain. Dozens of similar creatures, foreboding in presence and sickening in appearance, poured after it into the opening. Voices in the sea of men screamed in unadulterated terror as the creatures ruthlessly bounded toward the unwavering lines of rebel soldiers. Lain gripped his bow harder. He and the men beside him aimed their bows into the forthcoming onslaught.

"Hold your ground! Pikemen to the fore!"

Corious glanced quickly at Ree. His friend held no bow, but two hunting daggers had settled neatly into his meaty hands.

"Fire at the torgs!"

The diktat came clearly as another line of rebel arrows streaked from their masters' bows and found their marks on the massive torgs' bodies. A jumbled chorus of freakish yells rose from the rebels as the torgs careened blindly into their front lines. Corious watched in horror as the torgs were stabbed to shreds, but not before they had cleared a huge hole in the rebel ranks.

Ree smiled bitterly. "Isn't it an amazing thing? To watch so many good men fight and die for a lost cause in which they will gain nothing?"

Corious placed his hand on Ree's shoulder. "It is quite amazing also, when good men fight for a lost cause only to find it found and won. Open your eyes, and see that with the Almighty, our numbers are greater than theirs."

Ree eyed Corious, puzzled. Corious lifted the corners of his mouth in a weak smile. "Remember the tale of the man in Fal-Nunien who defeated one hundred invaders because he was defending his home?"

Ree took Corious's shoulder in his free hand and whispered sadly, "One hundred is not a very large number."

Their eyes burned, and Corious howled like a wounded animal as hundreds of Shalkans poured through the hatch after the torgs. Corious's shout was lost to the clamor as he was swept into the tide of moving men. The rebels' weary legs and grave hearts remained stalwart as they rushed into battle. Lain took the flag of Quantus Plain in his free hand, and as he raced forward, he shouted only three words.

"For Quantus Plain!"

Corious gave such a cry that his own blood curdled at its ferocity. The Shalkans dropped their rifles. The rebels clashed with the official lines, ripping their dark blue columns into bleeding masses. Taking four hidden knives from his boot, Corious placed them between the fingers of his right hand. He punched with his knifed fist and cleaved the enemy in two with the other. Stepping on a kneeling Shalkan and catapulting himself into the air, Corious landed on the hatch's staircase. He kicked a Shalkan off the stairs who teetered without the use of a recently mangled leg. Ree fought his way up to Corious.

"I like your ingenuity," he shouted over the clamor, gesturing to Corious's right hand.

Corious punched a Shalkan in the arm, robbed the official of his sword, and buried the steel into dark man's heart. Ree leapt past Corious, entangling himself with a fresh group of Shalkans that had pressed through the initial wave of rebel charges.

"Return to formations!"

Ree turned towards Lain. "The men do not want to pull back. They want to fight! We need to retake the field!"

Lain did not listen to Ree's suggestion but rather helped a wounded officer back to his men in the middle of the Great Hall.

"Let's have a peek," Corious said, gesturing towards the Shalkans beyond them.

Ree grinned, "I like that idea—" Two bullets screamed their way past Corious's head.

"Damn it!" Corious exclaimed nervously as he bounded down the stairs.

Rushing to where Lain surveyed the field of battle, Corious and Ree let their previous idea drown in the whiz of bullets. No sooner had the forces been mobilized when more Shalkans streamed in from above.

"Tell Boragheld to attack from behind," Lain yelled to Corious over the noise of clanging weapons.

"They'll be forced to use the back halls; if the enemy follows, they'll be led right to the infirmaries and women and children," Corious protested while ripping his knife from the back of a Shalkan.

"It is a risk worth taking. In fact," Lain paused to swish his sword through the middle of an approaching official who fell screaming to the ground, "make sure the others are well fortified. Do not release the women's army now. Tell Salene and Malov we will need them later."

"I swear to you I will not let one official go beyond the Great Hall, Lain. We will not need the women to fight," Corious promised.

"So be it. Go tell Boragheld my command."

Corious fought his way through the masses of people on the other side of the Hall, searching for Boragheld. Officials streamed through the small hatch while others smashed through the ceiling next to the entrance. The rebels would be able to handle a few officials at one time, but if more came in at once…Corious dreaded the thought of Jenny fighting. It was not that she could not; it was just that she was not battle hardened. Would she be able to find within herself the will to kill?

The battle intensified, and Corious could barely see Boragheld, no less reach him. The mayhem pressed Corious into the second charge of the battle, sweeping him inexorably away from Boragheld and postponing the delivery of the vital message.

Dumped in the center of the Hall by the tides of battle, Corious hastily loaded a bow deserted by its owner. Hunkering behind an overturned crate which served as his scrawny fortification, he sighted an arrow. A Shalkan with a black saber fought nearby. With a forward thrust of his arm, Corious shifted his comrades' attentions to the marked man. Almost instantly, three sets of arrows were trained on the Shalkan's head. At the count of three, they fired. Corious inspected his own arrow zipping through the battle's premises and nailing the Shalkan general in the eye. The eye popped from its socket with a splat. Another arrow landed somewhat lower than his, thumping into the official's right lung. Although the third arrow went slightly amiss, the general's wounds stole his life after torturous minutes of uncontrollable bleeding.

"Good shots, men." Corious thumped the two archers on the back though his stomach turned at the sight of the gore.

The men returned the congratulations with the same enthusiasm before loading their longbows and racking high the number of Shalkans on their casualty lists. Corious loosed several more volleys of arrows into the concentrated enemy masses. On his eleventh shot, he noticed with alarm that the navy and black masses had expanded like a sponge soaked in water. The heaps of Shalkan corpses had deceived him; victory did not grace the rebels. Assailed by an escalating horror, Corious realized the tides of the battle had turned.

The number of officials billowed to their fullest extent as they spread to fill the underground halls. Corious managed to maintain a façade of ease while placing several arrows through a Shalkan's torso. His offensive efforts did no good, and the officials converged on the rebels' easterly flank. As the Shalkans unraveled their wrath, the archers next to him retreated behind the central reserve-flanking units; Corious remained the sole defender of his position. Several of the advancing, blue soldiers suffered the effects of his arrows, choking on their own blood, but the number of bullets aimed at his head increased. By Corious's fifteenth shot, the Shalkans had breached the rebels' side units, and the last line of rebels toppled to their knees in agony.

Blood spurted across the walls in hectic design, and Shalkan warriors dragged rebel entrails over the floor in freakish delight. Some brought the gore to their mouths and stuffed it in their bloated cheeks. Corious could taste the bile in the back of his throat. *I will avenge my comrades,* he vowed. *And I will depend on my knives to scourge the enemy.* In one rushed throw, he heaved the steel into the Shalkans' line of assault. The sharpened metal caught the unwary officials in their upper throats. Their mutilation of the dead ceased, but the others faced Corious in an irrepressible rage. Dropping his bow with his heart pounding out of control, he wasted no time.

Before the ocean of blue-coated Shalkans could swarm him, Corious took a deep breath and charged.

He hurtled over a crate and slit the throat of the first victim. Seizing the next Shalkan's arm, as if dancing, Corious snapped it in two. With a flick of his sword, he dealt him the final blow before being driven back behind the crates. Chasing him, an official leapt onto a crate and fumbled with his gun. In an explosion of movement, Corious kicked the crate out from under the Shalkan. Seeking vengeance, a row of maddened officials loaded their guns in unison. Corious whipped his head back and forth, frantically seeking escape.

Fortuitously, ten of his potential killers crumpled and clutched at chests pierced by the precisely aimed arrows of the Riders of Meneas. They thundered past Corious and overran the Shalkans' position. At last, a reserve flank unit had been summoned from the back of the rebels' forces. Corious sighed gratefully as the familiar soldiers marching in their crimson and gold tunics came to his rescue. As he saluted them, Aban strode by him at the front of the line.

"Aban!" Corious shouted joyfully. "May the Almighty bless you! Victory shall be ours tonight!"

Aban broke into a knowing smile and saluted Corious proudly. During the small break from battle, Corious allowed himself to feel relief. Denying fatigue its desire to ease into his limbs, Corious grabbed his old quiver and bow, collecting his thoughts.

"Corious!" Ree's bloody, dejected, and dirty face appeared from the chaos of clashing bodies. "We need you to the fore now! We—we cannot hold long. Bring a reserve unit!"

Corious did not move even after Ree had disappeared into the confused mass of battle; his mind labored in overdrive as a sobbing figure ran to him. It was Jenny.

"Corious!" Streams of tears spoiled her pretty face. "My...my...my brother—the pub has been taken by Shalkans! There is a battle in there; no, there has been a slaughter! And your friend, the blind one, he led a unit into the carnage...but my brother," she sobbed heavily, "my brother was in there."

Corious cursed under his breath as a misfired bullet pinged off a wall to the left of him.

"Get back to the civilians Jenny! I cannot lose you, neither can your brother."

"But—"

"You must go Jenny. I promise you that we will find your brother. Please, Jenny," he pleaded. Even to himself, his words seemed hollow.

Whimpering, she nodded childishly and ran back through the closest hallway. Corious looked skyward. In the midst of battle, he knelt and prayed, for he knew not what else to do. When the last word left his lips, he drew his sword and careened through anyone, friend or foe, towards the pub, Tar, Jenny's dying brother, and the slaughter.

This was a battle Tar could fight. Nothing surrounded him but the enemy. For once, he had no fear of hitting his fellow warriors, and ever since the officials had raided the pub, Tar had had one sense of direction. His movement was forward, always forward.

Rolling over a table and a Shalkan with a shout, he brandished Lain's gift: his sword. Whistling a series of notes to Faylene, Tar struck while she came screeching to her master's aid. Harassing the Shalkan soldiers, she bought him the extra time needed to swing a stolen musket. His assault bashed an official's legs to a pulp, but he had no time to finish off his mangled victim. Brushing aside another official's groping hand, Tar slashed his sword in a wide circle. Abruptly, he perceived a hiatus in the Shalkan attack, and he listened intently. A hand rustled his shaggy hair.

"We've cornered them in the kitchen, Tar!"

Tar grinned at the reassuring sound of Malov's voice. "If we didn't," Tar remarked, "we'd have no place to chug ale or eat meat over the spittle. That right there is worth a war!"

Malov smiled half-heartedly before retaking command of her unit with Tar on her heels.

"We haven't won yet," Malov reminded him as they strode through the smoky room. "They just withdrew their immediate assault. We should set up a defense using the chairs and tables. Does your unit have enough arrows and bows?"

"Yes, but do you think it wise to slow the offense?"

"They might be able to overwhelm us with a direct frontal assault."

"We'll be receiving reinforcements?"

Malov grunted unhappily. "Don't count on it."

Before they could confer anymore, Tar heard the clangs and clashes of metal on metal. He and Malov steadily pushed the front lines towards the kitchen. He spun freely with his sword and knife in hand, cutting down officials before they could even handle the guns at their belts.

As he navigated around a table, someone from behind clipped his knee with a sword. Tar flinched awkwardly as he spun, his knee bursting with an acute pain. Tar limped behind another table and whistled for Faylene as he braced himself against the table for support. He heard the official circling behind him; he pretended not to notice. The man inched closer and exhaled noisily. Tar bent, and the Shalkan's saber whiffed over his head, throwing the man off balance. Tar lunged and caught the man fatally under the chin with his knife. He was safe, but the exertion had strained his sliced knee ligaments to their maximum capacity. Bright lights flashed as dizzy warning signals in his head. Barely retaining his consciousness, he limped back behind the cover of a table, hoping Malov could hold on her own.

The heat and the stench of gore clogged Ree's nostrils as he labored heavily for fresh air. Blue and grey dots swarmed before his eyes as the residual lactic acid circulated through his weary body. He had abandoned his armor. The necessity for speed had supplanted that of defense. As in the jungle, speed was his best protection.

Ree's and Lain's infantry brigades shook under the pounding; the Shalkans were gaining ground. Though the officials paid dearly for every inch of territory gained, their onslaught accumulated momentum. *There is no need to fear yet.* Ree had successfully transmitted Lain's message to Corious; with Boragheld's reinforcements, the rebels might be able to oust the Shalkans from the Great Hall.

Ree's reflexes gave him just enough time to twist out of the reach of a bayonet. Rapidly, he knocked the pointed weapon away with a broad sword that only a man of his build could wield. He swung it furiously in a circle and cleaved a Shalkan in half. Planting his feet firmly on the ground, Ree directed his attention back to the frontal assault. The lines of rebels faltered. *We cannot back down now.* As a concentrated volley of bullets hissed past his face, he rushed to the front lines and dove to the ground like a diver cleanly slicing the water's surface. Despite his finesse, a gritty bullet bit into the top of his ear. Ree grimaced, gritting his teeth while the pain consumed his ear like a wildfire. *Do not lose focus; do not lose focus,* he repeated to block the burning flesh from his mind. Scrambling to his feet, he tore apart the unprepared line of Shalkan riflemen. Hitting one man with the hilt of his gun, Ree then reversed the motion and drove the metal shaft of his sword through the unprotected torso of the man next to him. The distorted Shalkan writhed on the ground and died in a sticky, red pool.

Without pausing, Ree grabbed a dagger concealed beneath his outer tunic. With a hasty flick of his wrist, the knife spun from his hand. A vigilant Shalkan ducked in time, but the knife thumped into the lower gut of the commander behind him. Hurriedly sliding to his knees and holding a discarded metal breastplate before him, Ree's arms shuddered as five bullets thudded into his improvised shield. The fifth one shattered the abused armor into tiny fragments and spat the shards into Ree's face and shoulders.

"Go to hell!" Ree shouted as the metal blasted into his right cheek and mercilessly clawed his at face. He flung what remained of the armor at the enemy. *Where are the reinforcements?* An infuriated Ree was about throw himself once more into battle when Lain pulled him into a pocket of safety. Ree's torn face did not faze him.

"We need to hold a brief council," he panted. His sword dripped with dark drops of blood. "We must maintain a plan of attack. We should have had the Shalkans pinned by now. What happened?"

"I relayed the message to Corious, but I did not wait for his consent. I thought he would obey orders. Reinforcements should have been applied to our easterly side and flank by now."

Lain ran a dirty hand over his shaved head. "Follow me," he commanded. "I've put Marcelus and Perry in charge of our brigades even though they should be at the council. I have formulated a plan to keep the Shalkans at bay long enough for us to either receive reinforcements from the outside or to overtake the Shalkans ourselves."

Ree strode behind Lain, watching the brave men rush towards battle as he walked to safety. *How many of them will see tomorrow?* The first stone columns in the back of the Great Hall came into view, and the insane clamor of battle died gradually. Ree finally sheathed his sword and trudged behind Lain dutifully. Finally, Lain found the room and pushed open its door; a flood of torchlight met Ree's bloodshot eyes. Shelves of books and maps occupied the room, but the old stone floor had not been trod upon for many years. The makeshift council had violated the room's silence and its peace. Lain counted heads as Ree flopped despairingly into the nearest chair.

"We're missing Corious, Malov, and Captain Hans, but all else are present."

Ree perked up at the sound at Malov's name before a wave of sickening grief swept over him. He blinked twice and sunk into his chair. *She may not have been notified, or maybe she's safe with the rest of the civilians.* His mind snapped back to attention when Lain began to rapidly enumerate the specifics of his plan.

"What to do now, gentlemen, is the question that must be asked and answered. We simply do not have enough reinforcements to push them back from the way they came. If we cannot repulse their frontal assault, we must either retaliate from the eastern or western halls."

Ree observed intently as Lain studied an interior map of Quantus Plain.

"We have five sets of unequally numbered reinforcement units left. We might be able to encircle the Shalkans if we send men in brigades around the officials' flank. If they are repulsed, we would pull back and hope for the best. I do not have time to argue with you, but do you support my idea with at least half a heart?"

Just then, a messenger popped his head into the light of the doorway. "Master Lain!" He saluted hastily as he tried to regain his breath. "I have been sent to report that a force of our rebels led by the blind boy retook the pub! They've trapped the officials in the kitchen. They wish to burn the entire mess of them and then conduct a flanking assault to disrupt the Shalkans' flow of troops. They ask for your permission."

"We must seize this opportunity," Lain said; he did not face the messenger but rather the map of their underground fortress. "Captains shall return to their battle stations and follow our plan of action while Tar flanks the Shalkans from behind. You there, messenger," Lain said, pointing a finger at him. "Give my permission to Tar to carry his goal to the desired end. Waste no time."

The man dashed from the doorway, his footsteps fading into the sounds of the ongoing struggle. Lain addressed the dozen people sitting before him.

"That goes for you too. Tell Perry and Marcelus to hold their positions while the unit commanders of the westerly and easterly units push forward and around. We cannot afford to lose this battle."

Twelve chairs scraped against the stone floor as the unit commanders, lords, and captains exited the room in haste. With their mission at the forefront of their minds, they unsheathed their swords and stepped into the battle raging before their eyes.

Corious, Malov, and Tar each gripped a wooden shaft which, at the top, burned and flickered like a snake's tongue. The smoke singed their clothes, and the acrid smell made their noses scrunch in disapproval. The Shalkans had fortified themselves in the kitchen area; the previously busy cooks and kitchen hands now lay slaughtered beneath the debris and dead bodies. The rebel force had barred the entrance, sealed the stone wall with sticky tar, and trapped them.

"They have come, and we shall not let them leave." Corious spoke to the units of Tar and Malov. "Show them no mercy. Let them have the kitchen if they so dearly want it. Just leave it a burned heap." Corious's face was drawn.

When he thought of the mutilated, young body that was Jenny's little brother lying atop the heap of rubble, he felt no remorse for the official blood shed by his hands. The boy had been tortured, and there had been no final stroke to end his misery. Joining an injured but rejuvenated Tar, Corious stuffed his wildly burning torch through a small hole and ignored the startled shouts from inside the kitchen. The wood beams cracked as the room filled with smoke. Tar limped next to Corious, his clothes bearing the stains of battle. His shuffle did not escape Corious's notice.

Rushing towards them was the courier with his belated message. He coughed from the mushrooming smoke but managed to yell, "You have Master Lain's permission. Attack at will. Lain wishes you success."

"It's been taken care of," Corious responded, abandoning Tar in order to direct his ragtag band of rebels into formation. The courier nodded curtly before stepping in with Corious's men. "We will attack in lines of four and columns of ten. Seven groups in all. We'll give the signal for the all-out charge. About face, and march!"

The tramping of boots overwhelmed the forlorn sounds inside the pub as the rebels wound through the vacant room. They entered a ravaged but sparingly guarded hallway. It would lead them into the west part of the Great Hall—the part predominantly controlled by the Shalkans. Corious waved his sword, and his troops progressed into a jog as they neared the Hall. Shalkans yelled raucously in surprise as Corious raced forward, his troops melting out of formation as they poured from behind him. His boots clicked against the stone floor lighter and faster in the frantic sprint. He waved his sword once more, needlessly, and then careened into the cavernous Great Hall. Bullets zipped dangerously by his frame. Almost at the end of his feverish dash, Corious collided fearlessly with the regrouping Shalkan lines.

A wave of sheer adrenaline flew through him as he acquainted his sword with fresh Shalkan blood. Taken off-guard, the officials could offer little resistance.

Lowering his head, Corious bowled over an official. A sickening crunch in his shoulder lessened the vitality of his attack, and he faltered in his step. Flailing his arms to regain his balance, Corious helplessly found himself splayed on the floor. The opposing Shalkan struck, slashing his gun into Corious's exposed torso. In a shuddering paroxysm, Corious's stomach spewed its contents onto the floor. The repugnant smell of the vomit piling around his face compelled him to stagger to his feet. Swinging wildly, as though in a drunken swagger, Corious managed to maim his attacker.

Choking slightly as the hair fell in front of his face, Corious spat on the Shalkan whom he held at sword point. With a clouded look, he spoke quietly, "I will kill you."

The Shalkan's gun clattered to the floor. "I surr—"

Corious bashed the Shalkan in the head with his sword hilt. His stomach heaved again at the wretched stench and macabre scene before his veteran eyes. There was nothing glorious about killing; the glory of battle, both past and present, lived as a grim illusion.

Tar hobbled beside him. His sword showed signs of recent use. "Corious, our attack has succeeded at last. We must pursue the officials!"

Corious watched as though from a distance as Tar limped unwaveringly after the retreating Shalkans. Faylene gripped his arm; her crooked smile unnerved Corious. Tar was right: the Shalkans had not expected a renewed attack. The advantage had been torn from the Shalkans. *I am not needed.* Sheathing his sword, Corious trudged through the halls, away from the battle.

As men of action and duty, neither Perry nor Marcelus stayed behind the protection of their front lines. Perry, in control of Lain's regiment, defended their coveted position, but the dreadful deadlock dampened the men's spirits. No longer could his words of encouragement carry them forward.

Perry whipped an arrow from his depleted quiver, notching the sharpened shaft to his bow. Marcelus tackled an official as Perry released the arrow. Taking a second to reach its destination, the shaft connected with a Shalkan officer's flabby, lower jaw, causing the official to jerk sideways off the horse that he had brought through the widening hatch.

"Leave them leaderless and you may as well have killed them all," Perry muttered, smugly.

Marcelus laboriously threw a Shalkan off his back, sending him back into the sea of teeming men. Perry nocked his bow and rushed to Marcelus, who, being inundated with enemy sabers had little room to maneuver. He aimed hastily. The arrow spun crazily astray. Without Marcelus to destroy immediate attackers, Perry discarded the bow and brandished his shamshir. Upon seeing a fresh column of sleek and armed Shalkans, Marcelus sputtered a foul word while Perry gulped down the huge lump rising in his throat. The effort to keep his men organized and courageous was futile. Marcelus picked a forgotten knife from the ground, and with a growl, he sent it spinning at the approaching enemy.

"God there's a lot of them. Where are the rest of our units?" Perry complained to distract himself from the assailing terror.

Marcelus let out a satisfied grunt when his second knife finished the work which his first had started. The Shalkan fumbled to dislodge the two knives that had struck him. His inexperienced hands twisted the metal into his internal organs, and with a hideous scream, he died.

Official bullets answered the flight of the second rebel knife. Momentarily handing the treasured shamshir to Marcelus, Perry aimed with his bow. Despite the commotion, the arrow deviated only slightly from its course, rocketing into the shoulder of an official. Within seconds, the rebel lines collided with the frontal columns of Shalkan infantry. Perry grabbed his sword from Marcelus's sweating hand.

As the Shalkans battered the rebels from their firm, defensive position in the Great Hall, Marcelus spun his swords in dizzying whirlwinds. He took no time to admire his skill. The Shalkan before him wielded both a saber and a gun; Marcelus dropped a sword and drew his pistol. *I'll match you weapon for weapon.* Stepping backwards, he extended his arm. The Shalkan fell easily before Marcelus could even pull the trigger. Turning to glare at Perry, Marcelus found his comrade admiring the accuracy of his own shot from a safe ten yards away.

"Coward," Marcelus mumbled before raising his voice so Perry could hear him. "You are cheating, Perry! Fight like a man. Get a little closer!"

Perry said nothing but put another arrow through a Shalkan nearing Marcelus.

"Aauggh!" Marcelus roared in recurrent ire. He stopped. *What's going on?* The rebels had shifted and spread their lines thin, concentrating their numbers in the flanks. Rebels in the center fiercely united their army, but the Shalkan commanders did not order an attack. Perry strode to the stationary Marcelus and pointed. An officer on horseback swept around the Shalkan's front lines, reeling his men away from the battle.

"I don't like that man," he muttered as he aimed his bow.

Marcelus snorted. "You have too much fun cheating."

Perry aimed. "It is hardly cheating." Perry's arrow buried itself in the officer's head. Marcelus cringed as the Shalkan head snapped off its neck and as the official plummeted from his horse. Mayhem consumed the remaining infantry.

Marcelus grinned. "There is opportunity here," he declared fervently as he ran off.

Perry raised his eyebrows as his comrade zigzagged after the officer's horse. "Fool," Perry said admiringly as he loosed an arrow into the confused lines of Shalkan infantry.

Marcelus sprinted awkwardly towards the panicked horse. He hurdled over the copious heaps of dead bodies. He ducked and swerved arbitrarily, saving himself from the shots of the stanch Shalkan riflemen; the officials had terrible aim. Nearing the hysterical horse, Marcelus admired its rich, tan coat, black mane, and powerful lower legs. The eye coverings which had once protected the horse from the gruesome scene had fallen.

Marcelus pitied the scared animal. With one last stride, he leapt over the dead officer's body and draped himself over the rearing steed. The horse did not appreciate Marcelus's feat, and it took off like a bullet, plowing through the Shalkan lines. Marcelus howled in earnest, laboring to fully mount the horse. After burying his hands in the thick mane, he finally pulled himself into a sitting position and found the reins. Once he had established control, Marcelus hastily tied a scrap from his shirt about the horse's head to shield its eyes. He silently thanked the Almighty as the horse slowed to an easy gallop but then rescinded his thanksgiving as the Shalkans trained hundreds of guns on his head. Marcelus spurred the horse ahead, bouncing madly through startled faces. He smiled subtly as the Shalkans parted before him.

"Hya! Heayah!" he cried, directing his steed in a semicircle. With his shamshir, he cut a graceful arc in the air, cleaving heads from bodies. Clearing his way to the widening gap between the rebel and Shalkan lines, Marcelus kicked the horse. "Come! Let us take the field of battle and claim it for ourselves! It is ours and always will be ours! Hyeah! Come with me!" Marcelus slowed to a canter as the Shalkans limped back to their organizing lines. He watched as the begrimed rebel army regrouped in the center. The men were ready to vanquish and conquer, but Lain rode from the back of the Great Hall.

"Marcelus!" Lain thundered. His voice overpowered the suddenly quiet Hall. "Captain Marcelus," he repeated, saluting his friend as he fit a helmet over his head, "I thank you for your leadership and for Lord Perry's leadership in my stead. You are each to take command of a flank unit. You specifically are to meet with Corious and conduct a counterattack. Do you understand and concur?"

Marcelus spoke for everyone. "We concur!" The men rallied to their leader.

"To vengeance and to victory!" The men loosed a rowdy whoop. Lain raised his sword above his head and rode to the fore of his troops. "For your brothers!" Lain called, and the echoes of his cry reached his ears even through the barrier of his heavy, metal helmet. "For your family! For your lives! For peace!"

His men shouted so earnestly and vigorously that they drew Lain into the momentous charge. He galloped ahead on his white spotted horse, waving his sword in front of him like a deranged berserker. Meanwhile, the Shalkans braced themselves, prepared to keep the charging rebels at bay.

Pleased to find the left flank primed and ready, Marcelus galloped to his men while the rifle bullets and rebel arrows whizzed by in rapid exchanges. Each side fought to clear the battlegrounds. Locating the three units of which he was to take command, Marcelus saluted and dropped from the back of his newly acquired horse.

"Greetings, gentlemen and lieutenants."

The lieutenants saluted and sheathed their drawn swords. "The men are ready, Captain," the shorter one announced. "Give the word, and we will have tucked another victory under our belts by nightfall."

"Is that so? Well, since you organized these men, I want you to lead the two units behind mine, the ones which support my leading unit, understood?"

The men scampered to command their divisions.

Marcelus saluted the men on the front lines and brought the archers to the fore. *We'll organize*, Marcelus decided, *then we'll strike them as lightning does water. Won't that be a shocker?*

"Draw weapons!" His rebel lines moved in unison as the infantry unsheathed their swords and as the archers methodically loaded their bows. A volley of musket fire exploded around him, propelling rock fragments and rebels into the air.

"Archers, fire!" Marcelus waved his hand while pointing his sword. "Loose the arrows into their ranks!"

Arrows spilled from the rebel units, and Shalkans slipped to their knees as their lives drained. Marcelus bit his lip, waiting until the tension mounted unbearably to voice the command. Issued from a parched throat, it was a laughable yell, but it struck a cord in the hearts of the rebels, and they sprung from their formations into a mad flow of sprinting soldiers. Marcelus strove forward, spearheading the push.

Smashing a hole through the once-solid ranks of armored soldiers, he ran an official through and dragged him along on the floor until he could free his sword. Repulsed by their headless comrade, the Shalkan defenses broke as the rebels advanced. Marcelus waited for the infantry to fill the fissure which he had nicely cut for them. Catching a glimpse of the shorter lieutenant, he shouted for him to direct his unit to the left. The lieutenant paused to register the command and was shot twice in the chest.

"Blast it, that bast—" Marcelus never finished his sentence, for he felt a strange pressure against his sternum. He gasped for breath as he felt the second and then the third explosions shatter his breastplate. Gasping in pain as wretched, whirling visions flocked before his eyes, Marcelus studied his tunic. His hands began to shake. His stomach turned upside down as he discovered shards of metal sticking from the cloth of his shirt; his hands were damp with fresh blood. Kicking his horse weakly, he fled, choking on his thickening saliva. A fiery sensation bloomed in his abdomen. The pain intensified, but his concentration sharpened. With a new determination, he ripped the pieces of breastplate from his ravaged skin.

"I have a debt to repay. They ask for their deaths!" Marcelus whispered in anger as he spun his sword above his head in a frenetic display of resolve. His troops roared despite their dying masses; their fanatical captain would lead them.

"Push forward! We are condemned if we stay still. Push forward and make them die by the touch of our steel!"

Marcelus tossed aside caution along with his pulverized armor. The Shalkan guns fell steadily silent as the rebels rallied and broke into wide columns, rolling the Shalkan flank like it was a dirty carpet. To those who had nothing to lose, the Shalkans were a hollow enemy.

One soldier next to Marcelus saluted him merrily. "You know Cap'n Marcelus, this isn't very gentlemanly like, but it sure is nice to win!"

Marcelus laughed; they were no longer content with a simple retreat. Only the ruin of the entire Shalkan force could satisfy them now.

Corious stopped at the pub. The fire had weakened into isolated spurts of flame. Wiping his smoke and dust-stricken eyes, he spit inside the doorway. Whether or not it was moral, he had little regret for what he had done. He knew he was shirking his duty; Lain had entrusted him to specific units. He had simply walked off.

Searching for Jenny, he wandered through the smaller, interlocking stairs and hallways. The ceiling above him rumbled with cannon and troop movements exceeding any number he might imagine. He stepped down a stair. A torch toppled, and a crash resounding in the Great Hall several circuitous corridors away extinguished its flame. Corious scooped the ashes back into the handle. As he rested it between its two prongs, he hoped the light bearer would see better days.

Corious awkwardly felt his way through a passageway devoid of light. Passing huddled masses of people, he nodded to them. They stared back in fascination; whether it was because he still lived or because he had left the battlefield, he did not know.

A young boy hushed his whimpering sister. "Cap'n! Are we winnin' our fight in the Great Hall? Those dark men gonna' come down on us soon 'nough, right?"

Corious answered neither in a reprimanding way nor in a confident one. "Young sir, many, many men wielding the saber are dying upon it today."

The boy's face crumpled. Corious did not reply; he continued walking. He walked to find Jenny. They knew why he walked.

"She's gone inside," one gangly boy said, pointing to a door.

Corious pressed his lips together. "Yes."

He found the door partially open. There, on the bed, was Jenny. She sat on the edge, surrounded by her weeping brothers and sisters. They clung to her, but only she remained in his sight. Leaving his sword and scabbard outside the room, Corious heard his footsteps resound against the stone floor of the room. Jenny stifled her tears. He forced himself to look her straight in the eye, and when she saw his determined but gentle gaze she spoke quietly.

"Captain, you come to me when the time is most dire and when Lain needs you most. Why?"

Corious took off his cape and knelt to embrace her on the bedside. Jenny broke into an emotional sob, and she laid her head upon Corious's shoulder. She drenched his soiled shirt. He let a tear squeeze between his closed eyelids, and he stroked Jenny's hair.

"Never mistake my love for you, Jenny. Please, never forget it either."

Jenny did not reply, but buried her head deeper into Corious's shoulder. His encircling arms did not leave her; he could not move when Jenny needed him the most. *This is what life means; this is the glory I want in life.* He lifted Jenny's head gently by her chin and turned to sit on the bed beside her. The children moved aside for him, oddly quiet as though they realized the moment's significance. Corious had no concept of time, and for precious minutes he breathed in the peaceful smell of Jenny's hair. It was a frozen moment, and he did not want it to end. But her hand melted into his, and he felt her slender fingers turn his face towards hers.

"Corious, your heart tells you to stay here so it may beat alongside mine, but," her voice cracked, "you are a captain of a great people, and you belong not with a woman when battle rages. It is your duty to save our people. Please, go, for me."

Corious's lips touched Jenny's, and he held her once more before rising.

"I will return to you, Jenny." He paused to retake his weapons, and then he dashed from the room and into the smoke-filled hallway. Ashes crunched beneath his feet, and he dragged his fingertips against the blackened wall.

"The Cap'n returns!" one of the younger boys cried as Corious reappeared. "He goes back to battle!"

"Aye," Corious called, "to battle! Pray for Quantus Plain and her warriors."

"Yes Cap'n," the young voice called back to him. "Momma, Cap'n Corious says to pray to the Almighty!"

"Yes, that is good." The voices of the women faded; they were not important.

"What good is the Almighty if captains do not show up to lead their troops."

Corious stopped in his tracks.

"Ree..."

"You abandoned your troops, Corious." An exchange of fire outlined Ree's figure. "I will believe in no Almighty unless I come from this battle unscathed. I will most likely die before sunrise, and my only hope was to die beside a friend."

"Don't say that, Ree." Corious ground his teeth. "No one will die."

"Why did you leave us? Did you see there would be no winning? Did you know that we would all fall here?"

"Stop it," Corious bellowed. "We're going to attack the flank and surround them, do you hear me? We're going to push them back!"

"The troops have been forced to the second corridors. Our charge failed when there was no one to attack the flank. That plan is over and done. You weren't there, Corious."

"Don't put this on me, Ree." Corious shook. "Get out of my way." He tried to push by, but Ree did not move.

"Since when have friends swapped blows?" Ree asked sadly.

Corious halted, and his eyes closed. The moment lingered in an almost palpable, painful tension before Corious found his voice. "I'm sorry, Ree." He hung his head. "Allow me to fight with you once more. I swore to Lain I would not let one dark man leave the Great Hall alive. I wish to keep that promise."

"Then to our deaths!"

Ree turned, running through the sepulchral halls, and Corious followed, his boots leaving hard indents in the settled dust.

"To our deaths, then," he echoed.

"Hold, men!"

Lain's troops faltered under the onslaught. Tar's men had issued from the pub and joined Corious's recently arrived troops.

"There will be no retreat," Tar informed his men as they marched from the pub into the second corridors towards the battle. "If the dark men chase us past this hall, there is no escape; we will be trapped. Roken has led the women and children back into the fourth corridor, but once the officials take the second, they have won. Our only choice is to repulse them. Is that clear?"

"Yes, Sir," his troops called from behind him.

"Good, for the sounds of battle approach, and my blood boils with excitement. Tell me when I can wield my sword without fear. Remember, our threadbare lines have encouraged our retreat. We must overcome our weaknesses."

"Now," alerted one of his men. "The enemy is before us!"

With a bloodcurdling yell, Tar bounded forward. He no longer feared battle. It was the one place where his blindness no longer hindered him and where he was no longer useless. His men depended on him, and they gave him space to swing freely. Tar's sword connected and slid off metal. Grinning, he listened to everyone's footwork in front of him. It did not matter whether it was careless or intricate; every movement Tar calculated and analyzed. Perfecting his form, he straightened the arm brandishing his sword. Whistling for Faylene as he rid the Hall of another Shalkan, he anticipated her swooping wings and shrill cry. The forces behind him swelled.

"Men, forward, march! Archers, release!" Corious had come.

"Tar, I am impressed." Ree had accompanied him.

"Aim more to your left. You don't want to end up stuck by a friendly arrow."

Tar whipped his sword to the left, and he heard the choking of another Shalkan.

"You took my man."

"Sorry, Ree, but please don't talk too much; it might distract me."

"As you wish, warrior," Ree answered stonily, but Tar detected a hint of pride in the hard voice.

The air left Tar's lungs in a grunt as he struck. This time, something stopped his sword. He heard the heavy boots scrape against the floor, and he moved parallel to their direction. Intuition warned him to be careful, and he whistled again for Faylene. Shrieking, she landed on his arm and then flew off, attacking something he could not place. Hooves hit the floor. In alarm, he leapt away.

"I've got this taken care of," Ree yelled to him. Running alongside the rearing horse, Ree watched in amazement as Tar easily avoided the careening creature and then rushed again into battle. "Don't let them route you, men!"

"Aim for the rider!"

Arrows flew from all directions to hit the rearing horse in the chest. The horse stumbled, and the rider slipped off the saddle, plugged with arrows. The rebels cheered.

"Nice work, men!" Corious shouted before he joined Ree.

"So we fight again side by side."

"It's the only way I like to do it."

Ree and Corious cut through officials as a rapier cuts through grass. Their strokes improved as they fought and rediscovered the rhythm of the jungle. Losing track of time, the two felt nothing—not the sweat rolling off their faces, not the smells of smoke and dirt and blood, and not the sore muscles that yearned to stop. In imitation, their men began to pair in twos or threes, abandoning their traditional formations.

Baffled, the officials began to falter and fall. The rebels neared the middle of the hall, and their distinctive cry could be heard behind the thin line of officials separating them from Perry and Marcelus. Sweeping to the right, Ree caught glimpses of Perry and then heard Faylene's piercing cry. Worried, Corious came in Ree's wake and then witnessed as Marcelus, stained with blood, plunged through the officials with a greeting.

"Tar! Ree and Corious! How fares your battle down there?"

"Well, Lord Marcelus! Is that your own blood?"

"There is no victory without sacrifice. Shall we meet Lain? I haven't seen him lately."

"Aye, sounds like a good plan. Are the officials out of the second corridor?"

"Mostly, and those that aren't should beware, for the women warriors roam those areas and are more vicious than ever. Have you seen them fight?"

"No, what of Malov?" Ree asked suddenly.

"I hear she leads them well, but I would not entangle myself with a woman warrior if I were you, Ree," Marcelus sincerely advised.

"And why not?"

"She might be stronger than you, and it's never good to encourage them, the women you know, to be stronger—they'll take advantage of that."

Ree smiled wryly and tucked his worries about Malov into a corner of his mind; he did not have the energy to think about both himself and Malov. He, Corious, Tar, and now Perry and Marcelus led a unified force, and the officials melted before them. Leaderless, causeless, and surrounded, any semblance of their resistance rapidly dissipated.

Boragheld and Lain careened through the dwindling officials. Tar had already torn ahead, providing a brief lull in which Corious could catch his breath. The minute was precious and savored. The memory of rest was kept in Corious's mind to enjoy later, for the taste of victory was ready and sweet upon his tongue.

"Do you believe in an Almighty now?" Corious called to Ree as they pounded ahead.

"The battle is not over yet," Ree replied grimly, rushing to hew down the officials. "That's fifty-one under my belt," Ree said nonchalantly as he worked his sword through the air in perfect form. "And that's fifty-two."

"That's it?" Corious said in disbelief as he struggled against three of the enemy.

"Why, how many have you to claim?" Ree asked dryly.

"About the same," Corious grunted as he threw an attacker to the floor. Using his armor protected elbow, he slammed it into an official's chest and ran his sword through the last remaining official. "But now I think I have you beat."

Ree's reply was masked by an excited rebel cry.

"There's Lain and Boragheld yonder!"

A neighing of horses reverberated against the walls of the darkening halls, signaling the rebel advance. Slipping around the other rebels before him, Corious raced to the front line. Not fifty feet from him, Lain bore down upon the Shalkans from his horse. Hacking his way through the cornered officials, Corious's attention was once again directed upward by Faylene's piercing cry.

"The officials flee up the hatch! Archers, to the fore!" Corious enjoined.

The officials scattered. Like small spiders climbing up their web, they struggled to get through the broken hatch. Archers shot and hit most of their targets, and two or three arrows pierced the falling victims. The rebel forces seemed to multiply in light of the smaller enemy.

"At last, victory has touched these halls," Lain exclaimed. "After them! Up the hatch, rebels. Chase your foe!"

In an exuberant charge, the rebels hurdled over dead bodies as they flew up the ladder. The first to the ladder was Tar, and he raised his fist as he threw open the hatch. Bursting through the opening was not his fist, however, but rather the snout of an enormous, black cylinder. It met him eye to eye, but he saw it not.

"Tar!" Ree screamed, "Cannon!"

Confused, Tar reached out his hand and touched the barrel. His eyes opened wide as the clink of the cannon being loaded registered in his mind. Hollering, he jumped from the ladder, taking some of the others with him. In a detonation of colossal proportions, the rebels withered and fell. Blackness settled.

Hideous cries and Lain's voice calling for a retreat overwhelmed the rebels. Men ran and dragged the injured behind them as blasts carved giant holes in the Hall's floor. Corious pounded to the front, trying to find Tar, and Ree directed men behind the columns of the back hall. The siege of Quantus Plain had taken an unexpected turn.

Chapter 11

Smoke clouded Redael's vision. "The entire field has been taken!" he muttered to himself in amazement. Riding in the shadowed edge of the vegetation before the river, he sedulously memorized the numerous positions of the officials, at least those he could determine through the heavy artillery fire and through the black sails which had beaten them to their destination. Black and gray lines of endless infantrymen spanned the plain before him. Wreckage from the one ship that had hit the barrier rose from the depths of the water and floated upon its surface. Like shrouded wraiths, the ships guarded the river.

Into the dismal air, he lifted his arm. His men in the trees flexed their arrows on the strings; he let his arm fall. Arrows zigzagged randomly and haphazardly across the river. They cut through the sails and dropped like rain into the ranks of Shalkans across the river. Several of the enemy slumped unnoticed to the ground before a perceptive captain turned.

With his eyes, the Shalkan scoured the ghostly apparitions of the ships before rumbling something in an abrasive, guttural tone. Answering volleys of bullets lurched into the trees. The officials scanned the bank, but after several minutes of no return fire, the dark men lowered their weapons and returned to their ranks. Everything had gone as planned. Redael nodded to a man hidden in the brush before him.

With the gesture, the rebel slunk forward. Joining the others situated at the bottom of the bank, he drew his sword. When his foot broke the surface of the water, Redael signaled. The archers showered another round of arrows upon the enemy; more dark men fell. Slinking low to the ground, the rebels advanced across the river. The water rippled about their knees, and the black sails hid their presence. The water reached their necks. Holding the swords above their heads, they swam around and under the hull. Nothing stirred.

Stealing downriver, three other groups dipped into the murky water. Focusing on the opposite side of the bank, Redael trained his eyes on the spot where the men would rise. As his arm dropped yet again to his side, arrows spurted from the trees. Angrily, the dark men returned the fire, but their inaccurate shots collided mostly with the sleek, black hulls in the river.

Curses and aggravated grunts filled the air as the officials on land curiously pulled an arrow from one of their men.

"This is rebel doing!" one roared.

"Where are they?"

"Go find them!" one who was obviously the leader yelled, shoving two men towards the river.

The two officials eased themselves to the edge of the river; they were the bait. The commander waited anxiously; no shots were fired. The doomed Shalkans shifted from foot to foot. Redael's tongue slid over his front teeth nervously as his men rose from the river and plastered themselves to the other side of the bank.

"Get closer!" the official demanded in a harsh, grating voice.

Snarling, but obeying, the officials took another step; the top part of their boots hung over the edge.

"Now!" Redael whispered to himself.

In a volatile, vicious struggle, the rebels dragged the officials into the river, triggering a round of fire from the enemy's back lines. As the bullets showered harmlessly into the water, the rebels strangled their victims.

"What is this rebel trickery?" the leader rasped. "Eliminate them! Cover the river!"

Several pairs of officials darted to the bank and lowered themselves from the higher ground; this time the skirmish was bloody and loud. Redael cringed as the ships woke from their slumber and as men issued onto the decks. With skilled bows, the rebels in the trees shot hurriedly; they did not wait for Redael's signal. An entire line of officials marched to the edge of the river, and those who escaped the arrows loaded their guns.

With a wave of his hand, Redael summoned the men behind him. In unison, they rose and skulked through the brush. Redael led them, knife in mouth and sword in hand. The rebels, like water rushing over stones, flew over the embankment and into the river. Arrows drenched the ships with straight shafts, and covered by the fire, the rebels lurched from the river onto the wet mud. The atrocious sounds of battle awakened around him.

"For Quantus Plain!"

"Kill them!"

"For Quantus Plain!"

The men fought their way up the steep incline and clashed brutally with the flank of the officials. Using the primitive tactics Redael had taught them, the rebels bashed the officials. There was no fair fighting in war. With a rebel cry, he plunged into battle.

"There she is," Logan said quietly. "Let's take her back boys. Bring her starboard. Prepare the cannons."

"They are ready," Hitachi responded, glancing at his brother. Logan held his wounded arm, which was swathed in dirty strips of a shirt, awkwardly at his side. Though he swayed back and forth with every movement of the ship, he concentrated on the mouth of the river. The former slaves and remaining rebels scurried about the ship.

"Don't bring her over the barricade. I want to be able to back out of here," Logan commented. "We don't want to become broken shards of wood. If the defenses of Quantus Plain have fallen, our foe is greater than he once seemed."

One of the freed slaves kneeled before him. "The cannonballs have been heated, Logan of Quantus Plain."

"Stand up. Do not kneel to me. When we are close enough, Hitachi will give you the signal, then aim for the ammunition storage in the first ship. It will be towards the back. Actually, Hitachi, position the cannons for him, will you? You were always better at angles, and we can't waste these shots."

"Indeed. We only have one round of the heated balls ready."

"We approach. Go."

Entangled with the rebels, the officials were unable to utilize their guns. Swords and bayonets clanged against one another, and a terrible grating noise overrode it all. Overwhelmingly outnumbered, the rebels were being beaten into the ground. Redael desperately fought and commanded his men to do the same. The ships were loading the cannons.

Squinting through the small space between the porthole and the mouth of the cannon, Hitachi ransacked his memory. The ammunition room was in the back and center of the ship. Luckily for the rebels, the black-sailed ships had maintained a straight course into the river, and their target stared directly at them. Twisting the cannon slightly this way and then that way, Hitachi was finally satisfied. At that moment, he covered his ears and ran behind the giant machines screaming, "Fire!"

The heat from the detonation crawled up Redael's back; he leaned forward and then helplessly waited for the flames to devour him. They did not.

"The ships burn!"

Disconcerted, Redael stumbled forward. Fire raced across the river, leaping from ship to ship. Bodies and planks floated away from the battle scene. A lone ship rose against the sky unharmed. His men did not see the ship, and they cheered in anticipation.

"Hurrah! Forward!"

The small band of men remaining surged forward, and the officials shrieked in rage as fire exploded in the middle of their lines. Chaos reigned. Redael hurriedly took a head count. Too many men had died; too many had suffered. They had to vanish, retreat into the forest while there was still time.

"To the Halfast!"

Redael let the officials gain ground. Taking one, two, and three steps back, Redael's men fled through the flames sputtering instantaneously to life. Diving into the river, he swam past the scarred remains of the official ships: charred chunks of distorted wood. Crawling onto the opposite bank with sopping clothes and exhausted limbs, he narrowed his eyes. The single ship guarded the mouth of the river, its berth incessantly vomiting cannonballs.

"What's going on?" the muffled voice of a bewildered rebel asked.

"A cannonball must have hit the ammo storage in another ship, setting off a chain reaction." Redael paused. "Into the woods," he enjoined, pulling himself up the bank and into the woods. The officials had not bothered to plague the rebels beyond the line of fire, and so Redael studied the ship one last time. "Something is amiss," Redael muttered to himself.

"Why does the ship still shoot?"

"Perhaps they think we are still on the battlefield," another soldier chimed.

Redael neither disputed nor endorsed the suggestion. Instead, he busied himself by assembling his men in the woods. Disappointment screwed his insides into tight, grooved knobs of guilt. "We have done enough damage today." The tattered men were reflected in his bleary eyes. "I plan to meet the Commander at the forts. March, soldiers, but take heart. This battle is far from won."

Empty barracks with sunken eyes stared openly at the Commander. Crouched in the brush, he examined the burnt wood and weakening walls. The identical buildings were bathed in a mysterious mist. No guns challenged the rebels physically, but bloated cadavers accosted their desire to enter the derelict structures on the river. Waves slapped against the rock and reminded him of their shallow, watery protection. The range of the sleeping ships' cannons would not extend this far.

A rustling in the brush froze his body motionless, but his eyes searched madly the area before him. A head and body popped up from the leafy vegetation which scaled the side of the fort.

"Curse them!" the man sputtered angrily.

The Commander's eyebrows knit together as the man continued.

"Burning and killing and burning! That's the extent of Shalkan ability," the man complained bitterly. "This is the last of the tree farms," he lamented, dropping an armful of crops and slamming his fist through the air in frustration. Anger and desperation were etched in his every feature.

He is a rebel, a one armed Pan who has seen his share of battle. The Commander chose the time to stand. "Rebel," he called. "Do not fear," he added when astonishment registered on the man's face. "I am called the Commander, cousin of your beloved Lain."

The rebel's eyes widened. He knelt, but the Commander's biting voice cut him short.

"Do not kneel, men," he said, permitting his army unit to rise behind him. "What is your name, rebel, and in what service do you engage?"

The rebel had little choice but to answer. "I am Roth, and I am a cook."

"Good, you will enter into the forts as our cook while we strengthen our position and prepare to attack." As the soldiers entered the forts, he approached Roth. "Do you know if the cannons are left?"

"I believe so," Roth looked uneasily at the forts, "but I suspect they are not in working condition."

"What is your business far from the fighting and dying of your brothers?"

"I escaped to the tree farms in order to salvage food for the men when the tunnels collapsed." A passionate rage overtook him. "I barely escaped with my life, but the tree farms are burned and destroyed." He continued, "I am grateful to align myself with you and fulfill my duty to Quantus Plain."

"And I to you."

With the Commander's acceptance, Roth trashed formalities. "If you don't mind me asking, what are your plans for these forts?"

"I do mind, but I plan to restore them and give the officials a pummeling from behind."

"The entire plain will rise up against you!"

"If I am able to divert but some of those evil men from Quantus Plain by giving my life, then so be it."

"If I had your bravery or foolishness then every man would follow me."

"Find that bravery then, for it lives in the hearts of all men thrown into evil times."

The fort reeked of smoke and ashes. Walking pensively through it, his every preoccupied step sent the ebony dust spiraling into the air never to settle. Faint smells of Roth's cooking penetrated the scent of war. The Commander rubbed his prickly chin. A scar jumped over the edge of his chin, and hard, vertical lines pressed against his face in the form of high cheekbones. His brawny appearance accented his leadership, and his men trusted him.

He thought of battle. The forts accommodated the rebels. While the buildings had been damaged, they remained a necessary component to his plan. To hold

JULIE AND RYAN DICKERSON

even one of the forts, he would need more men, but he would not receive more. He would have to spread his lines thin, creating the illusion of having a larger army than reality granted. Unfortunately, Roth had been right: the Shalkans had left little ammunition. The rebels knowledgeable about such weaponry employed their skill to fix them. The Commander watched these proceedings but said little, for his mind had wandered, recalling and rehashing his first encounter with the Shalkans and the skeleton of his smoldering home.

Tar spat the ash from his mouth. A hand grabbed his forearm.

"Tar, thank God you're alive!"

"The officials, are they moving in?"

"You're the last one not behind the Great Pillars. Here, help me drag this wounded man back. Reach straight down and take hold of the ankles. Got them?"

Tar tightened his grip on the ankles slippery with blood. He felt disoriented. "How bad is he?"

"Not good."

Corious began to weave back and forth, delaying their arrival at the massive pillars but reducing the probability of being shot. "Duck!"

Falling to the ground, both Tar and Corious shielded their faces with their hands. Shots ripped through the air where their heads had been moments before. Almost to the pillars, they crawled on their elbows and jerked the injured man behind them. Scurrying behind the rebel line of defense, Tar leaned back in relief as the shots ricocheted off the stone. The cool, vast mass of rock comforted him, sheltering him from the impacts of the small, metal bullets. Below him, the earth accepted the noise of the cannons rolling through the hatch, the blood of the dead and wounded, and the tired, beating hearts of the living.

Ramshackle attempts at defense walls obsessed the men in the back hall. The crinkling of ravenously consumed rations mixed with the painful grunts of casualties who were loaded onto carts and pulled into the third corridor. Tar longed for the peacefulness of the healing room, the sound of the fountains gushing with water, the fresh bed sheets, and the cool, calm touch of a healer's hand. He could almost feel Roken applying the poultice and bandages to his injuries. Snapping from the phantasmal vision, Tar knew he should be thankful; he was not yet in that medical room, or rooms, as it had become due to the influx of injured. Someone offered him rations, and he thanked them but refused.

"I've already had some." It was a lie, but one that would fill someone's stomach.

The rattling of the cannons ignited his dread. Night had fallen outside, and the men were commanded to search for torches. Tar stretched his legs and then squatted, imitating the rebels who feared to stand above the makeshift walls of rubble and wood. The siege walls had been damaged in the cannon fire; their preparation had been useless.

Tar carefully worked his way around the cowering multitudes of frantic rebels stacking debris on the wall. Tar called for those once under his leadership to reform their lines. Other captains went about a similar work, and the result was staggering. The men knelt in depleted, haggard lines.

Lain's voice echoed above them through the cavern, commanding Boragheld's men to shoot at the officials filing into the Hall. Though the rebels were at their weakest, the officials did not charge as expected. Instead, they argued amongst themselves, labored to lower the cannons through the hatch, and gave the rebels time to fear and contemplate their fate.

Droplets of water slid from blades of grass as they brushed the against the marching rebels' legs. Hot and humid, the moisture in the air seemed to lie heavily on the soldiers, making subtle the jerking steps of a unified march. The dwindling Mali-Mali riders came next; an inordinate number of the spiders had deserted their riders upon arrival, scurrying deep into the jungle, rumbling and humming. Redael did not understand their departure, but he could not expect more from the giant spiders. They had a mind of their own and had never been bound in an official allegiance to the rebels; they had no obligation to remain and die in battle. What had surprised Redael was the willingness with which they had left.

The forts were in eyesight, and the Commander came to greet Redael. "How was your attack? Few men return," he commented as he ran his trained eye over the survivors.

"Our attack went not as planned," Redael replied gruffly. "We have sustained heavy casualties crossing the river and back, but we have been graced by some unexpected luck," his voice rose in anticipation. "Only one official ship haunts the river. Heard you the explosions?"

"I did, but this sharp bend makes it difficult to see farther down the river." Containing his joy, the Commander said severely, "Do you think the lone ship belongs to Logan and Hitachi?"

Images of men running valiantly across the sandy beaches promoted him to say, "Perhaps their madness has paid off. Hope returns to our attack. Soldiers enter the fort and arm it well," Redael said, waving his hand towards the fort. "Join with your brothers and let us hold the river."

"I plan on more than that." He did not detail his plan, and Redael did not ask to hear it. The faint sounds of cannon fire drifted to their ears. Grey, blue, and black uniforms covered the plain.

"Each cannon fired reminds me of the valor of Logan and Hitachi and those who follow them. I would like greatly to contribute to their attack."

The clinking of loaded cannons were heard from inside.

"They left the cannons?" Redael asked in disbelief.

"To their disadvantage. Shall I give the command to fire?"

Redael surveyed the river. "So be it."

Nodding slightly to the man awaiting his signal, the Commander folded his arms at his chest and smiled. The seconds dragged. Nervously, Redael bit his lower lip until a small dribble of blood trickled down the insides of his mouth; he could taste it on his tongue. His eyelids rested, momentarily closed; and then he heard the forceful release of the cannonball, and his lids flickered open. To avoid the fire, the dark men were forced to cower closer to the hatch of Quantus Plain. The Commander did not celebrate.

"We are not drawing their forces from the Plain," he growled. "Those cowards just rush to enter and kill our brothers faster." To Redael he said, "I am going to direct the attack. Will you be joining me?"

Redael bounded after him up the stairs which shook from the offensive attack. Arriving at the top of the fort, they stood surrounded by their troops.

"Aim for the core of Shalkan's dense center. As far as the ball will go, aim it there. We need to divide the masses," he stated as the men readied the cannons for another round.

Writhing, the shape of the black Shalkan heap changed and convulsed with every cannonball issued from the fort and the lone ship. Like a wounded beast, the dark men wavered, bewildered that such a forceful attack could come from the outside. The Shalkan captains searched for a scapegoat, and one saw the iridescent lights sparkling across the river.

"The forts! They've taken the forts, the dirty rebels," he snarled. "Attack! Kill them all!"

Pushed before him by the butt of his gun, the dark men moved swiftly under his command. Though many died in the onslaught, others easily filled their places, and the black beast did not slow. It hurtled to the mouth of the river, shooting and cursing.

"Crossing the river, are they?" the Commander grinned sadistically.

"This is what you wanted?" Redael questioned as the officials moved through the river. The Commander did not answer but watched in satisfaction as the troops diverted their attention from the center of the field to the fort.

"This is more than an attack! We will be overcome!"

Men chucked debris over the fort walls at the enraged officials who scaled the embankment and threw themselves at the singed, vertical wall. The dark men trampled one another, creating a ramp of bodies. Neither the cannonfire nor the rubble fended off the immediate attackers. The Commander watched this knowingly, and the ramp climbed the wall until living officials poured over the top of the fort.

Then he lunged forward desperately to stop the assault from clambering beyond the cannons. Redael joined him. Guns were fired, and rebels hit the floor to avoid the shots. Rising, they met the first set of officials. Redael jumped forward but incurred a minor blow to his leg. Gritting his teeth in pain, Redael withdrew his sword and struck again as his men came to his aid. Thrashing about, the officials died, stuck with several rebel swords.

But the others came like a bulging storm, expanding, enveloping, and wailing. Cannonballs and swords chucked bodies into the air, but the flow did not stop. The rebels could not hold them, and the officials pushed them back. The rebels retreated down the stairs, but there was no escape.

Ejaculations of joy tripped from the mouths of Logan and Hitachi as their shots dug flawlessly into the other ship. Small explosions ruptured the targeted ship from the inside, and almost instantaneously, the bedlam attacked the other frenzied ships.

"Fire at will," Logan commanded smugly. Fiery balls crossed the darkening sky and landed in the field, displacing officials as the ocean tosses about grains of sand.

"I hope Lain doesn't mind us messing the plain up a bit," Hitachi said humorously. "Afterwards, the craters pocketing this land will make for some interesting scenery."

"We'll tell him we discovered a breakthrough in landscape design," Logan grinned. "This was easier than I thought." He wiggled the fingers of his injured arm.

"Don't get too haughty now," Hitachi reprimanded, though he could not stop his own burgeoning pride as cannonball after cannonball erupted in the official ranks.

"We'll have them out of here by morning."

"Eventually, to be in range, we will have to go farther down the river."

"You're telling me to go over the barricade?"

"It was broken."

"But dangerous nonetheless," Logan countered.

"What do you plan on doing when we run out of ammunition? If we head upriver, we'll at least be closer to land. The officials won't dare try to attack us with the cannons going."

"When do you plan on doing this?"

Hitachi plugged his ears with his fingers as another cannonball descended towards impact.

"They're getting out of reach now." Hitachi looked wonderingly at the scene before him. "They seem to be retreating across the river! Our attack has been successful! Hoist the main sail! We make for up the river!" Hitachi yelled excitedly.

Sailors scuttled about the deck and swung expertly from the ropes, obeying orders. Veering harshly to the left, items strewn about the deck slid wildly to the other side, and Hitachi grabbed a railing for support.

"Sir, we are taking on water!" a voice called.

"How much?" Logan demanded.

"It's hard to tell."

"Will we sink before the ammunition is completely utilized?"

"No, I think not. We can last maybe an hour more."

"An hour?" Hitachi asked incredulously. "That's it? All that ammunition and it will run out in a few hours? By the Almighty!"

Logan rubbed his chin meditatively. "The dark men cannot be fleeing from our attack alone. Something must draw them from Quantus Plain."

"Rebels!" Hitachi exclaimed. "Redael and the Commander must have arrived! We must save them!" Without waiting to confer with Logan, Hitachi cried passionately, "Forward, full speed! Aim for the fleeing officials!" The ship belched cannonballs. As the rebels came into range, the dark men fired, and the men pressed themselves to the deck.

"The barricade lies ahead!" Logan warned. "We must slow down to avoid the debris." But no one heard him over the clamor, and the planks of the ship were ripped from their spots to unite with the river. Logan cringed as the ship dipped. The water slapped against the fissured hull, rippling around the jagged shards of timber. With every turn, the river steeped the rebels in water. Rocking the already unsteady ship, the cannonballs raced from the mouths of the cannons in quickening rounds.

"A half hour," came the voice of a sailor. "Maybe twenty minutes now."

"Get all valuable items off the ship," Logan commanded worriedly as the ship continued to sink. Rope, barrels of food, and other items were thrown over the rails and onto the riverbank not far away.

"The officials still press on," Hitachi voiced in amazement. He added uncertainly, "It is as if their numbers increase the more we attack."

"At least we have made a nice dent in their ranks."

"That is true, but it is not enough. We cannot save Quantus Plain by infantry with a mere dent in the enemy."

"The forts sustain their fire." The ship rocked precariously as the cannons loosed an additional round. Sailors in the crow's nest dropped from their heights and hurriedly crawled down the rope ladders.

"Ten minutes!" the informant cried from below.

"All those who can swim, jump over now! Those who cannot, hold to the planks," Logan said, wrestling his resisting body from a chair and favoring his wounded arm.

"Last volley!" the cry extended.

"So we run out," Logan alleged dourly. "Help me off, Hitachi."

Logan, Hitachi, and the rest of the sailors who popped up from the lower decks sped to the rail. Many dove in. Supporting Logan, Hitachi lowered a rope and scaled down. Logan used his good arm to carry his own weight, but he depended on

Hitachi to support him as he released and slid lower. When their feet skimmed the top of the water, they fell in with a splash. Rolling onto his back, Hitachi used one arm to stroke backwards while he cradled Logan with the other. Digging his nails into a rotting plank, Hitachi transferred his brother's weight onto the buoyant board. Together, they kicked to the bank. As they clawed into the muddy incline, the ship faltered. Hitachi watched gloomily as the ship creaked and groaned.

"Men, take a breather and then into the woods. We must hold the fort."

"If the fort is not overrun," Logan murmured pessimistically as he hauled his body onto the bank.

"Do not talk like that," Hitachi admonished as they dove into the vegetation for cover. "We were ready to give our lives."

"I did not think we would lose."

Hitachi hesitated and then reached for Logan's good hand and squeezed it. "Neither did I." He looked his brother in the eye. "But here, together, at the end of the rebel cause, we shall offer our remaining strength if the Almighty calls us to do it."

Logan released Hitachi's hand and with a sheepish grin replied, "Then what are we waiting for?"

"You never did take me seriously," Hitachi muttered as they crept through the brush.

"Well, if we don't make it, here's a cheer for my good brother, Hitachi," Logan replied honestly. "Where do you think those forts are?"

"Must be somewhere down river. I smell the smoke already."

"The men are ahead in the clearing."

Emerging from the brush, the two brothers turned as the tip of a torn, black sail touched the water. It was no longer full-bellied with the wind or proudly pulled taut.

"That's two bad experiences on a ship so far," Logan commented as he materialized from the foliage. "I don't think I'll be getting on a third."

Ruts from the crude wheels of barrels spread before them. They had been used to transport the items previously thrown overboard. Hitachi did not approve.

"The barrels will have to go. Take the coils of rope and ammunition. If there are other tools of value, hide them in the brush until we return. When going into battle, it is best to travel lightly." His eyes clouded. "I hear the shrill cries of the enemy and the faltering steps of our brothers. Into battle, men, with brave hearts, go! The fort, it is not far now. Yes, I see it ahead! But what is it that crawls over its walls?"

"The enemy is retaking what was once theirs."

"What should have never been there in the first place."

Mouths twisted open in the battle cries. They stirred men's souls and forced them to fight a battle already won, but not by them. Eyes squinted against the rising sun, shielding minds from darting rays; lids closed to block out the bloody scene, to protect the soul from watching as man killed man and as good died under the mounting tide of evil. Arms rose holding swords, resisting the lassitude that hung like weights from every limb, every muscle, and every fiber of their beings. The fists rose into the air alongside the shouts, defying the fate that most assuredly would be theirs, fighting desperately for a hope that had already passed away with the dead.

Vague, obscure shapes flittered and danced before his eyes. Like the ripped ends of a flag, they taunted him. Shadows of darker things to come, they laughed at him, tore at his back, screamed as they tried to claw into his mind. Prying with dirty hands, they probed for any weakness—any small chink in his defense. His face dripped with tears, sweat, and blood.

The men were not lost, but they were giving in, yielding to the forces of the darkness. They were struggling for air but swallowing water. Roken had seen many such faces, and some he had tried to save. Yes, this sight was familiar to him, but never before had he seen the expression on the face of Lain. Never before had he imagined that the servants of the underworld would ever attempt to take him. Once Roken had been a slave to them, his mind chained to their unbending will, but by the Almighty's grace he had been freed.

Standing in the middle of the medical ward with bandages in his hand, he was frozen. He did not hear what Lain said to him; the words were coming out rushed, slurred from the cut on his leader's lip. Roken only saw his eyes misty with the things that haunted him. Roken knew that face, but he could not help him. No, Lain would have to conquer his demons alone.

Fire burst outside the stone wall, caressing its lascivious top.

"Hold your ground men," Ree commanded dispassionately. His face was perfectly blank. "They are trying to break the wall, but it will hold. It will keep us until morning."

How long until morning? It seems so long, a hideous nightmare; I cannot wake. The soldiers' feet were stationed comfortably apart at shoulder width. Their backs were straight, their swords positioned perfectly. More fire, higher this time, ate at the wall, trying to come over it. The cannons exploded, but the wall did not shake. Built by the hands of a strong people, a determined people, it would not fail them. Faint vibrations and ululations whispered through the floor. The officials were determined too; they would not give up either. Violence did not bother them because they had long ago surrendered any feeling but hate, and that had consumed them until only their bodies were recognizable. The next lusty explosion caused the nerves of the soldiers to jump.

"The wall will hold," Ree reiterated. "Prepare yourselves." His eyes focused straight ahead, unwavering. "Prepare yourselves for the morning."

Do not worry until the morning. The wall will hold until then. Just rest, weary sol-

dier, rest. Stand sure but do not think too much, because thinking is dangerous. If you think too much you will begin to fear, and once you fear, you cannot stop. You can fight it or deny it, but it is better not to let it grab hold at all. Look at Ree, imitate his face. Let your mind go blank except for thoughts of the Almighty. Pray and pray and pray. Do not wander in your thoughts; do not think about your wife or your children. Do not wonder where they are or how they are. Pretend you are Ree; you are not tired, you do not hurt. Imagine you are Tar. You cannot see the enemy, but you know he is there. You will not see the horror or the ending blow, so you fight valiantly. Remember your cause. Be Corious, solid yet lithe, but do not drink of his fiery passion until the moment battle breaks upon you. See, he stirs, restless with waiting; he twirls his sword and looks at the wall achingly. But the wall will not break until morning; it will hold until morning.

Long hair loosed itself from hard buns and fell beneath the rims of helmets not made to sit atop the small heads and slender necks. The hair was tucked back inside by obstinate hands which were calloused from use. Lips parted beneath sad, stubborn eyes, and the women marched to war with the men. They went to die next to them, to die fighting for the same cause that they loved so well, to die for the sweet smell of life untouched and unstained by the dark forces of the world. So they would die for life rather than live in death.

"Archers, last volley!" Lain's voice called, haggard from overuse. He strained it to its breaking point. The burning arrows hit targets which were replaced by new ones. "Move positions," he commanded, escaping a cannonball hurled in his direction. The rebels had carefully avoided the fire, but they would be caught eventually, cornered and killed in their own Hall. "Behind the wall," Lain shouted, and his men followed him without question and without fear.

Shadows darted before his eyes, and he felt the ever probing hands. "Almighty, save me," he whispered. "His presence is near. Defend me," his voice rose, and his eyes closed as one in pain.

You cannot avoid me. Turock's face was in his head, the empty eyes sucking at everything that was Lain's. *You cannot last forever, you cannot hide forever. You know this; I know this. It will not be long before I see you again, and this time things will be different. I have given you a taste of the fate which will come, but things could be different.* He dangled the Faustian opportunity before Lain.

No. No, I chose long ago my path, and you chose yours. Our fate will not change now.

Then you will die like every one of the pitiful men you try to save.

Nothing the Almighty has made is pitiful. Be careful, Turock; you tempt my anger. I am not afraid of you, Lain of Quantus Plain.

"The archers return," Tar mused. "I hear the steps of their boots and the hoofbeats of Boragheld's men."

"It is near time they returned," Corious tossed his sword in the air. "The hour grows late, and we must prepare for the morning."

"We have time," Ree chided. "Morning is far off yet."

"Where is Lain?" someone called.

"Lain? He was with us moments ago," an archer called.

"Well, where did he go?" Corious demanded. "There are battle plans to make. More than half the night has been wasted."

An explosion ripped through their quarter, and the wall shook. The soldiers flew to the ground, covering their faces from the rocks that rocketed from their places. *How long until morning?*

The empty eyes were before him. The horrendous face was swathed in darkness beneath the helmet. The hideous vision held him still, and Lain could not reach for his sword. He kept his jaw firm and forced his frozen arms to move, forced his fingers to grab the hilt of the sword. It was as if the icy reaches of winter had cruelly frozen his thoughts. He fought back.

As Turock wielded his saber, Lain unsheathed his own. It was dreamlike. Dripping and wet, the dank and dirty cavern walls shielded him from the noises of battle.

"What good is there in trusting your Almighty now?" Turock's voice rasped through the air like a snake. "What good has your work accomplished when all you love perishes?"

Lain wrestled his desire to strike as the eerie voice slithered into his mind.

"Your wall is breaking. It will break very soon, and then your people will be left leaderless. You leave them to die." Turock's sword flashed dully before him. The point of the sword was not far from Lain's chest.

The air sped from his lungs as Lain lashed at the enemy, heaving the sword from his side and over his waistline to connect with the black saber. Easily, Turock pulled back his sword and swerved deftly.

"You are tired," Turock observed, goading Lain into a rage. "The battle has taken much of your former strength."

"That is a lie!" Lain shouted, lunging forward.

"You're wounded, and not just physically."

Gritting his teeth, Lain pushed the voice away, ignoring the blood rolling down his forehead. The red liquid oozed from a cut inflicted by a flying stone—a stone repelled from a failing wall.

"Back to the first corridor!" Eruptions from the cannons transformed pieces of the wall into deadly projectiles. They had to avoid being hit. "Ree, you cannot stand there forever!"

"I'll stand here until they make me move. I will not retreat."

"It's not a retreat," Tar yelled. "We're going to charge when the wall blasts open, but it's no good charging if the enemy is already upon you! Now move back!

Malov rushed forward, but Corious caught and restrained her. "Do not leave rank," he told her decisively. "Let him go. This is his battle." Tears streamed down her face. "You are strong, Malov. Do you hear me? You are strong," Corious's voice caught as Malov gripped him like a frightened child. "Do not fear for a hardened warrior."

Mortar rounds landed beside Ree, around him, inches from him. Standing, he did not move. He was not afraid of death.

"My God! He's not been touched!" The soldiers cried in amazement.

I will not believe in an Almighty until I come from this battle unscathed.

Corious gaped. Not a single stone found their mark. Malov loosened her grip, and Salene took her from Corious, leading her back to the others. Corious crouched on the ground and prayed for his friend, watching him between the volleys of fire and stone.

"How long does he plan on standing there?" soldiers called.

"Morning comes!" someone shouted. "See the light!"

"He's gone mad. There is no light in here but from the fire," someone else shouted back. "He's dying; ignore him."

Corious hushed them, and then there was no noise. The vibrations of the floor halted. "What madness is this?" he whispered. His every fiber screamed danger. And then the wall shook like a leaf tossed by a gush of wind. With a terrible grinding of stone, the cannon burst through the wall, its black snout sniffing out its prey. The stones showered down, and the soldiers hunkered under the corridor bulwarks.

"Wait until they come!" Corious shouted. "Wait until you see their faces!" Two more cannons fractured the wall on either side, and then the wall cracked like a brittle leaf being crunched under a ruthless foot. The enemy was before them, draped in gloom. The Shalkans marched, and Ree waited in the middle of the narrow hall, ready to meet them.

"Charge!"

With the last strength allotted to them, Corious and Tar lifted one last battle cry from their lips. The rebels were an arrow, with Ree as their poisoned tip. They sped towards the sinister target looming before them. Morning had come.

Even in the caverns the detonation could be heard. He knew the wall had fallen. He had to get to his people. With a warrior's scream, he rushed at Turock, all his intricate footwork forgotten. He had to get to his people. He had to get to them. The black saber whizzed by his face, and Lain's sword dug in the dark for Turock's flesh. Lain retreated from the cavern, his feet slipping and sliding along the wet floor. Turock had wanted to distract Lain. Lain had met him; he had failed his people.

"Chittahow choa ow."

The Mali-Malis galloped to their master who called them, leaving the rebels and darting through the forest. They came to her, and she stroked them gently, squatting on the ground. As they chattered excitedly, the ground trembled.

"The night obfuscates my vision," Aisii murmured. "Into what evil do you lead us, Shrie, Maiden of the Wood? To what fate do I bring my people?"

Aisii's words were not heard by Shrie, for with her entire body she was listening, searching for her brethren. The army marched, and the smoke and ashes settled onto it in accumulating layers. Shrie was suddenly consumed by the urge to run.

"Ready your weapons," Dashjmar cried.

"I smell the foulness of the enemy."

"Let us destroy them." Shrie's army sped forward, the thrill of the attack pulsating in its limbs.

Soaked in blood, Redael wondered vaguely if he had been injured. Too many dying men surrounded him; he could no longer distinguish their blood or their pain from his own. The battle raged about him; but for valued seconds, it did not find him. Catching his breath and clearing his face, he saw the officials, but he did not feel them. He did not feel the hot stink of their mephitic breath or the incisions of their pointed teeth as they burrowed into his flesh. He held out his sword, hoping that his dead arms would hold it straight and that he might take one official with him after he died. The floor was under him; his body was against it. The official atop him no longer writhed.

His vision turned gray, but then came the light—the piercingly soft, comforting light which beckoned him forward. *Well done, good and faithful servant.* The confusion of the battle and the besieged bodies disappeared in sweet relief and song. The crepuscular vision enveloped him. There was no more pain…no more suffering…It was his time.

The Commander saw Redael fall, but he could do nothing. He struck out in anger, in revenge, and then remembered his men. "Attack," he hoarsely called shoving an official from him. "Do not lose hope," he cried though he himself had lost it long ago. He ran his sword through the enemy but backed down the stairs; he vowed to make each step cost the officials dearly. His vision blurred. "Almighty, send us deliverance," he gasped.

Almost immediately, he felt a supple body at his side. An arm whipped back, and arrows gorged themselves on his attackers. He saw the pointed ears and the long, black hair.

"Tell me my eyes do not deceive me." He took a step up the stairs. An official fell.

"They do not." The green eyes glanced into his briefly. "Retake hope. The Maiden of the Jungle has come."

The officials began to melt before them. Logan and Hitachi cheered.

"We're doing good work, brother." Logan grinned, forcing himself to forge ahead. "The slaves fight somewhat fiercely don't they? It is amazing! They're actually retreating from the fort, and we've only just arrived!"

"Your presence alone is fearsome," a voice said amusedly behind them. The tattooed skin and the gold band on the muscular arm entered their vision.

"Dashjmar…" Hitachi's eyes opened wide. "Wh—"

The armies came into view: the people of straight, white hair and white faces, the snow creatures, and the tribesmen on lizards and Mali-Malis.

"By the Almighty," Logan stammered. "How—what brings you here?"

"We sweep left to Quantus Plain. Shrie can handle the fort," Dashjmar called, ignoring Logan's attempt at a greeting. Waving his arm, the small group of men that Logan and Hitachi had once led fell into line with the great armies of ice and tribes people.

Logan and Hitachi found themselves swept up behind Dashjmar as Shrie and her people spouted from the fort like water from a fountain. They saw the red-robed figure, with a bow in her hand, jump from the top of the fort and lithely sprint down the ramp of broken bodies, shooting at her enemy. Rebels waved bloodstained swords and plunged into the river.

The fresh army from the north swept down upon the Shalkans and routed them. Swords swung and arrows flew. White and black, brown and gold, and red and orange hair shone under the same rising sun. Gleaming in the light, they struck down their foe and advanced, retaking the lands which were rightfully theirs.

Cannonballs ripped through rebel lines; the arrow grew smaller as the target became bigger. Officials streamed through the hatches and scrambled into battle. Smashing into the multiplying official forces, the arrow all but disintegrated. The men submitted to Ree's leadership, but they wondered where Lain had gone. Where was their leader when the last day of battle came to claim them?

Twisted braids of dark and light strands, the entanglement claimed the lives of the rebels. Both sides knew that the rebels were dying. Slowly but surely, the cannons would eliminate them. The increasing volume of Shalkans would soon march forward, utterly annihilating the rebel resistance. The women and children would be slaughtered as they fled from the back halls, and then the Shalkans would sweep across the rest of Kurak like a rising flood. For when Quantus Plain fell and the last rebel stand went down in flames, the gateway to Kurak would open for the bloody, stained boots of the Shalkan army.

The foul smell of the cavern was replaced by the stench of fire, death, and ash. Turock thrived in it as he fought the fight he had so dearly wanted for years. Lain's footsteps slid in exhaustion over the floor, and Turock noticed Lain's knees could barely bend.

Lain ducked to avoid Turock's perfected swings. He had to get to the Hall. The anxiousness ate at him, and he sought Turock's death eagerly. The armor on the front of Turock's upper right leg was coming loose. Lain did not suppress his leap of hope. Parrying the flawlessly executed thrusts and jabs, Lain rushed at Turock's legs; his sword connected with flesh and muscle.

Anger swelled within Turock as the black, hot blood dripped down his leg. Furiously, he cornered Lain. The saber was at Lain's neck, but when he swung, he hit the wall. Lain had weakly slipped beneath Turock's legs, but the horns on Turock's boots had ripped open the skin on Lain's face. Turock veered violently, and Lain's sword dragged stiffly and ineffectively along the metal plating.

Lain attacked again, but his blows were stopped by the dreaded saber. He could hear the battle clearly now. The redness of shame flowed into his face. Turock laughed and flicked his wrist as he arrogantly spun his saber. Lain feigned a blow to Turock's leg. Turock raised his sword as Lain struck, smashing the duller side of his sword into his enemy's head.

The rebels were at the pillars; behind that protection, they regrouped.

"Try to take the cannons," Corious ordered breathlessly. He knew the tired, dirty faces of the rebels would not last long. "To battle!" They loped jadedly towards the enemy. "Take the cannons!" he shouted in a swelling fury. "Take the cannons!"

As if their bodies obeyed the sound of his voice, the men shot to the first cannon. They strained forward, but most died with bullets in their sides. As a rebel choked on a well -aimed bullet behind him, Corious shoved a dead artillery man off the cannon. A moment later, the rebels fired the commandeered weapon.

Ree slew any official that ventured within a three-foot radius of the second cannon. Several paces away, Corious jostled the first, placing the entirety of his weight behind it. The cannon did not budge. A light flickered about the hatch, and an unexpected strength welled inside of him. The cannon moved, and then the light went away.

Begrimed Shalkan faces met his as Corious pulled aggressively on the fuse string. The cannonball removed the faces from his vision and buried them in a crater of fire. Abruptly, a cavalry unit of Shalkans tore through the defensive ring which the rebels had dearly protected for the last several hours. A cantering horse charged through the rebels while its rider's sword speared them. Corious bayed in anger. The Shalkan directed his horse towards him. Hastily grabbing the cannon's powder rammer, a long shaft with a cylinder fitted on its end, Corious executed his rash plan. Blocking the horseman's sword with his own, he then lashed out with the rammer. The unprepared horsemen tried to lean out of the way, but the improvised weapon hit him full in the face, snapping his neck sideways and killing him instantly.

Corious released the rammer as the dead officer dropped from the saddle and landed at Corious's feet.

Corious spat on the crumpled figure but quickly spun away as another horseman missed his head by inches. After regaining his footing, he stabbed upwards when the Shalkan rode past him for the second time. The sword twisted into the unprotected gut of the rider; blood and entrails sprayed from the wound. Corious coughed as he retreated from the horses' path and wiped the blood from his eyelid.

The broadside of the saber struck his back. As he fell, Lain caught himself with his hands and kicked at Turock before jumping to his feet. Lain thrust his sword, narrowly missing. The strike threw him off balance, and Lain's foot left the ground as his momentum carried him. Lain's outstretched arm and sword slid past Turock's black helmet. Victoriously, Turock stepped forward and led his saber in a graceful half circle.

Lain felt the cold metal enter his stomach. His feet slipped and staggered on the blood-covered floor. He groaned slightly as his head smashed into the ground. Turock ripped the saber from his opponent's gut. Fresh blood gushed between Lain's fingers, and he shut his eyes, writhing in silent agony. Each breath came like stabbing knives into his sweating chest and suffocating lungs. Opening his graying eyes, he saw the saber coming, and he weakly rolled. Turock missed, smashing his hand into the ground. With one hand, Lain weakly gripped his sword, and with the other, he grabbed the hands that wielded the black saber.

Turock tried to shake the dying man from his sword but only succeeded in pulling Lain off the ground and to his feet. Lain's vision went gray as dribbles of blood seeped from his mouth. He swatted at the enemy. Turock laughed at his feeble attempts. He knew he had won.

As a cannonball tore over his head, Turock cursed the stone fragments that pelted him. Lain used the brief moment to lift his arms. His falling weight drove him forward, and his arm twisted painfully as his sword ground through Turock's thick breastplate, tearing to pieces his enemy's beating heart. Lain gasped in anguish and then dropped to the ground as the blood continued to gush from his stomach. If the rebels did not win the battle, at least the Shalkans would be leaderless.

Ree and Tar fought desperately to stay the incredible onslaught of the Shalkans. Wave after wave of berserker infantrymen careened from the Shalkan formations and into the tangle of fatigued rebel warriors. Tar stood in the outside ring of the rebel's pathetic defensive. He slashed the tip of his sword against the face of an official before shoving another into the ground. Another rebel engaged the prostrate official, and Tar rolled out of the way as the upper half of a dead Shalkan dropped beside Tar's feet.

"There are too many! We should retreat!" someone begged.

But there was no place to hide. "What do we do when we are finally cornered?" Bitterness crept into Tar's voice. "I wonder how the Shalkans will remember us."

Ree grunted. "I do not think they care to remember anyone, but by God, they will remember us! By the time they deal us the final blow, we will haunt their memories forever!"

Tar girded his sword in grim recognition. Ree was close beside him, and the two let no official pass without forcing him to suffer a fatal wound. Tar fought on and on though his men were worn and soon eliminated. Behind him, a Shalkan cannon roared. Tar hit the ground as a chorus of pained yells echoed in his ears.

Tar scrambled to his feet. "How many of this unit remains, Ree?"

Ree scowled. "The cannonshot killed nine of our thirty men." Beside Ree, a warrior was shot in the head. "We have twenty now," Ree corrected himself harshly as he kicked an oncoming official in the knee.

Tar struck at where he had thought an official lurked, but the Shalkan had stepped leftward. Tar lost control of his footing as he groped for something to hold onto. The Shalkan raised his pistol.

Ree shouted Tar's name in escalating fear as the Shalkan's finger curled around the trigger. Ree dove at the official, and Tar screamed in mixed emotion as the official planted his foot. Ree closed his eyes as his right shoulder connected with the Shalkan's chest. The dreaded explosion of sound and gunpowder did not meet him. Ree, with eyes still closed, rolled in the pulverized stone and dust beside him. He stumbled.

Between the eyeballs of the murderous Shalkan was a feathered arrow. Another arrow of the same color and making zipped by his eyes and stuck a Shalkan in the hips. Ree turned to gaze at the column of strange looking warriors from whom the arrows came. The foreign soldiers marched into the Shalkan's confused mass. Tar slowly clambered to his feet and hobbled over to Ree who had dropped to his knees in sheer ecstasy.

"What happened?"

Any organization the officials once possessed dissipated when the tribal warriors, like a waterfall plummeting from the hatch, spread throughout the room. The tribe's presence received a glorious shout from the rebels' mouths.

"Men, hold your fire!" Corious cried jubilantly. Joy swelled in his heart, and then Shrie was next to him, hugging him one moment and firing her bow the next.

"You almost lose without me," she taunted, though at the sight of Corious's grubby face, her heart nearly burst with elation. For her entire life, she had been waiting patiently for this moment, and now it had arrived. *My people are united.* The thought very nearly brought her to her knees in thanksgiving. Corious reached out worriedly to support her. Falling happily into his arms, she abandoned her bow and her worries to the floor.

"Shrie?" He patted her head in brotherly concern.

She laughed freely. "No need to worry, Corious! We did it!"

He smiled down at her. It was as if nothing had changed. *Everything is as it should be.*

"Go say hello to Ree," Corious finally commanded. The sentence rolled from his tongue in delight. They were all together once more. Without delay, Shrie bounded over to Ree and embraced him as her warriors swarmed past them, marched beyond the pillars, and killed the remaining, dazed officials.

"You found your tribe at last," Ree noted, wrapping his arms around her. "Where are they going?" Ree studied Shrie. *It is too good to be true...rebels never reunite with lost family, they certainly do not win, and they surely do not experience pleasure in the midst of battle. Therefore,* his thoughts reasoned, *the jungle woman next to me is surely an apparition stemming from my overworked imagination.*

"They go to heal," Shrie answered sadly, affirming that her flesh and bones before him did exist.

"Because it's over now," Ree said in wonder, the reality of the moment finally hitting him. In a surge of uncontrollable emotion, he kissed Shrie on each cheek, picked her up, and twirled her in the air. Shrie soared above the remnants of battle.

"I see Tar has a hawk," she added approvingly when Ree set her down. She would have willingly tackled her blind friend in exchange for his greeting, but Tar's ferocious sword destroying the last of the Shalkan warriors kept her at bay. *But there no need to run to him, for Shrie has plenty of days left to spend with him. There is time now...time untainted by the threat of imminent war.*

"Yes," Ree announced proudly, "Tar has improved greatly in battle."

"As have you," Shrie said mysteriously, "for the wounds on your face and ear already heal, and otherwise you are unscathed."

Ree touched his face tenderly. "The Almighty," his hushed voiced acknowledged reverently.

Shrie scanned the room. There was one person left who she badly wanted to see. The potency of her desire conjured Lain's face to her mind; quashed hopes and years of longing no longer shrouded his image. *"We will see each other again,"* his voice echoed. She had come back to him, and he had waited for her. His presence would erase the agonizing years of separation. They would be together, and that was all that mattered.

"Where is he?" she asked aloud, and then the sobbing messenger was running to her. "Where is he?" She could barely maintain control of her voice. "Tell me you know where he is!" she demanded desperately. *Oh, Almighty, do not take him from me now! Please...anytime but now.*

"Lain," the messenger choked.

Shrie's face crumpled in despair, and she could not conceal it. She had to flee the horrible nightmare, and so she ran, her body leading her where her heart refused to go. The rebels dashed after her from the room, and Lain's bloody body lay before them in the hall. Diving to her knees beside him, Shrie draped herself over his broken body and gently cradled his head in her lap. Her entire being shook in anguish. Her only comfort lay in the black garments and shriveled corpse of the enemy that had haunted her love. Lain had conquered the demon as he had sworn he would, freeing himself from a life of dread.

"Lain," she called tenderly, stroking her shaking fingers over his jaw. She saw a glimmer of consciousness in his open eyes, but she knew better than to hope it would last. Behind her, tears welled in the eyes of Ree, Corious, and Tar as their hate for the Shalkans wilted. Nothing but the sacrifice and love of their leader swelled in their minds. Seconds later, Marcelus and Perry entered, and in anguish, Marcelus dropped to his knees by Lain's side.

"Shrie," Lain's eyes lit in recognition before his lids fluttered in pain.

"Wh-who did this...how...?" Perry stuttered, his voice shaking.

"Tell my people, I am sorry," Lain's voice rasped. He shifted his head to look at Shrie, weakly trying to lift his hand. *It has been so long since I beheld her beautiful face. Has it been eons since I last touched her or felt her arms in mine? It has seemed that long; for it has been as hard for her as it has been for me. She has persevered for all this time, and now she knows I cannot stay. Even for her, I cannot stay.* "Oh, Shrie, I'm so sorry..." The path of his tear cut through the caked filth as Shrie caught the faltering hand and brought it to her face; the precious touch of his skin against hers dulled the sharp pains shooting through her heart. "I do not have the strength," he apologized, laboring for breath. "My time here is done, though I would have liked to see the enemy routed..." His voice faltered.

"They have been." Shrie's confident words quieted him as her eyes darted to the dead leader of the officials. "Your men will lead the last charge in your honor. Corious, Ree, go. I will stay here and tell your great leader what happens."

No one moved.

"Damn them!" Marcelus yelled earnestly. "These bastards will pay. They shall pay!" He bent his head and shamelessly let his tears stream into the bloody pool at Lain's side. He grasped Lain's hand and squeezed it hard before taking off to where the last of the Shalkans remained. Like lost children, Corious and Ree bolted from the room soon after, and their shouts could be heard from where Lain lay as the last of his foes met defeat.

"Master Lain," Shrie called, pressing her lips tenderly against his hand. "Look at your people. They have won. They have won the war, just as you have won yours. Fear not their fate. You have done your duty on this earth. The Almighty will guide you to his gilded halls." She slipped his ring from her thumb and put it back on his finger. "You will always be the spirit of Quantus Plain."

Lain dropped his head back upon her lap but smiled. "Thank you," he murmured, and then his eyes closed in peace as Shrie's single tear fell softly upon his closed lids.

Corious walked silently towards the room with the others behind him. Dust swirled gently in the air, sticking to sweaty and bloodstained brows. He paused at the doorway; the once-proud doorframe sagged. Broken walls and crumbling stones were portholes to the hushed outside. Lain's heavy desk held its ground among scattered papers. Any weapons that had once graced the walls were gone, used in battle. Yet four corners supported a roof, and an illuminating glow rested serenely on the wall to which Corious had come.

Stepping respectfully over the scattered items, he let a small tear form and drop from his eye along with the many others that had been shed that day. Shrie clutched her bow tightly as she stepped delicately into the room, her head tilted slightly and her face grave. Tar came next, and then Ree. Everyone, the slain and survivors alike, in body or spirit, filled the room with his or her presence. Bending down, Corious picked up a stone and fingered it. The other inscriptions stood singularly against the stone. He unsteadily brought the hand that held the stone to the wall, ready to add one more mark. As the stone's tip came to touch the wall, Corious bent his head, unable to bring himself to dig the rock into the wall.

Wet lines graced Shrie's face as she fell to her knees in the room. So the hearts of men went with her, and their bodies followed in suit. Heads bowed, they stayed that way until they heard the clink of an object dropping to the ground. The fallen stone had failed to make its mark; it had been unsuccessful in completing its task. Then a strange and sudden joy came to them at the sight, and the vertical marks seemed to fade on the wall, though they remained in their hearts. A new age had come, one which they had to embrace without forgetting through what they had come.

The congregation drew aside as Corious strode through their midst and into the daylight. Rising, they too swept from the room, leaving it to bathe in the light of heaven.

So the people will meet the Almighty and have their peace.

So ends the second book and
Chronicles of the Insurrection